LUKAN

DOMINI HIGHSMITH

LITTLE, BROWN AND COMPANY

A *Little, Brown* Book

First published in Great Britain in 1993 by
Little, Brown and Company (UK) Limited

Copyright © Domini Highsmith 1993

A CIP Catalogue record for this book is available
from the British Library.

Typeset by Leaper & Gard Limited, Bristol
Printed and bound in Great Britain by
BPCC Hazells Ltd
Member of BPCC Ltd

ISBN 0 316 90417 1

Little, Brown and Company (UK) Limited
165 Great Dover Street
London SE1 4YA

Also by Domini Highsmith:

Leonora

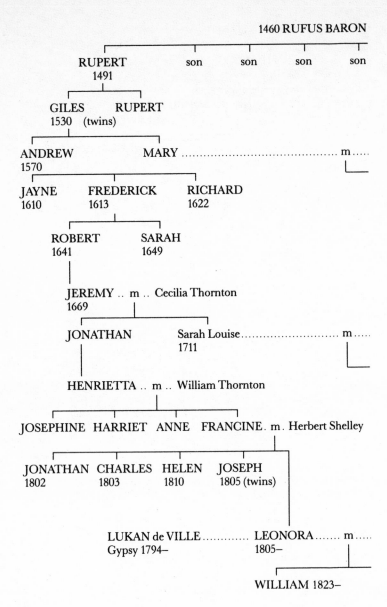

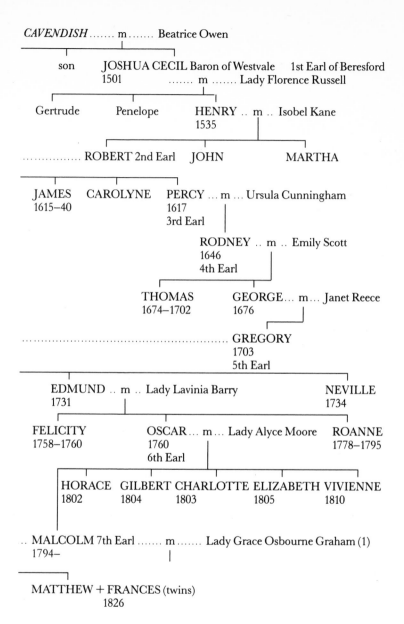

CAVENDISH .... m .... Beatrice Owen

son   JOSHUA CECIL Baron of Westvale   1st Earl of Beresford
1501   .... m .... Lady Florence Russell

Gertrude   Penelope   HENRY .. m .. Isobel Kane
1535

.... ROBERT 2nd Earl   JOHN   MARTHA

JAMES   CAROLYNE   PERCY ... m ... Ursula Cunningham
1615–40   1617
3rd Earl

RODNEY .. m .. Emily Scott
1646
4th Earl

THOMAS   GEORGE... m... Janet Reece
1674–1702   1676

GREGORY
1703
5th Earl

EDMUND .. m .. Lady Lavinia Barry   NEVILLE
1731   1734

FELICITY   OSCAR ... m ... Lady Alyce Moore   ROANNE
1758–1760   1760   1778–1795
6th Earl

HORACE   GILBERT   CHARLOTTE   ELIZABETH   VIVIENNE
1802   1804   1803   1805   1810

.. MALCOLM 7th Earl .... m .... Lady Grace Osbourne Graham (1)
1794–

MATTHEW + FRANCES (twins)
1826

CHAPTER ONE

I

3 a.m. 1st November 1823

Somewhere in the darkness a clock chimed. The woman, a servant, started at the sound. '*Oh Heaven help us, Heaven help us all!*'

Anabel Corey's plea was no more than an anxious little whisper. It fled with the draughts that breathed cold air from every corner of the ancient Hall. She shivered and drew her shawl more closely about her shoulders. She hated draughts. In her imagination they took on the shape of sinister, fleet-footed beasts of the night. They lurked unseen in secret holes and prowled deserted rooms and corridors throughout the dark hours in search of prey. The scuttling of draughts also reminded her of the vastness of that great mausoleum where she did not belong and would never feel at ease. This was a holy place. No matter how bloody and unchaste its history, Beresford Hall was built for an abbey and had its foundations set in consecrated ground. Small, ungodly people with their petty loves and spites were never meant to dwell within these

1

walls. Nor would their secret misbehaviours go unpunished. Adultery, like all sins, must have its price.

She wrung her hands together as she paced the shadowed corridor outside the sickroom, driven by a gnawing sense of mischief in the making.

'*Oh merciful Heaven*,' she repeated over and over again. '*Oh merciful Heaven have pity on us all.*'

It was All Hallows' Eve and Anabel Corey feared that the devil himself was roaming abroad, come to reclaim this night for his own dark forces. She could taste a scent of evil on the air. This was the withering hour, that curious time between three and four o'clock when everything in nature is reduced to its lowest and most vulnerable. It was the time of deepest melancholy, of cradle-deaths, of suicides and murders.

'*Oh, Lord, deliver us from the lowest and loneliest hour of this unholy night.*'

She stopped her pacing and lifted aside one of the heavy velvet drapes covering the windows. Outside the night was at its blackest. The moon had fled, leaving the sky pin-pricked with distant stars. Several bonfires still burned in the open spaces around Kingswood village and at the forest's edge, heathen fires lit by the superstitious to drive out witches, ghosts and goblins. Anabel shuddered at the sight of them. They flickered and spat on the dark earth like fiery embers raked from hell's grate and left to cool in the chill of that All Hallows' night.

'*... and keep us from our own folly ...*' She dropped the curtain. Its chain-weighted hem slid noisily over bare wooden floor boards. '*... and forgive us ... Oh please, dear God, forgive us all our trespasses.*'

She paused to press her ear to the sickroom door, her front teeth worrying her lip in agitation. Even the silence beyond seemed ominous. In a nearby alcove a young maid enjoyed the untroubled sleep of the innocent, unaware of the events in which she had become involved. No good would ever come of this wicked night. There would be a terrible toll exacted for its cruelties and its intrigues. The Lady Leonora had at last laid claim to her impossible dream, yet at what cost when she was

2

married but a few short hours and already an adulteress? In the bridal suite Lord Beresford's heir lay drugged with hemlock and tincture of opium while his beautiful young bride lay shamelessly abed with her gypsy lover. And while the revellers slept, replete with sumptuous hospitality, the body of the Countess of Beresford lay wickedly imprisoned behind the locked doors of her sickroom. And this, in Anabel's modest estimation, might prove to be the greater crime, the one to bring the wrath of God and the fury of men down upon their heads. The Countess's final seizure had remained a secret for almost thirteen hours, an infamous concealment. It seemed that Leonora's will would triumph even here. The embittered matriarch of Beresford Hall was silenced in death, as she had been in life, by a wilful slip of a girl driven by a vengeful ambition.

The elderly Lady Alyce Cavendish, Countess of Beresford, had despised Leonora simply for being the daughter of her husband's cousin, Francine Shelley. From the moment she first began to suspect that the cousins were lovers she set out to make their lives a misery. She defamed Francine at every opportunity. She refused to attend any social function to which the younger woman had also been invited. She even left abruptly any conversation in which the Shelley name was mentioned. Referring to Francine only as *His Lordship's whore*, she did everything in her power to have her rival ousted from respectable society. That she failed was due to her husband's considerable influence and social standing. Few could afford to offend him by snubbing the woman reputed to be his mistress, and few would risk insulting him by shunning his wife. Trapped in the middle way between the two, Francine walked a tightrope of respectability hung out across disfavour's abyss. Despite the odds against her she maintained that delicate balance for over twenty years.

Never content to punish only one where both were guilty, Lady Alyce set out to drive a wedge between Sir Oscar and his very powerful father, Edmund Cavendish. She even tried to set his own children against him, making them witness to her rages and her vicious, often sordid, accusations. When two of

Francine's sons were given an education at Sir Oscar's expense, and when the eldest, Jonathan, was seen to bear a striking resemblance to her favourite son, her vindictiveness increased ten-fold. She whispered lies that turned her son against his father, encouraged him to persecute his cousins and publicly to insult their mother's honour, and she made him vow that while he lived no Shelley foot would ever cross her threshold. That same unprincipled Horace Cavendish, if he were able to intervene right now, would light the torch to burn Beresford Hall to the ground rather than see Leonora made its mistress.

In the dark corridor Anabel Corey shuddered at the memory of those long, uncertain years. She had loved Francine with all her heart, not only as a servant loves a kindly mistress, but as a woman loves her dearest friend. That gentle lady had not deserved to suffer as she did.

Anabel pressed her hand to her lips and closed her eyes against the sudden sting of tears. That bitter vendetta had continued without respite for two decades, and when Francine died Leonora was meant to become the recipient of the countess's venom. But Leonora had shown herself to have more mettle than even her Cavendish relatives had suspected, and she had turned the tables on them all. And now the Countess too had breathed her last, so there was still a little justice in the world. Anabel offered up a simple prayer and tried not to think too harshly of the dead. It seemed to her that this family loved to the point of self-destruction and hated to the very brink of madness.

II

While Anabel Corey kept vigil outside the sickroom, the present Earl of Beresford, Sir Oscar Cavendish, rose from his bed and pulled on a robe of quilted silk brocade against the cold night air. Something had roused him from sleep, a dream perhaps, he had his share of those. Yawning, he crossed to the hearth of the great fireplace and used a fire-rod to prod life back into the dying embers. With a pair of polished brass tongs he fed fresh coal to the glowing cinders and watched the fire take hold. A handful of kindling sticks, added as a careless afterthought, encouraged the flames into hungry tongues that licked at the coals and sent bright sparks leaping and cavorting in a crimson dance across the blackened chimney stones.

He shivered as he knotted the silken sash of his robe more tightly. His legs ached and he felt his age more keenly than he had only a few short hours ago. He was a handsome man, still tall and elegant at sixty-three, still every inch the proud and stiff aristocrat. For the most part he enjoyed good health, but there were times when the night cramps kept him from his bed and a dull, persistent ache in his joints undermined his temper. His doctor had diagnosed rheumatism, that scourge of peasant and nobleman alike. Perhaps the rot of old age was setting in. He had seen it happen to other men, some of them up to twenty years his junior. First came the pains and night cramps, then the swelling of the joints and the characteristic stiffening that left the sufferer with a shuffling, old man's gait. For someone of Sir Oscar's calibre the prospect was especially depressing. He had always been active, preferring to run his estates personally rather than sit back in comfort and enjoy the fruits of other men's labours. He had no desire to adopt a lifestyle of slothful self-indulgence, to grow flabby of mind and body in a preoccupation with food and drink and frivolous young women. He still enjoyed riding the thoroughbreds from his own stables, hunting with his hounds, walking the extensive acres of forest and lush Gloucestershire countryside that had belonged to his family for the last three hundred years. Sir Oscar Cavendish was a man of action, loath to allow progressive lameness to rob him of his pleasures. He had a low tolerance for idleness. The likelihood of it being forced upon him by physical disability was totally abhorrent to him.

'Damn the cold,' he growled, seating himself close to the fire and rubbing his knees vigorously with both hands. 'Damn this infernal cold.'

5

A sudden gust of wind howled at the window, reminding him that the coming dawn would herald the first day of November. There would be apples and pears to store in the barns, meat to be pickled, beef and bacon to be hung and salted. Already the woods were thinned out. Doormice and snakes, lizards, slow-worms and toads were tucked away in their winter holes. Soon he and Malcolm and that man de Ville must arm their stoutest labourers and set about clearing bands of squatters from the plantations. If not discouraged early and with some firmness, wandering gypsies, fugitives and vagrant families would plunder his game and timber through the colder months. They had to be shifted, and soon, now that November was here. He rubbed his knees more gently as the fire's warmth began to penetrate. November 1st it was, All Hallows' Day, and already his rheumatism was at its worst. The season's damps and chills would not touch gently upon his joints this year.

He was dozing in his chair when a movement at the bedroom door disturbed him. He opened his eyes as a stoutly-built servant in a plain woollen dress bustled into the room carrying a tray draped in a stiff white cloth. She beamed a happy smile at the master, no hint of weariness on her cheery face.

'Here's your hot chocolate, Your Lordship, with just a dash of grated cinnamon. And here's your favourite sweet biscuits to spread with honey or crab-apple preserve.'

'What?' He scowled into the woman's plain, well-scrubbed features. 'But it's barely four o'clock in the morning, woman. Who ordered this? Who sent you here?'

'The Lady Leonora, Your Lordship,' she replied with a small bobbing curtsy. 'She told me I was to fetch a tray at the first sign of you stirring in the night.'

'But surely the Lady Leonora is still asleep in her bed?'

'Oh yes, Your Lordship, but with all that clearing up to be done, and the guests to fetch and bring for, and fires to rake and reset, and water to heat and carry to every room, and breakfasts to prepare ...' She paused just long enough to draw in a deep breath. 'Well, there's many of us what were up and about and working hard, long afore now.'

6

Sir Oscar scowled afresh at the rapid tumble of words. Undaunted by his stern expression, the woman smiled brightly and bobbed another brief curtsy before placing the tray on a small table close to the bed. A practised hand replaced the top covers across the sheets to protect them from the cool night air.

'Thank you,' Sir Oscar said, massaging his knees. 'That will be all.'

'Yes sir. I made the chocolate good and hot, and there's plenty for a second cup and more. Would you like me to bring a warming-pan for the bed?'

He shook his head. 'That won't be necessary.'

She curtsied again. 'Begging your pardon, Your Lordship?'

'Yes, what is it now?'

'Begging your pardon sir, but Her Ladyship Miss Leonora says you're not to sit too long in the night air without a rug to warm your legs.'

'Did she now?'

'Yes sir, and you're not to sit the fire out so as you catch your death of cold from the chill.'

'She said that too?'

'Oh yes sir, she thought of everything bless her kind heart, even on her own special day.'

'Quite,' Sir Oscar nodded. 'Quite.'

Still scowling thoughtfully, he watched her agitate the fire into new life and turn up the lamps before hurrying from the room and closing the door behind her. Then he rose to his feet, noting with some relief that the dull ache in his legs was beginning to subside. He flexed and relaxed his muscles several times, bending and straightening the knees to a slow rhythm. It was a simple exercise designed to return lost suppleness to the joints. He had no faith in it but persevered, still vaguely hopeful of a cure.

The chocolate was served in a china jug kept hot by a beautifully quilted and embroidered pouch. The spout protruded between the petals of a silken flower, trailing a rich aroma of cocoa beans and spices into the air. He poured a generous measure into his cup. It was delicious. He lifted the silver lid from the preserve jar and sampled its contents by the fingerful. His tongue detected a hint of clove and nutmeg in the crab-apple jelly, and perhaps just the merest trace of ginger to enliven the taste buds. The biscuits were crisp and fresh from the oven. Leonora had indeed thought of everything. He could not have wished for more satisfying fare or more timely a serving of it.

As he returned to his chair by the fire he caught sight of his reflection in the big oval mirror that stood in an alcove near the window. He was a tall man of well-balanced proportions and excellent posture. Although much of its strong blond colouring had faded to grey over the years, his hair was still thick and healthy and he kept it neatly shaped around his well-drawn features. Like his son he wore his hair much longer than the current trend of fashion dictated, bound at the back with a scrap of velvet ribbon to shape a tail that hung over his collar. His eyes were Viking-blue, above a long, straight nose, his mouth clearly defined over good strong teeth. The men of his family rarely lost their looks with age, and Oscar Cavendish was certainly no exception. He was an attractive man who still had the power to turn a woman's head or set a tender young heart a-flutter. He smiled a little wryly at his mirror-image. There was no mistaking the true Cavendish. Fair or dark, young or old, they bore the family imprint like a badge of office setting them apart from other men. His eldest son favoured the darker colouring, with eyes of a deeper, richer blue and hair the colour of freshly turned earth, but none would take him for anything but his father's son, a Cavendish at a glance. And rarely, perhaps only once or twice in a hundred years, the line produced the rarest of its breed: burgundy-haired and turquoise-eyed, arrogant, vengeful and infinitely sly.

The first of these had been Joshua, youngest son of an impoverished Scottish Baron. A forceful and ambitious young man, he pitted his wits against a treacherous King and proved himself the shrewder of the two. There were no half-measures for Joshua Cavendish in his quest for personal advancement. Although possessing neither wealth nor title of his own, he set his sights on taking the powerful Abbey of Beresford and all the lands and villages by which it was surrounded. He swore to have it for himself and, since it rested firmly in the King's gift, he would have it through the King's own generosity. Determined, single-minded, he cultivated that monarch and reaped a harvest worthy of a prince. To call him ruthless was to state the obvious. The only woman he ever truly loved was Lady Florence Russell, but he was without the means to marry and the lecherous Henry Tudor also wanted her. Seizing his opportunity, the wily Cavendish made his Lord an offer. He would marry the lovely Florence, at a price, and give the King free access to her bed until such times as his ardour ran its course. Scandal would then be avoided, the lady would be at the King's disposal and few but the favoured in royal circles would be one jot the wiser. No trustworthy historian would dare deny that the children of the marriage, Gertrude, Penelope and Henry, were as likely sired by England's monarch as by that newly-plumed First Earl of Beresford.

'And so our noble line was stained with the blood of English royalty.'

Sir Oscar chuckled at the observation, still capable of being mildly shocked by the cold-blooded antics of his ancestor. That act of dubious altruism earned the man his title and put the Abbey firmly in his grasp. It had all been a simple matter of priorities. He loved the woman but hungered for the Abbey, and in his callous way he took them both. Joshua Cavendish had been the first of the line with those distinctive sapphire eyes. Leonora, now Viscountess Cavendish, was the latest.

Sir Oscar shivered despite the warming effects of the chocolate. That beautiful young woman unsettled him. Nothing in her bearing or behaviour could be faulted, yet there was something about her, some quality only hinted at in her quiet strength and the effortless way she imposed her will on others. With her glorious eyes and captivating smile she touched upon his heartstrings and stirred the love he had always borne her mother. And yet her beauty caused his scalp to prickle, as if in warning of an enemy's presence. Was she, like the infamous Joshua before her, dangerously covetous of

9

the Beresford lands and titles? And was she, like him, willing to barter soul and truth and principle to get what she wanted?

Outside in the long corridor a clock struck the hour, its chimes muffled by a velvet hood so that guests sleeping in nearby rooms should not be disturbed at fifteen minute intervals. Soon the ebony of the night sky would start to recede from the east and the stars to fade and die before the gentle grey light of a new day. He sighed and stared at the bright flames dancing in the grate. The wedding had been a memorable affair despite the restrictions placed upon it by the Countess Alyce's long illness. Malcolm had been a proud man with his stunning Leonora on his arm, and she had looked and moved and smiled like an angel, making her husband the most envied of men.

Sir Oscar scowled suddenly and muttered a small profanity under his breath. That gypsy fellow had been there, of course. He was Malcolm's closest friend and ever society's favourite novelty, respected by the men and damnably popular with the women. The impudent heathen had danced with Leonora. Tall and elegant and gypsy-dark, he had taken Malcolm's bride in his arms and danced with her as if she were his own. Watching them at the time, Sir Oscar had felt suspicion rake its dagger-edge across his heart. The two had moved together like lovers, too close, too effortless, too much as one to be ought less than that.

'The devil take that gypsy,' he declared angrily, shaking his head to dispel the memory. 'It was illusion, pure illusion. Devil take the man for giving me such injurious ideas.'

Somewhere an owl screeched long and loud. Many who heard it would tremble in their beds, likening the sound to the mournful cry of a departing soul. Sir Oscar shivered again and drew his chair so close to the fire that his slippered feet rested perilously close to the hot ash and cinders that had fallen in the hearth. Sometimes his heart felt cold and leaden in his breast. The love of his life, his cherished Francine was dead and buried, her daughter newly married to his son, her most bitter rival struck down by a seizure. How far the world had turned in one short year. Their lives were altered now for

10

better or for worse, and it seemed to him that Leonora had played some subtle, ingenious part in all of it. He cradled his cup in both hands and sipped the cooling chocolate. He was a troubled man. His unease was vague and nameless, yet it gnawed persistently at his peace of mind.

III

The night owl's sorrowful screech was clearly heard from the apartment rooms above the old gatehouse. Here the great tower of Beresford Hall's West Wing, sombre relic of the original Abbey, rose like an accusing finger toward the sky. Its ancient stones concealed a thousand secrets and its history was stained with tragedies piled one upon the other down the centuries. Its massive foundations were reputed to hide the mutilated remains of a hundred innocents, those pious monks devoted to the Abbey, and a company of nuns seeking sanctuary from the terrible onslaught of King Henry's army. Trapped in the crypt by a drunken rabble of soldiers, all were slaughtered in an orgy of rape, desecration and bloodshed after the high stone walls were finally breached. The altar gold and the Abbey's treasure, along with the caskets of gold coin and precious gems brought there by the fleeing nuns, were never found. Not so much as a modest portion of it was ever uncovered, despite a frenzied search that left the main buildings in ruins. One legend said that the treasure was dispatched to Rome long before the army came, another that it had been interred with the victims in some remote subterranean repository. It was known that Sir Joshua, appalled by the carnage staining the King's gift, had ordered the underground tunnels sealed for all time with rubble taken from the ruined walls. Guarding this secret place was the sinister tower of the West Wing, with its tomb-like chapel and mysterious passages, its hidden sections of rough stone steps and dark monks' holes set

11

deep within its walls. Now the old gatehouse adjoining the tower had been renovated and enlarged, with a whole new suite of rooms whose main bedchamber was part of the old, long-abandoned tower apartments. And above it lay another room, a secret place accessible only by way of a hidden section of steps set deep into the tower's outer wall. Beyond the narrow stained glass windows of this bedchamber the night-owl swooped, still screeching, toward the ground.

'A hunting owl. It will be daylight soon.'

The voice of Lukan de Ville came as a deep rumble from the depths of his broad chest. It was a cultured voice, uncommonly rich in depth and resonance. He was sitting before a crackling log fire with his back resting against a chair of elaborately carved oak. He was naked. His long hair hung loose about his shoulders, straight and coarse and black as ebony. His dark, intensely handsome face was lit by reflections of amber-tinted firelight.

Between his bent legs nestled his mistress of a few hours, eighteen-year-old Lady Leonora Cavendish, the newly-married Viscountess of Beresford. She was the bride of Sir Malcolm Cavendish, heir to all the titles, honours and estates of Sir Oscar, Sixth Earl of Beresford. She was Malcolm's bride but she belonged to Lukan de Ville. She too was naked save for a shawl of fringed silver satin that hung over one smooth shoulder. Her hair was a cascade of burgundy-toned waves enriched with elusive hints of copper. It caressed her shoulders, back and arms, reaching her waist in rich and glossy splendour. Lukan touched it now with his big dark hand, and the simple gesture brought a smile to her lips. They sat without speaking, only the crackling of the fire intruding upon their comfortable silence.

Leonora Cavendish was a young woman of quite extraordinary beauty who possessed a strength of character equal to the lofty ambitions by which she was driven. In a few short months she had extricated herself from the mire of her father's debts to become one of the most admired, most talked-about women in the country. She had a flawless, peaches-and-cream complexion, a captivating smile and a body shapely enough to

12

inspire longing in any red-blooded man regardless of his age. More significantly, she had inherited from her maternal grandmother all that was most prized in the Cavendish blood-line. She sprang from the so-called lesser branch, that of the first Baron's eldest son Rupert, but she was of the self-same mould as Joshua. She had inherited his imperial bearing, noble features and fascinating, turquoise-tinted eyes, his mysterious power to impress, his undeniable charisma. And like him she had recognised her dream on sight and cunningly angled for it. She too had looked but once upon the splendour that was Beresford and vowed: '*This will be mine. As God Himself is my judge, one day all this will be mine!*'

'I must go,' she whispered now, turning her cheek to the hairy mounds of muscle on Lukan's chest. She touched a finger-tip to his neck, feeling the pulse trapped like a living thing in the warm hollow of his throat.

'Stay, my Lia.'

'I cannot, Lukan. I dare not.'

'Stay here with me.'

He closed his eyes and lowered his cheek until it rested on her hair. Even now the delicious scents of her assailed his nostrils and gently trespassed upon his most private parts. She had come to him in her wedding gown, eager, demanding and totally without shame. They had stolen this night of love with neither a twinge of conscience nor a moment's care for the consequences. Her husband had been Lukan's dearest friend since infancy, his brother in all but name, yet Lukan had betrayed his trust without hesitation in order to claim Leonora as his own.

'My Lia,' he said again, and pressed his lips to the top of her head. This woman had captured his heart as if by quiet magic, trapped him with her sweet snares one moonlit summer night in the tender darkness of the forest. Midsummer's Eve, the night of the Great Fair, and she, capti-vated by the scents and sounds of his wooded world, had allowed her steps to stray too far from the main forest pathway. By chance he had been on hand to pluck her from the approach of unseen danger. He had held her safely in his embrace, stifled her cries behind his palm and felt her strange and subtle magnetism quietly invade his senses. It seemed to him that in those moments she had bound him to her with invisible bonds. And later, in daylight, when he looked for the first time into her bewitching eyes, he had known that he was lost.

'I must go,' she said again, leaving his arms with a sigh of regret.

Lukan unfastened his long limbs from their comfortable position and rose to his feet in a single graceful movement. She watched him stretch the drowsiness from his body, letting her gaze travel over every taut, familiar inch of him. He was naked save for her gift to him, the ornate key that hung from his neck on a thick gold chain and nestled like burnished bronze against his dark skin. She smiled in satisfaction. Lukan de Ville was magnificent. His passions had ranged from tenderness to zeal and touched upon a whole spectrum of emotions between the two extremes. He had played upon her senses like a master craftsman and had still been prepared to surrender himself in turn to her demands. She doubted any woman was ever blessed with such a lover. He was a man of fascinating contradictions, this aristocratic gypsy, this gentleman rogue. He was sophisticated, educated, and yet beneath the civilised veneer there ran a myriad of dangerous undercurrents. There was something wild and unpredictable in his nature. He would never be fully tamed, not by her, not by any woman. That much could be seen in his dark, brooding good looks and arrogant coal-black eyes.

'Lukan is a genteel barbarian,' Malcolm had told her with brotherly affection. 'For all his refinements and accomplishments he is never more than a wink away from the barbarian. He is a secretive man, a mystery to us all, yet I would willingly trust him with my life.'

Lukan had been watching her closely. 'Your thoughts amuse you, Lia,' he said, his voice husky, his lips curving in a sensuous smile. Still standing, he rested his muscular forearm against one of the carved posts of the bed, looking back at her through half-closed eyes, uncaring of his nakedness.

14

She nodded. 'It has been a long and bitter battle between us,' she said.

'And a futile one.'

'Indeed. You swore from the first that I would belong to you, body and soul, before Malcolm Cavendish could take me to his bed.'

'And so you do, my Lia,' he reminded her. 'So you do.'

She tossed her head so that her hair shone with reflected firelight. 'I was so determined, so sure I could keep myself from you.'

'And yet here you are.'

'Yes, Lukan, here I am.'

'And mine,' he breathed. 'As you were meant to be.'

She nodded. 'Now we are one, you and I.'

He stepped away from the bed and placed his hands around her waist, drew her against him and bent his head to brush her lips with his own before asking, 'And now?'

'Hush,' she said, quickly pressing her fingertips to his lips. 'We have already tempted the gods as far as we dare. Only the present is ours to make of what we will. The future must remain beyond our reach.'

'No, Lia. The future is what we *will* it to be. Have you not shown that clearly to be so?'

She lifted and dropped her shoulders in a pretty shrug. 'I did what I had to do,' she said, remembering. 'When I realised that my future lay in the hands of those who would destroy me, I knew I must take control of my own life. It was a simple choice, misery or this. I simply chose the better of the two.'

'There was a third way, Lia. There was always a third way.'

She smiled and nodded her head. 'I know.'

'You might have been my wife instead of Malcolm's.'

'Yes, and forever mourned the loss of Beresford.'

He sighed. 'I watched you fight with a man's determination for what you wanted.'

'And I succeeded. I survived.'

'Aye, by shaping your own destiny. It is unnatural.'

Her chin lifted defiantly. 'Why so? Because I am a mere woman?'

He smiled. 'No, my love, because you are a mere mortal. Let us hope the gods forgive you the impertinence.'

She laughed at that and for a moment he shared her amusement. Then his face became serious. The laughter died on his lips and the brooding scowl returned. With his palm in the small of her back he drew her towards him and kissed her on the mouth. Warmed by the fire and by a night of shared passion, their bodies now pressed one against the other, the creamy white of her meeting the weathered brown of him. She made no protest when he drew her down to the rugs at their feet as, time and duty once again forgotten, she accepted him with a tiny gasp of pleasure.

Later they went up from the gatehouse via the hazardous Monks' Stair, that steep, tight spiral of steps set deep into the massive walls of the tower and only recently unsealed at Leonora's insistence. Like a single dark shadow the lovers stood together at the very summit of the ancient tower, the gypsy and his lady surveying the rolling Beresford acres as if looking out upon their own private kingdom.

The first fingers of dawn had begun to streak the sky with a wash of silver-gold and illuminate the dark-clad trees of the forest with an eerie light. The river shone white and flat as tin, and here and there the shadowed contours of the countryside were filled with a soft mist that gathered about its deep places like fallen clouds. The wind blew light and crisply cold, and as the colours of the new day deepened, the same panoramic view that had so obsessed Sir Joshua Cavendish three centuries earlier unfolded like a gift below them.

'All this is now mine,' Leonora declared with a different brand of passion in her voice. '*All this is mine.*'

'Aye, my covetous little witch, 'tis yours at last.'

She glanced up at Lukan's dark profile, now partially concealed as the wind whipped tendrils of his long black hair across his face. As she touched the key to their secret love-nest hanging like a trophy around his neck, the diamonds in her wedding ring were a cluster of glittering stars on her finger. Her heart was full, her body warm and satiated, and below her the whole world seemed to spread itself in mute supplication to her happiness. She drew his arms more tightly around her body, sighed contentedly and said again, 'Mine! And when Sir Oscar dies and Malcolm comes into his inheritance, I will be the Seventh Countess of Beresford. Then I will *truly* have it all.'

Even as she spoke the words she felt a stirring of shadows somewhere in the farthest reaches of her mind. A shiver of foreboding raced along her spine as an old gypsy woman's warning came back to her with unexpected clarity:

'*Beware the dream. Take care what you set your heart on, for it will surely be yours.*'

CHAPTER TWO

I

It was five o'clock and still she had not come. By now the sleepless Anabel was beside herself with anxiety. The strains and stresses of the long night hours had left her imagination totally ungoverned. She was almost convinced that a throng of scandalised aristocrats, led by Sir Malcolm and the Earl himself, was already storming through the house with murderous intent upon the lovers. She wrung her hands and cried out silently, 'For the love of God, Leonora, why are you doing this?'

Time after time she paced the draughty corridor on restless feet, muttering desperate, anxious little prayers into the darkness. A while ago she had heard the shriek of a night owl as it swooped in search of prey. It pierced her heart with dread. It was a cruel sound, perhaps of dead souls crying out in jealous rage against the living. She had covered her ears with her hands, wishing she had not heard it.

Somewhere in the house a loaded tray clattered to the floor, a woman shouted harshly and a door slammed. Although the brief commotion took place at a distance, it was loud enough to startle awake the timid Welsh maid who was supposedly keeping watch outside the sickroom door. With a cry she scrambled from her couch in the alcove, rubbing sleep from her eyes and muttering stammered excuses.

'P-p-please, ma'am ... beggin' yer pardon, ma'am ... I weren't sleeping ... not me, ma'am ... just resting me eyes is all ... honest to God, I weren't ...'

'Silence, girl!' Anabel hissed the words through clenched teeth, infuriated by the girl's casual disregard for the truth. 'May God forgive you for invoking His name in a lie!'

'Yes, ma'am. Sorry ma'am.'

'Go back to sleep. You're not needed yet.'

'Yes, ma'am.'

Anabel heard a series of rustling sounds as the maid scrambled back on to the couch and snuggled down beneath a heavy quilt.

'Beggin' yer pardon, ma'am ...?'

'Yes?' Anabel asked crossly. 'What is it?'

'Is Lady Alyce er ...?'

'What? Is Lady Alyce what?'

'Is she ... is she still ... I mean ... has something bad happened to the Countess?'

'Bad? Don't be foolish child,' Anabel snapped. 'Wherever did you get such an idea?'

'Dunno ma'am.'

'Go back to sleep girl. I'll wake you soon enough when you are needed.'

'Yes, ma'am.'

Anabel Corey closed her eyes and touched her fingertips to her forehead and chest, then to each shoulder in turn. Although this simple signing of the cross had never been part of her sketchy religious teaching, she hoped the ritual might add a little potency to the prayers she had been offering up throughout the night. Then she locked her fingers together and resumed her anxious pacing to and fro along the corridor.

19

Lady Alyce Cavendish, Countess of Beresford, had died of a seizure shortly before three o'clock the previous afternoon. Her death could not have been more untimely had the devil himself directed its course. She drew her last breath just a few short minutes before her eldest son Malcolm was due to marry Leonora Shelley, daughter of his father's cousin. By then Beresford Hall was bedecked with banners and huge displays of winter flowers, glowing lanterns, streamers and other such finery. The kitchens were a hive of frantic activity. In the Great Hall three hundred distinguished guests prepared to enjoy an event which, while opulent enough to satisfy even the most critical among them, was calculatedly modest in size. A clever balance had been achieved between the excellence of the occasion and the need to respect the sick. Amid the merriment it must not be forgotten that the Countess of Beresford lay stricken by a crippling illness.

It was Anabel who found the Countess and realised with dismay that she was dead. With a heavy heart she hurried to her young mistress's rooms to break the dreadful news, and there found Leonora already dressed in preparation for the long-awaited ceremony. She looked breathtakingly lovely. Her wedding gown was a fairy-tale thing of ivory silk overlaid with layers of shimmering rainbow gauze and decorated with hundreds of tiny, twinkling glass beads. Her mass of lustrous hair had been elaborately dressed with beaded net, fine pearls, miniature flowers and dried peacock feathers. Even her dainty gloves were trimmed with delicate silk blossoms and tiny mother-of-pearl buttons. Knowing that every eye would be upon her on this special day, she had been determined to make of herself a glittering spectacle never to be forgotten. She would be a vision in lustrous silver and glossy pearl, and when light from the famous Beresford chandeliers fell upon her as she moved about the Great Hall, a thousand sparkling beads would flash in her gown like so many tiny diamonds.

'It must be a gown fit for royalty,' she had insisted to the dressmaker who ran a team of skilful seamstresses. And so it was, a gown to make every man turn and stare and every woman want to weep with envy.

Nestling amid the delicate gauze flounces at her bosom, the legendary Cavendish Sapphire, that glowing gem now violet-blue, now aquamarine, now purple, echoed the elusive colouring of her eyes. Only the pale ivory orchid, a gift from Sir Oscar himself, waited to be pinned to her hair. The beautiful Leonora Shelley, society's latest darling and clever usurper of a dying woman's empire, was about to step from the brink of destitution to the lavish security of the Cavendish ranks. She was radiant, triumphant. Victory at last was hers. She had dreamed of being mistress of Beresford since she was ten years old. Like the Cavendish before her who had bent a fickle monarch to his will, Leonora had recognised her heart's desire at first sight and surmounted every obstacle to get it.

She received the news of the Countess's untimely death with a defiant toss of her head. She stamped her foot, flashed her sapphire eyes and obstinately refused to be robbed of a prize so dearly and so nearly won.

'I will not have it so,' she declared, her voice a hiss of indignation. 'I will not turn my wedding into a miserable funeral gathering for that hateful old woman.'

She had paced the room in distraction, the skirts of her gown swishing and rustling. She would not allow herself to be thwarted at this eleventh hour. If the marriage was postponed until a suitable period of mourning had elapsed, her chance of becoming mistress of Beresford might slip through her fingers and be forever lost. The wedding *must* take place as planned, while Malcolm Cavendish was totally besotted and the Earl so lowered by private grief that he lacked the heart to oppose the match. It must be now, before her consuming passion for the gypsy led her into ruin.

And so Leonora had insisted that Lady Beresford remain in the sickroom, her death unannounced, until after the wedding ceremony had taken place in the tiny private chapel set beneath the towering West Wing. Anabel was horrified by the very suggestion of such a plan. To turn a key on the dead, to leave a corpse unattended in a locked room, was for her a sacrilege, a violation of everything that was decent and honourable. And when Leonora, flushed and elated, emerged from the chapel to insist that the sickroom door remain locked until after the less formal celebrations, Anabel had found her every protest falling upon deaf ears. Hour after fearful hour had ticked by until the time of the evening ball with its grand gathering of dignitaries, its lords and ladies, its lofty politicians and fluttering socialites. The forty magnificent crystal chandeliers were ceremoniously ignited and the bride in her rainbow gown had dazzled the eye of every guest. She had been at her most beautiful when she took to the dance floor in the arms of her new husband's close companion, the handsome Lukan de Ville. Anabel had known the awful truth the moment she saw them together. It was in the look that passed between her mistress and the gypsy. The very worst was certain now to happen. The body of the Countess would be left to lie until morning while Leonora spent her wedding night in the arms of that black-eyed pagan. Anabel had seen the truth and shrunk from it with every fibre of her being, had seen it and yet been powerless to prevent that wicked, monumental act of folly taking place.

'Anabel? Anabel? Are you awake?'

The voice was husky in the darkness and accompanied by no more than the whisper of a fine satin shoe and a breath of distinctive perfume. Plunged back into the present with a start, Anabel whirled to confront her young mistress.

'Of course I'm awake,' she hissed. 'Did you think I could sleep this night? Did you think I could close my eyes for one moment upon your ... your *scandalous* behaviour?'

Leonora stepped forward to grasp Anabel in an affectionate embrace.

'Oh Anabel, dear Anabel, be happy for me,' she pleaded.

'Wickedness, sheer wickedness,' Anabel insisted, then sighed deeply as she returned Leonora's hug. 'Oh Leonora, you have taken everything you ever wanted. You have won the Earl's heir for your husband. You have made yourself mistress of Beresford Hall, just as you always vowed you would. Why must you take more? Why must you risk everything you have gained for that ... that gypsy?'

Leonora stiffened and removed herself from Anabel's embrace. When she spoke again her voice was low and had a warning edge to it.

'Anabel Corey, you have cared for me since I was a child and I will be forever in your debt for the love and loyalty you showed to mama. I will not forget how long and how well you have served us.'

'Then listen to what I say and . . .'

'Hear me out,' Leonora insisted. 'Despite our many differences I love you dearly, but there is one thing you must understand if we are to remain on good terms.'

'And that is?' Anabel asked coldly.

'Never question what lies between myself and Lukan de Ville.'

'But child, this madness will . . .'

'Never question it, Anabel.'

'For Heaven's sake, he is your husband's *servant*.'

Far from feeling insulted on her lover's behalf, Leonora laughed softly in the darkness. 'That is nonsense and you know it Anabel, and Malcolm himself would be the first to call it so. Servant indeed! That arrogant man a servant? Let me assure you that Lukan de Ville is not, nor ever shall be, *any man's creature*.'

Anabel wrung her hands together. 'He frightens me. I swear he's a devil sent to destroy you.'

'No, Anabel, I think not.' Leonora sighed and drew the older woman to the door of the apartments adjoining the sickroom. She shuddered as she recalled how much of the old gypsy woman's prophesy had already come to pass, and her voice was reduced to a troubled whisper when she added, 'I believe it is I who will one day destroy him.'

The sickroom was bitterly cold. A small casement window had blown open during the night to admit the chilly November wind and the fire had long since cooled and died. A draught from the wide chimney stirred the dead ashes, and the invading night air seemed to gather in wintry pools about the floor. Lady Alyce lay on her bed in the centre of the room between the open window and the empty grate. It was now 5.30 in the morning. She had been lying dead for fifteen hours.

The plump, fourteen-year-old maid supposedly caring for the invalid was once again sleeping soundly on her couch in the alcove along the corridor. She was a timid girl, chosen for this task because she was too terrified by the old lady's frozen features to venture too close to the sickbed. Leonora was cautious. She would have no witness to this night's events.

In her lengthy reign as mistress of Beresford, Countess Alyce had ruled her retinue of underlings with a dedicated absence of compassion. Her constant spites and vicious cruelties were inflicted upon all those who were unfortunate enough to come face to face with the real woman behind the carefully drawn facade of gentility. Such was the suffering she had wrought that none could be found to nurse her with a willing heart when the paralysis struck her down. Her every care and comfort had rested solely upon Leonora's goodwill and the large gratuities offered to reluctant servants in exchange for the very minimum of nursing care. The arrangement suited Leonora perfectly. The Countess could make no move without assistance, nor could she speak above a strangled whisper. For months she lay there, willing some curious visitor or servant to meet her furious gaze or lean close enough to hear her choking rage. They never did. Nobody questioned Leonora's sincerity and none suspected that behind the mask-like features and the guttural spasms of the throat lay a flood of accusations and complaints. Helpless in her paralysis but seeing, hearing and understanding everything, she watched Leonora turn the situation to her own advantage. And while everyone marvelled at the young woman's tireless and selfless devotion, Lady Alyce lay trapped in an isolation of her own making. All her life she had given nothing but pain to those around her and now she was to reap her just rewards. For want of a grain of sympathy she was forced to live out her final weeks in helpless frustration, nursed with feigned affection by the girl she had always despised as the witch-eyed daughter of her husband's whore.

Now Leonora wrinkled her nose as she drew the covers

back from the sickbed. She had little stomach for what she must do, but here was a task she dare not trust to others.

'Get a good fire started and the room warmed as quickly as possible,' she told Anabel. 'We must lay fresh covers on the bed and sprinkle the mattress with Tristram's water. And we must burn plenty of dried lavender and lilac flowers to sweeten the air in here.'

'I could fetch some of the perfume pouches from your closet and hang them about the room,' Anabel suggested, already raking cold cinders from the grate.

'An excellent idea. As many as you can find.'

'Shall I rouse the maid?'

'Not yet. Let her sleep until Sam Cooper returns from Oakwood Lodge with the doctor.'

'And the minister? Did you remember to send for the minister?'

Leonora nodded. 'I'm sure he will be here shortly. I doubt the good man will be sober, but the customary death-bed rituals will be duly observed, you may have no fear of that.'

'And not before time,' Anabel muttered, crossing herself once more and wondering when, if ever, she would see an end to all the dishonesty and deception.

'Why you should attach so much importance to such things is beyond me,' Leonora declared. 'To be honest, I find it more than a little ridiculous, especially in the present circumstances.' She glanced contemptuously at the bed. 'Who cares a fig for *her* immortal soul?'

'*Leonora!* That's a terrible thing to say.'

'It is the truth. Everyone knows the world is well rid of her. Your so-called Christian ritual will be a farce.'

'No matter, we must do what is decent,' Anabel said.

Leonora laughed harshly at that. 'And for the sake of decency we perform for the world like foolish players on a public stage.'

'Perhaps, but you know well enough that we are all obliged to keep up appearances.'

Leonora sighed, resigned despite her objections. 'You are right of course, we must, but has it never occurred to you that these *appearances* make hypocrites of us all?'

Anabel opened her mouth to comment but closed it firmly before the words were out. Instead she piled a stack of kindling in the grate and bent to place small pieces of coal around it. She was weary and had no wish to quarrel with her mistress. All she wanted was to have done with this night, to have done with it and never see its like again as long as she lived.

During the next half hour Leonora attended the Countess with meticulous care while Anabel brought fresh bedding and perfumes and raised a decent fire in the grate. Death had released the cruel grip of the seizure so that the face of Lady Alyce, so long contracted into a fearsome sneer, was now relaxed, almost peaceful. For the first time since August, when Leonora's bold intrusion at her garden party had induced the initial attack, the dignified features were relieved of their hideous grimace. The eyes, once bulging, were now gently closed, the hands liberated from their claw-like pose. The skilful application of a little powder and rouge brought an illusion of life back to the sallow skin. A layer of deep vermilion enlivened and fleshed out the lips, a few decorative combs and jewels softened the hairline and brightened the sombre countenance. For the final touch Leonora added a shawl of black and crimson Flemish lace, held across the still bosom by a brilliant ruby brooch. She draped the bed with a heavily fringed cover of gold and silver brocade while Anabel adorned the room with flowers and perfumed pouches from the adjoining apartments. Satisfied at last, she stood beside the deathbed looking down at the face of the woman who had stood so long between her dear mama and the happiness she might have known.

'Yes, you may have your day, Lady Alyce Cavendish,' she said quietly. 'You may have it, now that I have had mine.'

For a moment she stood without moving. Thoughts of her mother filled her mind. Francine Shelley had fought long and hard to keep her family together. She had struggled in vain to secure the futures of her children and deflect the consequences of her husband's insane extravagances. She had endured the hardships bravely and without complaint, yet in the end she had died despairing, her life snuffed out like a candle while she was barely into her fortieth year. Reduced to a state of poverty and disease, she was even to be abandoned in her darkest hour by Oscar Cavendish, the man she had loved for over two decades. Leonora closed her eyes on the memory. If only Francine had survived to see this wicked woman carried to her grave. If only she could have lived to see her daughter claim the very dream that she herself relinquished in the name of love so many years ago.

'You had Sir Oscar's name,' Leonora told the painted figure on the bed. 'You shared his home and bore his children, but you never touched his heart. It was mama who had his love. It was Francine Shelley, she *always* had his love.'

'Hush. Let it rest, child.'

Leonora started as Anabel laid a restraining hand on her arm. She pulled herself together with an effort, drawing her velvet cloak around her body to conceal the thin shift beneath.

'Poor mama. How she suffered . . .'

'But now it's over,' Anabel said firmly, even as Leonora's sudden grief plucked at the wounds in her own heart. 'We must let her rest in peace. We must let them *both* rest in peace.'

'Both?'

'Yes, my dear, both.'

'Equal in death?'

'And in the sight of God.'

'What rubbish,' Leonora said bitterly. 'Mama had more compassion for the beasts of the field than this woman ever showed for her fellow human beings. How can they possibly be equal in the sight of God?'

'He has His reasons.'

'Is He blind then? Can He not see what lies between the sinner and the saint?'

'Hush child, those are blasphemous words.'

'And what of the Countess? It seems to me her whole life was a blasphemy.'

'Let it lie,' Anabel urged. 'Don't torture yourself with regrets, child.'

27

Leonora's shoulders rose and fell in a deep sigh. 'I sometimes think more harm is done in the name of love than ever
could be inflicted in hatred. Oh, Anabel, why does love always
seem to come in equal measures of joy and pain?'

'Because all things have a price, Leonora. Nothing in life is
free. You more than anyone should have learned the truth of
that.'

Leonora nodded and issued a long, unhappy sigh. 'I have
achieved so much,' she whispered. 'I have been granted everything I ever wanted at the cost of everything I ever loved.
Mama is dead, my elder brothers have been forced to flee their
father's army of creditors, and my twin, my poor dear
Joseph . . .'

'Hush child! And for Heaven's sake stand your ground. Be
as strong now as ever you were forced to be in the past. We are
all of us lost if you should stumble now.'

Leonora turned her head to look back at Anabel with a
bleak expression on her lovely face. It seemed that all the pains
and losses of the last few months had suddenly risen up to cast
a dark shadow over her happiness. The anguish in her eyes
would have frightened Anabel were she not so certain of the
unquenchable courage with which this spirited young woman
was blessed. Leonora was as brave as she was beautiful. She
had a will of iron and a heart that could be moved from sentimentality to icy ruthlessness in a flash of her turquoise eyes.
She was a determined woman born into a world designed
specifically by men for the enjoyment and privilege of their
own sex, and so her individuality and her often formidable
strength of character were ever a source of anxiety to those
who loved her. Had she been born a man, none would have
questioned her arrogance or dared begrudge her one scrap of
the happiness she had stolen for herself.

The fortitude that had sustained her this far now lifted
Leonora's head and brought her body proudly erect. She
flashed Anabel a brief but brave smile, turned from the bed
and strode towards the door.

'Send word to me when the doctor arrives,' she instructed.
'Offer him refreshment and bid him wait for me here. He is

28

not to examine the Countess unless I am present, and you must be very careful what you say to him. As far as you are aware, Lady Alyce has suffered a fatal seizure and I have gone to break the sad news to my husband. The rousing of the rest of the household is to be left to the Earl's discretion.'

In the adjoining room she paused just long enough to conceal her glittering wedding gown behind the dark draperies protecting the contents of a deep clothes closet. Then she gathered her cloak about her body and stepped into the dimly lit corridor, there to move like a swift and silent shadow towards the bridal chamber in the east wing.

II

Sir Malcolm Cavendish was sprawled across the big bed with his face pressed into a mound of soft white pillows. His left arm was bent at an awkward angle and pinned beneath his body, his right hung over the edge of the mattress so that the backs of his fingers rested in the thick pile of a bedside rug. He was naked save for a shirt of fine white linen and his long, muscular legs had become entangled in the sheets while he slept. He was still fast asleep, his lips parted, his breathing hoarse in the otherwise quiet room.

Leonora entered without a sound and tiptoed to the bed to look down at her husband of but a few hours. His hair had fallen across his face in untidy strands. It was a rich chestnut brown in colour now that last summer's sun-bleached streaks of blond had faded. A layer of stubble coarsened the skin of his cheeks and lay dark across his upper lip. His was a fine face, not startlingly attractive like that of Lukan de Ville, but very handsome none the less. It was the face of a Cavendish, strong and evenly shaped, with a long, straight nose adding much to its aristocratic profile. That he loved her and trusted her implicitly she had no doubt, and in a gentle, sisterly way she loved him too. She felt a surge of pity and hated herself for it. Pity was a dangerous sentiment. It could lead her to underestimate the man, to forget that he too was a Cavendish with a dark and potentially violent side to his nature.

'I swear I will do everything in my power to make you happy,' she vowed, brushing her fingertips across his brow. 'And I will love you as much as I am able. I will Malcolm, I really will.'

She knew she would not regret her marriage to this man. As his wife she would be mistress of Beresford with private apartments of her choosing, a carriage and horses for her exclusive use, and as many servants and rooms as she required. She would have such gowns and jewels as she had hardly dared dream of, a personal fortune, a title, status, *power*. And she would have Lukan. *She would have Lukan.*

Smiling a little, she flung off her velvet cloak before setting her attention to more important tasks. She retrieved a covered wine goblet from the table close to the bed and poured what remained of its contents into an extravagantly decorated plant container standing in a corner of the room. Then she cleaned the inside of the goblet with a napkin, added a little fresh port which she swished around and poured away, then added more and sniffed it carefully. Only then did she return it to its original place, satisfied that no tell-tale traces of hemlock and essence of opium remained.

'Now for the *virgin's water*,' she muttered as she hurried into the dressing room. Once there she unfastened her pretty night shift and allowed it to fall to the floor in a heap. She pulled a fresh shift of embroidered silk from a drawer and shivered briefly as it slid over her naked body. Then she reached to one of the back corners of the same drawer and pulled out a small, unmarked bottle. This she uncorked and shook gently until a small amount of its contents spilled in deep pink stains on the fallen shift. She smiled at the result, reminding herself that many a marriage had stumbled at the first hurdle for want of a little foresight and a few drops of port wine and cochineal.

Returning to the main room, she shook the bottle over a section of the bed's underlinen and drew a heavier cover over the stain. By her calculations the young doctor from Oxford would soon be arriving at the house, roused from his bed by Sam Cooper. As one of the lesser guests he had been invited to stay over at the Earl's favourite lodge some two miles or so from the house. Leonora had chosen him because she could rely on his eagerness to please Sir Oscar and his dependence upon the goodwill of the family. Her summons would bring him here without delay, but there was yet time to brush her hair and braid it neatly over one shoulder, then pull on a robe of dove-grey silk trimmed with palest sable. She used a little charcoal to outline her eyes and a tiny amount of oil to add lustre to the dark lashes. A fine powder, cleverly applied, disguised the deep flush that had given her cheeks their pretty, tell-tale glow. She was satisfied that the unusual brightness of her eyes would be interpreted as unshed tears for the loss of the Countess.

Before waking Malcolm to prepare him for the news of his mother's death, she poured a large measure of pleasantly scented liquid into a clean glass. This was an old country remedy to comfort the head and brain, a mixture of wood-sage, rosemary and borage infused for several days in a good canary wine, to be sipped as often as the sufferer desired.

'Malcolm. Wake up, Malcolm.'

He stirred in his sleep, muttered something that might have been her name, then buried his face still deeper in the pillows and lay quite still. Leonora placed a hand on his shoulder and shook him firmly.

'Wake up, Malcolm. Stir yourself.'

'Huh? What is it? Leonora? Oh, my head.' He spoke into the pillows, his voice thick with sleep. 'What time is it?'

'Almost dawn,' she told him. 'Please make an effort to stir yourself, my dear. I have here a drink to ease the pains in your head.'

Malcolm struggled on to his back, his eyes still tightly closed and both hands pressed to his forehead. He groaned loudly and complained, 'By the gods, Leonora, I feel wretched.'

She smiled and adopted a stern expression. 'As well you might sir. You drank far too much brandy and mulled wine,

31

and I did warn you not to finish the *entire* bottle of Madeira.'

He hauled himself into a sitting position, scowling deeply. 'What? I drank a whole bottle of Madeira?'

'Yes, my dear.'

'After brandy and mulled wine?'

She nodded. 'I do believe you drank a hearty toast to every member of the Cavendish family born during the last 350 years.'

'I did?' He shook his head, winced and groaned again. 'I must have been insane. I never drink to excess.'

'It *was* rather a special occasion,' she reminded him.

'Yes, but to drink like that on our wedding night ... I must have been dead drunk when I ... when we ...' At that moment he caught sight of the stained area of sheet uncovered by his movements. He looked up at her with an expression of remorse in his deep blue eyes. 'Oh, Leonora, can you ever forgive me?'

'Please don't apologise,' she reassured him.

'But to drink so heavily and then ... Oh, my dear, you must think me a brute, a boorish drunken brute.'

Leonora lowered her eyes modestly and shook her head.

'Forgive me?' he asked again, touching her hand.

She nodded, still avoiding his gaze. This was the measure of Malcolm Cavendish, that he should exhibit such genuine concern for her feelings. Her own father had inflicted his lusts upon a fragile wife with never the smallest care for anything beyond his own gratification, but this gentle man would never allow himself to sink to such depravity. He was too good to treat his wife as an inferior partner in the marriage bed, a mere vassal to be used or ill-used according to his carnal appetites.

'I'll try to make you happy,' she said sincerely, repeating the words of the vow she had made while he slept. She wished with all her heart that she could promise instead to give him the devotion and fidelity he deserved.

'I know you will,' he replied, 'And as my lady you will want for nothing.'

'You and your father have already given me so much. Never did I anticipate such generosity.'

32

'And all this is just the beginning, Leonora. I hope you may always have what your heart desires.'

'I hope so too.' She smiled and guided the glass of sage wine to his lips. She waited until he had finished drinking and set aside his glass before taking his hands in hers and looking deeply into his eyes.

'Malcolm my dear, there is no easy way for me to say this. There is news from the sickroom. Bad news, I fear.'

'My mother is worse?'

'I'm sorry.'

'Another seizure?'

Leonora nodded her head. 'I have sent to Oakwood Lodge for your friend, the young doctor from Oxford. I expect him very soon, but I doubt he can do any more than confirm what we already know.'

He paled. 'You mean . . .?'

She squeezed his fingers. 'Yes Malcolm. She died an hour ago.'

'Oh *hell*!'

'Reverend Thorpe is with her at the moment because the servants have been unable to locate Reverend Evans. She was not alone when it happened. I was with her during her last hours.'

'You were there in the night?'

'I was. She needed company. I could not refuse her even on our wedding night.'

'I should have been there too. It's unforgivable that you were left to cope alone.'

'I did try several times to wake you,' she told him. 'I'm afraid you were impossible to rouse.'

'But you could have asked Hammond to help you.'

'We gave him the night off, remember?'

He groaned and raked his fingers through his hair in a distracted gesture that touched Leonora's heart with sympathy. It had not been part of her plan to add guilt to his grief. She was simply holding fast to her story so that no part of it should fail under scrutiny. The facts of his mother's death must never be allowed to come to light.

'You must not blame yourself for being absent,' she insisted. 'You know how withdrawn she had become in her illness. She refused to see anyone, and in the end I believe she was too ill to recognise even you, Malcolm. The final seizure came so swiftly I doubt she was aware of it. She went with neither protest nor distress, you can be sure of that.'

He nodded. 'And we have you to thank for that. Bless you.'

'I did what I could. She had been kind to me.'

'Perhaps, but in these last months you have repaid her many times over for any kindness of hers.'

Leonora smiled her slow, mysterious smile. 'As God is my judge, I gave the lady no more than she deserved.'

Malcolm drew her into his arms and held her there. He was saddened by his mother's death but Leonora knew he would not weep. Lady Alyce had been a distant and indifferent mother. What little affection she had to offer had always gone to Horace, and in his absence even that had turned to hatred. Few tears of honest grief were likely to be shed on her account.

With her cheek resting against Malcolm's chest Leonora recalled how only yesterday she had forced the old lady to hear a long-concealed truth.

'Two sons I have stolen from you,' she told her. 'One by deceit and now another by marriage.'

The woman's eyes had widened at that, her throat making spasms of attempted speech.

'An outraged young girl put her pen to two anonymous letters and you, dear lady, believed the worst of him. I knew your son to be as odious and vindictive as yourself, but guilty of unnatural practices? No lady, I think not.'

Again the choking sounds as Lady Alyce tried to give voice to her protestations.

Leonora had pulled no punches. 'You pampered him, you encouraged the very worst of his many vices, but sodomy was the one crime you could never forgive. It is a hanging offence and the scandal of it would have destroyed you. So you disowned and disinherited him. He was your favourite and you cut him off, cast him adrift on foreign soil like a despised outcast. And for what? For sodomy? Oh no, he was never

34

guilty of that, Lady Alyce. That was pure and wicked invention on my part. I wrote those letters. I created the void between you and your son, and I did it because I hated both you and him.' At that point she had paused to wipe the dribbled saliva from the Countess's chin before adding, 'My family has suffered greatly at your hands, but when I am wed to Malcolm I will consider any debt you owe us well and truly paid.'

Now Leonora lifted her head and looked into her husband's troubled face. Her conscience was clear where Alyce Cavendish was concerned. She touched his cheek and smiled and said again, 'Believe me, my dear, I gave the lady no more than she deserved.'

CHAPTER THREE

F or a long time Lukan de Ville, keeper of the Earl's wood-
lands and forests, stood alone at the tower's summit,
staring grim-faced into the distance. His eyes were narrowed
against a wind that whipped his long hair about his face
and plucked at the edges of his heavy cloak. He gripped the
rough stone parapet so tightly that his knuckles became bloodless and the sinews were raised like bands of steel along his
powerful forearms. A night that had seemed endless in its
delights had now vanished with cruel swiftness. What had
represented an eternity of pleasure only a few hours ago might
now have been tasted and spent in the winking of an eye.
Leonora was gone and he could not find it in his heart to
welcome this new day; not while her perfume lingered in his
nostrils and the heat of their shared passion still warmed his
blood. She had left his arms for her husband's bed, for
Malcolm's bed. She had offered Lukan paradise with one
hand and hell with the other and he, caught in a trap from

which he could not hope to escape, must teach himself to live in peace with both. It was a trap of her own forging. Even before she pledged herself in passion to him, the woman he adored beyond reason had contracted herself in law to the man he revered above all others.

'Aye, lady, and which one of us do you betray this night, the man you married or the man you love?' He ground the question through clenched teeth and the words were snatched up and carried away by the wind.

'She betrays us both,' he shouted after them, 'and God knows if she were anyone but Lia I would kill her for it.'

With a final grunt of frustration he turned and strode to that part of the ancient wall which enclosed the Monks' Stair, the only remaining access to the uppermost sections of the tower. He stepped sideways into the concealed opening and descended rapidly, his steps sure and confident on the roughly hewn treads. In the darkness his palms pressed outwards against walls of pale Cotswold stone set a mere chimney's width apart. Here and there were tiny apertures, each no more than a slit between the stones or a jagged hole carved in antiquity. Like poor men's windows they permitted a sliver of light and a breath of morning air to penetrate the gloom. The pillar around which the steps turned so tightly was smooth and rounded, as much by the hands of holy men as by the tools of stonemasons. The treads were worn and treacherously narrow at the newel's edge. As he descended he thought of those long-dead monks who had used that route to reach the tower's summit, moving like hooded shadows across angled rooftops, using a whole chain of lost pathways and priests' holes to reach the farthest corners of the abbey.

Eventually his probing fingers found a larger opening set at such an angle that it was unlikely to be discovered by mere accident. Even a lamp would cast its light in such a way that the hole was overlooked, or judged to be no more than a shadow-fall against the paler stones. Lukan moved sideways as if to step into the air, ducked his head and was inside the newly renovated apartments over the ancient gatehouse. Here a gloomy stone antechamber gave way to what was once the abbot's study, a room now claimed by Leonora as her own. He paused, drew in a deep breath and expelled air from his lungs in a long sigh. This was where they had spent the night together, where she had dropped her wedding gown in a shimmering heap beside the great four-poster bed and come to him naked. He closed his eyes and sucked in a long, deep breath as thoughts of her stirred the smouldering embers of his passion. As he exhaled he breathed her name, imagining her nakedness.

'Lia ... Lia ...'

He left the bedchamber by its only exit, the same low aperture by which he had entered, dropped downwards in the gloom and paused again at a similar opening. This was the bedroom of Leonora's private apartments, similar in style and decor to the one laid out above it. On the far side of the apartments the reinstated main staircase spiralled less severely down to ground level, its upper flights still sealed as they had been since the tragic fire of 1640. Lukan knew the story well. A spilled oil lamp in the gatehouse kitchens ignited a pile of kindling logs. Some say it was done by a house dog left untethered, others that it was the work of a vengeful or envious hand. Whatever its cause, the fire had quickly spread until it was pulled by up-draughts into the enclosed staircase. Feeding on carved wooden panels and mouldings, oil paintings, stair rugs and wall hangings, it became an inferno. Sir Robert Cavendish, Second Earl of Beresford, had struggled heroically to reach his wife and crippled daughter, both trapped in their upper rooms. He was struck down when several roof supports collapsed, and would have died there but for the courage of his eldest son. James battled through the heat and smoke to find his injured father, dragged him free and carried him to safety on his back. Then he too was lost in a last desperate attempt to rescue his wife and infant sons. Along with four brave manservants and five young maids, an entire family perished that night, robbing Sir Robert of everything that was dear to his heart. The loss left him so broken in mind and body that, a whole year after the tragedy, he struggled to the top of the ruined tower and hurled himself to his death. Grief and pain had wrecked his spirit, but it was the burden of his guilt that finally destroyed him. He had been personally responsible for closing the hazardous Monks' Stair when the new staircase was installed. He had paid the masons well to seal up the holes and passageways where a child might wander and come to harm. How could he live with the knowledge that had he not done so, had the ancient priests' holes and steps remained accessible, every member of his family and staff might have been spared?

Lukan scowled grimly in the darkness. Here was another example of the way the gods made sport of proud men. The family line continued through Sir Robert's youngest son, the notorious Percy, who had languished in the arms of a local whore while better men than he had perished in the blaze. He withdrew from between the legs of a whore to become the worst Earl of them all, the man who managed to bring the prosperous Earldom of Beresford to the very brink of ruin. The fortunes of this family were rooted in tragedy and nurtured on the extremes, from best to worst, to be found in a man's character. Of all the things that marked him out as special to his breed, this was perhaps the key to the *true* Cavendish, that he could trace his history through a quagmire of death and intrigue, of hatred, loyalty and grand passion, all the way back to its bloody beginnings.

Lukan left Leonora's rooms and continued downward to ground level. Here the old steps ended in a tiny room that smelled of age and dust and damp earth. In the walls ahead of him and to his left were two large rectangles of stone marking the handiwork of those masons employed by Robert Cavendish. One had given the monks access to the underground chapel, the other was thought to have been the mouth of a tunnel which once led under the old gatehouse and its cobbled courtyard to the main buildings beyond.

In the wall to his right was the low, arched doorway through which he had entered the tower for his tryst with Leonora. He used the key she had given him, turning it with surprising ease in a lock as old as the tower itself. The door was so short that he had to bend almost double in order to pass through, and so heavy that it swung on its newly-oiled hinges to slam with a clang behind him. It had the sound of a prison door, solid within the old stones. It reminded him of his sister's words, and of the curse supposedly brought upon him by the ill-starred timing of his birth.

'You are a chime-child, Lukan,' Rebecca so often reminded him. 'Born on a Friday, you were, just as the church bells chimed the noon hour. 'Tis a curse. It means you are destined to be hanged or murdered.'

'Foolish superstition,' he whispered, shaking his head. Only half of him was gypsy. His other half dismissed old lore as child's talk.

He had stepped into the dense shadows ever present at the secluded western end of the house. Here the embankment loomed higher than the head of a mounted man. It leaned towards the tower wall, a great mass of earth restrained by tree roots and half-buried boulders. It hid from view the family crypt on its far side, and it created a deep and narrow channel between its near edge and the west wall of the house. This tunnel-like pathway was still known as Monks' Walk and was reputed to be haunted. It was an eerie place overhung with the whispering, restless branches of trees whose roots protruded from the embankment like sinister pale tentacles. Barely wide enough to accommodate a light-weight gig, it was unevenly enclosed and set with such rogue roots as would trip man or horse in the darkness. Monks' Walk stretched as far as the house was deep, ending in a jungle of thick bramble and over-grown ironwork that long ago had led pious holy men to the sepulchre by way of secluded gardens and shaded walkways. Amongst the wealth of superstition attached to Beresford Hall were tales of ghostly apparitions haunting the Old Walk, the souls of butchered monks and violated nuns still restless after three long centuries.

Twin shadows stirred in the darkness and two cold, damp noses nuzzled Lukan's hands in silent greeting.

'Gillan,' he whispered. 'Garvey.'

The ever-patient wolfhounds had waited through the night for their master to return, lying like quiet sentries on either

40

side of the door. They had been bred for their height and speed as well as for their hunting skills, and for the quick intelligence that made them far superior to other dogs. Lukan had done the rest by skilful training, and he had the satisfaction of knowing that these tall, calm, obedient creatures were priceless. He patted both coarse-haired heads in turn, tugged at the warm ears with affectionate fingers. Then hounds and man suddenly tensed, alerted by sounds coming from the area between the terraced gardens and the stables. Lukan covered the short distance between the Monks' Door and the angle of the West Wing in a few strides. He stopped at the corner and peered into the darkness through narrowed eyes. He was a man of the forest. His senses were keen and his sharp black eyes were practised in the art of spotting a moving shape or separating a single shadow from its neighbours. Now he could make out a figure moving across the lower lawn, weaving in and out of flower beds and skirting clumsily around islands of tall rose bushes. It was a man blinded by the deceptive play of light on shadow created by the fading night, a man uncertain of his steps in Beresford's unlit open spaces. Lukan glanced to his left where, beyond the darker bulk of the gatehouse, chinks of light showed in several windows to indicate that parts of the household were already up and about. The great house was stirring itself for another day, but the figure making its way across the gardens was not a part of that activity. Whoever the man was, he had no business to be here on the western terraces. And if he was an intruder with villainy in mind, his target was obviously the Earl's stables.

With the wolfhounds padding silently at his heels, Lukan moved away from the tower wall and hurried down the terraced slopes toward the lower orchards. By making a wide detour to avoid crossing open ground, he arrived unseen at the door of the main stable just as the man came out again. He was a young man, broadly built and modestly dressed. He walked backwards towards the stable door, coaxing a reluctant chestnut mare, newly saddled and bridled, from her stall. As Lukan appeared in the open doorway the man bumped into him and jumped sideways with a cry of alarm, '*Holy Mother of God!*'

The mare rolled her eyes and whinnied softly. With one hand the man clutched at her reins, with the other he snatched a knife from his belt. The small oil lamp swinging to and fro at ceiling level glinted on the long blade and illuminated his startled features. Lukan saw a clean-shaven face, youthfully freckled, topped by a thatch of dark ginger hair that grew unchecked in all directions at once. Round blue eyes stared at the silhouette now framed in the stable doorway. Fright, not boldness, forced him to stand his ground. The hand clutching the knife was trembling too much to be of any real use to its owner.

'Who's there? Is that you, Mr de Ville?'

'Aye, Sam Cooper.'

'Lord 'elp us, sir.' The young man's shoulders sagged with relief. 'I didn't hear you come up.'

'It was not my intention to be heard,' Lukan told him.

'You scared the life clear out of me.'

'So it would seem.'

Lukan stood with his hands on his hips, waiting to hear what the other had to say about his presence in the Earl's stable with a saddled horse in tow. Sam Cooper eyed him anxiously. He still had the advantage. He was armed and would not be shifted from his course. Even as he bobbed his head respectfully, his shoulders squared and he gave no sign that he intended to relinquish his weapon. He was new to Beresford. He had not yet learned to trust this man of the forest who could move without making a sound and whose black-as-night eyes seemed to stare right into a person's soul.

Lukan smiled in the darkness. He recalled how bravely this same young man had stood his ground on the Drive of Oaks a few short weeks ago. Thinking to protect his mistress from a wandering vagabond, he had raised his whip to the big gypsy and vowed to thrash him soundly unless he stepped aside and allowed the carriage to continue on its way. He was a good lad, strong and well-grown for his tender years and as loyal a servant as Leonora could hope to find. He had come to the family's London home as a groom hired by Leonora's father, and he had proved his worth a dozen times since then. It was much to his credit that he remained steadfast to his young mistress throughout the rapid collapse of her family's fortunes. He had served her loyally, often without hope of payment, through long weeks of hardship and heartache.

'I mean you no harm, Sam Cooper. Put up the knife.'

The voice was low and completely without edge. There was menace enough in this quiet man without the need for heavier tones.

The groom licked the dryness from his lips and cautiously replaced the knife in his belt. Then he drew more firmly on the reins of the chestnut, cleared his throat and said, 'I'll be on my way, then.'

'Will you now?'

Cooper cleared his throat again. 'Aye, if you'll be so kind as to step aside, Mr de Ville.'

'Where are you going, lad?'

'Oakwood Lodge, sir.'

'Surely not on that mare?'

'Aye,' Cooper said again, glancing from man to beast with a puzzled expression on his face. 'She's mine, sir. My own horse she is, given me by Miss Leonora ... er, by Her Ladyship, that is.'

'And she's a fine mare, I'll grant you that, but hardly fit for night-time riding. It's still as dark as pitch out there.'

'Sir?'

'Too dark to travel,' Lukan said. 'You'll not be setting out before full light?'

'Reckon I can't wait until daylight, sir. I got business at the Lodge, urgent business.'

Lukan glanced toward the east, where a pale band of light was struggling to push back a sky that was heavy with cloud and still dotted here and there with stars. An inexperienced mount, inexpertly handled, would endanger a rider's life in such uncertain light.

'Then at least hold off another hour,' he suggested.

Cooper shook his head. 'I can't do that, sir.'

'Then you are either an obstinate fool or a much braver man than I, Sam Cooper,' Lukan observed. 'I'd not try to reach Oakwood in bad light on that animal.'

'Needs must,' the young man insisted. 'It's the Countess, you see, Mr de Ville. She's been taken ill with another of them seizures and Miss Leonora says I'm to bring back the visiting doctor without delay. Urgent, she called it, *urgent*.'

'In that case I must go in your place,' Lukan decided. 'I will take the swifter route through the forest and . . .'

'No sir, I mean, you can't do it, sir.' Cooper was upset by the suggestion that another man should seek to shoulder his given responsibility. He shook his tangle of ginger hair. His pride and reputation were at stake. 'Beggin' your pardon, sir, but 'tis my own task, given me in person by the mistress 'erself.'

'And I am about to relieve you of it.'

Lukan tilted his head, almost smiling. 'You doubt it?'

'No sir.' Cooper tightened his grip on the mare's reins as she sidestepped, wary of de Ville's hounds. 'I'll not be passing on my given duties to another, thanking you kindly for the offer, sir.'

'But the Lodge is a good two miles away,' Lukan reminded him. 'How do you plan to find your way there in the dark?'

'By following the road, sir. Aye, that's what I'll do, I'll follow the road.'

'You'll be fortunate if your mount doesn't take fright and toss you in a ditch at the first rustle or cry of a night animal.' Lukan reached out to stroke the horse's face. 'She's highly strung. She'll bolt if an owl hoots or if a leaf slips underfoot. Think again, lad. You'll not make Oakwood on this animal.'

Once again Sam Cooper looked from the man's rugged profile to the mare's nervous eyes and twitching ears. He shifted his weight from one foot to the other. He was a perfect example of his class, unused to making decisions and oafishly uneasy in the company of his betters. Lukan might have shown his amusement but for the other's fierce pride and rigid loyalty to Leonora. Instead he strode into the stable and set about transferring the saddle from the chestnut mare to the sable.

'But Mr de Ville . . .?'

'Don't argue, lad,' Lukan warned. 'I too have my reputation to consider. I'll not be held accountable should you come to harm for want of a decent mount. You'll be safe with the sable. Give her a steady rein and she'll get you to Oakwood Lodge without mishap. When she stops at the crossroads, ease her towards the right-hand fork and she'll carry you right to the gates of the Lodge. She knows the way well enough. There's nothing out there can spook this brave old lady.'

'But she's Sir Malcolm's horse,' Cooper protested.

'Aye, one of the many.'

The youngster shook his untidy head. 'Nay, I'd best not take her, sir. I couldn't just ride off on one of Sir Malcolm's own horses without so much as a by your leave or ...'

'Don't argue, lad.' Lukan checked the straps on the saddle and reached a bridle from one of the stable hooks. 'I'm giving you leave to take her.'

'I don't know as I should, Mr de Ville.'

'Look, I'm giving you the use of a decent mount. Do you question my authority to do that?'

'No, sir.' Sam Cooper shook his head vigorously and repeated in apologetic tones, 'No, sir, it's not that, sir.'

'Then hold your tongue, lad.' He led the sable outside and handed over the reins. 'Now be mindful of my instructions. Just a steady rein and don't try to race her. Let her set her own pace. It should be full daylight and safer travelling by the time you're ready to start back with the doctor. You're a brave lad, Sam Cooper.'

'Beggin' your pardon, sir, but Miss Leonora says I'm not to be called a lad no more. I be nineteen now and bigger and stronger than most at my age.' He swung himself into the saddle and turned his head to look down at the older man with an air of studied confidence. 'I be a grown man now, Mr de Ville.'

Lukan nodded and offered his hand. He was pleasantly surprised by the strength of the youngster's grip.

'A grown man and a brave one,' he conceded solemnly.

'Thank you, sir.'

Lukan turned away quickly and slapped the mare's flanks to speed her on her way. Amid the creaking of horse-leathers

45

and the crunch of hooves on the cinder path, Sam Cooper did not hear the low, husky chuckle of laughter following in his wake.

As the dark horse and its rider moved out of sight, Lukan returned to the stables, unhooked the oil lamp and began to make a search of the stalls. He made soft clucking sounds with his tongue and spoke gently to the horses as he moved in and out of their stalls. He knew each animal by name and temperament, and he derived much satisfaction from their calm and trusting response to his presence. Only the big, half-wild grey refused to submit in full to his gentle domination. Starlight Warrior was more spirited than any stallion out of the Cavendish stables. He would be mastered but never tamed, so that every confrontation between man and beast became a battle of wits and a test of strength and skill. Although of uncertain temperament, the stallion was one of the Earl's finest racers. And now it belonged to Lukan. Malcolm had given it to him for plucking Leonora from its path when it bolted at the Midsummer Fair. It was a fine gift indeed, and the unpredictable nature of the beast was in this case ideally suited to the mercurial spirit of its new master.

Now Lukan moved lightly from stall to stall, still soothing the animals with his voice as he deliberately scattered the looser piles of straw with his feet. As he had anticipated, his search revealed the stable boy curled up in the warm straw of one of the farthest stalls, fast asleep. It was the same boy he had seen working with the dairy cows the previous day. He had encountered him again at the wedding celebrations, fetching and carrying for the guests until late in the evening when most of them were in bed. He nudged sharply at the sleeping form with his boot and the lad sprang to his feet, groggy with sleep and clearly sick with fear. He gaped up at Lukan, then cast his glance beyond him, expecting to see his master. Exhaustion had left dark rings below his eyes. He looked thin and poorly nourished. The present Master of the Earl's Horse was a hard man. He drove the children in his employ as harshly as he drove the men.

'What's your name, lad?' Lukan demanded.

'Charlie, sir. Charlie Pickles.'

'And how old are you?'

'How old?' The lad puckered his brows together over the bridge of his nose and considered the question. 'Dunno to be sure, sir. 'appen ten or eleven year, I reckon.'

'Well, Charlie Pickles, you'll be whipped like a cur if your master returns to find you sleeping away your stable watch.'

'Yes, sir.' The boy twisted a misshapen felt hat in his fingers. The boots he wore were several sizes too large for his feet and had rubbed crimson patches around his skinny ankles. There were so many stray bits of straw clinging to his shabby clothes that he looked more like a scarecrow than an employee of the Big House. Watching him, Lukan felt the tension relax from his own features. Compassion made a softness in his eyes.

'It's a hard world, Charlie Pickles.'

'What's that sir? Oh, er ... yes, sir, I reckon it must be if you say so, sir.'

'Do you know who I am?'

'Oh yes, sir. You're that Mr Devil from the forest yonder.'

'*De Ville*,' Lukan corrected sharply. 'The name is Lukan de Ville.'

The boy nodded his head frantically. Fearing the consequences of his error, he gripped his hat more tightly and hunched his shoulders as if bracing his skinny body for a rain of blows. 'Beg pardon, sir,' he muttered in a small voice. 'Didn't mean no harm, sir.'

'Relax, boy. You have no reason to fear me. Never in my life have I raised my hand to a child.'

The boy looked incredulous.

'What sir? *Never* sir?'

'Never,' Lukan said emphatically.

Charlie Pickles blinked his eyes several times, his mouth gaping open. Then his thin body relaxed and the merest hint of a smile touched the corners of his mouth.

'What, not ever? Not even once?'

'Not even once.' Lukan grinned and ruffled the untidy mop of hair. 'When your master gets back, tell him I sent the sable

47

mare to Oakwood Lodge on an urgent errand for Sir Malcolm.'

'Yes, sir.'

'And you'd best stay awake for the rest of your watch.'

'Yes, sir.'

The skinny little lad was staring up at him through frightened eyes, and it suddenly occurred to Lukan that he must seem like a giant by comparison. In his voluminous dark cloak and with his long black hair hanging loose about his shoulders, he surely resembled some fearsome creature of the night to a nervous country child freshly plucked from sleep. He offered the lad a grim smile, then turned and strode toward the stable door, angered by the presence of that exhausted little boy where he should have found the Master of the Horse.

In the chill of that first November morning he turned his steps toward the forest. The wolfhounds paced him, springing along beside him with that graceful lope peculiar to their breed. They were watchful and alert, ears dropped, senses straining for the whispered word, the small movement of the hand, the sudden command that might send them racing off over meadow or hill.

Lukan breathed deeply through his nostrils, sucking the scents of earth and forest into his lungs and expelling them, warmed and sifted, back into the air. He could feel an easing of the jealousy that had set its cutting edge into his heart the instant he and Leonora parted. She had not, after all, gone to Malcolm's bed to offer herself to him as his willing and dutiful young bride. Instead she must have gone directly to the sickroom and there found the ailing Countess in need of a doctor. Once again the consummation of the marriage would have to be postponed. Lukan would not end this night of bliss in bitter imaginings, torn between love and jealousy. There would be no nuptial delights for Malcolm to enjoy while his closest friend, the guilty one, crept away like a thief in the night.

'I have no reason to hate you, my friend,' he said, thinking of Malcolm still married in name only. 'Not today at least. Not today.'

He began to grin as he strode across the lower meadow. He

wanted to yell her name out loud, to have it carried on the wind to every corner of the earth so that no man would doubt his joy of her. His stride increased in pace to a canter, and from there to a sprint that sent the hounds darting on ahead like slender grey shadows scudding across the grass. Lukan followed, running for home like a man with demons snapping at his heels, sucking at life itself with every breath. As the familiar trees of the forest's edge loomed closer he pushed himself harder, aiming for his limit, feeling the big muscles straining in his thighs and the powerful beat of his heart filling his chest as he ran. With a cry of elation he crashed through the trees and was immediately enveloped by the eerie stillness of the forest. He dropped into a low squat, clenched his hands into fists, threw back his head and roared at the top of his voice, '*Lia!*'

The sound echoed and bounced and danced its way among the trees. Late-returning night animals scuttled indoors in alarm while early risers, their eyes and ears not yet adjusted to the dark morning, rushed for the nearest cover. With a final sigh the sound was gone, and Lukan stared after it with an odd sense of having lost something precious.

'So, Lukan, the deed is done?'

He came erect and turned quickly, his breath still coming in rapid gusts. She was no more than a shadow, a soft movement amongst the foliage, a scent of dried herbs and crushed heather. This was his half-sister Rebecca Adams, a plain, swarthy-skinned woman some thirteen years his senior and as much a true gypsy as ever trod the open road. As his only living relative she had become his advisor and confidant, his would-be conscience and his sometime comfort. She was the only woman who had ever come close to knowing the secret man inside himself. Until Lia.

'Aye, Rebecca, it is done,' he nodded.

'Then you are a fool, Lukan de Ville.'

'And a happy one,' he grinned, flinging off his cloak.

'She will hurt you, Lukan. She will twist you to her will until your life and your senses are no longer your own. And then she will destroy you.'

49

'Aye sister,' he conceded, still grinning. 'But first, before all else, *she will love me.*'

'*Fool!*' She cleared her throat and spat upon the ground. 'Such is the value of that love compared to her ambitions.'

Lukan stepped towards her. The smile had faded from his handsome face and his breathing was back within his control. Nearby the waters of a stream lapped against the wooded bank, ice-cold and inviting.

'You judge her too harshly.' He almost whispered the words, but there was a warning in the altered tone of his voice.

'I judge her as I would a scorpion,' she countered.

'Have a care, Rebecca.'

'What? While you throw caution to the wind?'

'Lia is my love.'

'Yours?' she asked. '*Yours?*'

'Aye, mine.'

'No, Lukan. No! She is *Malcolm's.* She married him willingly, in spite of your pleas and your rages. And while she played the wanton in your bed she no doubt hoodwinked your best friend with those tried and tested feminine deceptions, hemlock and opium and a sprinkling of virgin's water.'

'Be silent, Rebecca. You are wrong. You judge her too harshly.'

'You blinkered fool!' she flared. 'How is *anyone* to judge such a woman?'

'Rebecca, last night . . .'

'Last night she lay down with a gypsy, and today she will use her wiles to convince her husband that he, in an act he will never recall, stained the bedlinens with her virginity.'

Lukan had begun to remove his clothes, tearing each item from his body and tossing it down on his outspread cloak. She watched him in the darkness, half-seeing, half-imagining the swell of his dark chest, the taut flatness of his belly, the heavy bulk of his manhood hanging used and empty between his legs. She had known he would love that spirited, sapphire-eyed woman. The signs had told her that destiny bound them one to the other before ever their paths could cross in the forest on Midsummer's Eve. She had known it, yet still she choked on the injustice of it all. The woman who already had all she could want in life had snatched away everything Rebecca Adams had ever loved.

'Why you?' she demanded. 'She could have any man she set her heart upon, so why must it be you?'

'Enough,' Lukan warned. His voice was low and dangerous. 'I will hear no more of this.'

Rebecca cleared her throat and spat again.

'She beckoned and you followed,' she said in disgust. 'You went to her like a lamb to the slaughter. Such weakness shames you, Lukan.'

He moved towards her, a dark shape naked in the cold November morning, and Rebecca had to will herself not to take him in her arms and confess her love. She checked herself with an effort. To find the manly scent of him changed, altered in some subtle way by the closeness of that other woman, would be the final twist of the knife already at her breast. And she knew beyond all doubt that should her half-brother suspect the true nature of her feelings, a wedge would be forever driven between them.

'Like a lamb to the slaughter,' she repeated bitterly. 'Willing and docile.'

Lukan stood with his fists on his hips, his black eyes glinting in the poor light.

'What is it that galls you so, Rebecca?' he asked. 'Is it jealousy?'

'What?' She shrank from his words, fearing he had touched upon the truth.

'Well? Is it?' he demanded. 'Is it jealousy? Do you begrudge me this happiness because you have none of your own?'

'That's fools' talk.'

'And do you hate Lia simply for her beauty, and because no man has ever turned his head to look with desire at *you*?'

The breath hissed through her teeth as her hand shot out to strike his face. Even in the darkness he caught it with ease, gripping the slim wrist in his steely fingers, bruising her swarthy skin.

51

'No more,' he growled. 'I will hear no more. It is done, Rebecca. Lia and I are one. You will live in peace with that or put the length and breadth of this forest between us. Choose now, woman, for I will hear not another word against something that was always meant to be.'

A moment later he was gone. As she massaged the fiery pain from her wrist Rebecca heard the soft sound of his body sliding beneath the icy waters of the stream without so much as a splash. She stooped to pick up the bundle he had made of his clothes and turned back towards the forest and its familiar pathways. Thin morning sunlight was beginning to fall here and there across the shining surface of the water, silvering every ripple. She knew he would swim until he reached the shallows a long way downstream, his dogs following at their own pace. She hugged the rough bundle of his clothes, tears stinging her eyes. She was past her youth, uncomely, and his sister; for this her hopes of happiness were forfeit.

Neither Rebecca the gypsy nor her brother looked back as they made their separate ways into the forest. She had read the signs. There could be no turning back for either of them now. The die was cast. The fateful cards were dealt.

CHAPTER FOUR

The announcement of the death of Lady Alyce, Countess of Beresford, brought an air of uncertainty to Beresford Hall. The wedding guests were unprepared for mourning. Those reluctant to offend by casting gloom over the marriage celebrations risked as much by seeming to make light of the family's grief. Caught in the narrow space between the two extremes, propriety made cowards of them all.

Leonora managed to snatch a few hours sleep late in the morning, but for most of the day she was on her feet, attending to guests and family alike, giving orders, making arrangements, placing her personal mark on the general running of the great house. It was a long and exhausting day for an eighteen-year-old bride suddenly plunged into the exacting role of mistress of Beresford Hall. Her reputation in top society hung upon success or failure here. Not while a single eye was still upon her would she allow her inexperience to show; not while her every word and gesture were the subject of other people's curiosity.

One of the day's many rewards was an opportunity to set a precedent that would permanently alter an item of Beresford tradition. The Countess had lain too long in her paralysis for anyone to suspect that she was about to die. Since the height of summer she had been bedridden, so those attending this late October wedding had not considered it expedient to pack mourning attire. Even before the death was officially announced, Leonora hurried to Sir Oscar's study with a request which, under the unique circumstances, he could scarcely refuse.

'It has my approval,' he nodded thoughtfully. 'And Malcolm is not against it?'

'Not at all, though we would not presume to do this without your full consent.' She spoke earnestly, as if drawing him into her confidence, but at the same time she was careful to stress her husband's involvement. 'We believe our concern must be for our guests and family, particularly the ladies, who are quite defenceless in the open arena of public opinion.'

'It was to be a joyous occasion,' he observed.

'Indeed, and since they are here by special invitation we can hardly send them home with their reputations injured. The moment we adopt deep mourning we render our guests improperly and disrespectfully attired. To attend a burial service wearing wedding gowns would be a serious breach of etiquette, while not to attend at all would be an insult.'

'I must confess the dilemma had not occurred to me,' the Earl admitted. 'Your tact and diplomacy are admirable, Leonora.'

She smiled. 'The Countess would have done as much, in my place.'

'I doubt that,' he told her, recalling his wife's often total disregard for the feelings of others.

'We believe my plan will save the day and set everyone at their ease, but it can only succeed if the Countess's closest relatives agree to participate.'

'They will,' he assured her. 'I will see to it.'

'Thank you.'

Following that conversation she was free to approach each

party of guests and, in a brief and intimate interview, assure them that on this occasion the wearing of black would not be required. As a token of respect she proposed they wear a band of braided black ribbon fastened about their upper arms. Even as she spoke, baskets of ribbon were being prepared and set on tables around the Great Hall. The gentlemen were invited to follow Malcolm's example by wearing a band of plain black cloth around the sleeve of their coats. So it was that several matters of importance were settled at a stroke. Her reputation was enhanced by her determined efforts to preserve the dignity of their guests, and her wedding celebrations were rescued from the misery of enforced mourning. She had managed to preserve some element of merriment which might otherwise have been totally lost and, with her generous supply of pretty satin armbands, she created a new chic amongst the ladies. Above all she had influenced one of the long-standing customs of the Cavendish family. Her personal mark was now inked indelibly upon the fashions and formalities of Beresford Hall.

Thus freed from the obligations of mourning, Leonora wore a superbly cut morning gown of cream silk trimmed with flounces of copper lace. In the afternoon she chose a gown of rich blue velvet with puffed and ribboned over-sleeves and a full skirt inset with panels of beaded embroidery. Through a delicate rosebud veil her eyes appeared huge and dark, her skin as pale as buttermilk. She offered a personal farewell to the short-term guests who were due to depart that day and were unable, or unwilling, to rearrange their plans at such short notice. As an extra touch she ordered suitable refreshment; a selection of cheeses, cold meats, sweet pastries, fruit and wine, to be packed and placed in each departing carriage. The fairy-tale bride had proved herself the perfect society hostess. Her stunning appearance, her tireless devotion to the Countess, her deep regard for the comfort of her guests, all these would be the favourite topics of smart drawing-room conversation for many weeks to come. Her success was absolute. The old Countess was dead and gone, and in her place emerged a most remarkable young woman. By popular opinion, Leonora Cavendish, mere daughter-in-law to the Earl, was already mistress of Beresford.

By four in the afternoon the last of the guests intending to travel that day had filled their warming-flasks, sealed their carriage windows against the cold and taken their leave. Those who remained kept mostly to their rooms or to the gardens, reluctant to intrude upon the family's private grief. In the quiet of the afternoon when luncheon had been cleared away, Leonora snatched an opportunity to rest in the old gatehouse apartments. She reclined on a firm sofa, her feet raised upon a padded footstool, her eyes covered by cotton pads dampened with soothing witch hazel. She had claimed these rooms for herself when their owner was first struck down by a seizure in August. Lady Alyce had chosen them for their convenient access to the old family chapel, where she had once spent long hours in religious activities so contrary to her cruel nature. Leonora had wanted the rooms chiefly because they were attached to the old tower, which held such a fascination for her. They also housed the Countess's secret hoard of journals and letters, those writings preserved and enlarged down the years to create a detailed history of the Cavendish family. There were five rooms in all, including the one in which the body of the Countess now lay. They were spacious rooms, warm and well furnished, and for the last three months their convenient setting had helped Leonora maintain her role as Lady Alyce's devoted nurse. It had been established from the earliest days of her illness that neither friend, family nor servant may approach the stricken Countess except through her.

'I will not allow it,' she had declared passionately to Malcolm. 'I will not allow these people simply to come and go as they desire, without concern for your mother's finer feelings.'

'Then it will be as you wish,' he had assured her.

She had pressed her point regardless of his assent. 'Oh Malcolm, I know her to be a woman of the deepest sensitivity. She trusts me to ensure that she is dressed and perfumed, with all evidence of her illness concealed, so that she may receive her guests in the proper manner, with *dignity*. How can I do this if visitors are allowed to present themselves at a moment's notice, whether she is prepared for them or not?'

'Leonora, I will attend to the matter immediately,' Malcolm had insisted, and only then had she been quite satisfied that she would have her way.

It was some time after this that Sir Oscar returned from his daughter's home in Cornwall to find his son besotted and Leonora firmly ensconced at Beresford Hall. Already wounded by the double blows of his lover's death and his wife's paralysis, his first visit to the sickroom had proved to be his last. He had averted his gaze from the mask-like sneer that was now Lady Alyce's face, had closed his ears to the guttural noises bubbling in her throat, but there was no escaping the evidence of her incontinence. She had lain helpless in her husband's presence, the bed-linens soiled, the air around her fouled, and he had been appalled by the experience.

Ever watchful for the smallest personal advantage, Leonora had been swift to capitalise on his repugnance.

'Would you have others see her like this, Sir Oscar?' she had demanded softly. 'Would you have them see her at her lowest and most helpless? If only I had been given a little time to prepare the dear lady for your visit, I might have spared both you and her this humiliation.'

Sir Oscar had been deeply shocked. 'I had no idea.'

'She recognises no-one, yet she is still a lady and her dignity must be protected.'

The Earl had readily agreed to her suggestions, and so Leonora had placed herself firmly between the sickbed and the door, between her would-be accuser and anyone who might be persuaded to take up that accuser's cause. In the name of dignity she was able to restrict all visits to those times when the patient's meagre powers of speech were subdued by hemlock or laudanum or both. Cold grey eyes had stared with hatred from their rigid features and nobody, not even the surgeon Sir Marcus Shaw, had suspected the truth of the matter. Now the Countess was dead and Leonora felt no twinge of conscience that her own actions had brought on the first of those crippling seizures. Even from her deathbed, Lady Alyce would have denounced Leonora simply to vent her spite against Francine.

'I'd give a penny for them.'

'What? What did you say?' Leonora pulled herself back to the present with a start.

'For your thoughts,' Anabel said. 'I offered a penny-piece for your thoughts.'

Leonora sighed deeply and lifted the dampened pads from her eyes. 'I was thinking about the Countess,' she admitted. 'I did her no harm, Anabel. I confess I hated her with all my heart, but I did her no harm.'

Anabel leaned over to pat Leonora's hand.

'I know that, child,' she smiled. 'Oh, you made wicked capital of her illness, but not once did you raise your hand to her or withhold the care she needed when it was in your power to do so. The comforts she received during her last weeks were far more than she deserved, and much to your credit, my dear.'

Leonora nodded solemnly. 'And she will be buried with all due respect and dignity.'

'Aye, my little madam, but only after you dared turn a key on the dead and leave a corpse unattended through the night, just to suit your own ends.'

'It was necessary.'

'It was wicked. And it will likely cause a haunting.'

'Oh, what nonsense, Anabel.'

'It will. It will cause a haunting. You mark my words, young lady. That restless soul of hers will roam these rooms for ever.'

'Then it will be in pleasant company, for Beresford Hall is crowded with ghosts, so I am told.'

Anabel shook her head. 'Make light of it if you will.'

'I will, since it is nothing but foolish superstition.'

'But no good ever came of turning a key on the dead.'

'Nor any harm, I'll warrant.'

'We'll see,' Anabel whispered, making the sign of the cross. 'Time will tell what harm has been done. We'll see, soon enough.'

Leonora sighed heavily and turned her gaze to the ceiling. Overhead were her bedroom, water closet and dressing rooms, and above them the secret place where she and Lukan had spent the night. A shiver, cold and swift, ran along her spine. She did not regret what she had done to bring about her marriage to Malcolm and make possible that stolen night of love with Lukan de Ville. Whatever Anabel's objections might be on the grounds of superstition and religious doctrine, Leonora would never regret one moment of the long All Hallow's night.

'Don't scold, Anabel,' she pleaded, pressing a hand to her brow. 'I am far too weary to tolerate your scolding.'

She allowed Anabel to place several extra cushions at her back and hand her a large tumbler of sage tea. She sipped the hot liquid, brewed as a tonic to help her endure so many hours without sleep.

'The velvet gown is particularly heavy,' she observed.

'But glorious,' Anabel smiled. 'You and your gowns will be the talk of all the most fashionable circles, just as you predicted. It was a wedding fit for royalty, a truly remarkable occasion.'

'Did it go well, Anabel? Are you sure? Did it go as well as I had hoped, as well as mama would have wanted?'

'Such false modesty!' Anabel smiled despite the firmness of her tone. 'As if you need the likes of me to confirm your success. You were superb, Leonora Shelley, and well you know it.'

'*Cavendish*,' her mistress corrected sharply. 'I am now Leonora *Cavendish*. The Shelley name must never again be spoken here.'

'Oh? And what of your three brothers, young madam?' Anabel demanded, defensive on their behalf. 'What name will you give to them if not the one they were born with?'

Leonora shuddered. 'Their father has sullied that name beyond redemption.'

'Nonsense, child, and when the boys return ...'

She stopped speaking as an adjoining door opened to admit a plump, tightly-laced maid whose ankles were two unsightly

59

mounds of flesh bulging between the tops of her shoes and the hem of her plain brown frock. She curtsied stiffly, wincing with the effort.

'Beggin' your pardon, Your Ladyship, 'tis His Lordship come to see the Countess.'

'His Lordship the Earl?'

'Yes, ma'am.'

Leonora rose quickly to her feet, pulled on a fur-trimmed robe and checked her reflection in the big mirror. Even at rest, her appearance could not be faulted.

'You may show His Lordship in,' she said.

The maid bobbed her head and shoulders in a makeshift curtsy. 'Yes, ma'am.'

Sir Oscar Cavendish strode into the room with his hands clasped behind his back and his brows furrowed. He was elegant in a dull red velvet coat, white linen breeches and darkly-patterned waistcoat. His face seemed pale and drawn, and his striking blue eyes were so heavy-lidded that he might have been weeping. Leonora offered her hand in greeting.

'I am deeply sorry, Sir Oscar,' she whispered. 'The Countess's death marks a great loss to us all.'

'Indeed, indeed,' he muttered.

When his eyes met hers Leonora saw the pain in them. Perhaps he had wept this night for his wife, but his real grief was for his beloved, his poor Francine. She found it impossible to hate this isolated man. He had loved unfailingly for over twenty years and then betrayed it all through pride and anger. That perfidy had broken his own heart and sent a very special lady to her grave uncomforted. Like most men of his breeding he could be arrogant and obstinate to a fault. It was those two inclinations, used at full rein against the innocent, that would cause him to repent his haste for the rest of his life. Leonora was touched with sympathy for his predicament. It was too late now to set the matter straight, to draw back cruel words, to act contrary to accomplished actions. She saw him haunted by regret, yet still she knew his pain would never meet the debt he owed her mother.

'I would speak to you in private, if I may,' he said.

60

'Of course, Sir Oscar. Leave us, Anabel.'

Anabel glanced anxiously at her mistress as she left the room. The Earl looked stern and she feared his mood on Leonora's behalf. Most of all she feared the outcome of any dispute there might be over how long the Countess had lain unattended after her fatal stroke. Not even the tender bride, burdened as she was by responsibility and bound by the demands of a healthy young husband, would be readily forgiven such neglect.

'May I pour you some tea?' Leonora offered.

'Thank you, no.'

Sir Oscar paced the floor several times before coming to a halt with his back to the fire and his hands clasped under the tails of his coat. Leonora seated herself in a straight-backed chair and waited. Her face betrayed no anxiety.

'I wish to speak to you about the letter,' he said at last. 'That old letter you found from your mother. She was writing to me about the child she was expecting and ...'

'My brother Jonathan,' Leonora reminded him softly.

'Yes.'

She met his gaze steadily. The lie was too important for her to falter over it now. The letter was locked away amongst her private treasures, and only she and Anabel were privy to the full story behind it. The child to whom Francine referred in those heart-rending lines was indeed the Earl's child, conceived in love but not in wedlock and named in the womb as Jonathan. Francine had married Herbert Shelley in haste when she discovered her pregnancy, and that in itself was an act of loving sacrifice. She could not bear to see her lover forfeit his wife and young family, his vast inheritance, his name, his father's love, for her. Within days of the marriage she wrote down her unhappy confession, begging Sir Oscar to keep their child a secret, but the letter was never dispatched to the man she truly loved. Their child was lost by miscarriage only days before her husband's child, the living Jonathan, was conceived, and instead of destroying the letter the distraught Francine had hidden it away in a secret place.

The Earl cleared his throat and cast around for words. He

61

knew nothing of any miscarriage, simply that Francine's child was born prematurely after a serious fall. He had been shown the letter twenty-one years after it was written, only weeks after Francine's death, and he had believed, as Leonora intended, that it proved one thing beyond all doubt: Jonathan Shelley was his natural son. For all those years he had suspected it and now he knew the truth. Francine's letter told him it was so.

'Did you, er ... have you ...?'

'Have I what, Sir Oscar?' Leonora prompted.

'Does Malcolm know of it?'

Leonora looked at her father-in-law steadily. Her hands were clasped in her lap, her head raised proudly, her expression betraying nothing of the rush of relief his words inspired. Her fears were groundless. She was not to be questioned about the Countess, after all. She met the Earl's steady gaze.

'I did not consider it my place to speak of it,' she told him. 'I judged it a personal matter to be kept between Jonathan and yourself.'

'Then Malcolm has not read the letter?'

She shook her head. 'Let me assure you that he does not even know of its existence.'

The Earl's relief was obvious. 'Thank you.'

She lifted her head proudly. 'Sir Oscar, common courtesy needs no thanks.'

'Perhaps, but you have my gratitude none the less,' he said. 'It is my dearest wish that your brother learn the truth of his birth from me. We shall have much to discuss before the rest of the family is informed and the matter made public.'

'You will acknowledge him as your son?'

'Of course I will.'

She smiled. 'Thank you, Sir Oscar. I believed you would.'

'Your discretion is much appreciated,' he told her.

'And totally unexpected, it would seem.'

'Forgive me. I had no way of assessing how you might deal with a matter of such ... of such ...' He made elegant gestures with one hand as if to pluck the elusive word from the air.

'Delicacy?' she offered. 'Sir Oscar, you were always swift to judge me as my father's daughter. Do you forget the good lady who was my mother?'

She saw by the pained expression on his face that her words had touched a rawness in him.

'How could I?' he muttered.

While he scowled down at the carpet she allowed a silence to grow between them. It was broken only by the crackle of flames in the fireplace and the muted sound of a clock chiming the hour in a distant part of the house.

'Is there news of Jonathan?' she ventured to ask.

He shook his head. 'Not a word. It is almost as if he and Charles walked out of the London house and simply stepped off the edge of the world.'

'They have gone to earth like hunted animals,' she said gravely. 'They believe themselves wanted men, felons in the eyes of the law. Sometimes I fear they will never allow themselves to be found.'

Sir Oscar stood erect and tightened his lips. 'They are innocent, and Jonathan must be told that he is my ...' He broke off, unable to give voice to words so long unspoken. Then he added more softly: 'My people will find him. They *must* find him.'

'Are you so certain of that?' she asked. 'Already there has been no word of them in three long months. They know that mama was forced to beg loans from you to finance father's gambling, and that not so much as a guinea piece was ever repaid. And they know that with her unwitting assistance he cheated you of huge amounts of cash before fleeing the country. When Jonathan hears that his biggest and most powerful creditor is financing this manhunt, do you think he will slow his steps long enough to ascertain the finer details of the matter? No, Sir Oscar, I fear he will run the faster, knowing that you are leading the hunt for him.'

Sir Oscar sighed heavily and lowered himself into an armchair. He was weary and it showed.

'This is a most unfortunate business,' he said, as if thinking aloud. 'What more is to be done, eh? What more?'

'Perhaps you should ...'

'*Hell and damnation!*'

The oath was so loudly and suddenly uttered that Leonora drew back in alarm. The Earl allowed his fist to rise and fall several times on the carved wooden arm of his chair. His eyes were tightly closed and his teeth clenched. At that moment he seemed barely in control of his emotions.

'Why?' he demanded. 'Why did the boy take fright? Why did he run away like a common criminal?'

'He did not take fright,' Leonora said firmly.

'He should have come to me.'

'As I once did, Sir Oscar? As I once came to you for help?' He would have ignored the frosty reminder but she pressed the point. 'I came to you on mama's behalf,' she said coldly. 'And you mocked me in the presence of your sons. You insulted me, accused me of lies and play-acting. So tell me, Sir Oscar, why should the son of Herbert Shelley hope to receive kinder treatment than his sister?'

'Jonathan is *not* that scoundrel's son.'

She lifted her head, determined to help her lie become his truth. 'You know that. I know that. Unfortunately, Jonathan does not.'

The Earl dropped his fist once again on the arm of the chair. 'So where is he? Why must he shame his noble blood by skulking in corners as if Herbert Shelley's debts were all that mattered?'

Leonora paled. 'His *liberty* matters. He had no choice. He was forced to flee.'

'It was a coward's act.'

She rose to her feet, her eyes flashing darkly. 'How can you say that?' she demanded. 'How can you hold my brother in such low esteem after all the sacrifices he willingly made for his family? He is a finer man than you know, Sir Oscar.'

'He has abdicated his responsibilities.'

'Not so. If you but knew the whole of it ...'

'*He ran away.*'

'He did *not* run away,' Leonora flared, flinging the words at him. 'And you, sir, would do well to remember how once you wrongly judged his mother in the same high-handed manner.

64

Remember too how you belittled me before your sons, how you scoffed when I told you mama was dying and desperately in need of your goodwill.'

She stifled the emotional outburst with both hands and turned her back on him. Hot tears sprang to her eyes. The grief she had thought better hidden rose up to fill her throat with a lump of painful proportions. She heard the rustle of his clothes as he rose from his chair. After a moment his hands rested gently, hesitantly on her shoulders.

'Forgive me,' he said awkwardly. 'I had no right to speak as I did.'

'Indeed you had no right sir, and no cause.'

'Forgive me, the words were uttered without due care.'

Leonora nodded and dabbed the tears from her cheeks with a tiny embroidered handkerchief. Her own weakness infuriated her. She had not suspected that her sorrows ran so close to the surface, that their banks could be so easily breached. She cleared her throat softly and managed to speak with a steady voice in spite of her feelings.

'Sir Oscar, for mama's sake, may I beg one favour of you?'

He lifted his hands from her shoulders and she sensed his wariness. He had already been much wounded by the begging and granting and withholding of favours.

'You may ask,' he said cautiously.

'Judge us without haste or prejudice,' she said.

'I beg your pardon?'

She turned to face him, her eyes bright with tears and her face ashen. But as well as sorrow there was anger in her. He could almost taste it. Few men he knew would dare to face him eye-to-eye as she did.

'For her sake,' Leonora demanded tightly. 'For Francine's sake, judge her children without haste or prejudice.'

'Is that all?'

'Yes.'

'A fair, calm judgment for you all?'

'It is the only privilege I will ever ask of you, Sir Oscar Cavendish,' she replied, and the words were spoken as a vow.

He stared back at her for a long time, jolted by the cauldron of hurts and angers, courage and sorrows he saw in her eyes. At last he nodded gravely, took one of her hands and lifted it gently to his lips.

'Why do I forget so easily that you too have suffered?' he asked.

'Because you will not forgive me for being the daughter of Herbert Shelley,' she said bitterly, knowing that she spoke only a fraction of it.

'Then I am a fool,' he conceded. 'I owe you much. When I feared that Malcolm would never fully recover from the death of his first wife, you rid him of that shadow and made him a happy man again. And you showed such goodness to the Countess.'

'Please.' She touched her finger quickly to his lips, a gesture robbed of its boldness by the sudden intimacy between them. 'You must never feel that you are in my debt. How could I forget how the dear lady took me to her heart when I was homeless and without prospects? You can be sure that I have nursed her out of the deepest gratitude and ...' She paused, feeling she might yet choke upon the lie, '... and *love*.'

Sir Oscar nodded, then glanced at the door of the sickroom and said, without enthusiasm, 'I should go in.'

'Of course. You will find her peaceful.'

'Ah, so the seizure has relaxed its grip?'

'Mercifully, yes. She looks almost serene.' Leonora dropped him a polite curtsy and watched him walk toward the door of the sickroom. Her mind was racing. She did not wish to forbear the moment, for here was an ideal opportunity to win him over once and for all. She had yet another ace to play and now was the time to show it. His hand was at the latch of the sickroom door when she called him back.

'Sir Oscar, there is something else, something I have kept from you in order to spare you further pain.' She watched him stiffen, wary of secrets and surprises, and she added, 'Were it not for the failure of your search for Jonathan and Charles, I would prefer to let the matter lie, at least for a while.'

When he turned his head she thought he seemed weary and resigned, and when she indicated the big armchair he

66

returned to it and seated himself without protest.

'Someone knows where my brothers are,' she told him.

He stiffened. 'What?'

'Someone arranged for a ship to carry them from England.'

'They were helped? And you kept this information from me?'

'I had to, Sir Oscar. Speaking out would have served no purpose, and to be honest I feared your reaction if you learned the truth.'

'Who was it?' he demanded. 'Who made the arrangements?'

Leonora swallowed and looked down at her clasped hands. 'A wicked man,' she said at last. 'A hateful, conniving man whose hand was in my father's affairs and whose greed was instrumental in bringing my family to ruin.'

He watched her with a frown. 'Are you serious?'

'Never more so.'

'And yet you say this same man helped my son to flee the country?'

'For his own ends. He merely used Jonathan. He used us all, including mama.'

'Tell me his name, Leonora.'

She hesitated, raising her eyes to his with as much assumed reluctance as she could muster. She must not appear too eager to touch a flare to this particular pile of dry kindling, even though she had waited so long to speak out against their mutual enemy.

The Earl's features had set like stone. 'Give me his name.'

'Fairfax. Nigel Fairfax.'

She saw the colour drain from his face as his eyes narrowed into cold blue slits and a pulse began to throb in his cheek. His fury was tangible.

'Nigel Fairfax? *Nigel Fairfax?*'

'Yes, Sir Oscar.'

'And what part has that jackdaw *dared* to play in my affairs?'

She watched his eyes, savouring his fury. 'Nigel Fairfax conspired to profit from your past generosity and my father's dishonesty. He encouraged my father to play the gaming

67

tables and make unwise investments financed by huge loans from the Fairfax bank. I believe they played him like a puppet at your expense.'

'At *my* expense?'

She nodded and watched him lean back in his seat, scowling as he surveyed her through hooded eyes. A practised movement of his hand invited her to proceed with her story. She took a deep breath. She had imagined this moment for many weeks, and she intended to enjoy it, no matter how painful the memories it stirred. The words were right there in her head, waiting to be said, and this time all she was required to do was speak the truth.

'As you know, Sir Oscar, my father stripped us of everything we had of value before he left. He had already obtained my brothers' inheritances, along with my wedding portion, by fraudulently inserting mama's signature on documents of release drawn up by the Fairfax lawyers. They even assisted him in selling the house, *mama's* house, as if it were his own. At the end her precious gowns and jewellery, her own family silver and her private collection of paintings and crystal were stolen from her. Even items of fine furniture were dishonestly disposed of to help line Herbert Shelley's pockets.'

The Earl nodded, listening intently as Leonora continued her story in a clear, unfaltering voice.

'He was also given several thousand pounds in cash in exchange for his signature on a marriage settlement drawn up between myself and his eldest son, Christopher Fairfax. He sold me.'

'He did *what?*'

'He sold me,' Leonora repeated bitterly. 'He sold his own daughter as any man might sell an animal at market, and to that odious Christopher Fairfax, that flatulent, bloated *toad* of a man ...' She broke off, shuddering, disgusted by the memories springing into her mind.

'Please continue,' the Earl prompted.

'It was agreed that the elderly Fairfax, to whom father was heavily in debt, would disregard his losses in father's favour and that Christopher would take me in marriage without a dowry. Mama would then have a comfortable home and the best medical care available. My twin brother Joseph, who is poorly sighted and not capable of making his own way in the world, would be given a safe position as junior clerk in the firm of Fairfax, Reece and Tilbury. In exchange for all this, Jonathan was required to sign papers accepting full responsibility for father's affairs so that the burden of his debts should not fall upon the Fairfax name. As part of that agreement, Nigel Fairfax offered Jonathan and Charles cash in hand and safe passage away from England on the next available tide.'

'And the offer was accepted?'

'Of course it was. How could they refuse when father's creditors were already at the door and the new owners of the house were threatening to evict us into the street?'

'*My God!*' It was a whispered oath, barely audible.

'They signed. It was the only way they could save us from total ruin, and don't forget that as a major creditor, Fairfax was in a position to have Jonathan arrested on the spot and thrown into debtors' prison in his father's absence. My brother was trapped. How could he walk away from such an offer and escape with his liberty? And what would have become of us had Fairfax had him arrested, as he was perfectly entitled to do?'

'By Heaven, this is scandalous!'

'As for myself,' Leonora continued, 'I too was ensnared by Fairfax treachery. The house and its contents were lost. Mama was dying. There was nobody to help us, nothing left to sell, no way to protect her from the open streets or the stinking Poor House.'

'So you agreed to marry Christopher Fairfax?'

She nodded. 'I did. What choice was left to me? What choice was left to any of us?'

'Dear God in Heaven!'

She looked up to see that the Earl had closed his eyes. She guessed he was reminded of their meeting in London, when she had gone to him in desperation and he had angrily returned her mother's keep-sake, the ring he had worn for twenty years as a token of their love. The events she had just related would never have taken place if he had then been motivated by compassion instead of anger. She could only guess at how deeply he now regretted his actions.

'God's curses on the Fairfax name,' he suddenly muttered.

'Indeed, Sir Oscar. I am aware that they have been a thorn in the Cavendish hide for generations, and I have no doubt that Nigel Fairfax beguiled my father into accruing massive debts solely for the purpose of elevating himself at your expense. They are no longer content to sit like squatters upon Cavendish land thanks to their ancestor's trickery. They sought to put Cavendish blood in their children's veins by the same foul means.'

'My God, if only I had known . . .'

'I tried to tell you,' she reminded him. 'You were too proud, too suspicious. You refused to listen to me.'

'I was aggrieved. I thought Francine had betrayed me.'

'That is exactly what you were meant to believe if Fairfax was to see his plans come to fruition. He knew your anger at being falsely played would overwhelm your affection for us. You were our last recourse and you refused us, as he knew you would. All through mama's last days Fairfax was hovering in the background like a vulture, gloating over his success, certain that soon he would be in complete control of your dying cousin and her children.'

'So it was *his* doing? *He* kept me from her, him, that villain, that Fairfax.'

She nodded. 'He played upon your suspicions.'

'And I obliged him.'

'Yes, as he knew you would,' Leonora sighed.

'I thought she had betrayed me,' he said again. 'How could I have been so wrong, so cruel? I refused to speak to her, and all the time she was dying, and that Fairfax . . .'

Leonora turned away. Speaking the truth at last had left her strangely chilled. She reached for a shawl and drew it about her shoulders, shivering as she did so.

'And you, Leonora?' Sir Oscar asked tightly. 'Did you marry my son knowing that you were betrothed to another man?'

Leonora rose from her seat and crossed to a large dresser in the farthest corner of the room. From one of its drawers she lifted a folded document bearing a bright red seal, and this she handed to the Earl.

'Because I still hoped to escape the trap I refused to sign my name to the agreement until the day of the marriage,' she told him. 'There is no legally binding document, no evidence that I agreed to the match, but here is proof of the Fairfax hand in your affairs, Sir Oscar. Here are the documents drawn up by Nigel Fairfax himself, signed under the greatest duress by Jonathan and witnessed by his brother Charles.'

'These are exact copies?' he inquired.

'Oh no, Sir Oscar,' she smiled a little bitterly. 'These are the original papers. I took them from the London offices by stealth in an attempt to sever the Fairfax hold on my brothers. I was successful, as you see, but ...'

'Go on,' he prompted.

Leonora swallowed the lump that had risen to her throat. 'While Anabel and I were absent from the house that day mama suffered a serious relapse and poor Joseph, terrified of illness, ran from home in a panic.'

'Leaving his mother alone?'

'In his fear, yes.'

'And that is how she died,' he said flatly, already aware of the fact. 'Alone, quite alone.'

Leonora nodded. 'And for that I doubt if I will ever forgive myself.'

'Nor I,' the Earl whispered hoarsely. 'Nor will I forgive myself for that.'

'And now my dear Joseph is also gone,' she said. 'There has been no word of him for weeks, and that too is my fault.'

'Come now, how can that possibly be so?' he asked gently. 'You and he were as unlike as any twins I ever saw, but you were devoted to each other. How can the fault for his leaving possibly be laid with you?'

'Because I told a lie,' she admitted with a deep sigh. 'There were so many people clamouring for settlement of father's debts, so many angry, threatening people. To deflect their attention from my brothers and to keep angry tradespeople from harassing us at the house, I began the whisper that Herbert Shelley had been left a fortune by wealthy relatives in Yorkshire. Like so many others, Joseph believed the lie and decided to go there and bring the man back to London to face his creditors.'

The Earl shook his head. 'A pointless exercise in any case. Shelley will never dare let himself be brought to book, not while certain charges of forgery can be laid against him. Here in England forgery happens to be a hanging offence.'

'Yes, I am aware of that, but I doubt if Joseph really understood the seriousness of his father's misdeeds. He believed the lie about his new-found wealth in Yorkshire and he left in the dead of night after voicing his plans to no-one. He was distraught and confused. He had no money and he left without a word of farewell to me.'

The Earl leaned forward in his seat. 'I'm sorry, my dear. I know you and he were inseparable.'

She sighed. 'Inseparable.'

Once again there grew a lengthy silence between them that stretched into several minutes. Then the Earl rose to his feet and solemnly held open his arms to Leonora. It was the gesture she had hoped for, the sign that at last this man was ready to set aside his natural suspicions and accept her into his family. Once she had feared that he would never forgive her for uncovering his darkest secrets, for witnessing his grief for Francine and for being the daughter of a man he despised. Now she stepped triumphantly into his arms and welcomed his warm, fatherly embrace.

'I will find your brothers, my dear,' he promised, feeling strangely unsettled by the perfumed softness of her hair and the firmness of her body against his own. 'Not just Jonathan but all of them. I swear I will find them all.'

'Thank you,' she said.

'And I thank you, Leonora. Had you been a vindictive young woman, had you hated me enough to keep me from seeing Francine's letter, I might never have known for certain that Jonathan is my son.'

'And can you forgive us all for allowing ourselves to be trapped by those dreadful Fairfax people?'

'Of course, my dear. And by the gods they will pay for the hurt they have inflicted upon my family.'

Leonora smiled and rested her cheek against his chest. She had worked long and hard to have Sir Oscar Cavendish override his uncertainties and declare himself her ally. Now they were joined against a common foe, and she in turn must shelve her private grievances against him. She would never forget that he had abandoned her mother in her very darkest hour, but she would do everything in her power to nurture this small seed of friendship. Her father-in-law was a shrewd and powerful man who must never be allowed to set himself against her. She would cherish him as an ally because she could never hope to match him as an enemy.

CHAPTER FIVE

I

On that gloomy day of his mother's death Sir Malcolm was determined not to neglect those tasks around the estate requiring his personal attention. In the afternoon he rode towards the Home Farm, allowing his mount to trot at its own pace along the narrow dirt track whose high walls separated the dairy buildings from the orchards. All the scents and colours of November seemed to reach out and touch his senses. Here were russets, browns and golds, and on the air the musky perfume of dead wood and wasting leaves. There was also the dark, earthy smell of the land turning back to itself for the colder months. By now only the oaks were still green. Not until the severe frosts came would their leaves blanch and rustle and tear off in the wind, leaving the great trees bleak until the turn of the year and the rising of the new sap. Country people like Lukan de Ville knew the oak as the thousand-year tree. They believed that at least 300 years were needed to bring it from acorn to full maturity. Then it stood its ground, solid and majestic, for 300 years and more before it began the three long centuries of its dying. *The thousand-year tree.* Surrounded by oaks as they were at Beresford, any might believe himself immortal.

Malcolm urged his mount on when it would have slowed its pace to investigate the hedgerows. The animal's warm breath was blown pale and frosted into the cold air. It was early but the light was fading. Already the colours of the orchards and meadows were beginning to blend into shadow. The coppery gold of a lowering sun trailed a final splash of brightness over the tips and edges of the forest.

A mood of quiet melancholy had dogged Malcolm all day. He felt groggy and slightly nauseous in spite of Leonora's herbal tonics. Even the lightly poached turbot he had been persuaded to eat at luncheon now sat upon his stomach in a leaden, undigested mass. His mouth was stale, with a peculiar metallic taste that no amount of perfumed waters could rinse away.

'Woah, boy! Steady-up there! Steady!'

He issued the order in a soft growl as his mount sidestepped a stoat that suddenly scurried across its path to vanish into a hole in the opposite wall. He stood in his stirrups to raise himself from the saddle until he could see over the left-hand wall into the meadows beyond. The wolfhounds were out, streaking a zig-zag course across open ground in pursuit of a hare. A series of high-pitched whistles told him that Lukan was some distance away, out of sight amongst the beeches that grew in a dense and stately wood within the forest. St Eloy's stream widened at that point to run slow and deep as it meandered a while on its busy route between the Wye and the Severn. He could almost imagine the big, sun-browned gypsy stripped naked, his long body cutting effortlessly through the water as if oblivious to its heart-stopping chill. The man was indifferent to physical discomfort. Many a fine gentleman's purse had been taken by wager at winter fairs until too many victories meant that none would bet against him.

Only once had he conceded defeat, one bitter January morning when the hills were white with snow and the ice on

75

the pond lay thick and strong enough for skating. A wiry Chinese acrobat from a travelling circus heard of Lukan's reputation and promptly challenged him to a test of endurance. Reluctant to participate but determined not to lose face, Lukan accepted, provided he was allowed to follow the challenger's lead. A frozen rain-barrel was rolled into place in the yard of the Dog and Gun, the Chinaman stripped naked, bowed to the crowd of onlookers, broke the surface ice with his fist and slid beneath the water. Bets were laid and doubled, cash and small items of value changed hands, promissory notes were hastily scribbled and pocketed. People gaped and wondered how long it would take for the blood to freeze in a man's veins. The Chinaman remained submerged for an incredible count of forty-seven before his seconds pulled him out half-drowned, half-frozen and almost senseless. At this point Lukan de Ville shook his head thoughtfully from side to side, then yielded up the ten-guinea stake with a bow of acquiescence.

'My compliments to you sir,' he told the semi-conscious Chinaman. 'I humbly concede that you have bettered me in this.'

Then he turned and walked away without so much as testing the temperature of the water. Ten guineas was small value on his comfort. He paid it willingly, content to remain warm and dry while his opponent froze himself into a stupor simply for the wager. It was Lukan who truly won the day, a wise man indeed to recognise his own limitations.

'How very like the man,' Malcolm remarked out loud, smiling at the memory. 'Gallant to let the Chinaman go first, ingenious not to imitate the folly.'

He was smiling still as he urged his mount to resume its steady pace between the hedgerows. Will Hynd, head keeper of the Home Farm, was waiting at the far end of the lane. He stood at the point where the farm's outer wall angled to the right, enclosing the ancient tithe barn, as old as the original Abbey itself. Will was a stocky country man in his early fifties. His legs bowed outward at the knees so that he boasted somewhat less than average height. He was shabbily dressed in mud-spattered boots and heavy outdoor clothes that stank of the animals he tended. He had a face like tree bark, weathered and broken up with lines. He grinned too readily, lacking the vanity to hide unsightly gums and an ungainly clutter of rotten teeth.

'Afternoon, sir,' he said, tugging at the brim of his hat with a filthy hand.

'Good afternoon Will.'

'Her Old Ladyship gone, has she?'

'Yes, Will, she died early this morning.'

'Aye, so I heard,' the man said, rubbing his chin to produce a sound like wire scrapping against stone. 'So I heard.'

He stepped back and leaned on his stout walking stick to watch Sir Malcolm dismount and drop the reins over his horse's head. Then the two walked side by side towards the farm gates while a dirty, bright-eyed dog ducked to and fro at their heels, herding them along like cattle. As they reached the yard Malcolm briefly turned his gaze back to the meadow. The sound of whistled signals told him Lukan was moving his hounds in the direction of the house.

'It's Nellie Dobbin, Mr Malcolm,' Will suddenly announced. 'Her husband told her not to go around talking of it to nobody else. He reckons they'll both of 'em likely lose their positions here if'n she don't learn to hold her tongue. And then that neat little cottage of theirs over Hill's Edge will be forfeit, that's for sure. If you ask me, all women have loose lips and it takes a man to shut 'em up, if'n he be a man at all. Still, I reckoned it was only right you should hear what she told him.'

Malcolm moved back, avoiding the man's unsavoury smell. 'Go on, Will, I'm listening.'

'Well, she reckons the old Countess, Lord bless 'er and keep 'er, didn't die this morning like everyone says she did.'

'I beg your pardon?'

Will grinned. His breath was sour. 'Nellie reckons she died yesterday afternoon.'

'What? Yesterday?' Malcolm tapped his riding whip in the palm of his hand. 'Don't be ridiculous, man.'

'Now that's just what I telled Harry Dobbin, Mr Malcolm, but his Nellie, she sticks to her story. Says she seen that Anabel Corey running out of the sickroom lookin' all hot and bothered and a-wringing of her hands. So Nellie nips in to see what all the fuss is about and sure enough, there's Her Ladyship, Lord bless 'er and keep 'er, dead as mutton in her bed. Nellie thought as how that Anabel Corey went to tell her mistress the bad news, but nothin' never come of it so maybe she kept her mouth shut after all.'

'And you say this was *yesterday afternoon*?'

'Aye, sir, shortly afore three o'clock, so Nellie telled her husband. She reckons your mother died afore ever you were wed, Mr Malcolm, and that it was kept quiet so as not to upset the fancy arrangements.'

'That's a monstrous suggestion!' Malcolm exclaimed.

Will Hynd glanced around to make sure they could not be overheard by the farm labourers. Then he shrugged his shoulders and lowered his voice before speaking again. 'All I know is what was telled to Harry Dobbin by his wife, sir.'

'But it's ridiculous. The Countess died today, at dawn.'

'Aye, so I telled him.'

Malcolm scowled down at the ground around his feet where scavenging chickens had left a criss-cross pattern of marks in the dirt. Two geese swaggered in by the main gate, their heads high, their manner grandiose.

'The woman was clearly mistaken,' he said at last.

'Aye, I telled him that, sir.'

'And to dare repeat such a story is both wicked and mischievous.'

'Aye.' Will Hynd nodded his grizzled head and puffed out his chest proudly. 'Telled him that too, I did.'

Malcolm pursed his lips, scowling. 'I'll speak to this woman personally. Where is she now?'

'Kingswood, sir. Went with Mrs Williams in the cart, she did. Won't be back yet a while.'

'In that case, have her brought to my study immediately after luncheon tomorrow.'

Will shook his head. Air whistled through his crooked

78

teeth. 'Beggin' your pardon, Mr Malcolm, but we're short-handed, what with all the wedding guests stopping over an' all. Nellie's having to lend a hand with the brewing and bread-making all day tomorrow. She won't be free until after second milking, if that be all right with you, sir.'

Malcolm was tempted to agree but caught himself just in time. Will Hynd had a compulsion to alter even the most trivial instructions rather than accept them without question. It gave him a feeling of power, a sense of superiority, to make of every order a compromise.

'No it is *not* all right with me,' he said firmly. 'You have my order, Mr Hynd. Send the woman to me immediately after luncheon tomorrow. And in the meantime she must be warned against repeating this wild story. If she persists in it ...'

He left the sentence unfinished, knowing that Will Hynd would colour it with suitable details. The imagined retribution, the dread of what might be to come, could be a subtle torture. It was often more effective than the punishment.

Will Hynd touched his forelock respectfully. 'Just thought you should know what's being said, Mr Malcolm.'

'Thank you for drawing my attention to it. I trust the matter will go no further?'

'Not a word to a living soul,' Will vowed, slapping his palm to his chest. 'And them Dobbins have been well warned to keep their lips sealed.'

'Good man. Now, what's to be done about this ailing dairy cow of yours?'

Will Hynd led the way across the wide yard toward a row of cow sheds, rocking his shoulders as his bow legs carried him forward in a rapid, lumbering gait. The dirty black and white dog pricked up its ears and whined softly in the back of its throat at the sound of a distant whistle. Even a hard-working farmyard cur, trained and obedient to its master, had moments when the call of freedom and wide open spaces filled it with the urge to race off in pursuit of the wild hares.

*

Closer to Beresford Hall, Lukan's whistle brought the wolf-hounds to heel and they loped along beside him, their tongues hanging and their breath frosting the air in white gusts. Instead of making his usual approach to the Hall he slipped through a narrow iron gate into the secluded walled garden set with tiny arbours overhung with cherry, birch and apple blossom. Here he and Leonora, protected from view by the lush foliage of summer, had shared many emotionally charged exchanges following her engagement to Malcolm. Without pausing to glance at familiar benches and ivy-clad arbours, Lukan strode across the garden, scaled the far wall with ease and dropped soundlessly into the cherry orchard beyond. From there he made his way through formal gardens to the Cavendish family tomb with its miniature towers of ornate sandstone and its ranks of fancy iron-work. Ahead of him now were the overgrown steps leading down to a derelict sunken chapel that was thought to be connected with the West Tower by a secret tunnel. To his right the embankment sloped steeply upward to form a natural hillock that sheltered the crypt from view. Beyond it the swift river twisted and turned on its way to Monks' Crossing. Lukan skirted the embankment and climbed a hedge choked with old bramble and wild hawthorn to reach the farthest end of Monks' Walk. Once there he walked in the shadows close to the Hall until he reached the tiny arched door that none would guess had been brought back into use. Checking that his movements remained unobserved, he lifted the key from around his neck and used it to unlock the door. Then he patted the heads of his dogs, stooped low and slipped inside.

Leonora was kneeling on a cushion before the huge storage cabinet in Lady Alyce's sickroom. Its doors and drawers were hanging open and many of its contents lay scattered about the carpet. She examined everything carefully before replacing it in the drawer, shelf or compartment whence it came. Only the papers were of interest to her. She wanted the deeds and titles, private letters, legal documents, accounts and record books, old journals and shopping receipts. She was gathering together everything the Countess had ever written and every item of correspondence received from family and friends. For Leonora the acquisition of information was of paramount importance. She had no personal history at Beresford Hall, no private niche to give her that sense of absolute security enjoyed by the members of great English families. She was an outsider who felt her vulnerability very keenly. By claiming this hoard of journals and documents accumulated over many decades, she hoped to acquire something of the Countess's rank and respectability. She needed to be part of Beresford's history, much more than simply the impoverished relation who had become Malcolm's second wife. By familiarising herself with the private lives and intimacies of other members of the family she would make herself a Cavendish not merely by marriage but in her own right.

Her task of searching the cabinet completed, she left Anabel to tidy away the last few items while she carried a pile of books and papers upstairs to her new apartments. The body of Lady Alyce had been removed to the candle-lit chapel below the West Wing. It would lie there until the burial, attended by a steady relay of servants and mourners. There was no shortage of good souls willing to watch with her through the long hours now that she could no longer fix them with her terrifying stare or beckon to them with her claw-like hand. The bed in which she had died stood stripped and bare, its bedding and mattress burned along with its pillows, bed-cushions and heavy brocade hangings. The atmosphere of the room was hung with wispy tendrils of blue smoke from several ornamental censers packed with burning frankincense to drive out the smell of death.

'I will be rid of her,' Leonora remarked from time to time. 'I will be rid of her, once and for all.'

In the bedchamber of the upper room she set down her burden on a dresser just as several scrolled documents began to slide from the pile. As she reached to retrieve the nearest one her movements suddenly froze and the breath caught in her throat. Trapped in the mirror was the shadowed image of a man. She whirled, letting the pile of papers and books topple haphazardly around her.

81

'Lukan!'

For an instant indignation flashed like fire in her eyes. He had come unannounced, of his own will, not hers. Then her heart quickened and she stepped into his arms, lifting her face for his kiss.

'Lia,' he breathed, and the rest of his words were lost against her lips as he kissed her with a passion undimmed by the night of love they had so recently shared.

'Lukan, this is too dangerous. I sent no word. You should not have come.'

He cupped her face in his hands. 'We're safe enough. Malcolm is with Will Hynd at the Home Farm.'

'But what of the servants?'

He sought her mouth with his. 'We are alone.'

'But the guests ... *the Earl.*'

He gripped her more tightly. 'Forget them all.'

She was wearing a robe of cream silk over her stays and petticoats. He slid the robe from her shoulders and bent his mouth to her breasts, drawing a gasp of delight from her.

'Lukan, no! We cannot do this,' she protested. 'Not here, not now.'

His lips were hungry and his breath was hot against her skin. His fingers worked deftly at the laces in her stays.

'No, Lukan,' she gasped.

'Don't fight me,' he growled. 'Not while your body says your need is as great as mine.'

'But we mustn't ...'

'By the gods, lady, I believe we must.'

He lifted her suddenly, flung her across the big four-poster bed and fell upon her like a savage. She was pinned beneath him, trapped by the hardness of his body and the crushing urgency of his lips. This time they spent their passions violently, he with his belt unfastened and his breeches ripped open in haste, she with her breasts lifted from her stays and her petticoats hitched up around her waist like a common serving wench taken in a bawdy tumble. Their gasps and cries of pleasure were subdued not by caution but by the pressure of their lips as each sucked hungrily at the other's mouth.

When at last they separated, it was to lie side by side, breathless and elated.

'Brute!' Leonora admonished with a smile. 'Where is my gentleman lover of last night, my tender administrator, my master craftsman?'

'You will find me a man of many faces,' Lukan grinned.

She pouted her lips. 'Today I find you common and brutish.'

'Aye, lady, according to your own desires.'

'You ravished me,' she protested.

'Aye, and well pleased you were with it.'

'Lukan de Ville, if you think for one moment . . .'

In one swift movement he grabbed her wrists, pinned her arms high above her head and rolled over to kneel astride her body. His hair hung loose, hiding much of his face and skimming, black and coarse, across her pale skin. He lowered his head to nuzzle her naked breasts, his tongue hot on her flesh. As she struggled to free herself her movements only served to bring her nipples, each in its turn, within convenient reach of his mouth.

'You brute!' she hissed.

'Wanton!' he countered.

'You took me with as much finesse as an animal.'

He threw back his head and laughed at that. 'Lady, before this love of ours can run its course I will have taken you a thousand different ways, and each one to your pleasure.'

'Run its course?' she echoed, flashing her turquoise eyes at him. 'Will it run its course then, like any commonplace love? Is there to be an end of it? Am I to be rid of you, one day?'

'*Never!*'

She narrowed her eyes. 'Not unless I will it.'

'Never,' he repeated, drawing his brows together in a deep scowl. His face was now only inches from her own, dark and brooding as he loomed over her. 'Never will you be free of me, Lia. Neither your fine husband, nor your vanity, nor your ambition will come between us. By the gods, not even the grave itself will part us now.'

As he released his grip on her wrists Leonora allowed her

arms to encircle his neck. The playful teasing was over. The laughter had gone from his eyes and he was deadly serious. Though at first he resisted her kiss, she drew his head down until their mouths met, at first with tenderness and then with a fierce possessiveness. With her passions already spent and cooled she was reminded once again that something more powerful burned between herself and Lukan de Ville. It went beyond desire and was, she feared, more dangerous than love.

II

Fairfax Manor was a rambling stone building of pretentious proportions erected in haste on land that had once been part of the Cavendish estates. The original section consisted of a larger-than-average two storey farmhouse constructed by simple craftsmen out of sturdy local stone. To this had been added a huge, fancy façade with a vaulted porch and paved walkway. The manor also boasted incongruous sandstone pillars and arched windows embellished with carvings and fronted by ornate balconies. Many extra rooms had been grafted on to the main building over the years, creating a hodgepodge of styles and tastes and ill-matched stonework. It had acquired a courtyard and a coach house of massive proportions, rambling gardens and huge orchards. Its long stretches of lawn were littered here and there with marble statues, fountains and follies reflecting some of the worst vagaries of fashion. Architecturally Fairfax Manor was an eye-sore, a blot upon the lovely Gloucestershire landscape. It was a tasteless jungle of bits and pieces. Like the family that built and named it, the manor house was a product of too much money and insufficient breeding.

'The v-villagers h-hate us,' Christopher Fairfax complained, lowering his great bulk into an armchair that creaked beneath his weight. 'They're n-not to b-be t-trusted. They ch-cheat us.

They s-steal f-from us at every t-turn.'

The rolls of fat around his chin were displaced by the stiffened collar of his coat so that the soft flesh quivered like pink jelly with every stuttered word. He reached out a large hand with pale, sausage-shaped fingers toward a tray of cakes and pastries on a nearby table. The hand hovered over a thick wedge of cold plum pudding, hesitated, then closed around a slice of apple tart dusted with fine icing sugar. He ate it quickly, biting through crisp pastry to the filling of firm, sweet fruit. Juices glistened on his lips and dribbled into the grooves and crevices separating the rolls of flesh around his neck. Crumbs of pastry and a snowy cloud of icing sugar spotted the dark fabric of his waistcoat. He pushed the last portion into his mouth and licked the juice from his fingers. He was still savouring the last mouthful as he reached for the largest slab of cold plum pudding on the plate.

Old Nigel Fairfax clicked his tongue in disapproval. 'You eat too much, m'boy. Far too much.'

'I'm d-d-depressed,' Christopher said.

'Nonsense. You're a glutton.'

'M-my heart is b-broken.'

Nigel Fairfax lowered his newspaper and scowled at his obese eldest son. The movement drew bushy grey brows down over his beak-shaped nose. His eyes were set like two small ink-dots in his scrawny face, and there seemed to be as much of him above as below them, for his head was domed, balding and darkly freckled. With his gaunt features, long neck and nervous movements, he resembled an aging, rather tattered bird of prey.

'Nonsense, m'boy,' he repeated. 'Broken hearts are the privilege of dry old maids and frivolous young gels. What you have is indigestion and what you need is a disciplined diet and a regular dose of Epsom salt.'

'Yes, f-father.'

The elderly Fairfax, senior partner in the banking firm of Fairfax, Reece and Tilbury, was a short, extremely slender man in his seventieth year. He favoured stiff white collars from which his neck seemed stretched to its stringy limits. The high

85

dome of his head was graced by a dusty old wig that had long since passed out of fashion. His preference was for black or dark brown clothes sparingly cut from a heavy woollen fabric bought in bulk at a reasonable discount. Nigel Fairfax was a frugal man in everything but the quest for advancement. The acquisition of wealth was the very cornerstone of his existence. All his life he had coveted only two things, great status and great wealth, and like his father and grandfather before him, he saw his tenuous connection with his Cavendish neighbours as a means of acquiring both.

'It d-didn't w-work,' Christopher lamented, in a voice resembling the wail of a moody child. He pursued his lips at a plump sugared tart, hesitated thoughtfully before taking the first bite. He continued to speak around the succulent sweetness filling his mouth. 'She w-was to be m-mine, *m-mine*, and th-the C-Cavendish took her. He had n-no right to d-do that. She w-was m-mine. We sh-should have m-made her sign the c-c-contract.'

'Stop whining, Christopher,' Nigel snapped. 'If you hadn't allowed the clever minx to steal back her brother's statement of liability, we would still have some means of recouping our losses.'

'You t-trusted her t-too. You sh-should have m-made her s-sign.'

Old Nigel glowered. 'When I think of the size of our investment, the massive loans we made to Herbert Shelley in order to get him firmly obligated to the bank ...' He broke off to suck air noisily through the spaces in his mouth long since abandoned by crumbled teeth. 'And the shame of it, to be out-foxed after all our efforts by that deceitful slip of a gel.'

'W-we sh-should have m-made her s-sign,' Christopher wailed.

Nigel Fairfax rose from his chair and crossed to a window from where he could see the darkening mass of Beresford Hall set against a sombre November sky. Christopher was right. He had been too confident, too sure of his success. He had overlooked the fact that she too was a Cavendish and therefore not to be trusted. He should have made her sign.

His tiny black eyes stared beyond the ivy-clad wall that marked the boundary between his land and the countless Cavendish acres. His grandfather had made no mistake when he procured that four hundred acre patch of prime land for his Fairfax heirs.

The facts were history now. Sir Rodney Cavendish, Fourth Earl of Beresford, was best remembered for two things, his extraordinary success in the political arena of his times and his consuming passion for the wife of his younger brother. When Lady Cecilia gave birth to a robustly healthy son ten months after her husband died of a wasting disease, the gravest of scandals was only avoided because Sir Henry had been nursed in his private rooms at Beresford Hall. The previous summer of 1696 had been long and balmy, resulting in record crops and increased lambing. These facts were used to support the claim that poor consumptive Sir Henry had rallied from the brink of death to impregnate his beautiful young wife. His elder brother, already the father of two grown sons to his Countess, took his fatherless nephew under his care and settled upon him a considerable inheritance. Much to the horror of his family he then went so far as to break the sacred Cavendish tradition of keeping the earldom intact. Against all opposition he divided off a section of land to settle upon the boy. Bitter legal battles ensued as the Earl's legal heir took steps to secure his own inheritance in full. In the glare of growing public scandal the young widow and her child were moved to one of the finer lodges, and the besotted Earl continued to lavish expensive gifts and a more than generous allowance upon his mistress and their son.

In due course the young Sir Henry, subject of so much speculation and controversy, grew into a boorish, self-interested young man dependent upon his doting mother and magnanimous uncle. By the tender age of eighteen he was known to be a liar, a gambler and a wastrel. At twenty-two he clubbed his best friend to death in a drunken brawl and inflicted irreparable damage upon the Earl's career and reputation as he struggled to extricate himself from serious prosecution. And at twenty-four, having claimed his modest portion of the earldom, the feckless young man produced his *coup de grâce*. In a fit of alcoholic pique following a quarrel with the Earl, he was persuaded to sign away his slice of the earldom in exchange for a handful of promissory notes. A man can wait a lifetime to benefit from such an opportunity, and one man did. The vital notes had been collected, over many years and at considerable personal expense, by an ambitious London clerk, one Roger Lampton Fairfax. By this patient stroke of cunning he became the first outsider ever to own a piece of the Beresford earldom. And he knew his rights in law. No man could legally reclaim his land, no price could buy him out against his will. Upon one shrewdly-acquired signature rested the Fairfax claim to a part of the wealth and prestige of Beresford. And now the ageing grandson of that wily clerk had failed to win himself a similar prize. He had allowed it to slip through his fingers for want of just such a Cavendish signature upon a document binding in law.

Old Nigel Fairfax turned from the window. 'You are quite right, m'boy,' he admitted, nodding his head the way a magpie nods as it struts across the ground. 'I was a gullible fool to take any Cavendish on trust. I should have made the filly sign.'

His father's admission did little to ease the misery in Christopher's already over-taxed heart. He watched the old man leave the room before struggling, with a good deal of huffing and puffing, to release his great body from the restraining confines of the armchair. As he rose to his feet a cascade of crumbs fell from his clothes to the carpet like a flutter of snow. He stooped to retrieve his napkin, wiped his hands and face and dusted the crumbs from his waistcoat. Then he burped noisily as he waddled through the double doors into the conservatory. The place was hot and humid due to the recent addition of several cold-weather heaters. Its atmosphere made his skin clammy and its heavy scents, blended with the smell of oil from the heaters, drew a protest from his bulging stomach. From the farthest windows of the conservatory he could see a group of riders approaching the lower meadow, their mounts moving at a leisurely pace. His heart fluttered briefly but painfully at the prospect of seeing Leonora amongst them, but the wave of hope died almost instantly. She was lost to him now. She was the wife of Malcolm Cavendish. To Christopher's father she had represented another priceless jewel snatched from the Cavendish coronet, a sturdy young woman of noble blood who might bear a dozen healthy children in as many years; *Fairfax* children. But to Christopher she had represented all his dreams and desires. She was young and luscious, spirited, cultured, intelligent. People turned their heads in open admiration wherever she went. Society loved her, men of all ages lusted after her. Owning her would have made him the most envied man in the country. Owning her would have recompensed him for every sexual humiliation in his past, every word of feminine ridicule he had been forced to bear. Owning her would have helped him forget all the grubby common prostitutes who insisted upon straddling him, at twice the normal fee, rather than lie under his overweight body.

Christopher burped again and rubbed his hands over his ample frontage. He could feel the wind gathering in painful pockets in his intestines, trapped in the space between a congested bowel and an over-stuffed stomach. He left the conservatory, glad to be away from the humidity that made his armpits clammy. In the other room he poured himself a brandy and returned his bulk to the armchair. From the deep inside pocket of his coat he pulled a large envelope and unfolded its crumpled edges with as much care as his black mood and his podgy fingers would allow. At least he still had her letters, the ones she would never see now that she had broken her promise to marry him, the ones from her precious brothers.

'You sh-shouldn't have d-done what you d-did, L-Leonora,' he stuttered. 'I'm th-the only one wh-who knows where th-they are, and I'll n-never t-tell. Not n-now. N-not ever.'

He smoothed the most recently delivered sheet of paper over his fat thigh. He was wondering how long it would take Jonathan Shelley to discover that his sister had married not

89

Christopher Fairfax under duress, but Sir Malcolm Cavendish after a whirlwind courtship.

'K-Keep away f-from the s-s-society p-pages, Mr Sh-Shelley,' he pouted sulkily. 'And I'll n-never t-tell her w-where you are. *N-never.*'

He licked his lips as he read the words again for his own pleasure. At the same time his hand reached out and his fat fingers hovered above the last two wedges of cold plum pudding left on the plate.

While Christopher drew what comfort he could from his food, Nigel Fairfax stood in his library before an open window, watching the wind move garden debris around the lawn in idle circles. He too had been reading a letter, a stiff, formally worded document demanding that any letters addressed to the Fairfax premises but bearing the name of Leonora Cavendish, née Shelley, be forwarded to Beresford Hall unopened. He scowled at his reflection on the glass. He wanted no animosity with Beresford. It was bad enough that his plans had gone so terribly awry and the purpose of them had been lost to his enemy's camp. He wanted no fresh war with Oscar Cavendish.

A tall man, stooped and shifty-eyed, entered the room and clicked his heels without lowering his head in a bow. His voice was weighted with boredom. 'You rang, Mr Fairfax?'

'I did, Stanley. You read well enough, so I believe?'

'Indeed I do sir.'

Fairfax indicated the document lying unfolded on his desk. 'A letter from those acting on behalf of the Earl of Beresford. Go ahead man. Pick it up. Read it for yourself.'

The man obeyed, holding the sheet at arms' length and straining his head away from it while he squinted at the writing through half-closed eyes. His lips moved as he read, and one eyebrow rose and fell with his understanding of each sentence. After a while he folded the letter carefully and returned it to the desk.

'Well?' Fairfax demanded, swivelling his long neck until he looked at the man behind him as a bird might, out of one small black eye.

'Sir?'

'Don't play the fool with me, Walter Stanley. Do you understand the letter or no?'

'I do indeed sir. It seems quite clear enough to me.'

'Well then? Have there been any letters, any messages of any nature intended for the lady my son had hoped to marry?'

Stanley shook his head decisively. His answer to that one had been ready for some time. The master was a mean old stick who never parted with a penny piece unless he could gain two more in return. He marked the level of brandy in the decanter and kept his bottles under lock and key, and like so many of his kind he would rather toss his cold meat to the dogs than see it go to a member of his household. Mr Christopher though was a bird of a different plumage. When he became drunk and maudlin he appreciated a sympathetic ear and an extra dish of something nice to satisfy his gluttony, and he was prepared to show his appreciation in coin. He was also inclined to be careless with his purse, and many a night had seen Walter Stanley handsomely rewarded simply by following in Christopher's drunken footsteps, picking up what had been left to fall. Of the two, father and son, Stanley knew who he would rather serve.

'I know nothing about no letters for any young lady, Mr Fairfax,' he said with sincerity.

'Nothing?' old Fairfax asked.

'Nothing at all, Mr Fairfax. I always see whatever arrives, being as how I'm the only one who can read apart from yourself and the young master. If something came for the lady I would know of it, and if I knew of it then so would you.'

'I hope so, Stanley.'

'Oh yes sir, it would be my beholden duty to pass anything of that nature directly to yourself.'

'Be sure you remember that.' Fairfax scowled, scratching his head so that his dusty wig tilted at a precarious angle.

'Oh yes, sir. Will that be all, sir?'

'It will. And shut this damn window, will you? There's a damnably chilly breeze out there today.'

'Yes, sir.'

Fairfax went to his desk and seated himself in a chair that dwarfed his tiny frame. One finger tapped idly at the folded letter. He wanted no truck with lawyers and their like, and he resented the implication that he would be so petty as to steal personal letters sent to a young woman by her brothers. Even so, he would have liked to have had something in his possession that Cavendish wanted, something he wanted badly enough to bargain for.

Chapter Six

I

The group of riders seen by Christopher Fairfax from the conservatory window was still passing close to the manor house boundary. It was making its way back to Beresford Hall via an ancient bridle path running close to the western boundaries of the Earl's estates. Here was the frontier where the two lands met, where the issue of that crafty clerk might stand upon embezzled soil, plucking the fruits of his neighbour's trees. It was a silent group, eight riders in all, keeping an unhurried pace. Two grooms from Sir Oscar's stables took the lead, followed by a pair of lady's maids, a governess passing middle age, tightly wrapped against the elements, and three ladies of quality.

Lady Charlotte, now Viscountess Morley of Cornwall, was Sir Oscar's eldest daughter, the one whose company he sought in times of stress or inner crisis. There was a calmness in her that could ease his troubled mind. It was echoed in the tranquil atmosphere of her home near St Austell in Cornwall, and in the calm behaviour of her children. Charlotte had made an admirable marriage. Her husband, a man of title, wealth and property, made no secret of the fact that he adored her. It was to their magnificent cliff-top home that Sir Oscar had retreated in late July and August, his mind unsettled by Herbert Shelley's treachery, his heart pained by Francine's apparent betrayal. It was upon those very cliffs, exposed to the fickle moods of sea and storm, that he had sought to exorcise his grievances. And while he pondered so, the woman he had worshipped for a lifetime died alone with neither comfort nor forgiveness.

Riding behind Charlotte was her sister Elizabeth, a pretty young woman of twenty whose intellect had failed to keep pace with her physical growth. For the most part she lived in a private world of her own making, far removed from the realities of life around her. Lady Alyce had been obsessed with the notion of keeping her middle daughter clean and properly groomed. She had her dressed in fine clothes that rarely survived their first wearing without mishap. An endless number of pretty bonnets found their way into flowerbeds and bushes or were plucked bare of their pretty decorations by their owner's restless fingers. To all outward appearances she seemed loved and cared for, but across Elizabeth's shoulders, back and buttocks was a criss-cross pattern of scars that told a different story. From time to time the girl was summoned to the chapel beneath the West Wing, there to be stripped naked and whipped at the altar by a mother bent on ridding her of the 'devils' responsible for her affliction. Sir Oscar Cavendish would have been horrified to learn that his feeble-minded daughter suffered ritualistic floggings at the hands of her own mother, the Countess of Beresford.

Now Elizabeth's fingers began to tug at the rim of her bonnet. Her elder sister brought her mount alongside, smiled and reached out to halt the restless fingers.

'Your hands are cold, my dear. Here, take my muff, the fur will keep you warm.'

'It's a pretty muff,' Elizabeth smiled, thrusting her hands inside. 'And warm and silky, like Tabby's kittens.'

The reins dropped, forgotten, from her grip. Charlotte took them up and moved ahead, leading her sister's mount.

The youngest and most vivacious of the Earl's daughters was Vivienne, just fourteen years old and one of the most envied pupils at her school for gentleladies in Cheltenham. She was a natural red-head while those who aspired to any kind of social standing dyed their hair the same fashionable shade of copper-blonde with which she had been gifted by nature. Her eyes were neither the true Cavendish blue nor the softer grey Elizabeth had inherited from their mother, but an interesting shade between the two. Lady Vivienne was known by her school chums to be resourceful and daring. She had a keen sense of adventure and a restless yearning for excitement. To her teachers these qualities made her virtually unmanageable. To certain young gentlemen of the stylish Cheltenham Set, she was a fiery red-head ripened before her time and would, given the opportunity, welcome the harvesting of her lush fruits.

Now Vivienne arched her back and eased her body into a more comfortable position in the saddle. She was weary of riding and bored with the solemn company she was forced to keep. Her eldest sister had little conversation beyond that of husband, home and children. And as for that fool Elizabeth, she was an embarrassment to be avoided at all costs, a half-wit who should be shut away in a lunatic asylum instead of being left to roam around exhibiting the family's shame with her stupidity.

'I am bored, *bored*,' Vivienne hissed through her teeth.

'*Ma cherie?*'

Vivienne turned in her saddle and caught the inquiring gaze of her governess Madame Michelet.

'Nothing, *Madame*,' she smiled, tugging on the frilled skirt of her riding jacket. Through her short veil she saw the woman's stern features tighten into an expression of disapproval. Vivienne had seldom known Madame Michelet smile. Indeed, it seemed to a young and frivolous girl of fourteen that the ageing French spinster dedicated her entire energies to a personal struggle against all things even remotely pleasurable.

Vivienne sighed in peevish discontent. In the distance she could see the stables and the large area of paddocks and yards at the side of the house. The big grey-and-white stallion, Starlight Warrior, was running loose in a small enclosure near the main stable. It pranced and reared like a pale phantom against a backdrop of stable buildings and darkening trees. A sly smile touched the girl's lips. If the big grey was loose then Lukan de Ville must be somewhere nearby. She sighed and felt a hot flush of pleasure colour her cheeks. As a child she had feared the strange and sinister gypsy, but now she had outgrown such foolishness. Now she was a woman and could appreciate him for what he was; frightening, exciting, a man to be likened to a dangerous, untamed beast. He was a handsome brute indeed, a half-bred gypsy with the airs and graces of a high-born gentleman, a creature of the forest and yet accepted, even admired, by men of breeding and refinement. She had seen how even the most genteel women lusted after him with their coy glances. She had seen the way he looked back at them from beneath his dark brows, his solemn stare no less inviting than his rare smile. And she had watched him at the ball after the wedding feast, impudently dancing with the bride as if it were his given right to lay his hands upon Sir Malcolm's property.

Vivienne shifted in the saddle, her lower body warmed by her thoughts. She still had her virginity, a useless thing that marked her as a child. Better to be possessed than to be chaste, her senses told her. Better submissive to a lustful man than playing childish games with some virginal and proper youth with little idea of what he was about. Lukan de Ville would be out there now, beyond the stable buildings, tending her father's horses. The sleeves of his shirt would be folded back over his muscular arms, the front left open to his belt. She could almost see his bulging chest, the coarse black hair, dark nipples and weather-browned skin glistening with perspiration. Her lips had dried. She licked the moisture back. Last night she had dreamed of Lukan. In her fantasies he pursued her relentlessly on his wild grey stallion, finally running her to earth deep inside the forest. Then he overpowered her with his brute strength, ripped the clothes from her body and ravished her without mercy. There had been no Madame Michelet to save her then, no wall of censure set between the helpless victim and the gypsy's lusts.

Behind her veil Vivienne smiled a secret smile as she slid the long silver hat pin from her plumed topper and concealed it along the narrow sleeve of her riding jacket. With slow and careful movements she began to work the pin beneath the saddle. Then she turned her mount's head toward home and jabbed the point of the pin as forcefully as she could into its flesh. With a snort the animal leaped forward, felt the reins slacken and the stirrups sting its flanks, and flung itself into a gallop across the meadow, heading for the distant stable buildings.

She shrieked in feigned alarm. '*Help! Oh help me! Somebody help me!*'

'*Hold on, Lady Vivienne! Hold on!*'

She heard the groom's shout and the startled cries of the women behind her. She was laughing now, urging the horse onwards, heeling its flanks in her determination to reach the stables well ahead of the others.

'*Help! Help!*' she cried at the top of her voice.

A young groom raced down a slope ahead of her, flapping the air with his cap and yelling as if to terrify the bolting animal into submission. Instead it veered sideways, almost dislodging her from the saddle, and suddenly she grasped the very real danger she had brought upon herself. She was no longer in control. She had neither the strength nor the skill to slow the animal or turn it from its headlong flight. It galloped blindly on, passing the gateway and the lower hedges, heading for the lofty orchard wall. Suddenly de Ville was there, moving from nowhere like a swift shadow, reaching for the reins, dragging the beast to a standstill, quieting and soothing with the deep, hypnotic timbre of his voice.

Taking fullest advantage of the situation, Lady Vivienne snatched off her hat to release her sparkling golden hair, uttered an anguished cry and slid elegantly from the saddle, right into Lukan's arms. He caught her with ease and lowered her to the ground as if she weighed no more than a small child. His body was hard and muscular against her own, his skin warm. The strong masculine smell of him, tinted with the scent of anise on his breath, filled her with an excitement beyond anything she had ever experienced. No callow, fumbling youth had ever made her feel like this. She was in the arms of a real man, and every pore in her body cried out for more of him. When he made as if to set her on her feet she swooned, eyes closed, and hung both arms around his neck. Her lips parted and her head fell back, exposing her pale throat like a gift. When moments later she heard the noisy approach of other riders she opened her eyes as if from a faint and smiled up into his dark face.

'Oh, Mr de Ville, oh Lukan, you are so *wonderfully* strong,' she cooed, '*so masterful*.'

His voice was low. 'Are you able to stand, my lady?'

'I think not,' she sighed. 'All my energy is drained away. Oh Lukan, I was so frightened. My horse suddenly bolted for no reason at all. It was dreadful. I might have been *killed*.'

Vivienne was still clinging to Lukan when Madame Michelet allowed one of the grooms to hand her down from her horse. She hurried forward to retrieve her charge. Tight-lipped and stiff with outrage, she drew the girl away after first fixing de Ville with a stare which implied that the fault for this dangerous incident might be set squarely with him. Lady Charlotte dismounted without assistance and eyed her young sister with a quizzical expression.

'Are you all right, Vivienne?'

'Oh yes,' Vivienne nodded, touching a hand delicately to her brow and leaning heavily on Madame Michelet's arm. She cast a sly glance at Lukan before adding, 'I'm perfectly all right *now*.'

'But what on earth happened? You are an accomplished rider and your horse is usually so obedient. What caused the animal to bolt like that?'

'Who knows?' Vivienne smiled bravely, then closed her eyes. 'Oh dear, I'm afraid I feel rather faint.'

Charlotte glanced at Lukan, caught the hostility of his gaze and signalled for one of the grooms to come forward. On her instructions the man lifted Vivienne and carried her toward the house. The second groom, a younger man, rushed forward cap in hand to make his apologies.

'I'm ever so sorry, Mr Lukan,' he said. 'She's a quiet horse is that one. Can't think what caused her to bolt.'

Lukan glowered. 'You were responsible for the safety of the ladies.'

'That we were, Mr Lukan, and we were keeping a careful eye on them, just like His Lordship told us to do. It happened all of a sudden-like, you see. One minute she's walking along nicely with the others and the next she's off like a bolt from a bow. I swear I never saw the like, Mr Lukan.'

'Something must have panicked her. A gentle beast does not bolt without cause.'

Lady Charlotte interceded, her voice brisk. 'It was an unfortunate accident for which nobody is to blame Mr de Ville. Since neither the horse nor my sister have come to any real harm, I see no reason why the matter should not be settled without fuss. Now, if you will be so kind as to assist Elizabeth.'

Lukan stepped forward to take Elizabeth by the waist and lift her down from her horse. When he set her upon her feet she smiled without looking at him directly. She held her head quite still while he straightened her bonnet and retrieved a tendril of well-sucked hair from her mouth. For a moment his rugged features softened and a smile curved the edges of his mouth. He lifted her chin until she looked at him.

'Did you enjoy your ride, my lady?'

She nodded vigorously. 'Oh yes. I saw a dead stoat in the hedgerow and a kestrel with a deformed foot and look, I found this pretty pebble by the river.'

He glanced at the stone in her hand. It was rough and dark and commonplace.

'It's a beautiful pebble, my lady,' he told her.

She pushed it into his hand. 'Here, I brought it for you.'

He closed his fingers around it. 'A charming gift. I thank you kindly for it.'

'Kiss,' she demanded. 'Kiss.'

Obedient, he bent his head to brush her forehead lightly with his lips. She giggled and ran off across the grass, lifting her gathered skirts a little higher than might be considered ladylike. He watched her go, compassion in his eyes.

Charlotte was perplexed by his behaviour. Such tenderness was at odds with his distance, his almost sullen manner, yet his fondness for the girl was unmistakeable.

'Thank you,' she said sincerely. 'My sisters and I are most grateful for your assistance.'

'My pleasure, lady.'

Lukan nodded a brief bow and turned away to attend to Vivienne's mount. His skilful fingers, working carefully over the animal's flanks, soon located the source of its agitation.

He called after her. 'A moment, Lady Charlotte, if you please.'

'Mr de Ville?' Charlotte turned, a maid hovering attentively at her side. When he made no move to approach her, she signalled the others to go ahead and returned to where the horses were still gathered. Lukan's hand was now extended towards her. A long and slender object rested on his palm.

'This pin was embedded beneath the saddle,' he told her. 'And look at this.'

He dipped his fingers under the saddle. They came away stained and sticky with blood.

Charlotte blinked her eyes. 'I don't understand.'

'But I do, my lady. This pin explains why a normally docile animal should suddenly bolt with its rider.'

'Embedded beneath the saddle? But it's a *hat pin.*'

He bade her take it. 'Indeed it is, and a cruel weapon with which to provoke a passive animal.'

Charlotte examined the balled silver head with its family crest and neatly engraved initials.

'It's Vivienne's,' she confirmed. 'I would like to know whose hand was responsible for this.'

'Then ask your sister.'

'What?' She looked at him closely. 'Mr de Ville are you suggesting that Vivienne *deliberately* injured her own horse?'

100

He lifted one dark brow, saying nothing.

'But why? To what end?'

Lukan merely smiled.

'Well?' Charlotte demanded, unnerved by his silence.

He inclined his dark head in a bow. 'Perhaps you will be kind enough to return your sister's property? Good day to you, Lady Charlotte,'

'Good day, Mr de Ville.'

She watched him lead Vivienne's horse to the stables while several grooms came running at his signal to take charge of the remaining mounts. She could not share her brother's fondness for Lukan de Ville. She found his manner disturbing, his stare a little too direct and knowing. And he was subtle. He had managed to accuse her sister of an act of wilful cruelty without speaking a word against her. And if Charlotte had found herself much moved by the tender way he handled poor Elizabeth, she had certainly noted his icy lack of response while Vivienne hung herself about his neck, intent on playing her coquettish games. He had not, by any means, encouraged that flirtation. Indeed his conduct was, as she had always found it, blameless.

With a sigh she turned and walked toward the house. She knew the man. He would not cast aspersions upon a lady's reputation lightly or without just cause. Nor had he made a verbal accusation which she would feel obliged to follow through. He had simply handed her the blood-stained pin, leaving her free to deal with the matter according to her own inclinations. But she had sensed a threat, an unspoken warning in his behaviour. Vivienne should be told of it. Such childish games lost all their innocence when adults were solicited to play. Even in silence, Lukan de Ville had made his feelings clear. He would not be trifled with.

101

II

Malcolm returned to his private drawing-room in the east wing shortly before dinner. He found Lukan already standing in the adjoining library, scowling as he scrutinised the spines of a row of books. His hands were clasped behind his back, his head lifted so that his distinctive profile was outlined against the paler background of the drapes at the far window. His hair was pulled back from his face and neatly bound to hang over his collar and down between his shoulder blades in a thick black tail. He was wearing a deep maroon coat over dark, straight-cut trousers and a colourful brocade waistcoat lined with silver silk. Against the crisp whiteness of his shirt his skin was honey-brown, his eyes as black as jet. He turned his head as Malcolm approached the open doors separating the library from the drawing room. His smile transformed him. It came sometimes with unexpected swiftness, lighting the grave features with a flash of big white teeth. There was true warmth, affection, and a hint of mischief in it.

'Good evening, my fine-feathered friend.' His gaze swept over Malcolm with a twinkle of amusement. He stepped back, his head cocked to one side, and eyed his friend from head to toe. 'Your new tailor is to be applauded. He has my compliments, though I doubt he shall ever have my patronage.'

Malcolm had anticipated his friend's mockery. He tugged at his velvet lapels and executed a slow, elegant turn. He was dressed in a rich blue coat of excellent cut and tasteful embellishment. His trousers were of white linen, piped in gold and tightly buckled below the knee. He was sporting a buttoned waistcoat with gold and silver stripes and a white shirt with fancy lace trims. He pirouetted proudly, then bowed with a flourish.

Lukan grinned. 'I fear you come too late, the ball was yesterday.'

'Indeed, but my fashion-conscious bride insists I dress the part while there are still so many guests around to mark my every defect.'

'I wonder that these guests of yours have nothing worthier to think about. They are at fault who criticise their host.'

Malcolm placed his hands on his hips and strutted foppishly about the room. His voice was deadly serious when he said, 'How can they criticise a host who is perfect? As you see, I am totally, *totally* without flaw.'

Lukan threw back his head and laughed. 'And modest to a fault, My Lord.'

'Take my advice, Lukan. If you hope to have a moment's rest from the rigours of keeping up appearances, never wed yourself to a woman like Leonora.'

Lukan's smile vanished on the instant. He was unexpectedly stung by the reminder. His voice had chilled. 'I'll do my best to remember that.'

Noticing nothing amiss with his friend, Malcolm crossed to a small table, selected a decanter and poured out two generous measures of brandy. For a moment he closed his eyes against a ripple of nausea. It passed almost at once.

'Seriously, my friend,' he continued. 'I do believe the time for you to marry is too long overdue. If for no sounder reason, marry to warm your bed and to put a thousand hopeful ladies out of their misery.'

Lukan accepted the brandy, turning the glass thoughtfully in his palms as he contemplated his reply. 'I am in no hurry,' he said at last.

'Sometimes you worry me, Lukan. In the last few months you have shown little interest in the pleasures of the fairer sex. What ails you, man? Are you already worn out and past your prime at twenty-eight?'

'Perhaps I fear to follow your example,' Lukan suggested. 'I'll not walk meekly into any pre-set trap of some young woman's making.'

Malcolm grinned at that. 'Oh, my dear Lukan, if marriage is a trap then it's a sweet one. I heartily recommend it.'

'Aye, I'm sure you do.'

Malcolm tasted his brandy, savouring its sweet sharpness on his tongue. Its fire, coming after, made his head swim. He pinched the bridge of his nose between a finger and a thumb, breathing deeply through his mouth. Lukan was quick to notice his discomfort.

'What is it? Are you unwell?'

Malcolm tried to shake the lightness from his head. 'It's nothing.'

'Liar, I saw you reel. Are you in pain?'

'A little nausea, that's all.' He smiled at Lukan's concern. 'I have no need of a nursemaid, Lukan. A decent brandy is the surest cure. Now tell me, did you find the time to check our dairy accounts?'

Lukan nodded. 'They seem to be in order.'

'And the stabling ledgers?'

'Ah, now they are a different matter,' he replied. 'I suggest we go over them together in closer detail, Malcolm. There are entries I am less than happy with.'

'Oh? That surprises me, Lukan. We both know Brunswick's a good man.'

'Do we indeed?'

'Of course we do. He came to us with papers of recommendation signed by Lord Hawsham himself.'

Lukan shrugged his shoulders. 'That doesn't seem to have deterred him from making counterfeit claims on his accounts.'

'What? Can this be so?'

Lukan nodded. 'He has a regular habit of claiming a man's wages of several shillings for a small boy's labours costing but a few coppers. Some labourers he claims for receive not a penny piece in wages. Others simply do not exist. By my calculations he also works only half the hours he registers, thereby pocketing twice the money he is entitled to.'

'Ye gods! The man is no better than a common swindler.'

Lukan nodded again. 'At five o'clock this morning I found the main stables supervised by a ten-year-old boy who needed the hard edge of my boot to rouse him from his slumbers. He did not stir while Sam Cooper prepared a mount for his journey to fetch the doctor from Oakwood Lodge, nor when I spoke at length with Sam on the matter. Indeed, I could have saddled up and auctioned off every animal in the stalls without disturbing him.'

'What? Was Brunswick absent then?'

104

'Aye, and eighteen of our horses, including Starlight Warrior, were dependent for their safety on a half-starved and exhausted little boy.'

'So where in hell was he, the Master of the Horse?'

'I hear he spent the night in Bishorne village with the wife of the local magistrate.'

'This is too much. I'll have his job for this.'

'I hope you hold off a while before you do,' Lukan said. 'It will be interesting to see what claims he makes for extra labour during his long absence.'

Malcolm poured another brandy and seated himself in a high, straight-backed chair.

'I don't understand it,' he said. 'The man came to us with the very best credentials.'

'He certainly did. I remember being very much impressed by them at the time, though I did wonder why Lord Hawsham wished to rid himself of such a paragon. I'll make a few discreet inquiries of my own on the Hawsham estates, if that meets with your approval.'

'Of course it does. And do it quickly, Lukan. Let's have this business dealt with as soon as possible.' He sipped his brandy, then shook his head and added, 'I just might horse-whip the rascal myself if your suspicions are proved.'

'They will be, have no doubt of that.' Lukan helped himself to a less generous measure of brandy. 'Did anyone tell you about the *riding accident* this afternoon?'

'Ah yes, I hear my little sister's horse bolted and you rushed to her rescue like the proverbial knight in shining armour.' Malcolm raised his glass. 'You seem to be our hero of the day once again, my friend.'

'The cause was not the same,' Lukan told him, shaking his head.

'But just as worthy, was it not?'

'I think not, Malcolm. Lady Leonora made no personal contribution to her own danger when Starlight Warrior bolted at the Midsummer Fair. The incident was not of her making.'

Malcolm's brow arched toward his hairline. 'But not so in my sister's case?'

105

'Not so. Lady Vivienne used the old hat pin trick.'

'What? She wouldn't!'

'I assure you she did.'

'The idiotic little fool!' Malcolm exclaimed. 'She knows horses too well to indulge in such tactics. I hope you took her to task on the matter?'

'I most certainly did not,' Lukan rejoined sharply. 'It is not my place to censure your sister's actions, however much I might deplore them. I brought the matter to Lady Charlotte's attention and now I'm bringing it to yours.'

Malcolm nodded. 'I'll speak to her. I fear she still has a childish appetite for attention.'

'There is more to this than mere attention-seeking, my friend. May I speak frankly?'

'Were you ever wont to speak otherwise?' Malcolm asked.

Lukan chose to ignore the gentle mockery in his friend's question. 'In my opinion there are three things your sister is quite urgently in need of.'

'And they are?'

'A chaperone with a strong hand, a tighter rein on her activities, and an early marriage.'

Malcolm looked back at him with a puzzled expression on his face, then his blue eyes twinkled with amusement and he began to smile.

'Why, I do believe she has a fancy for you, Lukan. By the gods, my baby sister has a fancy for him and the dashing gypsy gentleman is at a loss how best to handle it.'

'She is heading for trouble, Malcolm.'

'But she's only a child,' Malcolm reminded him. 'She is only just fourteen. Besides, if she has set her sights on you, my dear Lukan, then she shows uncommonly good taste for one of such tender years.'

'This is no laughing matter, Malcolm.'

'Ah but it is, my friend, so long as you keep your breeches buckled.'

Lukan was scowling now. 'Malcolm, will you please take this matter seriously?'

'Why on earth should I?'

'Because today she hangs *my* name upon her weakness, but tomorrow those same shortcomings will take her to one of the house servants or one of your own estate labourers.'

'What?' The smiled faded from Malcolm's handsome features.

Lukan met his inquiring gaze. It was not easy to tell a man that his fourteen-year-old sister was declaring herself available for a quick roll in the hay with any man determined enough to take up her challenge. He was familiar with the type. Young Vivienne had rubbed herself against him in unmistakeable invitation. And she had the look, the early signs of the wanton. She might rush unchecked into a passionate affair with the first man bold enough or stupid enough to risk the Earl's wrath. She might even prove to be the worst kind of tease, seducing a man with her coquettish games only to scream rape once she realised she had led him on beyond the point of no return. Whichever way she eventually jumped, the girl was brewing up more trouble than the earldom needed.

Malcolm was watching him. 'Lukan, be honest with me. What is happening with my sister?'

'I believe the problem may be nipped in the bud.'

'Problem? What problem?'

'*Potential* problem,' Lukan corrected.

'Malcolm scowled and swirled his brandy around the glass. 'Are you sure this is not merely part and parcel of her growing up and putting her feminine skills to the test? Young women flirt, you know.'

'Malcolm, she literally threw herself into my arms with an invitation most red-blooded men would have accepted on the spot.'

'She has a fancy for you,' Malcolm persisted. 'It's no more than a naïve flirtation. It's natural Lukan, innocent.'

'No, my friend, it is not innocent.'

'What do you mean? My God, has some man already ...?'

'No, I do not believe so.'

'Then what?'

Lukan sighed heavily. 'She's looking for conquests. She's making offers, promises she may or may not be intending to

107

keep. Some man will take her at her word, and soon, if she is not kept under firmer guard.'

'She has no mother to guide her now, not even a big sister to offer advice except when Charlotte makes one of her rare visits. She's just a child. She doesn't know what she's doing.'

Lukan smiled wryly. 'My friend, your sister knows exactly what she's doing.'

'But she's *fourteen*.'

Lukan shrugged his broad shoulders. 'It is a simple truth. Some women tire too soon of their virginity.'

'Damn it,' Malcolm growled. 'I had no idea.'

'You've had other things on your mind, my friend.'

'Yes, that's true enough, and now it seems the problem is acute, so I must trust your instincts.'

'My judgment is sound. That one needs careful watching.'

'Thank you. I'll see to it.'

'And I will do my bit. The word is already out that any man found alone with her will be dismissed on the spot, no questions asked.' He scowled into his friend's face. 'Malcolm? Are you sure you are all right? You look too pale and drawn for my comfort.'

'I'm fine,' Malcolm smiled. 'A little tired, perhaps, but well enough.'

Their conversation ebbed and flowed upon trivial matters before lapsing into an easy silence. Malcolm leaned back in his chair and closed his eyes. He was still troubled by pains in the head and a queer, unsettled sensation in his stomach.

Lukan stretched out his long legs and crossed them at the ankles, watching Malcolm through hooded eyes. How could it be so easy to betray him? How could he steal what Malcolm loved and still believe their friendship unimpaired? They had been as close as brothers all their lives, too self-contained for the Earl, who packed Lukan off to a school for young gentlemen two hundred miles away. He had believed that distance would dissolve the bond but he was wrong; the parting only served to strengthen it. Nothing had bruised or stained their special friendship in twenty-eight years. Then Leonora had stepped into their lives, and Lukan's love for her had brushed aside those years as if they were of no account.

Now Lukan cleared his throat and glowered angrily at his thoughts. It seemed to him that when it came to matters of the heart a man might cease to recognise the entitlements of his brother. More than that, in matters of the heart a man might cease to recognise himself.

Malcolm was beginning to doze in his chair when a maid entered the room to announce that dinner would be served at seven o'clock sharp and that Doctor Richard Winterton had arrived from Oakwood Lodge at Sir Malcolm's bidding.

'Business?' Lukan inquired.

'A small matter,' Malcolm yawned, rising to his feet.

'If it's private . . .'

'Not from you, Lukan,' he smiled, bidding his friend remain seated. He swayed slightly but quickly regained his equilibrium as his guest entered the room. 'Ah, Winterton, it's good to see you again. I believe you know Lukan de Ville?'

'Indeed, sir. Indeed.' The man pumped Lukan's hand warmly before dropping wearily into an armchair.

Doctor Richard Winterton, late of Romarsh Street, Oxford, was a short man whose bristling moustaches and receding hairline failed to conceal the youthful freshness of his features. His clothes hung upon his narrow shoulders with a touch too much tailor's padding and an inch or two of extraneous fabric in the sleeves. He had a ready smile, a somewhat reedy voice and an abundance of natural enthusiasm. All this gave him the appearance of a half-grown youth playing the part of an older man. He was in fact a competent thirty-year-old whose medical skills placed him amongst the best in his profession. He had known Malcolm personally for many years and had met Lukan de Ville on several occasions socially.

'My condolences, dear boy,' he said now, looking intently at Malcolm's pale features. 'I never had the pleasure of meeting the Countess Alyce personally, but I knew her by reputation. A fine lady. A truly fine lady. The ceremony takes place tomorrow morning, does it not?'

'It does,' Malcolm confirmed, pouring his guest a brandy. He eased himself back into his armchair with a deep sigh before clearing his throat, adding, 'It is about my mother that I wish to speak to you, Richard. You were summoned to the bedside quite soon after she died, were you not?'

'Within the hour, so I believe,' the visitor nodded.

'And you discovered nothing odd about the body?'

'Odd?' Winterton glanced at Lukan and raised one eyebrow quizzically. Then he leaned forward in his seat, his eyes bright with interest. 'I saw only a corpse, beautifully dressed and very carefully laid out, but a corpse none the less.'

'And dead for an hour?'

'At the very least.'

'Perhaps longer?'

'Perhaps,' Winterton shrugged. 'I was sent for some time after the fatal seizure had occurred. I had to rouse myself from my bed, dress and take a little breakfast before setting out for the house . . .'

'How long?' Malcolm pressed. 'How long might the Countess have been lying dead before you arrived to examine her?'

'Well, first of all let me say that I was not required to examine the lady, since it was clear that she was already dead. She had suffered a serious seizure, the last of several suffered in recent months. The only task required of me was to confirm the death. I was instructed that the family's own physician, Sir Marcus Shaw, was expected at the Hall and would carry out any examination he might consider necessary.'

Malcolm nodded thoughtfully. 'Quite, quite.'

Lukan rose from his chair and set down his glass next to the decanter of brandy. Some sixth sense brought a prickling of the fine hairs at the nape of his neck. 'Perhaps you should tell us what all this is about,' he suggested. 'Is there some mystery here?'

'There was nothing more to be done, if that's your concern,' Doctor Winterton interjected. 'Had I been in the next room at the time of the attack I could have done nothing to save her. Let me assure you, my dear Malcolm, that your lady wife did everything possible to make the Countess comfortable to the last. That the patient died was due entirely to the nature of the illness and not, I hasten to stress, to any fault in the nursing.'

'I have no doubts of that, Richard.'

'Then what?' Lukan asked. 'What troubles you, Malcolm?'

Malcolm raised and lowered his shoulders in a sigh before relating Will Hynd's story. At the end of it Dr Winterton and Lukan exchanged glances and the doctor indicated with a gesture that Malcolm should be given another brandy. Lukan obliged, then stood back and surveyed his friend with furrowed brows.

'Malcolm, that is the most ridiculous story I have ever heard,' he said at last. 'And by giving even small credence to it you insult the integrity of Lady Leonora.'

'I have already told you that I have no doubts as to the quality of Leonora's nursing,' Malcolm protested.

'Then what troubles you? Why is the good doctor suddenly brought here to give account of his findings and to confirm what you already know about your mother's death?'

'I need to know the whole truth,' Malcolm insisted. 'I need to know if my mother lay unattended in that room for fifteen hours while the rest of the house, including myself, made merry at the wedding celebrations.'

'What, left on her deathbed for *fifteen hours*?'

'That's what the woman said.'

Lukan shuddered. 'On whose instructions?'

'I don't know. Perhaps Anabel Corey ...'

'Without her mistress being aware of it?'

'I do not know,' Malcolm repeated wearily.

'Damn it, Malcolm, don't you see what you're doing? You're allowing the ramblings of a serving wench to cloud your judgment. Tell him, Richard. Tell our foolish friend that what he fears is simply not possible.'

Winterton nodded. 'Lukan's right, even though it is impossible to ascertain exactly how long a body has been lying dead when it is first examined. Its condition will depend on room temperature, stomach contents, general state of health before death ...' He spread his hands, pursing his lips thoughtfully. 'The death-rigour can take a full twelve hours to establish itself or come and pass away again in the same time.'

'Then the time of death cannot be proved?' Malcolm asked.

111

'This Dobbin woman's story cannot be dismissed as nonsense?'

Once again the doctor shrugged his narrow shoulders. 'There was a huge fire in the room,' he recalled. 'The windows were tightly shuttered and the atmosphere was hot and stuffy, with a strong scent of roses and dried lavender. In my opinion, had the corpse lain there for as long as fifteen hours, there would have been some signs of early putrefaction.'

'And there were none?'

'Not to my knowledge.'

'So you are quite satisfied that she died some time around dawn this morning?'

'I have already signed the death certificate to that effect, Malcolm.'

'Yes of course,' Malcolm smiled. He passed a hand across his brow. His head was throbbing again and the brandy was beginning to irritate his stomach. Having given voice to his concerns he realised how foolish his story must sound.

'Are you satisfied?' Lukan asked. His voice was unexpectedly cold.

'Perfectly,' Malcolm nodded. 'I simply wanted to be certain of the facts before I speak to the Dobbin woman after the funeral tomorrow.'

'Lady Leonora told you that she was at your mother's bedside when the final attack came,' Lukan reminded him. 'Was that not fact enough for you? Must you test her word against that of a common servant?'

Malcolm sighed. 'You are angry, Lukan.'

'I am amazed,' Lukan corrected. 'Amazed that a gentleman of your calibre should allow an ignorant serving wench to cast suspicion upon the integrity of his own wife.'

Malcolm began to rise from his chair. 'No, it was not really suspicion, Lukan. I was simply ... simply ...'

As he reached his feet his legs buckled, lacking the strength to support his weight. He lurched forward, glass and contents forgotten as he clawed the air for support. Lukan moved with alarming swiftness to grab him before he fell to the floor and, with the doctor's assistance, soon had him stretched out on a comfortable couch and covered with a rug. They rang for Hammond, who emerged from an adjoining room and in his calm, unhurried way set about attending to his master's needs.

Malcolm was shivering and his teeth were chattering. Even so his skin, the colour of parchment, was clammy with perspiration. While Richard Winterton checked his eyes, throat and pulse-rate, Lukan stooped beside the couch, his features tight with concern as he watched his friend's ashen face.

'What is it, Malcolm? What ails you?'

Malcolm tried to smile. 'Only a stomach upset. I've had a bilious headache all day. Everything I eat and drink seems to disagree with me.'

'What could have caused it? Have you taken something?'

'Not that I am aware of, though I must confess I took more wine than usual last night. Drank myself into a stupor, I'm ashamed to say. Perhaps one of the bottles was bad.'

'I have never known you to drink to excess, Malcolm,' Richard Winterton observed.

'Nor I,' Malcolm said, closing his eyes against a wave of nausea. 'And yet the truth is inescapable. Last night I became so drunk that today I have no recollection of the consummation of my marriage.'

'Perhaps you were so inebriated that it didn't happen,' Winterton suggested with a smile.

'It happened,' Malcolm replied flatly.

Lukan stood back from the couch with a brooding scowl on his face. He was recalling Rebecca's words about tricks with virgin's water and drugged men fooled into believing they had performed certain acts of which they had no memory. And he recalled the wine Malcolm had been given the night before, the wine Leonora had spiked with hemlock and essence of opium in order to leave her husband's bed for his own.

'Bad wine?' His voice was hoarse. He cleared his throat and said more clearly, 'Bad wine? Could that have been the cause, Winterton? Could he be injured by tainted wine?'

'Perhaps, but not seriously.' Winterton offered Lukan a reassuring smile. 'Don't look so anxious, man. Malcolm has the constitution of an ox. I recommend a sharp emetic to clear out the stomach contents, followed by a soothing cordial of laudanum and treacle to settle the discomfort. And tea, plenty of good sage tea with a little pinch of ground ginger.'

Dr Winterton rang for a maid and ordered her to bring plenty of hot water and mustard. Another girl was sent to the kitchens for the prescribed tea while a third was ordered to inform Lady Leonora of her husband's sudden collapse. That evening's dinner, he insisted, would have to go ahead without the presence of the newly-weds.

While waiting for Leonora to arrive, Lukan paced the corridor outside Malcolm's rooms. He marched this way and that like a caged animal, his fists tightly clenched and his face dark with concern. He strode to meet her as she hurried along the corridor. She would have ignored him but he grabbed her wrist and pulled her sharply to one side. He spoke harshly into her face, no trace of affection in him.

'Your husband is sick, madam. A little bad wine, the doctor thinks. Bad wine indeed! I must speak to you alone, urgently.'

'Not now, Lukan. I must go in to Malcolm.'

His voice was as cold as ice. 'Tonight.'

Her eyes flashed angrily. 'Let go of me, Lukan de Ville.'

'Not until I have your word,' he hissed. 'You will come to me tonight.'

'*Impossible*,' she flared, tossing her head. 'Now sir, will you be so good as to unhand me so that I may attend to my husband's needs?'

'Nay, I fear you have already done that, madam.'

'And for who's benefit was it done?'

'*Vixen!*' he hissed the word through clenched teeth.

'*Gypsy!*' she countered.

'Have a care, lady ...' Lukan gripped her wrist so tightly that she winced. 'We will speak of this tonight or Malcolm Cavendish will be asking how long his mother was left to lie on her death bed before the doctor was sent for.'

'What?' She paled before his eyes. 'Oh, my God!'

'Tonight, Lia.'

She nodded. 'The tower rooms at ten.'

Lukan released her wrist with a sudden, almost contemptuous movement. The marks of his fingers were livid on her creamy skin. She flashed him a look of pure fury before sweeping into the drawing room in a flurry of silk and lace and a whiff of perfume. He watched her go with a coldness in his eyes. Bad wine indeed! He was beginning to wonder if his sister Rebecca possessed more natural wisdom than he had been willing to allow. Perhaps she had been right all along. Perhaps he had lifted the lid of Pandora's Box when he won the heart of Leonora Cavendish.

CHAPTER SEVEN

I

The clock above the old gatehouse showed eight minutes past ten but the old chapel bell was still chiming the hour, a doleful sound, muffled and deep, as if drawn up from the bowels of the earth. A swift shape swathed in a black cloak crossed the courtyard at a rapid pace. It moved along an inner wall, found the gatehouse door and slipped inside. Once there, Lady Leonora lowered the dark hood from her hair and climbed the stairs on tiptoe.

Lukan de Ville was waiting in the upper bedchamber, his folded arms resting on the marble mantle above the fireplace, his eyes staring fixedly at the empty grate. He had thrown his coat across the big bed and unfastened his waistcoat. It hung loose, revealing a crimson lining, over his crisp white shirt. Encased in their narrow-cut trousers his legs were long, his hips taut, his belly flat and hard. He was built like the powerful hounds he kept; long, lean and muscular. For a moment Leonora paused in the doorway to watch him. She was still unable to turn her gaze in his direction without yielding to an inner shift, a quiet stirring of her most intimate emotions. It was as if he reached inside her with invisible fingers to fondle and toy with her most private parts.

She made no sound or movement but he sensed her presence. He moved his head just far enough to watch her from the corners of his eyes. His dark gaze devoured her, noting the creamy texture of the skin above her bodice, the dainty circle of her waist above her satin skirts. She saw his glance flicker to her throat, her mouth, her hair, and when at last his eyes met hers she was reminded with a jolt that her own emotions found their match in his. She could feel his pent-up angers as he watched her. From that angle his face appeared longer and more gaunt, his cheekbones high and sharp. His eyes were slits, wary and feline; a wildcat's eyes.

'How fares your husband, madam?' he demanded coldly.

She stepped inside the room, keeping a guarded distance between them. 'My husband is sleeping, thank you.'

'And his condition?'

'He is well enough.'

'Indeed? He will recover, then?'

She smiled a little. 'Of course he will recover. Really, my dear, your concern is grossly overdone. He has an upset stomach, nothing more. Believe me, he is in no danger.'

Lukan brought himself erect and stepped away from the fireplace, his face grim. 'I saw him collapse. He fell into my arms like an invalid, drained of his strength, his face the colour of death. What have you done to him, Lia? What price has he been forced to pay for your adultery?'

'*Our* adultery,' she answered swiftly. 'You were a willing partner in the crime.'

'What did you give him?'

'I have already told you.'

'Tell me again.'

She sighed. 'I laced his wine with hemlock and opium, a harmless mixture.'

'Harmless perhaps, but in what quantities, for Heaven's sake?'

117

'Only the mildest doses,' she insisted. 'I gave him nothing in excess, Lukan, only enough to keep him sleeping soundly through the night.'

'And to burden him with sickness,' he added sharply. 'And to bring about his total collapse. You were careless, Lia. In your haste to be rid of him you made a gross miscalculation of the dose.'

'I most certainly did not,' she contradicted. 'It seems he has a low tolerance for the mixture. How could I possibly know that? I gave him only a standard dose, and since I have no claim to second sight I trust I may be forgiven that mistake?'

'No madam, you may be forgiven *nothing*.' He stood with his feet apart, his big hands in fists upon his hips. 'You made him dangerously ill. You brought him to his knees with your harmless potion. How could you be so stupid? What were you trying to do, *poison* him?'

Her face blanched. 'How dare you?' she flared. 'How *dare* you say I tried to harm my husband? And what of yourself, Lukan de Ville? Last night you had no such noble concerns for his welfare.'

'Last night I had no idea.'

'Not so! Last night you did not care.'

'That is a lie. Now madam, have a care . . .'

She tossed her head and glared at him. 'Do not protest your innocence to *me*, sir. You knew well enough that he was lying stupefied. You spared him no thought then, did you? You were too busy bedding his wife to care a jot if his drink contained hemlock and opium or deadly poison.'

His voice was dangerously low. 'Madam, last night I was bewitched by a temptress.'

'*Liar!*' she flung at him, 'You were bedevilled by your own lusts, Lukan de Ville, your own base appetites, nothing more.'

'Aye, madam, lusts that were priced too highly if Malcolm must keep account.'

'You *hypocrite*!' She clenched her fists and yelled the word into his face, not caring how she provoked him.

He drew back, raising his hand waist-high as if to ward her

118

off. 'Have a care, Lia ...' There was a warning in his voice which she in her fury opted to ignore.

'*Hypocrite!*' she cried defiantly. 'You care nothing for Malcolm, *nothing*. You only want to take control, to lay down the rules and regulations of the game. You'll be content to make a cuckold of him, friend or no, but only on your own terms, not on mine.'

With a growl of anger he reached out and grabbed her by the shoulders and pulled her roughly towards him. Then he stopped, his face so close to hers that he could see his own reflection in the dark pupils of her eyes. The breath caught in his throat. He looked surprised, then closed his eyes and lowered his mouth to hers with a tenderness that belied the anger still simmering inside him.

Leonora accepted his kiss with a small shiver of pleasure. The mercurial swiftness of his moods excited her. Sometimes he moved from stillness into rage upon the instant. It gave her power of calm or storm over him. She lifted her arms to encircle his neck and leaned her body very close to his. She felt his quick response and this too was power in her hands. When he withdrew his lips he still held her so tightly that his words were muffled by her cheek.

'It frightened me, Lia,' he confessed, 'when I saw him so ill and heard him blame his sickness on tainted wine. It frightened me that you and I, who love him, could come that close to doing him real harm.'

'I know, my dear,' she soothed. 'I saw at once that you were sick with worry.'

'And with anger,' he admitted. 'Our passion for each other must not make us careless, Lia. I want to be sure that Malcolm is as safe in your hands as you are in his. Oh Lia, if ever I thought you meant to do him harm ...'

'Never,' she said firmly. 'You have my solemn word on that, Lukan. I love him too, remember, in my way. Neither by design nor default will I ever bring harm upon that dear man.'

He lifted his head to look into her eyes. 'Swear it.'

'I swear it, Lukan.'

He winced as if in pain. 'How can I let myself be torn

119

between the two of you? Loving you both will divide me. It will rive me in two.'

'No, Lukan, you must never let that happen.'

He released her suddenly. 'But how can it be otherwise when I love my friend as deeply as I love his wife? You are right, my Lia. I should be left to choke on my hypocrisy.'

'Don't torture yourself, Lukan.'

'Sometimes I dread what we have started, you and I.'

'Then you are a fool,' she said gently. 'You must not trouble your mind with fears of what may come to us tomorrow or the next day or the next.'

'Are you immune to such concerns, my Lia?'

She lifted one of his hands to her lips and kissed each long, hard finger in turn. 'Remember this, my dear; *sufficient unto the day are the evils thereof.*'

He laughed, a sudden sound, sharp and bitter. 'You quote the Bible at me? We meet in secret to discuss such sins as lust, hypocrisy, betrayal, and you seek to gentle me with words from that holy book?'

'I love you, Lukan.'

Her words were a simple statement spoken while she pressed his hand to her cheek and looked directly into his eyes. He gazed back at her, his expression softening as he searched her eyes for the truth behind her words.

'Aye, my lady,' he said at last, his voice a hoarse whisper. 'I know you do.'

He drew her back into his arms and held her there. Moments later they sprang apart at the sound of a soft but urgent rapping at the door.

'Miss Leonora! Miss Leonora!'

'What is it, Anabel?' she called out.

'The time, Leonora. Pay heed to the time.'

'Leave us, Anabel. But keep a careful watch. I'll be with you presently.'

'You should leave at once,' Lukan told her.

'Not yet. I want to stay with you a little longer.'

Lukan shook his head and gently removed her arms from around his neck. 'Malcolm is ill and Sir Oscar has taken to prowling the corridors at night to pamper his insomnia,' he reminded her. 'Go back to your husband. Tonight I will rest easier in my mind knowing that you and he are together.'

Her smile was teasing. 'Does that mean you would rather send me to Malcolm's bed than lie beside me here, in ours?'

He shook his head. 'Don't mock me, Lia. You know this marriage has sliced my heart to its core. Must you now rub salt into the wounds?'

With a sigh Leonora slid her arms around his waist and pressed her cheek to his chest until she could feel the patch of coarse dark hair hidden beneath his shirt. She loved the clean, outdoor smell of him. He bathed often and his clothes were laundered in forest streams and then stretched over bushes or hedges to dry. This left the fabric impregnated with the scents of sunshine and fresh air. He smelled of the seasons, of the open air, the forest.

'Forgive me, Lukan. I know this can not be easy for you.'

'Easy? *Easy?*' He laughed again, a small, harsh chuckle. 'Lia, it is barely to be suffered.'

She lowered her cheek back to his chest, blaming herself for his agony. Lukan, not Malcolm, should have been her husband. This gypsy was her love, her *grand passion*. He would willingly give her everything he possessed, but only Malcolm could have given her Beresford Hall. Too long she had been caught between the two. Hungering for both, she never would surrender the one prize for the other. She had surely tested Lukan to his limits by resolving to have both.

Now Lukan stood with his head bowed and his eyes closed, clasping her against him.

His voice was soft and low. 'When I hold you like this I forget everything.'

'What else matters, so long as we are together?'

'Malcolm matters,' he reminded her. 'As does Harry Dobbin's wife.'

She lifted her head, half smiling. 'Who?'

'Nellie Dobbin, the young woman who came from the dairy to help you nurse the Countess during her illness. She was

121

kept on by Anabel Corey to fetch and carry for you during the wedding preparations.'

'Ah yes, she's small and young and very pregnant. She feared to look at Lady Alyce's face lest her unborn child be born wearing the same dreadful grimace. Yes, I remember Nellie.'

Lukan stroked her hair as he spoke. 'It seems she told her husband a disturbing little story which he promptly took to Will Hynd on the Home Farm.'

'Yes?'

'And today Will Hynd felt obliged to pass the information directly to Malcolm.'

Leonora drew back her head a little. She was smiling, but her quick mind raced ahead of the trouble she sensed was about to be revealed.

'What story?' she asked softly. 'How could the talk of servants be of interest to Malcolm?'

Lukan released her from his embrace and watched her smooth the bodice of her dress with both hands. It was an unconsciously sensuous movement. 'This Nellie Dobbin told her husband that Anabel Corey rushed from the sickroom in a panic just before the wedding. When the girl crept in to satisfy her curiosity she found the Countess lying dead on her bed, struck down by another seizure.'

Leonora licked a sudden dryness from her lips. 'Dead, you say?'

'In her opinion, yes.'

'And?' she prompted.

'She claims that the death was then concealed, that the sick-room door was locked and guarded so that the wedding might take place as arranged.'

'I see.' Leonora gave no outward indication of the lump suddenly constricting her throat.

Lukan seated himself on the bed and allowed his fingers to caress the mounds and hollows of the eiderdown-filled cover.

'Her story is that the ceremony, the feast, the dance, the supper were all allowed to go ahead while Lady Alyce lay behind that locked door. According to her, the corpse lay

122

unattended until the alarm was raised this morning.'

'So many hours?'

'Aye, and that would mean that while you and I were taking joy of each other in this very bed, the Countess lay on her deathbed without so much as a corpse-candle to light her way from this world to the next.'

'And all this was told to Malcolm?'

'Aye, told in full, and the shock of hearing it must have added to his grief. He sent for Dr Winterton at once to discuss the matter.'

'The doctor? Richard Winterton? But why?'

'Because he wanted to be certain of his facts before he speaks to Nellie Dobbin after luncheon tomorrow.'

Leonora paced from one side of the room to the other, her brows furrowed and her fists tightly clenched. 'Does Sir Oscar know of it?'

'Not so far as I am aware.' Lukan sighed and leaned back against the pillows with his hands clasped behind his head and one leg balanced across his bent knee. 'Her story is obviously fanciful in the extreme, but Malcolm knows what mischief can be set abroad if such fancies are allowed to go unchecked.'

'And he intends speaking to her tomorrow?' Leonora interrupted. By now her pacing had become agitated and her face intent. 'After the burial?'

'After luncheon was what he said, and the burial will be over by then.'

'Are you sure of that? Did he definitely say he would speak to her *after* luncheon and, not before?'

'I know what I heard, but why . . .?'

She interrupted sharply. 'And what exactly did the doctor say?'

'That it was nonsense, of course.'

'Are you sure, Lukan? Are you absolutely certain that the doctor did not doubt my story?'

'Story? *Story?*' He lifted his head from the pillows and swung his feet to the floor. 'So she *did* die earlier than you reported. Ye gods, I suspected as much. You only agreed to meet me here tonight when I told you to expect to be questioned on the matter. What happened, Lia? Did she die while you and I were together, is that the truth of it? Did we stay too long at our pleasures? Was she dead when you returned to the sickroom at dawn?'

Leonora stopped pacing the room to face him in exasperation. Her voice was harsh. 'For Heaven's sake, Lukan, will you please stop questioning me and tell me exactly what Dr Winterton said to Malcolm?'

'I have already told you that. The story is a nonsense. How could the old Countess have lain dead for *fifteen hours*? The very idea is too preposterous for words.'

'And Malcolm believed that?'

'Of course he did, after I persuaded him that no gentleman worth his salt would consider taking the word of a servant girl against that of his own wife.'

Leonora's head jerked up. 'You told him that?'

'Of course I did.'

'So the doubt was already planted in his mind? He actually suspected me, so that you felt obliged to speak on my behalf?'

She saw the shadow pass across his face. 'Suspected you of what, Lia?'

'Of leaving his mother. Of going ahead with the wedding. Of concealing her death.'

'But Lia, you did *not* conceal her death.' There was a cutting edge to his voice that revealed his desire to convince them both of the fact. She made as if to turn away from him. He jumped to his feet, caught her by the arm and forced her to look him in the eye. 'Nellie Dobbin was lying, Lia. Tell me she was lying.'

Her eyes flashed. 'You have no right to question me.'

He pulled her against him. 'Tell me,' he insisted. 'Tell me you are innocent of this.'

Leonora struggled in vain to free herself, then lifted her head defiantly. 'All right, all right. You shall have the whole truth, and may it please you to hear it.'

'Ye gods, what are you saying?'

'Of course I left her there. What else was I supposed to do?

124

Was I to abandon my wedding just twenty minutes before it was due to take place? Was I to turn my celebrations into a funeral and all my happy guests into mourners?'

His fingers tightened around her arm and his features took on a grim tautness. 'Do not tease me with flippant games, woman. This is no playing matter. Confess that this is nonsense.'

She chewed upon her lower lip. 'If only I had known there was a witness. But I didn't know, I didn't even suspect.'

He shook her roughly. 'Stop it. No more. Tell me the *truth*.'

'Why should I waste my breath?' she flared. 'You have the truth already from Nellie Dobbin.'

'What? I don't believe it.'

'Then you are a fool.'

When she tried to break free Lukan held her fast, and when he spoke again his voice was thick with incredulity. 'Is this the truth? Is Nellie's story true? The Countess died before the wedding took place?'

'Is it the truth,' she told him.

'And you deliberately concealed it?'

'I did.'

'Ye gods! You simply locked the sickroom door and left her there?'

'Of course I did.'

'For fifteen hours?' Dismay hampered his voice. 'You left her there in that locked room *for fifteen hours*!'

'She was dead, Lukan. She was *dead*!'

He looked toward the big four poster bed, shaking his dark head in disbelief. 'All those hours, you and me, here in this very bed, laughing and loving together, and all the time ... all the time ...'

'For Heaven's sake, Lukan she was *dead*!' Leonora flared, snatching her arms free of his grip.

His voice was a growl. 'And death must be respected.'

'To what extent? Should we offer a corpse priority over the living?'

'Aye, if needs demand it. The dead must be given their due rights and rituals.'

'Fine sentiments, sir, but no corpse will ever benefit at *my* expense.' She made the declaration with a haughty toss of her head. 'And remember this, Lukan de Ville, any crime of mine is also your own. It served *your* pleasure well enough to let the old woman lie until a more convenient time.'

Her words shocked him. 'Madam, would you make me party to this wickedness?'

'Not I, sir. You made yourself a party to it.'

He stared back at her with an unreadable expression on his face, then shook his head from side to side in quiet disbelief. 'Oh, my Lia,' he said at last, his voice low and husky. 'How can you be at once so tender and so cruel, so caring and so ruthlessly conniving?'

'Because I am a survivor,' she said with icy emphasis. 'I do what I must, Lukan. I fought too hard for Beresford to be pipped at the post by a wicked old woman who chose my day, my very moment of glory, to make her final exit from the world.'

The anger drained from him. 'Oh Lia, Lia, sometimes I find myself appalled by the strength of your will.'

'I never promised you it would be otherwise.'

'I know that.'

She sighed. 'I am as I am.'

'Aye, and I must love you in spite of it.'

'You'll not change me, Lukan.'

'I know that, too.' He raised and lowered his shoulders in a sigh. 'So, what is to be done about the Dobbin girl?'

'I will deal with the matter personally,' she said. 'And Malcolm will never suspect I had a hand in it.'

'How on earth do you propose to manage that?'

'Through the husband. I'll do it through the husband. Quickly, Lukan, fetch him to me.'

'What?'

'We must strike the anvil while the iron is hot. Bring him to me.'

He glared at her. His temper, slow-burning but turned to quick-silver by her presence, flared afresh. 'I will do no such thing!'

'Lukan please, I need to speak to him now. Please ...'

126

He shook his head. 'Madam, I am not your messenger.'

'Oh, why must you be so proud? Fetch him. I must see him right away. Do it for me, Lukan.'

His eyes flashed darkly. 'I most certainly will not, madam. Let your hired hands run your errands, for I'll not place myself at your disposal. Make use of the yokel, Cooper, since it pleases him so much to do your bidding.'

Leonora smiled at his hostility and reached up to touch his lips with her fingertips. 'And would it not please *you* to serve me, Lukan?'

'No madam, it would not.'

'I think you are a liar, sir,' she whispered.

He took her by the waist and pulled her towards him with a sudden jerk that made her gasp. When he bent his head to kiss her she nibbled his lips with fierce little bites and then soothed away the sting of her teeth with a damp tongue. Her fingers twisted into his hair and tugged sharply to guide his head while her mouth sought his with a hunger that surprised them both. She felt his passion flare and was herself aroused, as much by the delicious pain of their kisses as by the powerful sexual force that flared between them.

At last he gripped her waist tightly with both hands and with a determined effort set her away from him. A tendril of dark hair hung over his face and his chest rose and fell with his heavy breathing. She reached down to cup his swollen genitals in her hands and smiled in satisfaction. He licked his lips, tasting his own blood on them.

'Witchery,' he said hoarsely.

'Love,' she corrected.

Lukan bent his body so that his hips drew back beyond her reach. His gaze travelled over her and his mouth curved in a slow smile that had its echo in the twinkle of his black eyes. Then he stepped quickly away from her and snatched his coat from the bed. He flung the garment over one shoulder as he strode for the Monks' Stair. In the tiny doorway he paused to look back at her. The smile had vanished from his face when he said, 'Heed me well, madam. I'll not be made to run your errands or carry your messages to and fro.'

127

'Perhaps not, but I think you will come running when I call.' Her smile was brilliant, her gaze challenging.

'Aye, just as you will run to me when I need you. But know it and know it well, there'll be no mistress and vassal here.'

She tossed her head. 'Nor master and maid.'

'As lover, friend or enemy, I'll stay your equal.'

'As I am yours.' She mocked him with her smile. 'It seems we are agreed.'

'Aye, we are agreed, but have a care, my Lia. I'll not be made use of and I'll not bow meekly to your will.'

'Nor I to yours, Lukan de Ville,' she declared, lifting her chin in silent challenge. 'Nor I to yours.'

He turned, stepped into the angled recess and was gone. Leonora started after him, his name on her lips. She was tempted to call him back, but checked herself almost at once and hurried instead to the main door. She found Anabel waiting outside on the stairs.

'Send for Sam Cooper at once,' she instructed.

'What, now? At this time of night?'

'At once,' Leonora repeated. 'Have him wait for me downstairs until I'm finished here. I am not to be disturbed.'

'Leonora, what are you scheming?'

'Just do it, Anabel.' She closed the door and slipped the bolt in place. Then she moved back to the bed, smoothed the creases from the cover where his boots had rested, and waited.

He came without a word, as she had known he would, just reappeared and leaned casually against the wall, watching her through narrowed eyes. She met his gaze with equal arrogance. They were like enemies, weighing and measuring the opposition. At last he thrust out a hand, palm uppermost in invitation. 'Come.'

She mimicked him, mouthing the word, and stubbornly stood her ground. It was an impasse, neither one prepared to give an inch in the other's favour. For a long moment he glowered fiercely. Then he pushed himself erect and took the smallest step in her direction. It was enough. Accepting that most grudging of concessions, she ran to him laughing and threw herself into his embrace.

128

II

Lady Vivienne took an early dinner in her rooms that night. The long ride and crisp fresh air had sharpened her appetite, though she insisted that the incident with the bolting horse had left her bruised and shaken. When Charlotte arrived unannounced, she found her younger sister lying on a couch, claiming to be fatigued and reluctant to discuss the incident.

'Yours, I believe?' Charlotte said coldly, holding out the pin as if it were something unpleasant.

Vivienne shrugged. 'Perhaps. I have so many.'

'It has your monogram.'

'Then I must own it, I suppose.'

'It was found beneath the saddle of your horse.'

Vivienne shrugged again. She examined her fingernails with studied indifference while her sister moved about the room in awkward silence.

'What you did was both cruel and dangerous,' Charlotte said at last. 'You might have killed yourself.'

'Would you have cared?'

'That question is not worthy of your intelligence, Vivienne. You know I care about you. We all do.'

The younger girl sighed and pouted her lips peevishly. 'I feel like a prisoner here. My every movement is watched and measured and restricted. You have no idea how I suffer, Charlotte. I could scream with boredom. Why must the whole world treat me like child?'

Charlotte tossed the hat pin on to the couch. 'Perhaps because you behave like one.'

Vivienne dashed the pin aside. 'It was not my fault. That foolish animal bolted without cause.'

'That is a lie, Vivienne.'

'And I suppose you intend telling father all about it?'

'Not if you promise me faithfully that such a thing will never happen again.'

'All right, you have my word on that.'

'No more silly games?'

'If you insist, *dear* sister.'

'And stay away from Lukan de Ville.'

Vivienne looked up sharply. 'How dare you speak to me like that?'

'Because I know you, Vivienne. Because with the help of that hat pin you wickedly conspired to be alone with him. I saw the way you draped yourself around his neck, moving against him as if you were no more than a strumpet, and gazing into his eyes.'

'You're jealous!'

'That is nonsense, Vivienne. And for your information Lukan de Ville has no interest in children.'

Vivienne jumped to her feet and faced her elder sister with her fists clenched and her eyes flashing. 'I am *not* a child.'

'That is the way he sees you.'

'He does not, and to say so is a lie, a spiteful lie.'

'It's the truth. Heed my warning, Vivienne. Do not play games with that man.'

'It's jealousy. I see that now. I see the *real* truth, dear sister, you want him for yourself.'

Charlotte's hand shot out in a reflex action that caught her sister full across the cheek. She gasped, more shocked than pained, and shrank from Charlotte's quiet anger.

'You have said more than is sufficient,' Charlotte declared calmly. 'We can either end this matter now, to my full satisfaction, or I can take it to your father and your brother. The choice is yours.'

'You wouldn't!'

'Try me and see.'

The girl nodded, clutching her blazing cheek. Her voice was small and she did not meet her sister's gaze. 'Very well. It seems I have no choice but to do as you say.'

'No games, no foolish talk, no contact with the gypsy?'

'Yes. I agree. I'll do whatever you say.'

'Do not test me in this, Vivienne. Give me the slightest cause and I will inform father of your deplorable behaviour.'

Vivienne nodded again. After a moment Charlotte turned and swept from the room, closing the door firmly behind her.

Peevish and frustrated, Vivienne clenched her fists and contorted her face in a grimace, then stamped her feet in a tantrum and stuck out her tongue as far as it would stretch.

III

Madame Michelet was fast asleep, oblivious to all but her own dreams, when Vivienne crept from her bedroom almost two hours later. The girl was wearing an extravagant ball gown purloined for the occasion from Charlotte's wardrobe. Lacking the fuller proportions of her sister's figure, she had been obliged to add a considerable amount of padding to the bodice of the gown. It pushed her young breasts upward and outward, and she was well pleased with her handiwork. With a little more daring than skill, she had powdered her face and reddened her cheeks and lips with brightest rouge. When she studied her reflection in the long glass she was delighted by what she saw, convinced that she looked mature and sophisticated. Tonight she was no longer a child but a stunningly attractive woman, and tonight she was determined to be desired by every man who turned his gaze upon her.

A single lamp had been left burning in the spacious, beautifully furnished drawing room which she was forced to share with the woman acting as her temporary watcher and companion. Through a haze of her sister's perfume, liberally applied, she noticed the smell of scorched milk still hanging in the air from Madame's supper. A few small flames flickered sleepily in the grate and the tall clock in the corner marked time with its sombre tick. With a tantalising rustle of skirts she crossed to the other side of the room to press her ear to Madame's bedroom door. From beyond came the sound of the French woman's deep, nasal snores keeping the gentle rhythm of her slumbers. With a smile Vivienne lifted her skirts and hurried to the main door of the apartments, turned the big key in the lock and slipped outside.

There were several private parties underway in the drawing rooms of those guests and family members who had stayed on after the wedding to see the old Countess laid to rest. Scores of people, some of whom had homes within an hour's ride of Beresford Hall, stayed on to take full advantage of the Earl's generosity. Oscar Cavendish and his Countess had always entertained on a lavish scale, and the new Mistress of Beresford seemed determined to continue in a similar vein. It was an added bonus for many that the custom of wearing mourning dress had been waived in the special circumstances. Some had sent post haste for more appropriate gowns and suits while others were making use of the Hall's army of seamstresses. But most were content with the sheer novelty of attending the burial of an important member of society attired in frivolous wedding apparel.

Vivienne paused to tap softly at one of the doors further along the corridor and was admitted almost immediately by a laughing, dark-haired girl with mischievous brown eyes and lips that pouted prettily when she spoke. This was fifteen-year-old Marie Tay-Broughton. Her mother was a French aristocrat of exceptional beauty, her father old and sick with gout but, in Marie's own words, wonderfully wealthy. She pulled her visitor into the room and twirled daintily to show off her gown.

It was not to Vivienne's taste. 'How absolutely charming,' she enthused, thinking it more suited to a child than to a young woman hoping to charm her way into the heart of a Cavendish.

'Well? Do you think your brother will like it? Will he consider me pretty enough for his tastes?'

'Of course he will,' Vivienne smiled. 'And why should you worry if he does not? There are any number of cousins and second cousins for you to choose from.'

'But Gilbert is the one I like. And besides, I can not possibly flirt with them *all*.'

'Why ever not?' Vivienne asked with a wicked smile. 'Believe me, I intend to do exactly that.'

'Really, Vivienne, you entertain the most capricious fancies of any girl I know. Only this very afternoon you were protesting your undying affection for that oh-so-handsome but *terribly* frightening gypsy person who works for your father.'

'Lukan de Ville,' Vivienne said, tugging at the front of her gown to lower the already plunging neckline. 'Oh, I love him desperately, as you well know, but not so desperately tonight. No, tonight I shall forget all about Lukan de Ville and offer my love to someone else.'

They were laughing as they set out arm-in-arm to sample the first of the drawing room parties. In spite of her re-assurances, Vivienne doubted that even Marie Tay-Broughton, with her sweet looks and effervescent personality, could distract poor Gilbert from his present melancholy. He was the youngest of Vivienne's three brothers, a shy young man of nineteen. She believed he was secretly in love with Leonora and was heartbroken that she had married his brother. A year ago Leonora might have been glad of him, but fortune had suddenly tipped the scales against her and the doting Gilbert was snatched from her reach. When the balance shifted for a second time it was Malcolm whose heart she captured, leaving poor Gilbert to lick his wounds and wish his brother well.

'And with whom will you flirt tonight?' Marie was asking now.

'Someone *exciting*.' Vivienne sighed. 'He must have decent looks and manners, and he must have wit enough to entertain me, but most of all he must be *exciting*.'

Marie laughed prettily. 'There'll be excitement enough for you if Madame wakes to find you vanished from your bed yet again, painted and powdered and off to join the late night revellers.'

'A pox on Madame,' Vivienne declared with a snap of her fingers, and both girls collapsed into peals of mischievous laughter. As they hurried along the corridor arm in arm, Vivienne recalled the heated exchange with Charlotte. Tonight she was determined to show that she was no mere child to be so chastened by an elder sister.

In rooms just off the Great Hall a group of boisterous young men from Stroud were playing faro against an equally rowdy group fresh from the gambling houses of London. Competition was strong on both sides as one of Lord Faversham's nephews grew more and more reckless while the amount of his losses increased. He had already forfeited a small fortune at the tables, and now side bets were being placed on how long it would take the older, more experienced gamblers to ruin him completely.

The atmosphere around the tables was charged with fervour mingled with a quiet desperation. It had a taste of its own that sent thrills of anticipation coursing along Vivienne's spine. Only last year a young man named Jeffrey Wallace, the son of a respected land-owner from Carlisle, had actually shot himself through the head after losing a fortune at Boodles. At the last play he had no less than twenty thousand guineas riding on a single card, the black Queen, and when the game was lost he politely excused himself, withdrew to a private room on the first floor and blew his brains out. That incident had been the talk of London society for many weeks. It had cast the shadow of infamy over every person who had known Jeffrey Wallace or had gambled with him in the past, and it had glorified, in terms of common gossip, all who had dined or played at the club that night. How Vivienne wished she could have been there. How she longed to find herself caught up in that kind of drama, that kind of *real* excitement.

Finding her element in the forbidden, Vivienne glided from room to room and from group to group, a pretty butterfly lighting here and there in search of the sweetest nectar. Her eyes shone with pleasure and her scooped neckline daringly revealed her proud young bosom to advantage. She felt men's eyes upon her and gloried in their admiration. None would take her for a schoolgirl tonight, not while she wore that borrowed gown and behaved with such self-confidence in adult company. She raised her glass to all who caught her eye and swallowed her wine with what she hoped was the speed and enjoyment of one fully accustomed to taking alcohol.

An enormous cheer went up from the tables. Men pounded their fists and stamped their feet, women squealed with delight, and for a moment or two Vivienne became caught up in the sudden wave of euphoria generated by the turn of a single card. Lord Faversham's nephew had saved his fortune and his good name by a nine of diamonds. Vivienne moved away as the gambling continued, vaguely disappointed by the outcome. There would be no hasty suicide at Beresford tonight.

She was beginning to feel the heady effects of the wine when she became aware that a tall, well-dressed man in a cut-away velvet coat had been watching her closely for some time. She frequently contrived to catch his gaze, always turning her head away at the last moment and smiling coyly until he threaded his way through the crowds and arrived at her side, as she had known he would. Now she accepted the fresh glass he offered, smiling and fluttering her eyelashes over its rim. She saw that his face was interesting rather than handsome. He had dark eyes deeply set in a long face, straight brown hair and sparse side whiskers. She guessed him to be in his late twenties or early thirties. He lacked the brooding magnetism of Lukan de Ville, but the omission did not disappoint her. This man was available, obviously found her attractive, and he was bold. His gaze seemed to strip the clothes from her body with its frankness. She felt the blood rush to her cheeks in a hot flush.

'Roger Reece,' he told her with a brief bow. 'And you are Vivienne Cavendish.'

'Oh? Do you know me, sir? Are we acquainted?'

'Not exactly,' he smiled, 'but what man in all England could fail to recognise the most desirable of Sir Oscar's daughters?'

'You flatter me, sir,' she said, lapping up his praise the way a cat devours cream.

'I speak as I find.'

'Too boldly, I believe.'

'The truth is ever bold,' he whispered, placing his face very close to hers.

Flushed with pleasure, Vivienne gulped her drink and was left holding an empty glass. Her escort reached out to a passing waiter and soon she was sipping a bittersweet liquid that heated her insides in the most delicious manner.

'Are you a friend of my brothers?' Her words sounded oddly slurred to her own ears.

Roger Reece grinned sheepishly. 'I doubt that.'

'A friend of my father, then?'

He laughed out loud and she giggled loudly in response. His hand slid daringly around her waist. She could feel its heat through the fine fabric of her gown. His lips nibbled at the lobe of her ear, his breath more warming than the wine.

'My sweet little Vivienne,' he said, holding her very close. 'Your father would not recognise my face, since I am not known in these parts, and yet he would surely have his men horse-whip me off the premises if he discovered me here. In fact, any member of your illustrious family would have me hung, drawn and quartered rather than breathe the same air as my humble self, of that you may be sure.'

'What nonsense,' Vivienne laughed. 'But how exciting.'

'It's perfectly true,' he assured her. 'I am forbidden to set my feet upon Cavendish soil, yet here I am, eating at your father's table and enjoying the fruits of his famous cellars.' He nibbled her ear again. 'And falling helplessly, irretrievably in love with the most beautiful of his daughters.'

At this point he pulled her against him and pressed his lips to hers, forcing her lips apart and filling her mouth with his hot tongue. She gasped as her breasts were crushed against his chest and he grasped the plumpest parts of her buttocks with both hands. When he released her she was quite breathless. The room swam before her eyes and she forgot the gambling, the food, the other guests. All she knew was the warm glow of a man's desire and the intoxicating effects of the wine. She swayed and giggled, and once again the man's possessive hands were touching and caressing her body. A fresh glass was pressed into her grip and she drank from it greedily, even though the liquid tasted so bitter that her mouth smarted at its contact.

'So what am I then?' he demanded, his breath like fire against her neck and throat. 'Am I a highwayman? A thief? A murderer?'

136

'A highwayman!' she exclaimed shrilly. 'Oh, what in the world could be more exciting than a real highwayman?'

'Ah, but I am much, much worse,' he said solemnly.

'Oh do tell,' she begged. 'Do tell.'

'Whom does your father detest beyond all reason?'

'I have no idea. Tell me, oh do tell me.'

'Think, my dear. What man, what family, what *name* would he die rather than acknowledge in his own home?'

Realisation slowly percolated the haze of alcohol. 'Oh! Oh!' She almost shrieked in her excitement. 'You are a Fairfax. You are a *Fairfax*.'

Her companion bowed, grinning. 'Indeed I am. Roger Reece Fairfax at your service, Lady Vivienne.' Once again his palms were hot on her body. 'And now I am a desperate man. I must see you again and soon, away from here, *alone*.'

'But my father would be furious,' she squealed.

He released her quite suddenly. 'I thought you liked me.'

'Oh but I do,' she giggled. 'Don't scowl so sternly. Oh, this is all so tremendously exciting.'

'Perhaps you are afraid to be alone with me,' he suggested.

'I am not afraid of anything.'

'So, you will dare to meet me again, *alone*?'

'Well . . .' She hesitated, released a loud, unladylike hiccup and giggled again.

'I knew it,' he said sharply. 'You *are* afraid. I thought you were a woman, as sophisticated as you are desirable, but now I see that I was wrong. You are just a child, just a timid little girl.'

'I am *not* a child,' Vivienne cried, stamping her foot with such force that she splashed the remains of her drink down the front of her gown, where it produced an unsightly stain.

Roger Fairfax pressed his advantage. 'Then swear to meet me tomorrow at two o'clock, in the arbour in the upper orchard garden. And come alone.'

'Tomorrow? The orchard garden?' She sounded doubtful.

'Two o'clock. If you *dare*.'

She hiccuped and giggled loudly. 'Of course I dare. I dare *anything*.'

'Then you'll come?'

'Of course I will.'

'If you fail me I will laugh at you and mock you for the child you are,' he warned.

'I am *not* a child,' she repeated peevishly. 'I will come. I will, I will.'

The next thing she knew she was dancing, whirling dizzily around the room supported by strong arms that lifted her right off her feet. The room was spinning, a blur of movement that left her eyes unfocussed. Eventually she felt a couch beneath her as a voice, urgent and familiar, cut into the nebulous haze of her understanding.

'Vivienne! Wake up, Vivienne! Where have you been? What has happened to you? Are you ill?'

She struggled to rouse herself, only to find the room tilting at a sickening angle. She found to her dismay that Roger Fairfax had vanished into the mass of shapes heaving and undulating around her. She felt her stomach churn most disagreeably. Something hot and vile washed up into her throat. The room had become stiflingly hot and so noisy that she could barely distinguish her own voice amid the tumult.

'I feel wonderful,' she lied, wishing she had not ordered the maid to lace her stays so tightly. 'Oh Marie, this night has been so *exciting.*'

'What on earth have you been drinking, you silly girl?'

'Champagne. Wonderful, glorious champagne.'

Marie sniffed at a glass and winced. 'If this is champagne my father is the Moor of Venice,' she retorted.

'I care nothing for champagne and blackamoors,' Vivienne announced with a theatrical sweep of her arm that almost toppled her from the couch. 'Tonight I have met a dangerous highwayman who has fallen madly and passionately in love with me.'

Marie adjusted her friend's gaping bodice. 'I see no highwayman.'

'He was here and he *adores* me. We have an assignation. Oh, it is just too exciting for words.'

'Do try to keep your voice down, Vivienne,' Marie remonstrated. 'Everyone is staring at you.'

Vivienne giggled loudly, pressed a finger to her lips and spoke in a conspiratorial whisper that could be heard by anyone curious enough to listen.

'His name is Roger ...' She broke off, giggling again. 'But no, oh no, if I reveal his identity my father will have him hanged, drawn and quartered for daring to be here.'

Now she felt herself lifted from the couch and supported on both sides as the huge double doors of the room came rushing towards her.

'I have a lover,' she sang as she was hurried from the room by several of Marie's friends. 'I have an assignation. Isn't that just too exciting for words?'

CHAPTER EIGHT

I

It was dark and very late when Roger Reece Fairfax entered Fairfax Manor by the conservatory door. He found his cousin Christopher sitting before a dying fire, nursing a pot of steaming hot chocolate and a bowl filled with sugar-dusted cubes of Turkish delight. There was an empty plate nearby and a scattering of pastry crumbs lying on the carpet around the chair. The two men exchanged glances, one morose, the other scornful.

'Feeding your face again, cousin?' Roger asked, glancing with distaste at the mounds of flesh quivering beneath the other's chin. He poked a finger at the vast overhang straining against a quilted night robe. 'One of these days you'll eat so much you'll burst at the seams. And what an explosion that will be. My god, we'll have to scrape up the bits and bury you by the bucketful.'

'You w-wouldn't m-mock m-me, Roger F-Fairfax, if y-you knew how m-miserably I s-suffer.'

'The only suffering you do is on behalf of your disgusting gluttony.'

'I w-was un-unhappy, and wh-when I-I g-get unhappy I n-need t-to eat.'

His cousin sneered. 'Dinner was over hours ago. You should be in your bed, sleeping off its effects, not down here stuffing your face with sweets and pastries.'

'I c-couldn't s-sleep,' Christopher stammered. 'I w-was w-worried about y-you.'

Roger laughed out loud and poured himself a drink. 'You? Worried on *my* account? Do you honestly expect me to believe that?'

'I w-was t-too.'

'Rubbish! If you had thought of me at all you would have been green with envy, not sleepless with concern.'

'You w-were over th-there again. You w-were at B-Beresford Hall, m-mingling with the b-b-bona fide g-guests.'

Roger held his glass to the light, studying its contents. He was amused by the note of petulance in his cousin's voice.

'Of course I was over there,' he admitted boastfully. 'Nobody knows my face, so why should I not enjoy myself at the Earl's expense? It is so very gratifying, my dear Christopher, to eat his food and drink his wine and roll with his serving girls between fine linen sheets.'

Christopher sucked back a dribble of saliva. 'You s-seem to f-forget that C-Cavendish is our enemy.'

'But that's the pleasure of it,' Roger laughed. 'He hates us, so while I steal his hospitality I thumb not only my nose but my bare arse at him.'

'Y-you'll b-be s-sorry,' Christopher warned, pushing such a mass of sweets into his mouth that his cheeks bulged. 'S-sooner or l-later s-someone w-will r-recognise you and th-then you'll b-be s-sorry.'

'But not before I toss the ultimate insult into the face of our high and mighty neighbour,' Roger grinned. 'And before I'm done, the entire country will know of it. Every gossip in England will hear of the manner in which Roger Reece Fairfax exacted payment in kind for past Cavendish affronts against this family.'

141

'W-what? W-what d-do you m-mean? W-What p-payment in k-kind?'

Roger placed a hand on each arm of Christopher's chair and leaned over until their faces were so close together that he could smell the sweetness on his cousin's breath.

'I mean, my obese cousin, that I have succeeded where you so miserably failed.' He took a handful of sugared cubes from the plate and stuffed them one by one into Christopher's mouth as he added, 'I have landed myself a Cavendish filly.'

Christopher's eyes widened. 'W-what? W-what?'

'The empty-headed Vivienne, Sir Oscar's youngest daughter, has fallen victim to my undeniable charms. That's more success than you ever had, eh, cousin?'

Christopher grunted and began to splutter. 'I d-don't b-believe y-you.'

'It's perfectly true. And don't dribble that sticky mess all over the place. Where are your manners?'

'Vivienne? B-but ... b-b-but she's a child, a s-schoolgirl.'

'And begging for it. She's ripe, Christopher. Some man is sure to pin her to the mattress before she sees another birthday, and why should it not be me?'

'Y-you w-wouldn't d-dare.'

'No? Would you care to lay a wager on that?'

'C-Cavendish w-will k-kill you.'

'Only if he catches me.' Roger shoved another sweet into his cousin's mouth and added, 'She's already tasted the lure and found it to her liking. Believe me, that silly young baggage will suck upon more than a baited hook before I send her back to her pompous father with my compliments.'

II

Several of the larger outbuildings were being used to accommodate the extra staff hired to help with the wedding celebrations. The barn where Sam Cooper had his bed was one of these. The nights were filled with assorted body noises, the snores and bickerings and other sounds of weary men tight-packed in rows against the walls. He found himself sharing his own small corner of the loft with a group of men from Kingswood. They were bawdy, hard-drinking labourers who teased him for his shyness and mimicked his London accent for their amusement. Their casual country ways offended him. In intimate matters they were as free and careless as the animals of the field, performing their bodily functions with not the slightest degree of modesty. On their first night in the loft the youngest man had pulled up the skirts of a kitchen maid and climbed between her legs during a game of cards. He relieved himself swiftly and without embarrassment while keeping one eye on his gambling companions and the other on his own cards. After that Sam pinned a makeshift curtain of old sacks to the rafters between his bed and theirs. Its presence was the source of much hilarity amongst the other workers but Sam, determined upon his privacy, insisted on it.

At eighteen, Sam's experience of women was limited as much by opportunity as by the awkwardness of his manner. When Freda Wardle, the candle-girl, offered to spend the night with him he was stunned by his good fortune and too uncertain to suggest a tumble in some dark, convenient corner of the estate. He felt obliged to sneak her up the ladder to his bed, but only when the heavy snoring of his neighbours told him they were soundly sleeping. Despite the makeshift blanket, the dearth of simple privacy in the loft inhibited him. He feared the threat of sudden and very public exposure to the labourers' ridicule. As a result his eager expectations proved far in excess of his actual performance. That which took so long to achieve was at first impossible to maintain, and when sheer physical desperation drove him into her, it was spent with unseemly haste. He slumped beside her, crimson with humiliation, muttering quiet curses.

'Oh hell! Oh hell and Satan's fire!'

Freda Wardle voiced no complaints. She liked him anyway, she told him, and besides, she was in need of somewhere warm to lay her head. The bed she was meant to share with another girl was otherwise engaged by that girl's conquest for the night. She was kind to Sam. Tomorrow she might deride the young gun that took such lengthy administrations to load and then went off on a hair-trigger, but for tonight she swore contentment. Sam Cooper wrapped his limbs around her plumpness, forgot his shame and slept the night contentedly.

Much later he was roused from his slumbers by a hand shaking his shoulder, a gentle intrusion but insistent. He tried to brush the hand away, only to find that it returned to the spot with the dogged persistence of a housefly at the jam pot. A small voice whispered its urgent message into his ear.

'Wake up, I'm sent by the mistress to fetch you.'

At the sound of the voice Sam scrambled from his bed in such haste that he twice struck his head on one of the angled roof supports. He muttered softly as he fumbled in the darkness to identify the tangled items of his clothing. As he struggled into his shirt his fingers were unwieldy things with a will of their own.

'What did the mistress say?' he whispered.

'Didn't see her. Miss Anabel said I was to fetch you to the old gatehouse and you was to wait there for the mistress.'

The lad who brought the message was a small scarecrow in ragged clothes and over-large boots. He set down a lighted candle, yawned and scratched at his scalp with both hands.

'I've seen you before, lad,' Cooper observed, hopping on one leg as he struggled into his trousers.

'I reckon so, Mr Cooper.'

'Aren't you Charlie Pickles, Mr Brunswick's lad?'

'Aye, s'right.'

Sam managed to get his trousers on, then rummaged around on all fours, searching for his boots.

Freda stirred and sat upright on the mattress. She was naked and her eyes were sticky with sleep.

Sam moved the candle so it no longer set her plump pink breasts in vulgar spotlight. 'Go back to sleep,' he told her.

'Where you going?'

'The mistress has sent for me. Go back to sleep.'

Freda lay back upon the mattress in such a way that Sam was obliged to move the candle yet again. He returned his attention to the task of dressing himself in a space too small for a grown man to stand upright.

'What's it like then, Charlie Pickles, belonging to the Master of the Earl's Horse?'

The boy shrugged. 'I work where I'm put.'

Sam nodded. 'I reckon the wages'll be good. Better'n kitchen or beer-house wages. Earl's a fair man when it comes to paying out, and no mistake.'

'Not to me he ain't. I don't get nuthing.'

'Come off it, lad. A-course you do. Everyone here gets wages.'

'Not me,' the lad said. 'I get bread and ale for scivvying in the kitchens, milk for dunging out the cowsheds and a bit of butter, if'n I'm lucky, for helping in the dairy. I can even pick up an egg or two if Mr Hynd needs me to fetch and carry for him around the farm, or keep watch while he's in the barn with a wench.'

'Kitchen scraps? Is that all you're given for a day's work?'

'Aye, 'cepting when your lady married Sir Malcolm and I was sent to run errands and clear away dishes and such. Got meself a whole sixpence then, I did.'

'Good for you, lad.'

'Nay, it weren't mine,' Charlie said. His eyes had widened. He seemed amazed by the very suggestion that his earnings should find their way into his own pocket.

'What do you mean it weren't yours?'

'It weren't.'

'You just told me it were.'

'No I didn't.'

Sam wagged his finger at the lad. 'Yes you did, Charlie Pickles. You said you earned that tanner clearing dishes and running errands.'

'Aye, I did, but that don't make it mine to *keep*, do it? Any coins I get from jobs and errands and the like has to be given over to Mr Brunswick. I'm his lad, see? What I earn is his by rights.'

Sam Copper frowned. 'That don't sound right to me,' he said, scratching his head thoughtfully. 'You sure he don't pay you proper wages?'

'Not one penny-piece,' Charlie insisted. 'He says His Lordship won't agree to paying out good money to runts like me what can't match a grown man's labours.'

'How does he pay you, then?'

The lad shrugged again and thrust his hands deep into his pockets. 'I get to sleep in one of the empty stalls. Nice and warm it is in there, softer than the bare ground, and all. It prickles though, does that bedding-straw. Prickles me something fierce it does, some nights.'

'Is that all you get for working seven days a week for Mr Brunswick? For doing night-watch and grooming and carrying hay and cleaning leathers and shining brasses and fetching water and mucking-out? Is that all you get for it?'

'Aye.' The lad's forefinger rummaged vigorously inside his left nostril. He withdrew it, examined the results with a scowl and wiped his finger clean on the nearest beam. 'Aye, and I'm to think meself lucky for that, Mr Brunswick says.'

Cooper nodded grimly and fastened the last button on his coat. He found he had a hole left over, groped about until he located the solitary button passed over in the operation, and with a sigh unfastened the coat and began again. After this he knotted his scarf at his throat and raked his fingers through his hair, harnessing the worst of it. Then he dusted his cap by slapping it against his thigh and settled it firmly on his head.

The sound of whispered voices halted him as he was about to leave the loft. He lifted the candle so that an arc of flickering light was shed across his bed. Freda was lying close to the sacking curtain, her eyes still tightly closed and a smile lifting the corners of her mouth. A thick, very hairy forearm protruded from below the curtain and a grubby hand, calloused and sinewy, sampled the fleshy pinkness of her breasts.

Sam moved the light away. He knew he had seen the last of Freda Wardle the candle-girl. He had given her no reason to be there when he returned.

He signalled for Charlie Pickles to go on ahead and followed close on his heels. He could sympathise with the lad. Mr Brunswick had a reputation for cheating the people in his charge. He was a harsh man who often made his workers toil beyond their strength for extra coppers to feed hungry families. He preferred to hire youngsters, even for the heavier jobs, because children took what they were given and worked where they were put. They didn't argue about the workload and they were too scared to complain when he made them do a man's work for a pittance in coin. Hiring and firing was a power that put big profits into some men's pockets. They didn't care that the likes of Charlie Pickles were worn out doing double labours for food that was never enough to put back into them all that the work took out.

Sam considered all this as he followed Charlie down the ladder from the loft and across the main section of the barn toward the doors. He held the candle high and both stepped with care over sleeping bodies curled or stretched out in every available space.

'It don't sound right to me,' he muttered thoughtfully. 'It don't seem fair. I reckon Miss Leonora would want to be the judge of this. Aye, I reckon she'd want to hear for herself about Charlie's situation.'

He knew the trap young Charlie had fallen into, the treadmill he was on. For the likes of him it was drudgery until he dropped. Such a life would dig him an early grave and force him into it. Or else despair would make a felon of him. Along that very path, but for the grace of God and the kindness of his mistress, Sam Cooper too would even now be treading.

Despite the lateness of the hour there was a small furore in progress when they reached the steps of the old gatehouse. The doors stood open and several lamps were lit. It seemed to Sam that many agitated ladies were left dancing around in the cold while Anabel Corey barred their way to the building. She marched to and fro across the threshold, wringing her hands and shaking her head. Her mistress, she said, was delayed because of a private matter. From time to time she glanced up at the soaring tower above the old grey gatehouse. Then she would close her eyes, cross herself with great reverence and utter a mumbled prayer. On the steps some servant girls were huddled in their shawls, stamping the cold from their feet. They were all talking at once of how poor Lady Vivienne had been carried to her rooms in a state of collapse. An older maid in black skirts added to the story or subtracted from it, as the talk dictated. She was in charge, she said, and had the facts first-hand.

Also present was the foreign woman, Madame Michelet, who always seemed much older than her years. Her mouth was small and pinched and her eyes viewed every man, regardless of his age or inclination, as a beast, a despoiler of young women. Clearly tonight some matter had distressed her. Even so, she managed to appear prim and stiff in her tight little bonnet and matronly overcoat. Her voice was shrill with indignation, thin with sufferance.

Sam Cooper and his ragged companion held back from the doorway. They exchanged a glance that was also a silent agreement before choosing a suitable spot in which to wait. Here they could be seen from the gatehouse without making themselves a part of its present activity. Neither was willing to be sucked into so turbulent a gathering of ladies.

Out of the corner of his eye Sam noticed a vague shape break free of the night-shrouded West Wing. He saw it cross the open ground near Monks' Walk and vanish into the darkness near the orchard wall. It was a tall figure, swift and agile. As it disappeared into the night it issued a long, low whistle not unlike the call of a night-flying bird. Almost immediately two big grey wolfhounds raced up the sloping lawn and along the upper terrace. It was an eerie sight, the two of them like phantoms, swift and soundless. As the gypsy and his animals were swallowed into deeper shadow, Lady Leonora appeared on the inner staircase and stepped into the light. She swept regally to the open doors of the gatehouse. Her appearance brought a sudden hush upon the group.

'You're to stay with me,' Sam whispered, grabbing Charlie by the collar when he would have darted off to his warm stall in the stables. 'Mistress'll want to have words with you.'

148

'What for?' Charlie squirmed and wriggled but found himself held fast. 'What does she want with me? I only did what I was telled to do. I ain't done nothing wrong.'

'No, I reckon you're a good lad, Charlie,' Sam assured him.

'So get your hands off me, Sam Cooper.'

Sam gave him a yank. 'Hush up. She'll want to pay you for your trouble.'

'Pay me?' The lad was still. His mouth fell open and his eyes were wide. '*Pay* me?'

'Aye, and what she gives you will be yours to keep.'

'What, honest?'

'Aye, lad. I'm no liar. Come on with me.'

Together they moved forward and hovered self-consciously on the perimeter of the group. There they watched and listened as Lady Leonora skilfully extracted the kernel of hard fact from the softer fruits of the commotion. It soon became clear to the eavesdroppers that the mistress was needed at once on the other side of the house. The Earl had decided to take a late supper in his son's rooms and Sir Malcolm was demanding the company of his wife. In another part of the house the Lady Vivienne had hoodwinked Madame Michelet and left her rooms for the dances and the gaming tables. She had amused herself in the most unsuitable company and consumed sufficient alcohol to render herself senseless. This was the last straw as far as Madame Michelet was concerned, the final outrage in a list of many. She declared the girl un-governable, wilful, disobedient. She would pack her bags and depart for France immediately, with or without the Earl of Beresford's leave.

Leonora dealt with the problem calmly, speaking a few words to each woman in turn and somehow managing to defuse the situation almost without effort. When she spotted Sam Cooper a little way beyond the group she beckoned him into the gatehouse and drew him to one side. He obeyed, still clutching the bony shoulders of his small companion. In a lamp-lit corner far from the door he stood perfectly still, his nostrils flaring as he tried to inhale the delicate perfume she was wearing. She spoke to him in a whisper, her lips so close

149

to his ear that her warm breath sent a chill along his spine. There was a faint scent of anise on her breath and he wondered where he had smelled it before.

'Go to the cottages over at Hill's Edge,' she said. 'Find Harry Dobbin and bid him attend me here tomorrow morning at first light. It is important that I speak to him in private *before* the burial ceremony takes place. And bid him speak to no-one of the meeting. He must be sworn to secrecy on pain of dismissal.'

'Am I to tell him all that, Miss Leonora?'

'All of it. And when your message is delivered I want you to leave confirmation of it with my maid Anabel. She'll be in the room attached to Sir Malcolm's apartments. Have you got that, Sam?'

'Yes, ma'am.' She stood so close that his cheeks grew hot with embarrassment. To save himself he shoved the skinny stable-lad between them, snatching the youngster's cap from his head as he did so. 'Er, this here be Charlie Pickles, Miss Leonora. He's one of them orphan mites you said I was to watch out for. I reckon this one's badly done to, and no mistake.'

'Is that so?' Leonora ruffled Charlie's hair and smiled into his work-weary face. 'Hello, Charlie Pickles. I think you and I are going to be great friends, don't you?'

The boy swallowed and nodded his head until strands of straw dislodged themselves from his hair. His eyes were as round as saucers as he stared at her. He found himself clutching a palm full of warm coins and tried to speak but his tongue had stuck itself to the roof of his mouth. He did not know how to answer such a question from a lady such as she.

Leonora drew Sam aside and allowed her hand to rest on his arm. 'Go now to Hill's Edge and remember, not another soul must know of this.'

'Will you want me here tomorrow then, with Dobbin?'

'Thank you Sam, if you are free by then I would prefer it.'

'I'll bring him at first light then, to the east side. And there's something I think ...' He broke off. He had been about to tell her that he had seen Lukan de Ville lurking in the shadows by the old tower. Now he doubted the wisdom of it. The man was her husband's friend, an honoured guest like any other at their wedding. He had no wish to trouble his mistress, upset Sir Malcolm or provoke the gypsy. He would let the matter lie. It was not his place to question the man's comings and goings upon Sir Oscar's property.

'Yes Sam? Was there something else?'

'No,' he lied quickly. 'Only about Charlie here.'

'It's late now. Tell me tomorrow.'

'Yes, Miss Leonora.'

She smiled briefly. 'Now to Hill's Edge. I am depending on you, Sam. Please do not fail me.'

Before he could protest that he would forfeit his life rather than fail her in anything, Leonora had moved away. He watched her approach the other women and usher them inside and across the spacious entrance hall. They left in more orderly fashion by the side door which led out on to the cobbled courtyard joining the gatehouse to the main part of the Hall.

'Cor!' Charlie Pickles stared after Leonora with his mouth sagging open and his eyes wide. 'Cor!'

'Hush, lad. Show some respect,' Sam told him.

'Cor!' the boy said again. 'She's just like one of them heavenly angels painted on church windows, only better.'

'Aye lad, only better, and don't you forget that.'

Charlie held out his hand, his eyes full of wonder. 'Look what she gave me.'

Sam grinned at the small fortune lying in the child's palm. There was a shilling there, at least, in smaller coin.

'And don't you go handing them over to that Mr Brunswick,' he said sternly. 'That's your money, personal like, and nothing to do with the likes of him. Come on lad, you can come with me as far as the kitchen door. If we're lucky there'll be a loaf of bread and some beef pudding in the crock, left by that nice Mrs Moston. Supper's always free to them as needs it, in her kitchen.'

'Cor, real beef pudding and nothing to pay for it?'

'That's right, lad. Now, straighten your cap and don't go

slouching around with your shoulders hunched. Lady Leonora likes her friends to have a good appearance.'

'Is she my friend now?'

'Certainly. She said so, didn't she? She has a fondness for waifs and strays what gets put-upon by cheaters.'

'Is Mr Brunswick one of them, a cheater?'

'Aye, and don't say I told you so.'

'And I'm to get proper wages now, off the lady?'

'Aye, if you deserve it she'll be good to you. She said you and she'll be friends, and so you will. She never goes back on her word doesn't the lady.'

Nodding his head, Charlie Pickles beamed with pride. He squared his small shoulders in manly fashion and smoothed the frayed lapels of his coat. He strode along beside Sam Cooper with a new air of dignity, though his over-sized boots hung from his skinny legs like leaden weights, scuffing the ground with every step.

Some time later he crawled into a pile of loose straw in one of the empty stalls in the main stables. In one hand he clutched his money, in the other a feast of buttered bread and cold, spiced meat pudding. In one of his pockets was a piece of cheese the size of new-laid goose-egg and just as fresh. For once in his young life he could count his blessings. He judged himself a wealthy man indeed.

He had no sooner got himself settled when the creak of the stable door brought him smartly to attention. He hurriedly concealed his treasures from sight beneath the straw and struggled to swallow a mouthful of meat pudding. The man framed in the doorway held a lamp above his head and stood with his legs placed wide apart, his whole body swaying from side to side as if he stood on the deck of a sea-going ship in heavy weather. He was a stout man, broad and whiskered and with a grievous temper.

'All's well, Mr Brunswick,' Charlie called out.

'You tellin' me the truth, lad?'

'Yes sir.'

Brunswick lurched forward, causing the tethered horses to sidestep and blow air anxiously through their nostrils. Charlie moved away from his stall. He would rather approach his master and risk a beating than let the man come to him and risk the loss of his new-found wealth.

'I've just been talking to the grey, Mr Brunswick. Keeps me awake through my watch, it does, talking to the horses.'

Now Brunswick loomed over him, the lamp still held above his head. His big-featured face was florid with drink, his greying hair untidy beneath a smart black hat. He was wearing a warm cloak of dark brown wool over Sir Oscar's blue livery. On his feet were expensive leather boots that few men in his position could afford to own. He glowered down at the boy.

'Done your work, have you?'

'Yes, Mr Brunswick.'

'All of it?'

'Yes sir.'

Without warning and at a speed contrary to his drunken state, Brunswick's left hand swung out to catch Charlie a flat-handed blow to his right ear. The lad sprawled sideways and landed heavily on both knees.

'And mind you stay awake tonight,' Brunswick growled. 'I'll not have no worker of mine sleeping away his watch.'

'No, sir ... er ... yes, sir.'

Charlie watched his master lurch back down the centre aisle of the stable to the big doors, then shuffle off into the night, cursing under his breath. Now the beamed stable was once again illuminated by no more than a lamp turned to its lowest setting so that it cast a small glow over the horses' flanks. He returned to his stall, safe in the knowledge that the master would not be back before daylight. His head was ringing and the tender skin of his ear burned like fire from Brunswick's blow. A sticky dampness on his left knee told him the fall had ripped the scabbed-over skin from a previous wound, causing it to bleed freely. He didn't care. Tonight he didn't care about *anything*.

Charlie was convinced that something special had happened to him that night, something that would change his life and render his lot more bearable. Suddenly he felt warm

153

on the inside, the way he had felt that day he sneaked into the kitchens and stole a ladle-full of hot soup from the pot and swallowed it in one hungry gulp. It was not the coins, nor the food, nor Sam Cooper's words that made him love the beautiful lady in the tower. He would have loved her anyway, the moment she smiled at him.

III

'Your wife should be here with you, not languishing in her own apartments on the far side of the house. Dammit boy, you are far from well and newly-wed to boot. The Countess is dead. What business can she have that keeps her from you at such a time and at this ungodly hour?'

The Earl was pacing a figure-of-eight path across the centre of the room, his hands clasped behind his back and his coat tails draped over his wrists. Weariness showed in his face and in the trace of a limp in his left leg where the rheumatism was most severe. His son was resting with his back against the scrolled end of a *chaise-longue*. His head was supported by a mound of soft pillows, his body covered by a warm quilt. Apart from looking heavy-eyed and in need of a good night's sleep, he seemed much recovered from his recent collapse. The vomiting had brought relief, and the warm buttermilk ordered by Leonora had eventually overcome his feelings of nausea.

'She works tremendously hard,' he reminded his father. 'There have been many unexpected letters to write and extra events to organise. No doubt she is working even now on the final arrangements for tomorrow.'

'No woman should be away from her bed at this late hour.'

'And I'm sure Leonora would be the first to agree with that, but you are forgetting that tomorrow will be an arduous day for her. We still have a great many house guests to be catered

154

for, father, and I believe the numbers are expected to double for dinner and the evening service. All this is a tremendous responsibility for an eighteen-year-old girl with little or no experience of such things.'

The Earl pursed his lips and shook his head as if to dispel the dark mood of his thoughts. 'You are right, of course,' he admitted. 'I can find no fault in her beyond that she was fathered by a scoundrel.'

Malcolm sighed. 'Why must you constantly reproach her for that fact?'

Sir Oscar shook his head again. 'Forgive me, Malcolm. I'm a suspicious old man. I may loath Herbert Shelley, but I confess I have no right, and certainly no cause, to criticise the man's daughter.'

'Thank you, father.'

The Earl paused to look sideways at his son. 'I suspect you care very deeply for the girl.'

'More than that,' Malcolm smiled. 'She means everything to me.'

Sir Oscar nodded. He knew how it felt to love a woman so deeply that all else in life took second place to her. He didn't want to envy the boy. Malcolm deserved this second chance at happiness after the tragic death of his first wife. He was grateful that his son would have something he himself had yearned for all his life, but still he envied the boy. What simple, quiet joy must fill a man's heart when the wife to whom he is bound in law is also the woman he loves.

Malcolm's voice cut into his thoughts. 'You look exhausted, father. It's late. You should go to your bed.'

'I'll wait.'

'Not on my behalf, I hope? I feel tired but perfectly well, and I swear that by tomorrow I will be my old self again.'

'I would rather wait.'

'As you wish.' Malcolm sipped the last of his buttermilk, then set down his glass and leaned back with a sigh. 'This is a peculiarly stressful time for all of us, is it not? We hardly know whether to smile or weep, to dance for the wedding or take up the black and mourn poor mother. I do so admire Leonora in her efforts to create a decent balance between the two.'

'Quite, quite,' Sir Oscar muttered, scowling as he resumed his pacing. A moment later he stopped again and asked, 'Is everything all right between the two of you? Have you er ... did you and she ...?'

'Did we what, father?'

'Dammit boy, you catch my drift quite well enough without the need to spell out every detail. You have no heir. You need a living son, and you abstained too long from a man's natural activities after poor Grace followed her last dead babe to the grave. Such abstinence is harmful to a man. It dulls his urges, weakens his potency. A man might even cease to be a man if he keeps himself too long from women.'

'You have no reason to fear on that score, father,' Malcolm smiled, recalling the stains on the bedlinen and his brief conversation with Leonora that morning. 'I may have been uncommonly drunk last night, but I can assure you I managed to perform my duty adequately.'

'I'm gratified to know that, but to be drunk on your wedding night! Shame on you my boy.' Sir Oscar squared his shoulders and applied his most formidable scowl to conceal the twinkle in his eye. 'Only a low-bred peasant needs that kind of liquid courage. Your nuptials must have been about as memorable as a quick turn in the hay with some faceless kitchen wench.'

Malcolm smiled. 'My wife makes no complaints.'

'Huh! Her silence is hardly to your credit, sir. The girl may own the mettle of a thoroughbred, but I doubt if even she would be outspoken on this subject.'

Malcolm received the remonstration with the same good nature with which it was given. His father would never know how close he had come to describing the events of last night. Leonora insisted that his advances had been neither brutal nor boorish, but she was too much a lady, he believed, even to hint that it was otherwise. He felt he had let her down. He had taken her in haste while too stupefied with drink to recall the act. Those stained linens were evidence not of the love he felt for her but of the lusts of a man too drunk, and too long without the comforts of a wife, to control his baser instincts. Such a thing must never be allowed to happen again. In future he would plan the event well in advance so that when she came to his bed or invited him to hers, she would find him a sober and considerate husband.

While the Earl paced and Malcolm pondered upon his failings as a husband, Leonora entered the apartments via a small anteroom and went directly to a full length mirror to examine her appearance. She had just come from Vivienne's rooms, where the foolish girl had been stripped of her borrowed gown and ill-matched jewellery, her powder and rouge and the entire contents of her stomach. She had been made to vomit copiously. Leonora had been sparing with neither the mustard nor the salt in her emetic. If any lesson at all was to be learned from the incident, Lady Vivienne must wake in the morning feeling so utterly wretched that she would never even dream of repeating it.

Now Leonora smoothed her hair over one shoulder and carefully buttoned her robe right up to her throat. She knew Sir Oscar and Malcolm had taken a late supper together. She could hear the occasional murmur of their voices in the next room, the soft tread of the Earl's boots as he indulged his habit of pacing the carpet. Malcolm would not dream of asking why she had left him to his own devices for so long, but Sir Oscar certainly would. He would be most eager to hear the reason for her lengthy absence.

Satisfied that her appearance left nothing to be desired, she moved quietly to the adjoining door and opened it just a few inches. From that angle she could see the couch where Malcolm lay and the figure of the Earl moving this way and that across the room. She wanted to time her entry to the second. By counting and measuring the Earl's strides she was able to judge the precise moment when he would be at his most distant. She wanted him on her extreme right with his back still turned to the door. At this point she burst into the room in a gush of endearments and apologies. Keeping her eyes fixed on Malcolm she rushed across the room to embrace him. She dropped lightly to her knees beside the couch, her skirts billowing prettily around her.

'Malcolm, my dear, are you quite better? I intended to be away no longer than a few minutes, but just see how the time has flown. What a night this has been. First poor Elizabeth had a frightening dream and refused to be comforted by anyone but myself, then Vivienne went missing ...'

'What? What's that you say?'

Leonora started and rose to her feet. 'Sir Oscar! Oh do forgive me, I did not see you. I had no idea you were here in the room.'

'Good evening, my dear,' he replied a little stiffly. 'Now what's all this about Vivienne? Missing, you say? Missing?'

'And safely found again, I hasten to add,' Leonora smiled. 'And I doubt she will think well of her adventure when she wakes tomorrow.'

'What do you mean? What adventure?'

Leonora hesitated. 'She is sleeping now. Perhaps you would care to speak to her tomorrow? She will be better able to explain than I.'

'I will accept the gist of it from you.'

'But it is not my place to ...'

'You are her sister now. Tell me what happened.'

'Well, if you insist.' She took Malcolm's hand very tenderly in her own, then turned to Sir Oscar with a sigh of resignation. 'I do so hate to be the bearer of unpleasant news, but I would rather you hear it from me than from Madame Michelet.'

'Unpleasant?' Sir Oscar cocked his head to one side.

Leonora nodded. 'I'm afraid Lady Vivienne dressed herself in one of Charlotte's ball gowns, made up her face with powder and rouge and crept from her rooms while Madame was asleep.'

'What? She did what?'

'She went out.'

'For what purpose?'

'To join the entertainments, I suppose.'

'What entertainments?'

'She wanted to join her friends at the gaming tables.'

'What? My daughter has been gambling?'

'No, Sir Oscar. I don't believe she went there intending to *sit* at the tables.' She sighed again and glanced at Malcolm for support. 'Vivienne is a lively soul and eager for excitement. She also has no head for alcohol.'

'Oh no!' Malcolm exclaimed. 'Is she drunk?'

'I'm afraid so,' Leonora nodded. 'It seems some man at one of the parties plied her with a mixture of champagne and brandy-wine until she was unable to stand unaided. Her friends found her collapsed on a couch and carried her back to Madame.'

'Who was the man? Was he one of my own people, a guest in my home? By God, I'll have him pay for this.'

'I'm afraid we don't know who the man is,' Leonora said. 'If I might offer my opinion . . .?'

The Earl nodded curtly.

'On this occasion she has come to no real harm, and I doubt she will forget the more unpleasant aspects of her adventure in a hurry. In fact, I'm sure she is already regretting the incident most sincerely.'

Malcolm hoisted himself into a more upright position on the *chaise-longue.* He was thinking of Lukan's concern that Vivienne was in need of a stronger hand. It seemed the warning was a timely one. Within hours of it she had painted her face and gone to the gaming rooms to meet with one of the guests. She had obviously succeeded in attracting the attentions of some man, but he had pressed with too much enthusiasm and she had saved herself by passing into a stupor. It was a damnable business. He would prefer his father not to be involved in it.

'A prank,' he smiled. 'She meant no harm by it.'

'But some man deliberately attempted to intoxicate her,' the Earl protested. 'And what guest in my house can be ignorant of either her age or her identity?'

'And if she was determined to drink herself senseless, what guest would know how to stop her?' Malcolm countered.

'You have a point there,' the Earl said, scratching his cheek. Then he turned to Leonora and demanded, 'What the devil was her governess doing while my daughter was putting herself at such risk?'

'Sleeping,' Leonora said. 'And in all fairness it must be remembered that Madame Michelet is employed as a teacher of languages and etiquette and as a temporary companion. She is not capable of playing chaperone to a girl of Vivienne's spirit. I am afraid it would take a much more determined lady than she to achieve that.'

'I'll not have the girl disgrace me in public.'

'I'm sure she has learned a harsh lesson,' Leonora smiled.

'I will speak to her in the morning,' the Earl decided. 'I will have the name of the man involved and I will have my daughter's full apology for this appalling behaviour.'

Leonora shook her head. 'I fear she will not be well enough to leave her room tomorrow.'

'*Not well enough?*' the Earl exploded. 'Madam, if she is well enough to make a public spectacle of herself then she is well enough to fulfil her family duties.'

'Whatever you say,' Leonora demurred.

'Perhaps you will be kind enough to inform her that I insist upon her presence at the morning service, her mother's burial, the procession, the set meals of the day and the evening service.'

'But Sir Oscar . . .'

He raised his hands for silence. 'Your loyalty is commendable but I will hear no more in her defence. My daughter is both headstrong and rebellious but, by the gods, tomorrow she will bow to my authority. She will make herself available to me at all times and she will conduct herself in a manner befitting her station in life. Do I make myself clear?'

'Quite clear, Sir Oscar,' Leonora conceded.

'Good, good.' He strode towards her, took one of her hands in his and patted it gently. 'And forgive my ill-temper, my dear.' He turned his head a little to look at her sideways on. 'Or are you the only person here who does not quake at the force of it?'

Leonora caught the twinkle in his eye and made no effort to suppress her amusement. 'But Sir Oscar, my dear father-in-law, the very prospect of your anger strikes fear into my heart.'

He grinned at that. 'Tosh, my dear. Utter tosh and well you

know it.' He kissed her cheek. 'And now I must go to my bed and leave the two of you to yours. I bid you both goodnight.'

As the door closed behind him, Malcolm lifted Leonora's hand to his lips and kissed it lovingly.

'Stay with me tonight, my dear.'

'Of course,' she smiled. 'My bed is already made up in the next room.'

'No, not there. I want you to sleep with me tonight.'

'But you are unwell, Malcolm,' she protested. 'I think Dr Winterton would not recommend that you exert yourself so soon after your collapse.'

'And the good doctor shall have his way,' Malcolm grinned, 'for I'll not be a husband to you tonight, my dear. I simply want you beside me. I wish to wake in the morning with my health and strength returned and my beautiful Leonora in my arms. Will you stay?'

Leonora returned his smile despite the small shadow that seemed to fall across her heart. She kissed him gently on the mouth and tried not to remember other lips, other arms, other passions. She must never allow herself to forget that she was Malcolm's wife.

'Of course, my dear,' she nodded, smiling at him with a brightness in her eyes like unshed tears. 'I will always stay with you when that is your wish.'

He looked into her eyes. His own were very blue and shone with sincerity. 'I love you very deeply, Leonora.'

'Yes, Malcolm, I know you do.'

CHAPTER NINE

I

It was morning. Leonora opened her eyes to find a pale strip of light just beginning to push its way through a gap in the curtains. She extricated herself from Malcolm's embrace and eased herself, inch by careful inch, to the outer edge of the mattress. Drawing the covers up behind her, she dropped her feet to the floor and eased her body from the bed, leaving her sleeping husband undisturbed. He had remained motionless for most of the night, sleeping away the strains and weaknesses of the day before. She expected him to awaken revitalised, ready to consummate their marriage with a clear head and in full control of his actions. He would be disappointed to find his bride, intent on fulfilling her own duties at this difficult time, already gone from the bed.

'Give me a little more time,' she whispered, smiling down at his sleeping face with genuine affection. 'I will be a wife to you my dear, but not yet, please not yet.'

With a sigh Malcolm turned in his sleep to embrace the soft

pillow now filling the place where she had lain. He would sleep for a long time before the arrival of breakfast roused him from his dreams.

Leonora slipped into the spacious anteroom and from there to the much larger room beyond. There she found the drapes already drawn back to reveal the deepening colours of a chilly November sunrise. The sky was hung with sombre rain clouds whose edges had become briefly trimmed with copper and gold as the sun pushed its way upwards against the horizon, bringing the new day. For a moment Leonora's attention was caught by the beauty of it: the blackened contours of the land touched with bright colour as if by an artist's brush; the dawn of a new day lighting upon the forest and creating a blue-grey haze out of the pockets of mist in the hollows. From the summit of the western tower the Wye would be a ribbon of polished slate with an entourage of lesser streams and brooks in glistening attendance. And from there the forest would be a deep velvet-black broken only by the glitter of dark waters reflecting the sky back upon itself through a canopy of leaves.

'Lukan.'

His name was no more than a breath of sound passing her lips. She smiled, warmed by the memory of him.

'Morning, Miss Leonora, ma'am.'

A chorus of feminine voices brought her back to the present. Several housemaids were busy filling a hip-bath with warm water and laying out folded towels before a huge coal fire. Under Anabel's supervision a pretty muslin pouch containing crushed herbs had been added to soften and sweeten the water. Little billows of steam brought the perfume to Leonora's nostrils. She unfastened the ribbons at her throat, her robe dropped around her ankles and she stepped into the bath. She lowered her body with a soft sigh of pleasure and closed her eyes while Anabel let another pitcher of warm water trickle over her back and shoulders. When at last the outer door clicked shut behind the maids, she opened her eyes and asked, 'Have you had word from Sam Cooper?'

'He'll be here presently,' Anabel nodded. 'He says he'll fetch Harry Dobbin personally before milking starts. Leonora, are you sure you know what you're doing? There'll be hell to pay if Sir Malcolm finds out about this.'

'There is no reason why he *should* find out,' Leonora said firmly. 'But I promise to keep the possibility in mind when I speak to Dobbin, if that will help allay your fears.'

'It will only allay my fears when we have an end to all this secrecy,' Anabel said, lifting a tendril of dark hair and rubbing Leonora's smooth shoulders with the pouch of aromatic herbs. 'It unsettles me, Leonora. I have nightmares just trying to keep account of all the lies.'

'Don't exaggerate, Anabel.'

'How I wish I did! I have a sick feeling in the pit of my stomach telling me that things might even be much worse than they appear. And as for that gypsy ...'

She broke off as two maids re-entered the room carrying a bucket of rinsing water between them. Leonora flashed her a warning glance. Too much was revealed in great houses in the hearing of the lesser orders. Too many secrets were voiced, angers and jealousies expressed, fears exposed or privacies revealed in contempt of some servant's lack of status. The army of minions required to sustain a house of any size was expected to carry out its duties with a quiet familiarity. Lesser mortals must not intrude upon the comfort of their betters. They must become as much a part of the rooms they served as was the ticking of a clock or the crackle of flames in the grate. They must remain as commonplace as the carpets underfoot and just as insignificant. How easy it was to forget that these were real people, with eyes to see and ears to hear. Their ambitions were humble when judged by the master's standards, but they were ambitions none the less, and dangerous. With hard work, poor breeding and low wages separating them from the affluence they served, they were like waifs with empty bellies in the midst of abundance. Thus their currency became the shadowed secret, the careless word, captured and carried away to be bartered for profit of any kind. A poor man might be hanged or transported for stealing from his employers, but careless talk came free and, depending on its substance, was often of the higher value.

As she stood to receive the big towel around her body, Leonora shivered in spite of the heat coming from the fire. She could be thankful that Harry Dobbin and his wife were simple people of the lowest orders. Given a little more intelligence they might have turned Nellie's discovery to more gainful service. Given a few more years of servitude they might even have exposed Leonora simply for the satisfaction of it. There is great power to be had in bringing down a lady of high rank. And it can be done so simply, with the destruction of the one thing she is unable to survive without: her good name. Nothing in life, Leonora knew, could make or break a person more swiftly or more certainly than the acquisition or loss of respectability. And few things, she was sure, could bring more gratification to a discontented human being than the sudden fall to ruin of his master.

'Thank you, Susan,' she smiled at the pretty maid who handed her a folded foot-towel. 'That will be all for the moment.'

'Yes ma'am.' The girl curtsied, then hovered in hesitation, biting her lower lip. She smelled of milk, a faint and sour-sweet odour that brought to mind the dribbles and spills and vomits of small babies.

'Yes Susan? Is there something else?'

'Well, beggin' your pardon, ma'am, will Miss Vivienne be needin' me again this morning? Only, I was told to wait for Madame Michelet to send word, but I got work to do as won't wait until later, ma'am. That Mrs Moston in t'kitchens gets ever so cross an' hot under the collar if she can't find all her pastry-maids when 'er ovens is stoked and fully heated.'

'In that case, you have my permission to return to your kitchen duties,' Leonora smiled. 'I will find someone else to take care of Miss Vivienne.'

'Thank you, ma'am.' The girl curtsied again. 'Only, she was a bit sick in the night and Madame didn't care to sit up with her, and that Peggy Johnson from Durston what should be waiting on 'er all day didn't turn up for work yet.'

'How ill was Miss Vivienne?' Leonora asked, recalling Sir Oscar's instructions that his daughter attend all the day's events, including the early service. 'Was the doctor sent for?'

'Oh no, ma'am. She weren't *that* sick. Just crying and moaning she were, and calling out for Mr Lukan like he would know how to cure her ills.'

Leonora's features froze. 'I beg your pardon?'

'Ma'am?'

'Did you say *Mr Lukan*?'

'Yes, ma'am.'

'And just how does Miss Vivienne come to know Mr Lukan?'

'Don't know ma'am, I'm sure.'

'I see. Does she know him well? What does she say of him? Do they meet in private? Does she contrive to be alone with him without the presence of a chaperone?'

Susan realised by the sudden change in her mistress's tone and manner that she had spoken out of turn. Her face coloured to the roots of her hair. She bobbed several small curtsies in quick succession, then hastened to qualify her words.

'If'n you please ma'am, I don't think she knows him exactly, not *exactly*. She's just took a fancy to him, and him so dark and handsome and all. Oh, there's not a lady ever came here what didn't take a fancy to our Mr Lukan.'

'Oh, I see. And are these ladies often successful in their pursuits?'

The girl appeared puzzled. 'Ma'am?'

Leonora sighed impatiently. 'These ladies who take a fancy to him,' she said sharply. 'Upon how many of them does he choose to bestow his favours?'

'What, our Mr Lukan?' The girl shook her head and smiled. 'Not him, ma'am. He don't ever pay no heed to 'em and that's for sure, but it don't stop 'em giggling and whispering and peeping over hedges to catch a glimpse of him riding by. It don't mean nothing bad ma'am. It's just them sighing after him and trying to catch his eye.'

'Including Miss Vivienne?'

Susan giggled loudly. 'Oh, *especially* Miss Vivienne ...' She clamped a hand over her mouth, too late to prevent the remark from slipping out.

166

'I see.' Leonora's voice was as lacking in warmth as was the expression on her face. She felt Anabel touch her arm, warning her to be aware of her own responses. She shook the hand away, compelled to hear more. 'And I suppose this man is flattered by the silly flirtations of well-bred young ladies?'

'He pays no heed, ma'am.'

'Yet they pursue him,' Leonora commented coldly.

'Well yes, but there's no real harm meant ma'am. Nothing improper like. And I happen to know as how last night weren't none of Mr Lukan's doing.'

Sure of these facts at least, Leonora said, 'I am gratified to hear that.'

'No, it was that other gent as made Miss Vivienne sick with drinking too much.'

'Oh? And which man was that, Susan?' Leonora was instantly alerted. She asked her question in a deliberately casual tone of voice, aware that the silly girl was flattered to have been singled out by her mistress for such a lengthy discussion.

'I wouldn't be knowing what he calls himself ma'am, but there's more'n one housemaid as thinks herself the only one to leave her door unlatched on his account.'

'*Susan!*'

Anabel's exclamation caused the girl to press both hands to her lips and stare at Leonora over her fingertips, horrified by her lack of control over her own tongue.

'Oh ma'am, I'm truly sorry. I never meant to go an' say things I shouldn't. I was only speakin' up for Mr Lukan after telling you about Miss Vivienne's callin' out for him an' chasin' after him an' all. He never done nothing wrong. It was that other gent, truly it were.'

Leonora pulled open a drawer and reached inside for a length of pale green ribbon. She held it aloft, letting it sway in the air before Susan's startled gaze.

'This is for you if you bring me the name of the man who was with Miss Vivienne last night,' she said more warmly, smiling again. 'And it must be the *correct* name, Susan. Nothing guessed or invented.'

'Oh, yes ma'am ... I mean, no ma'am.'

'And this must remain a private matter between us. Nobody else must know of it.'

The girl nodded vigorously and eyed the ribbon, eager to possess it. Her hand came up to touch the stray bits of mouse-brown hair protruding from beneath her bonnet, an involuntary movement born not of empty vanity but of a natural desire to enhance her femininity.

'Off you go then, Susan, and don't hesitate to ask to speak to me again, in private, when you have discovered the man's name.'

'Thank you ma'am.' Susan curtsied again and hurried to the door, where she turned for one last glimpse of the ribbon and curtsied yet again.

'Oh, and there's just one more small thing,' Leonora said before the door could close between them. 'In future I would like to know which ladies take a fancy to Mr Lukan, and to whom in particular he gives even the slightest encouragement. Do we understand each other, Susan?'

'Oh yes, ma'am. Yes ma'am.'

The girl beamed and hurried from the room. The instant they were alone again Anabel faced her young mistress with her hands on her hips and her eyes narrowed with exasperation.

'Heaven forbid! If looks could kill, *Lady Cavendish*, the expression on your face would have hanged you for a harlot the minute that girl mentioned his name.'

Leonora tossed her head. 'Nonsense, Anabel. I was simply concerned that the Earl's daughter should be weeping in the night and calling on the name of a hired man.'

'What rubbish!' Anabel retorted. 'I know plain jealousy when I see it. And I know you, Leonora Cavendish. There's little you can hide from me, in spite of all your newly-acquired airs and graces.'

For a moment Leonora looked haughty and aloof, then her features softened and she looked stricken like a child on the verge of tears. 'Is it true?' she asked. 'Do all the ladies throw themselves at Lukan?'

'Aye, it's true enough, though heaven alone knows what attracts them to the likes of him.'

'All of them?'

'Aye,' Anabel nodded, wrinkling her nose in distaste. 'Like bees to a honey-pot they are, and him no better than a vagabond wearing fine clothes and speaking with a gentleman's tongue.'

'But he cares nothing for them,' Leonora insisted. 'Nothing at all, *nothing*.'

Anabel shrugged. 'He's a man like any other man.'

'But mine,' Leonora asserted. 'He is *mine*.'

'Yes, that's true enough, while he has you.'

'What? What do you mean?'

'Grow up, child. You have no special claim on him. He's a man like any other man.'

Leonora turned away. The maid's words had been like a sword-prick at her heart, and now here was Anabel, reducing Lukan de Ville to the baser level of his fellow men. *A man like any other man.* The full implications of it stunned her. That Lukan must share her with Malcolm was a fact of life, a matter of painful circumstance that neither he nor she could alter, but that *she* should have to share *him* was unthinkable. It must not be. She could never share him, *never*! She would rather see him in his grave than have him take another to his bed.

Seeing her so troubled, Anabel placed her hand on Leonora's shoulder and said brightly, 'Vivienne is no threat to you. She is nothing more than a silly child.'

'Like Daisy Kimble?' Leonora demanded.

Anabel winced at the memory. 'Poor Daisy was the tool of your father's lust, a child in his service to be used as he desired,' she reminded her. 'Would you compare your fine gypsy gentleman to the likes of Herbert Shelley?'

'And Helen,' Leonora said coldly, ignoring the question. 'My own sister. She was a year younger than Vivienne when she ... when she ...'

'When your father corrupted her,' Anabel declared. 'And now you must stop this, Leonora. You must not torture yourself with such recollections. That gypsy is a black-hearted devil who beds the wife of his closest friend and calls it love, but as God is my judge, I'll not hear him made the equal of Herbert Shelley, at least not while he holds your heart in his two hands.'

Leonora smiled a little tightly. 'I never thought to see the day when you rose to Lukan's defence on even the smallest matter, Anabel. And yet we both know how right you are. For me even to speak of them in the same breath is unjust.'

'Aye, I'll give him that. There's few enough can match his reputation.'

'He is held in high esteem by all who know him. Even Sir Oscar finds no fault in him.'

'Aye, he's a good man, so they say.'

Anabel made the comment grudgingly as she began to lift, brush and coil Leonora's hair with expert fingers. She was hoping now to let the subject drop. She had no wish to know what dark thoughts might be gathering in her mistress's mind. In that brief conversation with the maid Leonora had revealed the potency of her jealousy. Lukan de Ville belonged to her and her alone. One single episode of carnal intrigue on the gypsy's part would be sufficient to sever his hold on her. Another man's wife she might be, but she was too proud by half to let herself be used by *any* man for his occasional gratification. When in time de Ville succumbed to temptation his fine lady would discard him without compunction. Anabel smiled a little grimly as she worked with fine pins and a long length of beads to dress her mistress's hair. Neither she nor Leonora would ever be secure while Lukan de Ville figured so hugely in their lives. She feared him too much to carry false accusations against him, but she would watch and listen and hope that human nature would bring a rapid end to this dangerous situation. Sooner or later that arrogant gypsy would show himself blessed with the weaknesses of a common man, and then they would be free of him at last.

Leonora touched a light layer of powder to her face and used a delicate smudge of charcoal to outline her eyes. She found herself still remembering her sister Helen, already plump and full-breasted at thirteen, a spoilt, self-centred child with the body of a young woman and an unnatural craving for her father's admiration.

'It was the night I met Lukan,' she said aloud. 'When I fled from the Lodge and lost my way in the forest. Perhaps if I had not seen them, father and Helen … perhaps then …?'

'Hush, child, try not to dwell on such things.'

'I found him then, or he found me, that night I wandered off into the forest.'

'You said yourself that it was meant to be,' Anabel reminded her. 'And besides, I swear that gypsy was put there by the devil himself on the day you were born. He was always there, waiting just out of sight like a hungry black spider lurking in its web.'

Leonora ignored the unkind comparison. Her mind was elsewhere. 'I wish I had not seen them, Anabel. Such monstrous sights, once seen, can never be erased from memory. They remain in sharpest clarity while sweeter, more precious things begin to fade.'

Even as she spoke the words, the image of what she had stumbled across rose clear and detailed in her mind. It was Midsummer's Eve, the night before the Great Fair, and they were staying at Oakwood Lodge as Sir Oscar's guests. Her brothers were out enjoying the local festivities while their mother lay ill and exhausted in her upstairs rooms. Leonora, tingling with excitement and acutely aware of a certain magic in the air, had been too restless to doze in her room as intended. She had gone downstairs, pushed open the door of her father's apartment and seen them together. Herbert Shelley was sitting on a chair with his clothes in disarray and his face a flushed and fleshy mask of lechery. Helen's gown was open and she was naked to the waist. She stood between Shelley's legs, smiling with pleasure as she cupped one of her breasts in both hands and fed it, nipple first, into her father's eager mouth.

Leonora shuddered. 'I will not share him, Anabel,' she suddenly declared. She shook her head in an effort to dispel the unwanted images that caused her flesh to crawl. 'To lose him now would break my heart, yet never will I share him.

171

Never, under any circumstances, will I share Lukan with another woman!'

II

Harry Dobbin was ushered into Leonora's sitting room by a stern-faced and openly disapproving Anabel. He stood on the luxurious carpet cap-in-hand, his gaze travelling in wonderment from one item of elegance to another. He found himself surrounded by such trappings of opulence as would awe a common labourer unused to seeing beyond the kitchens of a great house. He licked his lips. He had heard such things described by the women who cleaned the gleaming grates and fetched the wines and polished the glittering silver. He had heard of them, but he had never thought to see such things for himself. It humbled him. In that place of riches and splendours he felt himself a worthless intruder.

Leonora watched him bow his head respectfully while keeping a measured distance between his dusty boots and the hem of her deep blue gown. He was a strong, muscular young man with weathered skin and pale, intelligent eyes. His clothes were shabby but reasonably clean. Even his blonde hair, hanging long and poorly trimmed about his neck and collar, seemed regularly washed and obviously grew from a healthy scalp. She stared into his face until his gaze dropped to his boots and his cheeks coloured with embarrassment. She was reminded of her elder brother Jonathan, tall and fair-haired, strong and broad-shouldered, and of Joseph her twin, with his paler eyes and more delicate colouring. She glanced beyond Dobbin to Sam Cooper, who hovered discreetly in the background by the door, and she saw that he had anticipated this memory. He smiled his sad smile and nodded his encouragement, and for a moment he was no longer a servant but a friend who had travelled with her through the very worst of

172

times. He understood the sorrows she kept hidden inside herself. With an effort she returned his smile, and when she looked back at Harry Dobbin the imagined resemblance to her two brothers had vanished. He was just another young man with fair hair and blue eyes.

'Well now, so you are Harry Dobbin?' She allowed just the right amount of firmness to add authority to her voice.

'Yes ma'am, I be Harry Dobbin, right enough.'

'And your wife is Nellie, a dairy maid to whom I paid extra wages in exchange for help in caring for the late Countess?'

'Yes ma'am, and right grateful we were, an' all, what with the baby nearly ready for coming and Nellie not fit to work every day of the week like afore.'

Leonora smiled and saw the flush rise again to his cheeks. In the quiet room the ticking of the large clock seemed extraordinarily loud.

'Living from one day to the next must be quite a struggle for you,' she observed.

'I'll not be complaining, ma'am,' Dobbin replied. 'I work hard and earn decent enough money when the season's good. I'll not be complaining.'

'Then you are a wise man, Harry Dobbin.'

Leonora watched him closely. Under her scrutiny he shifted his weight from one foot to the other and back again. His fingers began to fidget with the rough cloth cap he held tightly in both hands. With a swish of her gowns Leonora moved to the fireplace and counted a further twelve ticks of the clock before rounding on the nervous young man with a stream of carefully chosen words.

'While the Countess lay helpless on her sick-bed, an extremely valuable diamond and ruby brooch was stolen from her person.'

His mouth fell open. She heard Anabel's shocked gasp in response to the unexpected announcement. After the briefest pause she continued, 'The theft of such valuable property from a dying woman is particularly callous. The family is most distressed. And now, Harry Dobbin, I believe your wife has actually admitted creeping to Her Ladyship's bedside while

173

my personal maid was absent from the room?'

'Yes ma'am, but ...'

'And since the brooch seems to have vanished during those brief moments, what am I to assume if not the worst?'

She lifted her hands and let them fall again with a deep sigh. Dobbin was staring back at her with wide, incredulous eyes. He began to shake his head from side to side as the full implications of her words became clear to him.

'Well, Harry Dobbin? What does your wife know about this matter?'

'Nothin' ma'am. Nothin', I swear.'

'But on her own admission she was there, actually inside the room at the time of the theft.'

'Happen so, Your Ladyship, but she didn't take nothing. Not my Nellie. She's no thief isn't my Nellie.'

'But she *is* a liar.'

'What, Nellie? Oh no, ma'am.' He shook his head again and tried to lick saliva back to his dry lips.

Leonora wagged a finger in his face. 'Your wife has stated that the Countess died at three o'clock in the afternoon.'

'Yes, ma'am.'

'*Before* my marriage to Sir Malcolm.'

'Yes, ma'am.'

'And that my maid Anabel wilfully concealed the fact.'

Dobbin swallowed and nodded miserably. 'Yes, ma'am.'

'On what evidence does she *dare* make such an accusation?'

He flinched before her anger. 'She says she saw for herself.'

'When? When did she see this thing for herself? When she crept into the sickroom to steal the Countess's brooch, perhaps?'

'No ma'am, she never ...'

'Ah, then she did *not* go into the sickroom to steal the Countess's brooch?'

'No ma'am, I mean, yes ma'am, she did go inside, but she never stole nothin' belonging anyone else.'

'Come, come, Dobbin. She is a poor dairy maid heavy with child and fearful of losing her employment during the time of her lying-in. She saw Anabel leave the sickroom for a few moments and crept inside to see what she could steal. She found the Countess lying helpless with a jewelled brooch pinned to her shawl *and she stole it.*'

'No ma'am. That ain't so.'

'How easily you people fall into crime. The temptation must have been irresistible.'

'No, ma'am,' Dobbin almost yelled. 'Please, I mean, beggin' your pardon, ma'am, but that ain't what happened.'

Leonora placed her hands on her hips and lifted her head angrily. 'Very well, Harry Dobbin, why don't you tell us what *you* believe took place in that room with only your wife as witness?'

On the other side of the room Sam Cooper was standing with his back to the door and his gaze lowered. Anabel was gripping the arms of her chair so tightly that her knuckles were bloodless. She was furious. The expression on her face conveyed mute opposition to the manner in which the interview was being conducted.

Dobbin met Leonora's gaze only briefly before her unfriendly stare discouraged him. He cleared his throat and began to speak in a small, troubled voice.

'With respect, ma'am, my Nellie says she saw Miss Anabel rushing out of Her Ladyship's room in tears just afore three o'clock. She went inside to see what all the fuss was about and the Countess ...'

'... had suffered yet another seizure,' Leonora cut in.

'Beggin' your pardon, ma'am, but Nellie reckons she were dead.'

'Oh, really? And how long has your wife been a qualified doctor, Mr Dobbin?'

'She ain't no doctor, ma'am.'

'An experienced nurse, then?'

'No, ma'am.'

'But she has obviously been trained to recognise the very small distinction between paralysis caused by a seizure and death itself?'

'Well, no ma'am, she ain't, but ...'

'But she thought that by accusing others of some crime she

might throw a veil over her own misdeeds?'

'No, ma'am, no.'

'Let me remind you of something, Mr Dobbin. I nursed the Countess myself all the months of her illness, and I *did* learn to distinguish between death and seizure. My maid Anabel, whom your wife glibly accuses of a wicked breach of her duties, has long experience in the nursing of invalids. Dr Richard Winterton, a respected man in medical circles, saw the Countess shortly after she died, and no lesser personage than Sir Marcus Shaw, the Earl's own surgeon, has examined the body and confirmed that death took place around dawn yesterday morning.' She paused. She could see his mind reeling from the onslaught of her words. 'Now I ask you, Mr Dobbin, could it possibly be that all these people are in error and that only *your wife*, who is incapable of reading or writing her own name, knows the truth of the matter?'

Dobbin wrung his cap. 'No ma'am.'

'So she is not speaking the truth when she says the Countess died *before* the wedding?'

Dobbin swallowed with some effort. 'No ma'am,' he muttered miserably. 'I don't reckon as how she can be, when you put it like that.'

'And if she is not telling the truth then she is obviously telling lies.'

'Beggin' your pardon, ma'am, but if my Nellie's made a mistake ...'

'A mistake?' Leonora repeated. 'Harry Dobbin, your wife has made serious accusations against my personal maid and most loyal companion, and since Anabel Corey only acts on my instructions, the finger of your wife's suspicion would appear to point directly at *me*.'

The man looked mortified. 'Oh no, ma'am, I'm sure she never meant to do that. Oh no, ma'am, that can't be. Never in a hundred years would my Nellie stoop to doin' such a thing.'

'But what she says is so damaging to my good name,' Leonora protested. 'I visited the Countess several times between the wedding ceremony and her death yesterday morning. I was actually with her when she succumbed to the

176

final attack. Am I to be called a liar by this ... this *servant*? Is my word, the word of a *lady*, to be held in doubt simply because your foolish wife has *made a mistake*?'

Dobbin blinked his eyes rapidly. He was sweating and the outer edges of his vision were beginning to blur, as if he might keel over at any moment in a dead faint. He felt trapped, suffocated, beaten into submission by words that carried weight enough to ruin his life for ever. Suddenly he was caught in a situation that was growing bigger and more frightening by the minute. He could see himself and Nellie dismissed from the Earl's employ for this, and the cottage at Hill's Edge taken from them just when they most needed a roof over their heads. Worse than that, he could see them arrested and carted away for the hanging offence of stealing a precious brooch from the Countess of Beresford herself.

'It won't do, Harry Dobbin,' Leonora told him in a softer tone of voice. 'A very valuable piece of jewellery is missing. Your wife admits to being alone in the sickroom against my express orders to the contrary, and now she invents this totally fanciful story to discredit Miss Anabel. No, Dobbin, it simply will not do.'

'Please, Your Ladyship, don't be too hard on us,' Dobbin pleaded, looking desperate. 'Nellie's near to givin' birth and not herself. She must have made a mistake. I'll see to her. I'll tell her she's made a serious mistake.'

Leonora frowned and pursed her lips. 'I'm not so sure that will be enough, Harry Dobbin.'

'Please, Your Ladyship. She's near her time and she's a good girl, is Nellie. I promise you she never meant no harm.'

Leonora nodded at that. 'I suppose you are right. And you can ill afford to lose your position here, can you? And there's the cottage, of course, and the patch of land that goes with it ...'

'Aye, we stand to lose everything. We'll be destitute.'

'But if she persists with her story either Sir Oscar or Sir Malcolm will be compelled to take action against the two of you.'

'They'll not be,' Dobbin insisted. 'I'll not let it happen,

Your Ladyship. I'll not let Nellie bear witness against Miss Anabel.'

'*False* witness,' Leonora corrected sharply. 'What she says amounts to a pack of lies. She must not be allowed to bear *false* witness against Miss Anabel.'

'No, ma'am.'

'But that still leaves the matter of the missing brooch.'

Dobbin shook his head emphatically. 'It weren't my Nellie, ma'am. She's a good, honest girl what never stole nothing in her life. I'm sorry it's lost, that I am, but it weren't her, ma'am, truly it weren't.'

'But she admits to being alone in the sick-room when the brooch went missing,' Leonora reminded him.

'No ma'am, I swear to God she wouldn't touch nothin' that didn't belong to her.'

'Then it sounds to me as if she did not actually go *inside* the room at all,' Leonora suggested with a smile. 'Perhaps she merely looked in through the open doorway, saw the Countess lying on her sickbed and *surmised* that she was dead. And if that was the case, she would not have seen the brooch the Countess was wearing and therefore could not be responsible for its theft.' She paused again, letting the words sink in. 'So, Mr Dobbin, how could she possibly be the thief if she did not go into the room?'

'That's right, Your Ladyship.'

Leonora knew she had him now. 'Why, the whole thing is perfectly clear to me now,' she said emphatically. 'Your wife did not step inside the room, she did not see Lady Alyce dead, and she did not steal the diamond and ruby brooch.'

Dobbin's features began to brighten with hope. 'No ma'am. That she didn't.'

'Well then, it would seem we must look for our thief elsewhere.'

'That's right, Your Ladyship,' Dobbin repeated, nodding his head frantically.

'However, this mistake has placed me in a very difficult position. I feel I must hold you personally responsible for her future conduct, for what she says and to whom she speaks on the matter. You may consider yourselves fortunate that I happen to believe her innocent, but if Sir Malcolm or the Earl should ever know of this ...'

She left the sentence unfinished. She had already unsettled his peace of mind, the rest he would do for himself. A man's own imagination could often be far more effective than actually stating the retribution he feared.

'You have my solemn word I'll see to her ma'am,' Dobbin vowed, touching his forehead where beads of nervous perspiration had gathered.

Leonora sighed. 'I fear it will not be easy for her to admit to Sir Malcolm that she spoke in haste about the death of the Countess.'

'No ma'am, happen not, but I'll see she does it. I'll make sure she tells His Lordship how it really happened, and how she made a terrible mistake, and how she never meant to cause no harm to anyone.'

'Thank you, Dobbin. Sam Cooper said you were a good man. I am very pleased with you.'

'Thank you, ma'am.'

Harry Dobbin was already backing towards the door, casting sideways glances at Anabel as he went. By now his hands were trembling so badly that when he reached the corridor he dropped his cloth cap and almost trampled it underfoot. Sam Cooper gave him a shove to hurry him along, then turned to speak to Anabel as she was about to close the door behind him.

'Miss Anabel, will you tell Miss Leonora that the Dobbins is decent church-going folk what work hard and keep out of trouble and don't get drunk or nothing?'

'Very well,' Anabel said sharply.

He held the door with both hands. 'Only I'm sure Nellie wouldn't go stealing no brooch from the old lady. And if'n she did I reckon Harry'd make her put it right back where it came from. Will you tell Miss Leonora that from me, Miss Anabel?'

'I'll tell her,' Anabel promised.

Sam beamed. 'I'm right proud to be working for a real lady like Miss Leonora. Heart of gold, she has, letting Miss Nellie off like that. Heart of pure gold.'

'Yes, Sam, I'm sure she has.' Anabel spoke coldly as she forced the door closed between them. Then she rounded on Leonora in a fury. 'Madam, you should be ashamed of yourself. Never have I witnessed such an outrageous performance of brazen, bare-faced dishonesty.'

Leonora smiled and dropped into a deep curtsy. 'Why thank you, Anabel.'

With a sigh of exasperation Anabel crossed to the big dresser and began pulling open one small drawer after another until she found what she was looking for. She faced Leonora angrily. 'And just what, may I ask, is this?'

Leonora had moved to the window. Her cheeks were flushed and her eyes bright when she turned to glance at the large diamond and ruby cluster nestling in Anabel's palm. 'Ah, Lady Alyce's brooch.'

'Yes indeed madam, the one you just accused Nellie Dobbin of stealing.'

'Anabel, I will not live with the fear that someone may speak out against me or that damaging rumours might grow concerning the death of the Countess. Drastic measures were called for if I was to silence this girl permanently.'

'Drastic indeed,' Anabel hissed. 'When your husband hears her story reversed and thinks her given to malicious gossip, he's likely to dismiss her on the spot and Harry Dobbin with her. And where will they be then, these human pawns of yours? Tell me that, Leonora, where will they be then?'

'I will see to it that they lose nothing,' Leonora cut in. 'Do you think me completely heartless, Anabel? Do you think I would allow them to be dismissed to a future of hardship and uncertainty on my account?'

'Will you have a choice?'

'Of course I will. Can you honestly believe that I would defend myself without a thought for them? If so, then you do not know me, Anabel Corey. You do not know me *at all.*'

With a toss of her head she gathered up her skirts and marched into the next room, slamming the door behind her. Anabel stared from the jewelled brooch in her hand to the barrier of the closed door. She knew that look on her mistress's lovely face; the flushed cheeks, the bright eyes, the quick, almost nervous smile. Leonora was exhilarated, flushed with a sense of power. She had taken a man of strong body and simple mind and manipulated him into believing dead was alive and his own wife was a liar. With rare audacity she had threatened to bring a charge of theft against the girl for describing what she had seen with her own eyes. It was blackmail, plain and simple, and neither Harry Dobbin nor Sam Cooper possessed the wit to realise what was going on.

'You're a wicked girl, Leonora Cavendish,' she said, pushing the Countess's brooch to the very back of the drawer and covering it with several other items. 'You're wicked and clever and without a scruple when it comes to winning your way. And that simple-minded Dobbin is another conquest you can add to your list. You fogged his mind and twisted him around until he didn't even know what he was thinking, and as like as not he'll come to love you for it.'

With a heavy sigh she closed the dresser drawer and made the sign of the cross from forehead to breast and across each shoulder. It was a futile little gesture. It would take much more than signs to make amends for all the sins that fell in pretty words from Leonora's tongue.

III

Will Hynd was hosing out the feeding troughs when Nellie Dobbin hurried across the yard towards him. She was wearing soft slippers that were stained and worn at the toes, and the lower part of her skirts were lank and dirty from skimming the floor of the dairy every time she bent down. She was a pretty girl, still light on her feet and attractive despite the burden of the child she carried.

'Beggin' your pardon, Mr Hynd,' she said, breathless from

her dash across the yard. 'My Harry says I'm to tell you it ain't true. It were all a mistake.'

'All a mistake, you say?' Will Hynd glanced up from his task, first to the slender ankles showing below the grubby hem of her skirt, then to the colourful bruising around her swollen left eye. He sucked air through his broken teeth and shook his head from side to side. 'Give you a black eye, did he?'

Her cheeks coloured. 'Only for me own good, Mr Hynd.'

'I'm glad to hear it. What ain't true?'

'What I said afore about the Countess.'

Will scowled fiercely. 'You said she was dead afore the wedding, Nellie Dobbin. You said as how *somebody* made it look like she was still alive and left her all them long hours without so much as a sitter with a candle.'

'I thought it were true.'

'But it weren't, were it? Thinking don't count for nothing when it's done by the likes of you, my girl. Thinking it don't make it true, do it?'

She shook her head and looked ashamed. 'I never meant no harm, Mr Hynd. It were all a mistake.'

'Well it ain't good enough, Nellie Dobbin. Mistakes is best kept quiet so as no harm's done by 'em. And if you ask me, tongues shouldn't be let loose to make words that ain't meant.'

She hung her head. 'No sir, that's what my Harry says.'

'Words ain't dogs with decent training, you know? You can't call words back and make 'em behave just how you tell 'em. You can't just turn 'em loose and then call 'em to heel saying it's all been a mistake and expect no damage done.'

Nellie dropped her head even further towards her chest and locked her fingers across the hard round lump of her belly. 'I know, Mr Hynd, and I'm right sorry, honest I am.'

'Sir Malcolm won't go easy on you for making a mistake like that. It puts everyone in a bad light, saying things like that. It makes lords and ladies look like they don't know how to behave proper nor how to look after their own.'

'I didn't mean no harm, Mr Hynd. I swear I didn't mean no harm.'

'Well I hope Sir Malcolm believes that.'

Nellie lifted her head. 'Maybe he would if you was to put in a good word for me, Mr Hynd.'

His grizzled features softened. 'Now what would I be wanting to do a thing like that for?'

'I'd be ever so grateful, Mr Hynd.'

'Would you, now?'

Hynd rubbed thoughtfully at his mouth and chin. The friction of calloused palm against stubble produced a grating sound loud enough to attract the attention of several hens scratching in the dirt nearby. They lifted their heads, eyes bright with curiosity. Hynd scattered them with a stamp of his foot, chuckling at their sudden panic. He continued to rub his chin as he eyed the girl's pretty, anxious face. He reached out to rub his knuckles across her belly.

'When you expecting to drop it?'

She shrugged. 'Last week, this week. Mrs Morton reckons it won't be here for two Sundays yet. It can't be soon enough for me. I'm sick of carting this lump around and feeling like me back's broke every time I try to sit still for longer than a few minutes at a time.'

'Did you say your Harry sent you to me?'

She nodded. 'He told me to come here and explain as how them things I said about the Countess was all on account of a mistake.'

'And did he tell you to be obliging to me if I put in a good word for you with Sir Malcolm?'

Nellie shrugged again. 'Not in as many words, but he didn't say not to.'

Hynd nodded and licked his lips. Nellie Dobbin had nice breasts and soft pink skin that was as plump as a breeding sow's in some places. In summer she had been around the farm a lot, doing odd jobs and looking after the orphan calves. When she wanted Harry nicely set up with permanent work she had agreed to let Will Hynd feel around her whenever the urge took him. Nellie was a good girl. She knew her place and she didn't try to change the natural order of things. She was well aware of how things worked between the likes of her and all the men, from gardener right up to gentleman and every rank falling between, who were rightful masters over her. And she knew that she was better off than most, at least here on the Home Farm where she wasn't just taken or given away according to the master's whim. There was a lot to be gained on both sides by simple bartering. Hynd got to grope and fondle the girls and in return they took what favours he could offer either to them or their menfolk. And sometimes he got to undo his pants and take more than a fondle, but only if the girl was willing and the trade-off was of her own making. He had his pride. He wouldn't count himself amongst those who used their position to force young women into doing what they didn't want to do. Besides, he was pushing sixty and well past the days when he could straddle a girl more than once or twice a month. He was happier with the lighter stuff that didn't leave him wheezing and exhausted, just a regular handful of plump young flesh and a taste of nipple now and again.

'Well, Mr Hynd? Will you do it? Will you put in a good word for me with Sir Malcolm?'

Will looked into Nellie's bruised face. Her left eye was completely closed. The other looked back at him with a pleading expression. He glanced around the yard, then showed the blackened stubs of his teeth in a broad grin and jerked his head in the direction of the back barn.

'Of course I'll put in a good word for you, Nellie.'

'Oh thank you, Mr Hynd.'

She too glanced all about her. Then she offered him a painful, lopsided smile and stepped lightly towards the barn. Hynd grinned and patted her rounded backside in appreciation as his bowed legs carried him after her at an eager lurch.

CHAPTER TEN

Between midnight and morning the Great Hall had been a hive of activity as troops of servants with ladders and packing cases took away those extravagant wedding decorations to be preserved for future celebrations. Every candle had to be removed along with the huge hanging garlands, silk flower arrangements, wax cherubs and beautiful silk butterflies with delicately boned wings. Life-sized wire swans, layered with swansdown and plumed with real feathers, were lifted gently into cases, packed with fine gauze and wheeled away on small carts to storerooms on the ground floor. In the wake of these workers came a second wave of servants bearing sombre drapes and dark mourning candles. Wreaths of flowers and leaves, cut from fabrics of copper, bronze, black and deep ruby, were set about the hall. Lanterns were hung with shaded glass, mirrors veiled with muslin. Even the forty crystal chandeliers concealed their bright splendour behind hangings of fine black muslin that shimmered and billowed in the updraught like the gowns of dancing ladies.

A number of long, darkly-draped trellis tables had been erected against the far walls, each sagging beneath a burden of food and liquid refreshment. Most of it had been prepared in the Earl's own kitchens, but many special delicacies had been brought to Beresford by cart and coach to satisfy the many connoisseurs amongst the guests. Here were whole barrels of oysters from Whitstable, the very best larks-tongues from Dunstable, genuine Richmond eels and delicious pork pies from Stamford and Bent's bakery in Melton Mowbray. Here too was a fine selection of Beresford's own produce; its poultry and game, freshly broiled fish, cold meats, spiced sausages, succulent kidneys and warm new bread. There were home-made ales by the keg, hot soups and puddings, sweet tarts and savoury pies, fresh fruit, biscuits and butter and, to refresh the palate, white wines, claret, tangy punch and crisp peppermint water. A collection of elaborate silver urns with fancy lids also graced the tables, each one emitting a tiny funnel of steam that smelled of tea or coffee, chocolate or buttered milk.

Sir Malcolm and his father had arrived early. They strode around the hall together, inspecting every table and solemnly receiving the bows and curtsies of waiting servants.

'My compliments to your lady,' the Earl said at last, nodding approval at his son. 'I doubt even the Countess herself could have bettered this at such short notice.'

Malcolm smiled proudly. 'I think Leonora would rather hear such praise from your own lips father,' he said.

'And so she shall,' the Earl nodded. He looked around the Great Hall once again, noting all the extra touches, the thoughtful details that produced the perfect whole. 'She has done a wonderful job here, my boy, a wonderful job.'

The hall was already beginning to buzz with a hubbub of people impatient to sample the fare and carry their compliments to Sir Oscar. Members of the immediate family, close friends, business associates and more distant relatives gathered together in small groups to eat, drink and gossip freely before the funeral observations began in earnest. Most of the gentlemen had managed to find or borrow a suitable coat or a sober pair of trousers. Personal trunks and wardrobes had been thrown open to accommodate the needs of those who had made the long journey from their homes without the slightest intention of attending a funeral. The women, of course, were a different matter. Freed from the obligation of sacrificing high fashion for drab mourning clothes, they appeared now in their brightest and prettiest gowns, hats trimmed with fresh or silken flowers, petticoats rustling, jewellery glittering. Despite the solemnity of the occasion there was a new excitement in the air. What woman does not dream of openly flouting convention while keeping her respectability intact? What woman does not yearn to fly her own colours in the face of strict tradition, safe in the knowledge that she will suffer no ill for the boldness? At every great function was the eye that saw, the hand that wrote or sketched, the spy who carried news of this gown or that hat or those manners back to the very heart of city society. Every woman in the room was aware that she might be spoken of in fine drawing rooms all over the country within hours of this hasty burial. Her appearance might even be described in some fashionable magazine, or her image captured for posterity within the pages of the *Illustrated London News*. And to this end they were all devoted as they displayed their latest item in vogue, the shimmering clusters of black velvet ribbon gracing their upper arms. Some were twisted and knotted into elaborate designs, others bound with fancy black lace, still others tied in pretty bunches of bows with hanging tails. Even the elderly ladies had risen to the occasion by braiding their ribbons with black beads or pinning them in place with brooches of dark ruby or polished jet. Silken flowers and feathers of every shape and size had been dipped, dried and dipped again in dyes made from charcoal or oil of tartar until the result was a glossy raven-black. These ladies had taken a small concession, a simple matter of convenience, and made of it a spectacle.

'Clever, clever, clever,' Annabel said in a whisper that was forced from one corner of her mouth. 'This is supposed to be a funeral. Is there nothing sacred, Leonora, nothing you will not turn to your own advantage?'

'Do not preach, Anabel.' Leonora had been staring up at

the great arched windows that had survived from the days when Beresford Hall was a rich and very powerful abbey. Even the meagre light of this grey November morning was enough to bring the stained glass images to life in bursts of vibrant colour. She had first seen them in high summer, when shafts of brilliant sunlight struck the glass and splashed its shapes and colours across the pale stone floor of the Great Hall. She had been a child then, but as a woman she was no less enchanted by what she saw. Beresford's stained glass windows were magnificent. No single building in the whole of England could boast their equal, and they were hers, part of the property that was now her home and would one day belong to her husband and their children and their children's children.

'Do not preach,' she said again, pulling her attention back to the woman at her side. 'These people came to Beresford to enjoy a wedding, not suffer a funeral. For most of them there has been too little time between the two events to send for more suitable clothes. What you see is a happy compromise, is it not?'

'What I see is a fashion-show,' Anabel retorted.

'Then it bears the Earl's stamp of approval,' Leonora said, spotting her father-in-law across the hall. 'You see? He too is wearing a black sash around his upper sleeve and he, of all those present, could have dressed more appropriately, had he so desired.'

'So he too is to be twisted around your little finger?'

Leonora smiled and inclined her head in acknowledgement as Sir Oscar caught her eye and bowed in greeting.

'Not Sir Oscar Cavendish,' she said tersely. 'Believe me, Anabel, I will count myself fortunate indeed when I can say with certainty that I have earned *his* trust.'

'Earned or stolen?' Anabel demanded. 'Truthfully now, would you wish to earn his trust or steal it?'

Leonora shrugged and smiled again in the Earl's direction. 'What do the means matter, Anabel, so long as I eventually gain my ends?'

Anabel looked at her mistress closely, noting a feverish

188

brightness in her oddly-tinted eyes. 'I doubt if you recall the difference between the two,' she hissed. 'And don't think I'm blind to your wicked little ploy.'

'And which ploy might that be?'

'To make a celebration of the Countess's interment,' Anabel said sharply. 'To turn her going into a cause for merriment. Just look at them all, showing off their finery as if they face a Grand Ball rather than a funeral. It's wicked and you know it, my girl. You ought to be ashamed of yourself.'

'Ashamed?' Leonora asked sweetly. 'Why Anabel, I believe I have exercised an admirable restraint, given the circumstances. If I had my way I would be hitching up my skirts and dancing on that evil woman's coffin.'

With a toss of her head she moved off to greet the family mourners, leaving Anabel shocked into silence by her parting words.

There were almost a hundred people in the room, many of whom would be asked to wait patiently in the cramped rooms of the old gatehouse while the service took place in the tiny chapel below. The Earl had decided that certain matters of protocol must be observed, including the long and tedious funeral procession that would carry the cortège through all the local villages. The common people must be allowed to pay their last respects to the great lady. The carriages were gathered and waiting in order of priority, with lesser mourners and more distant friends bringing up the rear. A large company of grooms, maids and manservants were on hand, each bearing a coat, cloak or warm rug to protect delicate shoulders and fine clothes from the elements. Outside the morning had grown bright and blustery, with brief showers of rain tossed from clouds that raced as if pursued across the heavens. Trees already stripped of their leaves shook their bare limbs in threatening gestures at the sky. It was a cold, uncertain day, a good day for a funeral.

Like a rook among swallows the Reverend Cedric Evans mingled with the other guests, a tall, stooped individual incongruous in his bleak and colourless attire. He had already received a most generous fee and a veritable banquet of additional gratuities in return for performing the wedding service. Now he found it difficult to maintain the solemnity of his features as he anticipated the weight of this day's profits. He paid dutiful homage to each member of the family in turn, even offering a few timeworn words of comfort to those young Cavendish children who barely remembered the stern, unloving old woman who might have been their aunt, their great-aunt or perhaps their grandmother. His eyes glinted with unspoken satisfaction and his smile, a little too plump and wet about the lower lip, had become fixed upon his face. His dry hands rustled like parchment as his palms rubbed against each other in constant movement, a mannerism many might have found less objectionable on the grasping fingers of a money-lender. Cedric Evans was vicar of the villages of Wotherton and Bishorne. He had no less than five large congregations under his jurisdiction and was held, by a not-too-modest annual retainer, to perform occasional services at the private chapel attached to Beresford Hall. He was a man desirous of material improvement, a man of firm and resolute ambitions. If his personal prosperity and steady promotion within the church meant kissing the shirt-tails of men like the Earl and turning a blind eye to the transgressions of the Countess, then so be it. He was not too proud to bow his head, nor too bashful to pocket a bribe, nor even too pious to turn a poor man's intimate confession to his own use. Many a would-be thief had lost his liberty and many a gentleman his honour in the welter of self-interest plying between the eye, the ear and the tongue of this self-seeking man of God.

Floundering in the wake of the Reverend Cedric Evans waded the lesser personage of the Reverend Tobias Thorpe, an honest man of correspondingly meagre income. His pockets were empty, his boots borrowed from a local gardener, his clothes donated by the poor people of his parish. Only his piety was his own. His worldly goods consisted of a run-down house attached to a near-derelict church, a long-departed congregation, a formidable wife and thirteen children of healthy appetite. A frail and unassuming man with a voice so lacking in substance that few people bothered to listen to what he had to say, the Reverend Thorpe had long since humbled himself before the unrelenting greyness of his existence. At home his own fledglings snatched the food from his plate, in his crumbling church he preached to empty pews, and hovering over his life like a hungry vulture was the Reverend Cedric Evans, ready to pluck away even the smallest particle of good fortune that chanced to come his way. He too welcomed the rapid turn-about from wedding to funeral. He had been instructed to remain at Beresford and was more than happy to do so, even though the presence of Cedric Evans left him with little else to do besides eat and drink, sleep off his excesses and eat and drink again.

Leonora met the Reverend Thorpe with a bright smile that only hinted at the depth of sympathy she felt for him. She was well aware of his position within the clergy. He was at the lower end of the pecking order, struggling to survive, grasping at crumbs in a situation he could no longer hope to improve. Every walk of life, every simple process of human nature could be witnessed right here in the glaring inequalities between Mr Evans and Mr Thorpe. Written somewhere within the mysteries were the rules that kept the stronger man ahead of the weaker, the pompous above the pious. And so the imbalance was continually maintained. The meek would forever inherit the earth, but never the fruits or profits thereof.

'Good morning Reverend,' she said, slipping her hand into his and feeling her own grip to be the stronger, the more substantial. In that swift movement she managed to conceal a small silk purse between his palm and hers. Five guineas it held, enough to keep the wolves at bay a little longer. She smiled again into his thin, astonished face before moving away to pay her respects elsewhere.

When she saw Lady Elizabeth sitting on a bench beneath one of the great windows, she immediately threaded her way through the growing crowds of guests to reach her side. The young woman looked sadly out of place, shy and awkward amid all the splendour of the Great Hall. She resembled a pretty wallflower left alone at some glittering occasion where everyone else was partnered. She was dressed in a frock of pale blue silk with pink sleeve inlets and matching flashes let into the bodice. The mourning ribbons from around her sleeve had been pulled loose and draped clumsily around her neck. Her bonnet lay crumpled in her lap while her fingers plucked distractedly at the ringlets in her hair. She was humming a simple nursery tune, her soft grey eyes staring into the throng of chattering people without seeing any one of them. She turned her head as Leonora sat down beside her and took hold of her hands to still their nervous movements. A frown plucked momentarily at her brow, then her eyes lighted with recognition and she smiled a welcome warm enough to melt any heart.

'Leonora, my dear and lovely friend Leonora.'

'Hello, Elizabeth. You look very pretty today.'

The girl frowned and cocked her head as if listening for a far-off sound. 'The rooks,' she said urgently. 'The rooks are circling the tower again. I saw them. They come and go by the highest windows, you know. I saw them with my own eyes. Their cawing makes my head ache.'

'You must not go up there, Elizabeth,' Leonora reminded her. 'You know the tower is unsafe and the Monks' Stair very dangerous. You made a solemn promise not to go up there again.'

Elizabeth looked dismayed. 'Oh please don't let me be punished again. Don't make me go to the chapel.' She pulled her hands from Leonora's grip and wrung them together in sudden distress. 'Mama knows. I'm afflicted, touched by the devil's hand. Mama knows best. I must be punished for it. I'm wicked, wicked.'

'No Elizabeth. Hush my dear, hush.' Leonora pulled the girl into her arms and rocked her gently, smoothing her tangled hair as she spoke. 'Hush, you poor thing. All that is finished now. It is over. There will be no more whippings, Elizabeth. You need never go into the chapel again as long as you live.'

Elizabeth brightened instantly. 'Never? Never ever? Never never *never*?'

'*Never!*' Leonora smiled.

'Not even when I go to the tower?'

'Not even then,' Leonora insisted. 'But it frightens me when you go into the tower, Elizabeth. I fear you will fall and hurt yourself. Listen to me, my dear. Malcolm has promised to have it made safe so that I may one day make my apartments up there, right at the very top, just as our ancestor Joshua did all those years ago. Then you may come to visit me just as often as you wish. Would you like that, Elizabeth?'

'Oh yes, Leonora.' She frowned suddenly, puckering her pretty face into an expression of distaste. 'But first we must drive away the rooks.'

'Of course. And you must be my helper when the time comes to furnish the new rooms. But first you must promise not to go back to the tower until the work is done. Will you promise that, Elizabeth?'

'Oh yes. Oh yes. She paused, touched a finger to her pursed lips, then smiled and chanted, 'Cross my heart and hope to die, if my promise proves a lie.'

Leonora sighed. 'Oh Elizabeth, you are so sweet and obliging, but I wonder if you will remember your promise five minutes from now?'

Elizabeth nodded. 'My hair is messy.'

'A little, perhaps, but it does not matter, dear.'

'I need a fresh bonnet.'

Leonora touched the ravaged straw in Elizabeth's lap and smiled. 'Yes, Elizabeth, I believe you do.'

In one swift movement Elizabeth reached out to hug Leonora so tightly that she could scarcely breath. Then she jumped up and darted away in the direction of the kitchens. Her bonnet tumbled to the floor, forgotten. When Leonora bent forward to retrieve it she found her action anticipated by a strong masculine hand.

'This bonnet could well be the remains of a goat's dinner,' a deep voice observed. 'Leonora, you have always shown the patience of an angel toward my poor sister.'

'Gilbert,' Leonora exclaimed, her face lighting with genuine pleasure. 'Oh Gilbert, it is so good to see you again. I feared you might leave for Scotland before I had the opportunity to speak to you again.'

Gilbert Cavendish took the hand she offered and drew it to his lips. He smiled as he watched her, and there was no mistaking the Cavendish in those dark-lashed, startling blue eyes. 'You look wonderful, Leonora. Are you happy?'

'Oh yes,' she nodded. 'I feel that life has suddenly given me everything I ever wanted.'

He smiled. 'Then I am happy for you.'

She saw the same sadness in his eyes, the same devotion that had once filled her with such covetous satisfaction. It seemed to her now that a whole lifetime had rushed by since she had thought his love a prize worth having. She had deliberately angled for it in the hope of winning for herself the Cavendish name, a modest title and a home in the shadow of her beloved Beresford Hall. As a poor relation she had set her sights quite high in aspiring to wed the Earl's youngest son. But that was half a year ago, before her comfortable world came crashing down around her ears, before her will to survive was so harshly tested.

'My dear Gilbert,' she said now, recalling how circumstances had first brought them together, then set him beyond her reach, then elevated her beyond his aspirations. 'I do believe I broke your heart.'

He smiled. 'I recall nothing in the past for which you could possibly have cause to reproach yourself. There was never an understanding between us. The fault was entirely mine. I took your friendship to mean much more than it did, and for that I have been sorely chastened.'

'Poor Gilbert, I had not the slightest inkling of your true feelings,' she said, knowing he would believe the lie. 'I valued our friendship and never once suspected that to you it meant something more, something deeper.'

He was still holding her hand. He looked into her eyes intently, quite oblivious to the presence of other people in the room. 'I would have told you, Leonora. I planned to ask you to be my wife that day we all picnicked together near St Eloy's Well. If word had not come that your father had absconded with my father's money ...'

'Please,' she said quickly. 'Give me no reminders of that

day.' She laughed away the memory and withdrew her hand from his. To change the subject she asked, 'Do you recall all the letters that passed between us before ever we met face to face? I believed my friendship to be with Elizabeth, and all the time you kept me entertained with letters that she could never hope to write.'

He nodded. 'And yet she delighted in receiving your letters and having me read them to her. She carried them around like precious things. I was afraid Mama would find them and forbid the friendship.'

'And so you intercepted each one and wrote to me in Elizabeth's name. It was a generous, loving thing to do, Gilbert.'

'A selfish thing,' he corrected. 'I looked for them each week, not for Elizabeth's benefit but for my own. Those pages were filled with warmth, affection and such humour that I came to count the days between each letter and the next. I must confess I envied her your friendship.'

Leonora looked away from the quiet intensity of his gaze. 'Poor Elizabeth,' she said. 'I have always been extremely fond of her. Something in her seems to reach out and touch me ...' She paused, touching the bodice of her gown with both hands, close to her heart. 'Right here.'

'That much is obvious.' He looked at her for a long moment, then bowed rather stiffly and added without smiling, 'I am proud to have you as a sister, Leonora. Malcolm is a lucky man.'

'Thank you, Gilbert.'

'And I want you to know that you will always find a friend, should you be in need of one, in me. You may call on me for anything, anything at all. I will not fail you.'

'Thank you, dear *dear* Gilbert.'

He bowed again and walked away from her. She watched him go with only the smallest pang of regret. He carried his disappointment like the gentleman he was, and there was too much goodness in him for it to mar his affection for herself or Malcolm. He was young, still only in his twentieth year, and with the resilience of youth he would soon recover. Another spring, another pretty face, and love would find him again.

For a while she sat alone in the bright sunlight shafting down from one of the stained glass windows, watching its reflected colours fall upon her skirts. Clouds scudded across the morning sky, their shadows shifting and altering the stains of colour nestling in the deep green folds of her gown. Staring down at sunlight and shadow on silk, she imagined clusters of spring flowers nodding their heads over lush green meadowland.

She found her thoughts turning to the three Cavendish brothers. Two had never borne her the slightest measure of ill-will while the third, Sir Horace, had set himself against her from the start. Two she had won to her side with love, but the other she had defeated in a cold and calculating act of vengeance. Horace Cavendish bore such a marked resemblance to Jonathan Shelley that they were often taken for brothers. It was a likeness she had played upon to help convince the Earl that he had sired the one as surely as he had sired the other. They were like two sides of the same coin, but while her brother was an honourable man, Horace Cavendish was in all respects a scoundrel. While Jonathan had many fine and admirable qualities, the Earl's middle son seemed possessed of every vice and evil, fault and failing ever visited upon a single Cavendish. Leonora hated him with a passion. She could look Sir Oscar in the eye and swear that Horace and Jonathan were brothers, but she would never let him forget that they were different to the core. They were no more alike than were a serpent and a prince.

'And just what schemes are you hatching now in that pretty head of yours, my lady?'

Anabel sat down beside Leonora with a sigh. She was wearing one of the new frocks her mistress had ordered to be made for her. The fabric had a fashionable plaid pattern in muted colours that were less austere than her usual choice of black or dark brown. It had a simply-cut bodice trimmed with lace, and full skirts over several petticoats. Her hair too had been dressed in a less severe manner that left a few curls and a little softness around her face and ears. The bonnet she wore was trimmed with silk flowers and dyed goose feathers and tied with a streamer of blue muslin.

'You look nice, Anabel,' Leonora said.

'What? Oh, go on with you.' She touched her hair and smoothed her skirts, suddenly self-conscious.

'It's perfectly true,' Leonora protested. 'You *do* look nice, and mama would be pleased that I have finally persuaded you to take some pride in your appearance.'

Anabel looked down at her hands, remembering the mistress she had served with devotion for so many years. At last she glanced at Leonora suspiciously and said, 'I saw you speaking to Sir Gilbert.'

Leonora nodded. 'Don't start your fretting, Anabel. We have nothing to fear from Gilbert.'

'You should never have toyed with his affections the way you did. Men bear grudges when women let them down.'

'Not Gilbert. He is far too sweet and forgiving ever to bear a grudge.'

Anabel tightened her lips and looked at Leonora sideways. 'This time you were lucky. It makes me shudder even now, just to remember how you led that boy around by the heart-strings with your sights already set on Malcolm and your heart firmly fixed on ...'

'Be silent.' Leonora snapped the warning.

The older woman lowered her voice. 'When will you learn that men are not to be trifled with? They have the beast in them and they make dangerous enemies.'

Leonora smiled wryly. 'They do indeed. I am reminded of a certain Cavendish who hated me when I was only ten years old, simply because he was a pompous oaf and I a pretty child too proud to grovel at his feet.'

'Horace!'

'Yes, the ghastly boy who became the detestable young man.'

'He was a hateful man, but he met his match in you, did he not, my girl?' Anabel pursed her lips and shook her head. 'Oh, I tremble even now to imagine how things might have turned out if he had done what he set out to do. You were only

197

fifteen when he tried to take you by force. If you had lacked the courage, or the strength, to fight him off . . .'

'And still I hate him,' Leonora said passionately. 'Do you realise his exile has lasted for two years and he is still disowned by his father? He is not free to return to Beresford even to attend his mother's funeral.'

'Aye, and it's no more than he deserves,' Anabel said. 'He was nothing but an animal. That foolish old Countess doted on her darling boy to the point of ruin, but even she turned against him at the end.' She leaned a little closer to Leonora and lowered her voice to a whisper. 'Are you aware that he left the country in great haste and with the Earl's own boot behind him, because of some *hanging offence.*'

She mouthed the last two words as if the crime they represented was too heinous to be spoken out loud. And so it was, for despite the fact that so many crimes carried the death sentence, few gentlemen of wealth and recourse were ever brought to face the hangman's rope. Even such serious charges as forgery and grand theft could be bought off with hard cash, and murder itself could be satisfied out of court if the price were right. Leonora smiled and remained silent while Anabel warmed to her theme.

'They say that what Horace did was so wicked, and so at variance with God's Law, that the old Countess cut him off without a penny and never so much as spoke his name from the day of his going to the day she died.'

'So I believe,' Leonora commented.

'And quite rightly, too, if you ask me. The Good Lord should have struck him down dead for the life of debauchery he was living at that fancy gentlemen's school of his.'

'Oh? Have you been listening at keyholes, Anabel Corey.'

'I'll have you know I have my information straight from the horse's mouth, or almost.'

'Oh?' Leonora repeated. 'And where might that be?'

'Agatha Bonnar. If you recall, she was Sir Oscar's housekeeper at the time all this took place. She actually carried the letter to the Earl in his drawing room. It accused young Horace of all manner of things; drunkenness, fornication, cheating in his school examinations, theft, bribery, even committing adultery with the wife of one of his father's most powerful political opponents.' She shook her head and made a tut-tutting sound with her tongue. 'He stole a necklace from that lady to pay one of his gambling debts. He forged the bill of sale and sold it to a goldsmith for five hundred pounds when it was worth five times as much. The lady threatened to take him to law for that. She had proof of it, though I doubt it helped her get her necklace back.'

Leonora felt her forearms prickle with gooseflesh.

'And that's not to mention the other, the real *hanging offence*,' Anabel whispered, knowingly. 'It must have broken the Earl's heart when that letter told him all about his son's wicked doings.'

'Indeed it must,' Leonora agreed. 'And now I would like to change the subject, if you don't mind. The service will take place in less than an hour and I prefer not to enter the chapel with my mind filled with the misdeeds of Horace Cavendish.'

'But who do you think sent that letter to the Earl?' Anabel persisted. 'Mrs Bonnar didn't manage to read it all, but says it was left unsigned. *Interested parties* was all it said at the bottom, but whoever it was threatened to have the whole business made public property unless Horace was immediately removed. And so he was, removed and dispatched abroad, just like that.' She snapped her fingers to emphasise her point.

Leonora reached up to smooth the hair in the nape of her neck. The sleeve of her gown fell back to create a pretty cascade of lace that half-concealed her face. Her lips were pursed a little as she recalled the events of which Anabel spoke. For years Horace Cavendish had lived like a debauched Caesar upon his own excesses, financed by an open-handed father and encouraged by a doting mother who was prepared to overlook any vice, any evil *except one.*

'I hated him,' she said aloud.

'And with good reason,' Anabel reminded her.

Leonora recalled the tuft of hair he had torn from her scalp and the insults he had piled upon her when she was a child of ten and he a strapping young adult of fourteen. They had not met again until she was fifteen and a guest at Malcolm's first wedding to Lady Grace Osborne Graham. Then he had made a drunken attempt to rape her in the gardens where she had sought to be alone for a short time. She had bitten his lip and bruised his nose with her head, and later he had given her a farthing, the basest of all coins, as payment for bearing his insults. Leonora had borne her grudges secretly until the day she was called to the bedside of her friend Estelle in London's Portland Place. There she had witnessed his cruelty first-hand. Estelle had been distraught. She was pregnant with Horace's child and pitifully desperate to please him in spite of his callous treatment of her. More than that, she was suffering from a terrible breast infection after Horace had persuaded her to prove her love by submitting to the barbaric fashion of nipple-piercing. Within days the metal wires had become deeply embedded in the swollen flesh, blackened and corroded. The result was a putrid poison that seemed to devour her breasts as it spread inside her body. Estelle died in agony, too loyal to name her secret lover, and Horace Cavendish collected on the cruelest of wagers. He had gambled heavily on the certainty that his besotted little mistress would do anything he demanded, even have her nipples pierced with wire rings.

Horace Cavendish could never be brought to task for that terrible deed, nor was it revealed that Estelle was expecting his child when she died. Leonora had been horrified by those events and outraged by Horace's appalling treatment of a respectable young woman who loved him deeply. She vowed to find a way to bring him to account, to turn his evil back upon itself. And this she did. It was a simple catalogue of his misdeeds, weighted with innuendo and resonant with the threat of scandal, that destroyed him. The *hanging offence* of which he was anonymously accused was sodomy, and the name left off the damning document delivered to the Earl of Beresford at his London home was that of Leonora Shelley.

A man in a dark coat and high white stock clicked his heels before Leonora and bowed stiffly. For a moment she struggled to bring her thoughts back to the present, then his name was

200

plucked from her memory and she switched on her brightest smile. This was Jeremiah Dick, secretary and confidant of Sir Giles Powell, one of the Earl's closest friends. He was a quiet man, a bachelor, clever with figures and well versed in the tricks and intricacies practised by lawyers. He was here for the reading of the Countess's will. Leonora offered her hand. When she had seen him last, a year ago, they had not been formerly introduced.

'Why Mr Dick, how nice to see you again.'

'My pleasure, Lady Leonora.' He smiled as he brushed her hand with his lips. Knowing little of the social skills in which she was so gifted, he took the greeting personally and was most flattered that this beautiful young woman remembered him.

'Is your room satisfactory?'

'Most satisfactory, thank you. May I congratulate you on your marriage to Sir Malcolm and say that I sincerely hope you and he will be very happy together.'

Leonora's smile was brilliant. 'You are most kind.'

'I was asked by Sir Oscar to bring you to the blue drawing room on the first floor. The family are gathered there for hot toddies before the service, and the Earl particularly wished to speak to you before they leave.'

Leonora rose from her seat and slipped her arm through his, and together they went up by the main stair. At the top she turned to glance back at Anabel, nodded her head and lifted her free hand in a carefully contrived gesture. Noting the signal, Anabel turned and hurried from the Great Hall without looking back.

Leonora entered the blue drawing-room ahead of Jeremiah Dick and although she went directly to Malcolm's side, her smile was intended to encompass everyone present. She sensed that prior to her arrival she had been the main topic of their conversation, but there was no hostility here. They welcomed her with smiles and nods of approval. Lady Charlotte and her cousin Sarah were sharing a sofa with Lady Vivienne, who appeared ready to burst into floods of tears in spite of her heroic smile. Other ladies sat or stood nearby: the

201

three Fitzwalters sisters, all close friends of the Countess, Lady Abigail her younger sister, and Anne and Mary her sisters-in-law. Sir Gilbert was standing with a large group of men and several ladies. Leonora recognised Sir Giles Powell and Sir Ralph Marr, Lord and Lady Mornington, related to the family by marriage, and Sir James Trotter and his lovely wife Lavinia.

The family had gathered together for privacy in one of the loveliest rooms in the house. Even on the greyest day its five magnificent south-facing windows, all hung with shimmering gold brocade, bathed the room with soft light and provided wonderful views over the Wye Valley. It was very French in style, with silk-covered walls, gold leaf cornices, matching pink marble fireplaces and delicate crystal chandeliers. Beneath their feet was a carpet of deep blue with a gold fleur-de-lis design, so richly made that it sprang like a lush summer lawn underfoot. Above their heads was a wonderful sculptured ceiling of such beauty that even its creator believed it to be his masterpiece.

As she curtsied before her father-in-law, Leonora was aware that her gown complemented her surroundings and that the colour of her eyes was deepened by the rich blue tones around her. Sir Oscar lifted her by the hand until she was standing.

'The funeral breakfast is superb,' he told her. 'And the day's arrangements are flawless. My guests want for nothing. Not even the smallest detail of comfort or protocol has been overlooked. By your efforts, my dear, you have turned a tragic situation into one of dignity and charm. On behalf of my family I thank you Leonora, most sincerely, for everything you have done to make this sad time a little easier for us all. Please accept this small gift as a token of our gratitude.'

As he finished speaking he handed her a long, slender box which she accepted with both hands. She heard a small ripple of applause and a murmur of assent and suddenly her cheeks became hot with embarrassment. She found herself deeply moved by the quiet sincerity of Sir Oscar's speech. She had not expected this. He was a fair-minded man who would certainly not allow her hard work to go unrecorded, but she had not expected this.

'Go ahead, open it,' he urged.

Her fingers fumbled at the clasp. She was aware of the other people in the room, the smiles, the warmth of feeling, and suddenly it seemed to her that all her scheming might have been for that one moment. These people were her family now and she was one of them. It was a moment she wanted to grasp and hold to herself for ever.

'Open it,' the Earl repeated in a whisper.

Leonora lifted the lid and looked into the box. As she did so the breath caught in her throat with a gasp and her vision blurred a little with sudden tears. Nestling on a bed of padded silk was the most beautiful necklace she had ever seen. It was priceless. Set into gold filigree work of exquisite craftsmanship were no less than twenty perfectly matched opals. This was her mother's necklace, the one Herbert Shelley had stolen and sold to help meet a gambling debt, the one Francine had treasured not simply for its beauty but because it had been a gift from Sir Oscar himself.

'But how . . .?' The question stumbled and died at the lump in her throat. Sir Oscar came to her rescue by lifting the necklace from its box and stepping forward to place it around her neck.

'More than twenty years ago I bought this trinket as a wedding present for my cousin Francine,' he said carefully. 'When it recently appeared on the market, how could I resist buying it again for her daughter Leonora?'

Their eyes met in a look that was charged with secrets and regrets, sorrows and forgiveness. She reached up to embrace him, pressing her cheek against his until she could no longer tell if the dampness she felt on her skin came from her tears or his.

'Thank you,' she breathed. 'With all my heart I thank you.'

For the next few minutes the room was noisy with talk and alive with admiration for both Leonora and the opal necklace. When a footman entered the room and presented the Earl with a large jewel-casket emblazoned with the Countess's monogram, Leonora held back until precisely the right moment before rushing forward with a cry of protest. 'No, no, not now, you foolish man. I gave specific orders that these were to be returned to His Lordship *after* the morning service, not before.'

The man gaped in confusion, not daring to reclaim the casket now firmly in his master's grip. 'I'm sorry ma'am. Miss Anabel said I was to bring them up here right away.'

'Then Miss Anabel was in error. Be so good as to take it away at once.'

'But My Lady . . .?'

The Earl raised a hand between them. 'I recognise this as one of the Countess's personal caskets, but we already have her jewels safely under lock and key, do we not? They were collected from her rooms only yesterday and all accounted for.'

'Not all of them,' Leonora explained. She dismissed the footman with a wave of her hand. 'Lady Alyce and I grew very close during her illness, Sir Oscar. She was a generous lady and took a great deal of pleasure in presenting me with small gifts from time to time. It made her happy to see me wearing the lovely things she could no longer wear herself.'

He glanced down at the box. 'And these are they?'

Leonora nodded. 'Every gift, every piece she ever pressed me to accept.'

'Then it seems to me that they now belong to you,' he said, offering the box. 'Why have them bought here?'

'Why?' Leonora looked aghast. She knew that every eye was upon her as she shook her lovely head and took a small step backwards. 'Sir Oscar, it is perfectly obvious that I can not hope to keep these things for myself.'

'I see no reason why that should be so. Our inventory shows that the family jewels are intact and Lady Alyce was free to dispose of her *personal property* as she wished.' He offered the casket again. 'If these were gifts from her, you should consider them your own.'

Again Leonora shook her head. 'I cannot possibly do that. I was only her nurse. I have no right to them.' She glanced at

Lady Charlotte, the eldest of the Countess's three daughters, knowing that she would not begrudge the gifts. 'I would not dream of holding you to Her Ladyship's promises. These are beautiful things, trinkets and little treasures that should go to her own daughters.'

The Earl smiled. 'It seemed she had come to consider you one of her daughters, Leonora.'

'Oh, but I couldn't . . .' She glanced at the casket. For weeks she had been wearing jewellery belonging to the Countess and looking upon it as her own. She had been careful to choose only the lesser known items, avoiding obvious family heirlooms and those pieces renowned for either their colourful history or their prohibitive cost. Beneath that polished lid was a wonderful collection, coveted things she had shrewdly held back when the Countess's personal effects were collected for the inventory. Knowing that the Countess's private collection would not be known to the clerks, she could have remained silent and kept them for herself, or argued that they were indeed hers by gift, but Leonora was no thief. Lady Alyce hated her and had given her nothing, and if she could not claim these jewels by persuading Sir Oscar himself to give them over publicly, then she would not claim them at all.

'I think you should keep them,' Sir Oscar repeated. He glanced at his daughters. Charlotte nodded her agreement while Vivienne shrugged, uncaring. Gilbert and Malcolm too were nodding. The Countess had been an extremely wealthy woman. Such trinkets as these her daughters had in plenty.

Leonora offered one last protest. 'Oh I couldn't. Poor Lady Alyce was so ill, perhaps too ill to appreciate fully what she was doing.'

'Then give me the pleasure of performing the small task on her behalf,' the Earl smiled, handing the casket into her arms. 'These are for you, Leonora. Please accept them as part of my wedding gift to you.'

She beamed, holding the casket to her bosom and feeling the opal necklace lying warm and heavy against her throat. Once again she had played a part and triumphed in the role. The jewels were hers. This fabulous collection now belonged entirely to her. Here were huge diamonds, rubies, sapphires and emeralds, glittering necklaces, sparkling rings and earrings, gem-encrusted belts, delicate pearl drops and brooches too heavy with priceless stones to hang upon anything but the stoutest fabric. This treasure would be her *real* security, her safeguard against the awful poverty that had once seemed bent on overwhelming her. She alone knew the true value of that casket of so-called trinkets. While this family looked on without questioning her sincerity, she had claimed in feigned innocence the spoils of all those long weeks spent nursing the hated Lady Alyce Cavendish. She had earned her prize and made herself a very wealthy woman. As a final toast was proposed to her and Malcolm's happiness, it seemed to Leonora that the ground beneath her feet had become a little less uncertain.

She rang for Anabel and had the locked casket returned to its chest in her private rooms, then turned her full attention to the task of playing hostess to the grieving family. As they began to gather in readiness for the service, she overheard a snippet of conversation between the Earl and Mr Jeremiah Dick that added the final flourish to an extremely rewarding hour. They had drawn aside from the main group and were standing behind her high-backed chair, unaware of her proximity.

'But what of Sir Horace?' she heard Mr Dick inquire in hushed and rather reverent tones. 'He was always her favourite child. She loved him. He has expectations.'

'He has precisely *nothing*,' was the Earl's whispered reply. 'No provision was made for him in Lady Alyce's new will.'

'None at all, Sir Oscar?'

'None,' the Earl confirmed. 'At the end she thought fit to cut him off without so much as a penny-piece. The boy is disinherited. He will receive nothing.'

'But he was promised the Yorkshire Estates,' Mr Dick protested. 'He believes he is to have the lands, the property, the income.'

The Earl shook his head. 'Not according to the terms of her last will and testament. I understand you are aware of the circumstances resulting in his estrangement from his family, Mr Dick? His mother was deeply wounded by his behaviour and died without forgiving him his sins. He is to receive nothing, and I will thank you to inform him of that fact.'

Jeremiah Dick bowed low as Sir Oscar moved away. He was not a happy man and Leonora did not envy him the unsavoury task that had been thrust upon him. She would not have cared to be the one to break the news to Horace Cavendish that he had been deprived of his inheritance, though she would gladly have been a fly upon the wall when he received it.

She carefully fingered her wide-rimmed hat to release the attached veil and draw it down over her face. She complimented herself on having had the foresight to include the pretty scrap of decorative black lace. It would conceal the glint of triumph in her eyes and the smile of satisfaction on her face.

CHAPTER ELEVEN

I

He was a solitary figure at the Kingswood crossroads, a dark-clad man on a tall black gelding, half-hidden beneath the branches of a massive oak. Slung over his back was a double-barrelled Forsyth fowling piece that carried enough priming powder for twenty to forty shots. Sheathed at his belt was a heavy twin-edged hunting knife with a bone and brass handle. He used no saddle, and while at rest his powerful legs hung well below the gelding's belly, their length seeming to add inches more to his already considerable height. The collar of his coat was lifted high against the morning's chill as he waited in the pool of shade beneath the tree. His wolfhounds stood well back against the hawthorn hedge like two sentries. He had been waiting there for the better part of an hour.

Beresford Hall loomed in the distance to his right, its ruined tower ragged against the sky. To his left an arch of ornately wrought iron straddled the road, parts of its open gates embedded in the hedgerows. Here the distinctive Cavendish coat of arms reminded the visitor over whose land he travelled, and the family motto, intriguing in its wording, stood out against the sky in letters of twisted metal.

'*In truth, avarice in all men lies.*'

From where he waited Lukan viewed the letters in reverse. He studied them as he had done so many times before. The motto was contrived by Sir Joshua Cavendish, to whom the old Abbey had been gifted by King Henry VIII. That first Earl had surely known the taste of avarice. It was the force that drove him on to greatness, and with self-knowledge he had coined the motto. Had he recorded simple truth, that greed lies deep in every man, or did he claim that avarice makes liars of them all?

Beyond the gates was open country dotted with farms and cottages of honey-coloured stone. The land was brushed with the auburn tones of the season, and everywhere there were trees. Some, like the ash, were already stripped bare, their fine autumn foliage plucked by November's relentless fingers. Oaks grew like islands in the valleys or stood alone in solitary splendour. Here was the rook-haunted elm that might drop a limb suddenly and without warning, the only tree to die from the heart outwards. Here too the maple and witch hazel, ragged but brilliant in the remnants of their autumn scarlets, crimsons and corals. Every slope was cloaked in shadowed beech, in cedar, rowan, wych and holly, meeting the sylvan wilderness of the forest.

'This is mine,' Lukan smiled, and his ebony eyes glinted with satisfaction. 'Let the noble earls of Beresford measure their wealth and be glad of it. While this is mine I am a richer man than any one of them could ever be.'

He scowled suddenly, dark brows furrowing over his long nose as a tightness born of uncharacteristic envy hardened his handsome features. The deep contentment of his life was altered. Now Malcolm was the richer man by far, for he had Leonora as his wife.

He watched the funeral procession make slow progress along the Drive of Oaks. An easterly wind carried the sound of the horses' hooves back towards the house. Thus they came on in silence, feathered plumes bobbing, dark garlands dancing, hot breath frosting the air. It was an eerie sight. Two riders in Beresford livery set the pace, and behind them the canopied hearse with its side-panels of engraved glass glittered and gleamed in the morning's wintry brightness. It was a slow, soundless cortège bedecked with the sombre trappings of woe, a show of grief carried by carriage, coach and cart.

His horse sidestepped suddenly. He moved his knees and hissed a soft sound between his teeth. 'Easy. Raven. Easy.'

The gelding snorted and pawed the ground, ears twitching, nostrils flared. The dogs moved forward, sniffing the air. Lukan watched the dark hearse draw level and pass, seeing himself, his horse and dogs moving in distorted reflections across its polished surfaces. He looked for her carriage, saw a window curtain lift and a face appear. Lady Vivienne smiled and fluttered her eyelashes, and just beyond her Leonora turned her head to look in his direction. Her face was framed by a hood of soft white fur, her eyes dark with their mysterious colours. She met his gaze as lovers often do, abruptly, as if each had called the other's name out loud. It was no more than a glance, but one so full of love and longing that for an instant he was shaken by its intensity. Then she seemed to look right through him as she brought her defensive barriers between them. She became remote, untouchable, indifferent. Her manner declared that no claim of his upon her heart would ever prove her downfall. She would not be caught unguarded, with her passion in her eyes.

The cortège turned left at the crossroads and took the downward slope towards Kingswood, where the villagers would already be gathered to pay their last respects. Hats would be removed, heads bent, eyes lowered, but none would shed a tear for Lady Beresford. This was but an intermission in their labours, a common ritual to be observed. If the event held any personal interest for them at all it was this: that the Countess was dead and they might glimpse the pretty lady who was to take her place.

Lady Vivienne held the window sash aside to watch him as

the carriage made its turn into the Kingswood slope. No man had ever looked at her with such disinterest. She wanted him the more because of it.

Lukan nudged his mount into a trot, moving back along the lengthy procession of assorted conveyances. He had seen a rider approaching at full gallop, coming from the forest across rough open ground in a course as straight as an arrow. He narrowed his eyes, trying to identify the rider across the distance. Only a fool or a desperate man would attempt to cross that region of ditches, brambles and half-buried pitfalls in such haste.

The Earl's carriage was a closed landau in highly polished maroon with black and gold trim and the family coat of arms on its doors. It moved forward at a steady pace behind two matched pairs, hemmed in to front and back by carriages, restricted on either side by the narrowness of the road. Lukan came alongside and swung Raven around to match his pace with that of the carriage. Both Malcolm and the Earl had spotted the lone rider.

'It looks like Tom Meaching,' Lukan told them. 'He's one of my bailiffs from the centre plantations. Something's amiss.'

'Poachers?' Sir Oscar asked.

Lukan nodded grimly. 'Aye, there's little else would bring him over that ground at such a reckless pace. I'd best ride out to meet him.' He turned Raven off the road, ducking low over the horse's neck to clear the lower hanging boughs of an oak.

Tom Meaching was breathless and crimson-faced from the ride. He was also bare-headed, having parted company with his cap somewhere along the hazardous journey. He reined his horse. It snorted and pranced beneath him, stomping at the softer ground.

'Tis the poachers, Mr Lukan,' he yelled. 'A bunch of quarry men with nets and dogs and clubs. I saw one of 'em with a pistol.'

'Where are they?'

'Driving a stag and hinds through the old mine workings and along the thorn hedge to where they have their nets.'

'How many?'

211

Tom Meaching shrugged. 'Can't say for sure, Mr Lukan. Maybe six or seven. There's lots more of 'em camped way over by Duggan's Ditch, cutting and carting up the catch.'

'Damn their impudence,' Lukan growled. He swung back towards the Earl's carriage to find the men already out and shouting orders. Malcolm's voice rang clear and sharp above the others.

'Franks! Tyler! Morton! Get some men together and follow us to the old mine workings. Davies, we need more horses. Untie the dogs but keep them in hand. Get moving. Poachers are running a stag and hinds to ground.' He turned to Lukan, only to find his friend already galloping into the distance with Meaching's weary mount pounding behind.

It was the Earl who voiced Malcolm's fears as he swung lightly into the saddle of a borrowed horse. 'After him quickly. They'll not hesitate to kill him if he confronts them single-handed.'

He rode ahead with Malcolm, Gilbert and a handful of men who had been mounted for the funeral procession. Behind them the long parade of carts and carriages continued on its way as a score of riders, eager to join the fray, broke free and heeled their horses into the race across the countryside.

Riding well ahead of the others, Lukan reached the forest at full gallop and vanished into the trees by the twisting river path. He rode bent almost double, forcing Raven to maintain his pace in spite of the danger from protruding tree-roots and overhanging branches. He was grateful that the gelding was forest-trained and used to the rough terrain, a brave animal that trusted the judgment of its master. At a point where the land sloped suddenly upwards into impassable undergrowth, Lukan slid from Raven's back and plunged onward on foot, his dogs running close on his heels. It was some time before the sound of human voices and the unruly barking of dogs told him the poachers were just ahead of him. Several deer were being driven against a thorny, impenetrable hedge some nine feet high and five feet deep. It stretched for 400 feet along the edge of a ditch, forming a natural barrier against intruders. It petered out in lighter woodland around a small copse of hazel saplings just a few yards to the left, but that way had been barred by poaching nets.

Lukan measured the situation carefully, then retraced his steps for some distance before using his fingers to issue a long, high-pitched whistle not unlike the shriek of a hunting owl. It was answered almost immediately, telling him that Malcolm and his men had reached the forest's edge. He whistled again to make sure they had his position, then moved like a stealthy animal back towards the thorn hedge. In a small natural clearing seven poachers had managed to corner a mature stag. It was a beautiful beast, red-coated and muscular, with a huge head and magnificent antlers. It struggled against the wall-like hedge of thorn, hampered on all sides by nets or trees or rough patches of thicket too dense for it to squeeze through. It turned to face its pursuers, white-eyed but bold, its nostrils flaring and saliva hanging from its jaws in glistening white threads. Four hinds had been driven into the nearby nets and were held like helpless flies in a web, waiting for the kill. A fifth hind was already dead. Some of the poachers were bent over her, working with knives to hack her carcass into manageable portions, their hands and arms red-stained to the elbows.

Two men with hand-nets were closing in on the stag. They carried long stakes to which blades had been fixed, simple implements that could be carried openly, since no man could be arrested for owning a good blade and a stout walking staff. Lashed together the two became adequate hunting weapons, deadly and illegal. Their nets were small and stout and weighted with stones for accuracy when thrown. Step by step they stalked the exhausted animal, goading him deeper into the thorns in preparation for the kill. Menaced by men and snarling dogs, it heaved its massive shoulders against the hedge. There was no escape. Its coat was already matted with blood from a dozen small wounds collected in its frantic attempts to avoid capture. As the poachers and their dogs closed in, the great beast stood its ground, snorting and swaying its head defensively.

Keeping himself concealed from view, Lukan checked his weapon, loaded two cartridges and eased the hammers back.

There were four dogs in all, three hungry-looking mongrels and a powerful brown mastiff obviously bred for the dog-pits. The noise they were making would guide Malcolm and his men to the spot. The man leading the poachers was a mean-looking individual, short and stocky, with a thin blue scar running from hairline to chin, dividing his face into two unequal parts. He raised his pistol slowly, aiming at the stag's heaving chest, and Lukan knew that he could wait no longer for help to arrive. If he was to save the stag he must act now.

He saw the brown mastiff turn and sniff the air, scenting the presence of strange animals. He hissed a familiar command and the wolfhounds leapt forward like loosed arrows. In an instant they were upon the mongrels, tearing into them with such speed and ferocity that they scattered, yelping and howling, into the forest. The big mastiff turned upon the nearest wolfhound and bared its teeth, snarling ferociously. Gillan crouched, front quarters close to the ground, measuring the strength and courage of this new challenge. Alone he was no match for a heavy pit-fighter, and Lukan would have called him off but for the presence of his companion Garvey. Recognising the wolfhounds by reputation if not by sight, the poachers left off their bloody work and prepared to defend themselves against arrest. It was well known that Lukan de Ville was something more than just the Earl's keeper and preserver of the forests. He was also a true woodsman who would as soon see a poacher as a red deer slaughtered.

'I'll take the pistol, if you please sir.'

Lukan stepped into the clearing with his long-barrelled fowling piece aimed at the group's leader. One of the poachers immediately turned and ran , another dropped his knife as if it had suddenly scorched his fingers. Off to the right a movement caught his eye. Too late he heard the sound and saw the missile loom large as it approached. A heavy cudgel, expertly pitched, struck him a crushing blow to the cheekbone. As he staggered sideways his finger yanked the trigger by reflex and a shot was discharged with a thunderous retort that scattered bark and twigs from a nearby tree. The owner of the cudgel threw himself into the attack but reckoned without the speed of Lukan's reflexes. Even in his stunned state he reacted on the instant. He swung his weight to the right and a blow to the windpipe from the heavy rifle butt stopped his attacker in his tracks. Then he swung back to the left, shaking his head violently to clear his blurred vision. He was too late. The pistol was already aimed at his chest and the poacher's divided features were contorted into a grimace-like sneer as his finger closed around the trigger. The man spat on the ground and growled, 'Here's damning you to the devil, gypsy.'

Lukan gaped from the taut fist to the highly embellished silver work and fancy rams' horn butt. At that short range the .7 inch calibre pistol would blow a hole right through him. The prospect of death sharpened his mind to crystal clearness. When fired, those cumbersome Scottish pistols exploded in a flash of priming powder bright enough to startle a man from his aim. Between the strike of sparks from the flint and the ignition of the main charge was a short but vital delay, the hang-fire, long enough to scare off a deer, long enough to save a man's life. As the trigger drew back he hurled himself sideways and brought his own weapon around. He missed his footing, saw the bright flash as the powder fired in the pan, hit the ground elbow-first and yanked his own trigger home. The scarred man was thrown back against the trunk of a tree, screaming in agony as the upper part of his leg shattered and sprayed blood in all directions. The man with the crushed windpipe also fell back, his arms flailing, his belly blown open by the pistol-shot intended for Lukan. Then the clearing was filled with sound and activity as the first of the Earl's men arrived and set about rounding up the poachers. In the confusion Malcolm dropped to his knees beside Lukan.

'Are you hit?'

Lukan shook his head. 'Only by a cudgel. The pistol was a Scottish flintlock. I took advantage of the hang-fire and he killed his own man with the bullet meant for me.'

'You were damn lucky.'

'Luck had nothing to do with it,' Lukan growled. 'I was damn fast and had my wits about me.'

'Don't be a swaggering braggart, de Ville. Hold still. Let me take a closer look at that face.' His fingers probed the ugly wound on Lukan's cheek. Satisfied, he handed him a folded handkerchief and helped him to his feet. 'I don't think the bone is broken. You'll not die of your injury unless a poison sets in, and if you're lucky it will heal without a scar.'

'Ye gods, he must have pitched that cudgel thirty feet or more,' Lukan exclaimed, 'and he all but knocked my brains out. I swear I never saw a man more neatly felled.'

Malcolm glanced at the body lying nearby. 'I'm sure he appreciates your admiration of his skills. Can you stand unaided?'

'Aye, my head is clearing.'

'You might have been killed. You should have waited for the rest of us.'

Lukan looked beyond him to where the wolfhounds now stood up close to the stag, expertly marking its every move. 'I held back as long as I dared. Any longer and we would have lost him.'

Malcolm nodded, sharing his friend's sentiments. 'He's a beauty.'

'He's magnificent,' Lukan smiled.

Sir Oscar was panting but exhilarated as he strode into the clearing ahead of his men. They had four poachers caught and bound, their weapons and nets confiscated. A fifth was carried between two strong men, his foot and lower legs bloodied by the jaws of a steel trap. The mark of a man's club was on Sir Oscar's forehead but the weapon itself was in his fist, smeared with its owner's blood. When poachers stalked his land to steal his game, this Earl of Beresford was a fighter to be reckoned with. He scowled into Lukan's wounded face, then ordered his men to tear down the poaching nets. Once freed, the four trapped hinds took off at a sprint through the trees.

Lukan brought his hounds to heel with a snap of his fingers, and with their help persuaded the captured stag to move slowly towards the nearby plantation of hazel trees. Other dark shapes were just visible in the distance where the main herd was gathered in denser woods. The stag caught their scent and bellowed, tossing its great head so that its antlers jarred against the trunk of a tree and snarled amongst low-hanging branches. Then with a bound it was away, breaking free of the thicker trees and racing across semi-open ground to rejoin the herd. It paused briefly on the far side of the plantation, and turned to look back as if to ensure that it was no longer being pursued by hunters or their dogs. It lowered and rocked its head just once, then turned again and vanished into the forest.

When Lukan examined his hounds he found that Gillan had lost a half-moon of flesh from his ear and there was a trickle of blood on his lower lip. Garvey was bleeding from a deep bite on one shoulder that would require treatment if it was to heal cleanly. The plucky brown mastiff had not been so fortunate. It lay on the ground with its snout badly ripped and its throat oozing blood. When he knelt beside it and stroked its head it whined softly and tried to lick his hand.

'Easy, boy, easy. The fight's all over for you now.'

His fingers moved gently, expertly over the animal's body. They located several other wounds, including a deep hole in the groin and a serious bite to the chest that had broken at least one rib. The heartbeat was shallow and spasmodic.

Lukan shook his head at Malcolm. 'There's nothing to be done for him, except in kindness.' He took his big hunting knife and pressed the edge of the blade almost lovingly against the gaping wound in the dog's throat. There was no pain. It neither flinched nor whined, just watched the man who stroked its head and spoke in soothing reassuring tones. It was still watching him when its eyes glazed over and the unstable pulse behind its ribs fluttered and died.

The scar-faced leader of the gang of poachers lay where he had fallen, his right leg a mess of blood and bone splinters. He moaned softly as pain penetrated even to the deeply unconscious state where his mind had sought asylum from the horror of his injury.

'Will he live to stand trial?' Malcolm asked.

Lukan shook his head. 'It isn't just his leg. Part of his lower pelvis is shattered and there's leadshot in his groin. And he's lost far too much blood. He's finished.' He looked down at the double-sided blade still gripped in his right hand.

'Forget it, Lukan,' Malcolm warned. 'You may not dispatch a man as simply as you would a mastiff.'

From his position beside the wounded man, Lukan turned his dark head to look at Malcolm, his eyes narrowed to black slits. The man on the ground groaned again. Shock and loss of blood combined to grip his body with convulsions, causing him to shiver as if from extreme cold.

'He's dying,' Lukan said.

'I can see that.'

'And in agony. No man should be left to die like that.'

'You know the law, Lukan.'

The big gypsy rose to his feet with a sigh and sheathed his hunting knife. 'Aye, I know the law. It grants mercy to dogs but not to men.'

Sir Oscar stepped between them. 'We're ready to go after the rest of the poachers. Is there a problem here?'

Lukan smiled grimly and indicated the twitching, blood-soaked figure on the ground. 'Ask him,' he suggested bitterly. 'Ask *him* if there's a problem.'

They took nine men in all from the centre slopes and ran down fourteen more at Duggan's Ditch, three miles to the north. Most of them were quarry men looking to earn a fast profit, others were professional poachers hoping to make a quick kill and flee the area before the forest bailiffs could identify them. They were tough men and well armed, and all were prepared to kill or maim to avoid being taken. A number of freshly killed deer were found hidden in some old mine workings close to Duggan's Ditch, along with weapons, nets, traps and other evidence of previous hunting trips. The captured men were made to carry their spoils back to Beresford Hall, where the deer would provide meat for the Earl's table and the illegal equipment serve as evidence before the courts. Anyone found with nets inside enclosed land faced transportation to the colonies for his intended crimes, but one man had already died and another was unlikely to survive the day. The game laws were harsh and quite specific. These were hanging offences now.

Lukan watched from the edge of the forest as the Earl's men made their way back to Beresford Hall. It was midday and his stomach was beginning to growl with hunger. The morning's exertions had given him a ravenous appetite. He brought Raven's head around and steered him along the wide and easy northern path that would take him to within half a mile of his forest home. Rebecca would have a meal already cooking on the fire, and the small deer slung across Raven's shoulders, a mark of the Earl's appreciation, would provide them with tender venison for many days to come.

The hounds were well ahead when their behaviour told him they had run something to ground in the thicker foliage around St Eloy's Well. He was recalling Leonora's picnic at that lovely spot when Gillan padded towards him, dragging something heavy along the ground. It was a brace of rabbits, their necks broken and their hind legs strapped for easy carrying. Their bodies were still warm and had obviously been dropped by someone fleeing in fear at the sound of an approaching rider. Lukan slid from Raven's back, slipped two cartridges into his fowling piece and moved stealthily off the path. His silent hounds were now standing guard over a section of thick foliage. He pushed aside several branches and found himself looking into the frightened eyes of a man with a small hunting net slung over one shoulder. The man was crouched against the trunk of a tree with his arms clasped around a small boy no more than six or seven years of age, a thin little lad with huge, frightened eyes in a grey face. Two more dead rabbits told the story of the man's guilt. This too was a poacher on Beresford land, but a poacher of a very different breed. This man was hungry and was netting for the family pot. Not profit but hardship had persuaded him to risk life and liberty in the acquisition of stolen meat.

As Lukan stared at the lawbreaker he could almost taste his desperation. The hands that clasped the child were big hands, work-worn and protective. And they were trembling.

Without speaking a word Lukan dropped the brace of rabbits at the man's feet, turned on his heels and walked away. The law saw no dividing line between the hardened poacher seeking a fat profit and the poor man trying to fill an empty pot, but Lukan did. He saw the line and chose to live by it. He would not wield the power of life and death over hungry men, nor would he turn the letter of the law upon their children. If to do so was the law, he had no stomach for it.

II

He knew she would be waiting in the old gatehouse. Whenever possible Malcolm and his father maintained regular habits. In the hours between one o'clock and three they would be in his office on the eastern side of the house, making themselves available to the workforce. It was their policy to hear labour grievances and personal problems in private, where a man or woman might speak freely, without fear of incurring the wrath of a lesser master.

Leonora went to her room to rest immediately after a light luncheon, but minutes later she was hurrying to the tower rooms and Lukan, knowing she would come, had gone to meet her there. He stepped from the Monks' Stair into the shadowed bedroom, paused to listen at the far alcove, then lifted the curtain and stepped through into the drawing room where a fire crackled and spat in the grate. He tossed his coat into a chair and studied the autumn-stained view from the window. She came by the main stair minutes later. She gasped when she first saw him, then stepped into his arms and, no longer bound by feigned indifference, wept a little as he held her.

'Lia, my Lia, why the tears? Do you weep for a cudgel-blow that cost no more than a patch of skin and a little flesh?'

'I heard it all from Malcolm,' she said. 'You were almost shot, almost killed.'

He held her fast, touched by her concern. 'But as you see *almost* was not sufficient.'

'I might have lost you.'

'Aye, but here I am.'

She kissed his face and shuddered, unable to bring herself to touch the wound on his cheekbone. Above it the eye was swollen and discoloured. She pulled his face down to hers and pressed her lips against it. The skin was very hot beneath her lips.

'That eye will close before the day is out,' she predicted.

He nodded. 'So I am assured. That sister of mine insists upon treating the wound with an ointment made from sphagnum moss and garlic, with pounded chervil to assist the bruising. I swear her cures are often worse than the injury itself. I can suffer the cudgel-blow with a stout heart, but already I've come to dread the doctoring of it.'

'My poor Lukan.' She smiled up at him, her cheeks damp with tears. 'Is it very painful?'

He shook his head. 'I will not lie to you, my lady. It is not so fierce as it looks.'

Leonora took his hands from around her waist and, still holding them, seated herself on the couch and drew him down beside her. Her hands were pale next to his sun-browned fingers, like cream and coffee lying side by side.

'For the last two hours Malcolm has done nothing but sing your praises to anyone who will listen,' she told him.

He winced. 'And am I now to hear it all from you?'

'You certainly will not,' she retorted. 'I say you were a fool to go into the fray alone. You gambled with your safety and your life, and for nothing more worthy than a common stag. Now tell me sir, is that a fair exchange?'

'The stag would think so,' he grinned.

She would not share his amusement. 'How can any man call what you did *courage*? Lukan, the forest has as many deer as it has trees.'

'Ah, but this stag was magnificent,' he told her. 'Believe me, such a beast deserved the risks I had to take.'

'Perhaps to you it did,' she agreed softly, kissing her finger-tips and pressing them to his lips. 'But not to me, Lukan. For me nothing is worth the risk of losing you.'

He saw the brightness of fresh tears in her eyes and realised just how deeply her fears were rooted. Lifting her hand to his mouth he kissed the very centre of her palm and closed her fingers lovingly around it. He had kissed her that way in the forest on the night they met, and the kiss had been like a gift from him to her, a seal to bind one stranger to another.

'I've frightened you,' he said. 'Will you forgive me?'

She shook her head. 'I will not. You had no right to place yourself in such unnecessary danger, not now you have accepted the burden of being loved. I will not forgive you. I will not have you make light of it by risking life and limb for nothing more important than a common deer.'

'The *burden* of being loved?' he queried. 'Do you really see our love as an encumbrance?'

'Of course it is, of sorts. What touches one must also touch the other, and everything you do affects me now.'

'Then for your sake I must learn to be more cautious, my sweet burden,' he said, kissing her fingers.

'You must, Lukan, because nothing in the world could ever compensate me for your loss.'

'Nothing?' he asked, then glanced upwards to indicate the tower above them. 'Not even this?'

'Not even this,' she swore, and meant the vow.

He looked for the truth of it in her eyes, then said quietly, 'Then I am loved indeed.'

'Yes Lukan you are, and when I . . .'

'*Hush!*'

His hand came up in a quick movement to cover her mouth. In the sudden silence he cocked his head to one side, listening intently. His eyes narrowed and a pulse began to throb below the wound on his cheek. His whole body had become as taut as a coiled spring.

She heard it then, the sound that had alerted him. It was right there in the apartment, over by the curtained alcove leading to the bedroom. Something was moving in the shadows. Leonora's face blanched and her eyes went wide above his fingers as questions crowded one upon the other into her mind. Had the door of the gatehouse been open or locked when she arrived? Had Lukan in his haste left the Monks' Door ajar? Had someone lain in wait for them here, hoping to catch them together, to eavesdrop on their words of love?

Lukan signalled for her to remain seated, lifted his hunting knife from his belt and moved silently across the room. The curtain moved as he reached it, its brass rings clanking on their heavy wooden rail. Leonora held her breath. She saw the shape the instant Lukan grabbed it, heard the startled, child-like cry and his answering gasp, '*Elizabeth!*'

Lukan had grabbed her roughly, thinking her a man who meant them harm. Now he released her and she ran to Leonora. He strode after her and took her by the shoulders. 'I did not mean to frighten you, Elizabeth,' he told her, his voice low and soothing. 'You were hiding and you startled Leonora. She thought you were a brigand come to rob her of her jewels. Come here child, you mustn't be afraid of me. Did I hurt you?'

Elizabeth laughed and turned to hug him. Over her head he looked at Leonora, his eyes questioning. She shook her head in reply, not knowing what to say.

Elizabeth lifted her head and said, 'Kiss.'

He stooped to kiss her forehead and smiled when she giggled with delight.

'Oh, poor Lukan,' she exclaimed then, noticing his bruised face. 'Oh, poor Lukan. Did you fall down? Did you get all scraped and sore?'

'Only a little sore,' he assured her, looking at Leonora in desperation.

Leonora tried to gather her thoughts together as she watched the young woman reach up to touch Lukan's face. She had no way of knowing how long she had been hiding there in the shadows, or what incriminating words she might have overheard. Distracted, she said, 'Don't touch the wound, Elizabeth dear. You may hurt Lukan.'

Elizabeth immediately turned from him and grasped Leonora by the hand. 'No, no, no,' she sang.'I won't do that. I won't hurt Lukan because he's my friend and I love him more

223

than anything else in the world. You love him too, don't you Leonora?'

Leonora glanced at Lukan. He raked his fingers through his hair, then strode across the room and back again before stopping to look at her with his hands outstretched in a gesture of helplessness.

'You do, Leonora,' Elizabeth insisted. 'I know you do because you said so, and I know he loves you too. I saw him kiss you. He kissed me too.' She touched her forehead proudly with one finger. 'Here. He kissed me here.'

Pulling herself together with a start, Leonora led Elizabeth to the couch and reached for her silver-backed hairbrush. 'Now Elizabeth, I think I shall brush your hair until it shines,' she announced. 'And then we will go for a walk together in the gardens. Would you like that? Perhaps you'd like to wear one of my pretty new bonnets?'

'And your muff? The fur one with the pockets inside? May I wear it, Leonora? May I?'

'Of course, my dear, and after our walk we can have some hot chocolate with lots of delicious sugar and cinnamon.' As she spoke she made silent signals in Lukan's direction. She wanted him to leave at once, while Elizabeth's back was turned and her attention no longer focussed upon him. She needed privacy and a clear mind if she was to convince Elizabeth that what she had seen and heard was nothing more substantial then her own imaginings.

Lukan nodded and shrugged his shoulders as if by way of an apology. He knew the fault was his. He had been damnably careless. He should have checked the rooms more thoroughly before he stepped inside. All it needed was for one person to find him there, one enemy to watch him enter or leave her apartments using his own key, and he and Leonora were undone. And now Elizabeth had seen them together, Elizabeth the gentle innocent who could, without ever meaning to do them harm, blurt out the truth for all to hear and act upon.

'*Go!*' Leonora mouthed the word with some urgency. She was watching him through an oval mirror while keeping him and his reflection from Elizabeth's sight.

He kissed his fingers lovingly in her direction, then turned and reached for his coat. As he did so the main door of the apartment opened without warning and the figure of Sir Oscar Cavendish framed itself in the doorway.

'Well, well,' he bellowed. 'My instincts told me I might find you here.'

Leonora froze, the hair brush raised over Elizabeth's head, her eyes rounded in an expression of horror. Sir Oscar stood on the threshold with his hands on his hips and his face a mask of sternness. In the mirror the dark shape of Lukan de Ville moved back against the drapes, melting into shadow but still shockingly, scandalously visible.

It was the Earl who broke the stunned silence. 'Didn't startle you, did I my dear? I see my daughter has been making a nuisance of herself again. May I come in?'

'What? I don't think ... I mean ...'

Only then did she realise that the open door stood between him and Lukan, and that the spot her lover had occupied only a moment ago was now empty. Only a faint movement of the curtain betrayed his passing. There was no longer a dark, incriminating shape reflected in the mirror.

'Well, am I to be welcomed into this perfumed sanctuary of yours or must I go in search of more manly company?'

'Sir Oscar, you startled me!' Leonora exclaimed, her mouth so dry she might have been eating feathers. 'Of course you may come in. After all, these were your wife's apartments before they were mine.'

'I am intruding,' he said, striding into the room. To Leonora, hot with guilt, his gaze seemed to be everywhere.

'As you can see, I am merely helping Elizabeth with her hair,' she said.

He scowled at his daughter. 'She ought to be in her own room. She was seen in the orchard earlier, and I believe she has found a way on to the upper balustrades. If she cannot be trusted with her own safety she must be kept under tighter control.'

'Really, Sir Oscar, you make her sound like a dog in need of training.'

225

His scowl deepened. 'Indeed, sometimes I think my animals are less troublesome.'

Leonora forced herself to move the hairbrush in long, even strokes. She watched her father-in-law prowl the room and wondered if he might be noting the changes she had made, looking for reminders of Lady Alyce. At the door of the bedroom he stopped short.

'May I?'

'Of course you may.'

Her heart gave a sickening lurch. The concealed entrance to the Monks' Stair was on the far side of the room and she did not know if Lukan had found the time, or the wit, to reach it. One thing she did know: if he was found in her bedroom they were both lost. She heard the rattle of the curtain, then Sir Oscar stepped back into sight wearing a smile of approval.

'A pleasant room. You have made some admirable changes here.'

'I'm glad you think so.' She managed to return his smile as a wave of intense relief swept over her. He must have seen for himself that the place was unoccupied, the mattress bare save for a thin top-cover of fringed silk. If he had come here to spy on her, to monitor her movements during Malcolm's absence, he could have found nothing to feed his suspicions.

'My daughter Charlotte and her husband leave for Cornwall tomorrow,' he reminded her. 'Malcolm and I will travel to London for a few days on Beresford business. While there I intend to speak to Nigel Fairfax about the part he played in Jonathan's departure.'

'Thank you,' she said, grateful for the distraction. 'It has also occurred to me that you might wish to speak to Lady Fenwick on the matter.'

'Lady Fenwick? Lord Tewkesbury's widow? Why should I wish to speak to her?'

'Because her daughter Louisa followed Jonathan into exile.'

His face showed amazement. 'Louisa? That pretty little thing with the copper-gold hair and freckles? Are you sure?'

'Quite sure,' she told him. 'They were deeply in love and planned to marry until father's actions put an end to their hopes.'

'But I knew nothing of this,' Sir Oscar protested. 'I was under the impression that the girl was staying with relatives in southern Italy after a brief romance ended in disappointment.'

'That is the story Her Ladyship insists upon,' Leonora nodded. 'One could hardly expect the Dowager Duchess of Tewkesbury to admit the truth. The Duke was virtually penniless when he died, so she was counting on Louisa to make a good marriage. The poor woman must have been mortified when her only daughter fled the country with the son of a wanted man.'

'Damn it all,' the Earl said. 'The girl could not have made a better match.'

'Indeed, but as yet the Duchess is unaware of that fact.'

'Then she must be informed of it without delay.' He clasped his hands together under the tails of his coat and rocked back on his heels a few times, frowning thoughtfully. 'Well my dear, this sheds an entirely different light on things. If the Duchess has received word from her daughter, it is quite possible that she will know exactly where Jonathan is to be found.'

Leonora nodded. 'And she will be eager to share the information with you, once she is convinced that Louisa has not eloped with a disgraced young man hard-pressed by his father's debtors.' She watched him for a moment then said, 'May I ask if you intend to tell her the truth?'

'Not yet, my dear. Not until I have spoken to the boy.' He held out a hand to his daughter, whose fingers were plucking at the bristles in Leonora's hairbrush. 'Come Elizabeth, it's time you were back in your own room.'

'I want Leonora to take me,' Elizabeth pouted.

'As you wish, if she agrees to come with us. Leonora?'

'Of course,' she smiled. 'Let me fetch a wrap.'

'Lukan hurt himself,' Elizabeth suddenly declared. 'He fell down and hurt himself, but Leonora kissed it better.'

'I beg your pardon?' There was curiosity rather than suspicion in Sir Oscar's voice.

Leonora's heart seemed to miss a beat. She forced herself to smile and hastened to grasp control of the situation.

'I certainly did,' she laughed, placing one of her own bonnets on Elizabeth's head, distracting her with its profusion of ribbons and pretty silk blossoms. 'And I kissed your father's bruise better too, just the way I kiss you whenever you fall down and hurt yourself, Elizabeth.' She smiled brilliantly at the Earl, shrugged her shoulders and added in a whisper, 'Some of the stories surrounding this morning's events were quite distressing, so I promised to distribute my magical healing kiss to every man, woman and beast who suffered injury in the fray.'

'Including myself,' he noted, touching the area of light bruising on his forehead.

'But of course, Sir Oscar,' Leonora laughed. 'In fact, if I recall correctly, your name came second on the kissing-list.'

'What, following that rascal de Ville's?'

'Certainly not,' she chided. 'Your name was second only to that of Blaze, Sir Gilbert's horse.'

The Earl chuckled grudgingly. 'An infant's game.'

'Quite, but reassuring to the child in question.'

'And yet hardly the kind of talk we would want overheard by strangers. I would advise you to discourage such games, Leonora. There is always someone ready to misconstrue an innocent remark or read ill where there is none. If the servants hear that you have been abroad kissing every able-bodied male involved in this morning's fracas, your reputation will be in shreds.'

Leonora agreed, watching Elizabeth with affection as she yanked the ribbons on her borrowed bonnet first this way and then that. 'Have no fear of that, Sir Oscar. I'm sure the game will soon be forgotten.' She handed him her outdoor cloak. 'If you would be so kind as to help Elizabeth with this, I will slip into the other room to fetch a wrap.'

She was outwardly calm but inwardly ill at ease as she hurried from the room. She could not know what answers Elizabeth might give if the Earl questioned her more closely. All she could do was keep them from being alone until she had fixed her invented story firmly in Elizabeth's mind.

Once inside the bedroom she crossed directly to the recess

in the far wall where the entrance to the Monks' Stair was located. He was standing in the darkness with his back pressed against the wall.

'By all the gods, Lia ...' He measured a meagre inch between finger and thumb. 'We came this close ...'

His face was turned in her direction, and even in the deep shadows she was able to read the expression in his eyes. She reached for his hand and he gripped it tightly. No words were needed to describe what they were feeling at that moment.

'Tomorrow,' she said in an urgent whisper.

'Aye, lady.'

'Go now. Go quickly.'

She heard his light tread on the stair as she snatched a wrap from the back of a chair and left the room without a backward glance. She chattered brightly as she accompanied Lady Elizabeth and the Earl down the wider staircase to the lower rooms of the gatehouse, but behind the brightness her heart was sick with unease. How swiftly her hard-won happiness might have been snatched away, her new sense of security plucked out by the root. They had come within an inch of disaster. Only the Earl's good manners and the angle of the open door had prevented a confrontation between him and her lover, and only the quickness of her own wits had transformed Elizabeth's damning declaration into a childish game. She and Lukan had been but a heartbeat away from total ruin and such a situation must never be allowed to repeat itself. Much more must be done for her protection and his. She was no longer just another powerless and dependent young woman doomed to enjoy or endure whatever the day might choose to thrust upon her. She was Lady Leonora Cavendish, Viscountess Beresford, and she would not trust her destiny or Lukan's to the fickle whims of chance.

CHAPTER TWELVE

I

Anabel paled when the events were recounted to her.
'My God, the Earl would kill him for making a cuckold of his son!' she exclaimed.

'I know that.'

'And what of Malcolm? Surely he would see this affair as betrayal of the very lowest kind.'

'I know that too,' Leonora said with a sigh.

Anabel tightened her lips. 'You play with fire, Missy. And when you are burned, as you must surely be, then we are all undone.'

Leonora reached out to take Anabel's hand. 'There must be times when you hate me for the power I have over your life and well-being,' she observed almost sadly.

Anabel shook her head and smiled grimly. 'No child. I love you as I loved your dear mama before you, but you frighten me as Francine never could.'

Leonora looked at her in astonishment. 'You *fear* me?'

'Of course I do,' Anabel said with exasperation. 'I fear your passions Leonora, your angers, your ambitions. You have a strength of will that sometimes terrifies me. Most of all I fear your obsession with that gypsy. Nothing but harm will ever come of it. Mark well my words child, you will see us all in hell on his account.'

They were seated side by side on a small couch in one of the bedrooms adjoining Malcolm's private suite. They were both in sombre mood. Even while they spoke, Nellie Dobbin was standing head bowed in one of the other rooms, suffering the cutting edge of her master's temper and wishing she had not allowed her tongue to run ahead of her common sense. She had learned that *truth* was not a thing to be held up and recognised with any real certainty. Truth shifted and changed according to circumstance. It was not a thing for the likes of her to brandish before her betters, thinking it would protect her against their wrath. It evaporated too easily and, as with all the finer things in life, the lower orders could ill afford the luxury of it.

'I will be scrupulously careful in future,' Leonora said quietly. 'I will take whatever steps are necessary to protect myself against discovery. From now on, the gatehouse must be kept locked at all times. The roof entry to the tower must be bolted from the inside. I will have a servant's bell installed with a discreet bell-pull in the lower rooms so that you may warn or summon me as the case may be. No-one must ever enter my private rooms again unless I have ample warning of their intentions.'

'It's all very well for you to say that Leonora, but what can we do about poor Elizabeth?'

'Poor Elizabeth was the sole cause of all this,' Leonora reminded her. 'She is like a mischievous child who creeps around in the dark and conceals herself quietly in small spaces so that none would imagine themselves spied upon. Heaven knows what else she is likely to reveal about what she saw and heard today. Her absence caused her father to come in search of her, and it was only by a stroke of wondrous good fortune that he found her in full view when he opened the door to my

231

room. Had it not been so, had he taken but a single step across that threshold ...' She paused to shudder at the memory. 'Elizabeth in her innocence could be my undoing. She must be kept out.'

'It will break her heart. You know how she loves the old tower.'

'We must be practical, Anabel. Parts of the tower are still little better than derelict. Elizabeth risks injury every time she wanders around those empty rooms and dark stairs by herself. For her own sake, as well as for mine, she must be kept out.'

'It will break her heart,' Anabel repeated, shaking her head sadly.

'Then so be it.'

'But it's so cruel,' Anabel insisted. 'Lord knows she has few pleasures in life, and now you plan to take this one away from her.'

Leonora's turquoise eyes flashed darkly. 'Would you rather I continue to risk exposure, just for mere sentiment's sake? Should I indulge Elizabeth at our expense, and to the devil with caution?'

'But she needs to wander free. How can you love her the way you do and even *think* of bolting the doors of her own home against her?'

'There is no other way.'

Anabel withdrew her hand from Leonora's with intended sharpness. 'Is it any wonder that I fear you?' she asked. 'For you it is so simple. You push people around like pawns to satisfy your own whims. I don't need second sight to see where all this is leading, do I? One by one you will sacrifice those who love you on the altar of this wicked affair.'

'There is no other way,' Leonora repeated.

'Yes there is, and well you know it.'

With a sigh Leonora rose to her feet and crossed to one of the windows. She was wearing her favourite high-necked robe of ivory silk. It rustled softly as she moved. Her hair was piled lightly on top of her head and held in place with a single decorated comb. She wore no jewellery but her diamond wedding ring and the huge Cavendish Sapphire at her throat. From the

232

window she could see a long, curving sweep of lawn marked here and there with shaped flower beds, ornamental set-pieces and fountains now drained and idle in preparation for the winter months. Fallen leaves scurried about like frantic little animals amongst the topiary. Beyond the lawns she could see the stooped figures of men out working in the fields, and down by the lower meadow two fine heavyweights bent their massive shoulders to the yoke as they hauled a load of timber from the forest.

'I cannot give him up,' she said at last. Though spoken almost in a whisper, her words rang out with a truth that would not be denied. She could no more turn from him than from the air she breathed.

'Then what is to be done?' Anabel asked.

Beyond the window the breeze had freshened. It made windmills of the trees and gusted charcoal-coloured clouds, gilt-edged with sunlight, across the sky.

'I must find a way to strengthen my position here,' she said. 'I must make absolutely certain that the benefit of any future doubt will always fall to me.'

'Oh yes? And just how do you intend to make that so? By witchcraft?'

'No Anabel, I will do it by making myself a perfect wife and the most gracious mistress Beresford has ever known. And I will start by giving Malcolm that which he desires most, an heir.'

'What?' Anabel sprang to her feet. She gaped at her young mistress, astounded to hear her speak such words. It had never occurred to her that Leonora would even consider such a thing at this dangerous time, while two men shared her love. The prospect of a mistake, of Leonora being delivered of a black-eyed, swarthy gypsy child struck horror into her heart. 'How could you?' she cried. 'How could you even *think* of it?'

'Because it is the better way,' Leonora said as if only now convinced.

'And how will you be certain that you bear an heir and not a gypsy bastard?'

'Don't think me stupid, Anabel,' she snapped. 'You know

233

as well as I that there are preventatives available and remedies to induce the monthly courses. Believe me, I am scrupulously careful. I have to be. How else would I dare lie with a man whose child could never pass for ought but his?'

'Then you will need to take your remedies forever.'

'Not so.' Leonora shook her head. 'My courses are blessedly regular, so with careful planning and measured abstinence I can easily manipulate events to my advantage.'

Anabel was furious. 'You are a wicked, conniving creature. Must I remind you that your marriage to Malcolm Cavendish is not even *consummated*?'

'A minor detail,' Leonora smiled.

'*Minor?*' Anabel laughed harshly. 'And will you name it so if the rumours about him are true?'

Leonora rounded on her. 'Rumours? What rumours?'

'They say your husband is impotent.'

'What?'

'Can you say otherwise?'

'But it is nonsense, malicious gossip.'

'Can you?' the older woman demanded. 'Admit the truth. Can you say otherwise?'

'No, not yet, but ...' Leonora stopped and frowned deeply. 'What exactly do they say about him?'

Anabel touched Leonora's arm. She was frustrated by the girl's high-minded plans but unwilling to take too firm a stand against her. When she spoke again her voice was calmer, her expression softened by sympathy.

'How much do you know about the events surrounding the death of his first wife?'

'Very little other than that she suffered two early miscarriages and then died in childbirth during her sixth month.'

'And that's all you know?'

Leonora nodded. 'Is there more?'

'Indeed there is, and the story is not a pretty one,' Anabel warned. 'They say he had to watch her die a slow and terrible death while her dead babe decomposed inside her. She was a fragile girl already weakened by her earlier failures. She was into her sixth month when they realised that the baby had died and begun to decompose, but she survived it by a full week, Lord knows how.'

Leonora shuddered. 'Could they not take the child away?'

'Only by cutting, and that would have killed her for sure. Poor Malcolm had nothing to gain in either case, for it was a certainty that his wife was doomed. He passed the final decision to her parents and they agreed to send the doctors away. He kept his promise to stay with her to the end, even though the stench in the room eventually became so bad that servants refused to enter.'

'Good grief, that is horrible ... horrible.'

Leonora put a handkerchief to her mouth and tried not to picture the tragedy. She had known the story in outline but now the details sickened her. Her heart went out to the gentle man she had married.

Anabel continued with her story. 'Malcolm blamed himself, they say, since it was his need of an heir that killed her. All this took place two years ago, but rumour has it that he has touched no woman since.'

'But I must have a child,' Leonora said. 'I must have a son, a future Earl. Have I come this far only to take my place in history as the barren wife of Malcolm Cavendish? No, Anabel. I *must* provide Beresford with an heir.'

'Not if the rumours are true, my girl. You may have convinced Malcolm that the marriage is already consummated, but that is likely to be as far as your deceits will take you. You will bear no child of his if he is impotent.'

'But there must surely be a cure for such an affliction,' Leonora said passionately. 'Herbal remedies, drugs, simple feminine persuasion. He is a young man, strong and healthy. Oh Anabel, there *must* be a cure.'

'Then you'd better find it my dear,' Anabel said with feeling. 'Find it before it is too late, before that gypsy lover of yours puts his own dark cuckoo in Malcolm's empty nest.'

They fell silent then. Anabel watched her mistress's lovely profile as she stared out at the darkening November landscape. Perhaps the plan was not so wicked after all. A child might be the answer to all their ills if it could be got from the right man. Where would the gypsy stand in Leonora's affections once she had a child to occupy her time and cement her lofty ambitions? And where would Leonora stand in his esteem when she began to swell and grow ungainly with Malcolm's babe?

They were still standing near the window when Malcolm entered the room with a tearful Nellie Dobbin shuffling at his heels. His eyes met Leonora's and softened. There was a tenderness in his smile that touched her heart.

'Nellie Dobbin wishes to offer her most humble apologies for daring to question the integrity of your staff, Lady Leonora,' he said, using a formal tone of voice. 'Is that not so, Nellie Dobbin?'

'Oh yes, Your Lordship.' She curtsied in a comical sideways manner to accommodate her protruding frontage. Then she lifted her bruised and tear-stained face to Leonora. 'I'm sorry, ma'am. I made a mistake and said a lot of things that weren't right and I'm truly sorry and I won't ever do it again, not ever.'

'I'm glad to hear that, Nellie. What happened to your face?'

'Oh that? It ain't nothing, ma'am, just my Harry teaching me a lesson for me own good.'

Leonora was saddened by the girl's flippant dismissal of her injuries. 'He beats you for your own good?'

'Oh yes, ma'am. Black an' blue all over I am from slacking in me work and being too loose with me tongue.'

'That will do, Nellie,' Malcolm told her.

'Yes, Your Lordship, sir.' She turned back quickly to Leonora. 'But I never stole nothing, Your Ladyship. Honest to God I didn't. Cross me heart and hope to die. I never stole nothing.'

Leonora smiled and nodded her head, then Malcolm gestured towards the door and Nellie made several more apologetic curtsies on the way out. Leonora stared after her. Nellie was content to believe that her injuries were not the result of her husband's ill-treatment but of her own short-comings as a human being. Harry Dobbin would never think of himself as a harsh or cruel man. He was just an honest labourer who loved

236

his wife and was determined to train her into decent ways.

'That poor girl suffers hurts and humiliations for speaking the truth and then counts herself fortunate not to be branded a thief,' Anabel whispered. 'I hope you are pleased with your handiwork, Leonora.'

'It was just a threat,' Leonora hissed.

'And it worked, didn't it? She has suffered a beating from her husband and a reprimand from the master and been forced to declare herself a liar. I reckon she has paid most dearly for your peace of mind.'

'I intend to make it up to her, Anabel.'

'Oh yes, I'm sure you do, but tell me something, my fine young madam. What would you have done if she had refused to retract her story and insisted that the Countess was dead all those long hours? Would you have carried out your threat to have her taken for a thief?'

'There was no question of that,' Leonora told her. 'I was convinced she would be persuaded to retract.'

'But if you had been wrong ...?'

Leonora threw up her hands in exasperation. '*For goodness sake be silent, Anabel!*'

'Don't vent your spleen on me, child,' Anabel returned. 'You should ask yourself and give a truthful answer, if you dare. Just how far would you have gone to silence that poor girl?'

When Malcolm returned to the room Anabel was peevishly pounding the mound of couch cushions into shape. Leonora immediately dismissed her with instructions that they were not to be disturbed. She watched her husband pour himself a drink and stare at her over the rim of his glass. He was still shy in her presence, still awkward and uncertain, yet the world beyond that room knew him as a different kind of man. To them he was tough and uncompromising, slow to anger but with a temper most men feared. They knew him as a strict master, fair in judgment but swift to punish any disobedience among his workers. His scarred knuckles bore witness to innumerable fist-fights and the long, fine scar on his neck was one of several inflicted by the sword. By reputation he was Lukan's match in most things, a fearless man respected for his courage, and yet he was so marked by the death of his first wife that he had withdrawn into himself for two long years. He was, like all men, many faceted.

In those few moments Leonora looked at her husband as if for the first time and saw him for all the things he really was, for his many strengths as well as his hidden weaknesses. She had won his heart, but loving her would never make a weakling of him. There was no doubt in her mind that he would pamper and indulge her in the name of love, and no doubt that he would kill her with his bare hands if her betrayal ever came to light.

He frowned suddenly. 'What is it, Leonora? Why are you staring at me like that?'

'I hear you are leaving for London tomorrow.'

He nodded. 'That's right. We have some pressing business there. I expect to be gone for two days, three at the most.'

'Then I suggest we make the most of what time we have before you go.'

He tilted his head to one side, a quizzical movement that reminded her, with an unexpected stab of pain, of Lukan.

'Leonora?'

She smiled, holding his gaze. Her fingers came up to the buttons of her robe and unfastened them one by one. When the last one fell free she shrugged her shoulders and the robe slithered to the floor. Then she reached up to pluck out the curved comb so that her hair fell in a tumble over her pale skin. His eyes travelled over her body, drinking in her beauty. Then he set down his glass and stepped forward to take her in his arms.

II

Lukan rode down from the upper slopes at full gallop, his powerful thighs gripping Raven's flanks and his long hair flapping untidily behind him. He found the ride exhilarating. There was a hint of rain in the wind that stung his skin and caused his eyes to smart. He had been to the camp of a band of gypsies suspected of poaching fish and fowl, a small ragamuffin group travelling up from the Welsh hills. They were on their way north for the winter and had camped to repair a damaged cart and bury an old man killed by a poisoned dog bite. Lukan had stayed to help them mend the cart and then seen them on their way. Strangers were less than welcome at Beresford at this time of year. Sir Oscar wanted neither thief nor vagabond wintering on his land, snaring his animals and cutting his trees for fuel.

Raven slowed his pace as the ground levelled out beneath his feet. He pranced a little, tossing his glossy head in the stiff breeze that was plucking at his mane. A high whistle brought the wolfhounds alongside, another sent them streaking on ahead, swift as greyhounds, tirelessly eager to test the limits of their speed and stamina.

He was passing the old brick ice-house when he saw the woman. She was running, first along the paved terrace at the front of the house, then down the steps and across the upper lawns. She wore a long hooded cloak that parted at the front with every stride to reveal a splash of soft pink skirts with a frosting of white petticoats below. At first he thought it might be Leonora, but an instant later knew he was mistaken. This girl was clearly young and quick, but she lacked that certain grace of movement that was the hallmark of the true thoroughbred. Leonora had it in every movement, every breath she took. It set her apart from the commonplace, even amongst these aristocrats of Beresford. It was an extra something that was at once elusive and yet instantly recognisable, even from a distance, and it was something few other women seemed to possess.

Curious, he brought Raven's head around and urged him toward the orchards. The young woman was too far off to have noticed him. She ran lightly across an open space that still bore the stains and scars of an ancient maze, and when she reached the other side she vanished behind a high hedge of evergreen. When he saw her again she was slipping into one of the walled gardens via a narrow wooden door set into an arbour wall. Lukan nudged Raven into a trot, steering him on a more northerly course that would bring him out on the far side of the garden where the wall was lower and less dense with foliage. At the sound of his whistle the wolfhounds swerved in a wide arc to follow, running neck-and-neck across the open ground. The cloaked figure had entered the very pretty orchard garden, where visiting children were encouraged to play, safe from the dangers of ponds and ornamental fountains. It was the smallest of the gardens and the only one overlooked by the house since a pair of oaks had been felled to clear the view. Lukan had guessed that she was Lady Vivienne, and that she was going there to meet someone. He urged Raven along the narrow pathway beside the garden wall, then up the sloping embankment from where he had an excellent view of the meeting place. No sooner had he stationed himself there than a well-dressed man entered by the west gate. There was a brief murmur of voices and a little coy laughter, then the couple embraced and the hood of the cloak fell back to reveal Lady Vivienne's gleaming copper-blonde hair. Suddenly the man's hands seemed to be everywhere at once, grasping at her body while his mouth sought hers. The embrace seemed coarse, with no affection in it, though Vivienne moaned and sighed as if enraptured. They sprang apart, startled and guilty, when Lukan's deep voice bellowed from the embankment.

'Lady Vivienne! I believe you are expected at the house!'

Both figures turned and ran in opposite directions, Vivienne to the farthest corner of the garden, pulling her hood over her hair and attempting to conceal herself within the dark folds of her cloak. Her companion made a dash for the nearest gate and was surprised to find himself confronted by a mounted man and a pair of huge grey dogs.

Lukan stared down at the man through narrowed eyes. He had seen him somewhere before. The long features and dark, deep-set eyes were familiar, but for the moment he was unable to fix a name to them. The man made several attempts to pass

240

along the narrow footpath before bracing himself defiantly with his fists on his hips and an arrogant expression on his face.

'Remove your animals, if you please sir. I wish to pass.'

'I'm sure you do,' Lukan growled. 'Your business here is clear enough. Are you aware that the young lady you were so roughly handling just now is the Earl of Beresford's fourteen-year-old daughter?'

Roger Fairfax glowered back at him. He knew this wild-looking man by reputation, and he was determined not to bow to his conceit. 'I am not answerable to you, sir. Be so good as to allow me to pass.'

'Your name, sir,' Lukan demanded. He nudged Raven's flanks and the gelding stepped forward. The man stood his ground.

'I repeat sir. I will not be answerable to you.'

'And would you rather answer to Sir Oscar?'

'On what grounds sir? Really, I find your behaviour quite outrageous.' He stepped back as Raven moved forward. 'I know you sir. You are Lukan de Ville, the Forest Keeper, and I suspect you have no jurisdiction here. By what right do you question one of Sir Oscar's guests?'

'Guest?' Lukan asked, towering above the man, his hair whipped about by the wind. 'I believe you to be more tres-passer than guest. I'll have your name sir, if you please.'

Fairfax glowered back at him. 'I think you will not.'

'Then Sir Oscar will.'

Knowing he could not risk a confrontation with the Earl, Roger Fairfax cast about him for a means of escape. He found none. The path was too narrow, walled to one side and hemmed in by a steep embankment on the other. The horse and rider blocked his escape in the direction of the Hall's extensive open gardens. Behind him the path snaked through woodland to the meadow and from there to the western bound-ary and Fairfax Manor, but he could not bring himself to turn and run like a common criminal. He was too proud for that and too fearful that the rider or his dogs might run him down. Instead he forced himself to smile and tried the soft approach.

'Come now, de Ville. Why make such capital of so trivial a matter?'

'I doubt the Earl would name it so.'

'The Earl need never know of it.'

'You are in trespass sir. He will have to know of it.'

'But surely we can settle this between us? After all, we are two men of the world and this was but a meaningless flirtation, nothing more.'

Lukan bristled, offended by the man's impertinence. 'Let me remind you sir that the Earl's daughter is not public property to be lightly enjoyed by those who creep around like felons behind his back.'

Fairfax grinned but his eyes were hard. 'You flatter the lady. I would have sworn the opposite of that.'

'Then you are no gentleman sir.' Lukan leaned forward, his forearm resting across Raven's neck. He was watching the man's face closely. He saw a likeness there, a family stamp that prompted him to ask, 'Are you a Fairfax?'

'Not I sir,' Fairfax hastily denied. 'The name is Reece. Roger Reece, at your service.'

'I have a mind to charge you with trespass.'

'But I am here at the invitation of the Earl's daughter,' Fairfax protested. 'And that is all I have in my defence. I want no public scandal, but if I am forced to name her to protect myself ...' He spread his hands in a gesture of help-lessness.

Lukan watched him closely. This Roger Reece was not about to place any lady's interests above his own. A warning might suffice to nip this petty romance in the bud.

'You would be wise to stay away from Lady Vivienne,' he said.

'Indeed? And if I do not?'

Lukan leaned forward, glowering. 'Then you would be unwise in the extreme.'

'Do you threaten me sir?'

'Aye sir, I do.'

Fairfax grinned. 'What's this? The Forest Keeper playing chaperone to an over-heated schoolgirl?'

Lukan had heard enough. 'You will harness your tongue sir, if you please.'

Fairfax laughed out loud. 'Ah, *now* I see the truth of it. You worry that I'll taste the ripest fruit ahead of you. That's it, you want the little tartlet for yourself.'

Too late he saw the gypsy's features tighten and the big hands close themselves into fists. He had said too much. The tall black gelding pranced forward, its breath hot and damp on his face. Fairfax jumped back, raising his hands to protect himself, but the animal came on in response to the smallest pressure from its master's knees. Its snout touched his coat, then he felt the weight of its head against his chest. The animal then began to butt him in the breastbone, at first gently but soon with a severity which left him winded. He blustered a protest, only to find himself shoved backwards at such a pace that he almost lost his footing. This whole thing was preposterous. The gypsy meant to trample him to death.

'Damn you sir,' he shouted. 'I'll have you clapped in irons for this.'

'I think not,' Lukan replied, his face impassive.

'Damn you ...'

A tree root tripped him and he sat down heavily on the damp ground. As the horse came steadily on he was forced to scuttle backwards like a frightened crab, unable to regain his feet while the powerful hooves pranced on either side of him. Then with a roar he managed to fling himself sideways, clawing at the muddy verge with both hands. He scrambled to his feet and, not even attempting to negotiate the steep and slippery embankment, turned on his heels and took off down the path as fast as his legs could carry him.

Lukan chased him as far as the woods beyond the Home Farm. There he stopped to watch the fleeing figure head for the western boundaries, scramble over a stone wall and vanish into the thicker woodland beyond. He had been no forest man, with his light-weight boots and fine linen, and his soft pink hands had not a day's real labour to their credit. Since the only place of any standing in that area was the grotesque manor house, Lukan guessed that the lady's caller either

243

dined at or waited upon the Fairfax table.

He turned Raven's head back to the narrow pathway, ducking his head to avoid the leaning sycamore which grew on the bank but dipped its branches over the orchard wall. In summer it shaped a leafy canopy hung low as if concealing the entrance to some secret place. In winter too it cast dark shadows and gave the path an air of mystery. He found Lady Vivienne waiting for him at the little orchard garden gate. She stepped in front of him, her hands on her hips and her head tossing this way and that in indignation.

'You have no right,' she hissed at him. 'No right to interfere in my affairs.'

'I have every right,' he replied softly. 'I am here to protect the Earl's property.'

'Exactly! His woods, his game, his horses.'

'His property,' Lukan repeated.

'That does not include me, you arrogant gyp ...'

'Enough!' He cut her off before the word was out. 'Guard your tongue, lady.'

'I will not! I will not!'

He reached down to lift her hair from her neck where the marks of her brief encounter were red and unsightly on her pale skin. She tossed her head.

'Don't you dare put your hands on me, Lukan de Ville.'

'I have not the slightest wish to touch you lady,' he said coldly. 'Neaten your gown and hair and hide those marks of lust or the whole family will have evidence of your intrigue.'

'How dare you?' Vivienne stamped her foot. 'How dare you speak to me like that you ... you ...'

He turned Raven's head, intending to continue along the path towards the house. She stepped in front of him, barring his way. She was smiling up at him now, fluttering her eyelashes as she rocked her shoulders from side to side.

'Roger Reece accused you of wanting me for yourself. Is that true, Lukan? Well is it? Do you want me for yourself?'

He leaned forward to look more closely into her flushed and undoubtedly pretty face. She smiled up at him, thrusting her plump young bosom against the front of her gown as if to offer him the ripe fruits of her youth. She stirred no flicker of desire in him. All she inspired was the urge to cool her ardour in the nearest pond. He nudged Raven forward but when she insisted upon barring its way the gelding lowered its head and pawed the ground. At Lukan's command it would walk against a man or any other obstacle, but like his wolfhounds it was trained to sidestep women and children.

Vivienne licked her lips, smiling. 'You want me, don't you, Lukan? Admit it. Reece spoke the truth. You want me for yourself.'

He spoke softly and without emotion. 'Lady, I have not the slightest interest in you.'

'I think you are a liar sir.' She smiled coquettishly. 'And a poor one at that.'

'No lady, I speak the truth. I have no interest in you.'

Her smile faltered. 'You lie.'

'Believe me I do not.'

'But you can't mean that.'

'On the contrary, I mean every word of it. Now, lady, if you will move aside and allow me to pass, I have more pressing matters to attend to.'

'More pressing matters?' she echoed. 'You insult me sir! More pressing matters? How dare you say that? How *dare* you?'

He jerked the reins and heeled Raven's flanks. The gelding lowered its head and began to prance backwards with dainty steps. Vivienne refused to allow him that avenue of escape.

'You will remain sir,' she insisted shrilly, her features contorting with anger. 'I have not yet done with you.'

Lukan glared at her. 'Have a care lady. Any closer and the horse may trample you.'

'Do you think I care about that? Oh Lukan, if only you knew how much I ...'

'Lady, be warned, I will hear none of this.'

'But you want me, I know you do.'

Now she was pacing him along the path while his horse stepped backwards and he attempted to fend her off with words.

'I will hear none of this,' he said again.

'Oh Lukan, please, *please* . . .'

A sudden movement close by prompted him to glance beyond her. The figure of Sir Oscar Cavendish appeared in the gateway of the orchard garden not four paces away from them. The expression on his face showed clearly that he had overheard every word of their exchange.

'Look to yourself! Your father's here!' Lukan hissed.

Vivienne froze. The colour drained from her face and her eyes widened in horror. Her hands flew to the tell-tale marks on her neck, then down to the front of her gown. In one movement she ripped the bodice open to the waist, exposing her under-shift. Then she turned and ran from him, and with a cry flung herself into her father's arms.

'Oh father, father,' she wailed. 'This awful man, this . . . this *gypsy* has attacked me. He tore my gown and kissed me against my will.'

'Silence!' the Earl roared. 'Be silent!'

'But I want him punished. I want him punished.' Her sobs were loud and pitiful as she hung on his neck, feigning collapse. 'He tried to rape me. Oh father, that dreadful gypsy tried to rape me.'

The two men stared at each other over her head and Lukan knew he would not be required to deny the charge. Her words and his responses had been self-evident. Sir Oscar himself was witness to his innocence.

Slowly the Earl unfastened his daughter's arms from around his neck and held her away from him, his big hands on her shoulders. His frosty gaze took in the flushed condition of her face, the lover's bites staining her neck, the self-inflicted damage to her gown. After surveying her thus for some time he raised his hand and struck her such a heavy slap to the face that she was thrown to the ground. Lukan was shocked. He went to dismount but Sir Oscar raised a warning hand to stop him. Then he stooped and pulled his daughter roughly to her feet.

'Look up there,' he snarled into her startled face. 'Up there at the old nursery window. What do you see?'

Now genuinely sobbing, Vivienne looked at the window

246

and clamped a hand over her mouth in horror. There, looking down at her with cold, unfriendly faces, were the witnesses to her wrongdoing, her sister Charlotte, her brother Gilbert and the sour-faced Madame Michelet.

'We saw it all,' the Earl explained. 'We watched the whole sordid business from its beginning. I came down here to fetch you back, only to overhear what passed between you and de Ville. My God, have you no shame? Have you no ambition greater than to humiliate yourself in foolish game-playing?' He shoved her along the path towards the house and she ran from him, sobbing and clutching at her gown. Then he turned to Lukan and stared, ashen-faced, into his handsome, gypsy-dark features.

'Who was the man?'

'He called himself Roger Reece.'

'Do you know him?'

Lukan shook his head. 'He will not be back in any hurry. I let him go rather than have him defame the lady in his own defence. Another time I might not be so generous.'

'Thank you,' Sir Oscar said. 'And you may rest assured the accusations against you count for nothing.'

Lukan nodded. 'It is as well you overheard it for yourself. Had it not been so I would have found myself hard-pressed to prove my innocence.'

'I try to be a fair man,' the Earl reminded him.

'But not in this,' Lukan said, shaking his head. 'How could you be? What daughter of yours would stoop to such a thing? You would have hanged me first, *then* questioned her.'

'God damn it, de Ville, how was I to know?'

'I warned Sir Malcolm.'

'Then he chose to keep the matter to himself.'

'As I intend to do,' Lukan said with a curt bow. 'You have my word on that.'

Sir Oscar stared at him long and hard before saying, 'I am in your debt.'

'You owe me nothing, sir.'

'Oh yes I do.' Sir Oscar turned from him abruptly and strode along the path after his daughter, limping a little and muttering under his breath. 'Oh yes I do, damn you to hell de Ville. Oh yes I do.'

In the nursery wing Vivienne had locked herself in her room and was still sobbing loudly. Sir Oscar strode in, his face ashen. 'She tried to blame de Ville.'

'We guessed as much by what we saw,' Gilbert nodded.

'I heard it all down there. My God, she was no better than a common whore. She offered herself to him and he refused her. For that she would have charged the man with rape.' He paced the room, more distraught than angry. Inside him was a turmoil of emotions aggravated by memories and buried guilts. His daughter's actions had disgusted him, but most of all the buried, secret past had been disturbed. It rose up in his throat as foul as bile. A gypsy and a lady? God forbid! He would not wait to see that part of his family history repeat itself with her.

The others watched him pacing. They stood back in silence knowing that his rage, like the sudden belching of a volcano, would subside the swifter if left alone. Once vented, it often cooled itself at speed, to simmer and run in heated currents just below the surface.

'Pack her things,' he declared at last. 'She will travel to Cornwall with you tomorrow Charlotte, and from there to a school or relatives abroad as soon as suitable arrangements can be made.'

'Is that not a little drastic?' Charlotte offered. 'Perhaps the outcome of this unfortunate incident will be enough to ...'

He cut her off quite sharply. 'There will be no open discussion on the matter. She leaves Beresford tomorrow, and every hour that she remains she will be watched. Is that understood?'

He directed that question at Madame Michelet, who nodded and dropped him a stiff curtsy. She would not be sorry to see the last of Vivienne Cavendish. She had been fully paid at her own request and was already in possession of glowing references. Tomorrow could not come soon enough for her. Within the week she would be home in France.

248

III

Joseph Shelley hated Ireland. Nothing he had found there offered comfort to the exile. It was the place to which he had fled when his search for Herbert Shelley met with total failure and stubborn pride would not allow him to return home empty-handed. He had sailed to Dublin to escape his sorrows, to lick his wounds, to salve his guilty conscience, and every step of the way had been just one more small mistake upon another. Now he was trapped here, heartsick and penniless, dependent for his food and shelter upon the charity of nuns. Most of all he was lonely. In all his life he had never imagined that a man could live with such a crushing sense of isolation.

The crossing had been a nightmare, with seventy-two people packed like sheep into the hold of a stinking boat. Many of the passengers were ill with fever even before the boat set sail. The rest were either under-nourished or starving. All were to suffer horribly from seasickness during storms so bad that they were constantly blown off course in a crossing that eventually took four days to complete. Within hours of setting his feet upon Irish soil Joseph was struck down by the morbid sore throat. The port and city had been rife with it and he, hungry and weakened by the voyage, had quickly succumbed to infection. Even now, after so many weeks of idle convalescence, its effects narrowed his air passages and sometimes gripped his throat with steel-like fingers. It had left him with chest pains and a barking cough, yet he counted himself among the fortunate. He was alive. So many more had not survived the epidemic.

Joseph was a slightly built young man of eighteen, blond, blue-eyed and delicately boned. He had his mother's features, her pedigree from the noble line of Cavendish. Francine Shelley had been the blood-cousin of Sir Oscar Cavendish himself and he, Joseph, was the youngest of her three sons. He had failed her. He had failed them all and now he was trapped in a bleak country, nursing his regrets like precious things. He sat now in a small enclosed courtyard, huddled into a huge

249

black overcoat that swamped him with its generous dimensions. His legs and feet were covered by a rug, but still the air had reached him with its chill. It seemed to work its way into his bones, filling them with a dull, persistent ache.

'Winter again, old boy,' he said to the nervous Irish setter curled beside his chair. Lancer had also managed to survive the hardships of the last few months. He was thinner now. His coat had lost its healthy sheen, his eyes their bright alterness. In these hard times little could be spared to feed a hungry dog, even such a loyal companion as Lancer. He spent his days in idleness in sight of his young master, and whined sometimes as if he too were homesick.

It was mid November and the tiny convent of St Mary of The Rose was buffeted daily by high winds and driving rain. It was a draughty place in need of some repair, sadly neglected now that the population thereabouts had dwindled to a mere handful. The crops had failed three seasons in a row and faith alone, however well intentioned, brought little comfort to an empty belly. Twenty-three sisters had died that year alone, all of them buried in the crowded convent graveyard. Hunger had no regard for goodness and infection was no respecter of piety. Even the chosen, it seemed, were vulnerable.

Sister Benedict watched him from a nearby window. He was a strange young man, much given to moods of melancholy and worrying fluctuations of the appetite. Sometimes he went for days without taking so much as a morsel of food. It seemed to her that his times of fasting were acts of contrition, as if he did harsh penance for past transgressions. It pained her that one so young should be so burdened by remorse that even here, in the midst of hunger and hardship, he felt the need to deny himself what pittance was available.

She sighed and picked up a folded newspaper two weeks old. From her pocket she withdrew a letter bearing a heavy seal and addressed in a bold, rather spidery hand. She recognised the writing now and knew at a glance that it was not a woman's hand. She looked at it for several seconds, then thrust it back into the dark folds of her habit. She would try to raise his spirits before reading it to him. As she went to join him in the courtyard she was wearing a smile, though she had almost ceased to hope there would ever be happy news for him.

'Good morning, Joseph. It's a bitter day.'

'Bitter indeed, Sister Benedict. Was there a post?'

She hesitated, unwilling to lie outright. 'Perhaps tomorrow,' she suggested, and saw his shoulders sag beneath the great-coat.

He looked at her for a long time without blinking. His eyes were clear and large and very pale in colour. She had always thought them to be the eyes of either a blind man or a saint, and lately she had come to believe he might some day be both. His sight grew weaker by the day, it seemed, and every breath of cold or speck of dust affected them. He was softly spoken and suffered without complaint, a gentle creature cast adrift in a harsh, unfriendly world.

Sister Benedict was plain of feature and far too tall and heavy-boned to be considered feminine. She was worn and aged before her time by the demands and disappointments of her vocation, but the Good Lord had rewarded her a thousand-fold when He entrusted Joseph Shelley to her care. She had found him in late July in one of the worst of Dublin's ramshackle waterside buildings, a dying boy guarded day and night by a dog that could barely stand for want of nourishment. Lacking the means to obtain more comfortable passage, he had sailed from England in the stinking, airless hold of a converted fishing boat. Half-starved and deprived of fresh drinking water, he had arrived in Ireland on the verge of collapse to find the port seething with infection. When Sister Benedict found him he was in a state of delirium, sharing a mattress with two sick adults and a dead child in a basement room infested with vermin. She had brought him all the way to the convent by donkey cart, and by the Grace of God and the indulgence of the other sisters, he had survived.

'Would you care to have me read to you?' she offered.

He shook his head. On a plate beside him was a large crust of dry bread and a piece of cheese. Neither had been touched.

'There'll be turnip soup for supper,' she said cheerfully.

251

He smiled for her benefit. 'That will be nice.'

'I see King Charles of France has been unwell,' she said, attempting to interest him in the newspaper. 'Only two months a monarch and already the state of his health is speculated upon in the newspapers.'

'Perhaps you should pray for him,' Joseph suggested.

She nodded. 'Perhaps we all should. It seems to me these French are never satisfied. All they want is to change one thing for another, whatever the cost to themselves.'

'Perhaps you should pray for them too,' Joseph smiled.

'I see the Earl of Beresford's son has wed again, and what a spectacle it was, by all accounts. They say his bride is both beautiful and popular, a rare combination, don't you think?'

'Rare enough,' Joseph said without enthusiasm. 'He loved my sister when she had a fortune. How swift these noblemen change sides. They swear undying love when all is well, then fortunes change and love flies out the window.'

She laughed at that. 'You're a cynical one and no mistake. It pains me that life has been so harsh to you Joseph.'

'To me?' His laugh was bitter. 'Don't waste your sympathy on me, Sister Benedict. What about my sister Lia? Her father absconded, leaving his family to face ruin, her mother died of a horrible illness, her elder brothers fled in the night to avoid arrest and I ...'

She touched his hand. 'Hush now, Joseph. Don't do this to yourself.'

He drew his hand away, refusing comfort. ' ...and I, her twin and closest confidant abandoned her just when she needed me more than ever before. I was weak and peevish and cowardly in my grief. I wanted to punish her for not being there when mama died.'

'Oh, surely not ...'

'It's true,' he insisted. 'When mama had her last attack I was so terrified of what was happening to her that I ran away. I left her all alone. It was all so ugly and degrading and I had no stomach for it. I left the house and ran, just *ran*. I didn't even have the wit to fetch a doctor. Poor mama died alone because I was too afraid to stay with her. It was for that, for my own guilt, that I wanted to hurt Lia.'

Sister Benedict fingered the letter in her pocket. She knew how often, and how earnestly he had begged his sister's forgiveness. Perhaps this time she had heard his plea and asked her husband to respond with generosity. Joseph was speaking again as she drew the letter out.

'And in the end, poor Lia was abandoned. For all our sakes she gave herself in marriage to a man she loathed. And we, to save ourselves, simply handed her over like a sacrificial lamb to that bloated Christopher Fairfax. She bought our liberty at a fearful cost to herself.' He clenched his fists and turned an impassioned face to the sky. 'Dear God in Heaven, I pray my brothers have fared better with their freedom than I have fared with mine, or all poor Lia's sacrifices were for nothing.'

'Enough, Joseph. There is a letter.'

'A letter? From her? From Lia?'

'It bears the Fairfax seal.'

'Then open it, quickly.'

Sister Benedict broke the seal reluctantly. She looked first to the signature then scanned the letter with a sinking heart.

'Well? What does it say? Does she sign it?' He leaned forward in his chair, his face lit with hope and his eyes bright. Slowly the hope began to fade within the silence. He slumped back in the chair, despondent. 'It is from him.'

'From Mr Fairfax, yes,' she said.

'No word from Lia?'

'Perhaps she needs more time?' she suggested.

'You don't believe that any more than I.' His voice was flat, his face expressionless. 'Read it to me.'

Sister Benedict cleared her throat and began to read in a clear, softly-accented voice.

Dear Shelley,
My wife and I are in receipt of your letter dated October 18th last. Our response is as follows. A modest sum of money will be paid annually into the Dublin Bank on your account, on acceptance of which you will undertake to sever all contact with your sister. In default of this condition the payments will cease at once. No further correspondence will be entered into.

253

'Is that all?'

Sister Benedict nodded. It was a brutal letter.

'No word, no hint of forgiveness?'

'You have heard the letter word for word, Joseph,' she said gently. 'But things are not quite so black as they appear. The allowance is for thirty pounds a year, payable each November. There'll be money waiting for you in Dublin.'

'Leonora will have to pay her *servants* double that,' he commented bitterly.

The nun's heart went out to him for this compassionless rejection. She was reminded of the thirty pieces of silver paid to Judas Iscariot for his betrayal of the gentle Christ. Thirty pounds a year from an unforgiving sister. It seemed a fitting sum.

'It will be enough to pay for food and medicine,' she said. 'Enough to keep a roof over your head and a crust on your plate, at least.'

He nodded, then lowered his head and said no more. A moment later Sister Benedict dropped to her knees beside his chair, gathered his frail body into her arms and held him while he wept.

'*Joseph!*'

Leonora awoke with a start and sat bolt upright in her bed. Her forearms were prickling with goose-flesh and the hairs at the nape of her neck seemed to be standing on end.

'It's all right, my dear,' Malcolm soothed. 'You fell asleep and you were dreaming.'

'It was Joseph,' she whispered, blinking at the thin sunlight that slanted through gaps in the curtains. 'I heard him call out to me.'

'It was a dream, just a dream,' Malcolm reassured her.

Leonora lay back against the pillows, her face troubled. Malcolm had made love to her with his usual eager tenderness, but once again his efforts, and hers, had come to nothing.

'It will be better next time,' he had promised yet again and she, hiding her growing fears, had smiled and reassured him that it would be so. Now he sat writing at his desk, his face extremely handsome in the lamp-light.

'Malcolm?'

'Yes, my dear.'

'Do you believe that twins are joined at the heart?'

'I know there's something special in the bond.'

'It is a fact. Joseph and I have demonstrated it on more than one occasion. We have a special bond that binds us at the heart. He needs me now, Malcolm. I can feel it here, deep down inside myself. Joseph needs me.'

Malcolm smiled. 'You believe that only because you *want* to believe it Leonora. You were always the stronger of the two. You mothered him. You encouraged him to lean on you for the strength he lacked, and now you imagine that he can not survive out there in the big wide world without you.'

'How can he? He is all alone.'

Malcolm rose from his chair, approached the bed and stooped to kiss her tenderly on the forehead. 'There is more than a touch of Cavendish blood in that young man,' he smiled. 'He will survive.'

Leonora turned her head away. The gap between the curtains darkened suddenly as rain clouds raced across the sky. She stared at it, willing the sun to show itself again. She had been married to Malcolm for three weeks and she was fourteen days into a new cycle after her November courses. She would not go to Lukan again until the month's end. She knew her body to be at its most responsive, its most fertile right now, while she was in the very centre of her cycle. Must all that go to waste despite the depth of Malcolm's love for her?

She closed her eyes and felt the pain again, that special, poignant ache of loved ones separated.

'I love you, Joseph,' she whispered as Malcolm returned to his desk. 'Come home to me. Please come home.'

255

CHAPTER THIRTEEN

I

The first snow fell in December that year. It whitened the land and clung to the bare branches of the trees, twinkling like crystal. On clear days it was tinted a soft blue by the sky's reflection. On moonlit nights it seemed touched with a ghostly glow. Malcolm Cavendish considered none of this as he stood at one of the windows in the vaulted library. His hands were clasped behind his back and his face was grim. He was waiting for his father to finish reading the detailed report on Benjamin Brunswick, Master of the Earl's Horse. The man was undoubtedly a scoundrel. Here was proof positive of his systematic villainy against the position of trust he held in the Earl's employ. Money intended for the paying out of fair wages was finding its way into his own pocket. Boys were being employed for such stable duties as carried a man's responsibilities and often demanded a man's physical strength. Expensive leathers, tools and stabling equipment bearing the Beresford mark had found their way into unauthorised hands and claims had then been submitted for their replacement. Two wheelwrights in Kingswood and another in Stroud were being questioned by bailiffs concerning several branded items allegedly bought from Brunswick at half their market value. The Earl's own master blacksmith had provided a sworn statement to the effect that he had been ordered to produce or repair certain implements for which corresponding entries could not be found in the accounts. Neither these items nor their cash value could be accounted for.

'Jacobs, Dobbs, Hern and Clifford,' the Earl read aloud. He sounded puzzled.

Malcolm turned from the window. 'Horse breeders, father. We've bought from them all at some time or another. Read on.'

The Earl studied the pages for some time before looking up with a scowl. 'But it says here . . .'

'I know what it says.' Malcolm's voice was cold. 'We've been cheated, not once but countless times. The scoundrel has made a regular business of it. On the pretext of exercising some of our best stock he's ridden out to prearranged meeting places, put our stallions to inferior mares and pocketed the stud-fee.'

'What?' The Earl's face paled. 'He has *dared* to put my finest bloodline to stud for his own profit?'

Malcolm nodded. 'It seems Lord Hawsham suspected him for years but never actually caught him at it. In the end he simply let the fellow go.'

'And with glowing references as I recall. Why in Heaven's name were we not warned?'

'He had no proof. Brunswick had been in his employ, in one capacity or another, for two decades without so much as a stain against his character. He was trusted. He was allowed to keep his own stable records, which of course made no account of any discrepancies or illegal movement of stock. Then he began to drink heavily. He made enemies who muttered vague accusations against him, but nothing was ever proved and Lord Hawsham was loath to end their lengthy acquaintance on a sour note. In the end I believe he chose to offer

257

Brunswick the benefit of the doubt rather than condemn him on the word of others.'

'Then he was a fool!' the Earl exclaimed. 'Damn it, he has a moral duty to his neighbours to expose that kind of dishonesty in a working man. He had no business to cut his own losses out of sheer sentimentality and then leave someone else to bear the full cost of his negligence. I intend to see him personally on this matter. Damn it all, he could have prevented this.'

'Indeed he could,' Malcolm growled. He slapped his fist into his palm. 'Seven! In all we have bought seven ponies from Brunswick's breeders and never once suspected that they were such fine animals only because they came from our own select stock. The scoundrel helps breed animals at our expense and then advises us to buy the litter. He pockets the stud-fee, then sells our stolen property back to us and takes his own percentage on the sale. It's so galling, father. Such treachery sticks in the throat like fish-bones.'

The Earl was no less angry. 'And while he grows rich at our expense, he lowers the high standard of my stable by breeding on the highest bidder regardless of any pedigree involved. He must be stopped. This whole unsavoury business must be stopped at once. Do we have any reliable witnesses, men of good standing who will testify against him?'

'We certainly do,' Malcolm told him. 'Lukan went first to Lord Hawsham with this evidence and placed him under obligation to assist us. At his suggestion Hawsham agreed to enlist the services of his new Master of the Horse, who happens to be the younger son of your old friend Major-General Alexander Gasgoine.'

'Ah, young Teddy,' the Earl said immediately, nodding his head. 'I know him well. A decent enough young fellow, honest and straightforward. He's every bit as honourable as his father, so I believe.'

Malcolm nodded in agreement. 'He's also a brilliant card-player. Lukan discovered that much of Brunswick's ill-gotten profits are quickly lost at the gaming tables. It seems he has the taste but not the talent for it, so the method of trapping him was obvious.'

The Earl made an exasperated sound through pursued lips. 'So, once more I find myself cheated and robbed of money that will be thrown away on the turn of a card.'

'Gambling is a national pastime,' Malcolm reminded him. 'For some it becomes an obsession, and all obsessions, large or small, are costly to maintain.'

Once again Sir Oscar nodded his grey head thoughtfully. 'So what exactly was the plan they cooked up for Brunswick?'

'On Lukan's instructions, Teddy invited him to the tables at Morpeth's in Stroud and took him for 500 guineas in the first few hands. He knew Brunswick was short of cash in spite of all his double-dealings, so Teddy agreed to payment in kind by way of a special deal on Lord Hawsham's half-Arab mare. He was offered the best of the Cavendish stables for 600 guineas, leaving Brunswick a clear profit of 100 guineas.'

'The best?'

'Starlight Warrior.'

'My God, the nerve of the man!'

'He had just seven days to complete on the deal,' Malcolm continued. 'As instructed, Teddy Gasgoine made sure he had everything in writing and the signatures correctly witnessed. The money was paid in advance by traceable banker's draft.'

'The plan was airtight, it seems.'

Malcolm smiled. 'Indeed, we can always rely on Lukan to do a thorough job. He was ready to sit up all night and every night if need be to catch the man at his dirty work, but it never came to that. Brunswick knows his horses, but he obviously reckoned without the big grey's eccentric temperament. After a week of failures and excuses, he is now forced to admit that the stallion is too difficult for him to handle. Since Hawsham's mare may not be brought to Beresford openly, he has no hopes now of honouring the deal.'

'So, he has trapped himself in triplicate,' Sir Oscar observed. 'He has a gambling debt of 500 guineas which he is unable to pay, a written agreement which he cannot honour, and his own signature on a document branding him a criminal.'

259

'That's right, father, and those are but the first of many charges.'

'And the breeders?'

'I'm sure he will speak against them once he knows we have him, and even if he does not, their actions speak for themselves. No breeder can agree to lead his mares to stud in clandestine circumstances and claim to believe the transaction legitimate. And don't forget the foals. Their papers, when we have them all from Brunswick, will show no signature of yours or mine to substantiate their claims of pedigree. I think we can safely assume that Jacobs, Dobbs, Clifford and Hern will be out of business once this affair becomes common property.'

'Good, good,' Sir Oscar nodded. 'And Benjamin Brunswick will be hard-pressed to defend himself when it is shown that he has abused every aspect of his high position here.' He looked closely at his son, scowling. 'Damn it, this matter touches on the personal. I am disinclined to leave it solely in the hands of the law.'

'Then leave it to me,' Malcolm replied. 'I swore to horse-whip Brunswick if Lukan could prove the charges against him and, so help me, I intend to keep my word.'

The Earl nodded. He wondered if he himself had grown too old to take his whip to a felon caught red-handed. He doubted it. He still had the strength of arm and passion enough for flogging, though now he was content to leave the task to Malcolm. He had not flogged a man in thirty years, and even now he shuddered at the memory. No human being should ever feel such rage, such murderous intent upon another, that even the felon's death brings no appeasement. 'We need another Master of The Horse,' he said aloud, dragging his attention back to the present.

'We have one,' Malcolm told him.

'Since when? I have not hired a new man.'

'Father, we already have the finest man available and well you know it. Give the job to Lukan.'

The Earl shook his head.

'You refuse?'

'I most certainly do,' the Earl said coldly.

'But why?'

'Because he also happens to be the best forest and game keeper in the country.'

'True enough, but that is not a valid reason for refusing to install him in Brunswick's stead.'

'Don't argue with me, boy,' Sir Oscar said. 'I can not spare Lukan from his forest duties.'

'Then let him do both,' Malcolm insisted. 'You know he already keeps a keen eye on the stables. How else would we have known what Brunswick was about, but for him?'

'No,' Sir Oscar said flatly. 'I need him in the forest.'

'Give him the job, father. We both know he deserves it.'

'No! I will not have that man as Master of my Horse.'

Malcolm threw up his hands in irritation. 'Why not?' he demanded. 'Why must you be so obstinate in this? Can you not abide to give him even that small title, *Master of The Horse*? Are you too proud to give a half-bred gypsy his true worth?'

'Damn it boy you have no right to speak to me like that.'

'Why, father? Why have you hated him since the day he was born? Why have you always tried to stand between me and Lukan, despising our special friendship? He's proved himself to you a thousand times over and *still* you refuse to own him for what he truly is.'

'Don't question me, sir. I have my reasons.'

'Then I demand to know them,' Malcolm flared.

The Earl bit back his rage. 'Since when have I been answerable to you?'

'What grudge can you possibly bear against him?'

'The matter is settled, sir,' the Earl said, glowering.

Malcolm faced his father angrily. 'My God, sir, you can be obstinate when it suits you. You're content to measure the worth of others in proven honour and honest sweat, but with Lukan it must always be in *blood*, and even that is not enough for you. Why, father? What has he ever done to you that you should count him less than other men?'

'*Enough!*' He'll not be Master of The Horse, and there's an end to it.'

'You fraud, sir! You know he has been so for years. It's time

261

you gave him coin and credit for it.'

'The answer is no,' the Earl said firmly.

'Give the man his due,' Malcolm persisted. 'Surely you owe him that much?'

'What? How *dare* you speak to me of debts unpaid?' the Earl exploded. 'Damn it, I'll not be lectured by my own son.'

'And I'll not be shouted down by my own father when we both know that what I argue makes the better sense,' Malcolm yelled back. 'Give Lukan the job. He's earned it. It's his by right.'

Sir Oscar drew back as if struck. His face whitened and his voice dropped to a brittle whisper. 'Right?' he echoed. 'By *right*? What right do you dare speak of, sir?' He shook his head and spoke through his teeth, and there was fury in his eyes. 'Your gypsy has no rights here.'

The words took Malcolm by surprise. They were spoken with such coldness, such unwarranted hostility. He stared his father in the eye for many seconds, recalling the efforts that had been made to keep himself and Lukan apart during the years of their growing. All their lives it had been so. The Earl's money had paid for Lukan's fine eduction, his testimony had secured him the de Ville inheritance as Forest Keeper of Beresford, his life-long patronage had made a gentleman of him. And yet his hatred for Lukan was often a tangible thing. It made no sense to Malcolm that his father could be so dutiful a guardian for twenty-eight long years and in that time give neither word nor hint of friendship to his charge. There had to be some pressing obligation somewhere in the past, an obligation or a guilty conscience. Keeping his thoughts to himself, he bowed stiffly to his father, turned and strode from the room, slamming the door behind him.

Sir Oscar stared after him, his anger tempered with regret. It was always Lukan. On those rare occasions when he and Malcolm suffered a clash of temperament or a strong difference of opinion, Lukan de Ville was always at the heart of it. He could not fault the man and there the kernel of his chagrin rested. Lukan had too much of his gypsy father in him to be forgiven for it, and yet too much of his gentle, high-born mother to be despised without reserve. Sir Oscar had made a deathbed vow to keep that lady's child from harm and see him raised a gentleman, and she had died, leaving the debt with him. Loving the mother, hating the brat, and struggling to find a middle course between the two emotions, he had seen one error follow upon another each adding its own dead weight to his burden of guilt. All those years ago a lovely young girl had died and the gypsy who loved her was flogged to death in a frenzied and monstrous attack. Lukan's presence was the cross Sir Oscar bore for that. He would not, could not, bear it with a generous heart.

'I kept my promise.' He spoke the words aloud. 'Damn it, I swore to keep him from harm, but I did not undertake to have him here at the house as Master of The Horse.'

Malcolm found Lukan in the farthest stall of the main stable building, grooming Starlight Warrior with a confident and steady hand. The wolf-hounds were curled up together on a bed of straw, resting after racing hares in the lower meadow and the elm plantation. Lukan looked up with a smile as his friend arrived. His face and hair were dark against the stallion's pale flanks.

'So Malcolm, how did your father take the news?'

'Fiercely,' Malcolm replied, striding the full length of the stable until he was close enough to Lukan to converse comfortably without fear of falling foul of the big grey's unpredictable temper.

'And what of you?' Lukan asked. 'You look upset. Did Sir Oscar blame you for this situation?'

Malcolm shook his head.

'But you have quarrelled,' Lukan pressed, knowing his friend too well to mistake the signs.

'Aye, we quarrelled. Ye gods, I doubt the devil could be more obstinate.'

'Unless the devil also is a Cavendish.' Lukan grinned, but briefly. 'Tell me, was I the cause of it?'

Malcolm shrugged. 'I wanted him to set you up in place of Benjamin Brunswick.'

'You asked on my behalf?'

'Of course I did.'

'And he refused point-blank.' It was not a question but a simple statement of fact.

'He did.'

'And you are surprised?'

'No, not surprised at all, but I thought he might see reason in the end.'

'You never should have raised the subject with him.'

'Lukan, you know if it were mine to give ...'

The dark eyes narrowed. 'I never asked you for it.'

'No, you never did, but even so ...'

'Nor did I ask you to set yourself against your father on my behalf,' Lukan reminded him, scowling deeply and brandishing the horse-brush to illustrate his point. 'Don't ever beg, my friend. Don't ever beg the smallest thing of *anyone* on my account, for if you do, you can be sure I'll not thank you for it.'

Malcolm pursed his lips and nodded his head grimly. Then he heaved an exaggerated sigh and kicked out at a stool that stood nearby. It clattered across the smooth stones and came to rest against the heavy wooden beam at the stall's entrance. The sudden sound alerted the hounds and caused Starlight Warrior to dance in his stall and show the whites of his eyes. Lukan soothed him, speaking in a low murmur with his face very close to the animal's own, a thing no other man would dare attempt with that particular beast. After a moment he tossed the brush he had been using at Malcolm, who caught it easily.

'Hard work is a certain cure for peevishness,' he said. 'Take off that fine jacket and roll up your fancy shirt-sleeves. I could use some assistance here.'

'Not me,' Malcolm demurred. 'I have more pressing business. Where is the Earl's Master of The Horse?'

Lukan shrugged and selected a brush with softer bristles with which to polish the grey and white coat of the stallion to a high sheen.

Malcolm righted the stool and seated himself upon it, prepared to wait until Brunswick showed himself. 'Even with the best of intentions I seem to be at loggerheads with everyone today.'

'Everyone? Come now, surely you exaggerate, sir? There must be someone in this world with mettle enough to endure your company, though I'm damned if I could put a name to him.'

They laughed together, then fell into an easy silence. Malcolm had always liked this particular stable building. It had a dank, familiar smell about it. It was very old and mainly built of timber cut from the forest and utilised without benefit of plane or sander. Massive oaken beams divided each stall, and above them a warren of timbers, each one crossing or supporting or leaning against its neighbour, created a spider-web world in the darkness below the roof. He and Lukan had played there as boys, hiding from the Earl or from their tutors, swinging and scampering like rats among the timbers. As young men they had learned to leap up and grasp a particular cross-beam, then swing themselves like acrobats up into the gloom and vanish from view before a footfall on the gravelled path could become a hand upon the door-latch.

He was still recalling those happy, difficult days when the main door was suddenly flung back on its hinges and the figure of a man loomed large against the snowy backdrop of the outdoors. The horses twitched and fretted for a moment, then blew down flaring nostrils and were still. Brunswick swayed a little on his feet, squinting into the gloomy interior.

'Pickles!' He bellowed the boy's name. 'Jump to it Pickles! Heed your master, boy, or I'll thrash some obedience into you!'

He lurched into the stable. Framed in the rectangle of daylight from the open door, he looked as if he had just emerged from a deep sleep in some convenient hollow. His clothes were dishevelled and his hair uncombed.

'Pickles!' he yelled again. 'Jump to it, runt, before I break your miserable neck!'

At the far end of the stables Malcolm remained seated and Lukan continued to groom his stallion with long, even strokes. As Brunswick approached his eyes quickly became accustomed to the gloom and he saw them there. His features set themselves into a mask of suspicion.

'Oh it's you, Your Lordship. And Mr Lukan too. Up and about nice and early, I see.'

'Good morning, Brunswick,' Malcolm said. 'Fine boots you're wearing.'

'Aye, the best.'

'And a magnificent overcoat. You seem to spend your wages wisely, Mr Brunswick.'

The man nodded. 'Aye, I'll not deny I likes a bit of quality on me back, and I knows how to spend me money to advantage.'

'With enough left over for the gaming tables, so I hear.'

'That's true enough. I enjoy a wager now and then. And where's the crime in that?'

'Ah, now *that*, Mr Brunswick, is what I'm here to speak to you about,' Malcolm said evenly, rising to his feet. His riding whip was in his hand. He tapped it gently against his left palm, testing its weight and flexibility.

Brunswick stood before him with his feet placed wide apart, his hands on his hips and his chest thrust out. Malcolm could smell stale food and liquor on his breath and wondered when the man had last used a mouthwash. He could have struck him down right there and then to satisfy his simmering rage, but he wanted to play the moment out, to make him sweat. He wanted to see that arrogance deflated.

'Do these names mean anything to you, Brunswick?'

'Names? What names?'

'Lord Hawsham?'

'Ah yes, His Lordship. Worked for him for nigh on twenty years I did and left his service with high recommendations.'

'The highest,' Malcolm agreed. 'And Teddy Gasgoine?'

Brunswick licked his lips. 'He's the new Master of The Horse, the young'n what took my place at Hawsham Hall.'

'How about Clifford, Hern, Dobbs, and Jacobs?'

Brunswick licked his lips again. He glanced at Lukan, who continued to groom the stallion as if the other men did not exist.

266

'Aye, I know 'em. Them's breeders. We've dealt with 'em all at some time or another.'

'So it would seem,' Malcolm responded in a friendly tone. 'And then we have Job the blacksmith and Mr Delany the farrier, and Daniel Davey who deals in second-hand saddles and leathers.'

He watched Brunswick's face, saw the features tighten and the throat muscles flex as he swallowed with obvious difficulty.

'I know 'em all, so what?' he said at last.

'They are all prepared to testify against you,' Malcolm told him. 'You're finished, Brunswick. All your little schemes and dirty dealings are out in the open and you are *finished*.'

'What? It's lies, all lies. I'm innocent. I've not done nothing wrong.'

'You'll have your chance to say so to the courts.'

'The courts? But you'll not have me arrested, Your Lordship? Nay, you'll not have me arrested?'

'You can be sure of it.'

Brunswick began to bluster. 'But you can't. There's nothing to charge me with. There's nothing that'll stick well enough to come to court.'

Malcolm smiled and counted on his fingers. 'Theft, falsification of records, disposing of stolen property, obliteration of the Earl's mark for your own personal gain, forgery, running an illegal stud. I wonder how many of these are hanging offences? Three, would you say? Four, perhaps?'

'You'll never prove it,' Brunswick blurted, taking several steps backwards as if he intended to make a run for it. 'You'll never prove it. It'll just be your word against mine and . . .'

'I have all the proof I need,' Malcolm assured him. 'That deal you made with Teddy Gasgoine was a trap, Brunswick, and in your greed you walked right into it. You even signed the proof yourself, remember?'

The man cast around for an avenue of escape and, finding none, squared up to Malcolm with one last bluff. 'I'll not stop here to have my integrity doubted. I'm leaving. You can tell His Lordship the Earl to keep his wages. I'll not be spoken to like this by some young whipper-snapper with a fancy title.'

'And a horse-whip,' Malcolm pointed out. 'A title *and* a horse-whip. The bailiffs are on their way, Brunswick, but before they take you away in chains, I have a little score to settle on my own account.'

Brunswick glanced at the whip in Malcolm's hand, then at the long-pronged pitch-fork standing against one of the stall beams. He backed away, shrugged off his heavy overcoat and snatched up the fork.

'You raise that whip to me and you'll regret it,' he snarled, stabbing at the air with the fork so that its sharp, curving prongs came within inches of Malcolm's face. 'They can only hang me once over, and they'll have to catch me first, before they can do that. Throw down the whip and stand off.'

'Don't be a fool,' Malcolm said. 'You've lined your pockets at our expense for long enough. The least you can do now is give yourself up and take your punishment like a man.'

'Not me, young sir. I'll not be flogged by any man.'

'It will not serve you to do me injury. The bailiffs are on their way. You'll not get past them and the chances are they'll shoot you if you try.'

'Happen so,' Brunswick growled, lashing out with the fork so that Malcolm was forced to duck his head to avoid the prongs. 'But at least I'll have the satisfaction of drawing your blood, you self-opinionated bastard, afore they take me.'

Lukan chose that moment to clear his throat loudly as a reminder of his presence. The sound startled Brunswick. He stared first at Lukan, then back at Malcolm, suddenly uncertain of the position. He knew he had no hope of taking on both men together, that he was as good as dead if the gypsy took it upon himself to intervene. After only a moment's hesitation he threw down the fork as if it had suddenly grown hot and burned his fingers. He spat into his palms and, noting that Lukan had returned his attention to the grey, prepared to defend himself against his master.

Malcolm was tall and slender, muscular enough, but lighter and far less bulky than the bull-like Brunswick. He tossed his whip aside and pulled off his jacket, then raised his fists in challenge to the man. Brunswick grinned and licked his lips, certain that he could beat the young aristocrat in an even fist-fight. He was wrong. The only blow he managed to inflict was a glancing punch to Malcolm's shoulder that did little more than scuff the fine linen of his shirt. Ungainly and un-disciplined, he flung himself this way and that in an attempt to overpower the lighter man with his size. Fists flailing, grunting with pain and frustration, he suffered one damaging blow after another until his face and clothes were reddened with blood. On Malcolm's part no single blow was wasted as, with calcu-lated precision, he battered the bigger man into submission.

Lukan looked up from his task in time to see Benjamin Brunswick buckling under a rain of neatly delivered punches. This was Malcolm Cavendish at his best: calm, ruthless and virtually unstoppable. Lukan was reminded of the age-old saying, *beware the fury of a quiet man,* as he watched his friend at work. He was seeing again the cruel underside of Malcolm's seemingly placid character. And then it was all over and the bigger man was lying senseless and spread-eagled on the ground, his face a battered mask. The jaw and nose were ob-viously fractured, and even as he lay in the dirt the damaged flesh was swelling up to distort his features further.

'Nice work,' Lukan said.

'He asked for every blow. The beating was long overdue.'

'Aye, I'll grant you that.'

'And by the gods, my friend, I confess to feeling all the better for it.'

'I doubt if Brunswick does.' Lukan brought a bucket of water, waited for Malcolm to clean the blood from his hands, then examined his knuckles carefully. He reached up to take a small, stained, papier-mâché tub from one of the beams, scooped out a fingerful of its contents and smeared it over Malcolm's hands. 'Massage it well into your hands. It will soothe the chafing and keep the skin over your knuckles from splitting.'

Malcolm sniffed at the sticky brown substance and wrinkled his nose in distaste. 'It stinks to high heaven. What's in it?'

'Don't ask,' Lukan said, grinning as he replaced the lid and

269

returned the tub to its niche above the beam. 'Use it and be glad of it, but do yourself a favour and curb your curiosity as to its contents.'

The bailiff was Martin Stocks, a Chepstow man. His cheerful, florid face was half-concealed behind a thick brown beard. His voice was thunderous, coming as it did from a barrel-shaped chest of over-generous proportions. It was a voice much envied by local tradesmen and auctioneers, by vicars, foremen, schoolteachers and the like. He drank two brandies with the Earl and took his instructions first-hand before joining Malcolm and Lukan in the stables. There he found his prisoner slumped on hands and knees before the horse trough, his face and head submerged. The water in the trough had turned a deep bloody crimson.

'Seems to me like he won't be giving us trouble on the journey,' he bellowed at his two assistants, nodding approval at the injured man.

'He won't be givin' much of ought by the looks of that face,' one of them replied.

'Now Herbert,' returned the bailiff, wagging his forefinger and speaking as if to a pupil in the trade. 'In my experience the rougher the justice the sharper the lesson learned. A busted jaw has a powerful sobering influence on a man. There's nought like a broken bone or two to knock a poor sinner like this one back on to the straight and narrow path.'

'There's not much straight and narrow to be had in Newgate prison, Mr Stocks.'

'Happen not, Herbert, happen not,' the bailiff allowed, shaking his head so that the bristles of his beard dislodged a layer of dust from his lapels. 'But food for thought is what he'll have in plenty, thanks to the young master here.'

Just then the semi-conscious Brunswick uttered a moan that caused the water in the trough to froth and bubble around his face. The bailiff stooped over his own well-rounded frontage, grabbed the kneeling man by the hair and dragged him away from the water.

'Now then Mr Brunswick, we'll not have you drown afore your fair and legal trial.'

'I reckon I'd as soon be drowned as hanged if I were him, Mr Stocks.' The man call Herbert wiped the sleeve of his coat across his damp nostrils and carefully examined the outcome. 'Leave him be. It'll save on carting fees from here to Newgate.'

When Malcolm and Lukan left the stable, the bailiff and his men were still discussing the matter of their prisoner's fate in solemn tones. They both saw Leonora standing at the library window with her father-in-law, her gown a splash of vivid red against the snow-swept walls. She smiled and graciously inclined her head, then watched the two friends walk together toward the Home Farm. Both were tall and of athletic build, both long-limbed, handsome and very masculine. She looked at Malcolm and felt her heart grow warm with affection, but when she looked at Lukan something leaped inside her like a living thing that loosened and moistened her most secret parts with an urgent sense of longing. As he walked away she found her gaze drawn to the width of his back and the long thick tail of hair hanging between his shoulder-blades. Below the leather jerkin his buttocks and thighs were firm and muscular and achingly familiar. And this, for her, was the vital difference between the two men in her life. She loved her husband, but she *wanted* Lukan.

II

It was the sixth of January when she knew. The twelve hallowed days of Christmas were gone and the last traces of decorative greenery hastily removed so that no goblins could hide themselves there. It was shortly after dawn when Leonora slipped from the old gatehouse to walk a while on the quiet terraces. She had been awake for hours, watching the moon recede as morning crept in to light the snowy hills. Then she had watched the whole of Beresford materialise like some fairy-tale place out of the misty darkness. Thin white ice began to glitter on pool and pond as one by one the stately trees

271

revealed themselves in stark black silhouette against the sky. Slowly the tower and Hall came into view, casting a frozen shadow at their back. It seemed to her a perfect winter dawn, bathed in its own chill magic.

She still wore a thin silk night-shift beneath her cloak as she stepped into the open and sucked the sharp, clean air into her lungs. Her slippers made soft crunching sounds in the snow and her cloak, billowing behind her, left a frosting of displaced crystals in her wake. The day was dawning clear and bright and crisp, with sunlit orange stains around its edges and late-fading stars strung out like diamonds in the blue. She was learning to love the long cold weeks of winter. The scenery was magnificent, the days rose-tinted, gold or blue or steely-grey in colour. And every hue seemed to bring its own particular scents and sounds, and everywhere that special hush of winter stilled the landscape. The carpet of snow outside the kitchens was patterned with tiny footprints. Chaffinch, sparrow, missel-thrush and crow came every morning for a breakfast of soaked bread, following the robin whose voice was always the first to be heard after daybreak.

Today she knew. Today, with a woman's intuitive certainty, she knew that her place at Beresford would be safeguarded and her longings for a child fulfilled. Her monthly courses, usually as regular as the phases of the moon, were ten full days overdue, but even without this physical sign her female instincts would have told her she was pregnant.

Somewhere a lonely moorhen called, a mournful sound in the silence. In the sky above her a hunting kestrel seemed to hang on invisible threads, and from the distant slopes came the baa of sheep and the tender bleat of lambs. With a deep sigh of contentment she left the terrace and strolled to the far side of the tower where shadows huddled like nervous animals in the gloom. Here she found a single footprint in the glittering snow. It lay between the Monks' Door and the hunched shoulder of the embankment, dropped as if by accident, discarded and forgotten. She stooped to lay her palm on it, remembering, then smoothed away its edges with her fingers. Now a scattering of golden petals and waxen green leaves caught her eye. Here was a bed of winter aconite, that cup-like flower of wilful growth that thrived according to its own whims, caring nothing for the nature of the bed in which it rested. It sprang up immediately after Christmas, bloomed and died away again long before February's snowdrops thrust their pretty heads above the ground. It lived by neither law nor sense nor reason. It might survive in solitary tufts where nothing else would flourish, yet shrink and perish from the kindest nurturing.

'Wolf's Bane,' she whispered, giving the aconite its ancient name. Just then the tree above her head shuddered and dropped a spray of spidery snow from its branches. It fell like fairy-dust on to her cloak, melting into its warmth. She laughed softly and rose to her feet, shaking the hood from her hair.

'A glorious sight, my lady.'

His voice never failed to thrill her with its unexpected depth and resonance. She turned, still smiling, and looked directly into his black eyes. His breath, like hers, was frosted on the air.

'Winter Wolf's Bane,' she said again.

He held her gaze. 'I prefer the Monk's-Hood.'

'But that too is Wolf's Bane.'

'Aye but what a colour! Even the pretty violet pales beside it.'

Leonora smiled. He had often likened the colour of her eyes to the deep blue-mauve of the Monk's-Hood, and likened her temper to its deadly poison.

'Lukan.' She mouthed his name on a sigh.

His lips curved in a smile as he whispered her name. 'Lia.'

He had come upon her suddenly, for although sounds carried far within that stillness, she had not heard his step as he approached. He wore a wide brown cloak and beneath it coarse cotton breeches and a jerkin of softest leather. He had worn that jerkin when she first encountered him in the darkness of the forest. It had a warmth of its own and was impregnated with the scents of greenery and woodsmoke and the man himself. His hair hung loose about his face and shoulders, framing his head in a glossy black cowl. As ever, her senses quickened at the sight of him. Her gaze followed the heavy gold chain around his neck, rested for a moment on the ornate key that hung close to the buckle of his belt, lifted again to his dark features. He raised an inquiring eyebrow, she smiled and the deal was struck. And yet the encounter had seemed innocent enough. Anyone listening would have heard only a brief, polite exchange between the two. Anyone watching would have seen her turn abruptly and walk away from him, heading for the upper terraces. She lingered there a while to watch a jay, blue-grey against the bright white snow, then opened the old gatehouse door and stepped inside.

Anabel was already awake and about her duties. Hot chocolate laced with cinnamon was waiting on a tray and a healthy fire crackled in the grate. Leonora bade her bring a shovel to scoop up the hot coals and carry them upstairs to her secret bedroom.

'Upstairs? Why on earth would you want to ...' She broke off as the obvious occurred to her. 'Oh no Leonora, not today of all days?'

'What better day?' Leonora smiled. 'A perfect morning, a certainty of happy news, and the man I love to share it all with me. What more could any woman ask?'

'I know what I would ask,' Anabel retorted. She looked more closely at her mistress. Already there was a glow about her, a radiance. A few more weeks was all they needed. Time itself would set the balance straight. Let the gypsy take his pleasure while he could. His days were numbered.

'The fire, Anabel,' Leonora reminded her, and the older woman, muttering loud complaints, shovelled out the burning coals and carried them upstairs.

When Leonora came up carrying two tankards of chocolate he was already there, squatting before a blazing fire with only a rug to hide his nakedness. The key to the Monks' Door hung over one of the carved bedposts, its chain bright gold against the rich dark oak. His clothing lay where he had dropped it in his haste to prepare for her arrival. She smiled and stood for a moment watching him. Then she set down the cups and knelt beside him, placed a hand on his bronzed back and allowed her fingers to travel along the deep hollow of his spine until they met the muscular tautness of his buttocks. He turned to look at her, and between his shoulder and his hair all she could see of his face were those elongated gypsy eyes with fire-light flickering in their black depths. She shuddered before his gaze. Sometimes it hurt to be this close to him.

'What is it?' he asked softly.

'I love you.'

He nodded without smiling. 'I know.'

They made love right there on the rugs before the fire. For a long time they simply lay with their limbs entwined, touching and tasting as if this were the first time they had come together as lovers. Then Leonora straddled his body, watching his eyes as she matched his movements with a gentle urgency and thought of nothing but her joy of him. His big hands reached up to cup her pale breasts, then his fingers slowly traced the contours of her body until they found the triangle of hair into which his manhood had been gathered to the hilt. He drew her down to cover her mouth with his, then turned his body swiftly until their positions were reversed and she was pinned beneath him. Her lips parted and her eyes half-closed, she gasped her pleasure and called his name out loud in her release.

'Madam,' he laughed as he rested himself beside her. 'I fear that cry was heard as far as Chepstow.'

Leonora stretched her body, savouring the afterglow of their love-making. 'Rooks and ravens,' she told him. 'The tower is alive with them.'

He shook his head. 'It sounded like a woman's voice to me.'

'A lady-rook then,' she conceded.

They lay together without speaking for a long time while she stroked his chest with gentle fingers. His eyes were closed, his lips pulled into a contented smile when she said into the silence, 'Lukan, there is news.'

She felt him stiffen slightly. He was sensitive to the subtlest changes in her moods, her thoughts, her tone of voice. He had

275

told her once that, as a resting man might know when the smallest cloud has passed between him and the sun, so he could see, or sense, or hear the changes in her.

'What news?' he asked at last.

'I am to have a child.'

She felt him shrink from her words, and then it was as if some impenetrable barrier had suddenly appeared between them. She tried to read his profile but could not. All she could do was wait for his response.

Scowling, Lukan rolled his long body into a sitting position and hung his arms over his bent knees, staring into the fire. After a few moments he tossed his head so that his long hair flicked back to reveal his face. He looked at her without a trace of affection.

'May I ask who is the father?'

She smiled. 'Malcolm, of course.'

'*Of course?*' he demanded. 'You share my bed while your husband is all but impotent and you dare to say to me *of course?*'

She touched his arm. 'Lukan, the child is his.'

'How can you know that?'

'I know it, Lukan.'

He clenched his fists. 'You cannot possibly be sure. You *cannot.*'

Leonora sighed and reached for her shift. 'I am sure,' she repeated firmly. 'We women have preventatives as well as cures, and my cycle can be measured to the hour. I chose our time together with scrupulous care. There can be no doubt. The child I carry is Malcolm's.'

Lukan nodded grimly and turned his face away. Firelight made flickering patterns on his hair and on his skin. 'So what must I do now?' he asked. 'Shall I stand meekly by while your belly swells with another man's child?'

'You will do as you must,' she answered gently.

He looked at her sharply. 'Aye lady, I will at that.'

She watched him jump to his feet and begin to pull on his clothes. She went to him, tried to penetrate his pent-up fury.

'Can you not be happy for me Lukan? I need this child. I

have plotted and schemed and even prayed for it.'

'Aye, Malcolm's child, not mine.'

'Yours?' she echoed. 'Yours?'

He glowered at her. 'Should it not be so? Have we not love enough to make a child between us?'

'But that is nonsense,' she declared, astounded by his words. 'How could I possibly bear a child of yours? A son of yours in Malcolm's bed? Good Heavens, Lukan, do you seriously think he would not know the difference?'

'What, between a good seed and a bad?'

'No, between a Cavendish and a *gypsy*!'

He snatched up his leather jerkin. 'Go on, pepper the wound with your cruel tongue, my lady, lest the gypsy forget his humble place in your great scheme of things.'

She sighed. 'Lukan, you forget that I am Malcolm's *wife.*'

'You married him for gain.' He flung the words at her.

'And for love,' she corrected sharply. 'I've never lied to you. You know I love him.'

'Aye, like a sister, and only for what he gives you.'

She sighed again, trying to curb her anger. She had not expected him to be this difficult. 'Stop this. Our quarrelling hurts us both and will not alter the simple truth that I am Malcolm's wife,' she told him.

He yanked on his boots and stamped his feet to settle the fit more snugly. 'Aye, his wife, but you were mine first.' He ground the words through his teeth. 'Nothing will change that, not man nor child. You came to me in love, you went to him in duty, and I'll not let you forget that while I live.'

He strode for the stair. She snatched the key from the bed-post and held it out to him.

'*Wait, Lukan!*'

He turned and looked at her coldly. 'For what?'

'The key.'

'Give it to your husband.'

Stung, she tried desperately to diffuse his anger with a smile. He stepped back as she approached him, watching her through coldly narrowed eyes.

'Please take the key, Lukan,' she said.

277

He shook his head. 'Lady, I have no more need of that key than you now have of me.'

'*Lukan!*'

As he vanished into the stair-well she heard him say, his voice sharp with bitterness, 'Look to your child and your husband from now on. By heaven, I wish you every joy of both.'

Chapter Fourteen

I

The man was as good as his word. Knowing the volatile nature of his temperament she was content to allow him the fresh storm of his anger, but soon she began to watch each passing day with growing concern. He neither came to her in person nor sent word. He avoided the house, altered his daily routine at the stables, even changed the times of his regular plantation inspections so that she could never be sure where he might be at any given time of the day or night. Each afternoon between the hours of one and three, while Malcolm and the Earl attended to estate business from their rooms in the east wing, Leonora pleaded the need to rest and locked herself away in her own apartments. There she prepared the room, the bed, the fire, perfumed her body and wore her prettiest shifts, always remembering to unlock the Monks' Door from the inside. Then she idled the hours away in restless anticipation, waiting for a guest who never appeared.

After two whole weeks of silence she took to pacing the front terraces in the hope of confronting him as he came or went from the house. She contrived ways and means of passing messages to him via Charlie Pickles or Sam Cooper, but these ideas never came to fruition. She missed him desperately but she was too proud to beg. She would not humble herself by pleading with him to visit her. If necessary she would match his stubbornness hurt by hurt and stand her ground until he came to her or not, as he might choose. She would not join the ranks of dewy-eyed ladies chasing the handsome gypsy gentleman like foolish moths drawn to a candle's flame.

'Damn, *damn* his arrogance,' she declared one day when yet another trysting-time had crawled by at a snail's pace without a sign of him. 'Damn his ill temper and his arrogance.'

'Have a care for your language,' Anabel said. 'You are a lady, not a serving wench.'

Leonora paced to the window and back again. 'Tell that to him while he leaves me waiting upon his pleasure.'

'He was never known to do what did not suit him.'

'He has always done as I desired, until now.'

Anabel made a small snorting sound and set down her needlework. 'That's nonsense and you know it. He did as *he* desired. He came to you so long as it suited him.'

'And now he tires of me, is that what you believe?'

Anabel shrugged. 'You know him well enough.'

Leonora strode from one side of the room to the other and back again, a storm of indignation and frustration raging inside her.

'How dare he humiliate me like this?'

'He dare.'

'I hate him.'

'So you say.'

'I mean it, Anabel.'

'Of course you do.'

'Why should I be expected to hold myself in readiness for him? From now on the Monks' Door will remain locked. If this is what he wants, so be it.'

Anabel smiled. 'So be it,' was all she said.

Her resolve faltered when she met him at the door of

280

Malcolm's apartments, leaving as she approached along the corridor. He bowed a brief, formal greeting and strode by her without so much as looking her in the eye. She could have wept. His anger, even his pain she could accept, but this complete detachment was unbearable. She felt that she had ceased to exist for him, as if he had closed a door inside himself and shut her out.

In the weeks following their parting Leonora channelled all her energies into preparing for the arrival of her child. She was forbidden to ride her horse or venture beyond the house unescorted lest she injure herself in a fall and miscarry her precious burden. Despite her robust good health her pregnancy filled Malcolm with concern and caused the Earl to have her closely attended every moment of the day and night. Her life gradually ceased to be her own. Every passing week brought some imagined hurdle to be overcome, and a host of anxious comparisons between herself and Malcolm's first wife.

'Poor Grace would have taken to her sickbed by now, my dear.' This reminder was often grudgingly said by those who had known the first Viscountess Cavendish. It was usually accompanied by, 'You look so well compared to poor, dear Grace.'

She learned to smile patiently when visiting aunts, cousins, neighbours and well-meaning friends of the family added similar comparisons. They often spoke of her as if she were not present, or pressed her with advice or dire warnings supposedly for her benefit. When Malcolm added his own fears to theirs she laughed in a kindly way and told him to accept the evidence of his own eyes.

'I am wonderfully well,' she insisted. 'The only thing that ails me is a headache from all the well-meaning advice and fearsome stories I am forced to listen to from other people. I am well. Believe it, I am well.'

Whenever she found the lack of privacy unendurable she took leisurely walks outdoors so long as the weather allowed. Anabel was her constant companion, and during her third month Malcolm insisted that two maids and a mounted groom accompany them on any journey beyond sight of the house, and that routes be planned in advance and strictly adhered to. Thus Sam Cooper became more dedicated than ever to serving his young mistress. He watched her as a hawk might guard its young, and was content to idle away his days at her convenience.

When forced to remain indoors Leonora passed the time in practising the pianoforte or the harp. She produced fine needlework, created elaborate and delicate rounds of lace with which to trim her gowns, made beautiful drawings of each season's flowers and herbs and grasses. Her journal became more detailed and her letters to social contacts more carefully worded. Every fortnight she wrote especially to Lady Caroline Rainer, whose ear for gossip and scandal had become legendary. The letters were innocently phrased and full of news from Beresford, the weekly out-pourings of a young bride to an older friend of some years' standing. Lady Caroline felt herself the most fortunate of women to have such direct contact with His Lordship's private hearth. Her social life had doubled in intensity on the strength of it, and she was rapidly becoming one of the most popular women in London. Top society ladies rushed to add her to their guest lists. Nobles of every rank were keen to lay a place for her at their table. Rarely did such a source of first-hand information concerning the secrets of a noble house become available to them. The new Viscountess Cavendish, with Lady Caroline Rainer as her mouthpiece, had become the absent darling of them all. What neither they nor Caroline suspected was that far from being open-hearted, Leonora's letters were worded with a craft and care deserving of a lawyer. Circumstances kept her apart from the best of society, but she held her position within its exclusive echelons by clever proxy.

Anabel chided her for her insincerity. 'How can you even pass the time of day with that frivolous woman?'

'She is useful to me,' Leonora said.

'But you know how she whispered against your mother and spread the news of your father's misdeeds the length and breadth of London.'

'I am well aware of that, but her talents now are working in my favour. Lady Caroline Rainer is my unwitting pawn in a game where I am determined to be queen. Every word she whispers concerning my family has been meticulously selected and put into her mouth by me.'

'I don't like it. Have you forgotten the doors that were firmly closed against poor Francine at the end? Have you forgiven all the cruelties?'

'I forgive nothing!' Leonora spat the words in sudden anger. 'You know me well enough by now to know that *I forgive nothing.*'

Despite her occasional quarrels with Anabel, Leonora became increasingly careful of her state of mind. She tried not to dwell on past hurts and was determined not to grieve for Lukan at the expense of her unborn child. No babe of hers would be nourished upon emotional stress and born with an anguished mind. She intended to enjoy her pregnancy and at the end of it be blessed with a calm and healthy child.

During February's high winds and bitterly cold days she began teaching Sam Cooper and young Charlie Pickles to read and write, and as the month progressed she added Elizabeth to her small but dedicated class of students. Despite her efforts, Elizabeth's grasp of the subject was severely limited, though she gained a great deal of pleasure from the extra attention.

For the most part Leonora found a sense of quiet satisfaction in the waiting, but there were times when she paced the long corridors like a caged animal, to and fro, this way and that on restless feet. She tried to avoid these darker moods by filling every day with varied activity. Brooding only encouraged a lowering of the spirits, and she was determined to avoid the trap of mourning her losses simply out of boredom. The success of this self-discipline was obvious to all who came into her company. They found her sound in health, serene and beautiful, and if there were times when her eyes filled with tears, or when she stared out at the forest with the look of one who grieved, nobody ventured to question what was in her heart.

II

Spring blossomed that year in a breathtaking display of colour and delicate textures. April brought the year's fresh start, with lambs, fox-cubs and young rabbits in plenty. The cuckoo's call could be heard above the noise of men cutting hedges and putting up new fences. The month came frosty and cold but departed in bright warmth, and in the woods only the tardy ash tree waited to come into leaf. Each day brought its own fresh ration of subtle alterations as springtime moved to fulfil its promise of a spectacular summer. It seemed to Leonora that she watched the seasons gently unfolding day by day, marking the steady growth of the child inside her.

'I miss mama so much, Anabel.'

She spoke the words one day while they were sitting in one of the shaded garden arbours where insects buzzed and butterflies flirted amongst brilliant May blossoms. It was a charming place, secluded and unspoilt. Leonora's words seemed all the more poignant because Francine had often spoken of this very spot, describing it as a little patch of heaven.

Anabel nodded sadly. She too had been thinking of Francine. 'I know my dear, but we must look to the future now, not to the past. It will be easier soon, when the renovations are complete and she can be brought here to lie at Beresford, where she belongs.'

'But she will never see my children,' Leonora said sadly. 'She will never know that they, her grandchildren, are to be the heirs of Beresford after all.'

Anabel took a deep breath which she expelled in a long sigh as she shook her head. A simple 'no' was all she said.

They fell silent then, Anabel with her sewing, Leonora with her book of poetry and both with their own private thoughts. At last Leonora sighed and said, 'I miss him, too.'

'I know. I see it sometimes in your eyes.'

'It's been so long.'

284

'It has, but it's for the best. You're safe now Leonora. We are *all* safe.'

'But at what cost? Am I to have all this in place of *him*? If so, the having of it comes too dear.'

'Oh yes? And would you rather it were otherwise?'

Leonora looked at her closely, willing her friend and confidante to recognise the pain, the gaping flaw in the apparent idyll of her life. 'Yes Anabel, sometimes I would. Believe me, there are moments when ...' She hugged the bulge beneath her gown and closed her eyes until the wave of emotion that had risen up inside her began to subside. 'Moments when the dream, wonderful as it is, does not prove worthy of the price I pay to keep it.'

Anabel looked at her sharply, leaned forward and lowered her voice to an angry whisper. 'That's rubbish, my girl, sentimental rubbish. Pull yourself together, Leonora. You have Beresford Hall and such riches and finery as you never dreamed of possessing. You virtually own this countryside as far as the eye can see. You have a titled husband who adores you and a child in your belly who might well become the Seventh Earl of Beresford. You already have everything you could ever want and more. How could you entertain the notion that he, that black-eyed gypsy, is worth even a fraction of all this?'

'Oh Anabel, if only you knew.'

'I know enough to say you're a fool to even think of him, Leonora. Let it lie, for Heaven's sake. Forget him. Leave the gypsy to his own dark doings and get on with your new life.'

Leonora blinked away a tear and felt a distant door slam closed somewhere inside her. She should have known better than try to air the raw wound of Lukan's absence. Its pain was something she must learn to bear alone. She forced her mind to focus upon the present. On a carpet of lush grass nearby, the two young maids sat with their heads close together, whispering and giggling like children at play. Their duties were lighter now and they behaved like grand young ladies as they followed dutifully after Leonora. Susan still wore the green ribbon her mistress had given her in exchange for the name of

285

Lady Vivienne's suitor. It was grubby now and creased beyond redemption, but the girl displayed it proudly, like a trophy. Beyond the arbour's angled hedges, out of sight but within calling distance, Sam Cooper sat in a patch of shade with one finger and his whole attention buried in the pages of a book. From a distance came the cry of a hungry infant as Nellie Dobbin, already pregnant with her second child, kept the first by her while she worked in the dairy. Leonora felt her own child stir inside her. She had so very much to be thankful for.

She saw him briefly at the end of May when she went to the river to see the Mayflies dance. Lukan himself had told her of this place: a quiet, leafy spot where the river slowed and deepened as it made a double curve beyond the meadow. She sat on a rug beneath a parasol, the grass around her coloured as far as the eye could see with brilliant yellow buttercups, scented mayweed, white dandelion clocks and crimson field-poppies. On the far bank a cloud of long-horned moths, known by children as fairy-moths, danced around the oaks and beeches in search of females. The woods beyond were saturated with bluebells, their scent overpowering the death-like perfume given off by the Mayflower's creamy blossoms. By now the water was blanketed in pretty crowfoot, their daisy-like heads floating and turning with the sluggish current and offering sanctuary to millions of dragonfly eggs. Above the water the Mayflies danced and drifted while chattering sand-martins darted among them, snatching them effortlessly from the warm air. The presence of the flies caused the trout to rise and over-eat, making the fishing plentiful and easy. Leonora marvelled at the simple cycle of events that was the very existence of these tiny creatures. Lukan had explained that the Mayflies crawled in murky water for more than a year before emerging into sun and freedom, there to dance their eerie dance of wings of gossamer for just a single day. That day was all they had. By evening they were mated and fell back to the water's surface in pairs to lay their precious eggs. After that they died of exhaustion or were taken by fish already bloated from too much feasting. She saw that it was just as he had described. They lay like fallen petals on the water, sad and beautiful.

'Good day to you, Mr Lukan sir.'

Sam Cooper's shouted greeting startled Leonora from her reverie. The sound of Lukan's name caused her heart to leap in her breast. She looked up to see him standing on the far bank, the grass long and lush about his legs. He wore a pair of tight breeches and the big, brass-buckled belt that held his hunting-knife. Apart from these he was naked. Bronzed and muscular, he might have been a creature of the forest as he stood there beyond a veil of drifting Mayflies with the summer breezes catching at his hair. She locked her gaze with his, silently begging his forgiveness and willing him to feel the void his absence left in her. She held him thus for but a moment before he turned and vanished into the heavy foliage of the forest's edge.

Anabel glanced at her mistress with mixed emotions. She hated to see that look of hurt and longing in Leonora's eyes. She was glad enough to have the gypsy out of their lives, but it infuriated her that the separation was only of his making. No man should own to that much arrogance, to keep himself from such a lady, ignore her messages and turn his back when she would have him stay. She gave voice to her annoyance.

'That man is nothing but a common lout who lacks the good manners to acknowledge the presence of a lady.'

Leonora turned to her with eyes that shone with unshed tears. 'I will go home now,' was all she said.

Two days later she went to see the Earl. He greeted her warmly, noting the changes in her shape, the rosy glow on her cheeks, the extra fullness of her breasts. His gaze rested momentarily on the slight roundness of her stomach, and there was pride and a certain longing in his eyes. This child meant as much to him as it did to Malcolm. It was new life, a welcome gain after so many losses. It represented fresh hope for the future.

Leonora was glad she had worn a gown that flattered rather than concealed her condition. She declined the seat he offered and came directly to the point. 'Mama was buried in the churchyard of St Augustine's in Kensington.'

'I am aware of that,' he said. 'I have been there several times and the plot is tended regularly by my housekeeper, Mrs Bonnar.'

'It is not enough,' Leonora said softly. 'How can it ever be enough? She should be here with us at Beresford. She should be with the ones who loved her.'

Sir Oscar nodded. 'Believe me, I have thought of it, Leonora, but to insist upon having Francine interred in the family crypt ...'

'Oh no, not there,' she said hastily. 'Not there. Not in the family crypt. She must not lie with Lady Alyce.'

'Then where?'

She smiled. 'I know the perfect spot for her.'

She then described her favourite arbour on the second terrace. It was set against the lower orchard wall, enclosed on three sides with ancient walls overhung with ivy and rambling rose. Its half-buried sets of steps led the walker through boughs of climbing creeper, between head-high hedges and beneath the branches of cherry and apple-blossom trees. In winter it was sheltered from the winds, in summer it became a haven of dappled sunlight where birds sang and insects hummed and delicate butterflies played amongst the blossoms. Sir Oscar knew the arbour well. Its simple, neglected charm was the result of his efforts to create an oasis of tranquility among the more splendid and more formal gardens. He could not count the times he had met his dear Francine there, among the fallen petals, far from the inquisitive eyes of guests and family.

He cleared his throat. When he looked at Leonora there was a brightness in his eyes that saddened her. His pain was still raw. Wounds healed with agonising slowness when it was guilt and cruel pride that caused them.

He nodded his head. 'She could lie beneath the trees. I recall how she loved to see the petals fall in springtime.'

'She loved it there. She often spoke of it.'

'Her little patch of heaven,' he said sadly.

'The place she would have chosen for herself.'

'A simple grave, nothing elaborate or too fancy.'

She watched him eagerly. 'A tiny headstone will suffice.'

'It seems to me to be the perfect plan,' he said, 'And who but a fool would be scandalised by it? For you to want your mother here is the most natural thing in the world, especially now that you are to bear a child. And since she is not to lie in the family crypt I see no bar to granting your wish.'

'Then you agree?'

'Consider it done my dear.'

'Oh thank you so much, Sir Oscar.' She ran to embrace him, felt him stiffen briefly before his arms encircled her and held her firmly against him. For a moment while his face rested against hers she sensed that his eyes were tightly closed and his lips compressed. She was wearing the perfume her mother had always worn, knowing he could not fail to be moved by it. His voice was hoarse when he lifted her hand to his lips and said, 'I'll speak to the gardener. He can prepare the plot and tidy the arbour in readiness. I think a simple blessing would be appropriate. Perhaps you would like to make the necessary arrangements with the vicar?'

'I would indeed. The Reverend Tobias Thorpe will do it admirably.'

'Thorpe? That timid little man with a hoard of children? Do we not normally favour the other man, Mr Evans?'

'Indeed we do, Sir Oscar.' She tapped his chest in playful admonishment. 'And while the clever rat grows fat on our favours, the poor church mouse must starve for want of work. I think mama would prefer the humbler man.'

He smiled. 'I do believe she would.'

'When is it to be? When will you bring her here?'

He kissed her hand again. 'Will Sunday suit?'

'Sunday?' she gasped. 'Sunday? But that is only five days from now.'

'Then I suggest you make haste with your arrangements.'

Leonora sighed and let her forehead rest on his chest. She had not anticipated this. Within the week her mother's remains would be here at Beresford, lying in the little arbour she so loved. Relief and gratitude washed over her in waves, making her feel light-headed. Sir Oscar led her to a chair and rang for Anabel, but by the time her maid arrived Leonora was quite recovered. She stood before him, beaming her lovely smile, then dropped into an elegant curtsy.

'Sir Oscar, you are truly the most generous of men. I will never forget this kindness.'

'If it helps you carry my grandson with a happy heart than I am amply rewarded, and besides ...' He stooped to kiss her hand yet again and whispered, 'It is a gift that all of us might share.'

The cortège arrived on Sunday morning shortly after dawn, three dark carriages bearing the Earl's insignia and drawn by dark horses in matched pairs. Francine's simple pine casket had been set in a box of highly-polished rosewood with brass handles and hinges and a simple plaque. It was taken directly to the library on the ground floor where a table draped in deep blue silk had been prepared to receive it. Candles were lit and flowers arranged to give the room a chapel-like ambience. Leonora was pale, bright-eyed and silent as the bearers filed from the room and closed the door respectfully behind them. She wept in private, her tears for the joy as well as the pain of that reunion.

'Lady Cavendish?'

The approach of Tobias Thorpe startled her. Her thoughts had been so lost in the past that she had not heard him enter the room. He looked at her now with concern in his tired eyes and only then did she realise that she had been sitting alone for almost two hours.

'Your maid is waiting outside,' Reverend Thorpe told her. 'Shall I call her to attend you?'

'Thank you, that won't be necessary.' She rose from the chair. The muscles in her legs were stiff from the long vigil and she had unwittingly allowed herself to become chilled. Her fingers slid over the polished side of the casket. Her mother had been dead a year and Leonora's wounds, like Sir Oscar's, had not even begun to heal.

She forced her attention on to more practical things. 'Is everything in hand, Mr Thorpe?'

'Oh yes, Your Ladyship. The ground has been prepared and the flowers arranged exactly as you directed. The blessing and burial will take place at two o'clock. I believe Miss Anabel would like to sit with your mother for a while. Is there anything else you'd like me to do for you? Anything at all?'

She shook her head. 'Just make sure she is not left alone, not for a single moment.'

'I will, Your Ladyship.'

She smiled at him. He was no taller than herself, a shabby man whose clothes, heavily impregnated with smells from the stove and cooking-pot, had been eaten by moths in several conspicuous places. He had the pallor of the undernourished and the look of one long used to suffering. It was time somebody took the man in hand, gave him a lift and set him on a more rewarding path.

'When you are ready to leave, my carriage will take you home,' she told him. 'I have taken the liberty of placing a few items in it that might be useful to you and your family.'

'Your Ladyship?'

'A few clothes for the children, a little wheat and sugar and cured meat.' She smiled and added softly, 'And a fine brandy with my compliments and my thanks.'

Tobias Thorpe hung his head. 'Your Ladyship, how can I ever repay your generosity?'

'Mr Thorpe,' she said sternly. 'I shall not forgive you if you so much as try. Luncheon will be brought to you in the next room shortly after noon. Don't hesitate to ring for Sam Cooper if there is anything else you require for your comfort.'

'Thank you. Thank you.'

When she offered her hand the man gripped it rather tightly and lifted it to his lips. She knew he was grateful for the work and desperately in need of his fee, but more than that he needed to be used. She could imagine few things sadder than a man with a vocation gone to waste. He had such a charitable, selfless heart. She had seen him on his knees giving thanks for this Heaven-sent opportunity, and it occurred to her that by employing him she had stirred a neglectful God into smiling upon His devoted servant.

Francine Shelley was buried in the arbour garden at five minutes past two that afternoon. The simple, poignantly worded blessing was witnessed by those who had loved her most, with three young visitors from Oxford standing proxy for her missing sons. When the mourners filed away Sir Oscar stayed. He sat on a garden bench while the coffin was covered with soil and the headstone set in place, then watched the gardeners cover the mound with flowers and tidy the plot before touching their caps and filing from the arbour. Alone with her at last, he placed a single rose beside her headstone and read aloud the inscription written there.

Francine Shelley. 1783–1823. Forever loved.

'Welcome home, my lady.' His vision blurred as a few hot tears spilled over from his eyes. He let them fall unchecked. There was no one to reproach him now for loving her.

As Malcolm and Leonora walked arm-in-arm across the upper lawn they saw the Reverend Cedric Evans hurrying from the house. Dressed in his customary black attire, holding his hat in place with both hands while his coat tails flapped behind him, he came head lowered and at a rapid pace. They barred his way when he would have rushed right by them, heading for the arbour.

'I must speak with His Lordship at once,' he blustered.

'My father is not to be disturbed,' Malcolm told him.

'But this is an urgent matter,' the Reverend protested.

Leonora squeezed Malcolm's arm. 'I think it is I the Reverend needs to see.'

'Sir Malcolm, I must speak with the Earl at once. My authority here has been placed in doubt by the employment of a lesser man where I should have been in charge.'

'Authority?' Leonora questioned. 'You have no authority here, Mr Evans.'

He addressed his reply to Malcolm. 'I have always been Sir Oscar's first choice. I should have been consulted.'

It was Leonora who answered the complaint. 'And why is that, Mr Evans?'

Again he looked to Malcolm. 'Sir Malcolm, if I might speak to you privately?'

292

'*Mr Evans!*' The lady's authoritative tone startled the man into giving her his fullest attention. He found her glaring at him through narrowed eyes, her anger quite apparent. 'I am not accustomed to being ignored, Mr Evans.'

'I beg your pardon, Madam, this matter is most urgent.'

'You will address yourself to me or hold your tongue sir.'

'Madam?' He made no effort to conceal his amazement.

'Mr Evans, you will speak to me, since I am responsible for the arrangements that appear to have unsettled you to the point of abandoning your good manners.'

He glanced at Malcolm, who offered no assistance. 'Madam?' he said again.

She glared and her tone was hostile. 'Sir, I have had my mother's remains brought here from London and laid to rest in a simple ceremony performed by the vicar of my choice. It is a personal matter, not to be criticised by the likes of you.'

'But Madam, the Earl has *always* used my services.'

'But I have not.'

'No Madam, but by tradition ...'

'Mr Evans, since when has tradition allowed you to question the decisions of those who pay your wages?'

The man glanced at Malcolm, rubbed his hands together with a distinct rasping sound and curved his lips in a servile smile. 'Sir Malcolm, I'm sure I can persuade you to ...'

Malcolm cut him off with a gesture. 'Address yourself to the Lady Leonora if you please.'

The man was furious. He had not expected to be dealing with a slip of a girl he considered better suited to decorate the place than to function in any serious capacity. He had already had his fill of Cavendish women. The Countess in her lifetime had sometimes proved more trying than even an ambitious man could be expected to endure. Swallowing his pride with difficulty, he turned to Leonora with a smile, still rubbing his palms together.

'I ask your forgiveness, Your Ladyship.'

'I will forgive you sir when you remember your position here.'

'I was in error. I stand chastised, Your Ladyship.'

293

'Let me inform you of this, Mr Evans. Neither I nor any other here is answerable to you.'

'Indeed, my lady and if ...'

'And if you dare to question me again sir, I will ask my father-in-law to act personally in settling the differences between us.'

Cedric Evans stopped smiling and looked distinctly uncomfortable. 'My lady, if I have given cause for offence ...'

'Indeed you have sir.'

'Then please accept my most humble apologies.'

'I will accept your undertaking that such a thing will never occur again,' she countered haughtily.

'You have it, Lady Cavendish,' he conceded.

'Good day sir.'

Her dismissal was abrupt and left him shaking with indignation. 'What an insufferable man,' she hissed, when she and Malcolm were beyond his hearing.

Malcolm chuckled. Caring little for the sugared insincerity of Cedric Evans, he had found himself enjoying the altercation. 'I believe you put him neatly in his place,' he told her.

'As if I would actually *pay* that creeping fool to whine over mama's grave for the sake of his own advancement.'

'I must admit, your friend Tobias made a decent job of it,' Malcolm conceded.

'More than that, he spoke to me at length about her character, her qualities, her hopes and disappointments. He even asked me to describe her to him in detail so that he might have a mental picture of her during the service. He actually wished to *know* the lady whose re-burial he had been asked to bless. Believe me, I would rather employ a hundred honest men of simple words than one bright cockerel with a slippery tongue.'

Malcolm laughed out loud at her description, and together they followed the others into the house.

III

It had been a beautiful spring and Rebecca Adams was content to spend the coming weeks of summer under her brother's roof. She chose to stay with him throughout the year rather than travel as she had done in the past, wandering with her own people beyond the boundaries of Beresford and the forest that was Lukan's home. Instead she chose to clean his house and tend his gardens, wash and stitch his clothes and prepare his food. She ingratiated herself into his life with every task she performed on his behalf. And sometimes when he tossed and turned in his sleep she soothed him with her words and her caresses, hating the woman whose name he spoke so often, and with such longing, in his dreams.

A sultry afternoon was slipping towards a still and golden evening. All the perfumes of springtime hung on the quiet air, and from the aromatic darkness under the trees came the distinctive scent of a nearby fir copse. In the leafy space near the well at the back of the house Lukan stood in a shallow tub of water, his face and hair frothy with soap as he cleaned himself from top to toe after working all day in the forest. His body was darkened by the sun and packed with solid muscle. There were callouses on his palms and pressure marks on his shoulders from the heavy weights he often carried. For weeks he had been driving himself beyond all reason, working the daylight hours away in an effort to ease his inner pain. She knew he still had longings for the woman he had turned his back upon. Nothing would ever alter that, but she hoped in time his passions would begin to ebb and flow, now fierce, now gentle, making the hurts more bearable.

She watched him standing ankle-deep in the tub, his hair and body streaked with lather. She could smell the soap from where she sat on the rim of the garden well. It was made from the common soapwart plant which flowered with pink scented flowers in late summer. Although suitable for all kinds of washing, it was valued especially for delicate silks and dark hair, for it left a sheen on both that could be achieved no other way. She could smell it too in the breeches she had been stitching and which now lay folded neatly in her lap, ready for him to wear. A rivulet of pale lather ran down his belly to his groin and lingered there, drawing her gaze, before streaming down his inner thigh.

'I saw the lady of the Hall today,' she ventured.

His hands paused briefly in his soapy hair but he offered no reply.

Rebecca's voice was light. 'She's in her fifth month and there's barely a sign of the babe in her. Slim as a thoroughbred she is, and I for one have never seen her look so well. Pregnancy suits her. They say she'll make a doting mother and fall for another child before the year is out.'

He cleared his throat. 'Then Malcolm is a fortunate man.'

'Aye, he'll not be seeing this wife weakened by miscarriages or poisoned by a dead babe trapped inside her.'

Lukan shook his head vigorously, scattering dollops of soap and a fine spray of water. 'He hopes for a son, an heir.'

'Aye, and she'll give him one sure enough, come August.'

'Is that a fact?'

'I said as much all along and now the old woman at the fair has confirmed it.' She caught the derision in his quick glance. 'Oh, you can scoff as if you know better, Lukan de Ville, but you've already seen for yourself that half of what she says comes true to the very letter of her words.'

'Aye, I'll grant you that,' he replied. 'But man could worry himself into an early grave over the half that doesn't.'

She watched him closely. 'Don't forget that you owe your fine position here as much to her as to me. When our father was killed I was only thirteen and you were a babe in arms, a half-child bred out of two camps and wanted by neither. I was all set to take you away and raise you as my own, far from this place, but the old woman bade me stay and I obliged her. She foresaw that your sworn enemy would eventually be the making of you, that his authority would shape your life for the better. And we have watched it happen, you and I. She spoke the truth. You *know* she spoke the truth.'

Lukan grunted and soaped his chest with both hands.

Rebecca gently pressed her point. 'And she was right about the uncommon bond between you and Malcolm Cavendish. Nothing in life will bring about its destruction. It will only be broken when one of you is dead.'

'Aye, but it was we who made it, Malcolm and myself. We made the bond, not some old hag with claims to second sight.'

'She was right about Leonora.'

'And so were you. So what? Anyone who knew me well enough might have predicted it.'

'Perhaps, but who else could have foreseen what that girl would have to go through in order to achieve all the things she wanted?'

'It's easy enough to be wise after the event.'

'No Lukan,' Rebecca shook her head. 'She spoke to Leonora at the Great Fair on the very day you met. She told her how it would be when not another sign existed to give warning of what was to come. You may choose to be cynical about these things but Leonora herself knows the truth of it.'

'Parlour games,' he scoffed. 'Tricks to earn a coin from gullible young women in search of an adventure and something to look forward to in their dreary little lives.'

Rebecca smiled. She knew him too well to take such words to heart. Her brother had a firm belief in destiny, in patterns woven for the individual at his birth that would colour his life until its final day. What he questioned was the power of others to read those patterns in another's palm or in his eyes or in his dreams. Lukan was a man alone who chose to find and follow his own destiny without benefit of signs and fortune-readers. He scoffed at much of what she said, but his own beliefs were simply more oblique and less readily available than hers.

'I also read the signs, Lukan,' she reminded him.

He smiled. 'But for the most part you are wise enough to keep your guesses to yourself.'

'I say that Malcolm Cavendish will have his son in late August.'

'But the child is not expected to arrive until mid-September,' he reminded her.

'August,' she insisted. 'First a son and then a daughter, just as you ...' She checked herself before saying more. She had always known that Lukan too would have two little ones, a son he would scarcely know and a daughter he would love and lose in a few short years.

'Just as I ...?' he echoed.

'Just as you would expect of such a fine young gentleman,' she added quickly.

'Then he is fortunate indeed,' Lukan said, unable to conceal the bitterness in his voice.

His sister frowned. 'Do you begrudge him that? He is your best friend and he has surely suffered more than his fair share of disappointments these past few years. Can you really begrudge him the happiness this marriage has brought him?'

Lukan rounded on her, his dark eyes flashing. 'You can be certain of it, woman. Friend or no friend, I begrudge him every minute, every *second* he enjoys with her.'

She rose to her feet and said angrily, 'You always were a fool. You torture yourself by hungering for something you can never have.'

'Torture *myself*?' he echoed. 'Ye gods woman, do you fancy for one minute that what ails me is *self-inflicted*?'

'This grief of yours cannot go on.'

'Tell that to her!'

'Forget her, Lukan,' she pleaded. Forget the Cavendish woman.'

He laughed at that, a bitter, sharp retort. 'I fancy it would be easier to forget to breathe.'

'Then find yourself another,' she insisted. 'Stop living like a monk on her account. Only another love can remedy a past love's sting. Heal yourself. Go find another.'

Scowling, he lifted a bucket of cold water above his head and tipped the contents over himself. She watched the water chase the soap from his body, leaving it sleek and dark and glistening in the sun. She had never seen a man so beautiful, never wanted a man so much, and yet her love knew neither joy nor satisfaction. It was a curse. She would have plucked it from her heart if she were able, but instead she nurtured it by living in his house, the faithful elder sister dedicating her life

298

and energies to his needs. The hypocrisy of her own words rang in her ears, striking a hollow chord, '*You torture yourself by hungering for something you can never have.*' That sisterly advice would have been better applied to her own unhappy situation.

Lukan stepped from the tub and leaned forward to wring the water from his hair. Then he flicked his head so that his hair slapped against his wet back and clung there, raven black against the brown. He reached for a wide-toothed comb but ignored the towel in favour of drying his body in the warmth of the sun. He was glowering, his train of thought reflected in his features. At last he strode over to snatch the breeches from Rebecca's hand. He grabbed his belt and boots, then kicked out at the tub with his bare foot, spilling his bathing water on to the grass.

'Damn it, woman, I don't need to be reminded that I live a monk's life.'

'I think you do,' she replied softly.

He shook his head vigorously. 'Nor do I need your incessant lecturing.'

'Oh yes, you need that too.'

He stood before her, naked, angry, unable to give vent to his frustrations. Then she saw his anger spend itself in a deep sigh. 'Rebecca, am I a stubborn man?'

'To a fault,' she said without hesitation.

'And moody?'

'Only from black to blackest.'

'As bad as that?'

'As bad as that,' she nodded.

'And yet you remain loyal, loving me in spite of it all?'

She licked her lips. 'Of course. You are my brother.'

On impulse Lukan dropped his clothes and boots and stepped forward to take her in his arms. He held her close, glad of her love but unable to express the quiet affection he felt for her. His feelings were based on the simple respect of a brother for his sister, on gratitude and trust and familiarity. He hugged her close in a rare embrace, then pressed his lips to her forehead the way he might have kissed the simple-minded Elizabeth. Then he released her, turned and walked away,

299

pausing only to pick up his pants and belt and boots. He was smiling when he raised his hand in a wave only seconds before the leafy forest closed itself around him.

'Perhaps you are right,' he called out from the greenery. 'Perhaps it is time I brought another woman into my life.'

Rebecca stared after him with tears in her eyes. Holding him like that, hard and naked in her arms, she had felt the forbidden passions flare up like sudden fires inside her. And to salt the wound she had seen his body's bland indifference to her closeness. While she burned with her secret and guilty need of him, he could hold her body against his own without so much as a flicker of response.

She lifted her apron and with it wiped the dampness from her eyes. She hated to think that her own words of advice would send him to the arms of another woman, yet half of her was glad of it, for his sake. She would rather see him bedded with a serving wench or one of the local whores than breaking his heart over the wife of Malcolm Cavendish.

CHAPTER FIFTEEN

I

Harriet Wyndham was a widow in her early thirties, a tall and slender woman of delicate colouring and immaculate manners. She was no real beauty despite her fine features and lovely, grey-green eyes, and yet men were instantly attracted by her magnetic personality. They found her an amusing and intelligent companion, attentive to their needs and sensitive to their moods, for Harriet genuinely enjoyed the company of the opposite sex. Though she possessed the social and conversational skills of a lady, her background was modest, her education adequate but basic. She was one of those fortunate individuals blessed with a natural ear for language and an eye for quality and style. She was also something of a mimic, and was thereby able to endow herself with all those airs and graces to which she had always aspired but was not in any way entitled. Although forced by circumstances to exist on a very limited income, her special talents allowed her to sustain a life-style of some distinction at her secluded country home. Lower Prescot Hall was a large, imposing house near Ledbury. Its main hall and drawing rooms were tastefully furnished, its wide main staircase hung with gilt-framed paintings and lit by beautiful crystal lamps, but here the façade of elegance came to an abrupt end. More than half the rooms in the house had been closed off one by one, their furniture and fittings disposed of to help meet the increasing costs of day-to-day living and maintenance of the property.

Harriet's apparently solitary life at Lower Prescot Hall was chaperoned by her close companion and lively social escort, her father Thomas Harding. He was now a retired and very distinguished-looking gentleman in his late sixties, a poor but practical man who had learned to accept his daughter's weaknesses along with her strengths. Behind closed doors it was she, not he, who ran their lives and painstakingly maintained their veneer of respectability. He would not confront her about the men who offered their business cards at the door, supposedly for *Mr* Harding's scrutiny, and were later ushered into Harriet's private rooms by an adjoining door. Nor did he question the gifts of money and jewellery that helped support their comfortable existence. The pattern of their lives had developed surreptitiously over the years so that his collusion in her affairs had neither been solicited at the start nor discussed between them since. As a poor man he had been compelled to accept that which he was powerless to alter. She had her appetites and he his needs, but between them they lacked the wherewithal to support either. So it was that, with a personal income barely large enough to meet the wages of his cook and butler, he preferred to let the matter of Harriet's income go unchallenged. Together they had once conspired to marry her off to a wealthy alcoholic who would eventually provide them with a lifetime's security. Their plans had fallen sadly short of their hopes and expectations, so now they simply conspired to survive.

Harriet's eight-year marriage to Reginald Wyndham had proved a sorry and scarcely profitable interlude in her life. He had been her senior by twenty years, a gloomy, hard-drinking man often beset by mysterious rages and periods of deep depression. Sheer determination on Harriet's part had finally prised him from the clutches of his domineering mother, but after forty-six years of iron-handed rule, the old woman was equally set upon maintaining her influence over him. She hated Harriet for having no fortune of her own and constantly rebuked her son for abandoning his dear mother after all the sacrifices she had made on his behalf.

'And not even a family to show for your folly,' she complained at every opportunity. 'No little ones, no dear sweet grandchildren to comfort me in my old age.'

Throughout the marriage she had made it quite obvious that she would never find it in her heart to forgive Harriet for ensnaring Reginald and then failing to provide him with the babies that were his right. He was his mother's only child and babies would have been some small compensation for the loss of him. The senior Mrs Wyndham visited Lower Prescot Hall on the first of every month to criticise the servants and the general running of the household, to complain about the food, bemoan the unchanging slenderness of Harriet's figure and lament the foolish whim that had inspired her son to marry such a woman.

'Better a homely bride and a brood of children than a pretty face and an empty nursery,' she would lecture, wagging her finger in Reginald's face and wondering aloud what his poor dead father would have made of such a sorry situation.

After every such visit the long-suffering Reginald would lock himself away for two or three days and succumb to a depression of the spirits, fleeing the weight of his inadequacies for the fog of an alcoholic stupor. It was not until the reading of the will following his sudden death that Harriet was in any position to retaliate against her mother-in-law's relentless airing of those real and imagined grievances. The old lady had been smug and self-satisfied in her role as the grieving mother set at last to see justice done. Her hand had shaped the terms of her son's will just as surely as her animosity was about to shape the widow's future. She knew that such a legally-tied legacy was, for a woman like Harriet, little short of a prison sentence.

303

'It is sufficient, even generous,' his mother announced for the benefit of everyone present in the room. 'After all, there are no children of the marriage ...' and here she touched a fragment of delicate lace to each eye in turn. 'A deficiency which undoubtedly drove my poor unhappy boy to an early grave.'

With all the dignity she could muster, Harriet Wyndham had risen to her feet and addressed the company of lawyers, bankers, clerks and family members. Hot tears glittered on her pale cheeks as she faced the woman who had tormented her so heartlessly for so long and who now sought to become her jailer.

'Mrs Wyndham,' she said in a clear and cultured voice. 'Any doctor worth his salt will tell you that Reginald was a drunkard who quite literally *drank* himself to death, and I'm sure we are all aware that he embarked upon that course many years before he met and married me.'

'Wh-what? Wh-what?' the old woman blustered.

'It is high time you faced the truth.' Harriet declared. 'The deficiency you speak of so callously was through no fault of mine. Your son was impotent. Our marriage was never consummated and every caustic remark of yours was one more wound that poor unfortunate man had to suffer.'

'How dare you?' his mother demanded, falling back into her chair as if on the verge of collapse. 'How dare you speak such wicked, *wicked* lies.'

Harriet's voice rang out clear and loud. 'I speak the truth. The fault was his, not mine. Your son was half a man, an impotent drunkard, and he blamed you for it, *you*.' She pointed an accusing finger into the old woman's shocked and ashen face. 'Your son hated you and who could reproach him for that? Only an evil, cold-hearted woman would set out to geld her own son, but geld him you did, and long before he took his marriage vows.'

With that she had swept from the room, leaving a horrified silence in her wake. The tears on her cheeks were genuine enough, for she was bitterly disappointed in the specifications of her husband's will, but much of what she had uttered in that room was blatantly untrue. Reginald Wyndham had been anything but impotent and she had never known his sexual appetites to be adversely affected by excessive drinking. On the contrary, there were too many occasions when Harriet had been deeply offended by his licentious appetites, but now the man was dead and who but she could know the reality of it?

The truth of the matter was that she had married Reginald Wyndham knowing full well that she would never give him children. She had been pretty, vivacious and virtually penniless when they met at Newmarket during a fierce thunderstorm that sent the patrons scuttling for the first available shelter. There she had marked him out for the cut of his clothes and the obvious weaknesses in his character. She had set her sights on becoming his wife and worked relentlessly to trap him, not because she cared one jot for him but because he was a fool who might more easily be tempted into marriage. She lacked the income to maintain herself independently and, like so many others of her time, had quickly come to recognise the only avenues open to a woman in her position. She could make the slow, demoralising descent to the streets, where ill-use and poverty would rapidly destroy her attractions until she was content to sell her favours for a tot of gin or a warm pie on a freezing winter night. She could become a kept woman, vulnerable to brutality and desertion, ever fearful of the foul breath of scandal that might suddenly slam all doors against her. Or she could marry. While the choice was still hers to make, Harriet prudently decided upon the latter. Her quest, however, was to prove anything but simple. She owned neither dowry nor background sufficient to attract a man with the required means and social position yet she had in her romantic youth a notion that love itself would be her redemption. Young men pursued her and often won her over with charm and fanciful promises, but they always married elsewhere, their sights on finer or more profitable partners. She was barely seventeen when she suffered her first miscarriage and by twenty-one had ceased to torture herself by keeping score. Her final miscarriage, induced in hasty and unsavoury circumstances within a few days of meeting the man who was to become her husband, left her with a serious pelvic infection that had almost proved fatal. By this time she and her father were desperate to see her safely married. When Reginald Wyndham staggered into that enclosure at Newmarket to shelter from the rain, he offered a swift solution to their problems. Neither had considered it expedient to confess that Harriet was incapable of conceiving another child.

By that summer of 1824 her fortunes had once again reached a dangerously low ebb. She was fast approaching middle age and Thomas Harding had watched his own income dwindle with the slow demise of a shipping and storage company in which he held a small number of shares. Now that his wife and sons were dead Harriet had become his last resort, his only hope of securing some measure of comfort in his waning years. She was thirty-three years old and soon her obvious attractions would be spent and faded. She tempted providence every time she invited a man into her private rooms, for under the terms of Reginald Wyndham's will, one hint of scandalous behaviour would see her homeless and without so much as a penny-piece to call her own.

'The only possible solution to our predicament is another marriage,' Harriet informed her father following a particularly sobering visit to the manager of her bank. 'The money is running out for want of better handling and bigger invest-ments, neither of which we can possibly afford. Another six months will see our income almost halved by rising costs and increasing obligations. There is no other way. I must marry again, and quickly.'

Harriet was hampered at virtually every turn by the puri-tanical conditions laid down in her late husband's will. Lower Prescot Hall remained hers only for as long as she was prepared to live there as a respectable widowed lady. Her small allowance would end if she remarried. Her furniture, carriage horses and jewellery would all be forfeit. Thanks to the inteference of his mother, everything Wyndham had left to his widow was conditional upon the clause that she remain single and respectable. If she remarried, or if her reputation

306

became tainted, everything would pass in full to the mother-in-law who waited in the shadows like some hungry spider watching for its kill.

For Harriet the situation was rapidly becoming intolerable. Her reputation remained intact while she resided with her elderly father, but every half-year when the accounts were balanced she saw her meagre security slipping from her grasp. The house was shabby, many of its upper rooms damaged by damp where parts of the roof were in urgent need of attention. There was simply no money left over to pay for such items as repairs, improvements and replacements. The cost of maintaining the house and its extensive grounds was expected to be met out of her allowance, and since she already supported her father, a cook, a butler, three housemaids and a gardener-groom, she was finding herself increasingly hard-pressed to make ends meet. She was an unprotected woman looking to her future and determined to avoid the clutches of poverty. She must therefore cut her cloth according to her means and set her goals according to her capabilities. No lover, however generous, would ever provide her with security. What she needed was another husband.

Lukan de Ville was no stranger to Lower Prescot Hall. He remembered Harriet's father from his boyhood, when the man had been coachman to Sir Edmund Cavendish, father of the present Earl. And he remembered Harriet herself as a hot-blooded eighteen-year-old living at her aunt's school for young ladies in Cheltenham, a penniless young woman acting out the role of a wealthy young visitor from the big city. Years ago he had accepted an invitation to her rooms, long before she had met and married Reginald Wyndham. Their intimacy had been brief and their friendship, light as it was, had survived the indiscretion. After her marriage he and Malcolm had often carried Reginald Wyndham home from some gathering where he had drunk himself into a helpless stupor. Even then, as Wyndham's wife, she had made no secret of the fact that she still had a fancy for Lukan. There was a subtle understanding between them, an unspoken invitation extended by her and discreetly acknowledged by him. Like many couples who shared a mutual attraction, their seemingly innocent flirt-ations sprang from serious undertones. Ten years had passed since he last shared her bed, but he recalled her eagerness and the forthright way she demanded some gift in appreciation of her generosity. Lukan still preferred it to be so, to pay for his pleasures in simple currency that left no room for tears or emotional warfare. This new arrangement suited him. He had no taste for common whores or giggling virgins or unwashed gypsy girls. The woman whose bed he shared must be clean and wholesome, with decent manners and wit and intelligence enough to hold his interest. For a man in his predicament Harriet Wyndham was the ideal choice. She boasted no recent connection with Beresford Hall and she was by necessity the very height of discretion. She and her father were angling for another marriage, one that would compensate them for their losses, and so discretion had become the very code by which they lived.

'Do you care for this woman?' Rebecca had asked, and he had answered with another question, genuinely puzzled. 'Do I need to?'

On his first visit to the house Lukan announced himself to the butler as a shipping merchant with important business to discuss with Thomas Harding. When the brandy was poured and the butler dismissed, Harriet entered the room by an adjoining door which led to a very tiny drawing room over-looking open fields to the south side of the house. It was there that Harding wiled away the hours with a book or a bottle of claret while his daughter entertained her guests in private. When Lukan left he did so openly, with Harriet moving through the house by different doors to meet them in the hall and briefly play hostess to her father and his departing guest. The lady of the house must think of everything. Domestic workers had eyes to see and tongues to tell, and might be bribed as spies to watch their mistress. Harriet Wyndham would never fall on their account, nor would she be robbed of her petty inheritance for want of a clever performance for the benefit of her servants.

In no way was she cheated by her memories of the man. He

308

was still the lover whose graceful body and earthy, ingenuous hungers she had found herself recalling with such longing during the last ten years. He was stronger now, more muscular and energetic, yet experience had balanced that with a need to tap and savour every moment for the sensual delights it offered. Nor did he take his fill and leave her wanting, for not even in the heat of passion did he forget that Harriet was his partner in the act. Only when he was sure that she too had reached the heights was he content to bring the encounter to its conclusion. In her bed he was both master, friend and gentleman, now even more of each than in the past. As a lover she could find no fault in him, except perhaps the veil he kept between them even in their naked intimacies. It told her that she had little claim on him, that even while he held her in his arms he held another woman in his heart.

On one occasion Lukan brought her a gown-length of peach-coloured satin and several matched pieces of silver jewellery set with precious stones. The delight he saw in her eyes was as much for the value of the gift as for its beauty, but her need to judge everything in terms of ready cash did not offend him. He had taken to leaving extra guineas on her bedside table and bottles of brandy on the old man's desk. They did not discuss his generosity. Neither needed to be reminded that the gifts he brought and the money he left were by way of compensation for the little he was able to give of himself.

Harriet had been quite open with him concerning her plans to manipulate an elderly admirer into marriage. He used that topic to defuse the situation one sultry afternoon when she seemed on the verge of asking him to stay. Her friendship he held in high regard, but he shied away from the many small pretences and falsehoods that were to be endured when simple friendship aspired to romantic heights. He wanted none of it. The terms of their relationship had been agreed at the outset and he had no desire to alter them in any way.

'When is the wedding to be?' he asked, avoiding the admiration in her gaze.

She was lying naked in the crumpled bed, watching him as

309

he dressed. In the sunlight from her window he saw the occasional streak of silver-grey glinting in her soft brown hair and wondered where she would be five years from now if she failed to procure the protection of a husband. She stretched luxuriously. 'Soon, I hope. The poor old man is almost beside himself with frustration.'

Lukan smiled. 'Are you able to deny him, then?'

'Oh yes, indeed I am.' She stroked her hands down her body, cupped her breasts and sighed. 'I'm afraid his eligibility as a husband is the only thing that stands in his favour. The rest is barely to be tolerated. Augustus Sharpe is a singularly unattractive man.'

Lukan laughed out loud. 'You surprise me, Harriet. How can you find any man unattractive while he possesses such a fortune?'

'But he's older than my father,' she pouted. 'His skin is dry and wrinkled and he is uglier than a sow.'

'Aye, but I'll warrant his money is as pretty as the next man's,' Lukan teased, reminding her of the priorities involved.

She watched him pull his breeches over long, muscular legs turned to nut-brown by the sun. 'Lukan, the perfect man would have your body and Augustus Sharpe's wealth, but I'm afraid perfection is not on offer here.'

'So will you compensate yourself with lovers even after the marriage?'

She smiled and stretched her body luxuriously. 'Why not, so long as I am still young and attractive enough to enjoy the attentions of a real man?'

He buckled his belt. 'Can you be certain then that he will actually propose marriage and not some lesser arrangement?'

She nodded. 'He must. He knows now that he will have me no other way and besides, I have been both patient and cunning to a fault with this one. I teased him to the limit of his endurance, then suddenly submitted to his advances when he least expected it. As I anticipated, the long-awaited was spent and gone before my stays were off.'

'Ye gods, it never fails to amaze me what wiles you women

are prepared to employ to gain your ends!' he exclaimed. 'The poor man has my sympathy.'

She smiled, unruffled by his teasing. 'And now he is beside himself with regrets and totally inconsolable. He feels a failure and was cruelly deprived of that which he so desired, so he is quite desperate to repeat the exercise to better effect.'

'But you hold him off?'

'I certainly do.'

'How clever of you, Harriet.'

'I can ill afford to be otherwise, Lukan. Father has spoken to him man-to-man on the subject, explaining the difficulties arising from my late husband's will. I, of course, have tearfully confessed my weakness for the *irresistible* Augustus and my fears of losing my reputation and everything that hangs upon it.'

'Clever,' he said again.

'And now he ponders upon the problem while my father firmly keeps himself between us. He will not be allowed to trifle further with the affections of a helpless widow overwhelmed by his attractions. He either marries me or gives me up, it's come to that.'

'Then I wish you every success in snaring the old scoundrel,' Lukan told her honestly.

She tilted her head and peered at him from the edges of her eyes. 'And you, my dear. What do *you* hope for in the future?'

His face darkened at the question. She was watching him closely, her hair curling around her face and her eyes narrowed slightly in the bright light from the window.

'I care nothing for the future,' he said at last.

'Nonsense,' she smiled. 'Only an empty-headed imbecile cares nothing for his own future.'

He regarded her solemnly. 'Sufficient unto the day are the evils thereof,' he quoted, recalling Leonora's words.

Harriet laughed prettily and rose to a kneeling position on the bed. Her breasts were pink-nippled, full and firm, with delicate veins just visible beneath the surface.

'Oh Lukan, when did you become so serious?'

He shrugged. 'Was I ever otherwise?'

311

'You were good company once, amusing, witty.'

'And now?'

She pouted her full lips. 'Now you are a glum old thing, my dear. I seldom see you without that scowl of yours and you make love to me as if it were a duty.'

He scowled. 'If my performance disappoints you ...'

'It doesn't,' she said quickly. 'It doesn't disappoint me at all, though I doubt it brings you more than a release of pent-up energies.' She reached out to brush his hand with her finger-tips. 'Poor Lukan, she must have hurt you very deeply.'

His scowl deepened. 'What do you mean? Why do you make such a statement when you know nothing at all about my personal life?'

She laughed again. 'My, my, you *are* defensive of your privacy. Don't fret yourself, my dear, I am not yet privy to your closest secrets, much as I would like to be.' Her smile faded and she grasped his hand more tightly. 'You are changed, Lukan. Something bright and vivid has died inside you, and only a woman can do that to a man. Will you not talk to me about her?'

He shook his head and withdrew his hand from hers.

'Did she leave you for another?'

Again he shook his head, then offered her a smile so brilliant that it instantly transformed his sombre features. 'My dearest Harriet, there is no woman in my life but you, no pleasures to delight me but your own.'

'Liar!' she laughed, then snatched up his hand and drew it to her lips. 'But what sweet lies they are to warm a lady's heart. When will you come again? Will it be soon?'

Lukan winced inwardly at the question. They had promised to make no demands, no promises.

'Not before the end of the month,' he told her. 'I'll send my card from the inn as usual. Have your father return it promptly if the visit is not convenient.' On impulse he stooped to kiss her cheek. 'Don't bother to get up. I'm sure your father will be happy to show me out.'

She listened for their voices in the drawing room, the clink of glasses and the butler's bell. Then she pulled on a light robe

312

and padded on bare feet to the window to watch him go. He led his horse through the narrow pasture gate, sprang lightly into the saddle and urged the animal into a gentle canter. He had always been a solemn man, indeed his aloofness was part and parcel of what attracted her to him. But he seemed different somehow, as if he carried a secret burden that caused him constant pain. His body was as wonderful as ever, hard and tireless in its energy, but he used it now without his previous enthusiasm, out of necessity rather than honest passion. And afterwards it seemed as if he held the wrong woman in his arms and almost despised himself for being there. His loneliness was almost tangible. She felt certain in her heart that Lukan de Ville had loved too deeply and somehow lost the object of his affection. She could only guess at what breed of woman was capable of winning and discarding such a man.

Harriet's father entered the bedroom without knocking and went directly to the beside table. A neat pile of golden guineas had been placed between the reading lamp and a small vase of flowers. He picked up the coins and counted them, nodded his head and shared them equally between his two small waistcoat pockets. The bed was in a mess, its covers flung aside in an untidy heap and its pillows in disarray. He could see a damp patch on the lower sheet that seemed to mock both her respectability and his. He glanced at Harriet standing near the window in her nightgown, her hair untidy and her cheeks still flushed. The quicker old Augustus Sharpe could be hoodwinked into proposing marriage the better he would like it. He could not go on indefinitely accepting money and expensive gifts in exchange for his daughter's services. Their diminishing circumstances made a whore of her and a common fleshmonger of him. He wanted an end to it. He was living upon the generosity of his daughter's lovers and he hated every minute, every coin and favour of it. He was a proud man once and would be proud again, if only he could meet the cost of it. He had long since learned that simple self-respect was much too costly for his humble purse.

Later that afternoon, over hot chocolate and buttered

simnel cake, they discussed Augustus Sharpe and Harriet's hopes for an early wedding. Neither she nor Harding would be sorry to see the last of Lower Prescot Hall, though Harriet was loath to have it pass so easily into the grasping hands of Reginald Wyndham's mother. She had a mind to beg de Ville to come there on her wedding night and set a lighted torch beneath the door. It would delight her to see it razed to the ground, a prize no longer worth having when the old woman came to claim it.

'If you think for one minute he'd do such a thing you don't know the man as well as you think you do,' her father told her. 'He's half a gentleman is that one. The likes of him don't go running around the countryside setting light to other people's houses just to satisfy a lady's whim.'

'He would if it suited him,' Harriet smiled.

Her father nodded. 'Now there I believe you are quite right. I'd judge that fellow capable of doing anything that suited his own ends and standing as stubborn as Old Lucifer himself against anything that didn't.'

Harriet laughed. 'I do believe you like him father.'

'I suppose I do at that,' he confessed. 'I've always thought him worth a dozen of many who like to call themselves gentlemen.'

'Speaking of value, dear, how much did Lukan leave today?'

'Ten,' he said, peering into his cup.

'Ten guineas?' Her laughter was a pretty sound. 'Ten guineas indeed. Mr de Ville is a man of discerning tastes to spend so highly on a whore.'

'*Harriet!* I will not have you say such things.' Harding was genuinely shocked. Such talk offended him, even when he could see the merriment in his daughter's eyes. She leaned towards him, smiling unashamed.

'Don't be a prude, father dear,' she admonished. 'I earned that money lying on my back. What would you call me then, if not a whore?'

'Harriet, *please*!'

She chuckled softly and poured more chocolate into her

cup. Presently she rang for a maid and ordered more hot milk. When it came she topped up the silver chocolate pot, replaced the lid and covered the pot with a quilted warmer. Relaxing in their respective armchairs, father and daughter allowed a comfortable silence to fall between them. Then Harding said, smiling a little at the memory, 'I met his father once or twice, you know.'

'What, Lukan's father? The gypsy?'

He nodded. 'Daniel Adams. Now there was a wild man if ever I encountered one. Temper as quick and deadly as mercury, he had, but a good and honest worker for all that. He knew how to turn a lady's head without even trying, too, just like that son of his.'

'Was he as handsome as Lukan then?'

'Not by a *half*,' Harding said emphatically. 'Oh, he was dark and dashing enough, with those same flashing eyes and that jet-black hair, but he was never so tall and aristocratic-looking as his son turned out to be. Never had the manners either, him being a true gypsy with no education to speak of and no decent breeding. No, Lukan gets all that from his mother.'

'Did you ever meet her?' Harriet asked.

'Oh, yes, I met his mother. A pretty little thing she was, all frothy and soft like a proper young lady ought to be.' He smiled, closing his eyes as he recalled the way his heart had fluttered at the merest glimpse of her. 'She was the youngest, the darling of the family. There was even talk of her marrying into royalty, but that was before the gypsies came.'

Harriet set down her cup and peered quizzically into her father's face.

'Darling, according to common belief, Lukan's mother was the wife of a forest keeper over Chepstow way, a simple country woman of no consequence.'

'Nonsense. She was a beautiful, high-born lady with a fortune of her own and a pedigree as long as your arm.'

Harriet sighed, exasperated. 'But if that were so, why on earth would she be allowed to marry a forest keeper?'

'She didn't marry a forest keeper,' Harding told her crossly.

'She never went anywhere *near* a forest keeper. She ran away with the gypsies and lived with them for months until her family hunted her down and hauled her back, kicking and screaming, to the big house. Some said at the time that she and her gypsy lover were married all legal and proper.'

'What, she actually had the nerve to *marry* the man?' Harriet exclaimed. 'Good grief, her family must have been infuriated.'

'Indeed they were, though the clever little madam swore it was a lie when she realised they intended to find the preacher who wed them and have the marriage declared null and void.'

'Did they do that?'

'No, they were happy to accept her protestations. They did not want to believe that one of their own would actually stoop so low as to wed a gypsy.'

'So, what happened to her?' Harriet asked.

'She died in childbirth. Some said she refused to eat so much as a mouthful until she was reunited with her lover. Her family stood firm and so did she, so by the time the babe arrived she was too weak and sick to survive the birth. She only lived just long enough to give the boy his name, bless her.'

'The poor unhappy girl. How could they be so cruel to one of their own?'

'Pride,' her father said. 'Sheer pride. He was born between silken sheets, that Lukan of yours, and there's many a soul still living who will bear me out on that fact.'

By now Harriet was all ears. 'So then the family concealed the truth and gave the child away to avoid a scandal?'

'That's exactly what they did,' Harding nodded. 'Marcus de Ville and his wife were elderly and childless, so the boy was given over to them to raise as their own. It seems his mother had threatened to do away with herself before the birth unless her family swore a solemn oath to keep the babe safe and provide it with a decent start in life. Poor Winifred de Ville had little say in the matter, as I recall, though she came to love her gypsy stepson well enough in spite of his strange ways and devilish dark looks.'

'How do you know all this?' Harriet asked, reaching for the handle of the chocolate pot with a folded napkin. 'Will you have more hot chocolate?'

Her father leaned forward and watched the hot brown liquid spill steaming into his cup. 'I was there,' he said into the expectant silence. 'I have few skills to speak of any more, but I was a good coachman in my time and I was right there to see how they kept the truth of that affair from getting loose. That young man of yours was born on December 12th, 1794. Ask him, he'll verify the date.'

'So?'

'Sir Oscar, the present Earl of Beresford, had a younger sister called Roanne. She was seventeen years old when she died giving birth on December 12th, 1794.'

'What?' Harriet blinked her eyes as she stared at her father. 'She died as Lukan was born? Father, are you saying that the high-born lady who ran off with a wandering gypsy was the Earl of Beresford's *sister*?'

'I am indeed,' he nodded. 'And one of the women who helped with the delivery swore the girl's babe was as black as midnight.'

'Good grief.'

'A gypsy child without a doubt was what that woman said. The blackest eyes in all Christendom and hair as ebon as any raven's wing.'

'Good grief,' Harriet repeated.

'And the story didn't finish there. When Daniel Adams tried to claim his son they accused him of raping Lady Roanne and beat the poor man to death. There are some who swear that Sir Oscar Cavendish and his father Sir Edmund each had a hand in it. There's little real proof apart from the word of country folk with long memories, but it's a matter of record that Lukan was born as Lady Roanne died, though few would dare to call it a child-bed death in Sir Oscar's hearing.'

'And probably a matter of record that she and the gypsy were legally married, if the lady's first story is to be believed,' Harriet added. 'Was there a doctor present at the birth?'

'There was indeed, and several women too. They say Sir

Oscar roared like an enraged jungle animal when he saw his little sister dead and the gypsy brat still lying in her arms.'

'Well, well, well.' Harriet sat back in her chair with a smile. 'My handsome gentleman caller certainly is a man of mystery.'

Thomas Harding wiped a forefinger around the inside of his cup to catch the last smears of sweetened chocolate clinging to the porcelain. 'It was never on the cards that he would inherit, of course, but inherit he did when Marcus de Ville and his nephew were both drowned at Monks' Crossing in 1814.' He chuckled wickedly and offered his cup for a refill. 'The boy had been away getting a gentleman's education as promised, at the Earl's expense. How it must have stuck in Sir Edmund's craw to have his daughter's gypsy whelp claim 400 acres and a lord's living right on his own doorstep. And it must have cut both him and Sir Oscar to the quick to know that in their efforts to disclaim the boy as a Cavendish they had handed him legal rights over all the de Ville holdings.'

'Poetic justice,' Harriet said, chuckling softly. 'What an interesting story father. Why have you not told it before?'

Harding shrugged, replete at last after three cups of chocolate and two slices of simnel cake. 'The events are almost thirty years old and I have rarely been reminded of them. It was seeing him here these last few weeks that brought it all back to me. I sometimes see his mother in him and I wonder how it might have been for him if she had lived. Who knows, she might have defied them all and made him her legal heir. She was as strong-willed as the best of them, and those Cavendish women have always had their own fortunes to do with as they see fit.'

'So if her family had disowned her she could have lived with her gypsy in fine style and raised their son a gentleman?'

'Indeed she could, and surely would have done. She had the mettle for it.'

'I'm surprised Lukan has never mentioned this.'

Her father shrugged his shoulders. 'I doubt he knows the whole truth of his birth. Who would have dared repeat that story to him? Besides, there were so many different rumours spread about in the first few years that he probably dismissed

318

them all as idle gossip before he was even ten years old.'

'But shouldn't he be entitled to more than he has already? Does he have no claim?'

'To what?'

'To a share of the earldom, for Heaven's sake. Father, if what you say is true the man's a *Cavendish*!'

'No he isn't my dear. Not without a certificate of marriage between his parents. I suppose the most he can hope for is a legacy of sorts when the present Earl dies and Lady Roanne's story comes to light... *if* it comes to light.'

Harriet left her chair and moved to the big fireplace. She stared thoughtfully into the empty grate for some time before asking. 'And what of Malcolm Cavendish? Everyone knows that he and Lukan are as close as brothers. Does he know the truth?'

'Not a chance of it,' Harding said. 'I happen to know young Malcolm well. He's every ounce as stubborn and unyielding as his father or his grandfather before him. If he ever suspected that he and Lukan were blood-cousins, he'd have the truth made public and the man acknowledged as such, even though he defied his entire family to do it.'

'So the subterfuge continues thirty years on. Can any of this be proved?'

'Well, there are those still living who know the truth.'

'Ah, but people can be bribed to remain silent or alter their stories, especially after so much time has passed.'

'Does it matter?'

'It might, if I should fail to secure this marriage with Augustus Sharpe.'

Harding's eyes suddenly widened in horror. 'My God, Harriet, surely you are not contemplating changing your plans in favour of the gypsy?'

She laughed in his face. 'Of course not, you old goose. He'll never marry. The woman is not yet born who can bend that man to her will. However, perhaps we might capitalise on this information some other way, without involving Lukan.'

'What way? How can a story nearly three decades old be used to serve us now?'

319

'Well, it seems to me that if Sir Oscar Cavendish has kept this guilty secret for so long, he'll be reluctant to have it made public now. Think of it my dear. Would he want the world to pick over the details of his sister's shame? Would he want it known that his family, including the babe not yet delivered, shares its bloodline with a gypsy?'

'He most certainly would not.'

She shook her head, smiling broadly. 'A public airing of that old story would be no less scandalous today than thirty years ago. And don't forget that Daniel Adams was beaten to death without benefit of a legal trial. And if the two *were* legally married, who can say to what lengths Lukan might go in seeking compensation for the death of his parents and the withholding of his own entitlements?'

'My God, what unsavoury plot are you hatching in that pretty little head of yours?'

Harriet grinned wickedly. 'I believe Sir Oscar will want the matter kept secret,' she explained. 'And he might be persuaded to pay for the privilege.'

'Silence-money? Harriet, do you dare? What if he refuses to oblige?'

She shrugged. 'No matter. Powerful men breed equally powerful enemies. What he refuses to buy will be offered to the man who hates him most.'

'Would you be prepared to do that, for a profit?'

'I certainly would. What does it matter to me who pays, so long as *someone* does?'

Thomas Harding chewed his lower lip and said at last, 'You will need certain proof before you put it to him.'

'Of course, my dear, and in order to begin my search for it, I intend to gain access to Beresford Hall.' She stooped to kiss a damp patch on his forehead, then dipped her fingers into the pockets where he had placed Lukan's guinea pieces. 'And if we are to move in grander circles, I think it is time I took control of our finances.'

320

II

Within a mere two weeks Harriet Wyndham had managed to secure an invitation, of sorts, to a garden party at Beresford Hall. She did so with the connivance of her friend Lettice Holland, the elder sister of Sir Toby Holland. As the unmarried sister still living in the family home, it fell to Lettice to be nurse, keeper and chaperone to the Holland children, a varied assortment of tasks performed not out of love but necessity. It had long since been decided on her behalf that she would never marry. She was needed at home, and since her parents had failed to provide her with an income of her own, she was totally dependent upon the good will and generosity of her brother. Her sister-in-law, Lady Holland, was a sickly woman who had borne a dozen children, eight of whom survived. Now she virtually lived her life from her couch, beautifully dressed and pampered, holding court like a royal personage while the lives of her family revolved around her, each one of them fastened to mama by a short, tight rein. In Lettice she had found the perfect blend of nurse, companion and servant. The younger woman would never have her freedom. For want of even a modest income she was trapped for life.

The plan between Lettice and Harriet was a simple one. Lettice was to fall ill with stomach cramps on the day of the garden party, leaving her pretty young nieces dressed and ready but lacking the vital services of a chaperone. She would beg that the three girls be taken directly to Lower Prescot Hall with a note asking Harriet, supposedly a fellow guest, to take charge of them for the day. For her part Harriet would be fully prepared for the arrival of the Holland coach and would willingly undertake to chaperone the girls. In return she had promised to invite Lettice to stay over at Lower Prescot Hall when a certain Mr Archibald Davey, a cabinet maker from Wynchcombe, would also be a house guest. It was a neat and workable arrangement. Lady Holland would avoid disappointing her daughters and Lettice would have a private meeting with the young man she secretly admired. As for

Harriet, she would enjoy this long-awaited visit to Beresford Hall in the company of the charming Holland sisters. She would step from a crested coach into the higher echelons of local society. If she could not sway an old man to marriage with her newly-found status, perhaps the adventure would result in the acquisition of other admirers.

Her new outfit was ready with a day to spare. Lukan's gift had been expertly cut and stitched into an elegant gown with a neatly embroidered bodice and heart-shaped sleeves. It was modest in style, quite striking in its simplicity, and would be worn with a fringed and tasselled shawl of lined white silk. With an eye to future functions, she had ordered every scrap of left-over fabric to be made into a tight over-bodice which was to be decorated with embroidery, beads and sequins and would transform the gown for a more lavish occasion.

'Thank you Lukan,' she said, curtsying to her reflection in the long oval mirror in her dressing room. She wore the silver jewellery he had given her, each piece polished to a brilliant shine with fine ash and a soft cloth. In her hair were pale silk flowers. Her hands and arms were protected from the sun by long gloves and she carried a pretty parasol. Her father burst in on her, his face reddened by the effort of running up the stairs. He held out a note bearing the Holland seal and Harriet tore it open.

'The coach is on its way,' she told him, beaming. 'It worked, Father. Our plan has worked. The coach is on its way.'

CHAPTER SIXTEEN

I

Lady Charlotte Foulds and her husband Rodney, Viscount Morley, were visiting Beresford from their home near St Austell in Cornwall. They had with them Sir Oscar's grandchildren, three tireless, robust individuals determined to explore every inch of the earldom before their holiday was over. Their father was a large, ruddy man with bushy brown hair and a magnificent beard and side whiskers. He was loud and bold, with a laugh as sudden and as startling as a clap of thunder and a growl like an angry bear. Big and fierce though he was, his children had no fear of him and his wife, with her patient smile and loving nature, mothered him as tenderly as she did them. Her children were little replicas of herself, tall and Viking-blond, with steady blue gazes and a streak of stubbornness befitting their Cavendish ancestry.

'Lady Vivienne is not with you?' Leonora asked when they arrived, knowing that the girl had been travelling back and forth between her sister in Cornwall and her aunt in Paris, unwilling to settle with either long enough to endure the discipline of private tutors or the restrictions of yet another school for young ladies.

'She is not,' Rodney Foulds said with heart-felt relief. 'And I pity that aunt and uncle of hers when they've done making a bed of thorns for themselves on her account. They indulge her every whim and she will repay them in tears and strife if I am any judge of a woman's character.'

Charlotte threw up her hands in mock despair. 'You have been warned, husband,' she wailed. 'Any talk of my dear, sweet little sister on this holiday and I will personally see to it that you sample the bottom of the nearest fish pond.'

'Could she really have been that troublesome?' Leonora asked with a smile.

'She has been a *horror*,' Charlotte insisted.

'Oh, much worse than that,' Rodney muttered, mysteriously.

'So we have decided to give the devil his rest and not even *discuss* the matter, lest we talk ourselves into some drastic solution that cannot afterward be mended.'

'Aye, like cold-blooded murder,' Rodney nodded.

'Oh dear, oh dear,' Leonora said with a merry twinkle in her eye. 'In that case, I think it might be best if the offending name is not mentioned by any one of us again.'

From that first day the rapport between them was light and easy, and Leonora knew she would enjoy every moment of their lengthy visit to Beresford Hall. The children were an entertaining trio egged on by a rowdy, fun-loving father, and between them they brought a carnival atmosphere to the Hall. She particularly enjoyed the time she spent with Charlotte, finding her witty and intelligent and without that keen competitive edge she had come to expect in other women. Charlotte did not look on her as a rival out to steal her father's or her brother's affections. She accepted her as a new member of the family, one to be loved and cherished as her own. It was this aspect of Charlotte that Leonora found so endearing, this desire to ensure that the newcomer to Beresford was given a secure place within the family. Charlotte's sister Vivienne had been Lady Alyce's favourite and, like her mother, fickle and unpredictable with her affections. Poor Elizabeth was safely enclosed within her own secret world, so that Charlotte had grown up lonely, feeling like the only daughter among three sons. Now at last she had a sister she could talk to, whose company she could enjoy and whose affection she could depend upon. Right from the start she had taken Leonora to her heart, expecting nothing but kinship in return. For her part Leonora was drawn to Charlotte for many reasons, the most important of which was the sheer pleasure of being able to lower her defences and simply be herself. There were no secrets binding them together like prisoners sharing the same shackles, no guilts and regrets drawing and repelling them in an ocean of uncertainty. They had come together freely, two women with much in common and many similar interests.

One day they were walking together on the terraces when Charlotte broached the subject of her father's lifelong love affair with Leonora's mother. She did so with a disconcerting bluntness. 'Did your mother love my father as he loved her?'

'Yes,' Leonora replied without hesitation. 'She loved him to the end.'

'Were they lovers still?'

Leonora shook her head, unabashed by the frankness of the question. 'Not in a worldly sense. Mama was a woman of quite rigid principle. When circumstances forced her to surrender her true love and marry Herbert Shelley she swore to be a faithful wife. To my certain knowledge she kept that vow.'

'And yet their love survived. I saw him in the garden yesterday, placing a flower on her grave with such tenderness I could have wept for him. I don't know if it is a kindness or a cruelty having her here.'

'I'm sorry,' Leonora said. 'It was for my sake he agreed to have the body moved. I wanted mama here, where I could feel her close to me.'

'I know.' Charlotte smiled and then on impulse hugged her friend warmly. 'You have lost so much, Leonora, and yet there is no trace of bitterness in you. I think you are the bravest and

325

most admirable woman I have ever known.'

Leonora smiled sadly. 'Believe me, I own not half my mother's courage. You met her on several occasions, did you not?'

'Indeed I did, and liked her tremendously. You father though I never met. Tell me, was he the reprobate they say he was?'

Leonora looked into the distance where the day rested in a still, warm haze. 'Take the worst you have ever heard of him and double it, then you will have an inkling of the man.'

Charlotte stopped and slid her arm through Leonora's. 'You hate him. Forgive me for mentioning his name. Now is the worst of times to stir up old angers and hurts.'

'He is a worthless man who will pay dearly for what he has done to those I love.'

Charlotte was taken aback by the quiet venom in Leonora's words. She had misjudged her. There was bitterness there in plenty, although from what little Charlotte knew of Herbert Shelley, his daughter's hatred seemed quite justified.

'Will you answer me one question honestly before we change the subject of our conversation?' she asked.

'I will give an honest answer or none at all.'

'That is exactly what I expected you to say. Is Jonathan my father's son?'

Again that unexpected bluntness. Wishing to delay her reply, Leonora reached out to brush the backs of her fingers along the pale pink petals of a rose. Its perfume hung on the still air, heavy and sweet. At the same moment her child shifted its position inside her. She touched her stomach and smiled at the unborn. Truth and lie were merging now, as if she had altered her brother's parentage simply by wishing it so. She turned and took Charlotte's hands in hers.

'I believe I could confide in you about anything,' she said warmly. 'But in this case I must divide my loyalties and with-hold the entire truth from you. Your father and Jonathan have important matters to discuss, personal matters that only came to light after mama's death. I cannot betray your father's confidence but I will say this: a certain long-standing rumour has been confirmed and will be made public just as soon as Jonathan can be found.'

'Then it's true! He *is* my brother! I knew it. I think I knew it all along.' Charlotte made her declarations as one who had just received a pleasurable gift. 'And I realise now that my mother knew it too. How could he look so much like father and Horace and myself and only be our cousin?'

'The family stamp,' Leonora said. 'It is distinctive, even among cousins.'

'But not in Herbert Shelley's case,' Charlotte attested. 'That man was never capable of siring such a thoroughbred. Well, my dear, the sooner our brother is found and brought home the better I will like it.'

'So you do not object?'

'Object? Why Leonora, I am delighted. We will share him, you and I. He is my brother and yours too, and in my opinion that leaves us but a trifle short of being sisters. But tell me, is there still no news of him?'

'Not a word,' Leonora said, shaking her head sadly. 'We are all convinced that there must have been letters sent to me at the Fairfax house or at their business premises in London, but our lawyers say that Nigel Fairfax denies all knowledge of them.'

'Ah, but would the old crow tell us if such letters existed?' Charlotte asked.

'I believe so,' Leonora nodded. 'I understand that Malcolm and his father paid an unofficial visit to *Fairfax, Reece and Tilbury* some months ago, threatening to take the law into their own hands should it ever be discovered that letters addressed to me had been withheld. Since then the senior Fairfax has been reminded of the position at regular intervals. I doubt he would dare hold them back.'

'And the fat man, Christopher? What about him?'

Leonora shook her head. 'I cannot speak for Christopher. He is a jealous, embittered man. It has occurred to me that he might steal my letters willingly, in defiance of the Earl, if by doing so he could repay my trickery.'

They had come to the row of fountains on the lower terrace,

where guests lazed about in the warm afternoon sunshine, sipping iced drinks and eating syllabub. The grass was a brilliant green dotted with tiny blossoms, the sky a haze of shimmering blue above them. And all about, the famous Beresford topiary arose in stately splendour from lawn and terrace, every lush, sculpted bush a living work of art. Two riders appeared like shadows in the distance and Leonora's heart made a sickening lurch before subsiding under a shadow of disappointment. A second glance, even across that distance, told her that neither one of them was Lukan.

Together the Earl's daughter and daughter-in-law moved amongst the guests, making polite and friendly conversation and ensuring that everyone received their hostess's attention in equal measure. Charlotte was dressed in white and carried a pretty parasol to protect her pale complexion from the sun. Leonora wore a pale blue gown of finest muslin that, being gathered below her breasts, floated sensuously about her body with barely a trace of the mound that grew beneath. Full sleeves and beautiful detail around the neckline drew attention upwards, to her pale throat and lovely face. The grace of her movements and the lightness of her step belied the burden she carried. Anyone watching her on that beautiful afternoon would be hard-pressed to see that she was almost six months into her pregnancy.

As they approached a small group of people bending over a card table, a woman detached herself and dropped into an elegant curtsy. That she had been watching for them and had timed her greeting to the second was obvious.

'Lady Leonora. Lady Charlotte. I have been hoping for an opportunity to thank you for a truly memorable day. I have enjoyed every moment of it.'

'In that case I may count my party a great success,' Leonora smiled warmly. This was Harriet Wyndham, a widow from Ledbury, friend and sometimes chaperone of the Holland girls. She was a charming woman, gracious to a fault and very attractive, with soft brown hair that fell in pretty curls, bright hazel eyes and a mouth that smiled readily. Leonora liked her; Charlotte plainly did not.

'The woman is too inquisitive,' she explained as they moved away. 'She questions everyone she comes into contact with, even the servants and gardeners. It seems to me she is hungry for any snippet of information about our family's past, and such open curiosity unsettles me.'

'Perhaps she intends compiling a history,' Leonora suggested. 'She seems a sweet lady. I'm sure she means no harm.'

'I do not trust her,' Charlotte said with her usual candour. 'This morning my husband found her in the long gallery, searching for a picture of the Earl's sister.'

Leonora looked up sharply. 'His sister? Your father has a sister?'

Charlotte nodded. 'He *had* a sister. She died here at Beresford almost thirty years ago. She was barely seventeen, poor thing, and my father adored her.'

'She must have been a good deal younger than him.'

'Yes, he was eighteen when she was born, and when she died of a fever his family feared he would go mad with grief.'

Leonora was staring wide-eyed at her friend. 'I never knew. I never even suspected that he once had a sister.'

'That's understandable,' Charlotte told her. 'She died a few weeks before Malcolm was born, so there are few people living who remember her, and fewer still who would dare speak of her. We know better than to mention her name. There are no pictures, no mementos that I know of. It is as if she never existed, except in father's memory.'

'Oh the poor man,' Leonora said with genuine compassion. 'Has he always lost the ones he loved the most?'

Charlotte nodded again. 'And usually through some fault, some blindness of his own. Perhaps that explains why this search for Jonathan has become such an obsession with him.'

'What was her name?'

'Roanne.'

'Roanne, what a lovely name.' Leonora smiled and said the name again. 'Roanne. Was she as pretty as the name implies?'

'Oh yes, they say she was quite beautiful. She could capture a heart without effort and light up a room simply by entering it.'

'And you say Harriet Wyndham has been questioning the staff about her?'

'She has, though Rodney has firmly warned her off the subject. Let's hope her patent desire for social advancement outweighs her curiosity. For the moment at least she seems torn between solving that old mystery and keeping her name on your garden-party list.'

Leonora pricked up her ears at this. 'Oh? Is there a mystery then?'

Charlotte slotted her arm through Leonora's and touched a finger lightly to her lips. 'If you love Papa, as I believe you do, you will forget I ever mentioned Roanne.'

'While in the meantime Harriet Wyndham is left to rake over old embers where she will?'

'Oh no, we must not allow that to happen. If she pays no heed to Rodney's warning I shall speak to her myself.'

Leonora's mind was racing. She sensed intrigue here, something she should familiarise herself with. She also sensed a personal threat in Harriet Wyndham's interest in Cavendish secrets long since buried. Leonora was mistress here and she welcomed no outsider with designs of any kind, however petty, upon her territory. She recalled the chance circumstances that had first brought the woman to Beresford, the borrowed coaches, the recut gowns, and suddenly it seemed to her that here was an opportunist looking for something more than the inclusion of her name on the Beresford visitors' list.

'I think that I should be the one to speak to this woman,' she informed Charlotte lightly. 'When you and Rodney are gone from here she will feel free to resume her probings in your absence. Let me speak to her if it becomes necessary, then she will know that His Lordship has a permanent watchdog.'

'That sounds to me like a very good idea. While I am in Cornwall my mind will then be at rest, knowing that you are taking good care of Papa.' She looked toward the meadow and smiled. 'Look, there's Lukan bringing Elizabeth back from St Eloy's Well. She ran off again this morning with a basket full of raw flour and table scraps, including a chicken carcass, to feed to the frogs that live around the well. Sometimes I am convinced the poor child's wits get fewer by the day.'

Leonora was not listening. She was watching Lukan ride across the blossom-spangled meadow with Elizabeth sitting before him in the saddle and the wolfhounds trotting at his horse's heels. His hair was loose, lifting a little with the rhythmic movements of the horse, and his back was ramrod straight as he carried the hapless Lady Elizabeth home. Suddenly the pain of being so long apart from him was a physical thing that made Leonora want to cry his name out loud and rush into his arms. Aching to see him, to touch him, to hold him, she stood her ground in that very public place and wished him a million miles away.

'Well, well, and what have we here?' Charlotte was saying as they watched a figure move forward to greet the rider. 'It seems the gypsy and the widow are acquainted.'

Leonora felt the blood run cold in her veins. Lukan and Harriet Wyndham? Might it be possible? The man was alone and the woman undoubtedly attractive. Had he, in his isolation, turned for consolation to the lovely widow of Lower Prescot Hall? Leonora's whole being rebelled against the prospect. It could not be so. She could not bare even to think of him in the arms of another woman.

'How is Elizabeth? Can you see from here?' Her voice sounded absurdly normal to her own ears. She could see Harriet's feminine, silk-clad figure, her dancing brown curls and fringed white parasol, and Lukan bending sideways in the saddle to speak to her. He lowered Elizabeth gently to the ground and then dismounted, and as he led his horse away Harriet Wyndham fell into step beside him.

'They make a handsome couple,' Charlotte observed.

'A hasty conclusion on your part,' Leonora remarked coolly. 'According to Malcolm, he is a solitary man.'

'But human,' Charlotte grinned and issued a long, exaggerated sigh. 'Despite the brute in him he is a man, and *what* a man.'

'Why Charlotte, you surprise me. What a shocking, unladylike thing for you to say.'

331

'But true enough.' Charlotte smiled wickedly and re-slotted her arm through Leonora's. 'My Rodney is a pet and I would not change him for the world, but I did not cease to be a woman when I took my marriage vows and I can still feel just a *little* envious when I look at those two.'

'Really Charlotte, you should be ashamed even to think such things.'

'Don't be such a prude, my dear,' Charlotte laughed. 'You don't have to like the man to see how intensely handsome and alive he is. He is the kind of man women dream about from the age of fourteen, as Vivienne discovered, until they are in their graves. And if you try to tell me that you have never looked at him and felt your cheeks ... at the very least ... grow wickedly warm, then I shall call you a liar.'

Leonora forced herself to laugh at the remark. Concealed by the rim of her hat her gaze followed the couple as they walked together deep in conversation. And then, quite suddenly, that uncanny magnetism between Lukan and herself came into play. He raised his dark head and looked directly into her eyes as if she had called his name across the wide expanse of lawn lying between them. Every part of her reached out to him, willing him to see her still as his beloved, not as Malcolm's wife. For a breathless moment his eyes held her fast, then his gaze faltered as if drawn unwillingly to the unfamiliar shape of her gown. He bowed in her direction, a stiff, formal acknowledgement of her presence and Charlotte's, then briefly took his leave of the widow and swung himself back into the saddle.

'Handsome devil,' Charlotte hissed as he rode away. 'And just see how the widow watches after him. You mark my words, Leonora, that one has either claimed our gypsy gentleman or is in the process of ensnaring him.' She felt Leonora sway and grasped her arm more tightly. 'What is it? Are you ill? Good heavens, you are as pale as death.'

'I feel the heat,' Leonora muttered, leaning heavily on Charlotte's arm. 'Please help me inside.'

Charlotte looked around to find the senior maid, Anabel Corey, already hurrying across the lawn to assist her mistress.

The woman had been watching her closely, attentive to her needs even when the duties of the day did not demand it. She had seen the look that passed between Leonora and de Ville. More than that, she had seen the charming, brown-haired woman who stood unknowingly, and dangerously, between them.

At dinner that evening Malcolm dismissed Charlotte's suspicions as nonsense. 'I insist they are lovers,' she told him. 'I saw as much with my own eyes and so did Leonora.'

Leonora laughed lightly. 'What I saw was two people talking together for no more than two minutes,' she corrected. 'What you saw was, it seems, something quite different.'

'Well if they are not lovers then they *should* be. They seem ideally suited to each other.'

Malcolm wagged a forkful of succulent pheasant at his sister. 'You were always an inventive matchmaker, Charlotte, but this time you are quite wrong. Lukan has known Harriet for more years than I can recall. He also knows her father and was well acquainted with her late husband. Besides, if they were lovers I would be the first to know of it.'

'He has not spoken to you about her?'

'He has not.'

Leonora breathed a sigh of relief until Charlotte's next remark.

'That does not surprise me in the slightest. He is far too much the gentleman to actually *name* the lady with whom he is romantically involved.'

'You look for intrigue where there is none,' Malcolm laughed. 'You may rest assured that Lukan is not involved with Harriet Wyndham, though to satisfy your feminine curiosity I will say this: he knows that she would rectify the situation in a moment, given half the chance.'

'I knew it,' Charlotte grinned, clapping her hands together in triumph. 'I knew there was *something* between them.'

'Charlotte dear, Malcolm has already explained that there is nothing but a long-standing acquaintance between them.'

'Nonsense,' she insisted, then leaned across the table to peer into her brother's face. 'You say she has already made her feelings known to him?'

333

Malcolm nodded. 'There has been a certain understanding there for many years, an understanding, I hasten to add, of which Lukan has declined to take advantage.'

'He has turned her down?'

'He has.'

'In favour of whom?'

'In favour of nobody that I know of. Lukan is very discreet, even secretive in these matters.'

'Then how can you be so certain that there is still nothing between them?'

'He would have told me.'

'I think not.'

'You do not know him as I do.'

'I know enough to believe he does not live in celibacy.'

'Charlotte, really!' Leonora had been following the banter between brother and sister with interest. She was trapped in a dilemma, desperate to uncover a truth from which she shied in dread.

'He does not,' Charlotte insisted. 'He is neither monk nor unmanly. He is a man like any other man, with the same needs and desires.'

'I think this conversation has exceeded the bounds of common decency,' Malcolm said, only half-mocking. 'Ladies, may I suggest that we enjoy our meal and leave Lukan de Ville to enjoy his private life in *private*?'

Charlotte grinned and winked an eye at Leonora. 'I will drop the matter only if you promise to ask him for the truth of it yourself,' she said.

'What? I would not dream of it.'

'Why not, you are the best of friends, are you not?'

'We are, but even so I would not dream of putting such a question to him.'

'Very well,' Charlotte said, sitting back with a satisfied smile. 'Leonora and I will simply have to assume that what we saw today was a true representation of the facts.' She pursed her lips and shook her head thoughtfully. 'I wonder how long it will take the gossip to reach his ears, and how it will have been elaborated upon by then?'

'Charlotte Cavendish!' Malcolm's voice had a warning edge.

'Yes dear?' she asked innocently.

He scowled, knowing that she would have her way whatever his sentiments. 'Very well, I will ask Lukan outright if he and Harriet are lovers,' he conceded. 'And I hope for your sake as well as mine that I do not receive a punch on the nose for my insolence.'

The matter might have ended there had Charlotte not been so determined to get to the bottom of it. She pestered her brother at every opportunity until, almost a week after her initial query, he was at last able to relate his friend's negative response to the enquiry.

'And let that be an end of it,' he told her firmly. 'No more of your foolish speculation, if you please. Lukan was most emphatic about it. There is nothing between himself and Mrs Wyndham but long acquaintance and mutual respect.'

Lying in bed beside Leonora that night, however, he told a very different story. Lukan, he felt, had been less than honest with him.

'I have never known him to be evasive, yet he parried the question like a prisoner in the dock before finally giving me an answer.'

Leonora felt elation give way to dismay. 'Perhaps he felt that you had encroached upon his privacy,' she suggested. 'Even the closest of friends must keep *some* secrets from each other.'

Malcolm shook his head doubtfully. Lukan had weighed the question carefully before attempting to deflect it. It was not like him. He rarely volunteered information of that nature but neither was he in the habit of sidestepping a direct question from Malcolm, no matter how personal it might be. The black eyes had watched him almost furtively and he had sensed the presence of a barrier that should have had no place in their conversation.

'Do you think he lied to you?' Leonora asked as if reading his mind.

'I cannot be sure,' Malcolm confessed. 'If so it makes no

sense. Why on earth should Lukan feel he has to lie to me, of all people, about any feelings he might have for Harriet Wyndham?'

Leonora turned her face into the pillows, feigning drowsiness. Her eyes were filled with tears and she felt such an ache in her heart that she wanted to release it with a scream. 'Why indeed?' she asked, her anguished voice muffled by the pillows. 'Why indeed?'

II

Midsummer's Eve was uncommonly warm. The air was still and heavy with the scent of clover as a cloudless day became a sultry evening. Restless again, Leonora decided to visit the heronry to see the chicks. The herons' clacking, rat-tat voices could be heard from the house and their busy activities viewed from some of the upper windows, but Leonora wanted to see the young chicks at close quarters. She walked with Malcolm as far as the main stable enclosure and saw the two wolfhounds, Garvey and Gillan, waiting outside the gate for their master. Her heart leapt as they rose to their feet and loped forward to greet her. Malcolm instinctively raised his stick in her defence but the wolfhounds, never boisterous and excitable like ordinary dogs, merely leaned their shoulders against her skirts and nuzzled their faces into her hands. They came with her as far as the heronry and then, like silent escorts there for her protection, accompanied her back to the stable gate. She waited outside with Anabel, content to obey the Earl's instructions to avoid the potential hazards of the stables. She waited hopefully despite the many disappointments of recent months, but once again the man she looked for declined to appear. The familiar rumble of his voice reached her ears, she recognised the ring of his riding boots in the cobbled yard and that was all. His whistle plucked the dogs from her as if they were attached to him by strings and he left the stables by a rear entrance, leading Raven by the reins, avoiding her.

Standing alone with Anabel, Leonora clasped her hands over her swollen stomach and willed herself to conceal the turmoil inside her. She felt torn apart by her conflicting emotions. The child she carried was desperately important to her, and yet because of it the man she loved had closed his heart against her. In her selfishness she had assumed that he would share her joy in the child that was to secure her future and fulfil her dream. Only now was she beginning to understand how cruelly she had hurt him. Into a situation already charged with guilt and overshadowed by sorrow she had proudly thrust the presence of her unborn child, Malcolm's child. She had brandished it before her lover as a personal triumph, thrown the fact of it into his face and expected him to accept it without complaint. More than that, she had failed to realise that what she was doing would break his heart.

'Leonora!' There was a warning note in Anabel's voice. One of the maids was hovering nearby, wide-eyed as she anticipated the signal that would send her scampering off to raise the alarm that her mistress was ill.

'I am well. Do not concern yourself,' Leonora said.

'You should not have come here,' Anabel admonished. 'The stables are no place for a woman in your condition.'

Leonora smiled but her eyes were bleak. 'It's Midsummer's Eve,' she said.

Anabel nodded sadly. 'I know, child.'

Midsummer's Eve was the anniversary of Leonora's first meeting with Lukan de Ville. That first brief encounter, with its elements of mystery, danger and romance, had changed her life, her very destiny. She would not believe that now, just one year later, she had lost him.

The two women walked arm-in-arm back to the house, the maids close behind them, while Malcolm and Sam Cooper, deep in conversation, brought up the rear. Leonora did not look back to see the mounted man crossing the meadow at full gallop, heading for the forest with his fleet-footed hounds racing on ahead.

337

It took every ounce of her considerable powers of persuasion to convince her husband and father-in-law that she
should be allowed to attend the opening ceremony of the
Midsummer Fair. A brief appearance was all she asked. This
was the famous Great Fair, the highlight of the Beresford year
and the most important celebration in the whole calendar. For
Leonora it was special because so much of her future had been
decided there a year ago. It had been the last happy time her
family had shared together before disaster struck. It had given
her a glimpse of what the future held in store if only she had
the fortitude to grasp it and the resilience to hold on to what
she took. And more, it had provided the moment when she
and Lukan first came face to face and saw each other in the
light of day, the moment when they knew beyond all doubt
that they would be lovers.

'You may stay for the opening ceremony,' the Earl agreed.
'There have been rumours, and your presence there will still
any doubt remaining as to the health and safety of Malcolm's
heir.'

Malcolm roared with laughter at his father's words. 'So, she
has you convinced at last that the child will be a boy?'

Sir Oscar spread his hands, smiling. 'When the mother is so
certain, how can a mere grandfather say otherwise?'

'And if it proves to be a girl in spite of that?'

'Then your daughter,' the Earl declared, feigning fierceness,
'will answer to the name of William unless you, my boy,
undertake to try again.'

And so Leonora's visit to the Great Fair was decided upon,
and that night she barely slept a wink in her excitement.
Round and around in her head went the ancient rhyme,
chanted by children and adults alike as they jumped the dying
embers of fires for good luck or hid sprigs of willow beneath
their pillows, hoping to see the face of their future partner in
their dreams.

'Fairy's halo round the moon
Wish a wish and have it soon
Fire's ash, midnight's dew
Bring by day a lover true.'

338

She too had sung the rhyme a year ago and then, as now, her dreams had been filled with images of Lukan.

From dawn on Midsummer's Day the decorated carts trundled between Beresford Hall and Kingswood village. They carried the Earl's annual gift of potatoes for roasting, freshly baked bread, fruit from the orchards, cheese from the dairy and dozens of barrels of strong Beresford ale. The morning would be raw with the sights and sounds of the market place as cattle and sheep came under the hammer and farmers, breeders and peddlers fought to secure the day's profits. Among them would be poor men seeking fair payment for the season's labours, able-bodied men and women looking for employment, pickpockets in search of an easy purse. The whole area would be seething with gypsies and travelling performers, people of every skill, craft and trade, some from as far away as Bristol, Brighton, Oxford and London. They would find here a wealth of goods to buy or trade, from cattle and sheep to sewing thread, from candles and wicks to thorough-breds, from a fancy carriage and pair to a lowly servant. By long tradition the gentry arrived in the afternoon when most of the cattle and sheep had been disposed of. They came for the horse-trading and the games, the colourful stalls and sideshows, the races, wrestling matches, cock-fights and dog-fights. They came to buy up the quality goods of impoverished gentlemen, to lay wagers or strike some bargain in smuggled or stolen property, to hire young girls not for a willing arm but for the swell of a pert young bosom or the firm roundness of a nubile thigh. Most of all these people came to be parted from their money, and with temptation baring its breast at every turn, the contents of jangling purses rapidly changed hands.

For the occasion Leonora chose to wear a shot-silk cloak of midnight blue lined with flaming crimson silk and trimmed with a narrow gold and black braid. These were the Earl's own colours, and set around its hem was a pattern in braid made up of the Cavendish family crest. She had ordered the cloak to be made specially for just such an occasion. She wore it over a dress of palest blue so full and beautifully gathered

339

from the bodice that none but the most critical eye would note the changes in her figure. She decided that her hair would be dressed with the tiny glass beads she so loved for their twinkling colours, and with sprigs of imitation Wolf's Bane to echo the turquoise toning of her eyes. Secretly, she wore the flower for Lukan and knew that if they met face to face he would have no doubt of it. Later she saw in Malcolm's face that she looked stunning, and saw it too in Sir Oscar's smile of approval.

She travelled to the Midsummer Fair in an open landau with Malcolm by her side and Sir Oscar and Sir Marcus Shaw sharing the opposite seat. The four mile journey along the Drive of Oaks was a pleasure in itself. The trees were in full leaf and formed a canopy of green above them, dappled with sunlight yet cool and softly shaded. The narrow road was busy with farm carts, hand carts and burdened individuals making their way to the fair to sell or trade their wares. Groups of grubby children ran alongside, begging for coins or trying to snatch tit-bits from passing carts. The Earl's party was made up of two landaus and a larger carriage. Lady Elizabeth had been allowed to join them, but the servants had strict instructions to keep her from wandering off alone and losing herself in the crowds.

Leonora felt her excitement begin to mount as her landau lurched slightly on the steep approach to the village. Word of their arrival had sped ahead of them. They were greeted by tumultuous applause and cheers, and it was some time before they realised that the greeting was not for the Earl and his generous gifts to the Great Fair, nor for Malcolm his son and heir. Their cheers were for Leonora. She was the fairy-tale figure from the Hall, the fine young lady who had overcome great personal tragedy to marry the handsomest, most eligible nobleman in the country. She was also the first lady of Beresford in living memory who treated her servants as if they were human beings. She made sure her staff had decent wages and good living conditions, and she protected the women from the men in her employ. The people loved her for it.

Leonora acknowledged the deafening cheers with smiles

and waves. Her reputation had certainly not suffered from a particular incident that took place just after the Christmas celebrations. A thirteen-year-old maid-of-all-work was raped by a gardener who had climbed in through an open kitchen window. Leonora had been on her way to the tower when the man entered the main corridor by the servants' stair, his face scratched and bloodied and his clothes in disarray. Upstairs she had found the girl sobbing in the corner of her tiny room. She had been raped and beaten while the other servants, too terrified to intervene, had closed their ears to her cries. Leonora had been outraged. On her own initiative she had the man flogged and then dismissed on the spot without references. She ordered bolts to be fitted to the inside of every bedroom door in the servants' wing and several trusted senior servants to be made supervisors over the younger, more vulnerable girls. Then she let it be known that the smallest complaint of male harassment from any woman in her employ would be immediately investigated and acted upon.

'This cannot go on,' she told Anabel at the time, pacing the room while her temper simmered. 'I will not have it. I will not tolerate this casual abuse of women.'

Anabel had sighed and shaken her head. 'It is the way of things. The whole world is designed for the ease and pleasure of our menfolk and you, more than anyone I know, should be perfectly aware of how we women are placed in it.'

'Not here,' Leonora had declared passionately. 'Not while I am Mistress of Beresford.'

'But it has always been so.'

Leonora narrowed her eyes and hissed out the words, '*But not any more.*'

Anabel smiled indulgently. 'I understand your feelings child, but you cannot change the whole world, just because you wish it to be different.'

'Perhaps not, but I can change my own small part of it. Oh Anabel, this kind of thing disgusts me. We are surrounded by men, like my own father, who seem to think that every female has been bred solely for their own convenience. They do with us what they will. They believe they are the masters and we the slaves, and who will ever teach them otherwise?'

'Calm yourself child. Remember the little one you carry.'

Leonora's anger had been unyielding. 'From this moment on I will have it known that no woman under my roof will be molested by any man, be he servant or gentleman,' she declared. 'And if any guest, however important, dares to lay his hands on one of my maids I will have him tossed off the premises and publicly exposed for the scoundrel he is.'

Malcolm had neither scoffed at nor dismissed her high-minded ideas. He was a reasonable man and he was deeply concerned that incidents of that nature would be detrimental to his wife's peace of mind. What she proposed was unheard of, yet he would not deny her something about which she had such strong emotions. And so the precedent was set, and soon word spread beyond the Hall that on Beresford soil young women came under the protection of the Earl and his family.

Leonora was reminded of all this as she was handed down from the landau and led, flanked by her husband and Sir Oscar, through the press of cheering people. They went directly to a small podium hung with a fancy canvass awning and decorated with the Earl's insignia. She climbed the steps and moved to the low safety rail, where she stood with her head thrown back and her face lit with excitement. Sunlight twinkled with all the colours of the rainbow in the tiny beads in her dark hair. It lay a sheen as pretty as mother-of-pearl on the smooth, silken surface of her gown. From there she looked out upon a sea of faces, her nostrils assaulted by the mingled odours of roasting meat, cattle dung, hot fruit pies, wine, ale and the stench of men and horses. Her ears rang with sounds from human and animal throats, poultry squawking, children's shrieks, peddlers' calls, traders' songs and travelling singers and musicians. She sucked in the heady atmosphere with every breath. Her senses had been dulled and pampered too long, and she recharged them now with the intoxicating rawness of her surroundings.

Suddenly she became aware that her father-in-law had abandoned his customary speech as Lord of the Great Fair and was holding out the magnificent silver toasting goblet to

342

her. He was inviting her to complete the opening ceremony, to make the final toast on his behalf. She hesitated and heard the crowd cheer its encouragement. No woman, not even the late Countess Alyce, had ever opened the Great Fair. This was a tradition reserved for the Earl or his heir, and in their absence a close male relative of suitable standing.

'Take it,' the Earl said, reading her thoughts. 'Dare to be first.'

'Oh, I dare,' Leonora told him, and her smile was brilliant. 'Have no doubt that I dare.'

She grasped the handles of the goblet in both hands and held it high above her head until the cheering of the crowd became a roar. A group of women near the front started to chant, 'Lee ... a ... nora! Lee ... a ... nora!' Soon the call was taken up by the crowds until the sound of her own name rang in her ears like a tolling bell. Excited, elated, she drank from the goblet and raised it high above her head a second time, encouraging their cheers.

When at last she was steered down the wooden steps from the podium with several of the Earl's men forcing a way for her through the crush of people, she was beginning to feel light-headed and slightly ill. A man pushed past them carrying a long pole on which hung the bodies of several freshly-killed rabbits. Trapped on the warm summer air the smell of their blood reached her nostrils and she was forced to grasp Malcolm's arm for support. Minutes later they passed the pig-pens and her head swam with nausea. In the carriage she was handed a fan and a tiny bottle of smelling salts, both of which she managed to use with barely an outward hint of her discomfort. She would not have missed this moment for the world. To become the darling of the common people, even if she remained so only for the duration of the midsummer celebrations, was an accolade indeed. With all her skills she could not have engineered such a tremendous welcome, and Sir Oscar's unexpected generosity had taken her completely by surprise. It meant she had another important precedent to her credit. This day's events would never be forgotten. Lady Leonora, wife of Sir Malcolm Cavendish, had become the first woman ever to make the official opening of the Great

Midsummer Fair. Moreover, she had done so with the blessing of the people.

She rode back to Beresford Hall in the company of her husband, Anabel and the two maids. Sir Marcus and Sir Oscar had decided to remain at the fair and Malcolm promised to rejoin them there after seeing Leonora safely home. The Earl would be showing his famous heavyweights later in the day and was keen to look them over before the show began. As the open landau made the steep right turn at the crossroads, Leonora looked back through the wrought-iron gateway that bore the Cavendish insignia. Kingswood village sprawled at the foot of the hill, its collection of squat stone buildings blonded by the warm sunshine. Every inch of space between them seemed to have been claimed by makeshift stalls, carts, tents, pens of livestock and huge piles of dry goods. The village green and the grassy slopes leading down to the river were cluttered with similar structures and hastily erected animal pens. All along the riverbank people were gathering together in groups to eat food freshly cooked at the stalls and to fill their tankards from the Earl's barrels. Beyond the river she could see the gypsy caravans with their accompanying camp fires and hoards of ragged children. Last year the gypsy woman had told her fortune and she, Leonora, had lived out her words to the full.

'*You will love two men, one with your heart, the other with your soul,*' the gypsy woman had told her.

And Leonora, haughty and sceptical at seventeen, had tossed her head and asked, '*Is there a difference?*'

She smiled at the memory. She was older now and wiser by a year, and she had learned the difference to her cost.

Some distance along the Drive of Oaks the landau and its escort carriages were driven off the road to allow the Earl's heavyweights to pass. They clattered along in a group of twenty-two, all huge, magnificent beasts with massive shoulders, glossy coats and fluttering silken feathers at their ankles. Harnesses jangling, brasses gleaming, polished leathers creaking, they came on with steaming breath and tossing heads. Eleven liveried grooms kept them in charge, each one mounted and with a second horse in tow. In the lead was a tall, dark man not wearing the Earl's colours but dressed instead in a white shirt, high boots, maroon breeches and a soft, rust-coloured leather jerkin. His hair was tightly bound at the nape of his neck and his intense dark eyes looked neither to the left nor to the right. Leonora's heart leaped at the sight of him. His skin had the glow of summer on it and his hair seemed longer and more glossy. She noticed an unsightly wound on one muscular forearm and it pained her to think that he had suffered an injury without her being aware of it. Anabel squeezed her arm with both hands to alert her to the dangers of the situation. Sir Malcolm was sitting in the opposite seat, watching her for any signs of fatigue. One careless slip and her secret would be out. He must not see what shone so clearly in his wife's eyes when she looked at that gypsy.

The incident was over in a matter of seconds. The great heavyweights thundered past on their way to the fair and the landau was pulled back on to the open road to continue its journey. Beresford Hall loomed ahead, its stained glass windows and glittering fountains made crystal in the sunlight. Leonora saw none of it. Her thoughts were on Lukan, who had loved her once but now could pass her by without a sideways glance as if for him she no longer existed. At the main gatehouse she and her maids were set down and the landau turned around to carry Malcolm back to Kingswood.

She was crossing the paved main courtyard with Anabel in close attendance when she stopped dead in her tracks, feeling her spirits soar. She realised with a shock that she had seen a splash of mauve-blue at Lukan's breast, a sprig of flowers attached to his jerkin the way she had pinned the first sprig there so many long months ago.

'For you, my Lia,' he had told her then with laughter dancing in his eyes. 'For the colour of your eyes and for the sting of your temper I will wear this devil's-blossom over my heart. And when I do, be sure I think of you.'

'Wolf's Bane,' she whispered now, touching the silken replicas trimming her bonnet as her face lit with a brilliant smile. 'He remembered! He was wearing *Wolf's Bane*!'

345

CHAPTER SEVENTEEN

I

By mid-July Leonora had virtually confined herself to the house. There was no concealing her pregnancy now with carefully cut gowns and cleverly shaped bodices, no hiding the child she carried behind the flounces and folds of pretty fabric. She was nearing her eighth month, glowing with good health and still vain enough to want to attach a little mystery to her condition. There was also one consideration that rarely slipped far from the very forefront of her mind: she would not have Lukan see her like this. Since that last brief glimpse of him riding the heavyweights with a sprig of purple Wolf's Bane pinned to his breast she had known that they were still one, and that soon they would be lovers once again. She wanted no image of her pregnancy to be stamped upon his mind when that day came. There must be no memories of another shape, an alien aspect of her womanhood, to cloud his vision of her when she returned to him. She must be the same as before. In fact and in remembrance she must always be the same for him.

What had once been the cloister of the old abbey was now an enclosed inner courtyard with a rectangular pond, ornamental fountains and covered walkways hung with honeysuckle, passion flower and rich green ivy. The late Countess Alyce had given her famous garden parties here, those splendid affairs at which no expense was spared in order to make an impression on guests too wealthy and flamboyant to be easily astonished by grand displays. Leonora still had water-lilies floating on the pond. Drowned ladies, Elizabeth insisted they were, drowned ladies with their skirts and petticoats turned up and their pretty faces buried in the weeds beneath the surface.

She also had the water in the fountains dyed deep blue for best effect, and every recess set with hanging plants to create a measure of privacy for the occupants. Arches of trellis supported the plants and created charming archways through which sunshine poured to leave patterns in a pretty marbled effect on the ground below. In these final weeks the courtyard had become her personal retreat. She could take her daily exercise here or rest for long periods with her books or her needlework during the long hot days of summer. She could walk alone in the quiet cool of the evening, receive guests in the comfort of a shaded arbour, even dine here in the open air whenever she desired. The courtyard had a calming quality that she found beneficial, a protective stillness evoking those bygone days of silent, pious monks and murmured prayers. It had become her sanctuary, and only when she looked up at the lofty ivy-clad wall of the tower, with its slits of windows and cherished secrets, did she feel a twinge of sadness in that peaceful place.

On a glorious July day, Harriet Wyndham was shown into the courtyard by a very proud and solemn-looking Charlie Pickles. Dressed in a re-cut uniform of the Earl's colours and wearing boots that were a perfect fit for his small feet, the boy marched ahead of the lady until he reached the shaded arbour where Leonora waited. Once there he announced the visitor by name, bowed as low as was humanly possible whilst still retaining his hat, turned smartly and marched away with the comic gait of a little clockwork soldier.

'My dear Mrs Wyndham, how very pleasant it is to see you again,' Leonora beamed.

'It was gracious of you to invite me, Lady Cavendish.'

In separate arbours ladies of all ages sat with their delicate china tea cups and plates of dainty cream and chocolate cakes. There was a brief lull in their conversations, a pause for the turning of heads and raising of brows in the late-comer's direction. The talk only resumed its busy-insect drone after Harriet had curtsied and smiled a greeting intended to encompass them all.

'I will introduce you to my other guests when we have talked for a while in private,' Leonora promised. 'Come, seat yourself beside me in the shade and Anabel will pour you some tea. Or perhaps you would prefer lemonade?'

'A cold drink if I may, Your Ladyship.' Despite feeling a little out of her depth and unsure of herself, Harriet's smile did not falter for a moment as she settled herself in a well-padded garden seat and accepted the tall glass of refreshingly cold lemonade. She had not expected to receive this invitation. Throughout the summer she had used every ruse imaginable to place herself among the guests on the lush green lawns of Beresford Hall. She had bribed Lettice Holland at every opportunity, had even forced herself to risk social embarrassment by tagging along with friendly groups when no direct invitation was forthcoming. On one occasion, determined not to miss one of Leonora's garden parties, she had ridden the common mail coach as far as Kingswood and had set out to walk the four miles from there to the big house. As she had anticipated, the first private carriage bearing a guest to Beresford Hall was ordered to stop and offer the unescorted lady assistance. Its elderly occupant listened with a sympathetic ear while she explained how a shattered wheel-rim had delayed her carriage at the blacksmith's shop in the nearby village, and how no decent conveyance could be found in which she might complete her journey. She arrived at Beresford that day accompanied by no lesser personage than Sir Marcus Shaw, who took it upon himself to introduce her to several other guests of distinction. She left on the arm of doctor Richard Winterton, whose company was amusing but whose income was not to be taken seriously. Thanks to these craftily engineered connections her social life had been greatly enriched and her personal status much improved. She had come a long way in one short summer season, and she had achieved it all without the benefit of a single official invitation. Until now.

Leonora sipped her tea thoughtfully as she studied the smooth, attractive features of her guest. By now she knew a great deal about Mrs Harriet Wyndham. She knew about her childless marriage and the crippling terms of her late husband's will, about her hostile mother-in-law, her occasional lovers and her recent attempts to ensnare the ageing Augustus Sharpe into marriage. What she still did not understand was the woman's connection with Lukan de Ville. According to her informants, Lukan had visited Lower Prescot Hall a half dozen times during the last few months, staying just long enough to share a game of chess and a glass or two of brandy with Thomas Harding. One of Harriet's servants insisted that the mistress was never a party to these meetings, only joining the men for ten minutes or so at the end of each game. It was clear that Lukan de Ville was not Harriet's guest but her father's. He went to Lower Prescot Hall not to see the lady of the house but to pay his respects to the elderly gentleman living there. That information should have satisfied Leonora but in fact it came not half-way to doing so. How much of it was truth and how much lies? Keeping the truth from servants had become a way of life for her, and as yet she had no reason to suspect that Harriet Wyndham was any less artful than herself in that respect.

Leonora swallowed a sudden wave of jealousy and, following the example of Charlotte Cavendish, came directly to the point on another matter. 'You seem to have a special interest in Lady Roanne, my late aunt. May I ask why?'

A small patch of colour appeared on Harriet's cheeks. 'I am simply intrigued by the story,' she replied.

'Oh? And which story might that be? I understand there are many, and the majority of them are so fanciful as to deserve not a grain of credence from any person of intelligence.'

'And which one should I believe?'

Leonora returned her smile. The woman was clever. All summer she had schemed and plotted to ingratiate herself with the people at Beresford Hall while lacking every social qualification for doing so. Her courage and resourcefulness were to be admired. Leonora and Charlotte had watched her progress closely, marking every move and manoeuvre that brought her more firmly within the ranks of what was now known as the 'Beresford Set'. Her ingenuity was indisputable. What remained was to discover exactly what this ambitious woman was after.

'The truth of it is simple and, I fear, somewhat lacking in excitement,' she said. 'Poor Lady Roanne developed a high fever and died here at Beresford Hall when she was only seventeen. I suppose there is always speculation when a young woman dies in her bed at such a tender age. I believe some even said at the time that she was poisoned by a dish of mushrooms that were picked in error by an ignorant maidservant and prepared by a cook with poor eyesight.'

Harriet laughed prettily, then looked at Leonora directly and said, 'Some even whispered that she died in childbirth.'

'Childbirth? Ah yes, all empty-headed gossips seem to fall back on that solution.' Leonora sighed and shook her head sadly. 'Alas, how does any woman avoid such rumours?'

'How indeed?'

Leonora sipped her tea. She had suspected all along that Harriet was after the facts behind the thirty-year-old scandal, but even now Sir Oscar was so keen to keep them hidden that her own discreet attempts to uncover the story had so far come to nothing. She had seen the tiny headstone in the crypt and the pale patch where Roanne's picture had once hung on the wall in the Great Gallery, and that was all. The rest might well be documented somewhere in the hoard of books and papers making up the old Countess's journals, but as yet Leonora had shrunk from the arduous task of sifting, sorting, reading and dating that dusty chest-load of paperwork. Other than that her own inquiries had met with no success. If there really was a mystery here it had been expertly concealed.

'My father knew her,' Harriet said into the silence that had fallen between them. 'He worked as a coachman to the Earl and remembers the lady well.'

'Then perhaps your father is the one to whom you should be speaking,' Leonora suggested, knowing full well that it could only have been Thomas Harding's recollections that inspired his daughter to seek out the true story behind those old rumours.

Harriet shook her head. 'He knows only what was said at the time.'

Leonora laughed prettily. 'In that case he relies on gossip and foolish country talk and must have a great many interesting stories to tell.'

'Perhaps, but only one to which he attaches any credence.'

'Oh? Do tell me about it.'

'Forgive me, Lady Leonora, but I don't believe I should. You see, it concerns the date on which she died and I . . .'

'December 2nd 1795,' Leonora said on impulse, altering the true date to undermine the woman's confidence in what she had been told. It was an instinctive lie hastily uttered. If Harriet Wyndham's knowledge of events depended upon that one small fact then it must be taken away from her. Only the headstone existed in fact. All else was nothing more than idle gossip remembered by a drunken old man after three decades.

Harriet looked incredulous. 'December 2nd 1795?' she echoed. 'But that cannot be so.'

'I beg your pardon?' Leonora asked, feigning surprise. 'I can assure you Mrs Wyndham that the date on the stone is exactly as I said, December 2nd 1795.'

'Oh but I thought . . .?' Harriet paused with a frown. 'I was led to believe that she died a year earlier, and on the 12th.'

'How strange, but I assure you I am quite certain of the date. The poor young thing lies in the family crypt beside her parents.'

'May I ask if you have seen the grave for yourself?'

'Indeed I have, as recently as last October when the old Countess was interred. There is no mistake, believe me.'

351

'The mistake was mine. I have been wrongly informed.'

'Does it matter?' Leonora asked innocently.

'Of course not.'

'Then may I ask you to do me a special kindness, Mrs Wyndham?'

'Most certainly, and please feel free to call me Harriet.'

'Thank you so much. The kindness I ask is this: be a little more discreet in your curiosity about my family's history. My father-in-law, the Earl, is highly sensitive where such personal matters are concerned. He loved his sister deeply and he is not a man who forgets a sorrow easily. Please have a care in what you say. I would hate to see him hurt, or see such a nice person as yourself suddenly ostracised from our society for want of a timely word of advice.'

Harriet Wyndham stared into the deep turquoise eyes and felt a chilling layer of gooseflesh raise itself along her forearms. Was this a friendly warning or a threat? Was this very beautiful young woman telling her to drop her interest in Roanne Cavendish or else find herself put out of society and counted amongst the family's enemies? If so, the lady need say nothing more. Harriet's interest in Roanne had already been superseded by the pleasures of social advancement. Her plan to extract silence money from Sir Oscar had wilted when she first became aware of the very real power he and his family were able to wield over the lives of others. She would not play David to the Earl's Goliath, nor make an enemy of such a man for any price. She had acquired a taste for gracious living and wanted nothing more than to be part of all this. And now that she had actually received her first direct invitation from the Viscountess Leonora herself, her priorities had been well and truly reshaped.

She set down her glass of lemonade and folded her hands very neatly in her lap. 'Your Ladyship, I humbly beg your pardon,' she said. 'I am ashamed to admit that it did not occur to me that my childish curiosity might cause your family distress.'

Leonora hastened to reassure her. 'To the best of my knowledge the Earl knows nothing of your probing, though Lady

Charlotte has been made most anxious over your questioning of the servants.'

Harriet looked stricken, as well she might, since Charlotte and the Earl were known to be extremely close. 'Then I must go to her at once and beg her forgiveness.'

'There is no need,' Leonora smiled, moved by what she saw in the other woman's eyes. It still offended her that the quality of a woman's existence could depend so much on the good partronage of others. A word from Leonora now and Harriet Wyndham would be a social outcast. 'Allow me to speak to my sister-in-law on your behalf,' she smiled. 'I am confident that she will be placated.'

'Would you do that for me? I surely do not deserve such consideration, but I would be so grateful to you.'

'It will be my pleasure, and you may judge the matter closed with no real harm done.'

'Thank you, Your Ladyship.'

'Now Harriet, there is something more I wish to put to you, something of a personal nature.' She made a show of looking all about her to ensure that her words would not be overheard, then leaned over to place her hand on Harriet's arm. 'May I be blunt?'

'Of course you may.'

'You will not take offence?'

'Not where offence is not intended.'

'Good.' Leonora leaned a little closer. 'I understand that Mr Augustus Sharpe is rather keen to make you his wife. Is my information correct?'

Harriet's cheeks coloured hotly. 'Well, he has certainly given Mr Harding and myself certain hints that such a proposal might be in the offing,' she admitted.

'I see, and would you be prepared to accept such a proposal?'

'I do believe I might,' Harriet nodded. 'He seems sincere in his suit and I, unfortunately, am in no position to turn down an offer from so wealthy and respected a gentleman.'

'And there is nobody else you might prefer, no secret lover who has prior claim on your heart?' Leonora watched the woman's eyes, dreading what she might be about to learn, determined to have the truth.

Harriet laughed even as she thought of Lukan. 'My heart remains my own,' she said. 'As for my preferences, well, I might have wished for a younger and more handsome husband.'

'I'm sure you would, but there will be ample compensation with Mr Sharpe. I believe he is both wealthy and generous, a happy combination.'

'Happy enough for me,' Harriet smiled.

'Then I will encourage him to speak out on the matter. He really is quite besotted, I believe.'

'He is?'

'Certainly, but many men are cowards when it comes to braving marriage, and the older they get the harder it is for them to make the commitment.' She patted Harriet's arm and smiled her most disarming smile. She saw no reason to mention the fact that Mr Augustus Sharpe would wed himself to a serving wench if he suspected he might please Sir Oscar Cavendish by doing so. 'Leave it to us, Harriet. Once he has our assurances that his proposal will not be rejected, I am certain he will feel able to hurry things along to their conclusion. I think we may safely expect to see your engagement announced within the month.'

'Your Ladyship, I really do not know what to say. I find myself quite overwhelmed by your kindness.'

'Nonsense, I will be happy to help get you settled and to see you suitably escorted to my future functions. In the meantime let me introduce you to some people who have not yet had the pleasure of meeting you personally.' She rose from her seat and led Harriet by the arm to a small, flower-draped alcove in which were gathered several elderly ladies of quality. 'Ladies, please allow me to introduce my dear friend Mrs Harriet Wyndham.'

Within minutes Harriet was whisked away to meet the other guests and Leonora rejoined Anabel in her favourite arbour. Anabel watched her face.

'I see you are looking very pleased with youself, Leonora.

354

What secrets did you manage to extract from the widow?'

Leonora settled herself once again in her comfortable chair and sighed contentedly. 'I discovered very little beyond the fact that she, like all of us, has a keen sense of self-preservation. I have promised to speak to that old bag of bones Augustus Sharpe on her behalf.'

'I was not aware that matchmaking was one of your special skills, my lady.'

'In this case you can be sure it is. I want that woman married off as soon as possible.'

'And beyond the reach of Lukan de Ville?'

'Oh, don't sound so disapproving, Anabel. I am merely protecting what is mine.'

'Yours?' Anabel repeated the word with marked incredulity. 'You *dare* to think of him as yours?'

'Aye *mine*!' Leonora hissed through her teeth. 'You know I will never share him with another woman.'

Anabel replied in a sharp whisper, 'By Heaven, you are a selfish little madam when it suits you, Leonora Cavendish. She's a nice enough woman with no man of her own and nothing to look forward to but marriage to a doddering old fool more than twice her age.'

'Harriet Wyndham's misfortunes are not my concern,' Leonora said dryly. 'I will certainly not stand idly by while Lukan becomes the source of her consolation.'

'No, because you are as selfish as you are cruel. Let the gypsy have his time with her if she pleases him. Lord knows he gets little enough of *anything* from you.'

'I will not share him,' Leonora hissed.

'Then give him up.'

'I will not.'

'If not for your own sake do it for his. Do the decent thing for once, Leonora. Give him his freedom to love elsewhere.'

'Never!' Leonora clenched her fists and her face paled under the strain of suppressing her anger. 'Damn your good intentions, Anabel Corey. I will never give Lukan up, *never*.'

Several heads turned in their direction, inquisitive faces looking and listening for anything of interest. They saw only

355

the young Viscountess discreetly admonishing her companion for some misdemeanour of which only those involved were aware.

'All right, all right,' Anabel soothed. 'Calm down Leonora. Don't go upsetting yourself and unsettling the child. Have it your own way, since you refuse to acknowledge the value and good sense of any other.'

When the guests began to leave, Leonora walked with Harriet Wyndham to the small carriage that had been placed at her disposal. By now she had recovered her composure and was determined to add the finishing touches to her handiwork.

'I do hope we can be friends,' she said.

Harriet beamed. 'I can think of nothing I would appreciate more.'

'Except the security of an early marriage, perhaps?' Leonora suggested.

'Alas, we women are all too often forced to resort to devious methods for our own protection.'

'Indeed we are.' Leonora glanced sideways but saw nothing untoward in the remark. 'And now I must bid you goodbye until the next time. Will you accept a small parting gift from someone who has your well-being at heart?'

'Your Ladyship, you have already been most kind.'

'And now I wish you to accept my gift in the manner in which it is offered. Will you do that?'

'I can hardly refuse such generosity.'

'Good. I have had it placed in your carriage, and let us speak of it no more. Goodbye, Harriet.'

'Goodbye, Lady Cavendish, and thank you so much.'

She was handed into the carriage by Sam Cooper and had settled into her seat before she spotted the gift Leonora had referred to. Across the empty seat lay two beautiful silk and muslin gowns and a superb afternoon dress in patterned maroon satin. Beside them were two large hat boxes bearing the late Countess's distinctive monogram. Harriet gasped and wheeled to comment on the gift, but by then Leonora was walking back across the lawn on the arm of her personal maid.

She turned to wave as she reached a short flight of steps and Harriet, on impulse, leaned from the carriage window and, laughing happily, blew her hostess a kiss.

Anabel Corey could not deny that she was impressed. 'And so the trap is sprung and the bunny caught,' she observed. 'It seems the widow is now in your debt several times over.'

Leonora smiled as she watched the coach depart. 'A simple mortgage on my security, Anabel. I will know where I have the widow from now on.'

II

It was a cool and shady spot just off the main bridal path where Lukan chose to dismount and wave Thomas Harding on ahead. His face was grimly set as he lifted Harriet down from her horse. He was angry and made no effort to hide it.

'You are well aware of my feelings on the matter,' he reminded her. 'I dislike this sudden interest of yours in Beresford Hall.'

Harriet shrugged. She was disappointed that he had insisted on taking a ride instead of remaining indoors. She had missed him and now his anger excited her. It was weeks since they had last made love. Her body was hungry for his touch and moist with anticipation. 'My social life should be no concern of yours, Mr de Ville.'

They walked along the woodland path, leading their mounts beneath low-hanging branches bright with sunshine. His voice was low in pitch and heavy with meaning. 'Your social life, Madam, has already involved me in a barefaced lie, one I have been forced to offer the man who least deserves it.'

'How so?' she demanded. 'I have seen you there but once and spoken of you not at all. How could my visits to Beresford Hall have involved you in an untruth?'

'I was obliged to deny that you and I are lovers.'

357

She stopped and looked at him, her eyes dancing with merriment. 'And who, may I ask, has put you under such an obligation?'

'Sir Malcolm Cavendish. He asked me directly.'

'Then you should have told him to mind his own business instead of troubling himself with yours. What right has he to question you on such a personal matter?'

'The right of friendship,' Lukan said. 'He asked and I denied it to his face.'

'Well then the matter is concluded,' she said, smiling.

He scowled at her. 'I suspect that Lady Charlotte and Lady Leonora put him up to it. There has obviously been some gossip among the women. Perhaps, Madam, you have been less than discreet.'

She looked at him directly. 'Then think again, for I have been nothing of the kind.'

'Why would he ask me otherwise?'

Harriet mimicked his scowl. She was growing exasperated. 'I have a better question. What does it matter?'

'It matters to me when I am reduced to lying to a man I respect.'

'Then tell him the truth and have done with it, for Heaven's sake,' she told him sharply.

Lukan narrowed his eyes and breathed through his nose so that his nostrils flared. 'Can you really be as foolish as you appear?' he asked. 'Within the week Augustus Sharpe will be down on one knee begging you to marry him, and you will have Sir Malcolm and his lady to thank for it. How will they feel when they discover they have been tricked, that the lady whose case they have so generously pleaded is not quite the lady she pretends to be?'

'Ah!' Harriet pursed her lips in a thoughtful gesture. 'Now I begin to see the problem. Leonora asked me if there was a man in my life who might prove a bar to the marriage.'

'And you denied there was?'

'I did indeed.'

He shook his head, relieved. 'That lie will cost you dearly if she ever learns the truth.'

Harriet smiled and resumed walking along the path. 'I think you are mistaken, Lukan. You see a problem where none exists. Lady Leonora and I have become the best of friends this summer. This gown I wear is one of hers. She is extremely tenderhearted to those she calls her friends.'

'And deadly to her enemies,' Lukan said, falling into step beside her. 'Remember that.'

They had reached a clearing where tall, slender shoots grew from the stumps of felled trees and sunlight fell in eerie shafts across the mossy ground. Thomas Harding, who had ridden on ahead, awaited them there. He was pushing a small hip flask back into his pocket as they approached.

'Have you finished lecturing me for today, Lukan?' Harriet asked lightly, still hoping to persuade him to return with her to the house. 'May we now speak of more pleasant things?'

He suddenly caught her by the wrist that held the reins and spoke so that her father heard his words. 'Make no errors of judgment here,' he warned. 'You deal with dangerous people when you deal with them. And remember that nothing comes without a price. They have given you friendship, a place in their society, pretty gowns and bonnets, even a wealthy husband. Make sure you are not called upon to pay for those privileges in kind.'

'Really, Lukan, if you think for one moment that I ...' She broke off, wincing as he gripped her wrist more tightly. 'Lukan please, you are hurting me.'

'Have a care, Madam,' he said, his face very close to hers. 'Take warning from one who knows. If ever they suspect that you have been less than honest in your dealings with them, they will strip you back to the bare bones and toss you into the wilderness with nothing. There has never been anything more than friendship between us. Say it, Harriet, *say* it.'

'All right,' she cried, more hurt than angry. 'I'll say it. We are friends and nothing more. Now let me go.'

With a small smile he lifted her hand to his lips and kissed it with unexpected tenderness. His features softened and his voice became more gentle. 'Make sure they always believe that at the Great House and you'll be safe enough, Harriet. You

359

may expect your future husband on Friday morning. I wish you every happiness.'

'Lukan?'

Turning from her he bowed to her father before mounting his horse in a single practised movement. He stooped low on the far side of the clearing to avoid an overhang of leafy branches, and in a moment he was gone. Harriet looked after him with tears stinging her eyes. The parting was final. Lukan was a proud man. She had known in her heart that he would not stay to make a common cuckold of Augustus Sharpe.

'It's over,' she said at last. 'I've lost him.'

Her father shook his head as he led her to her horse and helped her into the saddle. 'He was never yours to lose, my dear. I'll miss him though. He has been good to us.'

'I'll miss him too,' Harriet said.

Thomas Harding took out his handkerchief and handed it up to his daughter without looking at her face. 'No regrets, my girl,' he said brightly. 'Friday morning, Lukan said, and I see no reason for a long delay, once the details have been agreed upon. I think we'll have you safely wed before the year is out.'

'To an old man,' Harriet muttered, as she heeled the pony's flanks and followed her father along the bridal path. 'To an old man. After Lukan de Ville, an ugly, wrinkled old man.'

III

That August was a month of thunderstorms. The tiny church at Judd, already abandoned by its congregation and rarely visited by its rightful vicar, was struck by lightning twice during the same brief tempest. The first flash halved the old steeple and flung its iron weather cock a quarter of a mile into the forest. The second struck the roof like a hammerblow upon a flimsy toy, shattering ancient beams and joists and leaving the church in ruins. The local people saw it as an

360

omen, divine wrath visited upon a godless gathering. They crossed themselves and locked their windows tight, and laughed uneasily at their own fears when the storm had passed. A serious fire broke out at a village near Hill's Edge and was fought throughout the night by men and women with buckets and barrels and a dogged will to snatch what they could from the jaws of the inferno. Four lives were lost that night and one man's livestock burned alive in a blazing barn before it could be freed. It was a strange, unsettled month, hot and still and with the air so charged that simple country people could sense the slightest change in the atmosphere.

Lukan rode to the edge of the forest at midnight. Beyond the oppressive canopy of trees the meadow stretched still and dark and silent. From there he could see the storm on the horizon, lighting the sky in agitated flashes, a battle royal in progress somewhere in the distance. He sniffed the air, his nostrils flaring. He could smell the coppery scent of the thunderstorm tainting the night's humidity with its presence. His dogs were restless, pacing without direction and panting in the still, unnatural heat. They too were alert to the sense of something powerful in the making.

'Easy Gillan. Easy Garvey.' His voice had a soothing tone and the hounds pricked up their ears and whined softly in response to it.

It was then he heard it, the first quiet rumble of approaching thunder. It was like the growl of a stirring beast, deep and ominous. Lightning flashed in the distance. Then there was a sudden clap of thunder loud enough to startle his mount so that it sidestepped nervously in the darkness.

'Woah! Go easy, Raven. Steady boy, steady now.'

He felt a breeze stir in the trees around him and knew the rain would not be long in coming. He began to count, measuring the time between each lightning flash and its accompanying roll of thunder. The storm was travelling fast, racing towards him from the north-east. He welcomed it. He wanted to meet it in the open, far from the trees of the forest. He wanted to feel its violence echo the storms inside himself. He urged Raven forward, heading out across the wide meadow in

361

the direction of Beresford Hall, watching the sky and waiting for its turbulence to reach him.

The flashes of lightning grew closer and brighter, the thunder much more fierce as the storm approached. A wind was rising, heavy with the scent of rain. He felt his scalp prickle and the skin along his forearms tingle with exhilaration as his dogs whined and his horse danced under him on nervous feet. The heart of the storm was almost directly overhead and a few large drops of rain were beginning to fall when he saw what appeared to be a figure standing at the very top of Beresford's ruined tower. At first he did not trust his eyes in the eerie and uncertain light, but then the sky was brightly lit by another sheet of lightning and he saw it clearly, a small, dark shape standing between the tower's pinnacles.

'*Lia!*'

He should have known she would be there. Like him she became moody and restless whenever a storm was imminent. Like him she needed to be outdoors, to be a part of the tempest, to feel the fear and the raw excitement of it. He moved his horse forward again, hearing the hiss of knee-high grasses swaying in the meadow, feeling the breeze, grown stronger now, plucking at his clothes and hair. What he saw up there was madness. Leonora was heavy with her unborn child. She had no business climbing the treacherous Monks' Stair and exposing herself to the elements from the tower's dangerous summit. As if to illustrate his fears a shard of lightning flung itself earthward like a heavenly spear, and as he watched it seemed as if some greater force were trying to strike her down from that high place.

'*Lia! Lia, get back from there! Get back from there!*'

His voice was snatched away by the same wind that now whipped his hair about his face in long damp tendrils. Startled, Raven whinnied and reared up so that Lukan, having benefit of neither bridle nor saddle, slid from his back. Thunder crashed almost directly above them and the horse, confused, whinnied again and spun away, heading for the familiar shelter of the forest.

'*Damn you woman, get back from there!*'

362

The words were shouted at the top of his lungs, but even without the storm he knew his voice would never have reached across that distance. He began to run through the grass as the heavens were ripped open and rain began to fall in a sudden torrent. He was drenched almost at once. Warm rain plastered his hair to his head and neck and stuck his cotton shirt to his back. Squinting through the hazy curtain of it he saw the tower set against the sky in brief, pale silhouette. The figure had vanished. He tried to shield his eyes with both hands and willed the sky to light itself again, but the eye of the storm rushed on to do its damage elsewhere, leaving only an echo of itself behind.

'*Lia! Lia!*'

With a great effort of will Lukan forced himself to stand quite still in the pouring rain, letting its wetness cool his skin and soothe his temper. He stood with his feet apart and his head bowed, eyes closed, teeth clenched. She had no right to put him through this. He had wished her dead a thousand times, but for her to climb up there in her condition and place herself at the mercy of the elements, on such a night as this, was a folly of unforgivable proportions. He lifted his head to the pouring rain and yelled again, '*Damn you, woman. Damn you to hell for what you do to me!*'

Leonora clung to one of the tower's four pinnacles, her arms encircling the hard stone in a desperate embrace. Rain lashed at her face and hands, stinging the tender skin. Wind dragged her hair in all directions and whipped her cloak and her skirts about her body in what seemed a frenzy of violence. She had stood too long watching the storm approach, and now that it was here she feared to release her hold on the stones and attempt to reach the shelter of the Monks' Stair. Lightning flashed around her and thunder roared and bellowed like an angry beast above her head. What had been a stirring sight, invigorating to the senses, now seemed a dangerous and fearsome thing.

'*Lukan! Oh Lukan, Lukan!*'

She sobbed his name into the bedlam of the storm,

knowing he would be out there somewhere, running with his dogs like some untamed animal of the night. So similar to herself, he too loved thunderstorms. She had witnessed his excitement as he felt the elements let loose above him with all the rage, the power and the passion of an electrical storm. And she had seen him turn his face to the lashing rain as if in supplication to gods she dare not even imagine. She clung to the pinnacle now as she would have clung to him had he been there beside her, feeling the stones as cold and hard as he had lately proved himself to be. The child moved sharply inside her, stretching its limbs, testing the strength of them. A shard of brilliant lightning speared the ground beyond the tower and she, fatigued and afraid, allowed herself to sink slowly to her knees. The storm had beaten her, but it had also released the flood-gates of her emotions. For the first time in long months she allowed herself to cry without shame. She wept for Lukan, who had so easily abandoned her, for her lost mother, for Jonathan and Charles, and for poor, weak Joseph who had lived his life in the shadow of a stronger, more dominant twin. Lashed and battered by wind and rain she wept for them all: for Sir Oscar, never able to hold on to that which he loved the most, for Lady Alyce, eaten alive by the terrible cancer of jealousy, and for poor Elizabeth, beaten and humiliated by a mother who believed her lack of wits was the mark of the devil. Leonora sobbed until she felt physically drained, and at the end of it she rested her head against the cold wet stones and said his name over and over like a prayer, 'Lukan ... Lukan ... Lukan.'

Anabel found her when the storm had passed and the rain was easing to a steady downpour. Disturbed by the sound of thunder she had risen from her bed and gone immediately to the next room to check on her mistress. Only when a frantic search convinced her that Leonora could be in no other place, had she dared brave the dark and narrow chimney that was the Monks' Stair and set her feet on the very summit of the tower. She found Leonora huddled in a corner, soaked to the skin and barely conscious of her surroundings.

'Oh you foolish, foolish child,' she cried. 'Whatever were

you thinking of to come up here on a night like this and the child all but ready to be born? God help us all if you give birth tonight. It will be a cripple or an imbecile, or blacker than the night itself, or scarred by lightning, or made stone deaf and slow-witted by all that thunder. It will be ruined, your beautiful child and Malcolm's heir, ruined by exposure to this terrible weather. Oh Leonora, whatever were you thinking of? Whatever were you thinking of?'

'Help me, Anabel.' Leonora struggled to her feet, leaning heavily on the older woman. 'Help me downstairs.'

'Walk behind me and take care with every step,' Anabel instructed. 'Keep to the outside where the treads are widest, but hold the newel stone for support. Go slowly now. Lift up your wet skirts. Heavens above, you're shivering and shaking fit to fall apart.'

Moving cautiously down the dark stairwell, they eventually reached the room that had been prepared for Lukan's clandestine visits.

'In there,' Leonora gasped. 'Let me rest in there.'

'I most certainly will *not* let you rest in there,' Anabel said sharply.

'Please, I am exhausted.'

Anabel held her back. 'Exhausted or no, you'll not lie down in that room tonight.'

'Please, Anabel.'

'No! Heaven forbid it, but supposing your child decides to be born tonight? How will we explain a second bedroom, deviously prepared and kept hidden from all but the two of us? And what risks will you take to meet that man again, once your secret love-nest has been discovered?'

Leonora swayed, struggling to keep her balance. Her clothes were made cumbersome by the weight of water they carried. Even her hair had become a burden. 'Anabel, I must rest.'

'A few more steps. Hold on to me. Just a few more steps and we'll be there. Careful now, take it slowly.'

At last she had her mistress on level ground again in the alcove of her bedroom where the entrance to the stair was hidden. She hastily stripped away the wet clothes and wrapped Leonora's naked, shivering body in a blanket. Then she settled her in an armchair before the dying fire, wrapped her sodden hair in a towel and rubbed her hands and feet vigorously to move the blood more swiftly through her veins. Within a half hour she had the dazed young woman safely in her bed, sleeping soundly and apparently none the worse for her experience.

For Anabel it was a long and anxious night. She added fuel to the fire in the grate and kept it burning low but steady throughout the night in case the shock of being caught in the storm sent Leonora into early childbirth. She checked the child every hour, slipping her hand under the covers until her palm rested on the bulge of her mistress's abdomen. The babe remained quiet but the storm, and with it Anabel's fears, ebbed and flowed until the sun came up.

To keep herself awake, Anabel rinsed Leonora's wet clothes in fresh water and hung them to dry in one of the gloomy back rooms of the gatehouse. With infinite care she smoothed the fabric through her dampened fingers, coaxing the creases out and the pleatings back into place. Then she flattened every scrap of lace, every trim and ribbon between her hands and smoothed the hems until they were quite level. In the kitchen she made hot chocolate and cut herself thick slabs of cheese and fruit cake, and all the time she kept the inner doors wide open and her ears cocked for her mistress's call. Sometimes her heart despaired of Leonora. She was more wilful than any young woman had a right to be. And she was clever too. Soon her suspected rival would be making a lengthy wedding journey through Belgium, France and Spain with an ancient husband, gone for months beyond temptation's reach. Once again the girl had got her way.

'Selfish and wicked,' she said aloud, chasing the crumbs of cheese and cake around her plate, catching them on the end of a moistened finger. 'But such an angel when she puts her mind to it, an angel like her poor dead mother.'

With the first light of morning Anabel allowed herself to fall asleep in the big chair by the hearth. She awoke to find the fire gone out and sunlight streaming in at every window. Leonora had slept soundly and awoke wanting nothing but warm sweet buttermilk for breakfast. She instructed Anabel to brush and braid her hair and bring fresh linens in preparation for the lying-in.

'It will be soon, today I think,' she said.

'And early, thanks to your foolishness, young lady. What in the world were you doing up there last night?'

'I wanted to watch the storm.'

'To watch it or die in it?' Anabel demanded. 'It was a dangerous thing to do, Leonora. You promised me faithfully that you would keep away from the tower and the Monks' Stair after your fifth month, yet there you were, climbing up to that awful place in a raging storm that might have blown you right over the edge. And what if Sir Malcolm's child had been born up there? By heaven, Leonora, I dread to think what damage you might have done.'

'Please Anabel, no more. Come, help me to the window. I want to see the day that will welcome my son.'

Anabel did as she was bidden, flinging the main window wide open to let the clear morning air come flooding into the room. It was a beautiful day. The sky was clear and blue, with tiny wisps of milk-white cloud hung here and there like freshly laundered linen pinned out to dry. The fields of green and gold were rinsed to gleaming perfection by the summer rain, the forest glistened, the river shone with reflected blue and the sun had shrouded itself in a golden haze.

'It's a beautiful day, Leonora,' Anabel smiled. 'Warm and clean and new.'

'It is indeed,' Leonora nodded, her hands cupping her abdomen and her face still flushed from the exhilaration of last night's storm. 'And I think this new day will be William's day.'

CHAPTER EIGHTEEN

I

Lukan was working with Malcolm in the fields on the day the child was born. Once a year the dull brown hills around Beresford Hall turned gloriously flaxen for a few short weeks, becoming vast golden lakes that shimmered in the sun and shifted in lazy waves before the warm late-summer breezes. He loved the scents and colours of the corn, its constant motion and its diverse sounds. Some nights during the reaping he chose to make his bed at the forest's edge and watch the harvest fields in moonlight. There were splashes of crimson poppies then, charlock and corn-marigold, and everywhere a gentle haze of silver on the gold. His wolfhounds had chased the scuttling fugitives, the voles and tiny field-mice, rats and rabbits who had managed to escape the yearly massacre. Those nights had been long and warm and wonderfully scented. Now the long, hard days of harvesting were at an end, the yield all but safely gathered in for another year. Beyond the hedges of the fields the entertainments in celebration of the harvest-home were already in preparation. Sticks were being stockpiled for the camp fires, bigger logs piled up to form makeshift seating. The same cumbersome carts that had hauled in the grain would soon be swept and decorated and returned to the fields to carry the labourers to Beresford Hall for the annual harvest supper. This year there would be long plum loaves on the table and rich plum puddings capped with brandy sauce. Every child below the age of fourteen would receive two pennies each, and every little girl a lucky corn-dolly to hang above her bed. The main hall was set with benches and trestle tables, lit with candles and well fortified with casks of home brewed ale. Just once each year the master sat down to feast with his man, the mistress with her maid, and hungry and well-fed alike would eat and drink their fill for harvest-home.

After the supper the labourers and their families would revel all through the night on open ground around the empty fields, feasting again on leftovers and fruit-of-the-orchard pies and harvest loaves. The campfires would crackle and spit hot sparks into the summer night, the music would play and the people would dance until dawn, careless of the night's sleep, for tomorrow was to be a holiday.

Lukan was restless. Naked to the waist, he worked with a long-handled scythe around the edges of the field, and each time he aimed the deadly blade he cursed the bond that still existed between himself and Malcolm's wife. Today she felt closer to him, more real, more substantial than she had seemed in months. He looked to the Hall, knowing she needed him, and felt the hopelessness of his situation become acute. Rebecca too had known that this would be the day. Somewhere in that vast house Leonora was giving birth to her first child and he, the one who loved her more than any man should ever dare to love, could have no part in it. He wanted to shut her from his mind and from his heart, to free himself from the prison of loving her, but instead he found himself struggling to feel her pain, to draw the suffering and the danger from her.

'Lia. Lia.' He called her name inside himself, grinding his

teeth together so the sound would not escape to shame them both. He had not held her in his arms or even met her gaze directly for seven months and suddenly the breach was unendurable. If he should lose her now, if she should die in childbirth as so many woman did, he knew his own life would no longer be worth living.

'Damn you woman,' he hissed as the scythe sliced home. 'Damn you for being Malcolm's wife, not mine. And damn my soul to hell for loving you.'

He saw a servant come for Malcolm, riding at full gallop from the Hall. Malcolm had been standing atop a hay cart, stripped to the waist and sweating in the heat as he paid homage to long tradition by helping to stack the last cartload of the year's harvest. He was brown and his muscles were sleek and taut, and the sun had bleached long streaks of golden blonde into his dark brown hair. Against a sunburned face his eyes were startlingly blue, and when he smiled, which he often did these days, his fine white teeth revealed barely a flaw.

Lukan stood up straight, rested the weight of his scythe on the ground and wiped the dampness from his brow with his forearm. He saw a labourer draw the master's attention to the approaching rider, saw Malcolm toss his hay-fork aside and leap down from the cart with cat-like grace. A moment later he pulled the man from the saddle and leapt up in his place. He rode to where Lukan stood.

'I need you at the Hall,' was all he said.

Lukan could not refuse. Without a word he dropped the heavy scythe, locked grips with Malcolm and swung up behind him. A short sharp jab to the flanks sent the horse leaping forward at a gallop, scattering field-debris with its flying hooves.

By the time they reached the Hall, the big, south-facing window had been draped with a cloth according to local custom. A lantern would be hung there when the lady of the house was safely delivered of a living female child, two lanterns together if it were a son. Seeing them the populace would have the news and know what celebrations to expect. The lights would burn for four days and nights, keeping their vigil over that crucial period in which the newly-born might sicken and die.

'I cannot bear this waiting,' Malcolm said, pacing his private drawing room, white-faced with anxiety. A manservant had brought them water for washing, towels and fresh white shirts.

'You need another brandy?' Lukan offered.

Malcolm shook his head. He looked sick, the way he had looked when Lady Grace lay screaming in her bed with only dead babies to show for all her efforts. 'How could I do this to her?' he muttered. 'After what happened to Grace, how could I inflict such a thing on Leonora.'

'The choice was hers,' Lukan reminded him. 'You said it yourself, she desperately wanted this child.'

'But if she dies ...? Lukan, if bearing my child should kill her ...?'

'It won't,' Lukan insisted, his own face grey beneath the sun-browned skin. 'Leonora will not die. She will not.'

Malcolm raked his fingers through his hair. 'My God, I doubt if I could bear to lose her now.'

'Stop it!' Lukan demanded, rounding on his friend with his eyes flashing angrily. 'She needs a strong man at her elbow, damn it, not a snivelling milksop!'

'Don't attack me, Lukan. You have no cause.'

'I have every cause if you are determined to buckle at the knees over this.'

Malcolm was shocked. 'What the hell, she might be *dying* up there. Have you forgotten so easily how Grace met her death?'

'Now you just listen to me, Malcolm Cavendish. Your wife is hale and healthy, and if she has courage enough to bear your child the least you can do for her is endure the waiting like a *man*.'

Malcolm flinched. 'I don't deserve that, Lukan.'

'Does she deserve a frail thing for a husband?'

Malcolm's blue eyes narrowed and a pulse throbbed visibly in his cheek. 'Did anyone ask you to speak your mind so freely, Mr de Ville?'

'Would you rather I lie through my teeth on your account, Mr Cavendish?' Lukan countered.

'A little sympathy wouldn't go amiss.'

'It's backbone you need right now, not sympathy.'

'Nor friendship either, if this is to be the tone of it.'

'Oh, to hell with . . .' Lukan bit back the sharp response and turned away abruptly. What was he doing here, so close and yet so painfully far from her, lashing out at his dearest friend because he himself felt wretched and alone? He took several steps towards the door before halting in mid-stride, certain that if he walked away now a rift would open up between them that may scar their friendship forever. He turned to survey his friend through narrowed eyes. 'I regret my outburst,' he said at last.

'Like hell you do.'

'I had no right to speak as I did.'

Malcolm remained inflexible. 'And since when did *right* concern you, Mr de Ville?'

'Damn it, man, I'm trying to apologise. That's not my wife up there. My words were callous.'

'Aye, and I should thrash you soundly for them.'

Lukan took a step forward. 'Oh yes? Do you fancy yourself capable of that?'

'Without a doubt, since I am the one offended.'

'And if your nose is bloodied in the battle how will you explain your brawling behaviour to your lady wife?'

Malcolm shrugged. 'The sword will suit my purpose well enough.'

'Then the sword it shall be,' Lukan agreed, bowing stiffly and indicating with a flourish the door leading to Malcolm's practice room. 'At your service, sir.'

The room was large and overlooked one of the smaller inner courtyards, with windows set above head-height and a ceiling that soared away into elegant sweeping arches. The walls were lined with a collection of swords and sabres, daggers, axes and foils of every description. Some were exquisitely mounted in French or Italian fashion, others sported elegant swept hilts and elaborate interlocking ring guards.

372

One weapon might be so over-decorated as to be virtually useless in a serious encounter while its neighbour, a plain thing with modest ornamentation, might be so battle-scarred as to boast a hero's history.

Malcolm flicked two light-weight practice foils from their racks, caught them in mid-air and with a swift turn of his wrist sent one of them swishing across the room in Lukan's direction. The gypsy reached out to pluck it from the air without effort, then both men adopted a half-stance with a hanging guard and watched each other's eyes. They wore neither face-mask nor breastpad for their protection, and yet they were known to fight like bitter enemies on occasions, for they were brothers to the core, with as much rivalry as love between them.

It was Lukan who set the tone of the encounter. He observed the brief courtesy salute and followed up with an aggressive flying guard not quite in character with his customary style of subtle swordsmanship. Malcolm stepped lightly back without a parry, then forward to close the measure. For the next few moments each man matched his skill, style and speed against the other, each seeking to deceive his opponent's parries. Then Malcolm took a quick step forward followed by a lunge, and the rebated point of his foil made contact with Lukan's shirt an inch above the heart.

'*Quarte!*'

'Lukan glanced down. He could feel the blunted steel pressed hard against his flesh.

'*Quarte,*' he conceded.

The bout began again in earnest, Malcolm determined to maintain his advantage, Lukan equally determined to relieve him of it. So the offensive passed smoothly back and forth and the clash of steel against steel rang on the air. Sir Oscar heard it as he entered Malcolm's private apartments by the main door. His son's manservant, Hammond, stood by the open door to the practice room.

'What's happening here?' the Earl demanded. 'I sent for Sir Malcolm half an hour ago.'

'He came at once sir,' Hammond explained in his slow and

very cultured manner. 'But he and Mr Lukan had a slight difference of opinion which they chose to settle here in the sword-room. Sir Malcolm has the advantage.'

'Damn their hot tempers. This is no time for practising their arms.' Sir Oscar took his son's coat and strode into the room, his boots ringing loudly on the polished wooden floor. The sound momentarily unsettled Malcolm's concentration. As he glanced up Lukan snatched his opportunity. He made several parries in quick succession followed by a step-in parry that brought the point of his blade against Malcolm's right hip just below the belt.

'*Octave!*' he declared.

'*Octave,*' Malcolm conceded.

Grinning now, they resumed their on-guard positions and prepared to continue the bout. Sir Oscar watched them gravely. They were too much alike, these two. They could be at each other's throats one moment and laughing together like children the next, quarrelling or playing games according to the moods they seemed to share. Sometimes they appeared to represent opposing sides of the same coin, a coin so clearly minted in the Cavendish mould. Each man bore scars the other had inflicted, and each would go to any lengths to support or overshadow, to safeguard, challenge, assist or better the other. They were evenly matched and equally rebellious, and both more handsome than honest men need be. Too much like brothers. The gypsy and Sir Oscar's son had always been too much like brothers.

He stepped into the field of play abruptly, confident that two such expert swordsmen would not be forced into a serious error by his presence. 'Gentlemen, put up your swords. This is hardly the time for game-playing.'

'Game-playing?' Malcolm echoed, scowling. 'We do not play at this father. We fight in deadly earnest, is that not so, my friend?'

'For my part, certainly,' Lukan replied with a bow.

Malcolm looked closely at his father. 'Is there news from the nursery?'

Sir Oscar nodded and held out Malcolm's coat. 'She's asking for you.'

'Is she all right? Is the labour going well?'

'Smoothly and without a hitch,' the Earl replied with a smile. 'It's over, Malcolm. She is a mother.'

Malcolm stared at his father for a long moment, the colour slowly drained from his face. Then he tossed his rapier to Lukan, snatched up his coat and strode from the room. Sir Oscar hurried after him, leaving Lukan standing there with the words still jangling loudly in his ears, '*She is a mother.*'

He left the room slowly, his feet as leaden as his heart. Leonora was well. She had survived. She was a mother. Relief swept over him and abandoned him almost in the same instant. Leonora was safely delivered of her child, but now that scrap of dependent life would surely keep her from him. He tried to imagine it suckling at her breast, tiny and helpless, an innocent thief to claim her heart, her time, her love.

In Malcolm's drawing-room he poured himself a large brandy and stood at the window to drink it. The lowering sun had stretched the shadow of the western tower right across the river, laying it chimney-dark upon the ground. The river glinted like polished steel, running deceptively calm toward the treacherous, half-submerged rocks around Monks' Crossing. After a while he set down his glass and went downstairs to the main hall where dozens of giggling, excited servants seemed to be running around in all directions at once. A man with a ladder was at the big south window, hanging a second lantern on the bracket.

'Mr Lukan! Mr Lukan!'

Sam Cooper, laughing, shook him by the arm, his excitement making him overfamiliar. 'Have you heard the news, Mr Lukan?'

Lukan turned from the window. The glow of the lamps had caused his eyes to smart. He saw Sam Cooper's face as if through a veil. 'Yes Sam,' he said softly, willing his mouth to shape a smile. 'They have a son. My dear friend and his lady have a son.'

He strode from the Hall and down the sloping lawns to the stable, where he coaxed a reluctant Starlight Warrior from his stall. He rode the stallion bareback and gave him full rein, using his powerful legs to urge the big beast into a gallop and at the same time keep himself seated. All around the cornfields groups of local people cheered and raised their cups to Sir Malcolm's newborn heir. Many of them stood with eyes agape as, black hair flapping wildly in the wind, Lukan de Ville raced the big grey stallion at a heart-stopping pace away from Beresford Hall.

II

They named their son William Lucas. He was a sturdy boy with healthy lungs and firm, well-proportioned limbs, as dark-haired and blue-eyed as his parents were. He was three days old when Lukan first saw him. He turned his small head on the pillow and looked at the man with eyes that were filled to the brim with that uncanny wisdom of the newborn.

'We named him William for one of the sons of the original Baron Cavendish, born in the fifteenth century,' Malcolm explained. 'And we named him Lucas for you.'

'For me? You named your son for me?'

'Of course we did,' Malcolm grinned. 'Don't look so incredulous, Lukan. It is the most natural thing in the world for a man to name his first-born for his lifelong friend.'

'I'm truly honoured,' Lukan said. 'But did your father make no protest at the choice?'

Malcolm scratched the side of his nose and looked a little sheepish. 'He might have done, were it not for Leonora's clever handling of the matter.'

'Oh?' Lukan's brow arched toward his hairline. 'Surely the lady did not insist upon it?'

'She did indeed, by subtlety and sheer persistence,' Malcolm nodded. 'She gave my father leave to name his grandson, then added your name, with a small variation so that neither you nor he could be offended by it. I have known you all my life and yet I was unaware that for you a personal name is not a thing for others to take and use as they think fit. Had we named him Lukan you would have been insulted, I am told.'

'That is the way of it.' Lukan nodded his dark head. Leonora had remembered. She had named her son for him, and with just a little care she had done so without offending his beliefs. 'It is indeed a deeply personal thing,' he said. 'A man's name can be given but must never be taken without leave. What one deems an honour in these matters another might consider an injury.' He looked down at the child and nodded again. 'Lucas. It is a good name, a good name.'

'Take him from his basket,' Malcolm urged. 'Hold him. See for yourself what a fine young fellow Leonora and I have made.'

'Not I.' Lukan shook his head and drew back, emotion tugging at the muscles in his throat. 'I have little fondness for wriggling infants.'

'What nonsense. I know you too well to believe that. Here, take hold of him.' Malcolm scooped the child from his cot and handed him over. 'William, my boy, here is your Uncle Lukan.'

The pride that shone in Malcolm's face as he held his son was touching to behold. There was a particular happiness in him that was a very special thing, as if the man had suddenly become complete. For a moment Lukan held his gaze, wanting to share this new aspect of Malcolm's life as closely as he shared all others. He wondered if it ever could be so. What man could love his best friend's wife and not feel torn apart by the betrayal?

'Uncle?' he asked, his throat constricting further.

'Yes, and soon to be much more than that, I hope. Here, take hold of the boy.'

William Lucas Cavendish, second heir to the lands and titles of his grandfather the Earl of Beresford, lay without protest in the big hands of Lukan de Ville. His bare feet beat a small tattoo against the man's chest and the back of his tiny head lay warm and soft against the calloused palm. He seemed to regard the gypsy with a grave, almost knowing expression.

Lukan puckered his dark brows and spoke as if to himself. 'It is believed that every babe is born with full knowledge of its previous lives, and that the gods in their wisdom seal its lips and fog its understanding.' He touched a dark forefinger against the child's mouth, fitting it to the delicate indentation in the centre of the upper lip. 'The gods have left the imprint of a finger here, where they bade him hush. See how he watches me, holding me with his eyes as if he knows me from another time, another place.'

Malcolm smiled and stepped away to observe a group of starlings feeding beyond the window, a seemingly casual movement designed to allow the other man a few moments of privacy with William. Leonora had schooled him well. She had an instinct for these things, a natural sensitivity to the customs and beliefs of those around her.

Without being fully conscious of his actions, Lukan bent his head to whisper a few brief words of welcome into the babe's right ear. Then he looked closely at the small face with its already finely-drawn features. 'Lucas Cavendish,' he said softly, testing the name and finding it to his satisfaction. 'Lucas Cavendish.' Then he pressed a silver coin into one of the tiny, grasping hands. This wise-eyed stranger was Malcolm's first-born son, Leonora's little one, and his presence seemed to mark the end of Lukan's fondest and most secret hopes. Leonora had surmounted yet another obstacle in her determination to found a dynasty at Beresford, and when her husband eventually inherited the earldom from his father she would become the most popular Countess ever to hold the title. 'She has her dream,' he told the boy in a whisper. 'She has her dream secured and nothing now will ever keep her from it, least of all the gypsy fool who loves her.'

When Malcolm turned from the window the boy was lying quietly in his basket and Lukan was gone without a word. Malcolm smiled a little sadly. If he could have claimed one wish at that moment it would have been for Lukan, that one day he too would love this much and know the special joy of fatherhood.

III

Rebecca watched her brother's moods grow blacker as the year came to its close. His visits to Lower Prescot Hall had come to an end long before the lady left England with her two old men, the ailing husband and the drunken father, for more exciting climes in Europe. That he missed the lady not at all she had no doubt. Not even Harriet Wyndham, with her soft brown hair and gentle eyes and creamy smooth complexion, could bind this sullen gypsy by anything but her availability.

'Has there been no village wench to catch your eye this season, Lukan?' she probed, eager to have whatever snippets of information she could prise from him concerning his private life. 'No poor man's daughter worthy of your interest?'

He laughed without humour. 'They are as plentiful as grass-flies for any man who has the taste.'

'And you do not have the taste?'

He shook his head. 'I do not.'

'What about the new Mrs Augustus Sharpe? Will she welcome you back at Lower Prescot Hall when she's grown tired of the clumsy fumblings of her old man?'

'Aye, I'll be free to come and go if it suits me.'

'And will it?' she asked. 'Will it suit you?'

He looked at her sharply. 'Do you think me destined to pick over other men's leavings for the rest of my life, Rebecca? Should I make a cuckold here, a cuckold there, until I've had my fill of creeping behind men's backs to bed their wives?'

Having no answer that might ease his mind, Rebecca went about her tasks, hoping to let the subject lie. She had been on the point of declaring a simple truth, that he was fortunate indeed to have tasted love in any flavour, however sharp or bitter its aftertaste. She was forty-two years old and still a virgin. She would have given her soul in exchange for the smallest morsel from love's table.

On his twenty-ninth birthday, thirteen days before Christmas, Lukan was called to stand as godfather to the Cavendish child, William Lucas. Rebecca helped him dress with extra care for the occasion. She brushed the hair back from his face and bound it in the nape of his neck with narrow braid, then smoothed it with her hands until it shone like polished coal. She cleaned the dirt from his fingernails and polished them with pumice until they were smoothly rounded and would not harm his godson's delicate skin. He wore a high white collar and pale lavender stock, a fancy velvet waistcoat, dark grey tailed coat and straight-cut trousers with side slits. He smelled of amber musk and bergamot, and that familiar hint of aniseed on his breath. Not since Malcolm's wedding had she seen him look so handsome, or so grim.

He had taken his place in the chapel and made the guardian's promises as he held the babe that divided him from the only woman he felt himself capable of loving. And the task had brought his spirits to rock-bottom. He left for the Beresford christening proud and self-assured. He returned like a wounded animal.

'It is the same,' he told his sister, slumped in the cottage doorway with a look of total disbelief in his eyes.

'You only need more time,' she offered.

'Time?' he asked. '*Time?* How many months of heartache should it take, Rebecca? It's been a year and nothing has changed, *nothing*. It is the same as that first day, the same.'

'Be patient Lukan. It will ease, eventually.'

He had rounded on her then, his features betraying his inner pain. 'Hold your tongue, woman! I've had enough of your empty platitudes to last me a whole lifetime. Don't you see what has happened? I am betrayed. Twelve months I've grieved the loss of her, a whole year of my life in mourning and for what? The wounds she left me with have not even *begun* to knit.'

'But they will, Lukan, in time.'

He acted as if he had not heard her words. 'She was there in the chapel, my Lia, unchanged by either marriage or mother-hood. She was as fresh and beautiful as the day we met, and those eyes of hers, those wonderful turquoise eyes. Ye gods! I swear they looked right into me, they *saw* the misery she left here.' He pressed the heel of his hand against his solar plexus as if to show where it pained him most. 'She saw.'

'Oh Lukan, my poor dear.'

Again he turned the bleakness of his gaze on her. 'All this, a whole year's yearning, and not the smallest part of *anything* is changed.'

Rebecca looked on helplessly as he strode into the vaulted cellar and rummaged in the darkness at the foot of the stairs, cursing the littered shelves and low ceiling. He returned with a bottle of brandy gripped by the neck in each hand. She set herself between him and the door.

'Lukan? Where are you going with those?'

'To drown my sorrows, woman.' He raised the bottles above his head and smiled bitterly. 'When all else fails, the bottle must suffice.'

'Don't be a fool,' she snapped. 'You are no drinker, Lukan. You have neither head nor stomach for it. Leave the bottles here.'

His smile faded and his features hardened. 'It works for other men. Why not for me?'

'Because what ails you cannot be cured by drunkenness, and well you know it.'

'Perhaps not, but for this one night at least I will lay down my head without thinking of her.'

'That is not the way of it, Lukan. Not for you.'

'Get out of my way, Rebecca.'

'Lukan, don't do this.'

'Once again you seem to forget that you are only my sister, not my wife,' he said angrily. 'Don't preach. Don't try to tell me how to live my life. Now get out of my way.'

He brushed her aside and left the house, slamming the door behind him. Rebecca moved to the window and watched him stride along the narrow pathway leading away from the house. Moments later the barn doors slammed behind him and his wolfhounds, finding themselves banished from their master's company and sensing that he was not himself, paced restlessly back and forth, whining uneasily. She stared at the old barn and shook her head.

'It will not help you,' she said sadly. 'You cannot close the

381

door on what you feel for her. Fogging your brain with alcohol will only ease the ache for a short time.'

She turned from the window and her shoulders rose and fell in a deep sigh as she looked around the room. The de Ville house was several hundred years old and stood in a beautiful spot close to the river, sheltered by the forest on all sides and yet open to the very best of the spring and summer weather. It was known locally as The Forest House, and there had been a de Ville as master there for as long as there had been a Cavendish at Beresford Hall. Its low ceilings were supported by huge oaken beams and finished with splendid plaster work, while many of the rooms were lined with the same linen-fold panelling that graced the walls of Beresford Hall. The main stair was magnificent, with delicately scrolled panels and every main support bearing the carved head of a forest beast. Here was the bright-eyed hare and its enemy the fox, the vicious wild boar, the wolf and the deer, the kestrel gripping its prey, the eagle spreading its great wings. Here too were carved representations of herbs and flowers, leaves and blossoms, acorns and delicate fir-cones. Every aspect of the great forest had been caught by craftsmen in the mellow wood so that each rise of the stair provoked a reminder of all that existed in such abundance beyond the leaded half-stained windows. Rebecca loved the house. It should have had a family, the voices of children, music and the sound of laughter in it, but she loved it none the less for its tranquility. This was Lukan's house, and like him it was dark and brooding, elegant, handsome and rather sombre. It too had its shadowed corners and unfathomable mysteries, and like the man himself it held Rebecca prisoner and scarcely even knew that she was there.

It was early evening and the sky beyond the trees had turned to black. No stars were visible, but from time to time fast-scudding clouds released a flash of moonlight that lit the surface of the river with brief and brilliant shimmers of silver light. Rebecca sniffed the air, then breathed more deeply, drawing the darkness into her lungs. There was frost in the air, but this December had been a sunny month, with bright, clear days and wonderful, star-spangled nights. She had a special fondness for the winter months, when every sunset was spectacular and every night sky filled with precious gems.

She was standing in the garden wearing a night shift and a large fringed shawl, her feet bare despite the chill, her long hair hanging loose about her shoulders. She had washed her hair in clear spring water and for over a week had combed it out three times a day with a comb dipped in oil of tartar. Now it was glossy and jet black, without so much as a trace of those tell-tale grey streaks that were a reminder of her advancing years. She touched her cheeks with the backs of her fingertips. The regular use of quince cream had kept her skin smooth and soft despite the ravages of the seasons, but there were lines of age deep-etched around her eyes and her skin was nutty-brown, not creamy white as she would have it. No amount of creams and lotions would keep that crêpe-like texture from a woman's neck once she had reached beyond her fortieth year. Rebecca looked toward the meadow and the Hall beyond, where lights from certain windows were just visible now that the trees were bare. She was as much a fool as Lukan in her own way, and she hated herself for being so love-lorn that she thought to compete with a beautiful young woman barely past her nineteenth birthday.

There had been neither sound nor movement from the barn for several hours. The wolfhounds waited in the shadows, refusing to be tempted from the door. A supper of mutton, roast duckling and cheese cakes cooled by the kitchen stove and a healthy fire crackled in the grate. The village girls who helped with the cleaning, cooking and laundry had long since gone to their homes, leaving a warming pan in the master's bed.

Rebecca went back indoors, took a pewter tankard from the fireplace and pressed the hinge with her thumb so that the lid sprang open. The warm, hotly spiced wine gave off a delicious aroma. She let the lid fall back with a snap and replaced the tankard on the hob to keep warm. She stared at it, her thoughts as much in turmoil as her emotions. The plan she had in mind had come upon her slowly, born out of years of longing and nurtured on empty dreams. At first no more than a foolish daydream, it had insinuated itself into her thoughts and like a deadly poison spread itself until all else was over-shadowed by its presence. Now it had grown into an obsession, a relentless driving force that she was powerless to stand against. If she was to satisfy that obsession she must act now, tonight, while he was off his guard. The perfect circumstances were suddenly here and now. She, the victim of a hopeless love, must grab whatever she could or else abandon her hopes forever.

She knelt on a rug before the fire and unwrapped a small twist of paper containing a fine grey-blue powder which she herself had dried and ground and carefully measured out. Muttering a soft incantation to whatever gods might wish to lend a hand, she tipped the powder into the tankard, closed the lid and swished the contents gently around. Then she used a long, thin fire-iron to pull a few hot cinders from the fire. Selecting one, she dampened her fingers with saliva and quickly lifted it, hissing, and dropped it into the tankard of spiced wine. The potion was prepared. Now all she had to do was make him drink it.

She entered the barn by its small side door, a lighted lamp in one hand and the tankard in the other. Around her shoulders she had draped a warm blanket to guard against the chills of the night. Raven stood quietly in his stall, a cover thrown across his back and his dark head bowed in rest. She found her brother sprawled on a bed of straw with his legs outstretched before him and his back resting against the far wall. One empty brandy bottle lay on the ground beside him while the other, its contents already well diminished, was still clutched in his left hand. Rebecca lifted the lamp and peered into his face. It was pale and still in sleep but his features were tense, as if beneath the blanket of alcohol he found no escape from the dreams that had troubled him for so long.

She set the lamp in a recess in the wall and dropped to her knees beside him. The meagre light threw shadows beneath his eyes and hollowed out his cheeks. Carefully she removed his boots and unbuckled the heavy belt from his waist. She leaned forward to cover his mouth with her own, kissing him hungrily, passionately, regardless of his lack of response. Then she gripped him by the chin and shook him roughly.

'*Lukan! Wake up, Lukan!*'

He groaned a protest and tried to turn his head away but Rebecca persisted. With her free hand she held the tankard to his lips and forced him to drink. She gulped a little of the stuff herself, needing the courage she hoped it would induce. Lukan's protests were feeble, and when at last his head fell wearily against her bosom she was content to hold it there as she stroked his face and whispered against his hair.

'Relax dearest. Relax and let the aphrodisiac take effect. You'll soon begin to feel better.'

'What? What's that?' he mumbled. 'Lia? Lia?'

'Hush, my dear, hush now.' She reached out to extinguish the lamp. Darkness rushed in, broken only by the odd shard of moonlight slipping through gaps in the dusty windows. After a while he stirred in her arms, moving himself against her.

'Lia, is that you Lia?'

'Hush. Come, lie down Lukan. Lie down beside me and relax.'

The drug was taking effect. She felt his body respond to the movements of her hands and the tension begin to fall away from him as the aphrodisiac in his drink warmed his blood and touched upon his senses.

'Lia,' he murmured. 'Lia, my Lia.'

'Yes Lukan I'm here. Lia's here.'

He nuzzled his lips against her throat. 'My God I've missed you, I've missed you.'

'Yes I know you have, I know.'

Rebecca slipped the nightgown from her shoulders. The breath caught in her throat as he kissed her skin and caressed her body in the darkness.

'Lia, oh God damn you Lia, you were gone so long.'

'Yes I know, but I'm here right now and that's all that matters,' Rebecca whispered. 'I'm here and I want you to love me, Lukan. That's right, oh yes, that's right. Love me, Lukan, *love me*!'

It did not matter to her that he spoke another's name or that he believed, in his drugged state, that he held some other woman in his arms. She had loved him all her life and knew that this one night was all she would ever share with him. All beggars could be thieves when hunger burned, and for these few precious hours of darkness she was determined to have his love on any terms.

She left the barn at dawn, hiding her nakedness beneath her shawl as she carried away the tankard that had held the aphrodisiac and the cotton night shift that had gathered the tell-tale stains of her virginity. Indoors she washed her body and brushed and braided her hair, then climbed into her own bed in one of the first floor bedrooms and slept soundly until well after daybreak. She sang softly to herself as she prepared a hot breakfast and left it on a covered tray before the fire. It was done. The die was cast and not even a lifetime of regrets or recriminations would ever call it back. She had irreversibly altered both their lives, and neither Lukan nor his fine lady at the Hall could take that away from her. She was smiling a secret, almost mysterious smile as she left the house to call her brother home for breakfast.

The wolfhounds had been locked in the empty barn. They streaked by her as she opened the doors, racing off into the forest as if in pursuit of some fleeing, swift-footed prey.

'Lukan? Lukan?'

She hurried to the back of the barn where she had left him shortly before dawn, lying in the straw with only a blanket between his body and the night's chill. She found the blanket and the brandy bottles flung in a corner. Raven was gone from his stall and the rarely-used saddle, a gift from Malcolm Cavendish, was nowhere to be seen. Rebecca felt the blood chill in her veins. He could not know, he must *never* know what she had done, and with what stealth and cunning she had brought about their incestuous union.

The wolfhounds returned home, whimpering and confused, at nightfall. Rebecca waited and watched for him throughout that day and the next, but he neither came nor sent word. When Malcolm Cavendish came in search of him on the afternoon of the third day she could tell him nothing, only that her brother had ridden away in the night without a word, leaving his dogs, his loyal and constant companions, behind.

CHAPTER NINETEEN

I

Try as she might, Leonora found it impossible to enter into the true spirit of things as Beresford prepared for the Christmas celebrations. A masked ball was being arranged, her first public function since the birth of her son on the last day of August. Her natural vanity dictated that she make the most of this opportunity to show off both her child and her perfectly restored figure, and there could be no doubt that she was much in need of the diversions a masked ball offered. But Leonora was also restless and unhappy. She found herself anticipating the forthcoming celebrations and yet dreading the pretences it would involve. It took great skill and effort to maintain a convincing show of light-hearted gaiety where none existed. There had been so many occasions when this special type of dishonesty was required of her that she had trained herself to switch on her reserves of social brilliance in an instant. But this time Leonora was unsure, uncertain of her own ability to conceal the darkness lying across her heart.

'You'll cope well enough when the time comes, just as you

always do,' Anabel assured her when she confessed to a measure of self-doubt concerning the Christmas ball. 'I have never known you to let yourself down before your public and I don't expect you to do so now.'

'But I miss him so, Anabel.'

'Nonsense. All you need is discipline and enough determination to keep that gypsy out of your life. You have your son to love. It was a fair exchange.'

Leonora had smiled sadly at those words. It was true, she loved little William with a fierce, possessive love and time had shown that she had indeed traded one for the other. Yet in her heart of hearts she knew that William's birth had altered nothing, that what she felt for him was a new thing, separate and extra to anything she had ever felt before. He dominated her life and brought her a very special kind of joy, but loving him could never fill the emptiness that seemed to yawn like a gaping chasm inside her.

She had not heard from Lukan. For almost a year he had kept himself from her as if they were strangers, indifferent and uncaring. So many times she had climbed to the top of the tower to hang a lantern in the tiny side window, facing away from the house so that its light could only be seen from the Forest House. The lantern was their signal, the small, sure light that told him she had need of him and bade him come to her. She hung it there but Lukan paid no heed. She had even tied a strip of ivory lace around the neck of one of his dogs and sent the animal bounding off with the whispered instruction, '*Home*'. He must have known it came from her but still he had ignored it.

'Forgive me, Lukan,' she pleaded sometimes, looking from her window to the forest and aching right down to her bones for want of him. 'Forgive me and love me still.'

Lukan had arrived at the chapel for the christening looking wonderful, exactly as she remembered him and yet somehow larger, more vivid, more substantial. He had deliberately avoided looking at her until the ceremony was almost over, choosing instead to keep his gaze fixed firmly on the tiny babe in his arms. Leonora had been deeply wounded. The cold civility of his manner towards her had been hurtful enough, but this detachment, this refusal to acknowledge her existence by so much as a glance had sliced like a sharpened knife across her heart. She had stammered through the brief service with tears pricking at her eyes, willing the ordeal to end so that she might escape to the privacy of her rooms. Then he had lifted his head until his eyes met hers and the impact of that long-awaited contact had been startling in its intensity. In that instant she had seen the unhealed rawness of his wounds, all his hurts and longings suddenly exposed as if the man were open to the core. He had seemed too big and arrogant and yet had been so vulnerable in his pain. Since then she had hung the lantern in the tower window for a full hour every night, but that stubborn, unhappy man refused to acquiesce to either her demands or his own emotions. That he loved her still she now had not the smallest doubt. That she returned his love had never for one moment been in question.

'He's gone,' Malcolm said flatly. 'Lukan has vanished.'

'What?'

Leonora felt the colour drain from her face, leaving her chilled and slightly nauseous. She had questioned the unusual amount of activity around the stables and the forest's edge, the movement of men in groups, some bearing lanterns and setting out on foot long after nightfall. And she had questioned Malcolm's growing preoccupation with those activities, his lengthy absences and moods of acute anxiety. And now at last she had an answer to the mystery. Lukan had vanished, gone, and those men out there were searching the forest for him. For a moment Leonora felt swamped by the sudden pounding of her heart. She imagined him dead, thrown from his horse in the darkness, mangled by a steel trap laid by poachers, murdered by forest raiders, drowned in the icy river, gone from her for ever. Out of the sudden blackness her recovery was swift. She smiled as brightly as she could, confident on the surface, sick with worry underneath.

'Come now, Malcolm, that friend of yours is a creature of the forest and a law unto himself. It seems to me that he is much given to moods of melancholy. Perhaps he is brooding somewhere and better left alone?'

390

Malcolm shook his head. 'It's been too long. Something is wrong Leonora, very wrong.'

'Well then, perhaps some pretty young filly keeps him from your company,' she suggested, smiling despite a sudden, unreasonable stab of jealousy. She placed her hand on Malcolm's arm. 'Come, sit beside me and tell me all about it. I simply cannot believe that there is real cause for alarm.'

'It's true,' Malcolm insisted. 'After William's christening he went back to the forest, drank himself senseless and spent the whole night in his barn. Leonora, in all the years I've known him I have never seen him drunk. Oh, we have sunk a bottle or two between us in our time and roused the city with our rowdiness. We've even drunk enough on occasions to deaden the pain while we tried to beat each other to a pulp with our bare fists, just to see who stayed the course the longest. But I never thought to see him brought to this, taking his drink alone, in secret, and to the point of stupor.'

'It sounds so unlike him,' she agreed. 'Did you speak to Rebecca?'

He nodded. 'I suspect she's as worried as I am, though she would never lower herself to admit as much. It seems she left him alone that night in the hope that he might sleep himself sober, but when she went to the barn to check on him in the morning, he and his horse were gone. Nobody has seen him or had news of him since then.'

'But the christening was almost two weeks ago.'

'Twelve days,' Malcolm corrected.

'But the dogs,' Leonora said. 'I saw Gillan in the lower meadow yesterday afternoon, and where the dogs are running, Lukan is never far away.'

Malcolm shook his head grimly. 'He left them behind. He actually locked them in the barn to prevent them following him. I'm keeping them tethered at the Home Farm and releasing them one at a time, so that if one dog finds him and does not return to its companion, the other will lead us to it. I also have men out searching the forest day and night in case he is lying injured somewhere. Those woods are littered with man-traps and crawling with thieves and vagabonds.' He rubbed his mouth and chin with his palm. 'He's been gone too long, too long. I fear for his safety, Leonora.'

'Have faith,' she managed to say, the blood already chilling in her veins. 'Don't give up hope.'

'I blame myself,' he told her.

'That's foolish. Lukan is his own man.'

He nodded. 'I know, but I also knew that all was not right with him. You saw him at the christening. You must have noticed how remote, how depressed he seemed to be. I certainly did. I knew there was something wrong and yet I did nothing to help him. Oh yes, I blame myself for this.'

'Malcolm, are you your brother's keeper?' she asked gently.

He looked at her sharply, his eyes very blue and troubled. 'Yes, Leonora, I am his keeper just as he has always tried to be mine, and I have failed him when he most needed me. He would not have stood idly by and watched the same thing happening to me.'

'Malcolm, please don't blame yourself. You have your own life to lead, your duties here at Beresford, your son.'

'Aye, my son,' he said coldly. 'But having a son to care for is no excuse for failing Lukan when he needed a friend.' He took both her hands in his. Concern had etched itself in deep lines on his handsome face. 'Leonora, if I have lost him after all these years ...'

'Have faith,' she said again, and felt hot tears on her cheeks. It was as if a heavy stone had settled somewhere in her chest. Lukan's absence and his silence were unnatural. She too feared for his safety.

Malcolm touched her tear-stained cheeks and looked at her, perplexed. 'You weep for Lukan?' When she nodded he drew her in to his arms and held her closely. 'You like him hardly at all and yet you weep for him. You have a caring heart, Leonora.'

That night Leonora lit the tower rooms with several lamps so that the light would be visible over a greater distance. She also ordered the lights of the house to be kept burning throughout the night to give Lukan direction if he were hurt and stranded somewhere in the forest. She could do no more than that, except to pray.

She rode with Malcolm to the Forest House at noon and waited indoors while the barn was searched again. The main room was lit by a huge log fire that cast colourful reflections over the polished woodwork and sombre furniture. The full width and height of the massive chimney wall was hung with metal traps and snares, springs, spikes, rods, wires and other vicious-looking accoutrements. The sight of them made Leonora shudder. Some of those traps were capable of crippling a man, of severing a leg or mangling it so badly that he bled to death where he lay. She could not bear to imagine that Lukan had stepped upon such a monstrosity and died for want of help, alone in the forest.

To one side of the fireplace stood the big, high-backed leather chair where Lukan often sat with his feet stretched out in the hearth, watching the flickering flames and quick red sparks created by the fire. A dark green jacket with a velvet collar hung from a hook near the chimney-breast, its polished buttons brassy-bright in the firelight. His high riding boots stood side by side in a corner and a pile of freshly laundered shirts were folded together on a nearby table. Faced with so many reminders of him, feeling his closeness and his absence in equal measure, Leonora was all but overwhelmed. She reached for Lukan's chair. 'May I?'

Rebecca shrugged. Her manner was less than friendly.

'Why did he leave so suddenly, Rebecca?'

The woman sniffed. 'You know as much as I.'

'Is there a woman, someone he might have gone to?'

Rebecca hesitated, torn between heeding his brother's wishes and wanting to hurt this fine lady who owned him, body and soul, as if he were her property. For his sake she bit down on her jealousy and shook her head.

'None that I know of.'

'Then he had no reason to leave as he did, without a word to anyone?'

Rebecca's guilt rose to her throat like bile. She swallowed hard and repeated, 'None that I know of.'

Leonora leaned back in the big chair and closed her eyes.

She could almost feel his presence there, enfolding her as surely as his arms had so often done. She was still sitting thus when Malcolm entered the room unannounced. His mood was brusque and prickly. He was deeply concerned about Lukan but cared little for the company of his sister. To him Rebecca Adams was just a dour gypsy woman who bore no resemblance whatsoever to the man who was her half-brother.

'Where is Raven's saddle?' he demanded sharply. 'The saddle, woman, the one I had my own saddlers make for him?'

She shrugged. 'He took it with him.'

'Are you sure? He took the time to saddle up his horse before he left? Can you be certain of that?'

Rebecca nodded her head. 'The saddle was there on the block beside the stall and in the morning it was gone with the horse.'

'And the saddlebags?'

'Those too.'

'And his winter riding-coat, the one with the hood and leather lining, where is it?'

Rebecca shrugged again. 'I suppose he took that too. He always left it hanging in the barn.'

'Damn it, woman,' Malcolm exploded. 'You know as well as I do that he rides bareback and rarely wears a coat around the estate. Are you telling me now that he left that night on a pre-arranged journey?'

'I'm telling you nothing,' she returned, uncaring of either his anger or his status. 'My brother is gone and that is all I know.'

'But not on a drunken whim, as you allowed us to believe,' Malcolm said hotly. 'If he took his foul-weather coat, his saddle and bags, and took the time to leave his dogs behind, then clearly he anticipated travelling far and being away for some time. Why in Heaven's name did you not tell me all this a week ago?'

'Because you did not ask.' She almost spat the words at him. 'You asked for him and I told you he was gone. I answered your questions honestly at the time. Don't blame the timber if the axe is blunted.'

Malcolm clenched his fists and sucked air through his teeth. He only managed to control his temper with a great deal of effort. 'Madam, is there anything more you can tell me about your brother's disappearance? Anything at all?'

Rebecca met his gaze with open hostility. This Cavendish and his wife had snared her brother between them. They had made a helpless prisoner of him. And loving them both, she knew, would one day be the death of him.

'Well?' Malcolm demanded.

'I can tell you nothing.'

'Which is exactly what you've told us up to now.'

'Will that be all, Mr Cavendish?'

Malcolm was seething with anger. He opened his mouth to speak but closed it again as Sam Cooper was shown into the room by a shabbily dressed village girl with dirty hands and a greasy apron. Sam clutched his cap in both hands, nodded a bow to Leonora and avoided looking directly at the gypsy woman.

'There's a man asking to see you, sir,' he said to Malcolm. 'It's one of Mr Lukan's men, Bennet, the one what works over at Fairfax Manor. Says he needs to speak with you and Sir Oscar urgently.'

'Where is he?'

'Over at the empty mine where the old yew tree was blown over last year. He says he daren't come in no closer on account of his being spied on by them at the Manor.'

'Did he say what he wants to see me about?'

Sam Cooper shook his head. He was watching Rebecca without looking at her face, keeping a measured distance between them. He had always been nervous around gypsies.

'It's a message he says he should have passed on to you a week ago but wasn't able to on account of them watching him all the time.'

'A message? From Lukan?'

'I don't know sir, but I think you should come right away. Bennet's scared they'll miss him at the Manor and find out he's been listening at key-holes on Mr Lukan's account.'

Malcolm turned to Leonora, scowling. 'The old mine is no

place for you Leonora, especially in those flimsy riding shoes. I think you should wait here until we get back.'

'Well yes, if Rebecca ...'

Her words fell upon deaf ears as Malcolm strode from the room. Sam Cooper hesitated, reluctant to leave his young mistress alone with the gypsy woman, but a nod from Leonora reassured him enough to send him hurrying after Malcolm. As the door closed behind them Leonora turned to Rebecca with a practised smile. She had been watching the woman closely and was convinced that Rebecca Adams knew, or *feared* she knew, the reason for her brother's disappearance. The suspicion brought relief to Leonora. She would rather have him gone of his own accord, even in these strange circumstances, than lying dead or injured somewhere in the forest.

'I'm very sorry, Rebecca,' she offered graciously. 'In his concern for his friend, my husband seems to have mislaid his manners. Do you mind if I wait for him here?'

Rebecca shrugged, clearly resenting the intrusion. 'Don't apologise for Cavendish manners on my account. He's hated me since he was only five years old and first discovered that his precious Lukan was not his brother but *mine*.'

'A child's envy. I'm sorry.'

'I don't give *that* for your sympathy,' Rebecca declared, snapping her fingers. 'The dislike is mutual, you can be sure of that. I care nothing for the likes of him or for ...'

'... for the likes of me?' Leonora finished for her.

'You people have no right to come here in your fine clothes and fancy jewels expecting hospitality from me.'

Leonora spread her hands and looked surprised. 'Hospitality? Rebecca, you have so far offered neither comfort nor refreshment and you seem determined to be barely civil in your conversation. Quite frankly, I think your hospitality leaves much to be desired.'

The woman bristled. 'I did not invite you to my house.'

'Lukan's house,' Leonora corrected.

'Aye, Lukan's house, and a grand lady like yourself has no business with a man like him.'

Leonora rose from the chair, reluctant to relinquish the

firmness that seemed shaped to the contours of Lukan's own body. She looked directly at Rebecca and tried to speak as one woman to another. 'I happen to love him very deeply,' she confessed in a whisper.

'Love?' Rebecca snorted. 'You dare to call it love?' She turned her head and spat into the fire.

'Yes *love*, Rebecca. Nothing you say can make it any less than what it is.'

'What right have you to love a man like Lukan?'

'I did not choose it any more than he did.'

'*Pish!*' the gypsy hissed, spitting again.

Undaunted, Leonora gently pressed her point. 'You of all people must know how it is between us.'

'I know only that you have a husband and a son and still you torture my brother with this obscenity you call love.'

'Obscenity? My God, Rebecca, what are you saying?' Leonora drew back, shocked by what she thought she recognised in the other woman's eyes. She began to pull on her gloves, smiling politely to cover her discomfort. 'I think I should leave now. We seem to have said a little too much on the subject,' she suggested.

'Aye, you can creep off back to your husband and his Cavendish whelp, where you belong.'

Leonora rounded on her angrily. 'Now you just listen to me for a moment Rebecca Adams. Neither Lukan nor I would endure this heartache if it were in our power to end it. Never for one moment did we want our situation to be like this.'

'Liar! You enjoy the power of owning him.'

'That's nonsense. Nobody *owns* Lukan.'

'What kind of whore are you, Lady Cavendish? You could have any man you wanted.'

'I am no whore, Madam. I want no man but Lukan.'

'But why?' Rebecca almost screamed the question. Her fists were clenched, her face contorted into an ugly mask. 'Why him? Why Lukan?'

'Do you think I have not asked that of myself a thousand times?'

'You are a thief, Lady Cavendish. You take what should be mine, *mine!*'

'Yours?' Leonora echoed in a whisper. 'My God . . .'

'You have no right.' The black eyes flashed with hatred, giving Leonora a glimpse of the unpleasant reality behind the cold hostility. '*You have no right!*'

'Have *you*?' Leonora demanded, determined to fling Rebecca's ugly revelation back into her face. 'How dare you brand my love for him obscene? How dare you call *me* whore? My God, you are his *sister*, his own flesh and blood. Have *you* the right to love him as you do?'

An abrupt and brittle silence dropped between them. It confirmed that guilty knowledge each now possessed about the other, with Lukan de Ville, unknowing, as the cause of it. Then Leonora turned and strode toward the door.

'I'll wait in the barn for Sir Malcolm and Sir Oscar. Don't bother to see me out, Miss Adams. I can find my own way.'

Rebecca watched her through the window, feeling angry and frustrated and hating herself for being so transparent. Like Lukan, she found her emotions ran dangerously close to the surface in Leonora's company. She glared at the lovely young woman in her elegantly plumed hat and russet velvet riding habit. A man from the Earl's stables had charge of the two wolfhounds, keeping them in control on short, stout chains. The animals nuzzled Leonora's hands as she approached. Even they, wild, stubborn things that acknowledged the authority of only one man, fell to fawning and wagging their tails like stupid lap-dogs whenever she was near.

Rebecca left the window and seated herself in Lukan's big chair. She cleared her throat and spat into the flames. She should have held her tongue instead of speaking out as she did. She had only succeeded in giving the younger woman a weapon to use against her. Would she tell Lukan what she had discovered? Rebecca thought not. The Cavendish woman was far too clever to burden her lover with an unpalatable accusation which she could neither prove nor justify.

Large flecks of snow were begining to fall: soft, temporary stuff that swirled about on a stiffening breeze and would leave no trace of itself upon the ground. It blew into the chimney, disturbing the soot and setting the flames a-dance. Rebecca narrowed her eyes and peered into the fire. She had read the signs. She was sure her brother was safe and well and would soon be home again on Beresford soil, but to whose arms, and to whose bed was he returning?

II

The man called Eli Bennet was a nervous, wiry individual with pale hands that fluttered about him like feeble, dying things. His face was thin and badly bruised, and where a front tooth was missing a deep gash on his upper lip was healing in a scar. Someone had recently given him a sound thrashing, a master, by the looks of it, for his frail hands bore no signs of having struck a counter-blow in his defence. He glanced this way and that, constantly on the alert for spies. It was with great relief that he saw the dark clad figure and heard men's voices as the Earl's small group picked its way through the trees to the old mine. Eli Bennet did not care for the forest, especially after dark. There was a terrible scar circling his right leg as a reminder of the perils that awaited a man there, hidden traps and snares that threatened life and limb with every footfall.

'I have little faith in the word of a Fairfax man,' Sir Oscar complained as they stepped with care across the overgrown mine workings.

'He's Lukan's man,' Malcolm reminded him.

'So he says, but he lives and works at the accursed Manor. No man can serve two masters.'

'He can if the price is right.'

'Then we should take what he offers us with a pinch of salt. I will not trust the word of a Fairfax minion.'

Eli Bennet watched them approach, his cap clutched in his hand so that a livid wound was visible through his thinning hair, marking his scalp from hairline to crown. It had bled a great deal and, not being properly cleaned and tended, had closed with dirt and hair and congealed blood inside. He bowed to both men, acknowledged Sam Cooper with the briefest nod and addressed his words to Malcolm.

'I could get here no sooner, Your Lordship. That man of Mr Christopher's, he beat me something savage for going missing last week, and all I did was run over here to see Mr Lukan for a few minutes. Gone not half an hour, I was, but that big Irish lout has eyes like a hawk and a terrible fierce temper. If he finds out I'm here talking to you ...' He looked about him nervously, wringing his cap in his hands.

'Speak out man. Why have you brought us here?' Sir Oscar's mistrust was evident in his tone. He glowered, intimidating the lesser man with his stare.

Bennet cleared his throat anxiously. 'It's Mr Lukan, sir. They say he's not been seen for more'n a week now. They say he's gone missing and can't be found.'

'That's right,' Malcolm said. 'What can you tell us about it?'

'Well it's like this, sir. I came last week, that night your boy was christened, Lord bless him and keep him in His care. Early morning it was, not four o'clock and the forest as black as pitch. I had something important to tell Mr Lukan. I found him up and about, swilling himself down with water from the well and smelling of brandy. Funny that, because I never knowed Mr Lukan to smell of brandy afore that night.'

'How long have you been in his pay?'

'A year sir, ever since Your Lordship's wedding, only not in his pay. I wouldn't never take coin or kind from Mr Lukan.'

'What's this?' Sir Oscar sneered. 'An honourable man who takes neither coin nor kind for his services?'

Bennet nodded vigorously. 'S'right, Sir Oscar. He found me in the forest with my leg caught above the knee in a spring-loaded game trap. Took it off me with his bare hands, he did, afore the gangrene could set in. Then he carried me on his back all the way to the doctor's house in Little Clearwell. I'm in his debt for that and always will be, long as I live.'

'I'm sure your gratitude is commendable,' the Earl said

without much conviction. 'So how *do* you repay his kindness?'

'With information, sir. He wants to know what happens up at the Manor and I told him what I saw last week.' He touched gingerly at the wound in his head, wincing a little. 'And that big Irish bastard gave me a thrashing for being away from my bed without good reason.'

Malcolm drew the man away from a gaping hole in the ground. 'Stand here, where the ground is firmer. Now, you came to Mr Lukan's house at four in the morning on the night of my son's christening? What happened then? What did you say to him?'

Bennet cleared his throat and lowered his voice. 'I told him they'd had a visitor that morning at the Manor. Gentlemen with a beard it was, dusty and travel-stained and tired enough to sleep on his feet, by the looks of him. Said he wanted to speak to *Mrs* Fairfax.'

'What? Are you sure of that?' Sir Oscar demanded.

'Yes sir. Mrs Fairfax was who he wanted and Mr Christopher got himself all worked up and red in the face and stammering fit to burst his buttons, but he never told the truth, that there weren't now and never was no Mrs Fairfax. Just said she weren't available and sent him on his way. Didn't even offer the poor young gentleman rest and refreshment, just saw him off the premises real sharpish like, him and that nasty Irish watchdog of his.'

'Who was the man? What was his name?' Sir Oscar stepped forward, a sudden movement that caused Bennet to shrink away as if in anticipation of a beating. 'You say he had a beard? What colour was it? Was he blond? Were his eyes as blue as mine?'

'Hold up, father,' Malcolm said, surprised by the Earl's outburst. 'What are you thinking, that it was brother Horace sneaking back home to play mischievous games at Fairfax Manor?'

The Earl checked himself with a start. He too was taken aback by his sudden show of emotion. He had learned not to put his faith in so-called fortune, except when it moved in total opposition to his wishes. He had his searchers out as far as

Europe and South Africa in search of Jonathan Shelley, yet it would not surprise him to find that the boy had passed unseen not four miles from his door.

'There is a chance the caller was your brother,' he said, thinking not of Horace but of the half-brother who looked so like him, Jonathan Shelley.

'No sir, it weren't Sir Horace,' Bennet told him, shaking his head. 'I know Sir Horace well. It weren't him, and it weren't his temper, neither, begging your pardon, Sir Oscar. Quiet-spoken this one was, an engineer by trade he said, light brown hair and beard and blue eyes, sure enough.'

'And you say he left the Manor without complaint?'

'Yes sir. He kept demanding, sort of begging, really, to be allowed a few minutes with Mrs Fairfax, but he didn't make no trouble. Left like a lamb when Mr Christopher threatened to have him arrested, but they had to help him up into the saddle, he was that travel-worn and weary.'

'His name?' Malcolm said. 'What was his name?'

'I never heard it sir.'

'Damn it. *Damn!*'

'But he left a calling card. I pocketed it to show to Mr Lukan, and when he saw it, off he went, quick as you like, just saddled his horse and packed his travelling bags and set out after the gent with the beard. Four o'clock in the morning and he rode out of here like the hounds of hell were snapping at his heels.'

'Did he say where he was going? Think man, think. Did he say anything, anything at all that might tell us where he is?'

'No sir, only that he had to find the man and bring him back.'

'Bring him back? What, here to Beresford?'

'Yes sir. I told him everything I heard, that the man had ridden for days and would spend at least one night at the Sun and Swan on the Oxford Road. And if Mrs Fairfax changed her mind it would needs be soon, because he was sailing for North America within the week, working his passage over. Only there ain't no Mrs Fairfax and there never were, nor ever will be, so it seems to me.'

'Thank you Bennet. If that's all you can tell us, you'd best get back to Fairfax Manor before you are missed.'

'Thank you sir. I'm really sorry I couldn't get away to tell you no sooner than this, Your Lordship, only I'm watched night and day and I only just heard that Mr Lukan was missing feared harmed. That visitor weren't no villain though, just tired and dusty, and him sent off without so much as a drink of water for his pains. It ain't right, the Lord knows it wouldn't happen nowhere else but Fairfax Manor.'

They watched him replace his cap and attempt to walk backwards, bowing and touching his forelock until the uneven ground began to hamper him so that he turned and scrambled off towards the western boundary. A moment later he was back, waving a scrap of paper in his hand.

'I showed it to Mr Lukan before he took off in the night. It's the gentleman's calling card.'

Malcolm stared down at the stained and crumpled business card. It bore no address, just the legend: *C. Thornton, Esquire, Engineer.*

'The name means nothing to me,' he said, handing the card to his father.

He gasped. 'Thornton, that was Francine's maiden name.'

'Francine? But I thought she was a Cavendish?'

The Earl shook his head. 'Her mother Henrietta was the Cavendish. She married a Thornton and Francine gave the name to her second son.'

'Of course. Charles Thornton Shelley. I remember Horace making light of his aspirations and saying he'd never have the wherewithall to set himself up. My God, he still believes his sister was forced into marriage with Christopher Fairfax.'

Sir Oscar nodded. 'And that I, as his father's major creditor, could have him arrested on the spot.' He sighed and shook his head. He must have been bitterly disappointed after risking his liberty by coming here. America is half a world away. He must have been desperate to see his sister before he sailed.'

'So, this card explains everything. This is what took Lukan away from Beresford on the spur of the moment, without a word to anyone. Charles had a ship to catch.'

'And almost a full day's headstart.'

'But he was very tired and that would slow him down.'

'And Lukan was barely sober, I believe.'

Malcolm scowled. 'He'll bring him back, father. I'm sure of it. If Lukan set out to bring Charles Shelley back then bring him back he will, you can be sure of that.'

The Earl closed his eyes. He looked suddenly very tired. 'And perhaps young Charles will lead us to his brother.'

'Brothers,' Malcolm corrected. 'Leonora's twin is missing also, don't forget.'

'Quite. Quite.' They began walking back towards Lukan's house by the river. Winter sunshine glinted through the bare trees, lighting the pools of mist that clung to the hollows. Sir Oscar held back a hanging branch so that his son could pass safely along the narrow path. 'Will you tell Leonora what we know?'

'I think not,' Malcolm said. 'I'd rather not raise her hopes until we know for sure that Charles has been found.'

'That is wise,' his father said. 'I wonder if Jonathan has already sailed for America? I hope not. A man could lose himself for the rest of his life on that vast continent. Little wonder my agents have failed to find him, even after all these months.' Striding along behind his son Sir Oscar suddenly stopped dead in his tracks, a perplexed expression on his face. 'Malcolm?'

'What is it, father?'

'You say the name on the card meant nothing to you?'

'Nothing at all.'

'You had forgotten then, that Francine was a Thornton?'

'Not forgotten father. I never knew the name. As I told you, I thought she was a Cavendish by name as well as blood.'

'But Lukan knew. He read the card and recognised the name.'

'So it would seem,' Malcolm agreed.

'But how? Who gave him such intimate family information?'

'Not I.'

'Then whom?'

404

Malcolm smiled and frowned at the same time, puckering his face in a comical manner. 'Father, I'm sure I have no idea.'

'Then how did Lukan de Ville come to know something that you yourself were unaware of?'

'Really father, what does it matter *how* he knew, so long as he recognised the name on the card and acted promptly to track its owner down?'

The Earl shook his head and fell into step behind his son as they continued along the narrow, twisting path. 'It matters to me,' he muttered under his breath. 'It matters to me how that gypsy knew our business.'

III

On December 23rd they took tea on the terrace by the last of the afternoon's light, sipping hot chocolate and steaming spiced wine in a quiet, sheltered spot some distance from the house. Leonora was wearing an ankle-length cloak of fine grey wool completely lined with fur. When lowered the hood fell lightly across her shoulders, when lifted it framed her face in a halo of soft white fur. Beneath the cloak she wore a simply-cut day-dress of cream silk that covered her from throat to wrist to ankle while hugging every curve and hollow of her firm young body. She was radiant as she played the hostess, her finest and most pleasurable role. On either side of her chair the big grey wolfhounds sat obediently, elegant accessories to the beautiful Lady of Beresford.

Beside Leonora sat Anabel in her neat brown bonnet and heavy woollen cloak, and across from her sat Malcolm and the Earl, debating a fine political point in discreet whispers. Sir Marcus Shaw had joined them in their walled recess, along with Sir Percival Hall, his wife Lady Agatha and their daughter Violet. In another recess further along the terrace, two handsome young military men, splendid in their colourful uniforms, paid homage to the charms of Lady Constance

Hayward and her extremely pretty cousin Lady Angela Stanley-Slaughter. Here and there other house guests, early arrivals for the Christmas celebrations, took the crisp air after a rich and heavy luncheon, strolling about in groups of twos and threes across the winter lawns. Some distance away a game of battledore and shuttlecock was in progress, while closer to the house a young man fingered the strings of a banjo for the entertainment of a group of admiring ladies.

Leonora sighed and watched the gathering mists. The sky was low with snow-filled clouds and even the nearby forest was lost in parts to the poor visibility closing in all around them.

She heard no sound, yet the wolfhounds lifted their heads abruptly, sniffed the cold air and sat like statues, every sense and sinew on the alert. Puzzled, she set down her cup and stared from one to the other, noting the lifted ears, bright eyes and twitching flanks. Suddenly they were off, leaping from the recess to streak over the lawns like true-bred racing hounds released from their traps. Garvey, heavier and more muscular than his companion, slithered on the grass, regained his feet immediately and raced in pursuit of the equally swift Gillan.

'Ye gods, just look at those animals go,' a male voice exclaimed from across the lawn.

'A hundred says the lead dog keeps the advantage,' someone else called out, and then more voices joined the betting.

'My money's on the heavier dog. A hundred guineas on Garvey.'

'Go to it, Gillan. Go boy, go.'

Leonora rose from her seat as the wolfhounds made the Avenue of Oaks and raced at full speed, now side by side, along it. She peered beyond them into the failing light, the hairs prickling across the nape of her neck and her scalp suddenly tight and tingling. The hounds were running straight as arrows now, and no wild prey held such a steady course. Out of the greyness in the distance came a slow-moving shape, a single rider on a weary mount.

'Lukan!' She breathed his name.

'A rider,' someone shouted. 'Half-dead by the looks of him.'

'Lukan!' This time the voice was Malcolm's. He came to Leonora's side, squinting through narrowed eyes into the mist. 'It's Lukan. My God, it is, it's Lukan!'

'Two riders,' a man yelled from the lower terrace. 'Two riders. The horse is double-mounted.'

Sir Oscar stood. 'Quickly Cooper, go fetch a carriage and warm blankets. And brandy, fetch brandy.'

'It's the gypsy! It's Lukan de Ville!' The chorus of voices sounded shrill on the crisp December air. There was a brief ripple of applause as the excitement increased, 'By the gods, it's him, it's Lukan de Ville!'

Malcolm took Leonora's arm and ran with her down the slopes. Others joined them, forming a lively group that surged forward to meet the riders. Ahead of them the wolfhounds passed the horse, swung round and passed again, racing a figure-of-eight around the trudging animal. No longer silent, they barked and yelped like ordinary dogs as they flung themselves first in this direction, now in that, in their excitement. Malcolm released Leonora's arm and ran on ahead. She could see Lukan more clearly now, hunched over Raven's neck, swathed in his heavy black cloak like some defeated monk riding out of the mist. Malcolm sprinted along the avenue, reached the horse, took up the hanging reins and eased the animal to a halt. As he did so Lukan swung his leg over Raven's neck and with a groan slipped from the saddle and into his friend's welcoming embrace.

Malcolm clasped his hands at the back of Lukan's neck and held them there, leaning forward as he did so to touch the other's forehead with his own.

'My God, Lukan,' he said at last, his voice hoarse with emotion. 'We'd all but given you up for lost.'

'Oh ye of little faith,' the gypsy muttered.

'Are you hurt?'

Lukan laughed without mirth, but his eyes twinkled. 'I don't know. Ask me again tomorrow.'

By now a small crowd of fascinated guests was milling about the standing horse, staring at the travellers and calling out the occasional greeting to Lukan. The wolfhounds nuzzled their master's hands and leaned heavily against his legs. Both were whining softly. Malcolm ignored them.

'I'm glad you're home, Lukan.'

'Aye,' was all he said.

'I see you caught your man.'

Lukan nodded. 'A Christmas gift for your lady.'

Though bruised and weary to the bone, he turned to help his exhausted companion from the saddle. The other man groaned and shook himself awake, pulling the hood from his head as he found his feet and stood there, braced upon unsteady legs, staring beyond Malcolm Cavendish with red-rimmed eyes.

'Leonora?'

She had been slowed in her dash to greet Lukan by Anabel's restraining hands. But for them she might have been so overcome with relief as to abandon her composure and demonstrate her true feelings right there in that public place. Now she came to a complete halt some distance off, her hood thrown back and her breath frosting the air. The second rider was standing now. He was tall and bearded and painfully familiar. As if transfixed the two stared into each other's faces, then the man took a few stumbling steps towards her.

'Charles? Can it be ...? Oh my God ... *Charles?*' Her fingers came to her mouth to stifle a sudden cry, then her eyes grew wide with recognition and she raced forward to fling herself into his arms.

While brother and sister clung to each other the gathered guests made the most of the entertainment by cheering and applauding the happy moment. Men argued cheerfully about the hasty bets they had placed while their womenfolk looked on with smiles and no little number of tears. It was some time before Sir Oscar Cavendish, limping and leaning heavily on his cane, hurried forward to join the group. He took in the situation at a glance, then tightened his lips and stood discreetly to one side of the reunion. There would be time enough to question Charles Shelley about the whereabouts of his brother. This was the first step, the first link in the chain that would lead the Earl to his missing son, but for the moment all he could do was stand aside and leave Charles to the tears and welcoming embraces of his sister.

Sir Oscar turned to Lukan and, too proud to voice his thanks, offered him a brusque, firm handshake. The gypsy nodded an acknowledgement. He looked as if he had passed through hell and out the other side. His face was gaunt, dusty and bruised and his body sagged as if his legs lacked the strength to hold him upright. He was leaning against Malcolm's arm and for an instant Sir Oscar was stung by the old pain, the old barb that was Lukan's very existence. He had wanted the man found, first for Malcolm's sake and then because Charles Shelley would lead him to Jonathan, but now his gratitude was tempered with regret. And that regret was something he had been forced to live with for almost thirty years. Once again the truth of it was as clear as crystal in his troubled mind. It would have served him better had he set his vows aside and smothered that black-eyed brat when it was born.

Leonora and her brother were still clinging to each other, laughing and weeping and kissing each other's faces. They remained that way until Sam Cooper arrived with a closed carriage and Charles Shelley was helped inside. The fatigued man was handed blankets, copper warming-pans and a small flask of the Earl's best brandy. Malcolm helped Lukan back into the saddle.

'I wish you'd come back with us to the house,' he said again, but Lukan shook his head and gathered up the reins.

'Tomorrow then?'

'Aye,' Lukan nodded. He had turned off the tree-lined avenue and was heading for the forest with his wolfhounds trotting beside him when Leonora called his name.

'*Lukan de Ville!*'

He reined in his horse and slowly turned to face her. She was framed in the doorway of the crested carriage, her cloak falling in soft grey folds around her and her dark hair lying soft against the fur-lined hood. Their eyes met for a moment. She bowed her head the merest fraction, Lukan did the same, and

409

then they turned and went their separate ways. It was no more than that, a trivial thing to any other eye, and yet Sir Oscar Cavendish felt their mute communication slice like a blade across his deepest fears.

'Father? Are you all right?'

'Why should I not be?' he growled.

Malcolm frowned, surprised by his father's unnecessarily sharp response. 'For a moment there I fancied you were taken ill.'

'Nonsense. How is the boy?'

'Worn out, but he'll survive.' He opened the carriage door and lowered the steps. 'Will you ride to the house with us?'

The Earl shook his head and waved the carriage on. The long walk in the cold would do him good. He needed the exertion to help clear the questions and suspicions from his mind. He looked out across the fields to where the gypsy made for home, head lowered and shoulders hunched, his mount as worn and weary as himself. Sir Oscar watched him through narrowed eyes, then turned and limped rapidly after the carriage and the colourful entourage of guests walking in its wake. He tried to shake the black mood from his shoulders. He had seen nothing, heard nothing, witnessed nothing to justify his fears, and yet it had been there, a secret thing, something intangible. He had seen it at the wedding a year ago, and now again today. Too much had passed between them in that glance.

He stopped to catch his breath as a light fall of snow was carried on the wind from some distant place, swirling and gusting to give an eerie, half-hidden quality to the scene of carriage and walkers moving slowly away between two ranks of dark, bare trees. He looked to his left to see the mounted man now barely visible in the distance, where a thickening mist shrouded the forest's edge.

'I'll kill you,' he hissed at the small figure. 'So help me God, I'll kill you with my bare hands, gypsy, if you dare betray my son, to bed his wife.'

Oblivious, Lukan headed for the forest. At the barn he pulled the saddle and blanket from Raven's back and left

410

them to lie where they fell. He trudged slowly to the door of the house and flung it open. Rececca looked up from the fireplace, her dark gaze taking in the whole of him. Though sick with relief, her expression revealed none of it.

'You're back then?'

'Aye, I'm back, and weary enough to sleep for a hundred years.'

She caught him as his knees began to buckle, helped him to the couch and pulled off his cloak and boots. With a sigh he slid sideways until his face was pressed into the velvet-covered cushion. He was fast asleep even before Rebecca lifted his legs to the couch and tucked a warm, hand-stitched quilt around his body.

CHAPTER TWENTY

I

A s a guest staying over at Beresford for the Christmas celebrations, Sir Marcus Shaw was on hand to offer Charles the very best medical attention available. He found the young man to be suffering from much more than simple exhaustion. He was sporting several deep cuts and nasty grazes, and when the travel-soiled clothes were stripped from his body his nakedness revealed such extensive bruising as could only have been inflicted by a severe beating. Several cracked ribs had been smeared with a balm of comfrey and woundwort and tightly bound with the remnants of a man's white cotton shirt. A knife wound across the back of his neck was deep but healing cleanly. The knuckles of both hands, opened to the bone in some places, gave mute evidence of the violent battle he had fought in his own defence.

'A press-gang,' he explained before Sir Marcus administered sufficient laudanum to silence him for several hours. He grasped Leonora's hands in a pathetically weak grip and struggled to keep his gaze focussed on her face. It was as if he feared to surrender himself to sleep lest he lose her again after their long and painful separation. 'A press-gang, not even Englishmen. Foreigners, they were, all of them.'

'Hush Charles,' Leonora said, resting a dampened cloth across his forehead. His young face was lined and drawn, his eyes bleak. He looked like a cruel caricature of her brother. 'Go to sleep, my dear. We can talk later.'

As weariness closed his eyes, his feeble grip tightened fitfully around her fingers.

'Leonora?'

'I'm here, Charles.' She leaned over to press her cheek to his. 'I will sit with you while you sleep and I will be right here when you wake.'

He licked his damaged lips and groaned, remembering. 'They caught us in a beerhouse, six of them and only three of us, and one a lad of sixteen without so much as an inch of man's muscle on him. We took a beating but he got us out of there. Lukan got us out of there. We would have been taken, but for him.'

'It's over,' Leonora soothed. 'You're safe now.'

'We've been on the road for days with not a penny-piece between us,' he persisted. He was like a child who picks at a sore, needing to recall the pain or the triumph that had earned it. His eyes suddenly snapped open and he struggled to raise himself up. 'He's hurt. His ribs. His shoulder. Jesus, he must be black and blue all over. Leonora, I never saw a man fight the way he did. He was like a wild animal, or a madman. I saw one sailor turn and run at the sight of him. My God, he even growled and snarled like a beast.'

'Please Charles, lay back and sleep. You're safe now.'

'Help him, Leonora. He saved my life and the lad's too. He gave you back a brother and he gave some mother back her runaway son. You must help him.'

'Don't worry, Lukan is in good hands,' she assured him. 'He has Rebecca to care for him, and her skills can match those of any doctor.' She glanced at Sir Marcus Shaw and smiled a small apology for the comparison. 'Now sleep Charles, sleep.'

413

At last he allowed his head to fall back on the pillows and relaxed his body with a shuddering sigh. Leonora stroked his face, watching his eyes move fitfully behind his closed lids. It was some time before he ceased muttering and his hands fell, limp and unresisting, from hers.

Employing a small army of carefully selected servants, Leonora personally supervised the nursing of her brother. She sat beside him for long periods, took her meals in his room, even slept in the adjoining dressing room. Her only absences were the short trips she made to the nearby nursery to spend time with her small son. For those first anxious days of his return, she kept loyal vigil at her brother's bedside until his fever subsided and a healthier colour began to chase the deathly pallor from his face. Throughout that time he tossed and turned at intervals, mumbling and calling out in his dreams.

'Coming after us ... keep moving Jon ... needs a doctor ... a better ship ... Oh God, take care of each other ... I'll follow ... I'll follow.'

After such an outburst he might sleep for one hour or six, deeply and without stirring, before the anxious whispers began again. In his delirium he relived the hardships of life as a fugitive, the terrible fight in the beerhouse, the agonising journey home when he and Lukan, both badly injured, were forced to trudge long miles on foot, riding turn and turn about to save the horse. And he relived that morning of two weeks ago when Christopher Fairfax, after callously informing him that his mother was dead and his sister unwilling to see him, turned him from the house without so much as a glass of ale to help keep out the cold.

Occasionally he would awake in a state of acute tension and begin to talk rapidly, as if his very life depended upon how many words he could utter before the laudanum once again took its effect on his battered body. Little by little, between the lucid moments and the delirium, Leonora began to piece the story together. She shared what she knew with Malcolm, Sir Oscar and Sir Marcus when they came to sit with her each evening, and together they were able to fit the fragments of

414

information into a clear, coherent whole.

Faced with a tidal wave of creditors clamouring for payment of their father's debts, cornered by the inflexible terms of the protection offered to their family by Nigel Fairfax, the brothers had fled by ship to Calais and from there to Paris. Lady Louisa Fenwick joined them as planned after leaving her mother's London home at dead of night accompanied by her favourite maid and carrying only her jewels, a few personal papers and a single change of clothes. Within days she and Jonathan were married in a simple ceremony at a small country church outside Reims, after which the maid reluctantly returned to England. From Reims they fled to Lyons, and from there to Marseille, Milan, Florence, Rome and Naples. Convinced that the Earl of Beresford, their father's wealthiest creditor, would spare no cost in tracking them down, the three young fugitives travelled a haphazard course around Europe for as long as they were able to keep moving. When their meagre funds dried up they were compelled to slow their progress and take whatever work became available to them. The boys worked as tutors, coachmen, accountants and fencing teachers. They taught English to French students, German to Italian students, French to the Germans. They worked in gardens, orchards and hayfields, mended fishing nets, groomed horses and laboured in vineyards. Deprived of the love and support of their families and determined not to live the rest of their lives in fear, the trio finally came to a momentous decision. They would sail for North America, where land was readily available and all a man needed in order to succeed was a strong arm, a clear head and a dream worth working for.

Leonora experienced a deep sense of pride as the story unfolded. Despite the many hardships, her brothers had refused to be beaten. Even when their letters home had been ignored, when they felt themselves abandoned to their fate, their fortitude shone through undimmed. It demanded a great deal of courage for three young people of their gentle backgrounds to set out with empty purses for a new world thousands of miles away. But fate had one more blow to deal them before they left familiar soil behind, perhaps for ever. With their minds made up and their passage guaranteed, Louisa fell ill and it was discovered that she was almost four months pregnant. In order to spare her the dangers and discomforts of a lengthy journey by steerage class, it was agreed that Charles would remain behind and follow them out when he could. The money raised on his ticket, plus his share of the trio's joint fortunes, was put towards securing a decent berth on a better ship and a regular supply of food for the journey.

'At first we were prepared to risk the journey by English timber ship, despite the horrific stories we had heard of hardship amongst passengers and vessels lost at sea through drunkenness of both captain and crew,' Charles explained. 'But when we discovered Louisa's condition we set our sights on one of the safer United States ships at almost four times the cost. We were desperate. We sold everything, the horses and saddles, our signet rings and pocket watches, the last of Louisa's jewellery. We had to think of the child, you see. We had to consider the child.'

So the brothers had reluctantly parted company for the first time in their lives in a venture that would set the entire Atlantic ocean between them. Poor Charles had been totally unprepared for the sudden lowering of his spirits that followed the couple's departure. For several weeks he worked as a casual labourer on the docks in an attempt to raise his own passage. He slept in cheap, dirty hovels, ate the poorest food, prowled the seething streets in constant fear of being taken by robbers, press-gangs or agents of his father's creditors. At last, worn out and lonely and still less than half way to achieving his goal, he took his courage in both hands and headed for England. Lonely, friendless, and desperate to see his family again before quitting Europe for America, he bought himself the cheapest available coach ticket to Oxford.

'An outside seat?' Leonora exclaimed when she heard that part of it. 'Oh Charles, the journey must have been dreadful in this bitterly cold weather.'

Charles nodded, sleepy after yet another dose of laudanum. 'It was, and space was at a premium, with men, women, baggage and small children all crammed together so tightly we could barely breathe. Still, it cost half the price of an inside seat and at least it didn't rain. And it was fast. We were able to make an average of nine miles an hour on some stretches.'

'You arrived at Fairfax Manor on horseback,' she reminded him. 'Did you hire the horse at Oxford?'

He nodded. 'At the White Swan, and with money I could ill afford to spend. Oh God, Leonora. I am so sorry about mother. So very sorry.'

'Hush Charles.'

'For her to die like that, penniless and despairing.'

'But she left us a precious legacy,' Leonora smiled sadly. 'One letter, one family secret that has lifted us all beyond the reach of poverty. We have the protection of the Earl of Beresford now, all of us.'

'But on what terms?' he groaned. 'At what cost?'

She smiled and kissed his brow. 'No terms, no cost. Thanks to mama's love, Sir Oscar's protection is unconditional. Now sleep, you stubborn man, and we'll discuss the details later.'

Sitting out the long hours by Charles's bedside, Leonora contemplated the many hardships and disappointments the brothers had faced since fleeing their home at the insistence of Nigel and Christopher Fairfax. While she had enjoyed a wonderful society wedding that gave her a title and security for the rest of her life, Johathan and Louisa had wed like peasants in a tiny country church on foreign soil. Their guests had not been glittering society people with noble pedigrees but curious strangers from the nearby village. Instead of a banquet their wedding breakfast had been a humble picnic on the edge of a hayfield. Their marriage bed had been a straw-filled mattress in the barn of a local farmhouse, lacking the refinements of either pillows or clean linen. Leonora was saddened by the comparisons until she recalled the love that had shone in Louisa Fenwick's eyes whenever she looked at Jonathan. That quiet, very likable young lady had surrendered her home, her family and her reputation in order to live like a wandering gypsy with the man she loved.

'I would rather live with him in his world, whatever and

wherever that may be, than be forced to live without him in mine,' she had declared, and soon enough had slipped away to prove the declaration was no idle jest. Now Leonora shuddered at the thought. She herself had narrowly escaped being confronted by the same decision. Had it come to that, she feared she might have done as much for Lukan.

'She's a brave girl, cheerful and uncomplaining. Our brother is a fortunate man Leonora, and a happy one. Already Louisa has proved herself the very best of wives.'

Charles told her this on the third day of his recovery, while she attempted to feed him an infusion of catamint to ease his internal bruising and a rich beef broth to help build up his strength. He was looking better. Malcolm's manservant, Hammond, had shaved away the shaggy beard and trimmed his untidy hair, washed much of the grime from his body and scraped the dirt from beneath his fingernails. Propped up against a mound of pillows, he explained that Louisa had written to her mother on numerous occasions, using an accommodation address in case the Dowager Duchess tried to have her daughter brought back to England by force. She asked only forgiveness and the Duchess's blessing on their marriage, but neither was to be forthcoming. Even when she wrote a final letter swearing this to be her last attempt at a reconciliation, Lady Fenwick had ignored her. Louisa knew she must stand firm. The risks she took in writing home were enormous.

'*We do not believe the Earl to be a vengeful or vindictive man,*' she had written, '*but honour means much to his family, and the offences against him are grave. We feel sure he will not rest until he has seen justice done, and since Herbert Shelley has vanished without trace, poor Jonathan must shoulder the whole burden and answer to Sir Oscar's wrath. Wherever we flee, it seems his agents are not far behind. I risk my husband's life each time I put pen to paper, and since we plan to leave for a new life abroad, I must beg you for the last time to give us your blessing. We can delay no longer than the month's end. After that may be too late for us. I pray you will not fail me.*'

'But fail her she did,' the Earl whispered to Leonora while Charles was sleeping. They were sitting in opposite chairs with an ornate card table set between them. Sir Oscar set down a red queen with a snap of his elegant fingers. 'I read that very letter when I visited Lady Fenwick some months ago. Louisa is disowned and disinherited. It seems the Duchess would rather lose her daughter's love completely than see a single social eyebrow raised against her.'

Leonora nodded thoughtfully. The Duchess had invented a brief and innocent romance between Louisa and a certain young gentleman of good family who was, unfortunately, quite unsuitable as a potential husband. Too discreet to mention the young gentleman's name, she would say only that he was a younger son and therefore virtually penniless. The Duchess had considered it prudent to remove her daughter to relatives in Italy in order to nip the friendship in the bud, and from there the girl had gone on to take the grand tour of Europe, which comfortably accounted for her lengthy absence. The story had gone in detail from her own lips and could not now, with dignity, be undone.

'Pride,' Leonora said sadly, fanning out the collection of playing cards in her hands. 'We put such excessive value on it, yet it not only brings us misery, it also has the power to destroy us.'

He looked at her sharply but found no hint of reproach or innuendo in her eyes. His pride had kept him from her mother's bedside when she lay dying. It seemed unlikely that she would ever forgive him for that, and yet there were times when he was sure she had, when he thought he saw as much in her eyes.

He set down the hand of playing cards he had been studying and declared, 'If only I could have seen that final letter from Louisa soon after it arrived. A month she kept it from me, *a whole month*!'

'Perhaps you should have told her more on your first visit. She obviously did not consider it in her own interests to expose the runaways and risk a public scandal.'

'I'll wager the lady regrets her secrecy now. I informed her that by marrying Jonathan Shelley, Louisa had unwittingly achieved a far higher position in society than any her mother could have got for her.'

'No more than that?'

'No more than that,' Sir Oscar said. 'She now knows that a firm link exists between her family and mine. She has it on the very best authority that Louisa has made an extremely good marriage, and yet she is unable to capitalise on the information. I will not have her preen herself in public at my expense. She will have the truth, and the freedom to use it, only when Jonathan is found, not a moment before. Damn her pride, that letter could have led us right to him.'

'We'll find him soon, when Charles can tell us more about their arrangements,' Leonora assured him. 'But might I suggest that you hold your agents off from approaching him? He'll be looking out for strangers and cautious of anyone who mentions his name so far away from home. A simple letter from his sister will suffice. He'll recognise my handwriting, and have no cause to go to earth again.'

Sir Oscar reached across the small table to pat the back of her hand in a fatherly manner. 'Don't worry, I will give the matter very careful consideration and talk over my plans with you before I put them into effect. Will that suit you?'

'It certainly will. Thank you.'

She smiled, that now-familiar softness in her eyes. They were joined, these two, tied not so much by friendship as by mutual interests and by the secrets each was party to. It was a strange alliance. Whenever he sought to confirm her affection as genuine she would find some way of demonstrating her sincerity as surely as if she had read his mind. And yet he remained unsure and hated himself because of it.

'I thought you women devoured the society pages of every newspaper,' he remarked. 'If that is so, why has Louisa Fenwick not read of your marriage to Malcolm and the birth of little William? So much has been written about you in the last year.'

Leonora shook her head. 'No Sir Oscar, I fear you misunderstand our feminine ways completely. Louisa will not even glance at the society pages. She is a young woman of nineteen who once enjoyed an enviable position in society, but now she has cast herself adrift from all that. How could she hope to build a new life whilst clinging to the frills and flounces of her past? No, she will not torture herself by reading about the friends and acquaintances who loved her once but would now cut her dead in public rather than risk becoming sullied by her present behaviour.'

Just then Chalres muttered and turned his head on the pillow. Leonora went to him at once, soothing him with gentle words, mopping his hot brow with a dampened cloth. At hourly intervals she fed him a few sips of tonic made from bitter wormwood mixed with rosemary, blackthorn and saffron to hide the bitter taste. The whole room smelled of dried lovage and lavender, crushed catamint and calamus root, and though a huge fire blazed in the grate, behind their heavy drapes both windows had been thrown wide open to the fresh, crisp winter air. She was attentive to her patient, seemingly tireless as she divided her time and energies between her husband, her son and her injured brother. The Earl watched her. Even now, more than a year after her marriage to his son, he could find not the smallest fault in her. She had proved herself the perfect wife and mother and endeared herself to everyone who knew her. If she was guilty of any misdemeanour she was gifted beyond words at concealing it. Had her mother before her shown such grit, such cool and calculating resolve in disguising her own involvement in Herbert Shelley's dishonest financial affairs? The thought shocked him. He shook himself, horrified that he had slipped so easily into condemning Francine and assuming her daughter's guilt despite the weight of evidence to the contrary. To cover his discomfort he pulled out his pocket watch, snapped the case open and scowled at the dial.

'I must be going. There is something I wish to do before nightfall.'

'Of course, Sir Oscar,' she smiled. 'Shall we finish our game this evening, after dinner perhaps?'

'Certainly, if you wish it.'

He left her quickly and returned to his own apartments where he changed into outdoor clothes and called for his horse to be saddled.

II

With his groom following a measured distance behind, Sir Oscar rode to the extreme western edge of his earldom and drew his mount to a halt. Running parallel to the bridle way were an ancient stone wall and a ditch made treacherous by the rich growth of foliage completely covering it in places. Beyond those twin barriers was a stretch of sparse woodland fringing several acres of uncultivated brush, and beyond that the ill-designed gardens of Fairfax Manor.

Sir Oscar raised himself in the saddle and viewed the house through narrowed eyes. No architect worth his salt would have put his name to that badly proportioned façade, and no builder of repute would own to erecting those ludicrous sandstone pillars and vaulted porch. It was so vulgar in design as to be an affront to the senses.

'Cavendish land,' he said aloud. 'That eye-sore stands on what is rightfully Cavendish land.'

'Sir?'

Tom Tyler the groom moved his horse forward. He was a watchful man in his late thirties, thickset and renowned for his brawling skills. When drunk he could recite every kindness of word or deed shown to him over the years by the Earl of Beresford and his family, and hard work and loyalty were his way of repaying the debt. An ugly scar marked his face from lip to ear on his left side, inflicted by the only Cavendish who had every treated him badly, the second son, Horace. True to his type, Tyler hated Horace with an intensity only equalled by his love for the Earl. Now he urged his mount forward, a deep frown puckering his rough country features.

422

'Ride down to the yew tree near the second fork,' his master instructed. 'You'll find a gap in the wall and a pack-horse bridge over the ditch. Go directly to the Manor and tell Mr Christopher Fairfax I will speak to him at the south gate immediately.' He handed the man a card on which was printed his full name and titles. 'Tell him the matter is of the utmost urgency. I will not be put off and I do not care to be kept waiting.'

'Very good sir.'

As the groom rode off Sir Oscar turned his horse toward the south gate, where both Cavendish and Fairfax properties met the dirt road linking the villages of Kingswood, Bishorne, Wortherton and Judd. He smiled wryly as he thought of the last, a poor, overgrown little place with crumbling houses and only a handful of settled inhabitants. That dying village whose name the manor had once borne was just one more example of Fairfax stupidity. On old Nigel's orders, the local stream supplying water to the village had been diverted to feed the ornamental fountains and flower-beds of the manor house. Judd was left with a tiny ditch that ran dry in hot weather, froze in winter and stank to high heaven most of the year. As Fairfax steadfastly refused to provide sufficient clean water, decent housing and fair wages for his workers, the old families were forced to move on in search of something better. Now Judd had become a haven for thieves and squatters, bands of poachers, fugitives fleeing from the law. Nigel Fairfax, who might have had a steady supply of loyal workers at his disposal, had created instead a squalid slum right on his own doorstep.

At the south gate cross-roads the Earl dismounted. There had been a great deal of rain in the last few days and the ground in places had become a muddy quagmire. Where the ditch turned and narrowed there was a gap, probably caused by animals, that allowed the overflow to run free and form a wide, muddy pond. He made a mental note to have the water cleared and the bank rebuilt before the worsening weather turned the whole area into an ice-trap for horses and vehicles alike.

423

It was a long time before Christopher Fairfax arrived, by which time the temper of his visitor had not improved. He came by open carriage, being too heavy and capriciously balanced to trust himself in the saddle. At sight of him, bloated and sweating in his haste to do the Earl's bidding, Sir Oscar was filled with disgust at the very idea that his son's wife should be coveted by this man. To his certain knowledge there had never been a Fairfax worthy to join the company of true gentlemen.

A surly driver with a streaming cold helped the fat man down from the carriage and stood off at a distance, coughing and sneezing noisily. Christopher Fairfax waddled forward, panting and mopping his brow with a handkerchief as if he had come the whole distance on foot.

'S-Sir Oscar. G-good to s-see you s-sir.'

Sir Oscar ignored the proffered hand. 'This not a social call.'

'M-my f-father is n-not ...'

'I am already informed that your father is in London, at his offices,' Sir Oscar cut in curtly. 'It's you I want to see.'

'It is?'

'Yes, I want an explanation, Fairfax.'

'W-what?'

'On December 12th a man came to you asking for his sister, whom he believed to be your wife. You told him she was unavailable and sent him away without benefit of rest and hospitality. That young man had travelled for days in the hope of speaking to his sister. You were callous enough to tell him that his mother was dead and his younger brother lost without trace, yet you lacked the decency to inform him that his sister Leonora is now the wife of my son. Why?'

'W-well ... er ... I d-didn't ... th-that is I d-don't ...'

'For Heaven's sake pull yourself together Fairfax. You treated Charles Shelley in the most brutal fashion and turned him from your door as if he were your enemy. I demand to know why you did that.'

Fairfax began to bluster. 'D-demand n-nothing of m-me sir, if you please.'

424

'You treated him abominably.'

'Th-that was m-my prerog-prerogative. The m-man w-was n-not invited.'

'He wrote letters. He was expected.'

'N-no. N-not true ... n-not true.'

Sir Oscar sighed. He knew the man was lying. 'I have come for the letters, Fairfax,' he said coldly.

The fat man took several rapid steps backwards and only avoided stepping into the muddy pool by a few short inches. 'W-what l-letters?'

'Charles Shelley wrote to his sister at your address. They all did, and I want those letters, Fairfax.'

The fat man shook his head and took another step backwards. The rows of soft flesh hanging below his jaw wobbled like layers of milk-jelly.

'N-no, th-there have b-been n-no l-letters,' he stammered.

'I believe you to be a liar, sir.'

'Y-you insult m-me ...'

Sir Oscar shook his head. 'I state a fact. You are a liar sir.'

'S-Sir Oscar, I will s-speak to my f-father about this.'

'Do that,' the older man said. 'But first allow me to reiterate what I have already told him. I *know* you are in possession of private letters from the Shelley brothers to their sister.' He jabbed his forefinger in the air as he spoke, making no actual contact but driving the nervous Fairfax backwards into the mud. 'And I will have your hide for it, Fairfax. Believe me, I will have your hide for what you are doing to my family. Those letters are private property and you have no right to withhold them. What's the matter with you man? Are you riven by petty spites because the lady was too good a catch to settle for the likes of you?'

Standing ankle deep in mud, Fairfax stuttered and wobbled and gradually began to turn a deep shade of purple. Drops of perspiration flew off as he shook his head. He waved his fists, in the air, spraying spittle as he shouted his reply.

'She was mine,' he yelled. 'She was p-promised to me, to m-*me*! Your son had no right to t-take her. She was mine, do you hear, mine, m-*mine*!'

With a final shake of his fists he attempted to turn but found his shoes stuck fast in the mud. He struggled to maintain his balance but failed, despite the frantic wafting of his arms. His eyes bulged, his mouth shaped itself into a tight oval and a moment later he flopped on to his back in the mud, his bulk dispersing the pool in all directions. His struggles to rise were to no avail. He simply lay there as helpless as a beached whale, gibbering in his frustration.

Disgusted as much by the man's unexpected outburst as by the sight of him floundering in the mud, trapped by his own obesity, Sir Oscar swung himself into the saddle and, without uttering another word, turned and rode for Beresford Hall.

He was still unsettled when he met Leonora for cards after dinner. Unwilling to return to the subject of Jonathan, he allowed his thoughts to brood upon that brief but telling contact she had made with Lukan de Ville on the Avenue of Oaks.

'You never ask after Lukan,' he said at last, watching her smooth the covers on the bed.

'Why do you say that? Is he not recovering as rapidly as Malcolm has been led to believe?' She sounded curious, no more than that.

He looked for something extra in her eyes, saw only the clear, unusual colouring of them. He shrugged. 'He's well enough, so I believe. You do not appear to think too highly of him.'

'Nor do you, Sir Oscar.'

'*Touché*,' he smiled, then shook his head and added, frowning, 'I confess to disliking the man intensely. Always have and always will.'

She smiled at his candour. 'I agree he is not an easy man to like, but he has proved himself a sound and constant friend to Malcolm over the years, and for that we must all be grateful. He also saved my life that day at the fair when Starlight Warrior bolted and I was too startled to step away from the danger.' She glanced down at the sleeping man, clean-shaven now and bathed free of the journey's grime. She smiled the way he had seen her smile at little William, as if her heart had

426

suddenly risen to her eyes. 'And now he has brought my missing brother home to me. Like him or not, I fear I will be forever in his debt.'

Sir Oscar stiffened, recalling the way the gypsy and she had managed, or so he had been convinced, to convey so much with a single look. 'I detest such obligations. They can be cumbersome burdens, especially for a woman. They are plagued with hidden dangers.'

'Dangers?' She blinked her eyes and smiled a little. She had an open, innocent look about her. 'Do you think the man *dangerous?*'

He scowled. 'Debt makes the giver strong and the taker vulnerable.'

'Not in this case,' she smiled. 'I am deeply thankful to Mr de Ville, of course, but any recompense he might require for his efforts must be addressed to Malcolm, not to me. Believe me, Sir Oscar, I do not find my feelings of gratitude either burdensome or in any way compromising.'

'I'm glad to hear it.'

'And certainly not *dangerous*!'

He shrugged. She was teasing him. He rose from the table, their card game forgotten, and clasped his hands behind his back.

'You worry too much, and without just cause,' she told him lightly. 'Whatever we two might think of him, Mr de Ville is a gentleman to the core.'

'He is a *gypsy*.'

'Be that as it may ...' Now she too rose from her seat, her expression suddenly serious. She drew in her breath and expelled it in a long sigh. 'Sir Oscar, I fear you see a problem where none exists, and in doing so you compel me, in all fairness, to defend a person whom I barely know and scarcely care for.'

'Of course I do,' he conceded on the instant. 'And such a thing is unforgivable. It was careless of me and I ask your pardon for it.' He offered her a small how which she acknowledged by inclining her head. 'However, there is one small matter ...'

'Yes? Please speak out freely if something is troubling you.'

He cleared his throat and handed her the calling card her brother had presented at Fairfax Manor.

'Charles Thornton,' she read aloud. 'To avoid arrest he has chosen to use his middle name, my mother's maiden name.'

'How did de Ville know of it?'

'I beg your pardon?'

'The name.' He watched her face, her eyes. 'He saw the card and recognised the name at a glance. I wonder how he came by that information?'

Leonora shrugged prettily. 'It seems likely to me that Malcolm has discussed my family with him at some time. After all, I am a Cavendish by blood as well as by name, and many people are keen to ascertain from which branch of the family tree I sprang.'

'Not Malcolm. I asked him, but the name meant nothing to him.'

'Oh? That surprises me.'

'And yet Lukan de Ville knew of it.'

Leonora frowned. 'Forgive me, but I don't quite understand, Sir Oscar. What exactly are you saying? Is there some mystery here? Do you suspect the man of some kind of underhand behaviour?'

She was looking at him with such openness, such blameless curiosity, that he mentally chastised himself for being a fool. And yet he would have sworn that her lovely gaze had not been quite so innocent when it met the heathen stare of Lukan de Ville. This girl had always kept him on a knife-edge of uncertainty. He felt that familiar prickling down his spine, supposedly a sign that somewhere in the world a foot had stepped upon the plot of land where his corpse would one day lie. It was an oddly chilling and unsettling experience, one he had never known until this lovely young woman came into his life.

He forced himself to smile. 'I suspect the man of anything and everything.'

'You worry too much.' She stood on tiptoe to kiss his cheek and her warmth, her scent, her potent femininity invaded his senses in a sudden rush.

'Perhaps I do,' he granted.

She cocked her head on one side. 'It's Jonathan, isn't it? What you are *really* concerned about is Jonathan.' When he moved as if to turn away from her she placed her hand on his arm and squeezed it gently. 'We'll find him soon,' she promised with a dazzling and quite disconcerting smile.

Sir Oscar covered her hand with his. She had an almost childlike way of deflecting his ill-tempers and putting a different name to his unease. What started as foreboding over her relationship with Lukan de Ville had been reshaped, put back upon itself. And she was right, he cared about his missing son and wished with all his heart that the prodigal sleeping peacefully in that bed could have been Jonathan Shelley instead of his younger brother. And still that look was present in her laughing turquoise eyes, deceit or innocence, he could not tell.

'Good night, my dear,' he said, touching his lips to her hand.

'Good night, Sir Oscar.'

Leonora walked with him to the door, closed it behind him and turned the key in the lock. Then she leaned her back against the door and closed her eyes as her body sagged with relief. The sigh she issued was almost a groan. Her father-in-law had been taken in by her show of innocence, just as he had been when Elizabeth had very nearly exposed Leonora and Lukan as lovers. She blessed every past necessity for deception, every practised social skill that had helped make such a convincing, open-faced liar of her. She passed a hand over her forehead as she crossed the room to check that Charles was sleeping comfortably. The existence of a grubby calling card, seen by the right person at the right time, had reunited them after more than a year apart, yet that same godsend might so easily have been her undoing. All the long hours spent lying in Lukan's arms, the whispered words in the darkness, the shared confidences, came back to her with a startling clarity. At any given time they might be no more than a slip of the tongue, a guilty revelation of some secret intimacy, from exposure.

429

Malcolm arrived much later to share a light supper with her before returning to his own rooms for the night. His gaze flickered over her, taking in the prettily embroidered cotton shift beneath the loose silk robe, the pale hollow of her throat and the rounded firmness of the breasts that suckled his baby son.

'You look lovely,' her told her, and smiled at the sudden rush of colour to her cheeks. Then his smile widened and he strode across the room to the alcove where Charles Shelley lay only half-aware of his surroundings. 'And you there, Mr Shelley. How are you feeling?'

'Sleepy,' was the whispered reply.

'Good. Plenty of rest is the very thing you need right now. Sir Marcus tells me he's quite pleased with your progress. He assures me you'll be up and about and fit to be put to work in the fields before the week is out.'

The joke was wasted on Charles. 'Lukan. Tell me about Lukan.'

Malcolm grinned. 'I saw him only this afternoon. He was sitting by the fireside with his ribs strapped and his right arm tightly bound across his chest, stinking of his sister's herbal remedies and growling about being reduced to the existence of a pampered lap dog. His mood is thunderous and his scowl enough to curdle milk at a hundred paces. In other words, our friend Lukan is virtually his old self again.'

Charles chuckled and winced at the same time. 'Damn it, don't make me laugh, my ribs won't stand it.'

Leonora stepped between them to remove several pillows from Charles's back and ease him down to a lower level. She shot Malcolm a stern look but her eyes were twinkling with amusement as she imagined the big gypsy confined to his own hearth and hating every minute of it. Then she frowned, recalling her heated exchange with Rebecca Adams. At least she knew that Lukan was in good hands. His sister would nurse him with a tireless devotion, and if that prospect caused Leonora's flesh to crawl, it was only because she had recognised the woman's fierce, unnatural passion for her own brother.

Leaving Charles to sleep again, she drew Malcolm closer to

430

the fire where their supper tray was set on a nearby table. She ate a little roast chicken and sweet breast of veal, followed by poached fruits in a rich cream sauce. Her night-time drink was fresh cow's milk, warmed and with a little honey added. Always careful with her diet, she had become much more fastidious since giving birth. She would have no wet-nurse suckling her son. In the big cities innumerable babies sickened and died each year at the breast of unwashed, uncaring women whose milk was tainted by bad food and alcohol, or by nipples left unwashed between one infant and another. Even in country areas where food might be more wholesome and the local ale less damaging to the system, a mother could never be sure what ills her child might swallow with a stranger's milk. Besides, Leonora was far too possessive of her son to watch him suckle at another woman's breast.

'I know that look. You were thinking of William.'

She nodded, smiling.

'He's a wonderful boy,' Malcolm declared. 'And father dotes on him. Already he's talking about making a handsome settlement on him for the future.'

'Sir Oscar is very generous,' she said.

Malcolm raised an eyebrow. 'Do I detect a missing *but* to follow that statement?'

In a rush of words Leonora told him what had passed between herself and the Earl. She expressed concern about his mood and supposed that no slur on Lukan's character had been intended. 'And there's something else,' she added. 'Something I should have told you a long time ago.'

Malcolm set down his cup and watched her closely, 'Go on.'

'Your father and I share a confidence,' she said. 'I made an undertaking to say nothing until he was in a position to discuss the matter fully with you. He is a good man and I was happy to keep his confidence. I still am, but it frightens me to imagine how you will judge me when you learn the truth of it.'

'Judge you?' he asked. 'Leonora, do you really think me capable of *judging* you?'

'I believe a wife should keep no secrets from her husband,'

431

she replied, looking him directly in the eye. 'I am torn between the two of you. Must I respect your father first and you thereafter?'

Malcolm shrugged. 'In this case it would seem you have no choice, unless you intend to speak out now.'

'Oh no.' Leonora shook her head. 'It is not my place to speak out on such a personal matter, not even to you.'

'And I respect you for that, but . . .'

'But I want you to understand that it has not been easy for me,' she added quickly. 'We share a secret, your father and I. You will know of it soon enough, and I only ask that you think no less of me for keeping it from you all this time on his behalf.'

Without getting up, Malcolm moved his chair away from the table and held out his arms for her to come to him. Leonora obeyed, allowing herself to be settled in his lap like a small child. He pressed his lips against the pale flesh of her neck, breathing her perfume and the echoing scent of rosemary in her hair. It seemed that only yesterday he left the church of St Michael and All Angels with his first bride on his arm and met the gaze of a beautiful young girl in the crowd, a girl with ruby-dark hair and eyes the colour of freshly-opened violets. He had wondered since if he could have loved her from that moment, when she was perhaps fifteen, a cousin he barely knew, and he was just embarking upon the tragedy of his first marriage. It astonished him now to consider what shifts and changes, sorrows and misfortunes it had cost to bring them together.

'I love you,' he whispered against her hair.

'I love you too,' she replied, and spoke the truth. She did love Malcolm, just as the gypsy woman had predicted, with all her heart. What she felt for her husband was tender and undemanding. That other love was worlds apart from it.

'I know about Jonathan,' he said.

She stiffened. 'What?'

'My mother told me years ago, during one of her infamous rages. I knew it was true. Why else would she hate your mother so? How else would Jonathan and my brother Horace

432

bear such a startling resemblance to each other?'

She stared at him aghast. 'You knew, and yet said nothing?'

'Like you I had my loyalties. Father paid for his education and watched his progress with a keen eye. He loved him the more because he looked so much like Horace and yet possessed all the better, more admirable qualities my brother so clearly lacked. What surprises me is that he never acknowledged him. In this day and age a man is not only respected but admired for openly supporting his off-borns. Indeed, I have an uncle who insists on raising *two* fine bastards in his own nursery along with his legitimate brood.'

'He didn't know,' Leonora said, shaking her head.

'What? How could he *not* know? He loved your mother, even his own wife was aware of that. How could he love her so and not be aware that he had given her a son?'

'Because she lied to him,' Leonora said, blessing her husband for his open mind and heart. 'It was only after she died that I came across the truth in her letters. Oh Malcolm, she loved him so desperately that she married Herbert Shelley rather than force your father into sacrificing everything for her.'

Malcolm looked shocked. 'Did it come to that?'

'It did.'

Malcolm rubbed his chin thoughtfully. They were discussing a time when he was just a child and Horace a babe in arms. He had not been aware that they had come so close to losing their father. He nodded thoughtfully. 'Yes, it makes sense. At that time he had a wife, two sons, and was heir to everything his own father possessed. My grandfather was an unbending man who put family honour and commitment above all else. He would have disowned his son and seen him penniless before allowing him to abandon his responsibilities in favour of a mere *mistress*.'

Leonora winced at the word, though it was the only one that truly described her mother's situation. In society's terms Francine had been Sir Oscar's mistress, and as such she could have been kept in discreet comfort for as long as he desired her. What would not have been tolerated was his determination to divorce his wife and marry her.

433

'Yes Malcolm, and mama knew exactly the stand he would take on her behalf once he knew about the child she was expecting,' she said. 'So for his sake she kept her pregnancy secret and agreed to marry Herbert Shelley, and a letter she wrote confessing all and begging the Earl's foregiveness was never posted. Mama was gentle and refined, but she was also strong-willed, stubborn and fiercely proud. Once she had made her bed she was determined to lie upon it without complaint.' A note of bitterness had crept into her voice. 'Sir Oscar always suspected but never knew for sure because she never told him.'

'And Jonathan?'

She shrugged. 'I do not think the truth will come as any great shock to him. He has been teased unmercifully all his life because of his resemblance to Horace. Your brother's hatred of him, and your mother's vehement hostility towards mama, must have nurtured the seeds of doubt in Jonathan's mind many years ago.'

'And you say there are letters?'

She nodded. 'Love letters from your father which she kept hidden for more than twenty years, her private journals, and that single letter confessing her pregnancy and vowing that if the child were a son she would name him Jonathan and love him as she loved his father.'

At this point Leonora rose from Malcolm's embrace and drew her robe more tightly around her body. She shivered not from cold but from the pain of being reminded of her mother's suffering. Twenty-two years after that precious love-child was conceived and miscarried, all the poignant fragments of Francine's story slotted together so cleanly that the lie could no longer be distinguished from the truth. Anabel knew, but she would never dare speak out and hope to be believed. Only Leonora had the full truth of it, and yet that unfinished letter written in anguish two decades ago said otherwise. The facts were made to seem as clear as crystal. Jonathan Shelly was the Earl's illegitimate son, and by her scheming Leonora had given back the love-child lost to her mother all those years ago. And now that Malcolm accepted it so readily, Leonora promised herself that she would never again entertain a thought to the contrary.

In the alcove Charles Shelley watched his sister and her husband bid each other an affectionate good night before parting. He closed his eyes, his head swimming with words and ideas he could barely comprehend. Jonathan the Earl's son? Their mother Sir Oscar's mistress? He groaned and his sister's hand was immediately upon his brow, her voice soft and urgent. He needed to know what was happening in all their lives, but not now. For now it was much easier to sink into the soft mattress and obey his sister's whispered instructions to sleep.

III

Leonora woke suddenly, and, anxious that Charles might have been calling out for her, hurried through the open doorway separating his room from hers. She was surprised to find him sleeping soundly, his soft brown hair curling across the pillow and his face relaxed and boyish in repose. She rested her palm on his upper chest and left it there for several moments. His skin above the strappings was cooler now. The fever had left him at last and his breathing was far more regular. She lifted the covers up to his chin and adjusted the bed drapes so that no draughts would reach him from the doorway or the windows. As she stooped to kiss his forehead the clock in the other room chimed the hour with three muted strikes. It was Christmas morning.

Leonora crossed to one of the windows and stepped behind the heavy velvet drapes so that cold air from the open window wrapped itself around her body in a frosty embrace. Her thoughts were on the future. Sir Oscar still had his suspicions about her but they were fragile, subterranean things with little real substance. His guilt outweighed them all, that and the

435

unerring goodness he had found in her this last year. His guilt and her virtue were the reins by which she kept the upper hand over that wary, cautious man.

Out in the dark, soft night sounds reached her ears; the cry of an owl, the rustle of wind-blown trees, the rattle of autumn debris still trapped somewhere in the guttering. Now she knew what had disturbed her sleep: *Lukan.* She had dreamed yet again of lying in his arms, of tasting his lips and breathing the clean, sharp, masculine scent of him. Those vivid images had warmed her blood and stirred the secret longings deep inside her. She closed her eyes and felt her nipples stiffen to meet the cold draught from the window. Suddenly her loins were tight and moistly warm, as if he touched her there with his mouth or his long, dark fingers. She wanted him. She wanted him right then with every fibre of her being. If she had needed confirmation of her feelings she had found it out there on the Avenue of Oaks. Seeing him ride towards her out of the mist like some black phantom emerging from the unknown, she had felt the aching need of him right to her soul. And when she had called his name and locked her gaze with his it had been as if the long months of her pregnancy and William's birth had never come between them. Not since that first day at the fair, when they had sealed their unspoken pact with an intense, heart-melting stare had Lukan looked at her like that.

She hugged her arms across her body and closed her eyes tightly. She ached to lie in his arms again. And she would, she would have him soon and to the devil with Oscar Cavendish.

CHAPTER TWENTY-ONE

I

On Christmas morning she burst into Malcolm's apartments while he and Sir Oscar were enjoying a hot toddy before their early morning ride. They rose to their feet as she swept past the elegantly attired manservant and presented herself, arms outstretched and head lifted haughtily, for their inspection. She was wearing a forest-green riding habit that buttoned under her chin and hugged her like a second skin before flaring over her hips to accentuate the hour-glass proportions of her figure. The skirts were full and beautifully pleated to allow the heavy fabric to swirl freely as she moved. In places a simple but effective decoration had been added in the form of a spidery spray of winter foliage picked out in the most delicate needlework. Against the green background the leaves seemed to shimmer in copper, gold and russet tones. The same leafy design crossed her bodice from left hip to right shoulder like a sash, with two isolated leaves falling across the upper part of her right sleeve and a third resting on her left cuff as if dropped there from a dying tree. She wore tight black gloves and a man's topper decorated with a sprig of preserved leaves in every autumn shade from vivid yellow to darkest ochre, held in place by a long sash of delicate black muslin. Her hair was brushed into a smooth coil and held in a black net so that it formed a neat oval across her back. Every detail had been meticulously considered. Even her earrings were of beaten copper shaped into oak leaves, and a miniature spray of leaves was embroidered on each of her gloves. Beaming, she pirouetted before them, knowing that from head to toe she was immaculately turned out.

'Wonderful,' Malcolm exclaimed, his face alight with admiration. 'Quite wonderful.'

She kissed his cheek and said, 'Merry Christmas, dearest,' then turned to Sir Oscar. He was smiling and nodding his head in approval. She pirouetted again for his benefit, then kissed his cheek with an enthusiasm that brought a flush to his face. 'And a particularly Merry Christmas to you, Sir Oscar. And thank you so much for the habit.' She twirled around yet again, swishing her skirts. 'It is exactly what I wanted.'

Sir Oscar spread his hands and his smile broadened. 'I simply settle the accounts, my dear and can accept no praise for any of this. The success of that outfit is in your own flair for design and in your needlewoman's exquisite stitching.'

'Why, thank you Sir Oscar. Do you really like it?'

'It is quite stunning, my dear.'

She turned her head coyly. 'And does it do justice to the huge bill you will shortly receive for the fabric and handiwork?'

'I will consider it money well spent,' Sir Oscar grinned,. 'Merry Christmas Leonora.'

Malcolm looked on with a puzzled smile. Leonora was up to something. Her eyes were dancing with mischief and her face was radiant. More than that, she was flirting with Sir Oscar so skillfully that the crusty old Earl of Beresford was quite captivated by her. She accepted the glass he offered and sipped the toddy without taking her gaze from the Earl's face. Then she suddenly set down her glass and crossed the room to slip her arm through Malcolm's.

'I have made an important decision,' she announced. 'Sir Oscar, you were quite right, I *do* treat my husband's best friend with an indifference he does not deserve.'

His brows puckered, disturbing his smile but little. 'Did I say that?'

'Indeed you did, and if not then you certainly caused me to give serious consideration to my attitude and behaviour towards the man.' She smiled up at Malcolm. 'Lukan is too ill to attend the ball tonight, so I have had a private banquet prepared for him to enjoy at home with his sister. I expect each of you to donate at least one bottle of brandy and several bottles of good wine.' With calculated cleverness she added with exuberance, 'And cigars, of course. He should have a whole box of your best cigars.'

'Lukan does not smoke,' Malcolm said.

'He doesn't?'

'Not even on special occasions.'

'Oh? You surprise me, Malcolm.' She pondered a moment, then snapped her fingers. 'Sweets then. Does he like sweets?'

Malcolm shrugged. 'I have my doubts, but you can be sure he will find sweets of any kind a sight more acceptable than cigars.'

'And a gift. Do you have a gift for him?'

'Of course I do.'

'Show me.'

'I will not, madam.'

'Don't be mysterious, Malcolm. Show it to me.'

'I will not,' he replied sternly. 'It would not be proper for you to see his gift before it is given.'

Leonora pouted a little but quickly recovered from her disappointment. She returned to her glass and sipped the warming liquid. 'And you, Sir Oscar, do you have a gift for Lukan?'

The Earl shook his head and smiled indulgently as if dealing with a well-loved child.

'My dear, I hardly think the man and I are on such terms as require the giving of gifts.'

439

'But this is Christmas, and he did bring Charles back at great risk to himself.' She pouted and lowered her head so that she was looking up at him through her dark lashes. She measured an inch of space between her finger and thumb. 'Not even a *small* gift?'

'Damn it all, my dear, is the brandy not sufficient?'

'Two bottles?'

'Two? But the man is not a heavy drinker and he does, I believe, have a decent cellar of his own. I think one bottle will suffice.' He saw her pout increase and conceded with a sigh. 'Very well, one brandy and one port, and let that be the end of it.'

She clapped her hands in pleasure, then hurried to the door. 'The group meets in twenty minutes in the main drive,' she reminded them. 'I suggest we part company with the other riders beyond the lower meadow where the bridle-path makes its second fork. We can pay our visit to Lukan de Ville and rejoin them at Kingswood crossroads.'

'Will you be coming with us to the house?' Malcolm asked.

'Of course. And don't look so surprised at that, Malcolm. I owe the man that small courtesy, at least. Tomorrow I shall be out distributing Christmas buns and pies to the sick and needy. If I can go happily amongst those unfortunates then I can certainly endure a few moments in the company of your fine gypsy and his sister. And besides, I am determined to see what gift you have for him.' She sank into an elegant curtsy, her eyes twinkling. 'By your leave, gentlemen.'

Malcolm and Sir Oscar returned her curtsy with formal bows and watched her sweep from the room. As Hammond stepped from the shadows to close the doors behind her, father and son turned to each other, both laughing and shaking their heads.

'Is she not amazing?' Malcolm asked.

'Quite amazing,' Sir Oscar agreed.

'And tireless. I doubt she sleeps longer than five or six hours at a time, and then lightly, like an animal, alert at the slightest sound.'

'And her temperament seems to be set on a more or less

even keel, not scaling the heights one moment and plumbing the depths the next.' Sir Oscar checked his appearance in the long mirror and reached for his gloves. 'Leonora has proved herself a valuable asset to us and we are fortunate to have her. Few women could have slipped so easily into the day-to-day fabric of Beresford the way she has done.'

'That's because she belongs here,' Malcolm told him.

'Oh?'

'She always knew it, right from her first visit here when she was only ten years old. She has harboured a passionate love for the place since that day.'

Sir Oscar's smile was suddenly without warmth as he began to smooth the fingers of his riding gloves one by one. There was always a shadow. Whenever he felt sufficiently charmed or impressed by Leonora to forget his doubts, the shadow fell. Had she been driven by a compulsion to establish herself at the Hall since she first set eyes on it when she was only ten years old? A Cavendish with a passionate love for Beresford was a dangerous thing, a force that could stir ambition to obsession and turn a saint into a black-hearted fiend. Sir Joshua had recognised as much. That covetous man had known exactly what he was doing when he coined the cryptic motto that was to grace his family coat of arms down the centuries: *In truth, avarice in all men lies.*

'Father?'

He looked up with a start to find Malcolm watching him. 'I was thinking of Joshua, the first Earl,' he confessed. 'According to family records, he was the first Cavendish to have eyes of that deep amethyst colour, just like Leonora's.'

'I can assure you the eye colouring is the *only* thing my wife has in common with that old fox,' Malcolm laughed.

Sir Oscar slapped his gloves against his thigh and strode for the door, struggling to dispel the shadow that had touched upon his peace of mind. 'I hope to God you're right in that, my boy,' he said but Malcolm, striding along the corridor with a large leather case under his arm, was already out of hearing.

II

There was a noticeable lack of seasonal cheer at the Forest House that morning. Lukan sat in his high-backed chair before the great fireplace, his features set in grim lines as he stared into the flames. One booted foot rested on the rim of a wooden bucket left standing in the hearth. One elbow rested on his bent knee so that his hand hung loosely, the fingers uncharacteristically idle. A heavy coat was draped across his shoulders, beneath which he was naked to the waist save for the bandages encircling his chest and pinning his right arm across his body. He sat very still, his thoughts elsewhere. He had been brooding there since dawn, silent and withdrawn.

Rebecca cleared away the breakfast tray, its contents virtually untouched. He had picked a little at the broiled fish and chicken broth, but other than that he wanted only fresh milk laced with honey, which he drank from a pewter tankard.

'There's to be a special ball up at Beresford Hall tonight,' she reminded him.

'Aye.'

'Will you go?'

'No.'

'Why?' she asked. 'Why should you not go? You are recovered enough, so long as you don't try to ride. I'm sure Sir Malcolm would oblige by sending a carriage for you.'

'No.'

'But you've not missed a grand ball these past ten years or more, Lukan. You should put in an appearance, at least. Let all those fancy visitors be reminded that Lukan de Ville is no mere servant but enjoys a place of high standing at Beresford Hall. Go Lukan. It is your right.'

He looked at her sideways. 'Right be damned. I'm in no humour to play the fine gentleman before a bunch of posturing socialites.'

She pursed her lips and frowned at him. 'You should make the effort. You ought be seen with the nobility. The Christmas

442

ball is an important occasion, and when you appear with your arm and shoulder bandaged they will admire you all the more. These people love a hero and it might as well be you.'

He shook his head. 'The place will be bursting at the seams with Lords and lesser nobles and every petty dignitary who could catch himself an invitation, all with their over-decorated ladies on their arms and hopeful offspring in tow. They will gorge themselves on a banquet fit for royalty, followed by splendid entertainments and the most spectacular fireworks display money can buy. After that they will crawl into bed at dawn and sleep the whole day. Believe me, Rebecca, I'll not be missed up there.'

Rebecca seated herself in a chair and took up her stitching, exasperated by his attitude. 'Will the lady herself not be expecting you?'

He looked at her sharply before saying, with heavy emphasis, 'I will not go to Beresford.'

'Suit yourself,' she shrugged.

Lukan turned his attention back to the flickering flames. His sister's hands fell idle in her lap as she watched his profile. She was wearing a brightly coloured shawl over her dull red skirt and dark, embroidered bodice. Her hair was brushed back from her face and held in place by pretty combs. She wore colourful earrings and bangles that made tinkling sounds as she moved. She had reddened her lips and added a little rouge to her brown cheeks, even enhanced the shape of her dark eyes with carefully drawn lines of soft charcoal. Lukan had noticed none of it. He rarely looked at her directly, and when he did she was unable to read what was in his eyes. Lately he had become more testy and remote than ever. Sometimes she deliberately set out to irritate him in order to provoke a reaction that would alter the crushing atmosphere of the house. She would rather face his anger, dangerous as she knew it to be, than be forced to endure his indifference. Right now she needed to know how much he remembered.

Still watching him, she took up her stitching again and said, 'Lukan, do you recall the night you slept in the barn, the night of young William's christening?'

443

'Aye? What of it?' The question was guarded, almost defensive.

'What happened to you?'

'You saw well enough.'

She shook her head. 'Not just the brandy. It was more than that.'

'Leave it, Rebecca.'

'That's no answer. I want to know what happened to you.'

His scowl deepened as he pulled his black brows down over the bridge of his nose and compressed his lips.

'I don't know,' he said at last. 'I remember being dead drunk and struggling to uncap the second bottle and then ...' He turned to look at her, his face troubled. 'Did you come into the barn?'

She met his gaze with ease. 'Me? Why should I? Do you not recall that you were alone the whole night?'

'There were dreams.'

'What dreams?'

He shook his head. 'Nothing, just foolish dreams. I am unused to alcohol in such quantities, and I suppose the brandy might have been tainted.' He scowled again at that, recalling the stupor inflicted upon Malcolm by hemlock and opium, and the after-effects blamed upon bad wine. 'If I didn't know better I would suspect ...' He left the sentence unfinished. The brandy had come uncorked from his own cellar. He looked back at Rebecca. The idea was preposterous.

'If you didn't know better you would suspect what?' Rebecca prompted uneasily.

He shook his head, deeply troubled. 'I'm not sure. It's just that ... Why should good brandy have such an effect on a man's mind and senses? Those dreams. My God, such dreams, *such dreams*!'

She saw him shudder and was shamed by the brutal honesty of that unconscious response. Even the half-remembered shadows of that night were enough to make her brother recoil in disgust.

She rose from her chair and placed her hand on his shoulder, easing him back so that his head rested against the

444

back of his chair. 'Rest a while,' she told him. 'And forget the dreams. They mean nothing, *nothing*.'

She was sitting outside in a patch of thin winter sunshine when the riders came. She watched them dismount near the barn, the Earl of Beresford and his son, the Lady Leonora and two grooms bearing a huge lidded basket between them. Rebecca's dark gaze flickered over them all, swept over Leonora's radiant face and beautifully-clad figure, moved sullenly back to the Earl. Very slowly, and without a shred of respect for these fine people, she rose to her feet and stood with her hands on her hips.

'Good morning Rebecca, and a very merry Christmas to you,' Malcolm offered.

'We make no fuss of Christmas day in this house, Malcolm Cavendish,' she responded. 'As you well know.'

'You might think otherwise when you see the gift Lady Leonora has prepared for you. Since Lukan is not well enough to attend our banquet, we have decided to bring the pleasures of our table to him.' He signalled for the grooms to carry the heavy basket forward. 'A miniature feast to delight the palate, for you and Lukan, with our compliments.'

Rebecca narrowed her eyes. 'We're no paupers to eat of your charity Malcolm Cavendish.'

The Earl was enraged by her remark. 'Now just a minute . . .'

'No father,' Malcolm cut in, but before he could say more, Leonora had swept past him and marched toward the front door. The glowering Rebecca barred her way into the house.

'Please inform Mr de Ville that we are here,' she said.

'He's resting. He's not wanting visitors.'

'*Tell him!*' Leonora hissed.

Just then a movement inside the house drew her attention. She looked beyond Rebecca and saw that Lukan had entered the hall. He stood by the stairs, his face in shadow but his gaze fixed firmly on Leonora. He did not smile. The coat hanging around his shoulders concealed little of the muscle beneath, and between the lower edge of the bandages and the top of his tight trousers was a band of warm brown flesh that she ached

445

to touch her lips and her breasts to. His gaze moved slowly over her, drinking her in, drawing her to him until she felt herself held so tightly she could scarcely breathe. Even with the full length of the hall between them they were joined as if by an embrace. She saw his shoulders sag in subjugation and she guessed that he, like her, had fought a tremendous battle within himself these past twelve months. And like her he had failed, because in that look they both knew they were bound as securely as they had ever been.

Pulling herself together with a start, Leonora turned her back on Lukan and the house, offered her husband a pretty shrug and said, 'Perhaps we should simply leave the basket and go. If Mr de Ville is not well enough to receive visitors ...'

'An error, madam,' a voice behind her said. 'Mr de Ville is more than happy to receive you.'

She did not turn as Lukan stepped from the gloomy hall to appear in full view before his visitors. She went instead to slot her arm through that of Sir Oscar Cavendish, and only then did she smile her most brilliant smile and greet Lukan with a small curtsy.

'Good morning Mr de Ville. We come to offer you the season's greetings.'

'Lady.' He bowed stiffly. 'I must apologise for my appearance. As you can see, a shirt and stock would hardly improve matters.'

Leonora smiled into his eyes and wondered if he had ever looked more magnificent.

'How is the shoulder?' Sir Oscar asked. 'Charles tells us it was badly dislocated in the fracas.'

'Well enough now, Sir Oscar,' Lukan nodded.

'And the ribs?' Leonora's hand was in the crook of his arm. He covered it with his own, a protective, possessive gesture.

'Healing swiftly.'

Malcolm slapped his friend cheerfully on the shoulder and Lukan immediately staggered and let out a roar of agony that startled them all. A moment later his slow, toothy grin divided his dark features. One long brown finger pointed into Malcolm's startled face.

446

'Had you,' he declared, his eyes bright with laughter.

'Damn it, Lukan, you had me convinced I had done you further injury.'

'Will a glass of milk set you to rights?'

'*Milk?*'

'Aye, *milk*. See to it, Rebecca.'

The gypsy woman stared sullenly after them as they trooped into the house, grooms and all. She hated them. She had sensed the currents that passed between her brother and the sapphire-eyed woman. It was like standing outdoors in the tension of a gathering thunderstorm, as if the world was made to hold its breath while greater powers prepared for a confrontation beyond their understanding. Before ever it destroyed her brother, that terrible power they toyed with might destroy them all.

She hurried to the kitchen where Lukan's milk lay warming in its bucket in the hearth. She poured the creamy liquid into three tall glasses, and as she added honey wished that it were instead a deadly poison. How swiftly he had risen from his sombre mood to greet his guests with a show of natural wit and pleasure the like of which she had not seen for weeks. And not for the benefit of his friend did he spring so lightly from his melancholy. Nor was it for the Earl, who honoured him with this visit to his home bearing gifts and goodwill. No, it was for *her*, the lady of the house who owned his soul. It was for *her*, because he knew she had at last come back to him.

She carried the tray into the main room, her features set with resentment. It pained her to serve these people, even with something as humble as honeyed milk. One of these so-called guests had been responsible for her father's death, another had stolen her brother's affections since childhood and the third, the woman, had learned to work Lukan like so much putty in her pretty white hands.

'Let the grooms wait in the kitchen,' Lukan told her.

'They can wait in the barn,' his sister said.

'The kitchen,' Lukan repeated. 'And give them milk, and bread and butter if they want it.'

'If you insist.'

She left the room with a frosty glance at Leonora and not so much as a nod of respect for the gentlemen.

'Your sister is as prickly as ever,' Malcolm remarked.

Lukan bowed politely. 'Allow me to apologise on her behalf. She has little use for matters of courtesy.'

Sir Oscar raised an eyebrow at the glass of milk in his hand. 'So it would seem.'

Leonora was fascinated by the house. She knew that it had once been a splendid hunting lodge maintained by the Abbot of Beresford, a place where royalty had rested and cavorted during hunting trips in the forest. When the Abbey was rebuilt following its dissolution and near-destruction, The Forest House was gifted to Richard de Ville, keeper of Sir Joshua's lands and forests, and to his male heirs for ever. Since then none save a true de Ville had either owned the house or managed the surrounding forest. It stood on Beresford land, less than a mile to the east of Fairfax Manor. Two miles south was the south gate, the crossroads and boundary-line where the two lands met. The house was spacious and surprisingly elegant in design, set in a beautiful position close to a quiet stretch of river. To stand in its grounds was to enjoy the full benefits of river, meadow and forest, with all the wonderful sounds and scents associated with the three. The house itself was like its master: dark, mysterious, brooding and impressive.

Malcolm's Christmas gift to Lukan was a pair of matching pepperbox revolvers, each with a cluster of six barrels, a concealed hammer and rounded wooden butts sporting fancy brass inlays. Both pistols had been stamped with Lukan's initials, and came in a presentation box of polished rosewood with a plain brass plaque bearing his full name and the date.

'Superb!' he exclaimed, caressing each one in turn. 'Superb!'

'Rather too muzzle-heavy for my tastes,' Malcolm remarked.

'Aye, but what craftsmanship. And how many poachers will stand their ground at the sight of one of these deadly beauties. One turn of the barrel cluster and you have a second shot ...'

448

He demonstrated rather clumsily, aiming the pistol with his left hand. 'And then a third, a fourth, a fifth, and a sixth.'

Malcolm laughed. 'True enough so long as the pan-covers remain tight, but once those springs begin to lose their tension your first shot will open every pan-cover and dump their priming on the ground.'

'Do you think I will not take care of such a gift?' Lukan asked. 'Or do you doubt my ability to keep my own firearms in optimum condition?'

'May I?' At Lukan's nod Sir Oscar lifted the remaining pistol from its box and examined it closely. 'Impressive. True, a little muzzle-heavy, but impressive none the less.' He turned the weapon and squinted at the fine words engraved along the outer edge of the brass trigger-guard. '*Samuel Davidson. Chepstow. 1780.* Could you not find the man a gift that was less than forty-five years old, Malcolm?'

'He found exactly what I wanted,' Lukan grinned, gripping Malcolm's hand and shaking it warmly. 'My thanks to you, my friend. And to you, Lady Leonora, for the splendid food.'

'And you may thank *me* for the brandy,' Sir Oscar said a little pompously. 'I note there are *four* bottles, no less, and all of them of the best quality.' He glanced at Leonora, met her expression of feigned innocence with a smile.

Lukan bowed. 'Then I am clearly indebted to you all.'

Sir Oscar raised the glass of honeyed milk to his lips, sniffed the contents and drained the glass at the first attempt. He followed the last swallow with a grimace of distaste. 'Indeed you are sir,' he remarked, staring at his empty glass as if it had contained a noxious substance. 'Indeed you are. Come Malcolm, the ride is waiting and my stomach growls for its breakfast.'

In the hall Leonora paused to run her hands over the carved head of a ferocious-looking wolf guarding the lower banister of the staircase. A little more than life-size, it faced the door with a savage, open-mouthed snarl. Its teeth were huge and sharp, its tongue lolling and its eyes alive, so beautifully carved that they seemed to glint with the frenzy of the kill. She glanced at Lukan, touched the wolf again to convey a silent message, then took Malcolm's arm and walked with him to the door.

'Thank you for the milk, Rebecca. I hope you both enjoy the food.'

'Charity,' the woman hissed, and for a moment Leonora thought she might spit on the ground to emphasise the word. Only a sharp look from Lukan prevented her from displaying her chagrin in that manner. Looking from Rebecca to her elegant brother, she felt again the incongruity of their blood relationship. The reminder made her all the more aware of the part she had come to play in their lives. There was a chasm too wide to bridge between the aristocratic young lady and the middle-aged gypsy woman who met her gaze with such open hostility, yet fate conspired to make them rivals for the love of the man who stood so firmly between them.

As the riders moved off into the bleak winter landscape, Lukan walked back into the house and crossed directly to the stairs. He ran his hands over the carved wolf until his fingers located the small velvet pouch resting inside its open mouth. He drew it out and tugged at its delicate draw-strings with his teeth, then dipped two fingers inside to lift out the contents. The heavy gold chain hung gleaming from his dark hand while the ornate key of the Monks' Door turned lazy, bronzed circles in the air. He closed his eyes and let the breath loose from his lungs in a sigh that left him empty, as one beaten into submission. When he opened them again he saw that a tiny piece of paper had fluttered to the floor. His heart quickened as he picked it up. One single word was written there: *Midnight.*

III

After a light luncheon and an afternoon in which the guests either slept, relaxed in the privacy of their rooms or engaged in only the most leisurely activities, the banquet preceding the grand ball began at five o'clock. Leonora had chosen winter as her theme, using hundreds of candles to enhance the cool beauty of the tables. Crisp white cloths had been embroidered with borders of Jack Frost patterns and fringed with tassels of silver silk to represent hanging icicles. Every table glittered with crystal glass and highly polished silver, with huge ice sculptures and crystallised fruits in shimmering glass containers. Tall branches cut from winter trees had been placed in white pots around the Great Hall, their branches dusted with icing sugar and hung with glass icicles. For colour there were displays made from winter holly with scarlet berries, long boughs of ivy, sprays of pale mistletoe with clusters of pearl-like seeds, fir cones coated with silver and gold and scarlet lacquer. The main attraction was a special winter scene erected in one of the alcoves and made almost entirely from carved ice. It contained a frozen pond with tiny marzipan figures skating upon its surface, a miniature waterfall and bridge, trees and fences shaped out of ice. The whole scene, although a work of art in itself, was surpassed by a breathtaking sculpture of Beresford Hall that stood in the background, as tall as a man and superbly detailed.

The banquet included peacock, pheasant, magpie, duck and guinea-fowl, all individually roasted and returned to their skins and feathers, to be served up on vast oval platters accompanied by plums, oranges and nectarines lightly poached in champagne. Larks' tongues were plentiful, as were lambs' hearts and tender breasts of veal that had been simmered in white wine with Christmas strawberries and other out-of-season delicacies.

Leonora's ball-gown was in shimmering silver silk, the bodice heavily embroidered and hung with delicate pearl drops. A flounce of lace petticoats showed below the scalloped hem of her skirts and was echoed in the froth of lace edging her scooped neckline. A necklace of pearls in a gold filigree setting lay against her pale throat, the large centre pearl in the shape of a teardrop hanging just above the swell of her breasts. This was Sir Oscar's gift to her to mark the birth of his first

451

grandson. In her ears glittered Malcolm's gift, diamond earrings of exquisite quality to match the precious stones in her wedding ring. They glittered and gleamed in the candle-light, flinging out tiny shards of colour each time she moved her head. Only Leonora Cavendish would dare flout convention by pairing bright diamonds with creamy pearls. Only she could have done so to such stunning effect.

Accompanied by his lifelong friend Sir Giles Powell, Sir Oscar moved from table to table, examining every dish and eavesdropping shamelessly on the conversations of his guests. He was gratified by their remarks. This ball would be the talk of London within the week and these tables, bearing such impressively-named dishes as *Beresford Swan*, *Cavendish Brandy Pork* and *Sir William's Peacock*, would be described and copied in many households. Later there would be dancing and other entertainments, but for the moment everyone's attention was focused upon the banquet. He recalled the harvest-home supper when the field labourers and their families had stood in neat ranks before these very tables, eager for their share. The poor had stood in line but the wealthy and well-fed made the banquet a noisy free-for-all, dipping their hands into everything and grabbing what they could before it was gone. There was a clamour around the tables as each guest jostled his neighbour for access to every delicacy on display. They were doing no more than enjoy the grandeur that had been set there for their enjoyment, yet there was, Sir Oscar noticed, something unseemly in it.

Sir Giles touched his friend's arm to draw his attention to a faded beauty dressed in such frills and flounces as would befit a frivolous schoolgirl attending her first public function. Lady Caroline Rainer, who in her busy lifetime had lifted the gathering and distribution of gossip to the level of a fine art, was carefully scribbling into a small notebook attached to her wrist by a ribbon. Sir Oscar moved closer and craned his neck in order to see over her right shoulder. The scent of powder, liberally applied to conceal a myriad of imperfections, irritated his nostrils until he was obliged to sneeze. Lady Caroline turned, her face flushing a shade of pink at variance with the patches of rouge staining her cheeks.

'Why Sir Oscar, how nice to see you again,' she cooed, dropping into a low curtsy. 'And Sir Giles too. How nice.'

'Lady Caroline.' Sir Oscar bowed over her hand. It was freckled and deeply veined, with a flat, dry palm. 'Are you enjoying the feast?'

'It's wonderful, pure ambrosia, a repast fit for the gods,' she enthused, obviously quoting her own scribbled notes. 'Oh I can hardly wait for Lady Littleton to hear all about *this*. Believe me, Sir Oscar, she'll be positively *green* with envy.'

'I'm flattered. And have you managed to solve the mystery?'

'Mystery? Mystery, Sir Oscar?' She smiled coyly, using her fan and glancing from one man to the other as she moved closer, loath to have other guests hear the conversation at first-hand.

'The mystery of the Beresford Swans, of course,' Sir Oscar said. 'They were all sculpted from ice by a skilled hand, but how on earth did they come by their subtle pastel colouring?'

Lady Caroline's eyes widened as she sensed an opportunity to score a first in the race to grab the most interesting titbit and deliver it, suitably embellished and dramatised, around the social circuit. 'Why Sir Oscar, I'm sure I have not the slightest idea.'

He smiled. 'As you can see, we have swans of pink, blue, green, white and orange, but the question is, how are they so delicately tinted?'

'Perhaps you will be so kind as to enlighten me?' She gazed up at him with a coquettish flutter of her eyelashes.

He tapped the side of his nose with a long forefinger. 'Lady Leonora's secret,' he whispered, and moved away, leaving Lady Caroline scribbling frantically in her notebook.

He found Leonora standing with an energetic group of people close to the main ice sculpture. Here was Sir David Phelps, who had his middle-aged wife committed to a lunatic asylum when she persisted in raising embarrassing objections to his stable of young mistresses. And here was poor Eustace Rodway, whose wife produced no less than five unwanted daughters before finally providing him with a son. He was ruining himself in his efforts to keep those girls in his own class by providing a suitable marriage portion for each of them. Daughters could be a terrible encumbrance upon a man. Their marriage partner conferred rank, but not for free. Everything, even love, had its market value.

Sir Oscar watched Leonora mingling with her guests. Her smile was radiant. She sparkled even more brightly than the priceless gems she wore with such aplomb. Other women paled in her company, dazzled by her beauty and overshadowed by her natural vitality, while the men who fell within her spotlight were obviously enchanted. Sir Oscar realised with a jolt that he was proud of her. Despite the recurring doubts and brooding suspicions he was proud to have this fascinating, much admired young woman in his family.

He managed to draw her aside to compliment her on her skills as hostess and organiser of the grand affair. 'Rarely have I seen such splendid dishes presented with such flair,' he said with sincerity. 'And what variety! Our guests are encouraged to gluttony by it all. Once again you have quite surpassed yourself, my dear.'

She smiled, a triumphant glint in her eye. 'Food is power,' she replied passionately. 'The fame of a man's house can be measured at his table, in silver plate, in porcelain, in crystal glass and in *food*.'

'Is that the way you see it?'

'Absolutely,' she nodded. 'What we set before our guests must gratify all the senses. The presentation of each delicacy must be perfection in itself. Shapes, colours, textures and aromas are just as important to the diner as the actual taste of any dish, and the more stimulated the senses the more certain the prestige. Food is influence, Sir Oscar. Food is *power*.'

At that point they were joined by a tastefully dressed young man in a blue velvet jacket and tight white trousers. Woven discreetly into his waistcoat was a fine silver thread that caught the light when he moved. He had been hovering around Leonora since the festivities began, following her from group to group and attempting to engage her in conversation. He was Sir Andrew Normandy, eldest son of Lord and Lady

454

Cobham, a handsome, engaging young fellow of little talent and few ambitions beyond the pleasures of the gaming tables. He had a younger brother who, at seventeen, had the makings of a brilliant politician and was already capable of running his father's huge estates single-handed. This one was a credit to his family and his noble lineage, already twice the man his brother would ever be, but Andrew was the rightful heir, the eldest son, entitled to everything, and nothing save an early death would alter that.

Now Sir Andrew appeared at Sir Oscar's elbow, bowed briefly and began speaking without taking his eyes off Leonora.

'Had the pleasure of meeting your second son in Paris, Sir Oscar. Thrashed him at the tables, I regret to say. Sir Horace Cavendish is, if you will forgive the observation, an uncommonly careless card player.'

Sir Oscar stiffened at the mention of his son's name. He wanted no talk of Horace Cavendish to mar the congeniality of his mood. He cleared his throat and asked tersely, 'I trust you enjoyed your stay in the French capital?'

The young man gazed adoringly at Leonora. 'Indeed I did sir. I stayed a month with Lord and Lady Granville at the British Embassy and they were kind enough to introduce me into Paris society. Those wonderful *grandes dames* Lady Jersey and Lady Cowper were staying for the season and I found them most generous with their invitations.'

'I'm happy to hear that. Come Leonora, there are people wishing to meet you. If you will excuse us sir?'

'What? Oh yes, of course. One small matter before you go Sir Oscar. Your son gave this to me at the Paris tables. He assured me that you will honour it without delay.'

Stiffly, the Earl took the small piece of paper and unfolded it. The handwriting was strikingly familiar. It was a promissory note for eleven hundred guineas. His smile was fixed when he said, 'I fear you have made a grievous error, Sir Andrew. Oscar Cavendish honours no man's gambling debts.'

The young man stopped grinning at Leonora and gave the Earl his full attention. He appeared quite stricken by the other's response. 'But Horace is your son.'

'No longer. It is common knowledge that I disowned him more than two years ago.'

'But he assured me ...'

'Then he lied, and I repeat sir, Oscar Cavendish settles no man's debts.'

'But sir, eleven hundred guineas is no trifle.'

Sir Oscar shrugged and stuffed the note inside the young man's waistcoat. 'Do I speak to a deaf man? Mark me well if you will be so kind, sir. This is none of my business and I have no intention of making it so. Go back to Paris and settle this between yourself and Horace.'

The young man looked crestfallen. 'Sir, I beg you to reconsider. This cannot be your final word on the matter.'

'Indeed it is.' When the young man started to protest Sir Oscar held up a hand for silence. 'And if you attempt to press me further, sir, I will have you thrown out. Come Leonora.'

Just then a group of players led the jugglers and acrobats into the Great Hall by way of the old north aisle, still partially intact behind the sweeping staircase. Sir Oscar used the distraction to steer Leonora away. In one of the deep alcoves on the far side of the stairs Malcolm had been drawn into a heated discussion with several men concerning the state of English politics. They were seated in a tight group, all staunch Tory men of differing opinions, all serious-looking individuals bent on airing their opinions.

'Let me draw your attention once again to Old Sarum,' one of them suddenly insisted, speaking above the din of entertainers and the clatter of diners. 'Old Sarum is little more than a hill and a few tufts of dirty grass, yet year after year it sends two members to Westminster. Two! What about the huge industrial towns like Manchester, Leeds, Birmingham, Sheffield and Sunderland? They are expanding at an incredible rate, with huge populations and not a single representative in the House.'

'And what of the men, women and children who toil for these great industrialists?' another countered. 'They are forced to live in squalor and have nothing to thank their wealthy masters for.'

456

'And you, I suppose, would rather they were toiling in *your* employ,' the first man said, rounding on his companion. 'You need cheap labour on the land and you resent the loss of good men to the towns.'

Here Malcolm cut in, his voice not loud but demanding notice. 'At least here in the country they have some measure of protection, sir. They have jobs, houses and a master they can tip their hat to twice a day. They know what they're about and where their loyalties lie. As bondsmen to the big industrialists they are just faceless and nameless units of labour, living and working like rats in dark holes for the benefit of a master they have never seen.'

A fist came down on the small table around which the chairs were set. 'All the more reason why they should be represented.'

'*If* they are to be represented,' Malcolm declared. '*If*. I think we are all aware that it will not be so, gentlemen. Only the masters, not the workers and their miserable families, will be allowed to benefit under the present system.'

Leonora and her father-in-law exchanged glances and moved on, neither wishing to be drawn into the discussion.

'I believe Malcolm's name has been brought to the notice of the Prime Minister,' he said cautiously. 'How do you feel about the possibility of your husband making a career for himself in the political arena?'

She smiled. 'I believe he will make a success of it and I am happy for him.'

'I fancy he'll soon be offered his first seat in the House now that the Duke of Marlborough has offered his support.'

'The pocket borough of Woodstock?'

'Ah, he had already discussed it with you?'

'I keep my eyes and ears open, Sir Oscar. Look there's Charles. Do you mind . . .?'

He smiled indulgently. 'Of course I don't mind my dear. You run along. It's time you were dancing.'

He watched her go, a shimmering figure in silver and white, too warm, too vital to be a genuine representation of snow and ice. Charles looked well. He was clean-shaven and resplendent in borrowed clothes, and as brother and sister moved off into the dance the joy of their reunion was evident in their faces. He felt a stab of envy, missing Francine and still many months away from a reunion with Jonathan.

Many of the guests continued to clamour around the dining tables in search of something new to delight their tastebuds despite the growing fullness of their stomachs. Sir Oscar watched them gorging themselves and knew that some had already visited the closets to vomit what they had eaten in order to make room for more. Watching them, he could see that Leonora had voiced a simple truth when she said that food was power.

He heard a peal of feminine laughter, too loud and too harsh to be ladylike. He recognised the voice that followed as belonging to his youngest daughter Vivienne, at home for the Christmas celebrations. She was holding court to a group of eager young men with all the confidence of a professional, and despite her expensive private tutoring he was dismayed by the hint of vulgarity in her manner. She was now in the sole charge of her aunt and uncle, Sir George and Lady Sybil Cottingham, both of whom were wealthy and inclined to indulge their niece in place of the child they had never managed to produce between them. They were at present escorting their niece on a grand tour of Europe. After a month in Switzerland they stayed three weeks in Naples before moving on to Rome, where they had remained for the last four and a half months. They were expected to travel on to Milan, then through Germany to Vienna, but somehow Vivienne always managed to persuade the elderly couple to postpone that stage of their journey. Sir Oscar could guess what attracted her to the place. Rome, he had heard, was a hotbed of gossip and scandal, a sordid place that young men might wish to frequent in a rush to further their worldly education, but which respectable young women should avoid at all costs.

'Papa! Dearest Papa! Come over here at once and be introduced to all my *dear* friends!'

Sir Oscar glared at her, appalled by the loudness of her voice and the familiarity of her manner. She was wearing a powder-blue gown cut very low at the front and laced around the bodice with a criss-cross of deep pink ribbons. Her eyes were a little too bright and her lips a little too red.

'Come *along*, Papa,' she called out, playing the part of the adored younger daughter who could do no wrong in doting Papa's eyes. 'Do hurry dear. I want you to meet my new friends.'

Sir Oscar Cavendish was not a man to let himself be manipulated for the benefit of a group of empty-headed socialites for whom he cared nothing at all, not in his own house and certainly not by his own daughter. Ignoring her giggling entourage, he caught Vivienne by the elbow and steered her quickly across the hall to one of the adjoining drawing rooms. Her Aunt Sybil was inside with several other elderly ladies. They looked up from their card game in surprise as Sir Oscar pushed his daughter into their company.

'Lady Vivienne will spend the rest of the evening with you,' he said curtly. 'I have no wish to see her in the Great Hall again this evening. If she is hungry, let her send for a tray.'

'But why, Papa? What have I done? Why are you so cross?'

He looked at her with a scowl, recalling how he had slapped her face and knocked her to the ground at their last confrontation. He was tempted to do the same thing again. He was not a patient man who suffered fools gladly. This daughter of his was a constant irritation, and like all things that displeased him he wanted her removed from his sight.

'You will do as I say,' he told her coldly.

'It isn't fair,' she shrilled. 'I am not a child to be ordered from my friends' company while everyone else is allowed to enjoy themselves for hours yet. It isn't fair. You would not dream of doing this to *her*. You would not treat your precious Leonora so unkindly.'

Sir Oscar glared at her until she blinked and lowered her gaze. Then he bowed to the elderly ladies, turned and left the room without another word.

Leonora found him at one of the punch bowls shortly before ten o'clock. 'Ah, there you are. I came to say good night.'

'So early? But the real festivities have barely begun.'

She smiled. 'Your grandson knows his mind and will not be kept waiting for his supper. Besides, I doubt I could remain on my feet for a moment longer if my life depended on it.'

'That's a pity. You will miss the better part of the ball if you leave now.'

'And glad I am of it.' She laughed, then looked up at him with a serious expression. 'Forgive me Sir Oscar, but to be frank I feel I am hovering on the verge of exhaustion. Malcolm has given strict instructions that tonight I am not to be disturbed under any circumstances. I really would like to leave now, if I may.'

'Of course my dear.' He placed his hands on her shoulders and kissed her warmly on both cheeks. 'You have done a wonderful job here tonight and for that I am very grateful. Sleep well Leonora. Will we see you at breakfast?'

'Luncheon?' she suggested with an apologetic smile.

'As you wish. Good night my dear.'

She smiled and turned from him, only to turn back with a small frown. 'Would you be kind enough to perform a small service for me?'

'Name it,' he said.

'Will you walk with me to the door and remain there for a few minutes until I have reached my apartments safely? Sir Andrew Normandy has grown more and more intense as the evening has progressed. I fear he may try to follow me out.'

'Not while I stand guard,' he said, taking her arm and leading her to the door. 'Sleep well, my dear. This night is a credit to your talents. Few noble houses can boast so skilled a hostess.'

'Thank you. Good night.'

Alone in the corridor Leonora touched her hands to the uncomfortable fullness of her breasts. The night had been endless but at last the ballyhoo of the ball was over and she was free to prepare for her meeting with Lukan. Just thinking of him brought a softening, a familiar loosening to her loins. She knew she would be taking a terrible risk in going to him on this of all nights, but go to him she would. Go to him she *must*.

460

Chapter Twenty-two

I

Anabel was waiting in the nursery, her face anxious and her skin reddened in places from sitting too close to the fire. Lady Elizabeth was sitting on a stool, picking at her apron and wincing as a sleepy young maid attempted to brush the tangles from her hair.

'Sam Cooper found her in the orchard an hour ago,' Anabel explained. 'Wandering about like a lost soul, she was. Looking for windfalls, so she said. Windfalls in *December*?' She lowered her voice to a whisper, leaned close to her mistress and spoke through cupped hands. 'And she was hanging on to that kitten of Vivienne's. Dead it was, poor thing, half its fur picked out and its eyes bulging as if the life had been crushed right out of it.'

'The kitten?' Leonora drew the older woman into a curtained dressing room and demanded in an angry whisper, 'Vivienne dared to give that kitten to Elizabeth after I specifically forbade it?'

'The very minute your back was turned,' Anabel said. 'And

461

the worst happened, just as you feared it might.'

'And just as Vivienne hoped it would,' Leonora snapped. 'Could you not have stopped her? Could you not have taken the kitten away from her?'

'Neither one,' Anabel said firmly. 'You know as well as I do that Vivienne would as soon have me dismissed as listen to anything I have to say. And as for Elizabeth . . .' She shrugged and shook her head. 'She simply grabbed the poor little scrap and ran off with it. There wasn't anyone could *catch* her, let alone take it away from her. She's a spiteful one, that Vivienne. She knew full well what would happen if her sister got her hands on that kitten.'

'She is indeed spiteful,' Leonora agreed. 'I fear she will not be content until she sees Elizabeth locked away in some horrid asylum for the insane. Well, I will not have it, Anabel. I will not have Elizabeth shut in some hell-hole just to spare Vivienne's selfish blushes.'

'But what can we do? This is serious, Leonora. When Sir Oscar finds out that she has killed another animal . . .'

'Why should he?' Leonora cut in. 'Why should he find out? Who is to tell him?'

'Well, Sam Cooper knows about it, and little Charlie Pickles, he was there.'

'Who else?'

'Nobody.'

'Are you sure? What about the maid in the other room?'

Anabel shook her head. 'Sam buried the kitten in a corner of the orchard and we said nothing to anyone else.'

'So who is to know what became of it?'

Anabel bit the knuckle of her thumb between her front teeth, pondering the question. 'Will you say it ran off?'

'Better than that. I'll say I took it away from her and lost it in the garden when it struggled from my grip. I'll swear I *saw* it run off and I'll ask His Lordship to speak to Vivienne so that she never does such a wicked thing again. She *knew* the kitten would not be safe in Elizabeth's hands.'

Anabel nodded but looked unsure. 'Are you sure you want to do this Leonora? I know how fond you are of Miss

462

Elizabeth, but it's not the first time, is it? There were the song-birds last year, and that fat brown puppy belonging to the Irish cook, and those new-born kittens she found in the hayloft. She's getting worse, Leonora. Perhaps you should tell her father.'

'No. I will not give Vivienne the satisfaction of knowing that her nasty little ploy has been successful.' Leonora winced and inspected the front of her bodice for milk stains. 'I must go to William. It's after ten, his feed is overdue.'

'So, we say nothing?'

'Nothing.' She paused to watch Elizabeth through a small gap in the curtain. The feeble-minded young woman was sitting obediently in her chair, her head bowed low and her hands making swift, distracted movements in her lap. 'We need more servants.'

'Leonora, we have a whole string of maids.'

'From now on they must work in pairs,' Leonora asserted. 'There must always be *two* girls on duty in the nursery, even when you are present.'

'Because of Elizabeth?'

Leonora nodded sadly. 'After this she must never be allowed near my son except in the presence of at least two other people. And she must never be allowed to hold him in her arms, is that clear?'

'I'll see to it,' Anabel said.

'And make sure she's locked in her rooms tonight.'

'She's locked in *every* night, as you instructed.'

'Good. Make that your last check before retiring. Did you light the fire in the tower rooms?'

'I did. I also aired the bed and put out towels and soap. I'll be going up later with a supper tray and some hot water.' She pursed her lips and sucked air through her teeth. 'Leonora, I wish you wouldn't ...'

Leonora turned and gave Anabel a brilliant smile. 'Don't bother to voice your fears, Anabel. There can be no turning back. I knew that from the beginning.'

'But it's been a year, a whole year. Surely you don't need to ... not after all this time?'

463

'Hush! If it were ten years or twenty I would *still* need him. You know exactly how I feel, Anabel. We quarrel only because you choose to close your eyes to the simple truth of it.'

She passed through into the other room, scooped her child very gently from his cot and stood looking down at his tiny, perfectly formed face. His dark blue eyes regarded her with a solemn gaze and one small hand reached up to touch her face as if in greeting. The sight of William could still astonish her. He was so small and beautiful he took her breath away. Every finger and toe, every crease and hollow, every detail of his strong little body was sheer perfection. Even now he was a very handsome child, dark haired, with dark-lashed blue eyes and a placid nature, his father's son in every way.

She signalled that Elizabeth should be taken back to her own rooms and the maid hurried to obey. Elizabeth held back at the door, reluctant to leave. Her fingers began to pluck at her hair, dragging out several fine strands by the root.

'Let me hold him,' she pleaded.

'Not tonight, Elizabeth,' Leonora smiled. 'It's time for bed now. Good night dear.'

'I lost my kitten. I want to hold the baby.'

'Good night, Elizabeth.'

Anabel and the maid helped coax her from the room with the promise of toasted mallows after supper, and by the time the door closed behind them she had forgotten her disappointment and was smiling again.

Alone at last, Leonora unlaced her bodice and offered her nipple to William's tiny rose-bud mouth. He sucked hungrily, his fists resting on her breast and his eyes looking directly into hers. Feeding her baby son was a joy she had not anticipated. The deep, rhythmic sucking at her breasts was uniquely sensual, and those times with him were more special, more intimate and fulfilling than she could have thought possible. In the quiet room she fed him without haste, concerned with nothing outside their shared time. She told him all about the banquet and the Grand Ball, described the players, the flutes and bells, the ice sculptures and flickering candles, the glittering array of guests swirling around the Great Hall like colourful flowers in a breeze. And through it all the infant watched and listened, his lips and tongue growing languid at the nipple, his eyes slowly drooping in sleep.

Savouring their closeness, Leonora held him in her arms for a long time before returning him to his cot. Then she placed her hand on his head, feeling the warm, pulsating softness of the fontanelle beneath her fingers. She had wanted this child for the security he would bring her within the Cavendish family. Only at his birth, and since, had she begun to discover what motherhood could mean to a woman. This was her son, her first-born child, and just touching him could raise a lump to her throat and fill her heart with such quiet satisfaction that it swelled to bursting in her breast. Watching him like this she could almost believe that she was the most fortunate woman alive, and that William Lucas Cavendish was the finest, the most beautiful child ever to be born.

II

She left for the gatehouse apartments at a quarter to midnight wearing a silk-lined cloak over her silver ball-gown. She had removed all her jewels and knotted a ribbon of silver satin around her neck so that its ends trailed against the creamy swell of her breasts. Her hair had been brushed until it shone, coiled into a chignon and set in place with a simple mother-of-pearl comb. Her body was scented with amber musk and bergamot, her hair with rose-oil, her breath with aniseed. Even her feet, so tired after the ball and the long build-up to the Christmas celebrations, had been bathed in scented water and massaged with aromatic oils.

'You look beautiful, like a young bride,' Anabel said a little grudgingly. 'Are you so certain he will come?'

'He will come.'

'With broken ribs and a dislocated shoulder?'

Leonora nodded. 'He will come.'

And come he did. Within minutes of her arrival at the gate-house he was there, stepping into the alcove from the Monks' Stair as silent as a shadow. He stood quite still, watching her. He was dressed as she had seen him last, in tight pants, high boots and bandages, only now he had a heavy brown great-coat thrown across his shoulders. Winter raindrops sparkled like gems in his black hair and the chain on which his key was hung gleamed warmly on his neck.

'You came,' she breathed.

'Did you doubt it?'

She shook her head. 'It's been too long, Lukan.'

'Aye, too long.'

They watched each other's eyes, faltering in the silence that separated them now as surely as the last long months had done. She blamed him for his stubborn pride, he blamed her for being Malcolm's wife and William's mother. At last she took a step towards him and said, 'I missed you.'

'Oh Lia, Lia.' Her name passed his lips as a groan. He closed his eyes and leaned his unbandaged shoulder against the wall, lifting his face so that his head met the cool stone. She knew every line and curve of his face, every gesture and movement of him, and because of this she felt his anger and his pain.

'I thought you hated me,' she said.

He groaned again. 'I believe I did.'

'And now?'

'Now?' He opened his eyes just wide enough to see her through his lashes. 'Now I have learned that love and hate are two sides of the same coin. They are a pair. They feed upon each other.'

'You have become cynical.'

'I am well taught, my lady.'

She winced at that and once again they let the silence take priority. Between them was the great four-poster bed, the crackling fire, the wolf-skin rugs, and more: a yawning chasm of uncertainty.

Leonora unclipped her cloak and let it fall to the floor, removed the mother-of-pearl comb from her hair and shook her head so that her long dark tresses tumbled down her back. He watched her through narrowed eyes, unsmiling, then pushed himself upright and shrugged the cumbersome great-coat from his shoulders. He extended his left hand, palm-uppermost, inviting her to close the gap between them, and Leonora went to him with a small cry of relief.

'Hold me,' she demanded. 'Hold me tighter, tighter.' She pressed herself against him, kissing his neck and bare shoulder, wanting to have every inch of her body touching every inch of his. 'Oh Lukan, if only you knew how I have longed for this.'

'I know,' he replied hoarsely. He clasped her to him in a strong, one-armed embrace, his mouth pressed into the curve of her neck and his big palm warm against her back. 'Ye gods woman, how could I not know?'

She turned her cheek into his chest, felt the rough bandages against her skin. 'Your shoulder?'

'Impeded only by these infernal bindings.'

'Then take the bindings off. Nothing must come between us tonight.'

He chuckled softly. 'You'll do as you will, my Lia.'

He released her, took the big hunting knife from his belt and offered it, hilt first, to her. She took it and severed the clusters of knots at his shoulder, chest and elbow. Then she returned the knife to its sheath, unbuckled his heavy belt and let it fall with a clatter to the floor. With a smile she led him to the fire and drew him down to the soft fur rugs where they had made love so many times before. Gently and slowly, pausing at intervals to kiss the exposed areas of bruising, she unwound the strips of linen from his arm and body. She kissed the hard muscle of his upper arm, then pressed a row of small kisses all the way down to his fingers. For a moment she held his palm against her cheek, feeling its warmth, its strength, and when she opened her eyes she found him watching her with such tenderness that she was almost pained by the potency of it.

They removed each other's garments with unhurried pleasure, and it was as if in doing so they peeled away the bitter hurts and aching loneliness of the last year. Naked, they knelt

467

in the thick fur of the rugs, facing each other in the flickering firelight, rediscovering the delights that had been lost to them for so long. With infinite gentleness he lifted her breasts to kiss each one in turn. The tip of his tongue teased each nipple until it stood proud and erect and eager for his mouth. In response she lowered her head to light the slow fuse of his desires with her lips and tongue. And then it was as if they had never been apart as their bodies met and locked in that consuming mutual passion that had bound them since their first meeting.

The nursery clock chimed four and still Leonora had not come. The maid was fast asleep in her curtained alcove, the child still slumbering in his wicker cot.

'Where is she?' Anabel fretted, wringing her hands in anxiety as she paced the floor. 'Why is she not here? What am I to do if she does not come?'

At five minutes past the hour she left the nursery apartments, locking the door carefully behind her. With both sides of her winter cloak held tightly across her body she ran on tiptoe along the main corridor to the servants' hall, cut through one of the guest rooms and out into the chilly inner courtyard. Here she paused, shivering in the moonlight. This was where the old Countess had presided like a formidable empress over grandiose garden parties attended by the very cream of society. Here Leonora Shelley, then a penniless seventeen-year-old determined to defeat the odds against her, had marched defiantly to meet her destiny head-on. The rectangular pond was drained now for the season, its tiled interior littered with winter debris, the ornamental fountains still, the shaded walks of scarlet honeysuckle and scented passion-flower now turned to barest green for the colder months. The pretty seats and tables had been taken indoors, the great peacock chair carried off to Leonora's private rooms. In the moonlit shadows Anabel could almost see the old Countess shocked into a seizure by Leonora's intrusion; the unsuspecting guests, the subtle, deliberate entrapment of Sir Malcolm Cavendish.

'A world ago,' she whispered, shuddering in the darkness. 'A whole lost world ago, and now she has erased that old glory and put her own name to the new.'

Anabel crossed the court-yard and hurried through to the gatehouse buildings, her footsteps making no sound on the carpeted floor. She locked the door to the gatehouse behind her, took up the small night-lamp and carried it up the wooden steps to Leonora's apartment. There was no sign of her mistress, no indication that she had been there. Anabel glanced at the ceiling and cocked her head to one side, listening. Upstairs was the other room, the room where Leonora and her lover kept their wicked trysts. Hearing nothing, she crossed to the far wall and lifted the curtain concealing the old stone alcove. To one side was the Monks' Stair, spiralling upwards and downwards in its chimney-like well, dark and dangerous to the unpractised foot. She went up with great care, feeling in the darkness for a firm footing before proceeding from each step to the next. Ignoring the black funnel of stone above her, she stepped off at the next floor and found herself in Leonora's secret bedroom.

In the dim light she could just make out the two figures lying side by side in the big bed, the Lady Leonora and her handsome gypsy lover. Intrigued, feeling herself drawn by a strange magnetism, Anabel moved into the room with her lamp held high. The fire still glowed dimly in the grate and several stubs of candles flickered here and there around the room, casting shadows that danced over every surface. The silver ball-gown lay in a heap on the floor, beside it his breeches and a mound of discarded binding-linen. She tiptoed close to the foot of the big four-poster bed and raised her lamp to view the occupants by its steadier light. As she did so a tremor of shock ran through her and the breath caught painfully in her throat. With her eyes wide open and the fingers of her free hand touching her lips lest a cry escape between them, she stared down at the lovers as if seeing them for the first time, and what she saw quite took her breath away. They were beautiful. The gypsy lay on his back with one arm thrown above his head, his hair coal-black against the white pillows,

469

his skin a rich, warm brown in the gentle light. He was long-bodied and tightly muscled, strikingly handsome in sleep and fascinating in his nakedness. Leonora lay in the crook of his left arm, her skin like palest cream and her hair fanned out in all its ruby-toned glory. She lay on her side, one arm resting across his body, one tender pink and white breast pressed close to where his nut-brown nipple lay in a bed of short black hair. Anabel was deeply moved by the sight of them. As separate individuals they were uncommonly attractive in their own distinctive ways, but together they were something else entirely. They were magnificent. There was nothing wicked here, nothing unnatural. This gypsy and his lady had surely been created for each other. Like night and day, like sun and moon, they were as God intended them to be.

She realised with a sudden jolt that his eyes had opened and he was looking back at her with a kindly expression. He moved his dark head a fraction of an inch, acknowledging her reasons for being there, then turned to Leonora without the slightest concern for his nudity. Anabel was aware of hidden muscles shifting along the length of him, of the solid flesh of his buttocks and the taut brown flatness of his belly. He placed the palm of his free hand on Leonora's cheek and pressed his lips to her forehead in an act of infinite tenderness. When he moved again her eyes were open and she was gazing at him from their sleepy amethyst depths. The look that passed between them said it all.

For Anabel those moments shaped a turning point in her understanding of her mistress's situation. It was as if she had worn blinkers that at last were stripped away. There was no evil here, no self-indulgent pandering to the base desires of the flesh. What joined these two was pure and bittersweet, a thing too deep, too powerful for any outsider to comprehend.

Realising that her presence now went unnoticed, she left the room quietly as she could and made her way back through the gatehouse apartments to the nursery wing. She felt chastened, almost humbled by what she had witnessed in that secret tower room. She had seen the gypsy in his other colours, cherishing the lady in his arms as something precious,

470

something truly priceless. She had glimpsed the beauty Leonora saw in him, had felt and seen their unique oneness.

'Like night and day,' she said in confirmation of her earlier thoughts. 'Different, inseparable, *the same*.'

The child was awake. He turned his head to watch her as she stooped over his cot. She bent to lift him into her arms, loving the sweet-smelling vulnerability of him.

Leonora came with a special glow about her that was more than just the after-effects of sexual gratification. She was alive and vibrant. She was Leonora at her very best.

Anabel watched her feeding the boy and smiling down into his tiny face. At that moment, having left her lover's arms to take her child to her breast, she seemed totally fulfilled.

'I understand it now,' she said.

'What? I'm sorry, Anabel. What did you say?'

'I said, I understand at last about you and Lukan.'

'Do you, my dear?' Leonora's smile was brilliant.

Anabel returned the smile. 'I swear I will never like it. I will always fear it for the damage it can do us, but I think I truly understand it now.'

Leonora reached out to take and squeeze her hand. 'That makes me happy, Anabel.'

'You love him.'

'I do.'

Anabel nodded. 'And he adores you. I saw it all tonight and I understood. It could not be the same with any other man, not even Malcolm.'

'I know that, Anabel.'

'You should have married him. You were meant to be together. You should have forsaken Beresford and married Lukan.'

Leonora nodded and whispered, 'I know that too.'

Leaving mother and child to their intimate time without intrusion, the older woman went through into the next room, threw off her cloak and slippers and climbed into bed. The sheets were cold and she was grateful for their chill. Her mind was filled with images that warmed her blood and brought a guilty flush to her cheeks. She had never looked at an

471

unclothed man before. Seeing the gypsy like that had reminded her with cruel sharpness that her own body had never been touched by a man.

III

There was a brook some way above the meadow. It meandered downward through a quiet copse and past a slope where willows hung their pale and slender branches to the ground. Here a lop-sided wooden bench stood overgrown with weeds and scarred by all the seasons it had witnessed since the last Earl set it there. It faced to the north, to the gently rolling Cotswolds and, looking leftwards, to the statuesque Malvern Hills, now little more than a purple haze in the distance. Charles Shelley rode beside the Earl. He was fully recovered now and growing restless in his enforced idleness. It was a crisp, cold afternoon and they had been out for two and a half hours. For a while they had dismounted to watch the cut thorn-boughs stripped of their shoots, laid horizontally and interlaced to form long, low fences between the fields. They had been discussing Jonathan openly but carefully, the Earl unwilling to reveal his secret, Charles equally reluctant to confess his knowledge of it.

'The decision should be mine,' Sir Oscar said again, half turning in the saddle. 'I say the decision should be mine.'

They had reached the bench. Charles dismounted, tethered his mount and stood looking out at the hazy view.

'No sir, it must remain with me,' he said. 'I have my brother's trust and he my word. I am not at liberty to pass responsibility for that to another.' He turned to face the man upon whose generosity he had been living for almost a month now. 'Sir Oscar, give me a letter sealed and signed by your own hand. Tell Jonathan your true reasons for wanting him back and I will undertake to deliver the letter, unopened, into his hands.'

472

The Earl scowled. How could he put what he needed to say into a letter? But Charles was adamant, respectful but determined not to betray his brother's confidence.

'Letters may be misplaced,' he said.

Charles shrugged. 'I can only swear to guard it with my life. Other than that, I will tell Jonathan of your kindness and our sister's happiness and hope that he will come.'

'He must come.'

Charles smiled, compassion in his eyes. He could not know how much he resembled his dead mother, and how the similarity stung the older man.

'But not at the hands of your agents, Sir Oscar. Let him come to you of his own accord or not at all.'

'Not at all?' Sir Oscar repeated sharply. 'You doubt he will come?'

'He respects you sir, as I do. We owe our excellent educations, our sister's happiness and our present turn of circumstances to your enduring generosity. And our mother loved you dearly, that much we have always known. He will come, I'm sure of it, but when, I cannot say. He has plans for the future, dreams that will not easily be set aside.'

'Tell him ...' Sir Oscar hesitated, then nodded as if a decision had been made. 'Tell him I am prepared to come to him.'

'To America?' Charles was astounded.

'To America,' the Earl confirmed.

Charles looked at him with renewed respect. It was clear that he had never known with certainty that Jonathan was his son, and just as obvious that the truth of it was now tearing him apart. That he had loved their mother there could be no doubt. He was an honourable man, a man deserving of Francine Shelley's love. He had guarded her reputation as he had sought to protect her children, and even now, when she was in her grave, he wanted to take to himself all that had been hers. Her eldest son would be proud indeed to call him father.

'Tell him,' Charles said, watching the other's eyes. 'Tell him your reasons, sir. Be frank and open, and he will come to you.'

The Earl nodded sadly, looking out into the hazy distance.

Then he remounted, turned the horse's head and rode for home.

Charles left for America on the seventh day of February. He was accompanied as far as the post-house on the Oxford Road by Sir Oscar, Sir Malcolm and his sister Leonora. In the comfortable interior of the Earl's crested carriage the small group travelled almost in silence. Although together still, their parting had already begun.

'Have I found you only to lose you again?' Leonora had asked tearfully when she saw his bag was packed. And he had vowed to respect his brother's wishes for a year, no more than that, and then return, with or without Jonathan, to Beresford Hall.

All too soon they reached the bustling post house where he was to board the speedy post-chaise for London. Thankfully, there was little time to delay before the passengers were called upon to claim their places. Charles was to make this trip in relative comfort, protected from the elements in a well-sprung inside seat, free from the clutter of livestock and baggage and relieved of the very real danger of being thrown into the road with every lurch of the coach. At the last moment before he boarded, Sir Oscar handed him a sturdy leather pouch tightly buckled and with a sleek brass lock.

'For Jonathan,' he said. 'Keep it safe.'

'You have my word on that sir.'

'And here is the key. The money is meant for Jonathan and his family, but you'll find sufficient for your own needs should you become hard-pressed on the journey.'

'You have already been more than generous,' Charles smiled, indicating the purses packed inside his boots for safety's sake. 'I can not foresee the need to open the pouch, but I thank you sincerely for the offer.'

'Remember that there is a place for you at Beresford,' Sir Oscar said a little awkwardly.

'I know that and I thank you sir, most sincerely.'

'Take care of yourself.'

'I will sir, if you will undertake to do the same.'

Sir Oscar laughed at that, then shook the young man's

474

hand and embraced him briefly before turning away and climbing back into the carriage. He lowered the blind, unwilling to prolong that unwanted parting. He liked the boy and wanted him to stay, but more than that he feared to lose this one sure link between himself and Jonathan.

Leonora watched the post-chaise until its shape had dimmed and vanished into the winter mist and the clatter of the horses' hooves had long since ceased to reach her ears. He might return soon with Jonathan and Louisa, and with the little one when it was old enough and strong enough to make the long journey across the Atlantic ocean. He might never come back. A million unseen obstacles and fickle turns of fate might lie between these shores and the Americas. She trusted nothing, not even the strength of their own will, to reunite them across that hazardous distance. Dry-eyed, she felt the loss of him cut deep inside herself.

'*Bon voyage*,' she whispered into the distance, then turned as abruptly as the Earl had done and strode briskly back to the carriage.

IV

Rebecca could hear them in the other room, yelling and bellowing as they wrestled each other like two prize-fighters battling for a purse of gold. That room had Persian carpets on its parquet floors, swagged drapes at its mullioned windows and a superb plaster ceiling finely cut with Tudor emblems. Not a stick of furniture was there to complement its burled oak panelling and massive fireplace. A simple window-seat cut into the stone was where he sat sometimes, staring out at the secluded forest where deer and fox and even the bashful badger might pass within a few feet of the house. Beyond the open windows rooks were nesting now, every twig for every nest laid in place with a noisy conference of the whole flock.

Rebecca paused in the open doorway. Lukan and Malcolm were stripped to the waist and bare-footed, grunting as they tested each other's strength and speed in a wrestling match that was deadly serious. There had always been an element of warfare in their sport, a quest for superiority all the more keen-edged because they were so evenly matched in everything they did. They were of equal height and weight, both muscular, long-legged and slender-hipped. They even wore their hair in similar fashion, though Malcolm's dark brown tail, neatly bound in the nape of his neck with a black ribbon, was but half the length of Lukan's jet black main.

'The gypsy and the gentleman,' she said with quiet contempt. 'And who but a fool would wager upon which is which?'

She watched them lunge, growling, and grapple each other to the floor with such violence that they might have been the worst of enemies. And just as swiftly they were laughing and calling the bout a draw with none the winner and none the lesser man. When she walked away they were sprawled on their backs on the carpet, perspiring and breathless from their battle. She did not hear the request Sir Malcolm put to Lukan.

'I need you to speak to your sister on my behalf.'

'To my sister? To Rebecca? Malcolm Cavendish, must I remind you that you are a married man with a beautiful young wife? No sir, I will not proposition my plain-as-a-pudding sister on your behalf.'

'Fool!' Malcolm snorted, lashing out with his foot as Lukan's lithe body snaked beyond his reach. 'It's her herbal skills I would make use of, not her body.'

'And glad I am to hear that,' Lukan grinned.

'You mock me sir. I'll not have it.'

'Then do your worst, for I am past the effort.' He flexed each leg in turn, stroking the big thigh-muscles. 'I swear you fought me like a fiend unleashed, Malcolm. Do you bear me a grudge?'

'Of course not.'

'Then you have quarrelled with your father and you use me as your whipping-boy, is that it?'

476

Malcolm shook his head. 'I simply needed the exercise. Will you speak to Rebecca on my behalf?'

Lukan reached his arms above his head and stretched his long body in a feline movement. 'Why should I?' he asked lazily. 'You'll find her in the yard. Go speak to her yourself.'

'I cannot. The matter is too ... too delicate.'

Lukan opened one eye and grinned. 'Delicate?'

'It's personal. I could not speak of such a thing to a woman.'

It was the tone of his voice that alerted Lukan. Something was wrong here. He swung himself into a sitting position and watched his friend, seeing now the troubled expression in his deep blue eyes.

'What is it Malcolm?'

'My marriage,' Malcolm said, avoiding his friend's gaze.

'What? Ye gods! I could name a hundred men who would give their right arm to have your marriage, and each I'm sure could name a hundred more.'

'Aye, and each and every one of them would use the privilege to better effect than I am capable of doing.' Malcolm's voice had a bitter edge. He leaped to his feet and snatched up a towel that had been left folded on the window seat. He rubbed it vigorously over his face and neck.

Still seated on the floor, Lukan stared at his friend's broad back. 'What ails you, Malcolm?'

'Can you not guess? The problem is no stranger to my bed.'

'What ails you?'

Malcolm wheeled and threw the towel down. 'Damn it, must I spell out my humiliation by the letter? I'm impotent. I have a loving wife who never makes complaint while I am like a *brother* in her bed.'

'*Impotent?*' Lukan's mouth fell open in amazement.

'Aye, like a sick old man.'

'How long? Since when?'

'Since it was known that William was expected.'

'What? But that's ...' he paused and made a rapid calculation. 'That's thirteen months or more.'

'Do you think I need reminding of that?'

477

Lukan rose to his feet, shaking his head in disbelief. Leonora had not told him this. She had never uttered a single criticism, not a word to indicate that all was not well in her marriage. For an instant he felt elated in the knowledge that she was his alone, but then he pushed the notion aside, hating himself for it. At last he gathered his thoughts sufficiently to ask, 'How could this happen to you Malcolm? After Grace it was perhaps to be expected. When a wife suffers as she did and dies in childbirth, a husband's guilt may make him less than he once was, but now ...' He raked his fingers through his hair. 'Why now? Why now when you have the best of everything?'

'How can I answer that?'

'Do you not love her as you did?'

Malcolm laughed harshly. 'A foolish question, Lukan. As you must know, I love her to distraction. No woman could welcome me to her bed with more forbearance and compassion, and Heaven knows how much I still desire her, yet I am hampered by this persistent failure. Believe me, it is neither the need nor the intention I lack.'

'So all is well until the final gesture?'

Malcolm nodded miserably. 'At the first contact my erection retreats like a cowardly thing.'

'And she forgives you for it?'

'Aye, and has done since her pregnancy was known.'

'Then you are a fortunate man in spite of everything.'

'I am well aware of that.'

Lukan puckered his brows and began to pace the room with his hands clasped behind his back. 'You have always been a sensitive man despite your tough exterior,' he reminded Malcolm. 'It seems to me you feared too deeply for Leonora's safety while she carried young William. You withdrew yourself from the responsibility of giving her a child that might have cost her as dearly as it cost your first wife.'

'Fine reasoning, except that the boy was born five months ago and still the failure persists.'

'Have you not succeeded once?' Lukan asked. 'In all that time, not once?'

478

Malcolm shook his head.

'And she has borne it all without complaint?'

'Yes. There is a depth of affection between us that seems to survive unscathed despite it all, but this situation can not be allowed to go on. I believe there are medicines and potions that may help. Rebecca has knowledge of such things. Speak to her for me. I am rapidly becoming desperate, Lukan. I cannot expect a woman like Leonora to live a life of celibacy on my account. Thank God she is a woman of quiet passions.'

Lukan looked at him sharply. 'A woman of quiet passions?'

'Oh yes, despite the fiery look of her and the lust she arouses in young and old alike, Leonora is quite modest in her desires.'

'She is?' Lukan swallowed and cleared his throat, turning his face lest Malcolm read the expression on it. The words astounded him. He had never thought to hear his hungry, grasping wildcat Lady Lia described as quiet and modest in her desires.

'Will you speak to Rebecca?' Malcolm asked again.

'I will, this very day.' Without embarrassment Lukan peeled off his pants and tossed them into a corner. 'But first I'm for the river to wash this sweat away. Will you join me?'

'In *February*?' Malcolm exclaimed. 'Ye gods man, it's cold enough to freeze the ponds and rain-barrels out there. Were I to follow your peculiar habits I may never rise to my husbandly duties ever again. If you'll excuse me, I'll go home and take my bath like a civilised human being, warm and shallow and inhabited by neither fish nor fowl.'

He followed Lukan to the door, pulling on his shirt as he watched the sleek brown body leap the garden wall, race down the slope and pitch in a perfect arc into the icy river.

Rebecca watched from her window as Sir Malcolm mounted his horse and turned its head into the forest, following a narrow path that would bring him out at the highest section of the meadow. Minutes later she saw her brother pull himself to the river bank and shake the water from his hair in a spray of sunlit drops. He stooped to haul his wolfhounds one by one from the river and they, like him,

479

shook sprays of water in all directions. He ran to the house, shivering, and she was there to offer him a towel. His skin was turned to goose-flesh by the cold and the manly fullness of his genitals hung small and shrunken against his body. He rubbed the wetness from his hair, then handed back the towel and went to squat before the fire. Naked and brown, his buttocks tight and his hair plastered in wet streaks to his back he had become a gypsy once again. She watched him with longing, savouring the rare pleasure of seeing him like this, without the trappings of that other, unreachable side of him.

At last he lolled over into a more comfortable position on the hearth rug and gave voice to his thoughts. 'Malcolm needs your help.'

'He'll get nothing from me.'

'He has a health problem.'

'He also has a personal physician and money enough to buy a better one if he is no longer satisfied with the man.'

'He needs help, Rebecca.'

'Then let him find it with his own kind.'

'Rebecca, he has never given you just cause to scorn him as you do.'

She snapped her answer. 'He is a Cavendish and that's enough.'

Lukan sighed. It was an old, old argument. 'Then do it for me, because I ask it.'

She looked at him sulkily. 'What ails this precious friend of yours that he should seek my help?'

'Impotency.'

She stared at him, her face a mask of amazement. After a lengthy silence she asked, 'Is this a jest?'

He shook his head. 'No jest. Malcolm is impotent.'

'And he confides in you?' She laughed out loud, a coarse, unpleasant sound. 'He comes to *you*?'

'I am his friend,' Lukan reminded her.

'You are his *betrayer*,' she corrected.

He winced. 'That does not prevent me loving him.'

'No, but you love his lady more.'

'And you blame me for that? You knew it was to be. You

480

and that old gypsy woman between you had my fate decided and sealed long before I ever set eyes on Leonora.'

'Aye, I knew it, but I never welcomed it nor ever will.'

'Then just *accept* it, Rebecca. Resign yourself as I have had to do. I dislike the ill-will that has grown between us lately.'

'You have the means to end it,' she said bitterly.

'By turning from Lia?'

'Aye, if you've a mind to.'

His smile was regretful. 'It is not my mind that binds me to her, Rebecca.'

She looked contemptuously between his bent legs to where his genitals, now warmed, were hanging in their natural fullness.

He caught her glance. 'Nor that,' he told her. He touched his fist very lightly to his solar plexus and looked up at her with an expression that begged her understanding. 'It is here,' he said softly. 'It holds me here. I cannot leave her.'

Her shoulders fell. She sighed, 'I know.'

'Don't hate me for it, Rebecca.'

'I do not hate you, Lukan.'

'Sometimes it seems you do. You can be cruel.'

She scowled at him. 'Don't talk to me of cruelty, Lukan de Ville. You have the edge on anyone in that commodity.'

'I'm sorry you think that.'

'Aye, we will all be sorry before this thing is done.'

'Perhaps, but in the meantime will you help Malcolm?'

She laughed again, mocking him. 'Will I help him? You'd be wiser to ask yourself will you! I can provide the mixture, but will you give it to him with your blessing? If you leave things as they are you will be free to do with her what he's incapable of doing. She will then be yours exclusively and your betrayal of Malcolm Cavendish will be complete. Or would you rather hand him the cure, and with it the means to bed the lady while you wait your turn?'

He winced. 'You can be cruel,' he said again.

'Aye, think on it, Lukan.' She chuckled maliciously. 'I'll make the cure willingly enough, but will you have the stomach to take it to him?'

*

At that precise moment the object of their discussion was approaching the terraced gardens near the main entrance to the Hall. He came on foot, leading his mount at a slow pace. Some distance away Leonora frolicked on the winter lawns with two of the Earl's placid long-eared spaniels. The scene was idyllic. On a nearby bench sat Anabel Corey, muffled against the cold, and beside her the baby-carriage where the infant slept contentedly between the last feed and the next. Sounds were crisped on the chilly air; the ring of a hammer from the blacksmith's shed, the bickering of busy crows, the lowing of cows at the Home Farm. And the sweetest sound of all was that of Leonora's carefree laughter as she played with the two dogs like a happy child. She wore a velvet gown the colour of warm port wine, a hat with streamers and a short fur cape. She looked glowing and healthy, her breath gusting like pale smoke and her cheeks as rosy red as summer apples.

Malcolm stopped to watch her. At times like this he saw in her a hint of what lay in Lukan's nature, that same mercurial cocktail of almost saintly calm and devilish undercurrents. She too possessed a hint of hidden turbulence running just below the surface. It made him wonder if she, like Lukan, had a darker, earthier side that had yet to show itself.

When she saw him there she laughed and ran to kiss his cheek with childlike spontaneity, only to be gone again in an instant with the excited dogs bounding about her skirts. She was so full of energy, so alive, that he wondered if motherhood and a gentle companionship would ever be enough to satisfy her needs. At the moment he knew that no other man was compensating for the shortfall in their marriage. He would know instantly if she took a lover, because a woman like Leonora could not possibly conceal such a weighty secret. She was too honest and her gaze was too open, too tranparent. He would always be able to catch her out in a lie because she was so artless and unskilled in the practice of deception. She loved him, and only him. He had no doubt of that.

Just then she turned, laughing, to blow him a kiss which he pretended to catch in both hands. He pressed it to his lips

482

before blowing one in return. He was a fortunate man indeed for she was wholly his, despite his shortcomings. He knew all this and yet, as he turned to walk his mount to the stables, a nagging doubt cast shadows across his happiness. Leonora was his, but for how long?

CHAPTER TWENTY-THREE

I

Rebecca could hear her brother pacing the floor of his room, to and fro, this way and that, like a wild beast confined to a cage. His discomfort suited her. She wanted him to suffer. She wanted him to be torn in his heart between his own needs and those of Malcolm Cavendish. She had known from the start that he would love the Cavendish woman, and endure this obsession she must, but she would do everything in her power to see that he enjoyed his lady only at a price. Until today he had been happy in his reunion, happier than Rebecca had seen him for many a long month. He had a hearty appetite, slept well and smiled too much for a man of his singular disposition. He had changed. He was no longer the sullen, sombre companion with barely a civil word to offer. Lately he came home cheerful and amiable, sometimes behaving as if he were quite fond of her. Rebecca had often found his indifference hard to bear, but this bland, second-hand affection was no less intolerable. She begrudged him every smile, every sigh, every tiny moment of joy his lady had returned to him.

Now she rose from her chair to stoke the fire but paused, swaying a little with the fire iron in her hand. A wave of nausea swept over her. She dipped into her apron pocket and pulled out a piece of ginger root which she began to nibble at rather delicately, using her front teeth. After a while the wave of sickness began to subside, leaving the bitter taste of ginger in her mouth. She remained standing before the fire, her gaze marking his footsteps across the ceiling as he paced the room above her. He was making restless figure-of-eights diagonally across the room. She could almost see him up there, his hands clasped behind his back, his lead lowered, his brows pulled down into a deep frown. That habit of pacing sat like a stamp on him.

'Cavendish!' she hissed at the ceiling. 'Cavendish!' She made that single word sound like an insult.

She tensed as the tone of his pacing altered, and when the door of his room slammed with an almighty crash she busied herself at the hot coals with the fire iron. Moments later he flung himself down the stairs and into the room, hurling the door back on its hinges and filling the atmosphere with his private rage. He held out the jar she had given him and looked at her through narrowed eyes.

'It must be something else,' he growled. 'Not this. I will not give him this.'

'But you must. It is the best thing available,' she told him, adding, with just a touch of malice, 'But it must be used strictly according to the instructions.'

'You mock me, woman.'

'Nay, 'tis your own jealousy that mocks you, Lukan.'

He strode across the room, grabbed her hand and slapped the jar into her palm, closing her fingers around it. 'Then he shall make do with *second-best*, for I'll not give him this.'

'It is the only remedy I possess.'

'Then find another.'

'It will not be easy.'

'*Do it.*'

485

She shrugged and turned from him, concealing a smile. She had told him that Malcolm must use the potion nightly, without fail, and that his wife should massage it into the offending parts with such loving care that strength and purpose were persuaded to return. Lukan's imagination had done the rest. Just thinking of Leonora doing all that for her husband had driven him almost mad with jealousy.

'Perhaps you should leave well alone,' she suggested. 'Let your friend be content without his husbandly pleasures.'

He shook his head. 'He came to me for help.'

'Then give it to him.'

'Not this way.'

She shrugged again. 'There may be no other.'

'There must be. He trusts your skills.'

She rounded on him. 'Aye, as he trusts your friendship. As he trusts his *wife*.'

'Enough! Enough of this!' His fist came down with savage impact on a nearby table. Out in the hall the wolfhounds rose silently to their feet, padded into the kitchen and vanished through the open side door leading to the garden. Rebecca tossed the fire iron into the hearth and faced her brother. She placed the jar between them on the table.

'Take him the remedy.'

He shook his head, drawing back as if the jar contained a deadly poison. 'No, not that.'

'He is your friend. Help him.'

'She is my love, I cannot.'

'Then you are caught between two devils, Lukan.'

'Aye, much to your amusement it would seem.'

Rebecca smiled bitterly. 'Did you think it would be easy, loving her?'

He met her gaze, seeing a thousand hurts and resentments smouldering in her black eyes. He felt a sudden stab of guilt that was without recognisable foundation. Her hostility was intense, a personal thing between the two of them, and it had grown there without his knowledge. Deeply disturbed, he reached out to cover her hand with his own, but she snatched her hand away as if his touch had burned her skin.

'When did this happen, Rebecca?' His voice was softer now, his anger spent against her half-suppressed hostility. 'When did you come to hate me?'

She rubbed her wrist where his hand had briefly rested on it, wiping the skin as if to erase his touch. Then she shook her head but offered him neither a denial of his words nor a reply to his question. Instead they stared at each other across the table, Lukan aware of the animosity in his sister's eyes, she aware of the sudden hurt in his.

'I'll find another cure,' she said at last. 'A powder for his drink, a herbal tonic. She need not even be aware that he is taking it.'

'Thank you.'

'As for the rest of it ...'

'Yes?'

'You are mistaken.'

He shook his head. 'I think not, Rebecca.'

She licked her lips, then turned and walked away from him. At the door she paused with her hand on the latch, half-turned and repeated softly, 'You are mistaken.'

It was midday when he left the house again. He could hear Rebecca working at the well, hoisting the bucket on its creaking fittings, turning the big wheel as if no effort were involved. Recalling that she had recently been unwell with what she dismissed as a woman's complaint, he considered offering her a hand with the heavier work. The offer crossed his mind but did not reach his lips. She was as strong as a man and fiercely proud and would not thank him for his concern.

At the sound of his master's whistle Raven trotted out from his favourite spot on the quietest side of the barn. He came tossing his head and prancing in anticipation of a good long run. There was a hint of spring in the air: a sweet, crisp scent that neither Raven nor his master was immune to. It sharpened the senses, giving man and beast a restless desire to test their limitations. Lukan grabbed a handful of black mane and swung himself astride the muscular back. Once free of the overhanging trees he heeled Raven into a gallop across the lower meadow to the fields beyond. They cleared two hedges easily, almost came to grief at the third, splashed across the river where it slowed to a shallow stream at Middup's Mound. From there they pounded up the gentle slopes of the eastern pastures, shaping a wide horseshoe route towards the sheltered parkland skirting the hills. By the time they reached the final fence that separated the park from the open fields, both horse and man were labouring. Once inside the boundary of the park they veered to the right and, in a secluded grove of oaks, the panting horse slowed to a halt and the weary but exhilarated rider slid inelegantly from its back. Lukan sprawled on his back on the damp turf, spread-eagled, squinting up at the canopy of leafless branches set against a background of steel-grey sky. He was still lying there when he heard the sound of women's voices and the tinkle of familiar laughter in the distance. He scrambled into a crouch and scuttled crabwise to a nearby spot where, crouched in the foliage around the trees, he had a clear view of the long main pathway through the park.

'Lia,' he grinned, blessing the day's good fortune.

She was wearing red with a ruffle of white lace at her throat and walked purposefully along the path with a dark-clad Anabel struggling to match her stride. She was talking in an animated manner, using her hands in delicately expressive movements to illustrate some point she wished to make. He could see the sheen on her dark hair and a hint of brightness in her diamond earbobs. His eyes narrowed as he watched her and his smile, coming slower than his thoughts, divided his handsome face in a lop-sided arc.

'Really, Anabel, I do not see the point in concerning ourselves about something that may never happen,' she was saying. 'I have long since learned not to look a gift horse in the mouth, so long as it is given with a good heart.'

'It's a foolish risk to take,' Anabel insisted.

'Try telling that to the Earl.'

'You should have known better than to accept. You should have refused it on William's behalf.'

Leonora stopped with her hands on her hips. 'Refused it? Refused 35,000 acres on my son's behalf? Do you think me insane?'

'No, I think you a high-stepping, covetous little madam who sees her son's interests as her own.' Anabel mimicked her mistress's defiant stance. 'And what is more Leonora, sooner or later those 35,000 acres will be ...' She gasped and stared into the distance. 'What on earth ...?'

Leonora followed her gaze in time to see the rider bearing down on them from the far end of the pathway. He was doubled over the horse's neck until his hair and Raven's mane were indistinguishable from each other.

'*Lukan!*'

Leonora tossed her head and laughed out loud. Still standing with her fists on her hips, she turned to face the rider, unafraid. Raven's hooves pounded the ground, tossing bits of earth as he was urged forward at a recklessly fast pace. Anabel flung herself sideways with a cry of alarm but Leonora dared to stand her ground, laughing as she barred the way of the galloping horse. She knew that if the man misjudged the pace the horse would not. Raven was too well trained to run her down.

'Leonora!' Anabel screamed and covered her eyes with both hands.

At that moment Raven whinnied and veered to one side, and as Lukan leaped to the ground the momentum carried him forward at a run until he crashed headlong into Leonora. He caught her in his arms and together they sprawled on the grass beside the path. Over and over they rolled, laughing aloud like boisterous children, her hair breaking free of her bonnet and his legs becoming entangled in her skirts. Horrified by the spectacle, Anabel rushed after them.

'Stop that! Stop that at once! Someone will see! Someone will hear! Stop it! Stop it!'

Still laughing, Lukan struggled to his feet and hoisted a breathless Leonora after him. He kissed her passionately and she with equal passion wound her arms around his neck and returned the kiss.

'Stop it!' Anabel almost shrieked the words. 'Leonora Cavendish, stop that at once. Have you no shame, madam? And as for you, Lukan de Ville ...' She grabbed the sleeve of his shirt and tried to pull him away from Leonora, but as he turned to grin at her she saw such wicked mischief in his eyes that she shrank back, alarmed by it.

'Well now, what have we here?' He released Leonora and took a menacing step towards Anabel.

'Don't you dare,' she squeaked.

'Ah but I do dare,' he grinned.

'Don't touch me sir. Go away. Leonora ...?'

'I do believe I will kiss you, Anabel Corey.'

Aghast, she said, 'You most certainly will not!'

His grin widened. 'Ah but I will ... I must.'

'Don't you dare touch me. Get away. Shoo! Be off with you, you grinning black-eyed devil.' By now she was walking rapidly backwards with Lukan in hot pursuit. 'Get away! Leonora, make him stop this.'

But Leonora had covered her face with both hands and was laughing with delight. As Lukan made a lunge for her, Anabel squealed, turned on her heels and fled, rushing back towards the Hall as fast as her legs would carry her. Twice she dared to glance behind her, only to see him lurching after her with a comic gait his hands outstretched as if he meant to grab her by the throat. Not until she had reached the poplar trees at the far end of the park and she was barely able to draw another breath did she slow her pace and dare to look behind her for a third time. The devil had tricked her. By now he and Leonora were the full length of the drive away, running hand in hand in the opposite direction. She saw them leave the path and vanish into the trees, and almost at once the bright red flash of Leonora's skirts was lost from sight.

He led her through a maze of holly bushes, along a tiny winding footpath barely wide enough for each of them to pass in single file, across a tiny bridge over a brook and on into a small, sequestered grove. Herb Paris and Solomon's-seal grew here, and for several weeks of every year the ground around was carpeted in bluebells. He pulled Leonora to him, resting her back against the trunk of a great elm tree, leaning his body against hers. His big hands cupped her face, smoothing aside her breeze-blown hair and gazing so deeply into her eyes that she felt no part of her escaped his loving scrutiny.

'The ground is soft here,' he told her.

'And damp,' she said. 'My skirts will tell the tale of our encounter.'

'Then madam, this tree will be our bed.'

She slipped a hand between their bodies, fondled the bulge in his trousers and laughed seductively. 'What, here and now?'

'What better time or place?'

'My apartment in half an hour?' she suggested.

He kissed her long and hard, then took both her wrists in his hand and pinned them high above her head, against the trunk of the tree. 'It will be here and now,' he whispered hoarsely.

She caressed his lips with her tongue and pressed the lower part of her body against his. 'You have no measure of finesse, Mr de Ville. This is the stuff of common people.'

She felt him hoist her skirts with his free hand, felt his fingers hot and demanding on her inner thigh.

'The stuff of life,' he corrected, then released her hands and unfastened the heavy buckle of his belt.

II

She had William brought to the apartments after luncheon. When the maids were dismissed, the door locked and Anabel set on watch in the gatehouse, Lukan came down from the upper room to spend some time with his godson. The boy was now seven months old, a sturdy, inquisitive child with thick dark hair and black-lashed blue eyes. Already he bore a striking resemblance to his father, with the same steady stare and peaceful disposition, the same patient interest in the world around him. That he had inherited much of his mother's nature was also evident in the stubborn tilt of his

491

chin and the endearing tryanny with which he ruled the nursery in her absence. And on those rare occasions when William Lucas Cavendish was confronted by some obstacle to his desires, he proved himself to be both his father's and his mother's son in no small measure.

'He has the temper of a true Cavendish,' Sir Oscar had been heard to tell his friends with a certain pride. 'A true Cavendish.'

Now Leonora set the boy on his feet and, holding him firmly by the under-arms, allowed him to test his legs.

'He will be walking soon,' Lukan said with a grin. 'He has the muscles of a heavyweight. He'll be set to work at the plough before he's five years old if he continues at this rate.'

'Nonsense,' Leonora replied. 'My son is a thoroughbred, not a cart horse.'

'Your son is a beautiful child, my lady, a credit to his parents in every way.'

'Thank you, Lukan.'

Leonora handed the boy into his arms and watched the two together. William was fascinated by Lukan's long black hair and coal-dark eyes. It was often difficult to prise the hair from his grasping little fingers, his blacksmith's grip as Lukan liked to call it, and on more than one occasion an inquisitive finger had stabbed into one of his eyes before it could be avoided. She smiled as she watched them. Lukan loved the boy. In spite of the anguish he had suffered over his conception and subsequent birth, he loved that handsome little boy as if he were his own.

When Anabel came up with hot chocolate and a reminder that Sir Malcolm and his father would soon be finished with their office work, she was stopped in her tracks by the sight of them. Lukan was sitting with his back against the bed, one arm around Leonora as she sat beside him, her cheek against his chest. The future heir of Beresford was curled in the crook of his right arm, a strand of hair clutched tightly in his hand, his tiny face against the gypsy's cheek. It was a tender and a frightening scene. It sent such a shiver of foreboding through her that she almost dropped the tray she was carrying and only managed to set it down safely with a noisy clatter.

Leonora opened her eyes and inquired drowsily, 'Did you trip?'

'No, it's nothing.'

'Are you unwell?'

'I'm all right,' Anabel insisted. 'It was just a moment's clumsiness, nothing more.' She bent over them with an embarrassed smile. 'Here, let me take the boy. Drink your chocolate and be off with you, Lukan de Ville. The master will be here soon to see his son, and like as not the Earl will come with him.'

'Take him downstairs to the drawing room,' Leonora instructed. 'Bring the maids in from the garden and tell them to prepare for Malcolm's visit. I will be down presently.'

As she took the child into her arms Lukan reached up to touch his dark little head with his fingertips. Anabel shuddered. She would never understand how that fierce, unpredictable man could be so gentle, or how he could bear such love for another man's child. He unfolded himself and came erect in a single easy movement, towering above her as he touched the sleeping child again.

'Give him back to me. I'll carry him down while you go on ahead.'

'And what if you're seen?'

'Better that than you should stumble with the boy on those twisting steps. A fall would likely kill you both, Anabel.'

She looked stricken. 'Am I not to be trusted then?'

Lukan smiled and his eyes were soft. 'Your mistress and I have trusted you with our lives these last two years,' he reminded her. 'You must know how much we need you, Anabel.'

The woman's face coloured suddenly and she made an effort to avoid the warmth and intimacy of his gaze. She held her breath when he reached out to lift her face with a single finger placed beneath her chin.

'Allow me to repay you with small courtesies whenever I can,' he said. 'Let me carry the boy downstairs for you.'

'Yes ... er yes, of course.' She hurried out and Lukan, with a glance at Leonora, followed after her with the boy still sound asleep in his arms. When he returned a few moments later Leonora was sitting at her mirror, tidying her hair and freshening her face with cologne. He crossed to the table and poured himself a cup of chocolate.

'That was thoughtful of you, Lukan.'

'My caution was for William's sake,' he admitted. 'She is too old to carry him up and down those stairs.'

'Too old? But Lukan, she is only just into her forties,' Leonora protested with a smile.

'I think she had a dizzy spell just now.'

'When she clattered the tray? A moment's clumsiness, she said it was, no more.'

'Aye, and Rebecca says the same. They're of an age, those two, a *particular* age, according to my sister.'

'What nonsense,' Leonora laughed. 'I would have thought your sister was better informed than to entertain such notions.'

'My sister knows what she is talking about. She has begun to suffer similar moments of weakness. She insists it is her age that causes it.'

Leonora set down her hairbrush and watched him through the mirror. 'Is Rebecca unwell?'

He shrugged. 'I think her hatred of me is all that ails her.'

'She does not hate you, Lukan.'

'You would not say that if you could see the way we live.'

Leonora swallowed and said the words with difficulty. 'Your sister loves you, Lukan.'

He shook his head. 'She has become bitter. Her tongue has the sting of a scorpion and she suffers me with as much goodwill as she would suffer the presence of an adder in her kitchen.'

'I cannot believe that.'

'It's true,' he insisted. 'She was never of the sweetest temperament, but lately I have watched her begin to hate me. She has changed, Leonora. She cares little for her appearance and runs my house as if it were a hovel. Even her eating habits have changed. She either picks at her food like a spoilt child or

494

else gorges herself until she vomits. She is constantly chewing ginger root to settle her stomach but snaps at me if I enquire after her health.'

Leonora stared at him through the glass. She felt a sudden coldness, as if an icy finger had trailed itself along her spine.

'How long has she been like this?'

'A few weeks, six or seven perhaps.'

'Has she gained weight?'

'Indeed she has. She is sloppy and uncaring in her habits, and her clothes no longer fit her as they should. Believe me, if I was not already convinced that she will go to her grave a virgin, I might suspect that she was to have a child.'

He sipped his chocolate thoughtfully, unaware that the colour had drained from Leonora's face and her eyes had grown round with dismay. In her mind several things came sharply into focus before slotting themselves into place as neatly as a child's picture-puzzle. She recalled how he had described his drunken stupor on the night of William's christening, the blank spaces in his mind, the feeling of uncontrollable desire, the shameful, humiliating dreams. And she recalled how she had seen the terrible truth of Rebecca's feelings for Lukan in her eyes. A swift calculation added confirmation to her suspicions. Four months had passed since that terrible night in the stable, the night Rebecca Adams had slipped a powerful drug into her brother's brandy, the night she had conceived her brother's child.

Somehow Leonora found the strength to get through the next hour without mishap. She laughed when her father-in-law commented on her paleness, brushed off as nonsense her husband's fears that she seemed feverish and edgy. She played her part well, but when her son had been returned to his nursery and the gatehouse door closed upon the men, she went to Anabel, put her arms around her neck and wept as she had never wept before.

It was late afternoon before she was able to give voice to her distress. Anabel was careful not to question her. She held her close, comforted her with whispered words, stroked her hair

495

and rocked her in her arms as each fit of sobbing racked her body. At last, exhausted and red-eyed, Leonora went to her dressing room to rinse her face and returned some time later looking pale but self-composed.

'That night in the stable, the night of William's christening,' she began. 'What do you believe happened to Lukan?'

Anabel shrugged. This was ground they had covered several times. 'Like you I am convinced he was drugged.'

Leonora nodded. 'And Rebecca's feelings for Lukan?'

'Incestuous. I trust your judgment on that. You are a woman and you love the man. You would not invent such a thing.'

Leonora nodded unhappily. 'And why does a woman gain weight, develop bizarre eating habits and bouts of vomiting and have to resort to chewing ginger root?'

'Early pregnancy,' Anabel said with certainty. 'Ginger root is a common cure for the morning sickness, and those other things you describe are ...' She broke off, her eyes growing wide. 'Oh no, you don't mean ... you can't mean that she ...?'

Leonora closed her eyes against a fresh flood of tears and said in abject misery, 'Rebecca Adams is pregnant.'

'Oh my God! She didn't! Surely she didn't!'

'Oh yes she did. And it was a deliberate, premeditated act on her part. She drugged his brandy and crawled beneath his blanket in the night. And now she is to have his child, *Lukan's* child. It's *horrible*.'

Anabel gripped her mistress's hands. 'Keep a hold of yourself, Leonora. Does he know? Did he tell you all this?'

Leonora shook her head violently. 'He doesn't know. He must never know, Anabel. He has dismissed the possibility that she is pregnant because he is convinced that she would repel any man who took an interest in her. He still believes the horrors of that night were induced by dreams. If he knew what she had done, if he so much as suspected ...'

'He would kill them both,' Anabel finished for her. 'And rightly so. My God, this is the devil's work.'

Leonora moved away from Anabel to stare from the

496

window. Her face was ashen and there was an uncharacteristic stoop to her shoulders, as if some heavy, invisible burden had been placed there. Even her voice had taken on a stricken quality. 'That dried-up old woman has stolen from him the one thing he can never give to me. Anabel, *his child*. There is such love between us, yet we will never be allowed to take that love to its fullest conclusion while she, that woman, that *gypsy* . . .'

'And much joy it will bring her,' Anabel hissed bitterly.

But Leonora was not listening. She was staring out toward the forest, mourning the child she would never have and hating with a frightening intensity the woman who had contrived to thieve such a precious thing from him.

'I hope she dies of it,' she said at last.

'Now, Leonora,' Anabel warned. 'Never call ill upon another's head lest it fall instead upon your own.'

'I hope with all my heart she dies of it,' Leonora repeated. 'She's past forty and this will be her first confinement. I hope to God she dies of it and her misbegotten gypsy brat dies with her.'

Leonora was taken ill and kept to her rooms for several days following her discovery. She paced to and fro in acute distress behind drawn curtains, wept until her eyes were swollen, returned her food untouched and found herself unable to sleep for dreams that left her miserable and exhausted. She even began to avoid the nursery, unable to look into her son's eyes without seeing that other child and feeling as if something irreplaceable had been stolen away from Lukan and herself. Day by day her spirits sank lower and her health became less certain. Sir Marcus diagnosed a simple chill to the liver and prescribed a tonic made from agrimony and laudanum. Leonora feigned obedience and poured the tonic away the moment his back was turned. She had no wish to have sleep forced upon her. Each time she closed her eyes in search of rest she tossed and turned, tormented by visions of Rebecca and Lukan lying together in the barn with their limbs entwined and her own name on his lips. The dreams he half-remembered explained the episode in all its ugliness, and the utter distaste with which he repeated them was enough to indicate how he would react if ever he so much as suspected those 'dreams' of being reality.

He came to see her every day that week, the moment Anabel displayed the signal that the way was clear and Leonora was alone. Sometimes he held her while she clung to him, weeping, and he whispered words of love to her while she snatched what fitful sleep she dare in the safety of his arms. Anabel had never seen such anguish in a man's face. It seemed as if he never ate nor slept while the woman he loved lay so ill. Beneath the healthy darkness of his skin grew a greyness that was almost death-like. His eyes became huge and bleak, and by the end of the week his cheeks looked hollowed out, his features gaunt.

'I fear to lose her, Anabel,' he confessed one day while Leonora slept with tears still damp on her cheeks. He was sitting on a low stool beside the fire with his head in his hands. He and Leonora were so close, so much a part of each other that he had sensed her torment and, misreading even his own responses, feared that she was dying. It was then that Anabel had touched him for the first time. Standing beside him she reached out and rested her hand on his bowed head, feeling the strength and the warmth of him beneath the gloss of his coarse black hair. She had drawn back quickly, but he had raised his head to look at her and with his eyes acknowledged her self-conscious attempts to comfort him.

'You'll not lose her, Lukan,' she said.

'Can you be so sure?'

'Aye, I can.'

'But how?'

Anabel smiled. 'Because it doesn't suit the little minx to die just yet. There's too much she wants to do in this world and too much she still intends to have for herself. She's barely twenty years old, Lukan. She hasn't even *started* yet.'

He smiled at that. 'Bless you.'

'Just give her time. This thing will pass. I promise you, it will pass.'

And pass it did. Another day saw Leonora back on her feet,

despondency having at last given way to anger, nature's finest healer. On that first morning of April she flung off her depression like a soiled garment and rampaged through her apartments in a rage.

'Have my horse made ready,' she ordered. 'Bring me a riding gown and a heavy whip. I'll meet that evil woman face to face, and by the gods I'll see her in her grave before I let her do this thing to us.'

Dressed in a black velvet tunic and skirts, she mounted her horse without assistance and despite Anabel's tearful protests, set off at a gallop for the house of Lukan de Ville. Desperately afraid of what might happen if she forced a confrontation between brother and sister, Anabel pushed aside the small boy who had brought the horse and rushed to the stables in search of Sam Cooper. She found him saddled and prepared, expecting to accompany his mistress on her ride. Anabel told him breathlessly that Leonora had set out for the forest alone.

'She must be stopped. She is unwell and does not know what she is doing.'

Sam leaped into the saddle. 'I'll find her and fetch her back. Which way did she go?'

'Don't fail her Sam. She has not been from her sickbed but half an hour. She must be brought back to the house before she's taken ill again or missed by Sir Malcolm and his father.'

'Tell me which way she rode.'

'You must say nothing of this to anyone.'

'We're wasting time in talk. Which way did she go?'

Anabel reached up suddenly to grab him by the arm. 'Sam Cooper, can you be trusted?'

He looked more hurt than angered by the question. 'I'm capped you need ask it, Miss Anabel. I'll fetch the mistress safely back, you need have no fear of that, and I'll not be telling tales about it later.'

'You must stop her Sam. You must, for all our sakes.'

He nodded and heeled his horse forward, stooping to clear the lintel beam above the stable door. 'She'll be taking the forest path then, I reckon,' he said.

'How do you know that?'

He turned in the saddle to look at her with a solemn expression on his youthful face. 'Because it's the fastest route to Mr Lukan's house.' He looked at her stunned face a moment longer, then yanked his horse's head around and kicked the animal into a gallop across the meadow.

As Sam had predicted, Leonora reached Lukan's house via the dangerous but shorter and more secret forest route. In the clearing beside the gardens she leaped from her horse and marched, brandishing her riding stick, to the front door of the house. Without bothering to announce her presence, she opened the door and strode into the hall.

'Rebecca Adams!' She shouted the woman's name so loudly that her voice reverberated around the panelled hall. 'Come out and face me if you dare, Rebecca Adams!'

A very young, very shabby servant girl appeared in a downstairs doorway, curtsied nervously and dashed out through the garden door as if in fear of her life. Leonora raised her arm above her head and brought the riding stick down with tremendous force on one of the carvings supporting the lower banister.

'Come out and face me if you dare, Rebecca Adams!'

Her words rang hollow in the quiet house. She strode into the drawing room, found it grubby and neglected, then into the kitchens which were unkempt and smelled of damp. Upstairs the rooms were empty, most of them hung with dustsheets. The door of a water closet stood open to reveal large bunches of dried sage and lavender hanging from its ceiling. There was no mistaking Lukan's rooms, with the half-poster bed and fancy iron fireplace, lush carpets, high-backed chairs and row upon row of books. Such was the contrary nature of the man. He slept outdoors in barns or open fields, as much from choice as from necessity, but here at home he lived the life of a gentleman. His private rooms were beautifully furnished and scrupulously, almost fastidiously clean. The main room had windows on two sides, and from one of these she could see the rooftops of Beresford Hall and the upper floors of the west tower. From here he had a clear view of the windows of their secret room. If she lit a lamp and set it there he would see it from this window and know that she was thinking of him. She touched his bed and ran her hand over his flat, hard pillow, examined the book of poetry on his bedside table and consciously tried to drink in every detail of the room so that she could imagine him here whenever they were apart. There was a faint trace of lavender here, of aniseed and garden mint, and the fruity scent of pot-pourri from pouches hung here and there to maintain the room's freshness. Despite his dubious origins and often peculiar habits, his home was much as she had expected it to be. The windows were open, the bed linen clean, the dressing room immaculately tidy, with every garment neatly hung and every pair of boots cleaned and polished. For long moments Leonora closed her eyes and breathed in the familiar smells of him, but then she remembered the shabbiness downstairs and her purpose rose to the surface in a wave. Shaking off her sense of being close to Lukan, she strode from the room in search of the object of her fury.

'Rebecca Adams! Come out! Show yourself, damn you!' She heard a footfall on the steps outside and hurried to the stairs as the main door of the house was flung open. She stopped on the first landing. 'Lukan!'

'Lia! My Lia! Thank heaven you are well again.'

Lukan took the stairs two at a time and gathered her into his arms. He held her gently, burying his face in the curve of her neck. 'What is it? What on earth are you doing here?'

'I . . . I needed to see you,' she stammered. All her pent-up anger suddenly drained away, leaving her exhausted and acutely aware of her physical weakness. She leaned against him. 'Oh Lukan, I needed to see you.'

'But why? Who brought you here?'

'Nobody. I came alone.'

'But this is madness, Lia.'

'I know. I had to come.'

He stroked her hair and kissed her forehead and temples. 'It's madness,' he said again. 'Suppose you were seen? Suppose someone followed you?'

'I will say I came to see Rebecca. Where is she?'

'She's gone. She left the house nearly a week ago, taking her travelling bundle and her herb-basket. I doubt she is intending to return.'

'Gone?' She lifted her head and searched his face for details he might be keeping from her. 'Gone, and you did nothing to dissuade her?'

'Why should I? She has been dissatisfied for a long time and finally decided to make her own way in the world once again. That choice was always hers to make. I am not her keeper.'

'Did she leave no message?'

'None.'

'But you will make a search for her, or at least ask around the villages and fairs for news of her?'

'I will do no such thing.' He smiled and pulled her back into his arms. 'Lia, you forget that Rebecca is a gypsy. She has chosen to leave my home for the pleasures of the open road and in all honesty I cannot pretend I am unhappy to see her go. She has little interest in the running of the house and frightens away whatever help I manage to employ. And sister or not, I am convinced she hates me. Believe me, there was nothing to keep her here.'

Leonora clung to him, almost desperate to tell him the truth and yet knowing she must never, ever do so, for his own sake. Rebecca had gone away to have her child in secret, and she would surely not return to face her brother with the truth. Leonora must leave the matter there, but just as she had learned to pray when Lukan went missing, so she would pray now for the death of that unborn child. And she felt no guilt for feeling as she did. She did not welcome the prospect of living the rest of her life with the knowledge that Lukan, *her Lukan*, had a bastard child somewhere in the world, a child sired upon his own sister.

Into their intimate silence a man's voice suddenly said, 'Beggin' your pardon, Mr Lukan, sir.'

They did not spring apart; it was too late for that. They remained in each other's arms on the first landing, both aware that Lukan had left the main door wide open when he saw her horse and rushed into the house. They turned their heads at

502

the same time as Sam Cooper, cap in hand, cleared his throat and said again, 'Beggin' your pardon, Mr Lukan, sir.'

Lukan slowly stood away from Leonora and, keeping a protective grip on her elbow, led her down the stairs. His face was grim. The young man met his gaze with respect and just a hint of fear. 'Yes Sam, what is it?'

'I've been sent to take Her Ladyship back to the house, Mr Lukan. Miss Anabel fears she might fall ill, or be missed.'

Lukan nodded. 'As you see, Her Ladyship is well.'

'Yes sir.' He nodded politely to his mistress. 'Miss Leonora.'

'She came here to see my sister.'

'Yes sir, that's what I thought.'

Lukan glanced at Leonora. She shook her head in a brief movement and squeezed his arm reassuringly. Then her manner became brisk and very cool. 'Thank you so much, Mr de Ville, for your hospitality. Perhaps you will convey my message to Rebecca when she returns?'

'Indeed I will, Your Ladyship,' he said.

'And might I suggest that you employ a butler and house-keeper as soon as possible? I have the names and addresses of several reliable people and would be more than happy to assist you in that respect, should you require my help.'

'That would be much appreciated, thank you.' Lukan made a formal bow and walked with Leonora to the door. To Sam Cooper he said, 'See that your mistress gets home safely, and take the meadow path, well away from the forest.'

'Yes Mr Lukan, you can count on me sir.'

'I hope so,' Lukan said thoughtfully. 'I certainly hope so, Sam Cooper.'

He watched the young man help his mistress into the saddle and lead her horse along the short winding pathway to the river and the wider lower section of the meadow beyond. Then he returned to the house and went directly upstairs to his bedroom. From the window he watched them ride away, she in her figure-hugging black habit with skirts that billowed over her horse's flanks, and young Sam Cooper, proud and solemn beside her.

They rode back to Beresford Hall in silence, maintaining a steady but unhurried pace. Sam Cooper was attentive to his mistress, moving closer whenever a ditch or a section of rough ground had to be traversed. When they reached the orchards they could see Anabel running along the path towards them. She had been waiting anxiously between the orchard and the stables, and at first sight of them hitched up her skirts and broke into a dash. It was here that Sam Cooper reached for the reins of Leonora's horse and drew both animals to a standstill.

'May I speak freely, Miss Leonora?'

She looked into his troubled young face and smiled. 'Of course you may. You and I have been friends for a long time, Sam. You may say to me whatever you wish.'

He chewed his lower lip and looked uncomfortable. 'It's just that ... well, I don't think His Lordship will take too kindly to you going off to see that Rebecca Adams woman all on your own.'

'I fear you may be right.'

'Best not tell him then, Miss Leonora. I'll not mention it if you don't.'

'Sam, are you suggesting that we tell my husband an untruth?'

'Only a half-truth, beggin' your pardon ma'am.'

'And what half-truth did you have in mind, Sam?'

He frowned, gathering the facts together in his mind. 'I took you there. You asked me to ride with you as usual and I took you down there in the hopes of seeing the gypsy woman.'

'I see.' She chose her next words very carefully. 'And Mr Lukan?'

'It happened exactly as I saw for myself at the house.'

'It did?'

'Aye, Mr Lukan told you his sister was gone, so we came away.'

'And that is *all* you saw at the house?'

'Yes ma'am, you never left my sight for a minute.'

Leonora looked at him steadily, not sure how much he knew or for how long he had known it. What she did know was that she trusted him. She had taken him from certain poverty, treated him well, even taught him to read and write, and he had repaid her with unwavering loyalty. He would not betray her now, she was sure of that. She touched the hand that held her horse's reins. 'Bless you Sam. You have my gratitude.'

'As you have mine, Miss Leonora, and Mr Lukan's been nothing but good and fair to me since I threatened to take a whip to him on the Kingswood road three years ago.'

Leonora laughed out loud at that. 'And would you dare do as much again today, I wonder?'

He gave her a sheepish grin and shook his head. 'Nay, I reckon I'd sooner raise my bare hand to a savage beast than make that same mistake a second time.'

They were laughing together when Anabel reached them, and when Sam handed her down from her horse Leonora gave him the briefest hug and whispered again, 'Thank you, Sam.'

CHAPTER TWENTY-FOUR

I

Lukan was sitting with Anabel in the cramped but comfortable parlour of the old gatehouse. He had brought two parcels from Chepstow Fair, both wrapped in paper and bound with knotted string. One was a gift for Lady Elizabeth to be delivered personally when he took luncheon with Malcolm later in the day. No matter now hectic and demanding his duties, no matter how heavy his workload, the big gypsy never returned from the fairs empty-handed. There would always be something, some small token of affection, for his favourite lady, his little Elizabeth.

The second, more bulky parcel he placed on the table and began to unwrap with great care and solemnity. It contained a length of good quality dress fabric of a pretty summer blue with delicate pink rose-buds dotted here and there in a sprigged design. There were ribbons too, a bundle of them, all in soft pastel shades and varying widths and lengths. Anabel touched the silky blue fabric with her fingertips, perhaps just a little envious.

'You don't like it,' he said. 'I have made a poor choice.'

'Not at all,' she replied quickly. 'You've made a fine choice, Lukan. Any woman would be delighted to receive such a gift.'

'I did not buy it for *any* woman.'

She smiled. 'I'm quite sure you didn't, and don't worry, she will love it.'

'Nor did I buy it for Lia.'

'Not for her? But surely . . .?'

He looked surprised. 'You have obviously misunderstood my intentions completely, Anabel. These are not for Lia but for you.'

She looked aghast. 'For me?'

'For you,' he repeated. 'As a mark of my esteem.'

Anabel looked from the cloth to him and back again. No man had ever given her a gift of any kind before, and such quality as this had always been beyond her reach. She felt her cheeks grow warm as she wondered how much this man must see of her that others did not see. Her manner of dress was sober, even matronly, but in every woman there is a frivolous heart that yearns to possess the soft and beautiful, and Anabel was no exception. Had she been free to take what she desired from Chepstow Fair, this was the very stuff she would have chosen. Now she scarcely knew what words to say to express her thanks. His simple generosity left her speechless.

Without warning Lukan took the woman's hand in his and lifted it slowly to his lips. His kiss was warm and lingered on her skin, bringing a sudden crimson glow to her cheeks. He smiled his most wicked, lop-sided smile and winked one eye mischievously, then dropped her hand and walked from the room, leaving Anabel quite taken aback by his behaviour.

He had been waiting in the upstairs room for no more than a few minutes when Leonora arrived. She was wearing green, with a fancy belt encircling her tiny waist and a choker of fine pearls at her throat. Her face lit with delight when she saw him.

'You have been flirting with my maid,' she said with mock severity. 'Are you not content to enslave the mistress of the house but seek to conquer the servants too?'

507

'A length of pretty cloth and a few ribbons,' he said with a shrug of his shoulders. 'That's little enough repayment on the debt we owe to her.'

'It was a kindness she will not forget. You have a good heart, Lukan.'

'I do not need your flattery, madam.'

She looked at him sharply, surprised by his tone of voice. He was not smiling and his eyes were cold. Leonora stood on tiptoe to kiss his cheek and raised a questioning eyebrow when he failed to take her in his arms.

'I see you are angry, Lukan.'

'Aye, angry, if the word is strong enough.'

'Has Anabel annoyed you?'

'No madam, she has not.'

'What then?' She crossed to the dressing table and studied her reflection in the glass. Behind her his face was dark, his scowl intense. She smiled through the mirror, hoping to deflect his anger. She had already guessed at the reason for it. 'I do hope we are not going to quarrel, Lukan.'

'Not if you see the error of your actions.' It was a poor start to their discussion and he knew it the moment the words were out.

'You can be sure I will do nothing that is solely designed to pacify your temper,' she replied, still smiling despite the flash of indignation in her eyes.

'You know what troubles me, Lia.'

She did but would not admit as much. 'How can I know anything when you make a mystery of it?'

'I refer to this business of William's inheritance.'

'Ah, so that's it!' She turned to face him, leaning back against the dressing-table and smiling into his eyes. 'I am afraid the matter has been settled without the need of your opinion. The Earl has thought fit to settle the titles to his York-shire estates upon your godson. It is a welcome gift. You should be glad for him.'

'That land belongs to Horace Cavendish.'

'It most certainly does not,' she flared. 'His mother cut him out of her will so that his intended portion passed into the hands of his father, and the Earl of Beresford is free to dispose of his personal property as he wishes.'

'But not to William. Those Yorkshire properties should not be given over to William.'

'And why not, since everyone wishes it but you?'

Lukan watched her closely, trying to keep a rein on his temper. This woman could play upon his nerves and his sensibilities as skilfully as she played upon her pianoforte or plucked the strings of her harp. There were times when she seemed to provoke him for the sheer pleasure of it, with every word a device intended to bring out the worst in him. She was no fool. She knew his objections without the need to speak them out in detail, yet she would hear it all and give not an inch of leeway on his behalf.

'That land was promised to Horace,' he reminded her.

'And Horace was disinherited.'

'He still has rights.'

'Not so, not legally.'

'They were given as a birthright from his mother. He will surely consider himself morally, if not legally, entitled to them.'

'*Morally?*' she echoed, laughing in his face. 'You dare to mention morals and Horace Cavendish in the self-same breath? And since when have you concerned yourself with that man's personal interests?'

'Since his inheritance was given to my godson,' he growled.

Leonora sighed impatiently. 'Our quarrel is a circular one, Lukan. It is done. The Earl has chosen to will those lands to William.'

'And given you an income in the process. You stand to make a fortune on the transaction until young William comes of age and takes it for his own.'

'That is not an uncommon arrangement and you know it,' she snapped, offended by the implication in his words. 'What matters is that William now has his own inheritance.'

He stepped towards her, his eyes glinting. 'What matters, madam, is that William now has an enemy to be reckoned with.'

509

'A toothless tiger,' she corrected sharply.

'An embittered man,' he shouted back. 'And twice so when he hears of these events.'

'What of it?' she demanded, her temper rising. 'He dare not set his feet on English soil, nor dare he set himself against the Earl's grandson.'

'No? This is Horace Cavendish we speak of, woman. How will it be when he has had two decades and more to brood upon his losses? How will he feel when the boy is fully grown and makes himself the owner of land meant for his uncle?'

Leonora threw up her hands in despair. 'So, what would you have me do, refuse to accept the Earl's generosity? Give back the gift?'

'Aye, give it back.'

'What? You cannot be serious?'

'On the contrary, I am deadly serious. Give back the Yorkshire property.'

She stamped her foot. 'I most certainly will not.'

Lukan grabbed her roughly by the arms, tempted to shake her until her teeth rattled. 'Woman, you can be as obstinate as the very devil when it suits you. Give it back.'

'*No!*'

'Do it, or make your son the target of a man's hatred.'

'Never! *I* will protect my son from Horace Cavendish.'

'And how will you do that, you, a helpless woman?'

She struggled in vain to release his grip on her. 'Don't you dare assume I am subservient to him in any way. I do not fear that drunken oaf. I never feared him and I never will.'

Exasperated, Lukan shoved her from him. 'Then you are a fool. You do not have his measure.'

'Wrong on both counts, Mr de Ville. I am a fine match for Horace any day.'

'That is fanciful talk.'

'Is it?' she flared. 'Is it? And what would you know about the matter? Who do you think was responsible for his dismissal? Who wrote the letters condemning him as the lowest of the low? Who convinced his parents that he would hang on several counts unless he fled the country at a few hours' notice?'

510

'You?' He could only mouth the word.

'Yes me, the one you were so swift to disregard as a *mere woman.*'

He looked perplexed, suspicious of her argument. 'What in Heaven's name are you telling me, Lia?'

'It was all my doing, Lukan, and I can prove it. I have the original drafts of those damning letters. I can even show you samples of the self-same writing, my own hand carefully disguised.' She jabbed her own breastbone angrily with her forefinger. '*I* did it. *I* ruined Horace Cavendish.'

'No. No.' He shook his head in disbelief.

'Oh yes, it was me,' she said triumphantly. 'I watched a woman die in agony on his account and so I set out with calculated malice to avenge her death. I ruined him. I stripped that man of everything he held dear and I have savoured the sweet taste of my revenge for three long years.'

Lukan stared into her beautiful face, horrified by what he had heard. He stood so for a long time before shaking his head and saying, very softly, 'Oh Lia, let me pretend I did not hear all that.'

'You heard it Lukan de Ville, and now that you know what I am capable of, don't ever call me fanciful again. And never doubt for a moment that I will use whatever means I must in order to protect my son from that animal.'

Lukan slumped against a wall and groaned as if in pain. 'Is Horace aware that you have done this thing to him?'

She shrugged. 'He might suspect, but I doubt it. We hate each other enough apart from that, and more so now, I do not doubt, since I have wormed my way into his home and family.'

'So there is long-standing animosity between you?'

She nodded her head. 'It started the moment we met when I was only ten years old, and the years have only served to strengthen it. There can never be peace between us. Believe me, Lukan, should he ever cross my path again I would be more than happy to repeat what I have done.'

He nodded. His eyes were closed. 'I see. You will fight him then, if he challenges the gift?'

'With anything and everything at my disposal.'

'In open warfare with no holds barred?'

'I would indeed, and savour every blow.'

He opened his eyes to narrow slits. 'And leave my godson standing in the crossfire?'

'*I will protect him.* My God, have you not listened to a word I said?'

'Give back the land,' he growled.

'I will not.'

'Lia, don't burden the boy with this. Give back the land.'

'No. I can handle Horace if I must.'

He raked his fingers through his hair in exasperation. 'You, madam, will not be his chosen target. It is William we must fear for. The hatred of a Cavendish is not to be taken lightly.'

Leonora opened her mouth to counter his remark but stopped suddenly, her gaze fixed on his troubled face. In a flash of understanding she saw that he was not opposing her on a matter of principle or personal preference. Nor did he underestimate her skills in dealing with her own affairs. He was simply trying to protect his own. He was attempting to keep his godson and his lady out of harm's way, even looking ahead by twenty years to their future safekeeping. It was the most natural thing and she had misinterpreted it, thinking him merely disagreeable.

He watched her staring at him, puzzled as much by her sudden silence as by the strange expression on her face. 'Lia? What is it?'

'You love me,' she said softly, her eyes wide and round.

'What?'

'You love me.'

'What?' He balled both hands into fists and raised them to his head, growling with frustration. 'For the love of God, Lia, I have adored you since the day we met. You can be in no doubt of that when you have me in either a hell of anguish or sweet paradise and I endure it all for love of you. How can you stand there, looking at me as if you see me for the first time, and declare that I love you. Is this a new discovery for you? What ails you, woman? Have you gone quite mad?'

512

With a childish whoop of delight Leonora rushed forward and flung herself, laughing, into his arms. He staggered sideways, hoisted her from her feet and tumbled her across the bed. He was growling and snarling, rolling her this way and that in a fierce embrace while the sound of her laughter echoed in his ears. And then, just as suddenly as it had begun, the game was over and they were still. She lay beside him, her face so close to his that just by pouting her lips she could kiss his mouth.

'You love me,' she whispered and watched his eyes, certain that only he could understand how she had always known yet never fully come to terms with this truth.

'Aye, lady, I will go to my grave loving you.'

She could see herself reflected in the black pools of his eyes, a willing prisoner in the depths of him. 'And I in turn will love you all my life. I swear it.'

'But will you give back the Yorkshire lands?' he asked her in a whisper.

She shook her head. 'I will not even consider it.'

He kissed her then and moved his body closer, his hands seeking the warmer parts of her. 'No lady,' he murmured hoarsely, 'I never suspected for a moment that you would.'

II

During that spring of 1825 Malcolm and his father were much involved in the politics of the day. They disagreed endlessly on such matters as Sir Robert Peel's obsessions with Parliamentary Reform, the underlying tensions within the government ranks, Lord Liverpool's often dogged obstinacy and George Canning's brilliant, if not always timely, public oratory. They had their own individual opinions on the Combination Laws and the rights of common men to demand a fair return for their labours. Malcolm tended towards the view that wages would eventually find their own level in a competitive market, and that workers' combinations would prove useful in persuading reluctant employers to increase wages to meet and maintain that level. Sir Oscar agreed with that in principle, but feared the potential abuse of trade unions. They might be used to place even the fairest of masters under a kind of tyranny that would eventually drive them into bankruptcy. The grouping together of jealous, dissatisfied workers, some bearing real or imagined grudges against their masters, would produce a breeding ground for unrest. One spark would be all that was needed then, one clever man with a flair for leadership, and what a power for ill would be unleashed. A manipulative, self-interested individual might bring about strikes and riots to ruin his rival or change the very face of British politics, had he such a mob at his disposal.

'Dangerous,' he would mutter gravely. 'In theory noble, but in practice highly dangerous.'

'Then we must find the middle course,' was Malcolm's usual comment to such argument. 'The man and his master need each other equally. Both must be protected.'

While Malcolm's mind was set on politics and his physical energies directed mainly to the running of the estates, Leonora was happy to resume her round of garden parties and other such diversions. A dry, mild spring got the season off to an early start. She entertained her noble neighbours, opened her doors to visitors from abroad, received Sir Malcolm's political acquaintances and organised separate diversions for their womenfolk. She visited London as often as possible, her appointment book bulging with invitations, and while there she spent every waking moment fulfilling her social obligations. Often partnered by one or more of Sir Oscar's elderly friends, she attended glittering balls and colourful masquerades, special luncheons and dinners, levees and soirées given by the cream of London society. Her aim was to be seen at the most extravagant gatherings in the company of the most influential people. On one occasion she attended two balls in one evening, staying little more than an hour and a half at the first and changing her entire outfit for the second. The tongues wagged with a rare ferocity and she, with a tireless dedication to her task, managed to impart more impact on these short, hectic, scrupulously detailed visits than most women did in an entire season. Her greatest advantage was the fact that society did not know enough about her. She revealed herself in vivid, breathtaking snatches that always left her public wanting more. She was the mystery woman, the beautiful but poor relation of an Earl, the nobody who had stepped from obscurity to riches overnight. It was a self-made image designed to manipulate the higher echelons of society in her favour. Her carefully worded letters to Lady Caroline Rainer were common property, fuel for the gossip that guaranteed her fame and opened every door to her. She knew herself to be in complete control, the only woman outside royal circles who could maintain such a lofty position in society without making of it a full-time occupation.

'Sometimes I suspect there are two of you,' Lukan told her, when she had travelled up from London to receive important guests for dinner and still come to him fresh and energetic long after midnight. 'Or that you employ some dark and sinister means of fitting more than twenty-four hours in any day.'

'I'm happy,' had been her instant reply. 'And I never tire of anything that brings me happiness.'

He smiled at that. 'Then I must do my best to keep you so.'

'And so you will,' she told him. 'So you will.'

For them it was a time of joy and rediscovery, a time to cherish and strengthen the bonds that had been so cruelly tested in the past. Ironically, the child whose conception had driven such a wedge between them now bonded them more tightly to each other. Lukan loved him deeply. All the rage and inner turmoil had subsided, leaving him free to accept the child whole-heartedly. Nor did it trouble him to see his lady love her husband's child with such a passion. It was almost as if young William was his own, and Leonora knew it would cause him great pain when those carefree days of infancy came to an end, when William grew too old, too knowing, to be a party to their secret meetings.

515

One face conspicuous by its absence at Leonora's entertainments was that of Harriet Wyndham, now Mrs Augustus Sharpe. Earlier that year a formal letter had arrived at Beresford Hall informing the lady of the house that Mr Sharpe, already in his late sixties, had collapsed and died while staying over in Rome during his wedding tour. His widow would return to England at once and take up residence in his country home near Oxford. Harriet was wealthy now and free as she had never been before, and yet she replied to Leonora's letters with unexpected brevity. It seemed she truly grieved for the old man. She avoided company, discouraged friendships and rejected every attempt to draw her back into society.

'There's a guilty conscience there,' Leonora concluded when she received Harriet's regrets in response to yet another invitation. 'The lady's behaviour is too much out of character.'

'The proprieties must always be observed,' Anabel replied, quoting her mistress word for word.

Leonora tossed the formal apology aside. 'But not to this extent. She is too ambitious, and far too clever, to assume a level of mourning that is not required of her and risk offending useful friends in the process.'

'Would you rather she were here, making sheep's eyes at Lukan de Ville?' Anabel asked.

'If she's a rival, yes. I hate to have intrigues simmering just beyond my range of vision.'

'She is not your rival and never could be so.'

Leonora smiled, glowing with happiness. 'I know that now.'

Lukan received a letter from Thomas Harding in March. It informed him that Mr Augustus Sharpe had died of a heart attack in Rome and that Harriet would not be receiving visitors for some time. He was at once saddened and relieved by the news. It meant that he was not obliged to visit the house and expose himself to her attempts to involve him in her plans for the future. He was fond of Harriet and had no wish to offend her with refusals after the many intimacies that had passed between them, but at the same time he had few concerns for her state of mind. If she had chosen to mourn then that was her prerogative and she would hardly be inclined to prolong the process. She was too young and vital for that, too hungry for the many pleasures of life to keep herself withheld from masculine company. He dispatched a gift of good quality brandy to Thomas Harding along with a card bearing his condolences, and with that he felt his obligation had been fully discharged.

III

As another year's Midsummer Fair approached Leonora took an almost childish delight in the preparations. It was a special time for her. She loved the excitement and the magic of it, the carnival atmosphere weighted with tradition and superstition. And she loved this time because it marked the anniversary of her first meeting with Lukan, an event that had borne its share of drama and a definite hint of midsummer sorcery.

Determined to spend at least a part of this Midsummer Eve with him, she pleaded weariness and retired early, took a long, perfumed bath and slipped upstairs to their secret room. Lukan was already there.

'Do you remember?' he asked, as he drew her into his arms.

'Every moment,' she sighed. 'Every scent and sound.'

'I believe I loved you then, when I held you against me in that dark place in the forest, long before I saw your face by the light of day and you enchanted me with those forget-me-not blue eyes of yours.'

'We knew each other on sight,' she reminded him, shivering a little at the memory. 'We met in darkness, without identities, and yet when our paths crossed for a second time we knew with a single look that we were bound together as one.'

'Aye, we knew.'

She snuggled close and lifted her face for his kiss, holding him more tightly, more possessively than usual, as if despite her happiness she was afraid of something. He stroked her hair, sensing her uncertainty.

'Ebb and flow,' he reminded her. 'We have enjoyed so much these past months. We must not dread the ebb that is to come.'

'But I do. I fear it.'

'We cannot take the one without the other, my Lia. Sooner or later we must taste the sour that follows the sweet.'

'I want what we have to last for ever,' she insisted.

'And so it will, but it will ebb and flow as all things must.'

'Sometimes it frightens me.'

He smiled and held her close. 'I know. Sometimes it frightens me too.'

Following the precedent set a year ago, she was to attend the Midsummer Fair in the role once taken by the late Countess Alyce. This year the numbers were expected to be larger than ever. For weeks in advance of it there had been travelling people camping in the forest. Some of the younger men had formed themselves into bands that ran by night to pillage food and valuables from local farms and isolated houses. Sir Oscar had ordered groups of volunteers, led by his own forest bailiffs, to hear complaints and drive the robbers out. Against all sensible advice he had insisted on riding with the bailiffs, taken a fall from his horse and injured his hip and thigh quite seriously. Several weeks later the pain had not abated. Cold compresses and herbal ointments did much to ease the problem, but Leonora doubted that he would ever fully recover from the mishap. Come winter his rheumatism would invade the weakness, and then the cold would seep into the bones. He no longer had the resilience of his youth, but was obliged to walk with a stick and rest the injured leg whenever possible. Although he was too proud to make complaint, there were times when the deep-rooted pain of it was clearly evident in his eyes.

Lukan came to her briefly in the old gatehouse only minutes before she was due to leave for Kingswood. He was dressed for the fair, his huge brass belt-buckle gleaming, his leather jerkin softened with saddle soap, his hair a raven black against the crisp white linen of his shirt. He handed her a sprig of mauve Wolf's Bane to pin at his breast and she, knowing it was for her he wore it, happily obliged.

'Not a word, not a sign, nor a gesture,' he reminded her.

'I will be on my guard at every moment,' she promised.

'You must. Sir Oscar is both keen-eyed and sharp-witted, and he has lived too many years with secrets of his own to mistake what lies between us.' He stooped to place a kiss in the palm of her hand, closed her fingers lovingly around it, just as he had kissed her for the first time in the forest. 'Take special care, my Lia.'

Sir Oscar's party, preceded by the monogrammed black coach that had led the old Countess's funeral procession, arrived at Kingswood village to a tumultuous welcome. For the second year in succession Leonora mounted the dais and raised the goblet for the opening toast and this time, fully prepared, she played to the crowds with unashamed enthusiasm. She was wearing a gown of soft pink muslin with dark blue trims, ribboned at the bodice and cut low enough to display her smooth shoulders to full advantage. Her bonnet was bedecked with summer flowers so skilfully made that only the closest scrutiny could ascertain if they were real or false. Her hair was intricately laced with beads and wound into a net of silver lace that hung almost to her waist. A long dark ringlet hung at each side of her face, brushing her shoulders and dancing prettily with every movement of her head. A light parasol with a long silk fringe protected her skin from the hot sun and offered a little privacy from the constant scrutiny of curious strangers. She was glad of it when Lukan first came into view. He was sitting astride the big grey stallion, Starlight Warrior, walking the thoroughbred ahead of Sir Oscar's heavyweight, making a show of the best of the Earl's fine stables. He looked magnificent and very proud, and there was not one woman in a thousand who did not breathe a sigh or turn her head to mark his passing. For an instant Leonora too was captivated, but then his words came back to her: *Take special care, my Lia,* and she promptly lowered the parasol between them.

The fair was alive with its usual hubbub of frantic activity. Although her toast had marked the official opening, the trading and bartering, sideshows and entertainments, had been in full swing since dawn. Every patch of open ground not occupied by tents or stalls or pens was filled with Irish and Welsh ponies and horses tied shoulder to shoulder, and all about them freshly painted and decorated wagons filled the streets. Musicians, jugglers and acrobats wandered through the crowds, sharing the day with pick-pockets and card-sharps. There were animals in cages and in pens, songbirds and talking parrots, trained monkeys and dancing bears, performing dogs, strongmen and bearded ladies. That year a pair of Siamese twins, joined at the hip and shoulder and having only four whole limbs between them, were put on show in a tent on the edge of the village. For a tuppenny entrance fee the public could scream, grimace, laugh or faint at the sight of them. A sixpenny ticket would buy the right to watch them eat and drink, and for a guinea they would appear stark naked before as many curious eyes as were prepared to pay for the privilege.

Beside a large tent where glasses of ale, fresh drinking water and lemonade were on sale to the public, Leonora came face to face with the old gypsy who had foreseen the tremendous upheavals in her life. As the woman acknowledged her with a knowing smile and a nod of her slate-grey head, Leonora felt her scalp prickle and a rash of goose-flesh appear along her forearms. So much of what the woman predicted had already come about, and everything at a price, as she had warned. Every triumph, every gain had cost Leonora dearly. She had a husband now but had lost her brothers, she had a son but her dear mama was dead, she had a new life that her twin, her Joseph, may never share. And she had Lukan. What price would she one day have to pay for him?

She remained at the fair no longer than an hour, preferring to save her energies for the afternoon. By then most of the sheep and cattle would be sold and ladies and gentlemen of distinction would come flocking to the fair in their fine carriages. While Malcolm and Sir Oscar went off to examine the pens of livestock more closely, it was left to Gilbert, a rare visitor these days, to escort the ladies back to Beresford Hall. He was spending a week with them before travelling on to Cornwall to visit his eldest sister. Leonora found him much

520

altered, rather distant and perhaps even a little hostile. As they jogged homeward at a steady pace he expressed his concern for Elizabeth's welfare.

'It must be all of a year since I saw her last,' he explained. 'And I find the changes in her state of mind quite marked.'

'To us it has been a slow deterioration,' Leonora told him.

'But one you are aware of?'

'Of course we are aware of it.' She placed her hand over his and noticed with some surprise that he still trembled at her touch. 'We do everything we can for her, but we cannot make her well. However much we love her, Gilbert, neither you nor I nor the best doctors in the world can ever make her well.'

They rode in silence for a while before he said, 'I had a friend at school whose maiden aunt suffered a similar affliction. She eventually became unmanageable and had to be placed in a private asylum for the insane. She died soon after. By his accounts it was a nightmarish place.'

'You can rest assured that such a thing will not happen to your sister.'

'It might.'

'No Gilbert, not while she is so loved by all of us.'

He smiled without feeling reassured. 'When I saw her this morning she was sitting near the stable wall whispering to that battered, dirty old doll that she refuses to be parted from.'

'Battered and dirty it certainly is, but hardly old. Lukan bought it from the spring fair at Chepstow just a few short weeks ago. I'm afraid she has all but picked the poor thing to pieces.'

'I believe she must be watched now day and night?'

'A natural precaution,' Leonora nodded. 'We treat her as we would a child and watch over her for her own protection.'

Gilbert frowned as he digested her words. His time away from home had changed him greatly. He was broader of build, so much older and more handsome, no longer the open-faced young boy she might have married. He had grown a fashionable moustache and side whiskers, and maturity had given him that steady, observant stare peculiar to his family.

Under his close scrutiny she felt strangely uncomfortable, as if he were a stranger to her now.

'I suppose you see quite a lot of him?'

She held her breath. 'Of whom?'

'Lukan de Ville, my brother's favourite brother.'

She shrugged her shoulders. 'I see the man hardly at all. I believe he is kept busy with his duties in the forest. But what a strange way you have of describing him Gilbert: your brother's favourite brother. Do I detect a note of chagrin in it?'

'Not at all,' he grinned disarmingly. 'By now I am well accustomed to taking second place to a gypsy.'

'Gilbert?' Once again she placed her hand over his. 'What is all this? Has the man crossed you? Has he done something to upset you?'

'I simply do not trust him, and Horace believes ...'

'Horace? You are in contact with your exiled brother?' She tried not to sound overly concerned.

He nodded, unhappily she thought. 'I called upon him once or twice while I was in Rome recently, but you were not meant to discover that. I mentioned him in haste when it would have been wiser to remain silent. I hope you will not feel obliged to inform my father that I have gone against his wishes?'

'Of course not. I suppose what your father does not know he will not fret about.' Behind the smile her thoughts were racing. She had not been aware that Horace was in Rome. His sister Vivienne was also staying there, as was Harriet Sharpe when her husband collapsed and died. That place was a known hotbed of gossip and scandal and sordid pillow-talk. She dreaded to imagine what details of her own private life were already known to the man she despised so intensely. All this she hid behind her smile as she asked, 'How is your brother? I'm afraid I scarcely remember him.'

'Oh? I am surprised to hear you say that, since it seems he remembers you well enough.'

Again she smiled as brightly as she was able, determined to give nothing away without intention. She could only wonder what Horace might have told him about her. 'I remember him mostly for the strong resemblance he bears to my eldest brother. Is he well?'

Gilbert shook his head grimly. 'I'm afraid he is a very bitter man. He feels that his position within the family has been ...' He hesitated, searching for an appropriate word, then added, '... usurped.'

'Indeed?' she asked stiffly. 'Usurped by whom? Not by myself and surely not by my son.'

'No, of course not,' Gilbert said quickly. 'I am sorry, Leonora. I did not intend to imply that you ...' He shook his head. 'Perhaps *usurp* is the wrong word entirely.'

'Indeed it is,' she told him. 'Let us be brutally honest here, Gilbert. Your brother was sent from Beresford Hall because he earned his parents' censure, and from England's shores because he broke the law on several counts. Nothing of his was deliberately *usurped*. It would be a kindness to say that he fell from grace.'

'Ah, but did he lose his footing or was he pushed? That is the crux of it.'

'What?'

'Was he perhaps assisted on his way?' Gilbert placed his hands in front of him and pushed the air as if to shove someone away. 'Perhaps by some self-seeking gypsy to strengthen his own position at Beresford?'

'Lukan de Ville?' she asked incredulously. 'Horace Cavendish suspects Lukan de Ville of turning his family against him?'

Gilbert was nodding thoughtfully. 'He is convinced that his downfall was cleverly engineered and yes, he suspects de Ville of having had a hand in it.'

'Good grief!' Her astonishment was genuine. This was the last thing she had expected. It had never occurred to her that Lukan would come under suspicion for something she herself had brought about before she even knew him.

'And he certainly regrets that his Yorkshire inheritance has gone to young William. After all, the boy is his father's and his grandfather's heir, so his future is assured. He will want for nothing in life while his Uncle Horace struggles to survive.

523

The Earl's christening gift is perhaps the cruelest misfortune in that respect.'

'I sincerely hope he will not be so petty as to blame the boy for that?'

Gilbert shrugged and looked unhappy. 'I hear the gypsy was even asked to stand as godfather?'

Leonora winced inwardly. It had not occurred to them to consider asking Gilbert. 'You were away in Europe at the time,' she reminded him.

'Malcolm could have waited.'

'I'm sorry, I had no idea you were offended by the choice.'

'The fault is not with you,' he said softly. 'It is with me for imagining that Malcolm would choose a brother above a gypsy.'

'Oh Gilbert, I am so sorry.' She slotted her arm through his and rested her head on his shoulder. His feelings were hurt. He felt he had been rejected in favour of Lukan, and because of that he was ready to be persuaded that Lukan had had a hand in Horace's downfall. 'Malcolm would never willingly do you a wrong. It was a careless oversight on his part. Will you forgive him Gilbert, for my sake?'

The young man covered her hand with his and nodded his head. Her words were as oil poured on troubled waters and besides, he knew full well he could deny her nothing.

'I will never mention it again,' he promised.

'Nor brood upon it? Nor bear a grudge?'

He smiled, defeated. 'My dear Leonora, you may consider the matter closed and forgotten as from this very moment.'

It was late in the evening when she repeated every detail of the conversation to Malcolm on the strict understanding that he would not betray a confidence by challenging his brother. As she had expected, he was deeply concerned by the possibility that Gilbert might be about to throw in his lot with Horace Cavendish.

'If he does that he is as good as ruined,' he said. 'Horace will drag him down to his own level. Damn it, I will not have my younger brother's character damaged by that reprobate.'

'Then we must tether him here, away from the influence in

Rome,' she told him. 'We must keep him occupied and let him feel that he is a valued member of the family. May I suggest we make him manager of the Yorkshire estates?'

'Would that arrangement be to your liking?'

She nodded. 'He is young and needs to prove himself. This will offer him self-respect and valuable experience. He will have an income of his own and cash in hand to help his brother if he has a mind to. It will also encourage in him a sense of responsibility towards William. Our son may already have one Cavendish enemy in his Uncle Horace. We cannot afford to nurture another.'

'You seem to have thought of everything,' he observed.

'I have thought of little else since early morning.'

'My compliments, Leonora. I can find no fault with your suggestion.'

'Then you will discuss it with your father? Soon?'

He nodded. 'I'll speak to him first thing in the morning. Gilbert leaves for Cornwall at the end of the week and I think we would be wise to have the matter settled by then.' He looked up as the drawing room clock chimed the quarter hour. 'I expect Lukan will be here at any moment. Will you stay and take a glass of brandy with us?'

'Thank you, my dear, I'd rather not,' she smiled. 'I'm sure you two have much to discuss that will close my eyes with boredom. And besides, I do believe our son is expecting me.'

She met him in the hall, inclined her head and glanced at him briefly as she swept by. 'Good evening, Mr de Ville.'

He nodded, maintaining his rapid stride. 'Good evening, Lady Cavendish.'

At the door of his rooms Malcolm smiled good-naturedly. It would have pleased him to see his best friend and his wife become good friends instead of two strangers with not a scrap of affection to spare between them. Yet even as the thought came into his head he wondered if there could be any real truth behind it. Lukan de Ville was the handsomest, most enigmatic man he had ever met. Malcolm loved him as a brother, but when a man had a beautiful wife and could spend so little time between her sheets, even the dearest brother might become his enemy. The arrangement as it stood was the better way, especially under the present circumstances. There could be no brooding jealousies, no room for dark suspicion when a man and a woman displayed that amount of indifference towards each other.

The friends lingered over their brandies, reluctant to bring a pleasant evening to a close. It had been a long, hard day, a successful day. A great deal of money, horseflesh and livestock had changed hands at a profit. A great many happy bargains had been struck, and many a man would reach home that night with his purse improved. Leonora had hired a dozen young girls, country children of twelve-years-old or less who would now come under her protection until they came of age. She would train them at Beresford before finding them a safe position at one of the better houses, and word was out that anyone hiring a Beresford girl must treat her well or answer to Lady Cavendish.

'These children are hired by unscrupulous men and women for their own purposes, ill-used and then thrown out to starve or turn to theft and prostitution in order to survive,' Malcolm explained. 'There are men who make whores of orphans, who use them like animals at their drunken revelries and toss them aside even before the fair is over.'

'I have heard the worst of the stories,' Lukan told him. 'Your wife's kind efforts are to be admired, though I fear they can have but small effect upon a world in which a nine-year-old girl may change owners for a guinea and be used as the purchaser thinks fit.'

Malcolm nodded. 'But not the Beresford girls. They at least are safe from such debauchery.'

They discussed the merits of that year's Midsummer Fair at length and, over a second glass of brandy, the question of Gilbert and the management of William's Yorkshire estates was debated at length between them. At midnight Lukan made as it to leave, stopped at the door and dipped one hand into the deep pocket of his coat.

'There is another matter,' he began.

'Yes?'

Lukan scowled and selected his words with care. 'Some time ago you spoke to me on a personal matter. My sister prescribed a herbal tonic, a drink to be taken several times a day.'

Malcolm nodded. 'Since then I have seen a doctor and . . .'

'I seek no explanations,' Lukan cut in. He lifted a dark jar from the depths of his coat pocket, placed it on a table and stood back as if he found the thing distasteful. 'Rebecca left this remedy for you. It was overlooked, shut in a cupboard until now. She made it specially. It is said to be a certain cure.'

Malcolm looked embarrassed. 'It was good of you to bring it.'

'I believe it should be used regularly, not simply as and when required. If you no longer have a use for it then I suggest you dispose of it as it suits you.' He paused awkwardly then added, 'Let me know what Gilbert thinks of your idea.'

He left the room abruptly and strode along the corridor with his features grimly set and his fists tightly clenched. The sound of his boots rang out in the confined area, marking his progress until the slamming of the farthest door returned the long corridor to silence. Malcolm closed the door of his own room and, amused by Lukan's uncharacteristic awkwardness, uncapped the jar and sniffed gingerly at its contents. He was relieved when a pleasant aroma of blended herbs and perfumes reached his nostrils. Rebecca Adams had obviously been well instructed and had followed her brother's directions to the letter. Had she prepared so intimate an ointment in her usual country fashion, it might well have proved too pungent to apply, however acute her patient's need of it.

'Thank you, my friend,' he grinned, sniffing the jar as if it contained the scent of exotic blossoms. 'And may the gift soon place me deeper in your debt.'

Beyond the windows of Malcolm's apartment, Lukan whistled his hounds to heel and patted the coarse grey heads in turn as they approached. He saw the light in the window of Leonora's tower rooms and felt his heart quicken and his blood grow warm in anticipation of her touch. Between the two, the husband and the lady, he was at times unbearably divided. Jealousy and love had prompted him to withhold the remedy to Malcolm's impotence; conscience and love of a different kind had forced him at last to yield it up, albeit with a heartfelt wish for its failure. Now all he wanted was to have done with taunting and fretting his loyalties on the matter. The restorative would fail, of course. It must, *it must.* The possible outcome of his grudging generosity was too much for his mind and heart to contemplate.

By noon the next day Malcolm had begun to put the plans for his son's inheritance into action. Just as he had hoped, Gilbert was easily persuaded to accept full responsibility for the Yorkshire estates until such times as William was capable of managing his own affairs. The offer demonstrated a measure of trust that was as gratifying to the young man as it was unexpected. At last he was to be allowed to prove himself, to show his father and his elder brother his true mettle. As the youngest of three sons his expectations rested solely on the allowance settled on him through his dead mother's will, but in Yorkshire he would hold the purse-strings of a large and profitable estate. He would become a member of the landed gentry, a man of status who could well afford to maintain a respectable position among his peers. At a stroke his future had been assured, and the hard work involved in managing his nephew's holdings to the very best of his ability would help him avoid the threads of pity that drew him with such persistence to the sordid world of his brother in Rome. Even while heartily returning Malcolm's handshake upon the deal, Gilbert knew he would be despised for choosing to serve the interests of the new owner of all those lands once intended for Horace Cavendish. Within days of the agreement he left for Cornwall bearing gifts and letters and last-minute messages for his elder sister and her family. He hugged Leonora briefly as she lifted her head to kiss his cheek. Clearly, this latest shift in his fortunes would keep him away from Beresford Hall for long periods, but at the same time it would bind his future ever more firmly to hers. It seemed that fate was not yet ready to release him from her tender spell.

'He loves you,' Malcolm observed one evening when he and

Leonora were discussing the finer details of Gilbert's position in Yorkshire. There was neither reproach nor anger in his words. He had known of Gilbert's feelings from the outset.

'He will outgrow it,' Leonora smiled.

Malcolm shook his head and frowned a little. 'I wish I could be sure of that, my dear. We of the Cavendish breed can be stubborn devils in matters of the heart.' He reached for her hand and drew it to his lips. 'I will love you all my life and be glad of it, for you are mine to love, but I would not wish the same fate for my brother.'

'Time and distance will be the cure for Gilbert's pains,' Leonora assured him. 'Believe me, his youth and natural vigour will not allow him to brood upon his losses indefinitely.'

'Does he ever speak of it?'

'Never,' she said emphatically. 'Not by word or gesture would he willingly betray his feelings. He is a gentleman and he loves you too, remember.'

He smiled and opened his arms to embrace her. She came to him at once, dropping to her knees before his chair and kissing his neck as his arms encircled her. They sat in contented silence then, her head upon his chest, his cheek resting against her hair. Malcolm counted as precious these nights he spent with her. They planned their time together with great care, dining privately in his apartments or hers and retiring late to bed, replete with good wine, stimulating conversation and the many and varied pleasures they found in each others' company. They had not allowed his impotence to become a bar to their affection, nor had it robbed them of the tender intimacies that now marked the limits of love's physical expression. Their shared time was always special to them both. When she slept in his arms she did so out of fondness rather than wifely duty, expecting and demanding nothing beyond her husband's true and honest regard. Thus she was totally unprepared for the revival of sexual prowess that carried him far beyond the sleepy pleasures of other nights. Unplanned, unforeseen, the act of love was fully accomplished before any protest of hers could find its voice.

IV

In July there was a letter from Charles. He had reached
Quebec after several weeks on a British timber ship which
was, he wrote, unfit to carry cattle, let alone convey civilised
human beings across such distances. Stocked with only half a
cargo of salt for the Newfoundland fisheries, the captain had
ordered makeshift wooden berths to be erected between decks
so that passengers might be packed in to help make up the
shortfall. It was a common practice. The ships came laden
with timber but often sailed out again in ballast, empty,
unable to find sufficient coal or salt to finance the outward
trip. Paying passengers presented an easy solution to the
problem. Their meagre accommodation was provided cheaply
enough and they paid as little as two or three pounds for the
privilege of living like rats for weeks on end. They were
fortunate if they received sufficient fresh water for the journey
and often had their food supplies and personal belongings
stolen by other travellers. Charles described a horrendous
journey made in the most appalling conditions but, typical of
him, ended by giving thanks that Louisa had not been
compelled to endure a similar experience.

From Quebec he intended to press on after Jonathan,
perhaps across the border into the United States, depending
on what instructions his brother had left behind. He urged
Leonora and Sir Oscar to exercise patience. Jonathan still
believed himself a fugitive and may have travelled hundreds of
miles since first arriving in Quebec. Charles would try to
deliver his news and have letters of reply dispatched to
England before the St Lawrence River was closed by ice
between mid-October and mid-April. He sent his love to
Leonora and to little William, his sincere regards to Sir
Malcolm and Sir Oscar, and his deepest gratitude to Lukan de
Ville. It was a cheerful, well written and very welcome letter
which brought a joyous atmosphere to the house for several
days. Leonora saw Sir Oscar's spirits lift for the first time since

530

Charles had left Beresford. Having feared to lose his only link with Jonathan he now found himself four thousand miles closer to finding his son.

By the end of August the euphoria Leonora had felt for months was beginning to subside. She became restless and agitated, with rapid changes of mood and regular nightmares that caused her to resist sleep. According to her calculations, Rebecca Adams would soon be giving birth to her incestuous offspring. Leonora paced the floor in anxiety and prayed each night that neither mother nor child would survive the birth. She could not bear to think of another woman lying in Lukan's arms, cheating her way into his bed, giving birth to his child. To know that the woman was his gypsy half-sister had become a torment to her peace of mind. She dwelled and brooded upon it, torturing herself with her imaginings. But soon the fate of Rebecca Adams took second place to problems of her own.

'You must tell him at once,' Anabel insisted.

'I will do no such thing. I intend to keep it from him for as long as is humanly possible.'

'He'll know. He'll see it for himself.'

Leonora shook her head. 'With William I could have hidden it for months.'

Anabel dismissed that notion with a shrug. 'From Malcolm perhaps, but not from Lukan de Ville. He knows you better than you know yourself. One day he'll guess the truth and then there'll be the devil to pay because you tried to keep him in the dark.'

'I will not tell him, Anabel. I cannot. If he reacts the way he did with William ... Oh Anabel, I could not live through that again, all those long months without him, and the fear that he would find another love.' She pressed her hands to her blazing cheeks and shook her head, determined. 'I will not do it. I will not tell him. Not yet, not yet.'

'Then you must keep it from Malcolm too, and from his father, and neither of them will thank you for doing that.'

Leonora gave vent to her frustration by sweeping the contents of her dressing table on to the floor. 'I care not a jot for what they think and I care little more for this child I carry.'

Anabel narrowed her eyes. 'You will not think of destroying it? Not your husband's unborn child? Leonora, tell me you will not even think of doing such a thing?'

Leonora hung her head, defeated. There was a new life inside her, a tiny thing that had a right to live and grow and make a place for itself in the world. She would not, could not, raise a hand against it. Wretched though it made her feel, she would not harm her helpless unborn child. She shook her head. 'I won't,' was all she said.

The truth was out much sooner than she had hoped. Another week was all she had, a week of loving him with an almost desperate intensity until the bubble of her happiness was pricked. There was nothing violent or volcanic in it, no sudden fit of rage, no accusations. It was simply that the plug was pulled and all the good things of her life began to pour away.

It was early September. The forest already had a russet sheen with splashes of brilliant yellows, golds and flame. They could hear the crack of gunfire as the partridge was harried from field to field by sportsmen's guns, and the distant cries of men exhilarated by the thrill of killing. They had made love before a peach-wood fire whose scent now filled the room. Lukan had stroked her body with his fingertips, kissed and caressed every glowing inch of her, then wrapped her in a sheet and held her close. Later she watched him dress, hungry for every detail of his wide shoulders and taut brown buttocks, his long, muscular limbs. When he stooped to kiss her she pulled him down beside her and snuggled against him. Their silence had become a weighty thing.

'You are different,' he said at last guardedly.

'Am I?'

'Something has come between us.'

'It doesn't have to, not if you can accept ...' Her words trailed off into an anguished sigh. She felt him stiffen, felt a distance suddenly yawn between them. 'Lukan ...?'

'Another child.' His voice was flat.

She felt accused and found herself unable either to confirm

or deny the charge. Instead she froze, holding her breath, and for a moment it seemed that his response this time would be a calmer and more rational one. Then very gently he removed himself from her embrace and rose to his feet, reaching for his soft leather jerkin.

'Don't Lukan. Please don't do this.'

Ignoring her plea he buckled on his belt, his head lowered so that his hair, hanging loose, concealed his face entirely.

'Lukan, don't go.'

She spoke the words to his back. He left the room without a sound or a glance in her direction, dropped down into the twisting stairwell and was gone. She flinched as the heavy Monks' Door slammed shut behind him, the crash of it echoing right to the top of the tower. This time there was no anger to mask the pain of his rejection, no sting of recrimination to soothe the wounds. And this time there was no joy in her condition to compensate for the loss of him.

When Anabel found her she was kneeling on the floor, weeping as if her heart would break.

'I don't want another child to Malcolm Cavendish,' she sobbed. 'I want Lukan's child, the one Rebecca stole from him, the one I can never have.'

'Don't say it, Leonora,' Anabel pleaded. 'For heaven's sake don't tempt your fate by daring to give voice to such desires.'

In a frenzy of grief Leonora pounded her bent knees with her fists, then threw back her head and opened her mouth to release her misery in a piercing scream.

CHAPTER TWENTY-FIVE

I

The letters arrived in October, eight months after Charles had left Beresford in search of his brother and three months since they last had word of him. He had travelled up the St Lawrence River to Montreal, a distance of 180 miles, and in one of the many settlements which had sprung up outside the city, he and Jonathan were eventually reunited. Louisa was in excellent health after giving birth to a daughter, Marguerite, and both men had found no difficulty in securing well-paid work. Jonathan wrote that he was delighted with the news from England, though still reeling from the full impact of it. He told Leonora at length about his life since they had last met, of his sorrow at their mother's death, the joy of being presented with a beautiful baby daughter, the anxiety of learning that Joseph had been missing without trace for so long. And he told her of the deep sense of pride it gave him to know that Sir Oscar Cavendish was his true father. It was a long, emotional letter full of love and poignancy, the out-pourings of a young family man too long away from those he loved the most. What details he had overlooked, or was too modest to include, were to be found in Louisa's accompanying letter, and in the extra pages included by Charles. Leonora read them all several times, then went to the tiny garden where her mother lay buried and read them all again.

'You have a granddaughter, mama,' she whispered tearfully. 'And your son has the father you always wanted him to have. He is the Earl's son now and nobody but Anabel and myself will ever know the whole truth of it.'

When she heard Sir Oscar's tread on the gravelled path she slipped from the garden via a tiny footpath that wound downwards to the lower terrace and veered to the right toward the orchard wall. She did not remain to eavesdrop upon his private moments with the woman he had loved. He too had received a letter from Montreal, and from that day forward he was pledged to make no secret of the fact that Francine Shelley had given him a son.

The St Lawrence will be frozen until April of next year,' the Earl told them all at dinner. 'Whatever he decides to do will not be acted upon until then. We will not be seeing him until next summer, if at all.'

'He'll come,' Leonora said. 'Be sure of it, he *will* come home.'

When Leonora excused herself Sir Oscar sat back in his chair and regarded his eldest son closely. 'What do you make of it all, Malcolm?'

Malcolm grinned. 'As I told you this morning when I first had the news, it came as no real surprise to me. I'm happy for you father. I'm happy for all of us. Events could not have worked out better for us had they been planned in advance and exercised with true military precision.' He leaned forward and smiled into his father's sombre features. 'Francine was a beautiful and well respected lady and, to my certain knowledge, Horace and mother were the only people ever to hold her in contempt because of you.'

'And Herbert Shelley,' Sir Oscar said. 'According to Leonora, he made poor Francine miserable in every way imaginable. Perhaps he always suspected her of marrying him under false pretences. There is one thing you should know, my boy, something Shelley should know already if he has half the sense he was born with. There was no adultery as far as her marriage was concerned. She kept her marriage vows and never betrayed that husband of hers on my account.'

'I believe that, sir.'

'And I loved her,' Sir Oscar confessed. 'Whatever the rights and wrongs of this, my boy, I truly loved Francine.'

'Yes sir,' Malcolm said quietly, respecting his father for making the admission. 'I believe that too.'

Despite the happiness of making contact again with her brothers, for Leonora that second pregnancy was a joyless, unwanted thing. She struggled to love the child that was growing inside her, to make a place for it in her heart just as she must soon make a place for it in her life. She wanted to create a similar bond to the one that had existed so naturally between herself and William long before he was delivered, protesting, into the world. She tried, but Lukan always came between them. This time the sacrifice was too great. This time she could not love her unborn baby as she wanted to. Blaming it, resenting its untimely intrusion upon her happiness, she shut it from her mind and refused to speak of it, holding it to herself like a guilty secret. She threw herself into a frantic round of visiting and entertaining, often travelling great distances simply to show off a new gown or to practise her social skills before an untried audience. She travelled to Yorkshire with Gilbert to inspect her son's estates, a testing enough journey for someone in the very best of health. She did some hunting there with her noble neighbours, attended balls and dinner parties given in her honour, then travelled home in bad weather, urging her drivers not to spare the horses. Everyone could see that she was happy, but only those who knew her better recognised her so-called happiness for what it was. Leonora was living a lie, and by late November Anabel had begun to fear for her safety and the child's.

'Tell him,' she begged. 'For Heaven's sake put a stop to this insanity and admit to your husband that you are to have another child.'

Leonora stamped her foot. 'I will not.'

'Then give up this foolish passion for horse-riding and road travel. At least make some effort to safeguard your health and the babe's.'

'You worry without cause,' Leonora said haughtily. 'I am perfectly well.'

'You are four months pregnant Leonora.'

'I do not need you to remind me of that.'

'*Someone* needs to remind you,' Anabel insisted. 'If you should miscarry at this late stage ...'

Leonora laughed harshly. 'If I were to miscarry it would be a blessing, and glad I would be of it.'

Anabel's eyes widened as a terrible suspicion dawned on her. 'Is that it?' she demanded. 'Is that your plan, you wicked girl, to drive yourself so hard that the child miscarries? Did you decline to destroy it with remedies just so that you could murder it some other way?'

'What? My God, what a terrible thing to say.' Leonora's face drained of colour and she shrank from Anabel's accusation as if scalded by the words. 'You cannot believe that I would do such a thing.'

'Oh yes I can,' Anabel insisted. 'I would believe it of you, Lady Cavendish. I believe you capable of harming *anything* that set itself between you and your selfish desires.'

Leonora was astounded. 'Anabel, you cannot mean what you are saying.'

'I mean it,' Anabel retorted angrily. Then her anger softened a little and she added, 'Though I am ready to accept that his desertion has temporarily robbed you of your senses.'

Leonora sat down heavily and placed both hands on her stomach, her tear-filled eyes staring at nothing. 'Murder my own child, my helpless unborn? Oh Anabel, I couldn't, I swear I could never do such a thing.'

'Not intentionally perhaps,' Anabel conceded. 'But do it you will, my girl, unless this foolish behaviour is stopped at once.'

'I had no idea ...'

'No, you were too busy licking your own wounds, trying to

pretend they didn't hurt, to give a thought for the new life you carry. Right the wrong and ease the pain, Leonora. You need to share this burden for your own sake, and Malcolm has a right to know of it.'

'I'll tell him,' she promised, wiping tears from her cheeks. 'I'll tell him soon.'

'You'll tell him today,' Anabel said coldly. 'And if you fail then I will do it for you. My mind is set and I'll not go back on it, and I'll not stand by in silence while you take foolish risks with your life. Tell him today or I will do it for you.'

Faced with such an ultimatum and still in a state of shock following Anabel's assessment of her behaviour, Leonora took the news of her pregnancy to her husband. Malcolm was delighted, and both he and his father seemed to accept that she had made a common mistake in failing to realise that she was pregnant. Malcolm was able to confirm the dates with accuracy. They had travelled to London, stayed at His Lordship's house in Curzon Street and there, fortified by pills from his own doctor, a strong liquid tonic from a local apothecary and the special remedy prepared by Rebecca Adams, he had risen to the occasion and succeeded in impregnating his wife.

'It will be good to have a second son,' he told her.

'Or a daughter?' she suggested.

A month later Sir Marcus Shaw announced that they might both be right. She was not to have one child but two. As far as he could ascertain at this stage, Lady Leonora was expecting twins.

That night Leonora retired early and climbed up to the tower to look out over Beresford and the lovely Wye Valley. She tried to imagine the two small bodies growing inside her; her babies, her twins. The news had brought her little joy beyond the knowledge that she was unlikely to go full term and might deliver them as early as the end of March or the beginning of April. For that she was grateful. The sooner this pregnancy was over the better she would like it.

There was a moon that night, a pale, ineffectual thing giving out a watery glow that could not compete with the sharp, clear brightness of surrounding stars. It was a cold night, very dark and moved by an icy wind. She stared at the forest, willing her gaze to penetrate the darkness and find the glow that would be a light in his window. She saw nothing, but she heard the swish and rustle of the forest like the whisper of an ocean in the distance, and she was reminded of all the mysteries and secrets lurking in its depths. Somewhere out there his child was born two months ago. Had it survived? Had either of them survived?

'I hope you are dead, Rebecca Adams,' she said into the wind, and her words were snatched away as they were spoken. 'I hope you are dead and he will never know what you have taken from him.'

She came down from the tower when Anabel called, determined to allow the older woman to have her say in events from now on. She wanted her babies to have every chance, even while she fretted in her heart and brooded endlessly upon that other child, the one she *should* have had.

And so she resolved to do all she could to fulfil the debt she owed her unborns. She ate well and took daily exercise, drank plenty of buttermilk and honey, gave up her morning rides and cancelled all invitations that would take her more than an hour's journey from home. Once her distracted play-acting was over it became obvious to everyone that this pregnancy did not suit her as the first had done, but while she wept sometimes and seemed less vital, less happy than before, her time advanced without mishap and she remained in sound health.

Charlotte arrived during the second week in December to help with the Christmas celebrations, and she fussed around her sister-in-law like a loving mother hen. Leonora was glad of her company. She needed the distraction, the extra dimension to a life where only William was of any real interest to her.

'This isn't like me, Charlotte,' she confessed. 'Sometimes I feel so discouraged that I hardly care to leave my bed in the mornings. I weep for no reason at all and I find little joy in anything, and I feel such a fraud, when I have so very much to be thankful for.'

'I was like that with my second,' Charlotte told her. 'I could weep all day without reason and then cry all night because I felt so guilty. There's nothing we can do but see it through to the bitter end and hope the journey was worth it.'

Leonora smiled without amusement at those words. Nothing, as far as she was concerned, was worth losing Lukan. She felt empty and lost, tormented by the fear that this time she had gone too far, this time she had wounded him too deeply ever to warrant his forgiveness.

'Is there more, Leonora?'

'What? What do you mean?' She looked at Charlotte's handsome rather than pretty face, at the kindly, understanding eyes. 'What more could there possibly be?'

'I wonder if you are keeping something from me, something you dare not tell my brother, perhaps?'

'I'm sure I have no idea what you are talking about Charlotte,' she said, meeting the candid blue gaze with difficulty.

Charlotte placed a hand on Leonora's arm. 'It is no crime to be afraid, Leonora, and I respect you for keeping your fear from Malcolm after all he had to suffer on his first wife's account. Try not to worry too much, my dear. You will have the very best of care, and there is no reason to suspect that this confinement should be any less successful than the first.'

'But I do not ...' Leonora bit back her protest and lowered her head as if by way of an admission. If Charlotte had come to suspect her of harbouring a secret, she was welcome to put such an innocent name to it.

They sat together in the main drawing room during the hiring of extra staff for the Christmas celebrations. Malcolm had asked that a man and wife be found to take care of Lukan's house, a respectable couple selected from Leonora's own sources. She had access to some of the best domestic staff available, and at Christmas and other busy times they flocked to Beresford seeking well-paid work.

Charlotte was not confident that their task would be an easy one. 'He lives like a hermit in the heart of the forest,' she reminded Leonora, 'in a fine old house all but gone to ruin for want of decent management. It will be no easy matter, finding a decent pair to share it with him. The danger is that he will be forced to settle for the left-overs, the ones no other employer will accept.'

'Not while I am responsible,' Leonora declared. 'I will not be held accountable for a disaster in the de Ville household.'

Charlotte chuckled. 'From what I hear, the de Ville household is already something of a disaster, thanks to that dreadful sister of his.'

At this Leonora shuddered and felt a now familiar chill. She needed no reminder of Rebecca Adams. It was her dearest wish that there be no place for that wicked woman in Lukan's home once it was fully staffed and restored to its former dignity.

Mr Robert Armstrong and his wife Adelaide had been employed by the Plymouth Caldwells for seven years and presented glowing references as to their professional and personal qualifications. Leonora liked them on sight. Robert Armstrong was a tall, straight man of obvious military bearing, well groomed, with a fine moustache and a clear and steady gaze. There was a faded elegance about him, as if his present circumstances made it difficult for him to maintain the standard of appearances to which he was accustomed. His wife was short and stout, with shiny cheeks and greying hair. Her dress bore signs of having been turned and recut in places. Her slippers were darned, her bonnet skilfully retrimmed. The pair were extremely eager to secure the post and seemed particularly suited to it.

Leonora studied the letters of recommendation signed by the Caldwells, whom she knew quite well and respected for their honesty. 'These letters are two years old,' she said at last. 'May I ask what positions you have held since then?'

The couple glanced at each other. Mrs Armstrong looked anxious and began to wring her hands together. Her husband squared his shoulders and looked Leonora directly in the eye. 'We have lived on our savings, on what we had put by over the years, Your Ladyship.'

'For two years?'

'Yes ma'am.'

Leonora nodded and studied the couple thoughtfully. Of

those she had interviewed so far, these two were the only ones worth considering for the position. She had seen young men whom she suspected of wanting to profit from the local game and make sport of the local village girls. She had spoken to young women who would be happy to work for the handsome Lukan de Ville whatever duties might be demanded of them. She had even spoken to a well-starched, well-meaning couple who declared themselves *bent on showing the gypsy the error of his ways and planting the seeds of humility in his heathen household.* Lukan de Ville would have made short work of them all.

'Are you aware, Mr Armstrong, that the Forest House is rather more isolated than most, and that the gentleman entertains little and keeps irregular habits? I am informed that a great deal of careful reorganisation is required to bring his household up to the standards he demands.'

'We are well aware of that ma'am.'

'Are you acquainted with Mr de Ville?'

Armstrong nodded. 'I know him by sight, Your Ladyship. A tall, Spanish-looking gentleman as I recall. A man of few words and ... or ... rather forceful in his dealings with the rabble.'

'Indeed.' Leonora smiled at the description.

'And very nice manners,' his wife put in quickly, nodding her head eagerly. 'I met him too, and I recall his lovely manners.'

'Could you begin immediately?'

'Indeed we could ma'am,' Armstrong declared. 'Our baggage waits at the inn at Kingswood.'

'Very well, you will have my decision by two o'clock this afternoon. In the meantime I hope you will take luncheon here at Beresford. My maid will show you the way.'

'Thank you, Your Ladyship, we are very grateful.' The man reached out to squeeze his wife's hand, bowed and steered her politely from the room. When the door had closed behind them Charlotte turned to Leonora with a broad grin.

'You are a sentimentalist,' she said, wagging her forefinger in Leonora's direction. 'I believe you will recommend those

542

two simply because they are such a charming old pair. Do you believe their story about living for the last two years on their savings?'

'Oh yes, I believe it,' Leonora said. 'Their appearance bears that out and I certainly felt that Robert Armstrong spoke the truth. What I do not believe is that they endured those two years of idleness willingly. It would seem they have been unable to find employment despite such glowing references from their previous employers. I would be interested to discover why.'

'Will you recommend them to de Ville?'

'Certainly. I am an excellent judge of character, Charlotte. They are the perfect pair for the job.'

'On your head be it then, for I would not have chosen them,' she laughed.

Leonora sent word to the Armstrongs that their baggage would be collected from Kingswood and taken directly to de Ville's house, and that a letter of recommendation would be left for them at the main gatehouse. A carriage was waiting to deliver them to their new employment at their convenience.

'And in the meantime I will solve the mystery of those missing two years,' Leonora said. 'Beginning with a letter to Veronica Caldwell in Plymouth.'

They were interrupted some time later by the unexpected return of Robert and Adelaide Armstrong. The woman had been weeping and clutched at her husband's hand as if in terror.

'You wish to speak with me, Mr Armstrong?' Leonora asked.

'Yes ma'am. We wish to tell you the truth. Not that we lied to you, we wouldn't do that. We just didn't tell you everything.'

'And you wish to do so now?'

'Yes ma'am. You've been kind to us and treated us with respect, and we know Mr Lukan to be a good and honest man and a just employer.' He glanced at his wife and smiled reassuringly. 'So, we talked it over and we're both agreed you ought to know the truth.'

543

Leonora glanced at Charlotte. 'Please go on, Mr Armstrong.'

He cleared his throat and squared his shoulders. 'Well ma'am, these last two years we couldn't get employment anywhere because of how we left our last place.'

'The Caldwell's?'

'Oh no ma'am. We left there when Miss Veronica's new husband insisted on bringing all his own people with him. Cleared us all out he did, from butler right down to scivvy. Miss Veronica will confirm that, if you ask her.'

'I'm sure she will. What happened then?'

'Well, we took up positions at Lord Huddlestone's place in Kent. We were only there a couple of months when our son got himself into the most terrible trouble and might have been taken to prison if we had not helped him out. He's a good boy, hard working and sensible. Truly he is, ma'am, a good boy.'

'Then why was he in such dire straits?' Charlotte asked.

Armstrong acknowledged her question but addressed his reply to Leonora. 'He and his friend started a little printing business in London and were expanding nicely until his partner suddenly took ill and died, right there on the premises, and him no more than thirty-two years old. The widow's family moved in and grabbed everything for themselves, leaving our boy with orders he couldn't meet and debts he couldn't repay. As soon as the customers got wind of what had happened, everyone clamoured for what was theirs and demanded what they were owed right there and then. Nobody would give him time to pay or fresh credit to keep himself afloat. He was a brave lad. He might have survived if someone had lent a hand.'

'The poor-plague,' Leonora muttered. She was thinking of her mother and all the doors that were suddenly closed to her once word was out that Herbert Shelley had left his family destitute. The threat of the Poor House closes society's doors with sickening haste, so that loss of respectability through poverty becomes a crippling sickness in itself. It sets the sufferer apart and keeps him so. Nobody wants to lend a helping hand if doing so might taint him with the same

544

disease. It becomes a vicious spiral, always twisting downwards.

'Beg pardon ma'am?'

'Nothing.' Leonora shook her head. 'Please continue.'

'When he came to us we allowed him to take a few things from the house, things that wouldn't be missed right away because His Lordship had taken his family abroad and wouldn't be back for at least another month. It all went wrong. The man who took the goods on pawn recognised certain items and informed the police. Our son was arrested, we were dismissed and the business folded. That's the truth, Lady Cavendish, and we haven't been able to find work for two years because of it. We're not thieves. As God is my judge we never thought to rob His Lordship of a penny. It was just a loan, and every last item would have been back in place by the time he returned from his travels, if only that pawnbroker had remained silent. We tried to help our boy as any parents might have done, and we broke the law in doing it, but we are honest folk ...' He hung his head and lowered his voice to a whisper, '... honest folk.'

By now Adelaide Armstrong was weeping openly and Leonora felt her throat constrict with sympathy. Honesty was such a costly business. By being honest now they stood to lose the only employment they had been offered in two long years. Leonora waited until the woman had recovered, then handed the man the letter she had prepared. 'Please give this letter of recommendation to Mr de Ville with my compliments.'

'To Mr de Ville? But we thought ...?'

'I am satisfied that you and your wife are suitable for the post, Mr Armstrong. I do hope you will prove my confidence justified.'

'Oh, oh ...' The woman let out a choked cry and rushed forward to grasp Leonora's hand, falling on her knees and sobbing afresh. Her husband helped her up in a kindly, very gentle fashion.

'You won't regret this, Lady Cavendish,' he said. 'You have my solemn word on that.'

Leonora flashed him a smile of genuine pleasure. 'I do not

believe for one moment that I will, Mr Armstrong, and I wish you and Mrs Armstrong every happiness in your new life. Now, if you would like to follow Miss Anabel across to the main gatehouse, I think you will find a carriage at your disposal. And Mr Armstrong, it will not be necessary for you to repeat what you have just told me.'

'But what about Mr de Ville, Your Ladyship?'

'Let me assure you that your past misfortunes will be of no interest to him. He has placed this matter entirely in my hands and I happen to believe you will suit him admirably.'

'That's very gratifying, Your Ladyship, and we thank you right kindly for having this faith in us, but just supposing somebody speaks out against us and Mr de Ville discovers we were less than honest with him?'

'You need have no worries about that. The situation will be discreetly explained to him and I promise you will not be called upon to speak of it again.'

The couple exchanged glances, then Robert Armstrong looked at her with such an expression of gratitude that her heart went out to him. 'Bless you ma'am. You'll not regret this. You don't know what this means to us.'

'Oh yes I do,' Leonora told him gently. 'I know.'

'God bless you ma'am.'

They were at the door when Leonora called them back. 'Just one more thing, Mr Armstrong. May I ask if your son is now fully recovered from his misfortunes?'

The man placed his arm around the podgy shoulders of his wife and spoke softly. 'No ma'am. He was a quiet, home-loving young man, you see, not used to ruffians and hardship. That prison did for him, Your Ladyship. He hanged himself.'

II

In the New Year Leonora reached a decision over which she had been deliberating for weeks. She sat down at her desk on a crisp January morning and compiled a letter to Lukan. He would know what it had cost her to put her feelings down on paper. He, above any one, would recognise the desperation of her act and the awful risk she was taking. More than that, he would see by the wording of the letter that it was her own guilt she exposed, not his. Fearful that the letter might fall into the wrong hands, she revealed her own feelings without reference to any previous understanding between them. After several attempts she read the final version through and signed it. Her own seal offered the final incriminating touch. For her it was a personal commitment, and with it she was placing a weapon in the hands of an unpredictable and very angry man. The letter read:

> *Mr de Ville,*
> *Knowing that you despise me is a burden I must carry every hour of every day, but however honourable your reasons for hating me, be certain of this simple truth: I love you. Leonora.*

She found Sam Cooper in the kitchen garden, stacking logs against the north-facing wall. She drew him outside the gate and handed him the bound and sealed communication.

'This is for Mr Lukan. Will you take it?'

'Aye, I'll take it,' he nodded gravely. 'Them's satin slippers your wearing ma'am, not warm enough for a morning as cold as this. I'll walk you back inside.'

'Will you hand it to him personally?' she asked. 'Don't give it to Mr Armstrong or Miss Adelaide. Tell them it is from Sir Malcolm and you must give it directly into Mr Lukan's hand.'

Sam glanced down at her distinctive personal seal but made no comment on it. 'Into his own hand,' he said.

'Thank you Sam.' She hesitated, then pushed a velvet pouch into his coat pocket. 'And give him this. Now go quickly, and if he can't be found, bring back the letter and give it to nobody but myself.'

'I'll do that, Miss Leonora.'

'Thank you, Sam.'

He left at once for Mr Lukan's house. He was worried about his mistress. To him it looked as if she had been

547

weeping, and there were faint dark circles below her eyes that indicated sleepless nights. She was obviously not herself. She had come outdoors in satin slippers, regardless of the chill that might strike upward to damage her unborn babes or guarantee them gout or rheumatism in later life. He would have to speak to Miss Anabel about her. It was not his place to do so, but he would not stand by and watch his mistress catch her death of cold for want of more careful watching.

The Forest House had changed in many ways since he last saw it. The gardens had been cleared and several broken fences reset, and he could see that the yard outside the kitchen door had been relaid. The wolfhounds padded forward as he approached the house. He stood quite still, holding his breath as he waited for them to recognise him. Like guards on duty they hovered close by until the door was opened by Robert Armstrong and then, losing interest, the huge dogs loped back to their places in the yard.

Sam noticed a smell of furniture polish in the hall and several pieces of furniture that had not been there a few months ago. The big room on the right remained empty save for its many rugs and its collection of fencing foils, but the room next to it was now a magnificent dining room with sufficient seating for twenty people. On the left of the hall the drawing-room had been completely redecorated and refurnished. Its chimney wall was still adorned with every snare and weapon, every animal and man-trap to be found in the forest, but the rest of the room was changed almost beyond recognition. New drapes had been hung, new carpets laid, new furniture installed, and the lamps standing here and there were as fine as any that could be seen up at the big house.

Lukan de Ville was sitting before the fire in a high-backed chair that was obviously an heirloom, his long legs stretching right across the hearth, his sleeves rolled up above his elbows and a strand of thick black hair falling over one eye. He looked up slowly as Sam Cooper approached, regarding the young man through unfriendly eyes.

'I've brought a letter from the big house, Mr Lukan.'

'You could have left it at the door.'

548

'No sir, I was given orders to deliver it into your own hands or else take it back where it came from.'

Without smiling the man extended one hand to reveal his powerful forearms and thick wrists, and Sam Cooper stepped forward to place the letter in his up-turned palm.

'Thank you, Sam. Was there anything else?'

'Only this sir.' He proffered the pouch. Lukan stared at it but made no move to accept it. Eventually Sam let it come to rest on a nearby table. He knew what it contained. There was a key inside and Sam, like Lukan, knew which door it fitted.

'Anything else?'

'No sir, nothing else.'

'May I offer you some refreshment?'

'No thank you sir.'

Lukan looked at him very closely. Sam suspected that he was about to question him concerning the health of his mistress, but then the dark head nodded and he said instead, 'Thank you, Sam, that will be all.'

He was shown out by the elegant and very amiable Robert Armstrong, who informed him that there was a batch of freshly-baked apple pies cooling on the kitchen table if he cared to pass the back door as he left. Sam thanked him politely and licked his lips, then hurried to the kitchen via the herb garden, taking the longest route to avoid stepping over the lounging wolfhounds. As he passed the drawing room window it seemed to him that the big gypsy was just sitting there by the fire, staring at the unopened letter in his hand.

The kitchen too had undergone drastic alterations. It was clean and bright, with a huge dresser full of sparkling patterned dishes and glowing copper pans on every surface. The neglected stove had been blacked and polished until it shone like ebony with glistening silver trims, and every pot and pan gleamed and winked in the firelight. Even the flagged stone floor, so long the repository for all kinds of kitchen debris, was now scrubbed to its very corners and had a clean and mellowed look about it. Mrs Adelaide Armstrong was a smiling, pink-faced woman who looked at him as if he was the best thing she had rested her eyes upon all week. Sam snatched off his cap and stared at his boots, embarrassed.

'And who might you be, young man?' she asked, her big knife already poised above the golden crust of a plump apple pie.

'I'm Sam Cooper from the big house. I'm Lady Leonora's man.'

She laughed. 'And right proud you sound to be of that, and no mistake. Here, have a slice of pie.'

She slapped a generous portion into his hand. The steam from it was scented with apple and clove and cinnamon, and the hot fruit spilled over into his palm. He danced from one foot to the other, blowing the heat away.

The plump lady watched him eat, still smiling, then asked, 'How fares your mistress, Sam Cooper?'

'She's well enough, so I believe, considering.'

'It will be twins this time, will it?'

'Yes ma'am, so the doctor says.'

She handed him a cup of milk. 'Come on lad, eat your pie. Would you welcome another slice? Yes, I thought you would, strapping young lad like you. There's no need to feel bashful here. Will you tell your mistress the Armstrongs were asking after her? Lovely lady, she is, lovely, kind-hearted lady.'

'Yes, ma'am,' Sam mumbled, his mouth so full that the apple burned his tongue and the crust stuck in hot little pieces to his lips. He cooled his mouth with a gulp of milk and Mrs Armstrong promptly refilled his cup right up to the brim.

'I hope you'll come again Sam,' she said when he was leaving, and he had the feeling her invitation came right from the heart.

'Yes ma'am. There's ... er ... there's my friend Charlie Pickles,' he told her awkwardly. 'He's just a young'n really, but he's been learning to read and write and he's right partial to a slice of apple pie when he can get it.'

'Then you must bring young Charlie along too,' she laughed. 'And there's no need to bother Mr Lukan, just bring yourselves round here to the kitchen and we'll see what we can do for the two of you, won't we, Robert?'

Her husband had entered the kitchen by an inner door. He

beamed now and nodded his greying head.

'Thank you,' Sam said, walking backwards down the steps. 'I'm right grateful to you, Mrs Armstrong.'

He was grinning to himself as he passed the drawing-room window for a second time. He glanced sideways and what he saw gave him cause to slow his step. Lukan de Ville was staring at the now open letter in his hands, and Sam could just make out from where he stood that on the large sheet of mono-grammed paper were written only a few short lines. There was a good light coming from the blazing fire but the man's face was in shadow, his features further concealed by his untidy hair. Even so, it seemed to Sam that his cheeks were glistening, as if something in the note had brought tears to his eyes. As he watched, the gypsy put out his hand and let the sheet of paper fall into the flames. Then he doubled his body forward and cradled his head in his palms while his shoulders rose and fell in small spasms. He looked for all the world as if he wept.

Sam quickly turned his head and walked away. Some things were best not known, especially about a man like Mr Lukan. He rode back along the forest path, the quickest but not the most comfortable route between the two houses. Charlie Pickles ran to meet him as he approached the main stables.

'Mistress is wanting you in the old gatehouse.'

'Is there trouble?'

Charlie shrugged and investigated his right nostril with a grubby forefinger. 'Didn't see no trouble. She's wanting you, that's all.'

'Thank's Charlie. Hey, when did you last have a big slice of apple pie fresh out of the oven?'

'Not for a month or more,' the boy said sullenly. 'That Mrs Norris is fair enough with most things, but she keeps 'er best fruit pies for the gentry and gives little enough to the likes of me.'

Sam dismounted and handed the reins to Charlie. 'Cheer up lad. Mr Lukan's new cook says we're welcome at her kitchen door any time we like to go.'

551

Charlie's face lit with a grin, then became grave and scowling. 'She a gypsy?'

'Who?'

'His cook, her what makes them apple pies we're welcome to. Is she a gypsy woman?'

'Don't be daft, Charlie Pickles. The gypsy woman's gone these many months and won't be coming back. Mr Lukan got shot of her ages ago.'

The two were walking away from each other now, Charlie towards the stable leading the horse, Sam toward the old gatehouse. 'I'll come with you then,' Charlie called over his shoulder. 'When's baking day?'

'Whenever we like,' Sam called after him. 'Any day we like.'

His mistress was waiting for him in the gatehouse. He could tell by the way she whirled on her heels as he entered that she had been pacing up and down the way she did whenever she was agitated or angry. He glanced at her feet and saw that she was wearing the more sensible Hessian boots that would keep the frost from her babies. He would never have guessed that she had two babies due in just a few more weeks. She looked neither fat nor clumsy the way other women did at such times, just beautifully dressed in a different way and as graceful and light on her feet as ever. It was her anxiety that worried him, and those dark shadows under her eyes. He could hear Miss Anabel clattering dishes in the kitchen and wondered if she was aware that all was not well with their mistress.

'Did you see him?'

'Yes ma'am, I saw him and I put the letter right into his hand, just like you said I was to do.'

'What did he say? What message did he send?'

'No message, ma'am.'

'What? But what did he say to the letter?'

'Nothing, Miss Leonora. He didn't say nothing and he didn't send no message.'

She looked crestfallen, and he was suddenly reminded that this capable, sophisticated lady was really no more than a girl. She was several months younger than himself and the bravest, kindest person he had ever known.

'Are you sure?' she asked in a small voice.

'Aye, not a word.'

Sam hated himself for disappointing her. He remembered the day he walked into the Forest House and found them together, and the way Mr Lukan had held her arm in that protective way when he walked her down the stairs. Everyone thought there was no love lost between the two of them but Sam knew better. He knew how the gypsy came and went by the haunted door, and how Miss Leonora set a light in her tower window to bring him there. There was love between them, and now he understood that it had been there all those years ago when Mr Lukan had taken her off the carriage and Sam had dared to threaten him with a riding whip, long before she was promised to Sir Malcolm.

'Can you be sure he read the letter? Did you actually *see* him read it?'

'Yes ma'am, I saw him through the window when I was coming back from the kitchen. He read it right enough.'

She was watching his face, too open and too easily read to hide anything from her. 'And?' she urged. 'And?'

He paused, then said quietly, 'He burned it.'

He saw her eyes widen and her fingers come up to touch her lips. She made a tiny gasping sound that seemed to have a world of suffering in it.

'Miss Anabel!' he called out. 'Miss Anabel, come quick!'

He caught Leonora as she collapsed and lifted her into his arms as Anabel came rushing from the other room.

'Not here, Sam. Bring her to the nursery. Quickly, follow me.'

He hurried after Anabel, carrying his mistress as if she were weightless. They crossed the inner courtyard and slipped through two darkened rooms in succession before reaching the nursery wing via the servants' corridor. Once there he lay her gently on a couch and dropped to his knees beside her.

'I'm sorry, Miss Leonora,' he said, stroking her hand and staring at her with an unhappy expression on his face. 'I'm so sorry.'

Her eyes were closed as she moved her head against a

cushion and murmured, 'Oh Sam, was there nothing ... nothing?'

'I think he wept,' he whispered. 'I wasn't meant to see and I don't know for sure, but he put his head in his hands and I think he wept. Are you listening, Miss Leonora? Did you hear what I said?'

Before he could ascertain if she had in fact heard his whispered words, Anabel shoved him roughly to one side and took full charge of the situation. 'Out, Sam Cooper, away from here at once, the rest is women's work. Go fetch Sir Malcolm and tell him the doctor's needed.'

He felt a shiver of fresh anxiety. 'Are the babies to be born now?' She was pushing him backwards out of the room while he stared beyond her, watching his mistress moving as if in pain on the couch. He shook his head as if by doing so he could alter the natural course of things. 'No, Miss Anabel. They can't be born now, it's too early.'

'Aye, it's too early, and if you don't get out of here this minute it will be too late to help either her or them.'

He ran then, just turned on his heels and ran from the room. His footsteps could be heard stamping down the wooden stairs and along the servants' corridor, and the sound of his voice echoed through the house as he shouted for assistance for the mistress.

The suspected miscarriage was, to everyone's intense relief, a false alarm. Leonora had simply collapsed in a faint, perhaps because she had taken so little food at breakfast, and Sam Cooper's presence of mind had prevented the faint from terminating in a serious fall. They told Malcolm that she had been taken ill as she took her daily exercise on the terraces. Sam was only too willing to confirm the story rather than be called upon to explain his visit to the Forest House. Had that become necessary he was prepared to say that he had gone there simply to beg a slice of Mrs Armstrong's apple pie, preferring to suffer the consequences of that rather than betray Miss Leonora's trust in him.

'Thank Heaven. Thank Heaven.' Sir Malcolm Cavendish stood with his back resting against the wall. He had just

554

stepped into the hall after being informed by Sir Marcus that neither Leonora nor her babies were in any immediate danger. His eyes were closed and there was a layer of perspiration on his forehead.

A very uncomfortable Sam Cooper was sitting in a chair clutching his hat in one hand and a glass of port wine in the other. In his pocket was a golden guinea, the first he had ever seen at close quarters, his reward for acting so promptly in taking care of his mistress. The hall dividing the nursery rooms from the bedrooms was as wide as a room and so lavishly furnished that Sam became acutely aware of his outdoor boots and his grubby fingernails. The Earl and Sir Malcolm seemed to have forgotten he was there. He stared at the wine in his glass and shared their relief.

'I confess to being far from happy about her,' Sir Oscar said, pacing the room in spite of the pronounced limp that now demanded almost constant use of a cane. 'According to Marcus everything is progressing as normal and she is in good health, but anyone can see she's not herself. It worries me. Do you know what ails her?'

Malcolm shook his head. 'I understand that a lowering of the spirits is quite normal during the waiting months, even in an otherwise healthy young woman. I have already discussed it with Marcus and he suggests we simply watch her very carefully and see that she remains as calm as possible until the lying-in.'

'It cannot be easy for you,' his father observed.

'We must all forget what happened to poor Grace,' Malcolm replied. 'Leonora is glum enough already. If she suspects our concern, she may leap to the conclusion that Marcus has confided something to us that we are keeping from her. She is strong and healthy and the twins are doing fine, so for the present at least we must be content with that.'

Perched on the edge of his chair Sam Cooper listened to their conversation with a twinge of conscience and a fierce sense of loyalty. He knew full well what ailed Her Ladyship. Some awful thing had happened between her and Mr Lukan that kept them apart from each other when they wanted to be together. It must have been something serious to make her ill and cause that big ogre of a man to break down and weep. As yet Sam understood little about the mysteries governing the love between a man and a woman, but what he did know filled him with more fear than wonder. It seemed to him there was more pain than pleasure in it.

'Will you do that for me Sam?'

'What?' He leaped to his feet, splashing port wine down his pants. They had been watching him, speaking to him while his thoughts had been on Mr Lukan and Miss Leonora. He felt a guilty flush rise to his cheeks as he gaped from one master to the other in a small panic.

'It's quite all right,' Sir Oscar said. He smiled as if the lad had done no wrong. 'We are well aware that the incident must have caused quite a scare for you. You did extremely well, young man, and now my son wishes to know if you will be so kind as to show even more diligence in the future. Stay close to your mistress at all times, let her take your arm while out walking, watch out for any signs that she is unwell. Will you do that?'

'Yes sir. I'll do that right gladly sir.'

'Forget your stable duties,' Malcolm said. 'I'll set another man on at once to take your place.'

'Thank you sir.'

Malcolm smiled as he took the untouched glass of port from the young man's hand. He could see he was neither a drinker nor a conversationalist, and he knew he would be doing him a kindness by dismissing him. 'You did extremely well today Sam. You may go now.'

'Thank you sir.'

The nervous young man bowed himself out and reached the servants' corridor with a sigh of relief to be free of that elevated company. It was not for the likes of him to sit in a fine chair and drink port wine from a crystal glass with the likes of them. He fingered the guinea in his pocket and wondered if he dare return to the Forest House and ask Mr Lukan to send a message to the lady, just to put her heart and mind at rest. It wasn't much to ask if it would make her well again and take

556

that sad expression from her eyes. He suspected that the gypsy had not been to the haunted door since harvest time, and it seemed to him the long separation only served to hurt them both, each one being made as miserable as the other. The right and wrong of it did not occur to him. The sorrow in Leonora's eyes was all that mattered.

'I don't know what to do,' he muttered, wringing his cap between his hands. 'I don't know what to do to help her.'

In the end he knew he could do no more than stay close to her and protect her trust and be ready and willing to help her in any way he could. His courage was limited. He doubted he would ever find enough of it to speak out face to face with Mr Lukan on the subject.

CHAPTER TWENTY-SIX

I

Despite the rumours that had been circulating for months, the advertisement placed by Sir Oscar Cavendish in *The Times* of February 14th created a flurry of excitement. Money began changing hands all over London two days before publication when it was first whispered that a statement was to be issued through the pages of the press. Some speculated that the statement would constitute an emphatic denial, others that the Earl had at last decided to confirm what half the city had taken as fact for over twenty years, that Jonathan Shelley was his illegitimate son. Still others wagered upon a middle course, neither admission nor denial, designed to hamper wagging tongues without settling the issue either way. There was a tremendous rush to buy the newspaper on the day the account appeared, and at least fifty per cent of the buyers were more than satisfied with the outcome. Sir Oscar Cavendish, Sixth Earl of Beresford, acknowledged the young man as his son and rejected all attempts by creditors and tradesmen to make the boy responsible for the debts of his stepfather, Herbert Shelley. At the same time he offered his protection to Charles and Joseph Shelley and declared them free of all their father's unmet obligations.

'Let any man dispute it now who dare,' he growled to his dinner guests that evening. 'The brothers may count themselves part of this family, and anyone seeking to quarrel with any one of them must be prepared to address himself to *me*.'

London buzzed with the news of it for days. The history of that old near-scandal and Francine's hasty marriage to Herbert Shelley was aired afresh with many embellishments. Those who had kept her within their social circle boasted as much at every opportunity, while those who had ostracised her in favour of the Earl's Countess now found themselves with every reason to regret their choice. And all those who had closed their doors against her at the end were swift to deny that they had done as much.

Amelia Lacey fell squarely into the latter category. She and her husband Frank Alexander Lacey were wealthy and well-respected in the city, and they valued their social standing above all else. She was a woman of good breeding who had suffered disfigurement in her youth when the white lead and vinegar contained in the fashionable cosmetics of the day destroyed her complexion. Her face was now a mask created fresh each day with a kinder, gentler paint and powder. Her baldness she hid beneath expensive wigs, her scarred neck behind pretty lace ruffles. Like many women of her time, she had been cruelly robbed of the very beauty she had been at pains to enhance. Perhaps for that reason more than any other she was determined to maintain her good position in society. Leonora Shelley had placed her in an impossible position when she begged shelter for her dying mother during her last declining weeks. A room was all she wanted, a clean room with a comfortable bed where Francine could die with dignity after her home was so wickedly stolen from her.

'We must take her in,' Frank Lacey had insisted at the time.

'We will do no such thing,' Amelia had declared.

'We must, my dear. We owe that girl too much to turn away her mother in her hour of need. Have you forgotten so soon the debt we owe her?'

Amelia had not forgotten. It was Leonora Shelley who had comforted their seventeen-year-old daughter Estelle as she lay dying of a dreadful breast infection. And it was Leonora who helped conceal the fact of the girl's pregnancy as well as her mutilated breasts, so allowing her to go to her grave without so much as a stain upon her character. No, Amelia Lacey had not forgotten. She still possessed the ugly wire rings that had caused her daughter's death, and the brooch Leonora had refused to accept as payment for her discretion.

'One room is all she asks,' her husband had pressed. 'The Christian sanctuary of one small corner of our home. It is the least we can do.'

But Amelia had been adamant. To offer succour to Francine would be to fly in the very face of public opinion. The woman was brought to ruin by her husband and had obviously lost the long-standing favour and protection of her cousin the Earl of Beresford. Amelia could ill afford to make such a sacrifice. Whatever debt she owed Leonora would not be repaid by social suicide.

Now, two years on from those events, Frank Lacey carefully folded his copy of *The Times* and set it aside, then looked into his wife's expressionless face. 'We should have helped her then.'

'It's easy to say that now,' Amelia said through her tiny painted lips. 'It is easy enough to be wise after the event.'

'And now she is the wife of Sir Malcolm Cavendish and her brother the acknowledged son of the Earl of Beresford. She has the power to destroy us, Amelia, if she bears a grudge.'

'Then let us hope she allows the dead to lie in peace,' his wife said tightly. 'For her mother's sake as well as our own dear daughter's. She promised us faithfully she would say nothing to discredit Estelle. If she has any decency at all she will maintain her silence.'

'Ah, but see how things have changed since then,' Frank Lacey said, waving the folded newspaper in the air. 'Just see how things have turned around since then.'

Leonora was more than gratified by the Earl's very honourable public gesture. Wherever Joseph had fled to, he would be sure to learn of it sooner or later. He rarely taxed his poor eyesight by reading newspapers, but someone, somewhere, would surely recognise his name and rush to inform him that he was free to return to the family who loved him. It was just a matter of time, a matter of waiting for gossip and word of mouth to do its work. This had become her dearest wish, to have her brother back. She had taken care of Charles and secured Jonathan's future in a way her mother could never have thought possible. Now all that remained was for Joseph to come home and her family would be complete. Now that the matter had been made public she also felt a deep sense of satisfaction in knowing that Herbert Shelley, wherever he was hiding, would once again become a wanted man. No longer could his creditors pursue the sons in the absence of their father. Her brothers were free men at last, and Herbert Shelley must take sole responsibility for his crimes.

With two months still to wait until her lying-in, Leonora's health remained sound but her spirits did not improve. By now she was convinced that she had driven Lukan away for ever, and the prospect of that weighed heavily upon her. She rarely left the house but chose instead to spend her time writing, reading or sewing indoors. She had ordered rooms on the ground floor to be aired and furnished for her temporary use, and from there she could walk directly on to the inner courtyard where she had been in the habit of holding her garden parties. Sam Cooper and several labourers had worked long hours to erect a decorative trellis around the pond. This was to act as a barrier so that neither Leonora nor William, who had found his feet at last, might trip and fall into the empty tank. There were days when she spent much of her time there, pacing the walkways, making circuit after circuit in her restlessness. Charlie Pickles scoured the hedgerows and parkland for winter blossoms, the woods for mistletoe, holly and ivy so that his mistress might be encouraged to continue with her exquisitely illustrated floral calendar. She had in those bleak days little heart for sketching and even less for the more disciplined skills of water-colouring. Instead she accepted the boy's gifts with gratitude and sadly watched them perish in their vases.

Sam was her constant companion now, often reading to her in his faltering way, sometimes just listening while she talked about her family in the days before Sam went as second groom to the house in Garden Square. She never mentioned Lukan de Ville and nor did he. She had made it clear that what took place on that unhappy day in January was not to be referred to. He frequently wondered if she had understood his words that day and known that Lukan de Ville had wept over her note. And still he feared the consequences of giving her a falsehood by mistake. Better a comfort unreceived than something taken as truth when it lacked any sound foundation. As time went by the thing seemed more and more unlikely, that words on paper could have reduced that fearsome gypsy to tears.

Sam was present in the centre courtyard on the day Lady Vivienne Cavendish arrived unexpectedly from her aunt and uncle's rented house in Rome. She swept into the inner courtyard unannounced and still wearing her travelling clothes, a resentful, self-assured young woman with a purpose. Her coat was of burgundy cloth with fur trims and a hood, her hat a beautiful affair in red and black, with huge feathers and slender decorated pins. She looked mature and lovely after her time abroad, and marched through the courtyard to where the family gathered at tables in the shelter of the far wall. At sight of her Leonora half-rose from her seat, reminded of her own dramatic entry into that very courtyard three years earlier. She had come in search of survival and stayed to win an earldom, and now, for an instant, feared that another woman came to depose her.

The Earl rose to his feet, followed by Sir Marcus Shaw and Malcolm. In a nearby corner Sam Cooper jumped up and pulled off his cap.

'Vivienne!' Sir Oscar exclaimed. 'What on earth are you doing here?'

'Need you ask?' she demanded, tossing a copy of *The Times* on to the table between them. 'How could you do this to us, father? How *could* you?'

'You were warned,' he said curtly, offended by his daughter's attitude. 'You had a full explanation by letter.'

'What letter? I had no letter.'

'I wrote to you in Milan, and if you did not claim the letter it was to be forwarded to your next port of call in Germany.'

'We never reached Milan,' she said. 'We have not chosen to leave Rome for months. My aunt and uncle are too well settled to be uprooted and I am heartily sick of travelling from one place to another simply for the sake of making a fashionable *grand tour.*'

'You hate travelling and yet you made the trip here, in February? Damn it, girl, you have a contrary streak to your nature. Be seated and let us all get off our legs.'

Vivienne sat herself down in the nearest chair and faced her father with a defiant toss of her head. 'I will have an explanation if you please sir.'

'Then might I suggest we discuss the matter privately, perhaps when you have rested?'

She laughed at that. 'Privately? My dear Papa, *the matter*, as you call it, has already been discussed at every table in the English speaking world. We are a laughing-stock. At home and abroad we are the butt of every after-dinner joke and snide remark.'

The Earl took a deep breath and tried to make allowances for the circumstances. 'Look Vivienne, it was never my intention to embarrass any member of my family. I regret that my letter did not reach you, but I can hardly be held responsible for changes in your plans that you chose to keep to yourself.'

'But you *are* responsible for this,' she retorted, indicating the newspaper.

Leonora watched their faces. She could see that the Earl was exercising patience, respecting his daughter's right to express her feelings of shock and indignation. Malcolm's fists were clenched on the table before him and his eyes betrayed his pique at his sister's rude intrusion. She could also see that

Vivienne was arrogant and very angry, too much of both to benefit from either.

'This is humiliating,' the girl declared.

'It must be faced,' the Earl said gently.

'But why? Why did you have to admit to such a thing?'

'Because it is the truth.'

'And Jonathan Shelley is twenty-two years old,' she reminded him. 'Why was the truth hidden for so long, only to be flaunted now like a personal victory? My poor mama must be writhing in her grave at this disgusting turn of events.'

'Have a care how you speak to your father,' Malcolm warned.

'Your mother knew the truth before she died,' the Earl informed her.

His words inflamed her. 'What? My God! You *told* her?'

'I did. It was my duty, once I knew for sure.'

'And is that what killed her?' She jumped to her feet, tipping her chair to the ground with a clatter. 'I demand to know the whole of it. Did your confessed adultery kill my mother?'

Leonora heard Malcolm gasp and saw Sir Oscar stiffen as if he had been struck in the face. She laid her hand across his arm, hoping to hold back the reins of his temper. She needed to hear the rest of it. If Vivienne had come directly from Rome it was almost a certainty that Horace knew of his father's public announcement. It was in Leonora's interests to know exactly how the news had been received.

When there was no immediate response from her father Vivienne pressed on in blissful ignorance of her folly, her voice swiftly rising to a semi-hysterical whine. Her family had given her sufficient rope and she, faithful only to her own capricious nature, seemed bent on hanging herself.

'How do you think poor Horace feels about all this?' she demanded. 'How do you think it effects *him*?'

Here Malcolm cut in, smiling good-naturedly in an attempt to defuse a potentially explosive situation. Without rising, he righted Vivienne's chair and patted the seat. 'Oh come now, Vivienne. Don't waste your finer sentiments on Horace. He can hardly feign surprise at this particular disclosure, since he has claimed to know of it for years. At school he took a vicious pleasure in insulting Mrs Shelley to her sons' faces. He made no secret of his conviction that Jonathan Shelley was our brother.'

'*Half-brother*,' she corrected. 'And you are too much a fool to know what you are talking about.' When Malcolm made as if to rise she slapped his shoulder to shove him back into his seat, her volatile temper slipping beyond her control. She pointed an accusing finger at Leonora, her voice a shriek and her grey eyes filled with animosity. 'I blame her for this. First she creeps in from nowhere to feather her nest at Horace's expense, then his inheritance is handed over, lock, stock and barrel to her brat, and now *this*.' She snatched up the newspaper and hurled it into her father's lap. 'And what will become of *my* inheritance while she and her brother rule the roost at Beresford? Perhaps she has designs on seeing that too divided out amongst her litter of Shelley whelps?'

'Now just one moment . . .' Leonora began.

Vivienne rounded on her, her fists clenched and her eyes blazing. 'And who is to say you didn't have a hand in mother's death?' she screeched. 'She hated the Shelleys, she hated *all* of them. Never in a thousand years would she willingly have accepted *you* as her nurse and keeper.' She looked around at the others, wild-eyed and uncaring of the consequences of her outburst. 'She tricked my mother, don't you see? She tricked us all. That Shelley woman has wormed her way among us and now she seeks to install her brother also.'

'Enough! Enough!' The Earl sprang to his feet. 'By the gods, my girl I'll hear no more of this. This is your brother Horace speaking. He sent you here to play the viper's role on his behalf. He hides like a coward behind his sister's skirts and you have not the wit to recognise his use of you for what it is.'

'I too have rights here,' she insisted incautiously.

'I'll give you more than rights, my girl, if you let loose that tongue of yours with one more word.'

'I will not acknowledge your bastard as my brother,' she screamed into her father's face. 'And I will never believe that *she* had my mother's blessing.'

He raised his hand to strike her but Leonora, half rising, grabbed his arm and held on tightly.

'Get out!' he ordered. 'Get out of my sight before I strike you down where you stand!'

Vivienne stood her ground and for a moment it seemed that she would push her father's fury to its limits, but then she saw how far she had strayed from her original intent and realised that she had over-played her hand. She cast around for an ally and found none. Even Sir Marcus Shaw was on his feet now, as was the servant in the corner and the woman called Anabel, all staring at her as if she were a stranger, an unwanted intruder in her own home. Her anger spent and all her courage with it, she turned on her heels and fled from the courtyard.

Still holding the Earl's arm, Leonora pulled herself fully upright. As she did so she let her cloak fall open to reveal the bulge that would remind everyone of her condition. Both Sam and Sir Malcolm stepped forward to offer their assistance but she waved them aside, her face tight and pale. 'Must I defend myself against these charges?' she demanded of the Earl. 'Must I?'

Sir Oscar turned and looked into her eyes, and for a moment he was at a loss for words. Was it mere coincidence that Vivienne had voiced his own deepest fears, the dark suspicions that had once threatened to destroy his pleasure in his son's marriage and his grandson's birth?

'Must I?' Leonora asked again.

He shook his head, reaching for her hands. He wanted to believe in her innocence. All he had ever wanted was to be able to trust her, to believe in her innocence. 'Of course you need not defend yourself against such mindless accusations,' he said, wishing he could be as convinced as the words suggested. 'Such talk is nonsense, mischievous nonsense.'

Leonora leaned against him with a sigh and whispered, 'Thank you.'

'I'll see that Vivienne leaves first thing in the morning,' Malcolm said. His features were set in a cold expression and a

566

small pulse was throbbing visibly in his neck. Other than that his anger was contained.

'You will do no such thing,' his father countered. 'I will not have that venomous young woman under my roof for a single night. Show her the door.'

Leonora gripped his hands and shook her head. 'Please reconsider. Don't turn her from her own home without so much as a meal to break her journey. Please don't send her away like this.'

'No Leonora. This is not the first time your sympathy for Vivienne has been misplaced. I will not tolerate her presence here. She leaves at once.'

'Please,' she repeated. 'We cannot let her go unrested.'

Sir Oscar looked at her steadily, seeing only the pallor in her face and the deep concern in her eyes. 'Very well,' he finally conceded. 'She may stay the night at Oakwood Lodge. One night, Malcolm, and not an hour longer. See that she goes from there first thing in the morning.'

'I'll see to it,' Malcolm said, then turned to his wife and asked, 'Are you all right, my dear?'

'Of course she is not all right,' his father answered on her behalf. 'She is meant to stay calm and relaxed, not to be placed under attack by a mad woman. Look to your sister Malcolm, while I see Leonora safely to her rooms.' He patted the hand held in the crook of his arm. 'You are too soft-hearted for your own good, my dear. Most women would have wanted her off the premises without delay.'

Leonora smiled and leaned more heavily on his arm as they walked away from the tables. She felt she could afford to be magnanimous. 'I want no family quarrels on either my account or Jonathan's, Sir Oscar. Vivienne is young and head-strong, and much braver than I to risk provoking you in that way. I think you are right, her brother put her up to it.'

'And I think you are too soft-hearted,' he repeated thought-fully. 'It is not the Cavendish way to show such leniency toward an enemy.'

Leonora smiled again, knowing he had no inkling of the vengeful streak inherent in her own nature. She had gained a great deal from Vivienne's ill-advised invasion of their privacy. It was clear that Horace was exerting his influence over her, for that headstrong young girl was not clever enough to have formed for herself the suspicions she voiced so eloquently. The foolish creature could do little harm now that she had exposed herself as nothing more than the inept pawn of Horace Cavendish. Lacking the head for clever intrigue, she had set herself not only against Leonora but against her uncompromising father and her powerful elder brother, neither of whom were inclined to suffer her foolish tantrums gladly. Poor Vivienne would never learn to control her fiery disposition, the temperature of it was set too high for that. Whatever her prior intention in returning so dramatically to Beresford Hall, she could now only consider the visit a total failure. She would be allowed to cool her heels at Oakwood Lodge for a night, and then retrace the steps of her impetuous and ill-advised journey, unaware that she had actually done her sister-in-law a service. Leonora was warned that she had enemies in Rome. She would count on Sir Oscar's disfavour, subtly nurtured at regular intervals, to keep them there.

II

The news that so inflamed Vivienne Cavendish after setting the capital buzzing with speculation was not slow in reaching the ears of Herbert Shelley. In Munich he had styled himself Sir Herbert Wise, successful banker and gentleman of means, now retired and living quietly with his widowed daughter and her two-year-old son. In the three years since his hasty removal from England he had watched his fortunes dwindle with alarming rapidity. Gambling had always been his Achilles' heel. The thrill of the games and the need to play the peacock and live out his vision of his own importance might yet prove to be the ruin of him. For a whole year this self-styled gentleman and his small family had resided in the

568

better quarter of the city alongside royalty in exile, flamboyant society figures, professional gamblers and impoverished gentry, all boasting extravagant tastes and shallow pockets. These practised, skilful predators had fed upon his vanity and all but picked him clean before he found the will to extricate himself from their hungry clutches.

In desperation he fled to Vienna and took a much smaller house in more modest surroundings. Here he claimed neither title nor wealth to attract the interest of professional parasites. For months he was forced to live modestly and exercise a painful discipline over the amounts of money he squandered at the gaming tables. His fortunes made a brief upsurge when certain fringe investments, though risky at the outset, came unexpectedly to early profit. Some months later he suffered yet another setback when he attempted, with a rash indifference to his shrinking coffers, to repeat the process.

'You throw good money after bad,' his daughter Helen complained after every failure. Her rebukes were many and often cutting but she, whose interests fluctuated between the bedroom and the dining table, would fare no better if she held the purse-strings.

Apart from Herbert's manservant, they kept two maids, a woman and a girl, some cheap occasional help and a wet-nurse to attend the child. At sixteen Helen had learned to be no more than an indifferent mother and an uncaring mistress of her father's household, preferring instead to leave every chore to the servants. The birth of her first child and the recent conception of another threatened to increase her already ample girth two-fold, a prospect which troubled neither her nor her doting parent. She was voluptuous and greedy in her appetites, a fat, much-pampered, pretty child who still could do no wrong in her father's eyes.

Neither a change of identity, three long years in exile, nor the availability of Helen had reduced the carnal needs of Herbert Shelley. He continued to take his sexual pleasures where and when it suited him, using the women in his employ or buying his satisfaction on the streets. And yet his daughter was still his major source of happiness, as self-indulgent in matters of the flesh as she was at the dinner table, and as pliable as putty in his hands. She had given him a son and mocked him openly and with good humour for his disappointment. She knew, as he did, that a female would have better suited his particular tastes.

He received his copy of *The Times* for February 14th, 1826, by way of the girl who came each afternoon to help the cook prepare the family's main meal of the day. It was one of Herbert's little economies to take his newspaper several days late and well-fingered by its original owner, in this case a doctor whose premises were cleaned twice weekly by the same obliging maid-of-all-work. He was instantly incensed by the news from England. He rampaged through the house in a flaming temper, terrorising the servants and venting his fury upon everyone who came within range of it. His son, a nervous, overweight little boy, shrieked in alarm and fled to the arms of his nurse.

'A cuckoo in my nest,' Shelley raged, flinging the newspaper in Helen's direction. 'For all those years I nurtured a Cavendish cuckoo in my nest and gave respectability to a woman who was, it seems, no better than a common whore.'

'Sir Oscar paid you well for his bastard's upkeep,' Helen reminded him with quiet malice. 'And for Charles's welfare too, as I recall.'

Her father chose to ignore the insinuation in her words. 'Francine must have been pregnant on her wedding day!' he fumed. 'That fine, well-bred woman never once allowed me to forget that she had married beneath herself, yet she was spoiled before I ever laid a finger on her. She was pregnant, damn her, carrying her cousin's bastard when she made her solemn wedding vows *to me*!'

Helen pouted sulkily. 'And now my sister is Mistress of Beresford and my brother owned as the Earl's illegitimate son, while I must live in this god-forsaken place like an outcast. It isn't fair.'

Herbert snorted loudly at that. 'Your sister was always a crafty, conniving minx. She's too much like her mother, too much a Cavendish. By God, that strutting Earl of Beresford

570

probably sired her too.' Herbert's furious pacing brought him to the door. He turned the key in the lock and began to unfasten his clothes, still ranting and raving over the turn of events in England. 'My daughter Mistress of Beresford indeed! My son a Cavendish bastard! And Francine, my wife, *my wife*, bringing another man's brat into my bed. By God, a decent man should be amply compensated for injury of this magnitude. There should be payment in cash for the hurts and indignities those two have forced me to endure these many, many years on their behalf.'

Helen laughed as she began to unlace the bodice of her frock. 'That's nonsense and you know it, father. Besides, you had your chance three years ago and lost it. You snatched a pittance and ran for safety when you could have claimed a dozen times as much, had you but shown a little less haste and a touch more imagination.'

'Imagination be damned,' he spat. 'My creditors were like a wolf-pack at my heels.'

'And neither Jonathan nor Charles will be their scapegoat after this,' Helen said, indicating the crumpled newspaper. 'Your creditors can no longer be pacified with hopes of eventual payment on your behalf, and this scandal will surely stir them into fresh action against you. You promised we would return to England when the dust of your leaving settled, but how can we? How can we *ever* go back now? It will take much more than an altered surname and a fine new beard to keep you in anonymity after *this* disclosure.'

'Damn them! Damn them all for their dishonesty. I've lost a fortune here, a certain fortune.' Herbert's voice had become a high-pitched wail, his face a purple mask of anger. He reached out to fondle his daughter's plump white buttocks, kneading and knuckling the dimpled flesh. 'What a wealth of compensation has slipped through my fingers for want of an honest and timely admission from Francine Shelley of her guilt. My God, I'll not be forced to countenance such a scandalous state of affairs. I'll have my recompense for this. One way or another, I'll have my entitlement.'

Helen chuckled softly as she lay across the sofa with her

571

bodice undone and her eyes half-closed. 'You will never manage to extract a willing penny from any one of them, father,' she told him. 'But perhaps their dear little sister might succeed where you would surely fail.'

'You?' he sneered, staring down at her full, veined breasts. 'They would not even condescend to call you sister, swelled as you are with their father's brat and having a two-year-old at home that is both brother and nephew to them all.'

As her father hoisted himself on to the couch beside her, Helen smiled again and said, 'We'll see. When this babe is born I'll return to them a virgin, an innocent child whose only crime has been her steadfast loyalty to her father.'

'Oh, you clever girl,' he chuckled, nuzzling his face against her breasts. 'You clever, clever little whore to think of such a plan. And why not, my little innocent? If your sister and brothers have fallen upon easy times then you are fully entitled to your share of their good fortune.'

III

At Fairfax Manor, Roger Reece Fairfax and the grossly overweight Christopher were once again at loggerheads with each other. Together they resembled a comic illustration from some irreverent satirical publication. One cousin was tall and neatly built, an elegant man of moderate attractions. The other was as round as he was high, a breathless, featureless individual floundering beneath a mountain of obesity. The younger man, now aiming for a lucrative career in politics, was about to sharpen the teeth of his ambition upon the finer feelings of the banker.

'Y-you h-had n-no right,' the fat man stuttered in petulant, complaining tones. 'Th-that b-bureau c-contained m-my m-most p-personal p-papers.'

'You lying ape,' Roger Fairfax accused. 'That bureau, my dear cousin, contained another person's private letters.'

'Y-you had n-no right t-to t-take th-them.'

'As much right as you when you hid them there in the first place.'

'Y-you are a th-thief, s-sir.'

'And what are you?'

Christopher fell silent, his lower lip thrust out petulantly. 'H-how d-did you kn-know?' he demanded.

The younger man smiled. 'I simply used my common sense,' he said. 'It is quite obvious that those young men would wish to correspond with their sister, and equally obvious that you, my lovesick cousin, would wish to deprive her of the pleasure of hearing from them. I know you for what you are, fat man. Your disappointment has made you petty and cruel. While the Earl of Beresford makes his threats and old Nigel protests his innocence, those missing letters could only have been purloined by an interested third party. *You*.'

'W-well, it isn't f-fair. It isn't f-fair. And d-did you n-need to t-take a knife t-to the l-lock l-like a c-common house-b-breaker?'

'Would you have given me the key, had I asked for it?'

'I m-most c-certainly w-would n-not.'

Roger spread his hands and smiled triumphantly. 'Well then, I rest my case.'

Christopher waddled across the room to the ornate rosewood bureau with its neat inlays and fancy edging. He ran his hands over the slashes and splinters left behind by Roger's knife. 'You've d-damaged it b-beyond r-repair. It's r-ruined.'

'Nonsense, call in a craftsman and send the bill to me.'

'I w-want m-my l-letters b-back,' Christopher wailed.

'They are neither yours to receive nor mine to give.'

'W-what use are th-they t-to y-you? G-give th-them b-back.'

Roger shook his head. 'Not to you, my fat friend.'

'What th-then, t-to L-Lord B-Beresford?'

'Who else?'

'B-but you c-can't, you c-can't d-do th-that.'

'Oh don't look so alarmed, Christopher. I hate to see you trembling and wobbling like a jelly pudding deprived of its mould. Relax. Keep a grip on yourself. I suppose I will find some way of keeping you safe from his Lordship's wrath.'

'I w-won't a-allow it. I w-won't l-let you g-give th-those l-letters t-to Oscar C-Cavendish.'

Roger picked up his copy of *The Times* and waved it about as if to attract the attention of a half-wit. 'My God, Christopher, do you comprehend nothing outside your own petty disappointments? These letters are from the Earl's *son*. They are addressed to his daughter-in-law, the wife of his heir. How in hell's name did you expect to keep him from knowing about them?'

'He w-won't know u-unless you t-tell him.'

'Oh? Now there's a clever statement,' his cousin sneered. 'Do you think Jonathan Shelley and his brother Charles lack the tongues to speak of this?'

'I'll d-deny the l-letters were ever d-delivered h-here,' Christopher stammered. 'It w-will b-be th-their w-word against m-mine.'

'And who will the Cavendish believe, you fool, a Fairfax or his own son?'

Christopher's jowls wobbled and he seemed to be on the verge of bursting into tears. He rested his face on the comfortable cushions of his several chins and studied his meaty fingers, joining them with some difficulty across his bloated belly. He pouted his lower lip and it was damp and quivering. 'She w-was t-to have b-been m-mine. I had f-first c-claim on h-her. It isn't f-fair th-that M-Malcolm C-Cavendish t-took her.'

'Oh, for Heaven's sake, who promised you that life would ever be *fair*?' Roger demanded. 'It can only be what each man makes of it. Look, you made mistakes and lost yourself a filly, so why not go out and find yourself a replacement and be done with all this schoolgirl snivelling and moping. Find someone else, you idiot. One pair of thighs is pretty much like another when a man's blood is warmed.'

'I w-want h-her. I w-want L-Leonora.'

'Then eat your heart out, fat man, for you'll never have her now!'

Exasperated, Roger snatched up the bundle of letters and,

pausing only long enough to drain his brandy glass, strode from the room. Left alone with his misery, Christopher continued to study the fleshy pinkness of his hands and indulge the tremulous activity of his lower lip. When he heard the front door slam he crossed to the window and watched his cousin, enviously slim and agile, hoist himself astride his horse and ride away. Only then did he reach inside his coat for the letters Roger had failed to find when he broke open the bureau, the letters from Leonora's favourite brother, her twin. These were his real prize. He had watched the way she fawned over the boy, seen the softness in her eyes when she looked at him. She loved him best, and that would be Christopher's revenge.

He spread the pages out across the table and wondered if by now he knew every word of every letter by heart. With a shuddering sigh he reached for a bowl of battered strawberries dipped in sugar and coated with golden honey. He used a spoon to scoop one into his mouth, liked the taste and crammed in another before the first was eaten. A dribble of honey fell on one of the well-fingered sheets of writing paper. He wiped it away with one finger, then sucked the stain of sweetness from his skin. He was not beaten yet. He still had something left with which to hurt the woman who had destroyed his happiness. He would find a safer hiding place for these, a place where prying eyes and thieving hands would never find them. Joseph Shelley was the one she loved the most, and if Christopher Fairfax had his way she would never see her twin again as long as either of them lived.

While Christopher ate his battered strawberries and pondered upon the pleasures of revenge, Roger Reece Fairfax rode to Kingswood and from there dispatched an urgent note to His Lordship Sir Oscar Cavendish. At the Royal Oak he ate a fine luncheon consisting of best Severn salmon served in a savoury pastry basket, venison pie, plum pudding and several cheeses. After this he set his feet on a low stool and relaxed before a blazing fire with a half-bottle of unexpectedly decent sherry. He was joined there later by Percy Bell, a little, busy, balding man who was to be party to his meeting with the Earl.

Sir Oscar Cavendish arrived promptly at half past two in the company of his lifelong friend, Sir Giles Powell. The two stepped into the belly of the inn like kings into a commoner's humble parlour, imperious and full of their own importance. Roger stepped forward to meet them and, the introductions over, all four seated themselves at a quiet corner table. Fresh drinks were brought and poured and then the Earl, impatient of mysteries, came directly to the point.

'Your note says you are in possession of something which belongs to me, Mr Reece.'

The younger man nodded. 'Certain papers, Sir Oscar.'

'What papers?'

Roger Reece indicated the newspaper lying on the table between them, then looked at Sir Oscar intently. What he saw was an arrogant, insular man, a cold-eyed aristocrat with little concern and even less sympathy for lesser men. He saw the cause of his family's first prosperity, now too tightly kept under Cavendish rein to ever reach its full potential unless the breach between them and their neighbours could be healed.

'The matter concerns your son, Jonathan Shelley,' he said carefully. 'And I would first ask that you forebear to hear the whole of what I have to say, not just a part of it.'

Sir Oscar's eyes narrowed briefly. 'Is there good reason why I might not be inclined to hear you out?'

'Yes sir, there is. I am quite at liberty to lie and gain your favour, or speak the honest truth, and all of it, and risk your hostility. You, sir, must be the one to decide what tactic I should employ.'

'I want the truth,' Sir Oscar snapped. 'I have not come here to indulge in verbal gamesmanship.'

'Then you will undertake to hear me out?'

Sir Oscar bristled. 'Should I do less than that, since I am here at all?'

'Your reputation might suggest otherwise,' Roger smiled. 'If you will forgive me, Sir Oscar, the alacrity of your temper is legendary.'

Now it was Sir Oscar's turn to smile. 'All right, young man, you have my word, spoken before these witnesses here with us.

So long as you are prepared to speak truthfully, I will agree to hear you out.'

'Thank you.' He felt he had achieved a victory. Resisting the urge to smile again he sat back in his chair and surveyed the Earl with what he hoped was an open but not defiant stare. 'I allowed myself to be introduced as Roger Reece, which is but two thirds of my rightful name.'

'And the rest of it?'

'Fairfax.'

The air between them suddenly became charged. Sir Giles's involuntary intake of breath was for a while the only sound at the table. Old wars and new resentments could be seen in the Earl's features, mistrust in the slow narrowing of his clear blue eyes, iron self-control in the clenching of his fists.

'Continue,' he said at last.

The younger man obliged. 'I am the nephew of Nigel Fairfax and a man of politics rather than banking. I recently discovered certain letters tucked away in an unused file in the accountant's office of *Tilbury, Reece and Fairfax*. It seems they were delivered to my uncle's country home and handed over to a clerk in a well-meaning attempt to spare the feelings of my cousin Christopher. They were addressed, you see, to *Mrs Christopher Fairfax*.'

Sir Oscar's eyes were hard. 'Go on.'

'When I realised what had happened I brought the letters here and sent immediate word to you at Beresford Hall. To my knowledge, neither my cousin nor his father was ever made aware of their existence.'

'Do you expect me to believe that?'

'I expect nothing, sir, but I will remind you that I could have saved myself a good deal of effort simply by destroying them on sight.'

'And what, my I ask, prevented you from doing exactly that?'

Roger spread his hands and shrugged. 'I might have done so, had I not seen this copy of *The Times*.'

'Ah, now I see the truth of it.'

'I doubt that, sir. I doubt that very much.'

'Name your price, Mr Fairfax.'

Roger leaned forward, his own face set with indignation. 'Your judgment of me is hasty and unjust, Sir Oscar. I am a Fairfax, yes, but I own not an inch of disputed land, I employ no dubious clerks, I make no loans to foolish men and I have no stake in any quarrel with you. The letters are not for sale.'

'Then why am I here?'

'Because as a Fairfax I would not get as far as the door of Beresford Hall before your men attacked me, and I could hardly ask the Lady Leonora, to whom these letters rightfully belong, to meet me here as you have done today.'

'I repeat sir,' the Earl said tightly, 'why am I here?'

Well satisfied with his manoeuvres, Roger Reece Fairfax made a brief signal to Mr Percy Bell and the bound bundle of letters was placed upon the table.

'These letters have been opened.'

'Regrettably, yes.'

'And read by whom? The entire Fairfax workforce?'

'I am afraid I cannot answer that, Sir Oscar, at least not with any certainty,' Fairfax explained. 'However, I am of the opinion that the same clerk who concealed them was responsible for prying into their contents. He has, of course, been dismissed from his employment at my insistence.'

Sir Oscar touched the letters with one finger, his narrowed gaze still fixed on the younger Fairfax. He was meant to see this man as honourable, a man of principle, yet all he saw was a Fairfax. This one was of a pleasant outward manner without a doubt, even physically attractive but for his deep-set eyes and full, rather sensuous mouth, but he was a Fairfax none the less, and never was a Fairfax fit to receive the trust of a Cavendish.

'Your price sir, if you please.'

'I ask that you deliver them to the lady, nothing more.'

'Can I believe you mean that?'

Fairfax rose from his seat, smiling, and clicked his heels in a polite bow. 'Thank you for coming, Sir Oscar. I bid you good day. And to you, Sir Giles, my compliments.'

'Good day sir.'

Roger Reece Fairfax left the inn without haste and with a smile of satisfaction on his face. He came away from the meeting empty-handed, yet he considered himself the richer for it. His ambitions no longer included the maintenance of that old feud between two neighbours, since he was obliged to belong to the lesser side. Nor did he hope to snipe at the Earl through his daughter. He had parted her legs a hundred times in Paris, a pleasant enough experience but unprofitable, and he harboured neither hope nor itch to wed the wench. While Vivienne seemed bent on whoring her way through every pair of pants in Rome, Fairfax had found much bigger fish to fry. The wealthy widow, Harriet Sharpe, would suit his purpose admirably, if he could get her. Today he had taken the initial step towards his chosen future. Through Harriet Sharpe, and with the goodwill of Sir Oscar Cavendish, his daughter-in-law and her brothers, he might yet become the second Fairfax to improve himself at Beresford's expense.

When Fairfax and Percy Bell had left the inn, Sir Oscar shook his head in disbelief. 'What am I to make of all this?' he asked of his friend. 'A Fairfax offering favours to a Cavendish? There's mischief here, I feel it in my bones. He has lost much in the transaction. I would have paid him handsomely for these had he but named his price.'

'You paid the fee he asked,' Powell smiled, calling the land-lord over.

'What? What do you mean? What fee?'

Sir Giles sat back and puffed upon his pipe. 'The goodwill of the Earl of Beresford, especially toward a member of the Fairfax family, is worth more than a purse of gold, would you not agree?'

Sir Oscar pushed the letters into his coat and raised his glass, glowering at his friend over its rim. 'The letters were never his to bargain with, so he will find himself disappointed if he hopes to demand some future favour of me. I will never under any circumstances consider myself to be in debt to a Fairfax.'

Leonora received the letters with equal measures of joy and disappointment. There was no word from Joseph, not even a note to say that he was well. When she heard from Malcolm everything that had taken place at the Royal Oak, she suspected that there was more to the safe return of her letters than one man's wish to extract favour from another. The man at the centre of this was Roger Reece Fairfax, who possessed the barefaced audacity to walk into the Earl's own home, mingle with his guests, eat and drink from his tables and attempt to seduce his fourteen-year-old daughter. This was the man who had fallen foul of Lukan de Ville, had dared openly to oppose Sir Malcolm's policies on the Reform Laws and was now, according to Leonora's sources, paying court to the widow Harriet Sharpe. Taking all things into careful consideration, she was convinced there was more to the matter than met the eye.

'My sentiments exactly,' Sir Oscar told her when she voiced her fears. 'Believe me, my dear, the matter is already in hand. There is but one thing I mistrust more than an enemy, and that is an enemy calling himself a friend.'

Observing the proprieties, Leonora addressed a formal note of thanks to Roger Reece Fairfax at his club in Westminster, and for a while her brothers' letters were a welcome distraction from her self-imposed isolation. At first she read them through several times a day and constantly referred to their contents, but soon even these precious things were not enough to keep her inner suffering at bay.

'You must try not to fret for Joseph,' Malcolm told her one night as he held her in his arms. 'Fretting will hamper your recovery and will not bring him back before he is ready to come of his own accord.'

'Your father has sought to prepare me for the worst,' she replied. 'For the possibility that Joseph's long silence means he cannot, rather than will not, contact me.'

'In my opinion you would be better not to dwell on that.'

She turned in his arms to look at him. 'He is still alive, Malcolm. I know he is still alive.'

'Can you really be so certain?' he asked, stroking her hair.

She nodded and placed a hand upon her breast, then said with a sudden depth of feeling, 'So long as I can feel him here I know that he is still alive.'

'And while he lives we'll find him, however long it takes.'

'I know,' she said, 'I know.' But in her heart she doubted that they would.

IV

Leonora's twins were born on April 16th. It was not a difficult birth and there were no complications. The Honourable Matthew Cavendish came into the world at dawn, followed by his sister, Lady Frances, just twenty minutes later. By the time Sir Marcus Shaw arrived in a flurry of shirt tails and loose collars, the babes were wrapped in clean linen and bawling lustily. Leonora lay propped against a mound of pillows, exhausted and a little feverish. She examined her newborns in turn, counted tiny toes and fingers, measured bones and found not the slightest imperfection in their tiny bodies. They were both very fair with barely a wisp of soft blond hair between them, and they looked out through that mysterious blue veil all babies carry with them into the world. She looked at her twins and thought of Lukan's child, black-haired, black-eyed, born to a gypsy mother.

She wept a great deal following the birth. Anabel brought her leaves of borage to eat in a salad, supposedly a cure for sadness and a giver of courage. She made tonics of sage to encourage well-being, of chives to hamper the bleeding and thyme to induce restful sleep. And she watched over the newborns constantly, fearing the old tales of twin babes stolen by fairies in exchange for ugly changelings, or of one twin snatched away by elves whose womenfolk were often barren. She also feared the most common fate of twins who have but half the strength and fortitude of single babes and yet are pushed too early from the womb. She wanted them to live, and more than that she wanted Leonora to love them.

Within minutes of the births Sir Marcus Shaw paid off the midwife, declared the children small but perfectly healthy,

581

and by breakfast time the celebrations to mark their safe arrival had begun.

Malcolm rode to the Forest House at noon that morning. He found his friend a mile away, toiling to clear a ditch that was fouled by rotting foliage. There had been storms all winter, and swollen streams had rushed the debris from higher ground and settled it like plugs in narrow ditches. He approached the spot on foot, treading softly on the mossy ground. The gypsy was stripped to the waist, his legs braced one on either side of the obstruction, his powerful arms guiding the long-handled axe as it rose and fell in a steady rhythm. Muscles rippled across his shoulders and back with every movement, attesting the supple power in his long body. Without pause in his stroke he spoke with quiet threat.

'If you be friend, announce yourself. If you be foe you'll feel my axe's weight.'

'Not if I plant a bullet in your back, sir.'

Still holding the shaft of the axe in both hands, Lukan lowered its head until it came to rest on the tangle of roots and branches between his feet. He looked at Malcolm over one shoulder, his eyes long and narrow.

'You challenge me while I have this?' he asked.

'Bring me its equal and I'll gladly take you on.'

His mouth curved a little. 'Combat by axe?'

'Why not?' Malcolm grinned. 'It must be the only thing we haven't tried to kill each other with these thirty years.'

Lukan shook his head, smiling, and indicated the work still left undone. 'Would you have us hack each other to death before or after I free the ditch?'

'Neither, you fool. Come here and shake my hand. I've just been made a father twice over.'

The big gypsy set down his axe and sprang lightly on to level ground. Once there he grasped his friend by the hand and pumped it warmly. 'You are a lucky man,' he said.

'Lucky indeed,' Malcolm nodded. 'Fine twins they are, a boy and a girl, born at dawn. You'll think them tiny scraps of things, I'm sure, not half your William's birth-weight, but what a pair of lungs they have apiece. Already the nursery is a bedlam with their complaints.'

'Congratulations, Malcolm,' Lukan said. 'What are their names to be?'

'Matthew and Frances.'

Lukan nodded. 'Good names. They have my approval.'

'Thank God for that,' Malcolm grinned.

'How fares the lady?'

Malcolm's smile faded and he shook his head. 'Not good I'm afraid, not good at all.'

'Oh?' Lukan felt his blood chill but managed to keep his anxiety concealed. 'Is it the childbed fever? Is she ill?'

'Not ill exactly, not in a sickly sense,' Malcolm said, and in his concern he failed to notice the look of relief that passed over his friend's dark features. 'The birth was straightforward enough, even easy, according to those who witnessed it. It was certainly swift. The whole thing was over in a few hours and the twins were born before old Marcus was able to get himself from one end of the house to the other.'

'So what ails the lady?'

'I simply do not know,' Malcolm confessed. 'It is this persistent melancholia that settled on her early in the pregnancy. As yet there is no sign of improvement. She is proud of her babes and as loving as you would expect her to be toward them, but still she is tearful and depressed. Nothing seems to raise her spirits. I wish Rebecca had not gone away.'

Lukan frowned. 'There are other gypsies, other women with special knowledge of cures and remedies,' he reminded him.

'But not with your sister's skills, my friend,' Malcolm said with a smile. 'I believe I owe my twins to that cure you gave me.'

'What?' Lukan swallowed a lump that rose abruptly in his throat. 'Are you saying it was the remedy that made them?'

'You would have been a rich man, had you wagered on it,' Malcolm grinned.

Lukan's response was in direct opposition to his feelings. His grin was sudden, a flash of big white teeth against sun-browned skin. 'Then you are in my debt sir, and I'll not let you forget it.'

Malcolm's face was suddenly grave. 'Now I must have a remedy for Leonora, something to gladden her heart.'

'You'll find it,' Lukan said. 'Give her time, it is the finest healer of all for such ills.' He slapped his arm around Malcolm's shoulder and steered him back to the main path. 'And now you will take luncheon at my table and we will drink to your virility with a bottle of my best madiera.'

He saw the lanterns much later in the day, when Malcolm had returned to the Hall and the ditch was finally cleared of its obstruction. Damp and exhilarated after a long swim in the river, he walked across the meadow and saw the lanterns hanging against the special drapes in the big south-facing window. Two were set close together to announce that a living son was born to the mistress of the house, one hung alone below them, signifying a twin sister. And somewhere in that house the lady lay, weakened by childbirth and suffering a disorder of the soul.

'I too have suffered,' he growled through clenched teeth. 'Damn you, Leonora, I too have suffered a disorder of the soul because of you.'

In all the time he had been apart from her he had taken no other woman to his bed, made no contact with Harriet in response to her recent messages, sought out no comfort for his inner pain. He was a lonely man and desolate without her.

Feeling his isolation like a physical pain, he seated himself in the meadow grass and watched the wolfhounds bound like playful puppies all around him. April was always a special month, a time of fresh starts and new beginnings. In the woods only the ash waited to come into leaf, while dying beeches, wrecked by the winter storms, flowered to produce a new generation of seedlings. Farmers and their labourers were hard at work, cutting fences, putting up hedges, renewing the yearly battle to make and keep their livings. The young wheat in the fields was a tender green, rippling in the breeze like waves on water, silky-soft and with a silver sheen. Cattle and sheep were grazing in the meadow, cuckoos and lapwings called, and still a sudden frost could leave the grass white and brittle and a sudden shower turn it green again. It was the year's new start. What could gladden the lady's heart if April itself had already failed to do so?

He watched a group of Sir Oscar's men heading for the big house with rods and sacks carried across their shoulders. Dozens of rabbits hung from the rods as sagging flags must hang without a wind, and every man's sack was bulging with freshly killed fowl. There was to be jugged hare and pigeon pie on the menu, and tender rabbit portions glazed with honey, and blackbirds in an apple-cider sauce. Having neither the appetite for food nor the inclination to remain idle, Lukan glanced once more at the lanterns in the window, whistled the hounds to follow and walked away.

CHAPTER TWENTY-SEVEN

I

It was the end of May when Lukan found Sam sitting on a short flight of steps leading to the gardens, whittling with a sharp knife upon a piece of wood and muttering quietly to himself. He leapt to his feet as Lukan's shadow suddenly fell across him.

'Good morning Mr Lukan sir. Gave me quite a turn you did, coming up all quiet like that.' He glanced down at the man's stout riding boots and added in amazement, 'I swear I never heard so much as a footfall.'

'How fares your mistress, Sam?' Lukan's voice was very deep, with an accent that was neither Welsh nor West Country but a lilting combination of the two.

'As she was, Mr Lukan, as she was.'

'And the babes?'

Sam smiled in spite of himself. 'Oh, as lively as two piglets in a sack, if you'll pardon the expression, sir. She let me hold them once. Tiny little things they are, them being twins and born more than a month early, but they're strong as any two I ever saw, and no mistake.' The brightness suddenly faded from his eyes. 'I reckon you've heard all about Miss Elizabeth?'

Lukan nodded gravely. Malcolm had told him several days earlier, while he was still visibly shaken by the incident. Leonora had woken in the night to find one of her twins, then little more than a week old, missing from her cot. She roused Anabel and two maids before rushing out to find Lady Elizabeth at the top of the stairs leading to her own room, whose door had been left unlocked by a careless maid. She was cradling little Frances in her arms, weeping and bemoaning the loss of her kitten, and there was a very real danger that she would either crush the child to death or let it fall. It had taken all Leonora's persuasive skills to calm her down and, after mounting the stairs one cautious tread at a time, take the child away from her unharmed.

'Poor Miss Elizabeth. She didn't mean no harm, not really, but she can't be watched any more Mr Lukan. She's as cunning as a jack-rabbit when it comes to running off and she's not to be trusted with the little'ns, not after what she done to all them animals and birds and all them fish out of the big pond.'

Lukan looked off into the distance, thinking of Elizabeth with her gentle face, soft grey eyes and dangerously strong fingers. She meant no harm. There was not one ounce of meanness or wickedness in her. What damage she inflicted was merely an extension of her habit of picking at her hair, her gowns and her bonnets until they were in tatters, and her inclination simply to throw away anything that failed to hold her vaporous interest. She meant no harm, yet baby Frances might have been killed or maimed in what must have been a terrifying incident.

'She's to be locked up all the time now,' Sam Cooper said. 'Miss Leonora's had a set of rooms put aside for her on the other side of the house, with windows that don't open and lots of toys and things to keep her happy and people to watch over her day and night.'

587

Lukan turned his head sharply. 'Ye gods, is she not to have any freedom at all? Is she to spend the rest of her life a prisoner?'

'Bless you, no sir,' Sam said with a smile. 'She's let into the centre courtyard every day and taken into the grounds or the park whenever the weather suits. Miss Leonora wouldn't let her be forgotten, Mr Lukan. She loves Miss Elizabeth like a sister. She wouldn't ever let anything bad happen to her.'

'No,' Lukan conceded. 'Of course she wouldn't.'

'You love her too, don't you sir?'

Lukan nodded sadly. 'Aye Sam, I have always had a special fondness for her.'

'The doctors don't believe she'll ever . . .'

'Uncle Ookan! Uncle Ookan! Uncle Ookan!'

With a series of whoops and squeals of childish delight young William ran unsteadily down the terrace slopes, reached the top where Sam stood and fearlessly launched himself into the air with not a moment's hesitation. Lukan caught him easily, spun him around several times and hugged him while the fat little arms squeezed tightly around his neck. These days he did not see enough of his godson. He missed him. The boy was growing fast and Lukan often felt deprived of his share in it.

'I have two new babies,' William said gravely, describing the number with one finger of each hand.

'I know.'

'So big.' He cupped his podgy hands into an impossibly small measure. 'So big.'

'Aye, I do believe they are,' Lukan agreed with equal gravity.

At the sound of hurried footsteps he looked up quickly, half expecting to be confronted by Leonora. It was Anabel come in search of her small charge. She came to a halt on the grass beside the steps, her arms folded across her body as she glared at Lukan. He fancied he saw anger and sympathy alike battling for supremacy of her homely features.

'Good morning, Mr de Ville,' she said coldly. 'Sam Cooper, I think you are needed in the wood yard.'

'Yes, Miss Anabel, I reckon I am,' Sam said and hurried off.

'Well, Mr de Ville.'

'Well Anabel. The boy has grown.'

'All children do.'

'He's handsome, too.'

'No more than is to be expected.'

'How old is he now, eighteen months?'

'Nineteen.'

Lukan sighed and knew the conversation would not prosper. He placed his hand on the back of William's head and pressed the small forehead to his lips. He closed his eyes, feeling his nostrils flare at the sweet, familiar baby-scent. Then he set William on his feet and watched him gingerly approach the wolfhounds. Gillan and Garvey lowered themselves into a crouch immediately, as they had been trained to do in William's presence, and the fat little fingers fondled their ears and patted their big grey heads.

Awkward in the sudden silence, Lukan lowered his head and hung his hands from his belt by their thumbs. He kicked out savagely at a nearby stone. 'Must I ask, or will you volunteer the information?'

'I'll volunteer you nothing,' she said sharply.

He sighed again. 'How is she, Anabel?'

'Unhappy,' was all she said.

Another silence stretched itself between them. It was Anabel who broke it when she said, 'It's time the boy was taken back indoors.'

'Yes.' He crouched and extended his arms and William instantly forgot the dogs and ran to embrace his godfather with a chuckle of laughter. 'Be off with you now, for I have work to do.'

The boy allowed Anabel to lead him by the hand as he negotiated the short flight of steps. At the top he turned to wave his hand at Lukan, and from that angle he was the very image of his father.

'There'll be no message, then?' Anabel asked.

For a long time he held her gaze while a cauldron of

emotions seethed inside him. Then he muttered. 'No, there'll be no message,' and turned away.

Later that week Leonora was persuaded to walk in the park instead of spending yet another day in the central courtyard with only her son and two-month-old twins for company. By now the wooded areas of the park were carpeted with a hazy mist of bluebells and the air was sweet and heavy with their scent. Avoiding the tiny snaking pathways through leafy and secluded walks, Leonora trod the mossy main pathway with mixed feelings, hoping to find Lukan there and yet dreading the possibility that she might. She was wearing a saffron-coloured frock with copper lace at the throat and sleeves and tiny crimson flowers stitched into the bodice. Around its hem was a delicate quilting filled with small quantities of pounded and dried lavender, and a tiny heart-shaped bag tucked into her bodice sent the same perfume wafting into her face. She walked alone in thoughtful silence, with Anabel and Sam Cooper keeping a discreet distance behind her. Ahead the path stretched out beneath an overhang of birch and sycamore trees, some so heavily burdened that they formed a leafy tunnel in several places along the path. In the heavier soil of the park the great oaks grew, and where there was gravel, elms set down their roots. In the distance the path curved gently to the left, bending around and through the park on a two mile journey through woods of ash and copper birch and back towards the house. On either side of her the grass was lush and high, the flowers colourful and beautifully scented. Every few yards a single-width footpath meandered away to some picturesque spot just out of sight to left or right, tempting the wanderer to stray a while from the main path. Here and there the hedges were frosted with spiders' webs, dotted with red campion and white milkmaids. It was a perfect day set in a glorious month.

Leonora took a deep breath, held it for a long time and then breathed it out in a long, reflective sigh. She was drinking of summer's sweet, health-giving scents, trying to heal herself with the season's bounties. A butterfly, a delicate pale green hairstick, hovered a while among a cluster of poppies before settling gently on one crimson petal. She looked up and saw him then, a solitary, dark-clad rider approaching from the distance, horse and man framed by a canopy of lush green leaves. On either side of him the wolfhounds trotted.

'*Lukan!*' His name was plucked from her lips in a sigh.

She stood perfectly still, watching him approach at a steady pace, obviously unaware that she was standing on the path ahead of him. Then the horse slowed its pace and the hounds drew back as if suddenly called to heel. She stood like a statue with her heart pounding against her ribs and the breath trapped in her throat.

'*Lukan.*'

He was too far away to hear her call his name. She saw the tall black horse begin to prance this way and that, now coming on, now stepping back, its halting movements betraying the indecision of its master. Then horse and rider turned and began to move away, back in the direction from which they had come, Raven picking up speed with every stride. At one and the same instant she felt the stab of his rejection and the sudden soaring of her spirits. In the distance Raven first slowed his steps then came to a complete halt with Lukan sitting motionless astride him, hanging his head, defeated. For endless moments he remained so without moving, then he swung his right leg over the horse's neck and slid gracefully to the ground, facing her.

Leonora felt herself frozen to the spot. Behind her Anabel caught Sam Cooper by the arm and together they stood as if transfixed, watching the scene before them.

Lukan dropped the reins and signalled the wolfhounds to stay, and for a long time he simply stared at the slender, yellow-bright figure standing in the distance. Then he took a small step forward and so did she, and with that they were running towards each other, racing to close the gap that had lain too long between them. They came together at some half-way point and at last she felt his strong arms close around her, hard, possessive, wonderfully familiar. He lifted her off her feet, crushing her against him, holding her the way a drowning man might cling with his whole being to his rescuer.

'It's done,' Anabel said, shaking her head and glancing around her apprehensively. 'For good or ill, it's done.'

'Aye, it is and all,' Sam Cooper grinned.

The two had conspired together in these events. Anabel had persuaded her mistress to walk in the park while Sam, grasping his courage in both hands, had invented a lie to bring Lukan de Ville along the tree-lined pathway at precisely the right moment. They looked on now while the couple stood like a single shape, still clinging to each other.

Long minutes passed before they came apart and Leonora began the slow walk back toward the house. She turned to look behind with almost every step, to find him still standing there where she had left him, staring after her. She dabbed at her cheeks with a handkerchief, wiping away his tears and hers, and she knew that her world had suddenly been set back on its true axis. All this in one long, heart-rending embrace, and not a single word had passed between them.

II

As if by magic Lady Leonora, Viscountess Cavendish, was relieved of the depression that had lain so heavily upon her for almost a year. It was as if the storm clouds marring a summer's day were suddenly dispelled and the bright sun re-established in all its golden glory. She was herself again, dynamic and vivacious, and in her sapphire-tinted eyes was a radiance that seemed almost feverish. And with the restoration of her spirits came the stirring of old dreams, the re-awakening of old ambitions.

'Dare to be first,' she said aloud, testing the sound of it. 'That is what Sir Oscar told me when he conceded the opening of the Kingswood Fair to me. *Dare to be first.*'

Anabel was kneeling to attend to a small tear in her mistress's gown. She looked up with raised eyebrows and an expression of disdain. 'The man is quite mad to say such a thing to you, my girl. It would be more sensible of him to wave a red rag in the face of a bull.'

'I like it,' Leonora declared. 'In fact, I like it so much that I intend to have it placed on my personal seal and incorporated into my coat-of-arms. Let no-one ever be in any doubt that Leonora, Countess of Beresford, dares to be first.'

'Not Countess yet,' Anabel corrected. Her mending completed, she hoisted herself to her feet and wagged a finger in her mistress's lovely face. 'And for Heaven's sake Leonora, don't let others hear you make such a cruel, self-interested remark. They will think you impatient to see Sir Oscar in an early grave and Malcolm standing firmly in his shoes.'

'As indeed I am.'

'*Leonora!*'

Laughing in the face of Anabel's disapproval, Leonora grasped the woman's hands in hers and danced with her around the room. 'I will be Countess of Beresford,' she said. 'I will. That dream was born when I was ten years old and I first set my eyes on Beresford Hall. I will never surrender it, *never!*'

'And Lukan de Ville?'

'Dare to be first,' Leonora declared. 'If he cannot be my Earl then he will be my lifetime love, for I'll not give him up and I'll never risk the loss of him again.'

'Really? And may I take that to be a declaration that your family is now complete? Is there not to be another child for you?'

'Not unless he is the father.'

'*What?*' Anabel crossed herself several times in succession 'God forbid that it should ever come to that. Oh, Leonora, how can you say such a thing, even in jest?'

Leonora laughed a little too loudly as she flung back the curtains covering a deep alcove where several gowns were hung. It was but half a jest. Its roots were barbed and hidden somewhere in the very depths of her where love lay bruised by painful jealousy. Here was the one thing she could never have, the one thing neither riches nor power could buy. A child of his was something a common gypsy woman could call her own while Leonora, even as Countess of Beresford, must be denied the privilege.

'I love him,' she said softly, still standing with her hands raised to the drapes. 'I love him.'

Behind her Anabel crossed herself again and offered up a silent prayer. She could detect in that quiet, almost despairing statement more menace than might be found in any brash, impassioned outburst.

Lukan came that night. He stepped from the Monks' Stair into their secret room, dressed in a wide-sleeved shirt rolled up over his forearms, open to his waist and snowy white against his nut-brown skin. His hair hung loose about his shoulders, his pants were tight and buckled below the knee, his feet were bare.

'Gypsy,' she said softly, her gaze taking in every sensual inch of him. She wore a gown of white gauze, ribboned across the bodice and so delicately light it seemed to drift around her. She saw his black gaze drink in the sight of her.

'Lady,' he countered, licking a sudden dryness from his lips.

At last he moved into the room and took her in his arms, not grasping her against him now but holding her as if she were a precious thing, fragile and breakable.

'No more,' he said hoarsely. 'For God's sake, Lia, let there be no more of this ... this *torture*.'

'I swear it,' she vowed. 'No more, no more, I swear it.'

They made love atop the gold and silver coverlet, their bodies cooled by the quilted silk, their limbs entwined, their mouths, hands and eyes feasting on a banquet of erotic rediscovery. With infinite care he parted the folds of her flesh to reclaim the most secret parts of her with his tongue, then drew her nipples into his mouth in turn, tasting and tonguing until each one stood proud and erect from her pale breasts. She knew his body. Every breath, every sigh, every gesture spoke its needs so that she knew exactly when to guide him between her thighs. Then she arched her back, lifting her hips to meet his movements thrust for thrust until she felt that she would drown in the exquisite pleasure of having him inside her.

Much later they went up hand in hand to the summit of the tower where they had stood so often in the past, side by side, the gypsy and his lady. The night was warm and still, the moon so large that it bathed the dark landscape in a silver glow, lighting the river and the many streams and ditches with a mercurial sheen. The stars were as bright as gems against a sky of velvet black.

Leonora leaned against the stone parapet with Lukan at her back. His arms encircled her to grip the stone on either side of her body, trapping her where she stood. His head was lowered so that his warm cheek rested on hers, and she could feel his coarse black hair brushing her breasts.

'You know I love my husband,' she said.

'Aye, I know that, Lia.'

'It is a fact, I love Malcolm gently and with all my heart, the way I love my children. But you, Lukan de Ville ...' She nuzzled her face against his. 'You I love without compromise. You I love with my *soul*.'

'Aye, lady, I know that too.'

She thought of all they had and all they might have had if she had married him instead of Malcolm Cavendish, if she had dared surrender her dream of becoming Countess of Beresford. And she thought of Rebecca Adams and her child, her brother's child, incestuously gotten.

'If only we could have had our own child, you and I,' she said, tormented by a secret sense of loss.

'Lia, my Lia.' He turned her in his arms and kissed her mouth with a tender passion. 'How can such a thing ever be for us? We weep for the moon in wanting it. We have each other. Let us be content with that.'

'I love you, Lukan.'

'That much I will never doubt again,' he smiled.

'Does it still frighten you?'

'Aye,' he nodded. 'And so it should. It's a fearless, un-stoppable thing, this love of ours.'

She shivered and felt his arms tighten around her. They both knew now that she would never let him walk away from her again. She closed her eyes and lay her cheek against his chest, recalling that first time he had held her in the forest. He had smelled of aniseed, woodsmoke and leather then, just as he did now, and she tried to imagine how beautiful a child of his would be. As he bent his head to kiss her lips a sudden chill ran along her spine, bringing the old gypsy woman's words into her mind as clearly as if she heard them said afresh, *'Beware the dream, my lady. Take care what you set your heart on, for it will surely be yours.'*

Little, Brown now offers an exciting range of quality titles by both established and new authors. All of the books in this series are available by faxing, or posting your order to:

Little, Brown Books,
Cash Sales Department,
P.O. Box 11,
Falmouth,
Cornwall,
TR1O 9EN
Fax: 0326-376423

Payments can be made as follows: Cheque, postal order (payable to Little, Brown Cash Sales) or by credit cards, Visa/Access/Mastercard. Do not send cash or currency. U.K. customers and B.F.P.O.; Allow £1.00 for postage and packing for the first book, plus 50p for the second book, plus 30p for each additional book up to a maximum charge of £3.00 (7 books plus). U.K. orders over £75 free postage and packing.

Overseas customers including Ireland, please allow £2.00 for postage and packing for the first book, plus £1.00 for the second book, plus 50p for each additional book.

NAME (Block Letters) ....
ADDRESS ....
....
....

☐ I enclose my remittance for ....

☐ I wish to pay by Visa/Access/Mastercard

Number ☐☐☐☐☐☐☐☐☐☐☐☐☐☐☐☐

Card Expiry Date ☐☐☐☐